HEART OF STONE
VOLUME THREE

Books by K.M. Scott

Crash Into Me (Heart of Stone #1)
Fall Into Me (Heart of Stone #2)
Give In To Me (Heart of Stone #3)
Heart of Stone Volume One
Ever After (Heart of Stone #4)
A Heart of Stone Christmas (Heart of Stone #5)
Return To Me (Heart of Stone #6)
Forever With Me (Heart of Stone #7)
Heart of Stone Volume Two
Hard As Stone (Heart of Stone #8)
Set In Stone (Heart of Stone #9)
Silent As A Stone (Heart of Stone #10)
All of Me (Heart of Stone #11)
Heart of Stone Volume Three

Temptation (Club X #1)
Surrender (Club X #2)
Possession (Club X #3)
Satisfaction (Club X #4)
Acceptance (Club X #5)
Complete Club X Series Paperback

If I Dream (Corrupted Love #1)
If You Fight (Corrupted Love #2)
If We Fall (Corrupted Love #3)

Crave (Addicted To You #1)
Adore (Addicted To You #2)
Shatter (Addicted To You #3)
Claim (Addicted To You #4)
Addicted To You Series Paperback

In The Darkness (Project Artemis #1)
After The Storm (Project Artemis #2)
Behind The Scenes (Project Artemis #3)

Hard Work (Standalone)

Books by K.M. Scott writing as Gabrielle Bisset

Blood Avenged (Sons of Navarus #1)
Blood Betrayed (Sons of Navarus #2)
Blood Spirit (Sons of Navarus #3)
Blood Prophecy (Sons of Navarus #4)
Blood Craving (Sons of Navarus #5)
Blood Eclipse (Sons of Navarus #6)
Blood Ascendant (Sons of Navarus #7)

Stolen Destiny (Destined Ones Duology #1)
Destiny Redeemed (Destined Ones Duology #2)

Love's Master
Masquerade
The Victorian Erotic Romance Trilogy

HEART OF STONE
VOLUME THREE

K.M. SCOTT

HEART OF STONE
VOLUME THREE

Hard As Stone

Trouble. Playboy. Heartbreakingly gorgeous. Ethan Stone, the only son and spitting image of billionaire Tristan Stone, has a long line of women who would kill for a night with him, and rumor has it he's more than happy to oblige.

But Ethan has a problem. His family wants him to settle down. Why, he can't understand. But he needs to figure out a way to convince them he's given up his wild ways while at the same time living his life the way he wants to.

He has a plan, though, and Summer Carmichael, the quintessential girl-next-door, is perfect to help him. But Ethan better watch out or he might just find himself falling for exactly the kind of woman his family wishes he'd bring home.

Set In Stone

Driven. Sexy. Tressa Stone wants to take over the world. As one of Tristan and Nina Stone's two daughters, she's got the will to do it, and when she does, it won't be because of some man.

But you know what they say about best laid plans.

Killian Brenton has the world in the palm of his hand. The newest quarterback for a New York team looking to get back to the top, he's the toast of the Big Apple and can have his pick of women. All it takes is one look at Tressa and he knows she's the one he wants.

Catching her might be even harder than getting to the big game, but if he does, it will be worth far more than a handful of championship rings.

Silent As A Stone

Innocent. Sweet. Diana Stone, the last of Tristan and Nina's triplets, struggled from the day she was born. Never as confident as her brother or as strong as her sister, she was the brainy Stone child with her eye on one day sitting on the highest court in the land.

Until a horrible accident left her broken and trapped by her fears.

Cole Knight has known Diana for what seems like forever. Her brother's best friend, he's been told by Ethan that Diana is off limits since junior high. But he's been drawn to that forbidden fruit for years.

Once, Diana gave him her heart at a time when he needed it the most. Now, as he looks at her as a man and not a boy anymore, can he give her what she needs most so they can find happiness forever this time?

HARD AS STONE

CHAPTER ONE

ETHAN

"CALL ME," THE GORGEOUS BLONDE purred, smiling as she leaned over my chest to plant a soft kiss on my lips.

"Of course."

She rewarded me with a sexy wink before she turned on her heel and strutted out of my hotel room. My gaze drifted down her back, and I watched her beautiful ass sway seductively with each step, making my body come alive after far too little sleep.

Running my hand over my abs, I slid my palm over my hard cock and moaned. "Mmmm…if there was any justice in this world, I wouldn't have to get out of this bed and work."

I thought about the woman I'd spent the night with and a tiny lick of guilt nipped at me that I couldn't remember her name. Even if I wanted to call her, which I probably never would, what was I going to say? "Hey, gorgeous blonde with the great ass, what's up?"

Not exactly the way to get a woman in your bed. I mean, I'm good, but even I'm not good enough to tell a woman I can't remember her first name and have her back underneath me.

All the better anyway. Some things were meant to be momentary. I wasn't ready to settle down with any one woman yet, so why pretend?

I folded my arms behind my head and looked out at the world beyond my hotel room. I had to give my father credit. The man knew how to pick the best locations for his hotels. I'd never been in a single one of them that didn't have a view to die for. Today's offered the beach and the beautiful ocean water I planned to enjoy after a few hours of work.

Tristan Stone's Richmont Hotel on the southeast coast of Australia. Beautifully overlooking the crystal-blue waters of the Pacific.

I chuckled, imagining the marketing team Stone Worldwide paid to come up with that. The ads never mentioned my father's name, though. I added that part in because, in the end, that's exactly who the entire Richmont Hotel line belonged to.

Tristan Stone.

Squeezing my eyes shut, I pushed out any thoughts of my family from my brain. Lying in bed with a hard-on after a night of great sex was not the time to be thinking of them.

And then from the other room I heard the sound of the video phone alerting me that at any moment someone planned to ruin this perfect morning for me. Damnit. I forgot to turn on the away message before I fell asleep.

"Ethan? Are you there? I need to speak to you."

I scrubbed the last remnants of sleep from my face and rolled out of bed. Quickly, I slipped into a pair of shorts before I headed into the other room of the suite.

"Ethan? I know you're there. You didn't put on the away message, which I know you always do when you aren't around."

My sister's impatient voice echoed throughout my hotel suite. This was no way to begin the day.

As I turned the corner into the living room, I saw her. Tressa. With her dark hair up in a bun like she wore it so often, she reminded me of some librarian who spent her days in a stuffy back room poring over old books.

If only I'd put the damn message on before whatever her name was and I fell asleep.

"What do you want, Tressa?" I asked as I flipped on the screen so she could see me.

My sister opened her mouth and then closed it, grimacing at

me. "Jesus, Ethan. Did you get another tattoo? I don't think there's a square inch of skin left untouched on your torso."

Leave it to my bossier sister to be the one to call me. Too bad Diana wasn't the one staring back at me. Her I loved talking to.

"I'm guessing you didn't call just to comment on my tattoos. What do you want, Tress?"

She drew her dark eyebrows in and shook her head. "No, I don't give a damn what you do to yourself, Ethan. What I do care about is our mother and father, and that's why I called you."

Tressa always made it sound like she was the only one of the three of us children who gave a damn about our parents. As if, because I didn't live a stone's throw away from them, I'd somehow given up having any feelings at all about Tristan and Nina Stone.

"Since you're still being a royal—"

She leaned in and growled at me. "Don't you dare finish that statement, dear brother of mine, or I'll just have to tell Mom and Dad what I heard."

My mind immediately raced with the possibilities of what she could have found out about what I'd been up to. Lots of women. Nothing wrong with that, though. I was a healthy, red-blooded American male. A little too much partying. At least too much for my parents' tastes. Nothing wrong with a man having a good time while he could, right? That fight in that club a week ago. That wasn't so bad. It wasn't like I got arrested or anything. God only knew what she could be referring to.

Best to play it cool. Saying much of anything would likely give away my guilt.

"Uh-huh. So about Mom and Dad?"

Tressa grinned like a cat who'd just swallowed a canary. Obviously pleased with herself about something, she wiggled her eyebrows and asked, "So, how was your shoot last week?"

I plastered a smile on my face as once again my mind raced to piece together just what the hell she meant. Shoot last week? Nothing out of the ordinary had happened. I'd done my job, got some nice shots, and had a great time that night.

Same as always. So what the hell was Tressa getting at?

"Don't you have a job or something? I mean, you're twenty-five years old. Shouldn't you be at work now?"

My sister's face twisted into an expression of disgust. "It's six o'clock at night here in New York. You do understand that it isn't the same time around the world, don't you?"

I'd had enough of her for one morning. Reaching toward the screen to turn her off, I said, "Okay, bye. Nice chatting. Let's do this again in, say, another decade or so."

Before I could get rid of my sister from my hotel room, she said in her trademark snide way, "Imagine me hearing the awful news at the Morrison Gallery opening that our mother was dead and her dear son was in mourning over losing her so young."

Cringing, I stopped just before I turned her off. Damn.

"What do you want, Tressa? What's it going to take to make sure you don't say a word about this?"

A smile slowly spread across her lips. "I can't believe it. You actually used that line to get some bimbo into bed. Is nothing sacred to you, Ethan? That's our mother you're killing off to get a piece of ass."

"It wasn't like that. It was a misunderstanding, actually."

As I sat down in the chair in front of the screen, she laughed at my feeble attempt to lie my way out of this. If only Diana had been the sister to attend that gallery opening.

Unfortunately, she hadn't, and the sister who had stood staring at me with that look of judgment she seemed to always wear when it came to me.

"Let me see if I can figure out how it went down. You were talking to the flavor of the day and somehow the topic of your mother came up, and oops, you mistakenly said she died. Or maybe it was something more like bimbo du jour wasn't completely falling for your charms and you figured you needed a little something extra to convince her to jump into bed with you. Was that it, Ethan?

What's killing off one of your parents if it means you get laid, right?"

I pinched the bridge of my nose to forestall a headache that was beginning to form behind my eyes. "I said it was a misunderstanding. The person I was speaking to was talking about losing her mother, and I was consoling her when I said I'd be lost without my mother. That was it. She must have misunderstood."

Tressa laughed at my explanation. "And then you two just happened to spend the night together consoling each other."

The truth was far less appealing than my excuse. The model I'd shot that day had told me over a few too many drinks that her mother had died recently, and I'd sort of implied that I understood how that felt. Well, I'd done more than implied.

But not to get her into bed. Christ, I was a man-whore, but I didn't need to kill off my own mother to get a woman.

Closing my eyes, I asked, "What do you want to keep your mouth shut about this, Tressa? Tell me so I can get back to my life."

Just then I heard another voice and knew things had just gotten so much worse. "Why is it every time I see you, Ethan, you aren't wearing a shirt? Doesn't your job require you to wear clothes?"

I looked up at the screen and saw my mother staring back at me. Her blue eyes seemed to sparkle just like they had when I was a little boy. A hint of a smile told me maybe she wasn't furious with me.

"It's not even nine in the morning, Mom. Remember, I'm not in the country at the moment."

She nodded and gave me a warm smile. "Oh, that's right. How is the shoot going, honey?"

Smiling, I tried to stifle a chuckle. I'd had a great time, and very little of it had to do with taking pictures.

"Great, Mom."

She began to talk about the next time I'd be back in New York and abruptly stopped. "Did you get yet another tattoo?"

I looked down at my arms and torso and smiled. Lifting my left arm, I pointed to the sleeve I'd just had completed in the past month. "Yeah. What do you think?"

She didn't answer and instead simply smiled for a moment. "I remember when you were a baby. You had the softest skin. I used to blow raspberries on your belly and arms, and you'd giggle so cute."

Her reminiscing about my time as a baby made me roll my eyes. Twenty-five years old and she'd never accepted that I was a grown man. She seemed fine with my sisters, but with me, I was still her baby. Even though we were all the same age.

"Well, I better go, Mom."

Her expression turned dark, and she shook her head. "Not until we have a conversation about how disturbing it is for me to hear of my untimely demise, Ethan Stone. Imagine my surprise when I heard at the art museum opening last week that my son is telling people I've passed on. Perhaps you can explain what that's about?"

I sat silently, so she said, "You know, your father would be furious if he heard about this. He still thinks you should go back to school and finish getting your business degree so you can take over Stone Worldwide. I've made excuses for you because I like to think you're taking after me with your photography, but I'm not a fool, Ethan."

"I'm sorry, Mom. I'm sure the person simply misunderstood what I meant. I promise it won't happen again."

She smiled and shook her head. "Ethan, your father never resorted to these kinds of antics and never had to worry about attracting women. You've been blessed with his looks, so you don't have to act that way either to find a nice girl."

The last thing I wanted was a nice girl. Nice girls were boring. Time for some charm to get myself out of this.

"From the way he talks, there wasn't anyone before you."

She twisted her face into a disapproving grimace and shook her head again. "Don't try that flattery on me. I know you better."

So much for charm. "Things were different back then, Mom. You wouldn't understand."

"Things like that don't change, Ethan. I'll keep this latest issue between us, but if I get the sense that you aren't taking your job seriously, I will tell him."

"What about Tressa? She probably called him at work to tell him."

"She won't say a thing. Now be a good son and tell me we'll see you back home here soon."

"I will be, Mom."

She leaned in and frowned. "And tell me you'll find a nice girl and settle down."

I didn't want to lie to her face, so I smiled and said, "Love you. Tell Dad and Diana I said hi and I'll see them soon."

"I love you, honey. See you soon."

My mother walked away and Tressa's head popped up onto the screen. "I'll just add this to the list of things I can blackmail you with. Don't worry. I won't tell Dad. Unlike you, Ethan, I love our father."

Once more, I rolled my eyes. "Did I ever happen to mention that you're my least favorite sister?"

"It's less favorite, and yes, you've mentioned it once or twice. Now be nice and stop killing off our mother or you should expect the long arm of Tristan Stone to reach across the ocean and pluck you right off whatever beach you're spending your days lounging around on."

The screen went dark and I cracked my neck and shoulders before sighing in disgust. This was why I spent my time on another continent.

I knew my mother well enough to understand that her request for me to find a nice girl to settle down with was more than a hopeful wish. It seemed that my time as a single man enjoying life now had an expiration date.

But the last thing I wanted to do was settle down with anyone. I was only twenty-five, for God's sake. Why the hell did I need to stop living like I wanted to?

The answer to that was simple. I knew all too well what could happen if I didn't appear to be conforming to the life I was expected to live as the only son of Tristan and Nina Stone.

I also knew that perception was reality, so maybe all I had to do was look like I was settling down. My parents would be happy, and that would mean I could continue living my life like I wanted.

Pleased with my brilliant plan, I walked out onto the balcony and looked down on the beach below filled with gorgeous women in barely there string bikinis. All I needed to do was find one who could pull off the nice thing and make my family believe I was living the life they wanted me to.

And if she was anything other than a nice girl in private, all the better.

Chapter Two

Summer

For the third time in five minutes, Julia Carmon, the editor of *Belle* magazine and my boss, explained how important the beach shoot that day was to the May swimsuit issue eight months from now. I didn't need to have her lecture me yet again, but I knew better than to interrupt her. I'd done that once and had no intention of making that mistake a second time.

"I don't want any screw-ups, Summer. You make sure the models are on time for this shoot or you're going to have a lot of time on your hands. Do you understand me?"

She didn't have to threaten me with unemployment. I understood her just fine.

"Yes. You don't have to worry. The models and the photographer and everything will be perfect. I have this, Julia. You can relax and know that things are under control here."

"You better," she snapped. "If I have to jump on a plane and fly nearly a goddamned day to that damn beach, heads will roll, and yours will be the first one."

"You don't have to worry. I'll call you when it's all over, and I promise you'll be thrilled, Julia."

My boss gave her usual harrumph ending to our conversation and then the call ended without even the hint of a polite goodbye. And thus was my life. I loved my job, but I hated my boss. With a passion. Like the kind of hate you have when someone kills your entire family.

Well, not exactly that kind of hate. My hate for Julia was more like the kind of feeling you experience when you have to spend any amount of time around someone who is the most miserable and nasty person you've ever met. You know the feeling. Your stomach cramps up and makes you want to double over. Your chest tightens, and you want to tell them to go fuck themselves. With a red hot poker in the ass.

Yeah, that's what my boss made me feel.

I knew I had to pay my dues, though. This wasn't my first job out of school, and I understood full well how lucky I was to be the assistant to the editor of *Belle* magazine. This was one of the first rungs on my ladder to success, so I had to suffer through Julia and her constant mood swings for better things in the future.

Actually, her mood stayed the same with me all the time. Completely and utterly nasty. I might like it if her mood swung to something else sometimes.

I took a deep breath and let it out slowly. "The lower rungs are tough, Summer, but you're tougher. You can handle this."

In all honesty, the toughest part of the job was dealing with my boss. My responsibilities this morning involved making sure all the models got to where they needed to be on time and the photographer got all the pictures he would need. It wasn't exactly rocket science, and for a girl who'd graduated summa cum laude from Bryn Mawr, it wouldn't be hard at all.

I mean, how difficult could it ever be to corral a bunch of giant stick figures onto the beach? All I'd need was a single sandwich and I could probably lead them like the Pied Piper halfway around the world.

Chuckling to myself over my skinny model joke, I headed down to the staging area to begin gathering up the models. Today's shoot had five scheduled, which wasn't many at all. I hadn't checked the name of the photographer, but rarely did they present any problems. In fact, the only issues I'd ever had on any of these assignments was the rare model-boyfriend relationship blowup.

Those tended to be a nightmare, so I hoped we'd have none of that today. The last thing I wanted to deal with was some weepy model with her nose running all over her face or some despondent boyfriend who just found out he'd been replaced and his girlfriend just got around to telling him after he traveled halfway around the world to see her.

I stepped out of the hotel into the morning heat and saw three of the five models. So far, I was batting six hundred. Not bad.

Waving at the leggiest brunette I'd ever seen, I yelled over, "Emma, can you come over here?"

Naturally, she was named Emma. Trendy, ugly, older name perfect for one of the most beautiful women in the world. Only women who had been named by mothers channeling their hippy sides had names like mine.

Summer. I'd loved my name when I was a child. It was only when I got to school that I realized that nobody else was named after a season. I guess it could have been worse. That girl named Apple in my second-grade class had a long haul to look forward to with her name. Not trendy, old, or lyrical, it sounded stupid and offered no good nicknames. Who wanted to be called App?

Emma trotted over to where I stood and flashed me a perfect smile as she looked down at me and all my five foot six stature. She towered over me at nearly six foot, so I had to crane my neck to look up at her.

"Did you see Sarah and Ashley before you came down? We need to start on time. Have you seen the photographer yet?" I asked as the woman stared down at me with a vacant look in her eyes.

"I don't think so. Let me ask Maddie."

Before I could get her to clarify exactly what that answer referred to—the models or the photographer—she turned around and yelled, "Did you see Sarah or Ash this morning, Maddie? Summer's looking for them."

Maddie simply shook her head, making her blond hair swing around her shoulders. So much for her helping.

Emma turned back to face me and shrugged. "She hasn't seen them, either."

"What about the photographer?"

Suddenly, the vacant look in Emma's eyes disappeared, replaced by a sparkle I knew couldn't have anything to do with me since she was now looking over my head at something behind me. I turned around and saw a man as he strode through the hotel door. Tall, he wore a white button-down shirt and tan pants and looked like he belonged at a model shoot himself.

Just not one I had to manage.

"I think you have the wrong location. I saw a shoot a little further down the beach," I said as he paused to give Emma the once-over.

The man stopped gazing at her like she held the answer to some mystery he'd long pondered and smiled at me in a way that made me feel like I was melting. "I'm the photographer, but thanks for the compliment."

The photographer?

The idea that this guy had been blessed far too many times in life instantly ran through my head. Gorgeous looks and body, talent enough to snag an assignment with *Belle* magazine, and he got to work with models all the time?

He was probably the cockiest son of a bitch going, too. Ugh. Just what I needed. Was it so much to ask that this shoot go smoothly so Julia didn't tear me a new one afterward?

"Ready to make some magic, girls?" he said as he walked away without even giving me a chance to introduce myself.

Emma giggled and started to follow him out onto the beach, but I stopped her and asked, "Who is this guy? What's his name?"

She looked at me like I'd grown another head. "That's Ethan Stone. He's done some of the biggest shoots in the business this year. Shouldn't you know that?"

As the words *Fuck you, Emma* rushed through my mind, she turned on her heel and hurried over to where this Ethan Stone stood on the sand. Yes, I knew the name and what he'd accomplished this year, but I'd never seen a picture of him, so no, I didn't know that was him.

And I didn't need Emma the stick figure to point that fact out.

Sarah and Ashley came through the door behind me full of giggles and smiles and ran out to join the other models and Ethan. At least I didn't need to be model wrangler this morning.

"Okay, we've got the models, the photographer, the stylist, and me, your host for this lovely get-together. Models, please follow me to get changed into your outfits. We don't have all day, so let's get this going!"

BY THE TIME THE SHOOT had finished, I was questioning whether I really wanted to keep this job. Maybe it would be better if Julia fired me. At least then I could find a position that didn't involve so many models. Between getting them to the shoot and then making sure they did exactly as the photographer wanted, it felt more like directing recess at a daycare than managing a photo shoot.

Then again, the job did give me the chance to travel the world. That was a good thing. It was just what I had to do in those exotic places that I wasn't sure I liked anymore.

I made my obligatory call to my boss as I gathered up the last of the wardrobe changes and the sun began to dip below the horizon. At least I had good news to give her.

"Julia, the shoot went off without a hitch. The models looked gorgeous, and the pictures are going to be incredible. I just know it."

"Wonderful! Now tell me the truth. Did you have any problems at all? I want to know if you did, Summer."

She always asked that, and when I first began as her assistant, I used to tell her the truth. Now I was a lot smarter. Julia didn't need to know about the breakdown Ashley had that shut down the shoot for half an hour when she stubbed her toe on a shell and fell face first into the sand. She also didn't need to know that I was pretty sure Ethan Stone saw his job as his own buffet of potential women to have sex with, even if he did seem to have some talent at taking pictures.

Nope. She didn't need to know about any of the minor issues I handled all day. All Julia needed to know about today's shoot was that it had been a success. What it took to get it to that place could be kept behind the curtain like a magician's secrets.

"Nothing out of the ordinary that I couldn't handle. Trust me. You're going to love what we did here today. I can't wait to hear how you don't know which shot to use for the cover. It was that good."

"Excellent! Well, I want you on a plane and back here first thing Monday morning. We've got a lot of work to get done so that issue looks as good as you think it can."

I didn't protest her order to be back in New York not even forty-eight hours from that moment, even though just the thought of another twelve-hour flight made me groan. Since it was eight o'clock Sydney time, that meant I'd have exactly…

My brain was too tired to figure that out. All I knew was I'd have less than a day to relax before I had to go back to work.

The lower rungs are tough, Summer, but you're tougher. You can handle this.

Chapter Three

ETHAN

The hotel bar sat practically empty, even though it wasn't yet midnight. I'd worked far too fucking hard on the shoot that day to not enjoy myself, but at the moment, the only people who joined me were a middle-aged couple at the end of the bar who couldn't keep their hands off one another.

I gave the guy a wink as if to say, "Good for you, man," and told the bartender to get them both a drink on me. Although I wasn't enjoying myself, that didn't mean I didn't like seeing other people having a good time.

My conversation with my mother from earlier that morning settled back into my brain, and I sadly realized I likely wouldn't be having many more good times if I didn't find some way to fool my family into thinking I'd settled down. Twenty-five and they wanted me to act like I was twice that age. Christ.

Normally, I'd be taking advantage of the perks of my job and enjoying the company of one of the models by this point in the night. I would have given Emma a few extra smiles during the shoot, told her a few jokes afterward that would loosen her up, and invited her up to my suite. She would have said yes, we would have had a few drinks, and by now, I'd be balls deep in her and thinking there wasn't a fucking soul on this planet who had a better life than me. That's what I should have been doing instead of stewing over a beer that tasted like a wallaby's ass.

So instead of enjoying life as any man in his mid-twenties

"

deserved to, I sat there mulling over my options. It didn't take me long to figure out I didn't have many. I had two, to be precise. I could actually settle down with a woman and get married, which even thinking about made me feel like someone had their hands around my neck strangling me, or I could pretend to be settling down. Getting married was out of the fucking question, so that left option number two.

Pretending for my family so they could stop pestering me and go back to doing whatever they did when they weren't bothering me about giving up living.

All I had to do was find someone who could look the part of a nice girl for long enough to fool my family. She'd have a good time in the process courtesy of yours truly, and then when we parted ways, my parents and sisters would feel bad that I was all heartbroken and let me live my life.

The plan was foolproof. Now all I had to do was find the perfect girl. Since I'd be sleeping with her, even for a short time, she had to have something to attract me. More importantly, she had to appear to be nice.

Nice. Even the sound of the word in my head made me cringe.

I think I resented my father over this settling-down-with-a-nice-girl thing the most. From all the stories I'd ever heard, my mother was the quintessential nice girl when she was young, so she could be expected to think I should find someone just like her. My sisters had the same excuse, although I had a sneaking suspicion that Tressa was anything but nice when she wasn't around all of us.

And Diana? Well, she'd been a nice girl and what the hell had that gotten her? Nothing good.

But my father hadn't met my mother until he was nearly thirty, and there was no way in hell I was buying the story that he'd only been with nice girls all his life until he met the perfect one and married her. My sisters might have bought that story hook, line, and sinker, but I saw through that bullshit. He'd been left all that money and had private jets and expensive cars and he'd chosen to spend his time with librarians and nuns-in-training?

No way. Not buying it.

And yet, there he was singing the praises of this nice-girl nonsense with the rest of the Stone family choir almost as loudly as my mother. If I didn't have to busy myself with finding this mythical nice girl everyone thought I should be with, I'd hire a private detective to dig up dirt on Tristan Stone so I could finally know for sure my hunch about his life before my mother was right.

Then again, that would only hurt her if she found out, and as big a dick as I could be, she was my mother and I loved her. Even if she had the most asinine ideas about my personal life.

I took another drink of the shitty Australian beer I'd chosen and grimaced as it slid down my throat. No good-looking woman to get lost in and no decent alcohol in front of me.

This night was turning out to be nothing but shit.

Out of the corner of my eye, I saw someone sit down at the other end of the bar, where the middle-aged love birds had been before they headed up to their room. Maybe this night was looking up.

I turned on my stool and realized the person who'd come in was the girl from the photo shoot today. Not one of the models. Just the girl from the magazine. She wasn't bad-looking, though. She had nice hair. Brown and long, it reminded me of how my mother used to wear hers when I was little.

She ordered a drink and sighed heavily, like it had been a long day for her, too. She had handled the models pretty expertly, and except for that meltdown by the one who face-planted into the sand halfway through the afternoon, things had gone pretty smoothly. I had to give her that. Some shoots would have gone off the rails with one of five models bawling her eyes out, but this girl had taken control of the situation and I barely had to deal with it.

As I watched her take the first sip of what looked like some vodka drink, I thought about talking to her. Hell, it would be better than just sitting here alone. But for the life of me, I couldn't remember her name. Sunshine? Sunset?

Damnit. It was something having to do with nature, wasn't it?

"You okay down there? You look like you're having trouble," she said with a chuckle.

I waved off her concern and shrugged. "Yeah, I'm fine. Just a long day. Thought I'd stop in for a drink, but whatever the hell this is I'm drinking, it's not doing it for me."

She smiled sweetly and pointed to behind the bar. "They have other stuff. I'm sure they'll be happy to give you something else."

"Yeah. I should just do that. I don't think this beer and I are good for one another."

I waited for her to say something back, but she didn't and I still couldn't remember her damn name, so I stopped talking and took another sip of my disgusting beer. As it rolled over my taste buds, threatening to make me sick, a thought came to me.

This girl could work for my plan. She had the nice thing down pat. If only I could remember her name.

I ran through every damn nature name I could think of, sure it was something like that. Damnit! Why couldn't she have a model name like Emily or Alexis?

Then it came to me. Summer! That was it!

Fighting the urge to blurt out her name, I stood up and moved down the bar to take the seat next to her. She looked at me like she couldn't figure out why, but no matter. I had her name. That's all I needed.

"What are you drinking?" I asked as I waved the bartender over toward us.

Confused, she looked at her glass and then back at me. "Moscow mule."

"She'll have another Moscow mule and I'll have a Jameson and ginger."

The bartender nodded and headed off to make our drinks while I thought of something to say. My usual style likely wouldn't work so well with a nice girl. I tended to work on the principle that I'd gotten the go-ahead already so any conversation was simply a social lubricant to get the woman into bed. What I said didn't really matter, and it usually showed in crass double entendres heavy with sexual connotations.

I had the feeling none of that would help me with Summer, so I had to think quick. What did nice girls like? Jesus. I hadn't been with a nice girl since high school, and she wasn't nice for long after I got to her in the library after school one Friday afternoon.

Maybe the weather. Yeah, why not? Everybody had something to say about the weather.

"We were lucky to have a good day for the shoot today."

Literally the most boring thing to ever come out of my mouth.

Summer narrowed her eyes to a squint and gave me a pained smile as the bartender set fresh drinks down in front of us. "Yeah, I guess. This time of year this area usually has pretty nice weather. I could probably give you chapter and verse on it since the magazine researched it extensively in preparation for the shoot."

Oh, God. Please don't.

Damn, I needed to change the subject to something interesting before she started giving me details on the fucking weather.

"Yeah. So, you coordinate all the model shoots for *Belle*? That's a pretty big job, I'd think, right? The magazine's taken off in the past couple years."

Christ, this was like pulling teeth. *Ladies and gentleman of the jury, this is why I never go after nice girls. Who the hell wants to talk about this boring shit when we could be getting down to business upstairs in my hotel suite?*

Summer didn't seem bored at all, though. She took a sip of her drink and then nodded. "I'm the assistant to the editor, so I get to do all sorts of jobs. One day I'm on location making sure a photo shoot goes smoothly, and the next day I'm setting up meetings for my boss in and around the city."

I took a big gulp of my drink and held it in my mouth for a long moment before swallowing. "Sounds pretty important. I'm not sure I could do a desk job like that, but you seem to have a pretty good handle on it."

I'd never had a conversation go so bad so quickly. Tipping my glass back, I drank down the rest of my Jameson and ginger and motioned to the bartender for another. Maybe if I was drunk this would work better.

"Well, I guess if I had your talent I wouldn't have to do the desk job. But alas, I merely have my English degree from a well-respected school to pave the way for me."

Although I couldn't be sure, something in the way Summer said that made me think I'd just been insulted. She'd said I was talented, but none of the other words surrounding that seemed complimentary.

And then, before I could decide what she meant, she added, "I guess it doesn't hurt to have the Stone name, either, now does it? My last name doesn't carry as much weight, unfortunately, so I'm destined to have to work my way up the ladder of success."

Okay. That was definitely not complimentary.

I wanted to tell her how much a pain in the ass it was to have the Stone name. How being compared to Tristan Stone all the damn time had gotten old by the time I reached fourth grade. That, yes, I did come from a family with connections that had helped me get my first few jobs in the industry, but that wasn't how I'd gotten the job with *Belle* magazine.

However, I stopped myself. I had a plan here, and I couldn't let my bruised ego get in the way. I needed this girl to help me, so if that meant taking a few shots in the process, so be it.

The bartender barely set my drink down in front of me before I downed half the glass to keep myself from making a stupid mistake. Better to keep my mouth busy with drinking than defending myself to Summer.

Once I'd told myself for the fifth time that I needed to keep my head with her, I smiled and gave the whole situation a nonchalant shrug. "It probably doesn't hurt, but give me a little credit. You yourself said the shoot went great and your boss is going to love the pictures I took.”

She tried to speak, but her mouth dropped open. Shaking her head, she asked, “Were you spying on me when I was talking to my boss? That's not cool.”

“No, no. I was getting my gear all packed up and heard you. It wasn't like you were whispering. You were practically screaming it. You know, even though it's Australia, phones still work the same as they do back in the States. It isn't like you have to talk louder so your boss in New York can hear you.”

Summer's eyes grew wide as I spoke, and I wasn't sure she got my sense of humor. I made sure to finish with a smile, but for a few seconds, she just stared at me amazed.

Finally, she said, “You're quite the smartass, aren't you, Ethan Stone?”

“Sometimes. Usually people don't understand my humor, so I'm impressed you did. But my gut tells me you're a smartass yourself, Summer…” I hesitated for a moment and then admitted, “Sorry, I don't know your last name.”

She smiled and extended her hand. “I'm Summer Carmichael. From the Philadelphia Carmichaels,” she said in a snooty tone meant to make fun of her lack of status or my supposed status because of my family name.

Whichever she meant, it was funny and I laughed. “Nice to meet you, Summer Carmichael. Philadelphia, huh? My mother was born and raised right outside of Philly. Wait until I tell her I met another Pennsylvania girl just like her.”

Summer's eyebrows shot up into her forehead. “A man who talks to his mother about the women he meets in bars. Now that's a new one.”

“I'll leave out where we met and focus on your being from PA. Moms don't need to know all the sordid details.”

“I didn't think we'd gotten to anything sordid yet,” Summer said with a wicked grin I'd expect from someone far less sweet.

Maybe she did have a wild side to her, after all. That could work, too. I definitely wasn't against a nice girl in public and a freak in the sheets. All the better.

Chapter Four

Summer

What on earth was Ethan Stone doing sitting with me in the bar at the Richmont Hotel owned by his family? Why wasn't he upstairs in his hotel room, probably a suite, having sex with some hot model? Or two?

I'd done a little research on him after the shoot ended, and I had to say I was impressed. He'd definitely gotten more than a few breaks due to his parents' influence. Nina Stone's sculptures and exhibitions were known throughout the art world, and Tristan Stone's story was nothing less than heartbreaking until he met Ethan's mother. A billionaire left without a family due to a plane crash, he'd had money but little else.

Until he met Nina.

Their story had touched my heart, and then when I read about their three children, I had to admit it was hard not to like the Stone family. They weren't very different from my own family, except for the fact that they were ultra-rich. True, Tristan Stone had inherited his money, but he'd managed a successful business to make Stone Worldwide a giant around the globe. And he and his wife had raised triplets they adored, according to all sources.

Tressa, one of Ethan's sisters, took after her father and was soon to graduate with an MBA. Her future certainly held a position in the family business that made multi-billions a year in various ventures, including the hotel I was staying in. Ethan had taken after his mother artistically but chose photography over sculpture or painting. His parents had helped him get his break at first, but he'd made a name for himself over the past few years shooting models for magazines like *Belle* and seemed to be blessed with artistic talent just like his mother. He had another sister, Diana, but I strangely hadn't been able to find much information at all on her.

And all of this explained nothing about why he sat with me, of all people, in a hotel bar. Or why he claimed he'd tell his mother about meeting me. All of it made alarm bells go off in my suspicious brain.

A slow smile spread across his lips, showcasing how beautiful his mouth was. Straight white teeth and lips just the right fullness made me forget for a moment that I had no idea what this near-perfect stranger could want from me at that moment.

"Is everything okay, Summer?"

"Yeah. I'm fine," I lied, feeling the effect of the two drinks I'd had.

"Okay. I was beginning to think I'd done something wrong."

Damn. With every word, he seemed to get more charming by the second. No wonder there was a line of women who wanted to sleep with him long enough to stretch across Australia. Yeah, I found that out, too, while I was researching.

"No, no. I think I better go. I have an early day tomorrow."

I slid off the barstool and began to walk toward the door in a hurry. Tipsy Summer tended to do stupid things, and at that moment, all I wanted to do was press my lips against his to see if his mouth felt as good as it looked.

Behind me, I heard Ethan's deep voice say, "Was it something I said?"

Turning around, I watched him slowly walk toward me like a wild animal stalking his prey. Why was he following me?

"No. It's not that."

"Well, what is it?" he asked as he stopped in front of me.

"I just need to get back to my room," I lied.

God, this guy gave off a vibe that made me want to do things I shouldn't. It was a combination of confidence and power that was more intoxicating than the Moscow mules I'd drunk. And it would probably give me a worse hangover if I let myself enjoy it.

"Let me escort you back to your room," he said as the elevator doors opened and he followed me in.

We rode up to the second floor in silence, and as soon as the elevator doors opened, I rushed out and down the hall to my room. Never before had I wanted someone so badly and didn't know why.

Well, it wasn't hard to understand why. Ethan Stone was gorgeous. Great body, incredible looks, brown eyes I could get lost in. I'd always had a weakness for good-looking men, and it had never turned out well even once. And none of them were anywhere close to how stunning Ethan was.

Fumbling through my purse to find my room key, I felt him come up behind me. His presence was unmistakable. But why had he followed me?

It couldn't be possible that he wanted me. I didn't think I was ugly, but this man spent his time romancing models. I'd found that out in my research earlier that day too. So why was he standing right next to me?

Finally, when I found the key, I looked up to see him leaning against the doorframe and smiling. God, that smile was stunning. Everything about him was stunning.

"Everything okay?"

His deep voice washed over me, and I nodded, unable to answer without lying. I wasn't okay, and I couldn't blame two drinks on what I was feeling. I'd watched him all day and wanted him, but in a world full of models, I knew I didn't stand a chance.

But now that he stood next to me at the entrance to my hotel room, I wondered if maybe I'd been wrong.

Brave from the alcohol coursing through my veins, I smiled. "Yeah. Everything's fine."

And then I opened the door and looked back at him. My hormones must have taken over the speech center in my brain, and

I quietly asked, "Want to come in?"

My heart slammed against my ribcage as the words hung in the air between us and Ethan stood staring at me, not saying a word. Immediately, my mind began assessing the situation. The worst that could happen was he said no. And I'd feel humiliated for the rest of the night, probably salving my terribly bruised ego with more alcohol before I passed out. As for the best that could happen, who knew? I'd never done this before, so I had no idea what the result could be.

Except for flashing me a wicked smile, Ethan didn't answer my question and instead followed me into my hotel room. A million thoughts raced through my head. Why was he here? How did this happen? We'd just been having a drink together, and now he was standing there looking completely fuckable in my room.

Most of all, should I do what I'd fantasized about all day?

"So I hope you weren't planning on going to sleep," Ethan said, smiling in a way that said he knew exactly what I'd been thinking.

Then, as I stood there letting my gaze drift over his muscular body, he walked over to me and ran his fingertips up my arm. Goose bumps broke out across my skin in the wake of where he touched me as my nipples tightened in excitement.

What was I doing? I shouldn't even have entertained the thought of sleeping with him. If Julia found out...

While I tried to talk myself out of sex with Ethan Stone, he dipped his head so his lips brushed against my ear and said in a low voice, "Why so quiet all of a sudden?"

Oh, God, his breath rolled across my skin, making me weak with need. I struggled to answer him, muttering, "No reason."

"Good. You know, I saw you watching me today."

Something in the way he said that made me feel ashamed, and I pulled away, shaking my head. "Don't."

"What?" he asked as he reached out to take my hand in his. "Don't do what?"

I didn't want to be the only one in that room who had wanted this. I knew it was stupid, but to hear him say he saw me watching him made me feel pitiful because he hadn't been watching me.

Unsure how to answer his question, I closed my eyes and wished I didn't feel so insecure, but he'd been with model after model, so why was he there with me in my hotel room?

I felt him press his body to my back and I leaned against him instinctively, like everything inside me wanted to be closer to him. His mouth pushed lightly against the shell of my ear, sending a rush of desire through me.

"Tell me what you want, Summer."

I wanted everything he offered. The beautiful outside, the confidence, the vibration of his deep voice against my skin, the feel of his strong hands on me. Everything.

No words seemed to exist in my brain, and when I opened my mouth to speak, all that came out was a soft moan. A sweet ache settled into my body and made its way to between my legs. Pressing my thighs together, I let myself enjoy how good it felt.

My eyes still closed, I reveled in how his hands felt as they slowly slid down my arms and he wove his fingers through mine. Squeezing them, he brought my left hand up to his mouth. For the first time, I felt his beautiful lips on me.

I wanted to feel them on every inch of my body.

Another tiny moan escaped from my throat as he moved his hand up to my neck. Encircling it, he lightly teased just under my ear before dragging his fingertips down to my collarbone and then back up again.

"Oh, God…"

He sunk his teeth into my earlobe just hard enough to send a ripple of pain through it as he slowly slipped my dress down my body, leaving me in just my panties and bra. Cupping my breasts, he slowly planted kisses over my shoulder while he gently pinched my nipples through the fabric.

Every movement made me want him more, but he seemed to want to take his time, almost seducing me. Little did he know that I secretly fantasized about pushing him down on the bed and tearing his clothes off like a wild animal.

His hard cock pressed against the small of my back, practically teasing me with what was to come. I reached back and palmed him through his pants, and for the first time, Ethan let out a deep moan.

"I think it's time I took some of these clothes off," he said, stepping away from me.

I turned around to see him unbutton his black dress shirt. He let it hang open for a minute as he undid his pants to reveal black boxer briefs. The muscular body I'd guessed I'd see under his clothes looked even better than I'd imagined all afternoon. Tan and toned, Ethan Stone was a nearly perfect specimen of a man. But even better, across his chest sat an intricate, all-black Celtic-knot-design tattoo.

He slid his pants off and looked up at me, smiling as I watched him. When he shrugged out of his shirt, my eyes opened wide in surprise to see his chest wasn't the only part of him tattooed. The design continued down his left arm to his wrist and mixed with different images of a clock, some woman, a cross, and words I couldn't make out. On his right shoulder he had a tattoo of an all-black fire-breathing dragon.

As my gaze skimmed over his body in admiration of how gorgeous he truly was, I couldn't help but wish I had kept up with that workout program I had started last summer. Ethan's washboard abs put my much less defined and squishy midsection to shame.

I crossed my arms in front of my body to hide it, but I couldn't stay like that for long once he took me by the hand and pulled me to him. He seemed to be oblivious to my imperfections.

Then before I could say a word, he stuffed his hands into my hair and leaned down to kiss me better than I'd ever been kissed before. His soft lips pressed against mine as he tugged my head back just roughly enough to make my pussy run wet.

I moaned into his mouth, and he slid his tongue over mine to tease me with what he might do to other parts of my body with it.

More than anything, I wanted him to make good on that and more.

His hands left my hair and traveled down my body until they cupped my ass. Pulling me into him, he pushed his hips forward so his cock pressed just above my pussy. I'd never wished to be just a few inches taller more than at that moment.

I wanted to feel his cock in my hand, feel the hardness against my palm, so I slid my hand down his body and beneath those black boxer briefs and heard him groan. Looking up, I saw need in his dark eyes that thrilled me. I wrapped my hand around his cock and slowly moved up the shaft, feeling the silky skin against my hand. With every inch, that need grew until I reached the head.

Ethan closed his eyes and moaned, "Oh, God…"

Then in the split second as I thought about dropping to my knees and sucking his cock just to hear that sensual moan from him again, he spun me around and pushed me back onto the bed. Right before my eyes, he transformed from that sexy man who had seduced me from the moment he caught up to me at the elevator to a man with a singular goal.

To possess a woman in the most intimate way possible.

I'd never seen that look in a man's eyes before. Was sex always like this for him? I envied him if that was the case.

He stripped out of his boxer briefs, slid a condom on, and tugged my panties down my legs as I fumbled with my bra. I tossed it aside and watched as Ethan lowered himself down onto me. In one smooth motion, he kissed me long and deep while he pushed apart my legs with his knee. Then before I could catch my breath, he thrust into me slowly, inch by inch, until he filled me completely while his hands worshipped the rest of me.

My body surrendered to him even before my mind did, taking all he had as he pumped into me. I heard him say my name, but from the moment he began fucking me, I was lost to the ecstasy of the experience.

I ran my hands over his body, loving the hardness of him beneath my touch. His back muscles flexed with every thrust of his cock into my body, and he grunted in a way that made our fucking animalistic. I'd never felt like this with a man, and as much as I knew I shouldn't, I wanted more.

More of him. More of how he made me feel. More of everything about Ethan Stone.

CHAPTER FIVE

ETHAN

I OPENED MY EYES AND looked around at the room I lay in. It looked like my suite, but didn't Summer and I go to her room after the bar? Looking down at my chest, I saw her brown hair spread out over me, covering her face. As I tried to piece together the events of last night, she moved against me.

Slowly, it all came back. Yes, we'd gone to her room first—or more accurately, for the first round—but then I'd told her my room was more comfortable and we'd made our way up here to the penthouse. From then, it had been round after round of sex until we both collapsed onto the bed exhausted.

Summer lifted her head off my body and pushed her hair off her face. I'd seen supermodels first thing in the morning, and none of them looked better than she did at that moment.

"Good morning. Have a nice sleep?" I asked with a chuckle.

She sat bolt upright and tugged the sheet around her body to cover her. Why, I had no idea. After what we'd done all last night, I'd seen every inch of her intimately.

"Oh my God! What time is it? My plane leaves at eight," she said as she swiveled her head back and forth looking for a clock.

I looked across the room and shook my head. "I'm sorry to tell you you're not going to make that flight."

Summer buried her face in her hands and sobbed, "Oh, God. I have to be back in New York for Monday morning, and I'm never going to be able to do that now that I've missed that flight. My boss is going to kill me if I'm not in the office bright and early for work."

"Relax. It's okay. You can catch a ride back with me," I offered, hoping to make her feel better.

She looked up and twisted her face into a grimace. "That's a nice offer, but sitting in first class isn't going to get me back to New York any faster."

"I'm not in first class. I have the Stone Worldwide private plane. I'd planned to leave around nine today, so you'll come with me."

"A private plane?"

"Yeah. I'm happy to help. So relax. You'll be back in plenty of time. In fact, I'm going to call down to get some breakfast and then we'll head to the airport. Why don't you take a shower and when you're done, the food will be here."

Instead of making her happy, my suggestion did the opposite. She lowered her head and mumbled, "God, I must look a wreck."

I sat up and tilted her chin up to see her face. Shaking my head, I smiled. "You look great. I just figured a shower might relax you."

She forced a smile and stood up, tugging the sheet to cover herself. I pulled harder, though, and she ended up completely naked. Glaring at me, she said, "I needed that, you know."

"No, you didn't. I've seen every square inch of your body from half a dozen vantage points, Summer. Trust me. You don't have to cover yourself around me."

A blush crept over her cheeks, and she smiled shyly. "I'm going to take a shower."

And with that, she hurried away to the bathroom. I had to admit, I liked the view as much as I'd enjoyed everything else with her. And I'd been right. That nice girl had been a freak in private.

Leaning back against the headboard, I put my hands behind my head and thought about how to proceed with my plan. It had gone a little faster than I'd intended, no doubt. I'd figured we'd take it slow, get to know one another, and then she could meet the family. Since we'd launched into warp drive last night, I needed to figure out how to go from here. The end game remained the same. I needed her to help me convince my family I'd settled down with a nice girl.

All that had changed was finding out that behind closed doors, my nice girl was the best sex I'd ever had. I'd heard stories about nice girls rocking it in bed, but I'd assumed that was just lame guys lying to make up for the fact that they couldn't get models to sleep with them.

Everything I thought was wrong.

Maybe it was because she ate like a normal human being, but Summer had more energy during sex than any model I'd been with. It had been too damn long since I slept with a woman who could fuck for hours. She'd been a little self-conscious about her body at first, but she had no reason to be. So she was a little soft around the middle? I'd never really been crazy about how thin most of the women I slept with were anyway.

And even though I had a feeling most guys wouldn't believe me, my sexual escapades with models hadn't been as exciting as most people would have thought. Women used to being worshipped as gorgeous creatures tended to be pretty damn selfish in bed, sad to report. The sex was good, but it rarely made it to great.

Summer didn't suffer from that lack of interest in her partner, though. I'd forgotten how good a woman's mouth on my cock felt, but a few seconds of her going down on me brought it all back. Even thinking about it as I sat there in bed while she showered made me rock hard and ready for another round with her.

So the plan would continue, and it would include the added benefit of a nice girl who offered mind-blowing sex. I didn't think my life could get better, but I'd been wrong about that too. I had to give it to myself. Not only was my plan brilliant, and the person who came up with it equally as amazing, but my choice of Summer to join me in my plan was nothing short of genius.

This was going to work out beautifully.

✦   ✦   ✦

TWENTY HOURS LATER, THE STONE company plane landed at Teterboro Airport in New Jersey. In that time, Summer and I got to know each other better than I knew practically anyone but my best friend and my sisters. I found out she cries at sad movies and then apologizes for being silly and crying, which was way more charming than I would have thought it could be. I found out turbulence terrifies her, but she doesn't cry when she's scared.

And to my surprise, I found out that it was possible to spend nearly an entire day with a woman and have a good time that didn't include being in bed with her. I couldn't remember the last time I enjoyed being with someone as much as I did with Summer on that flight. We laughed, she cried at a few movies, and it felt like I'd known her all my life.

I was sorry our time alone ended, but I planned to have more. But as she prepared to leave, she turned toward me and took a sledgehammer to all my plans.

"I need you to promise me you won't tell anyone what happened between us, okay, Ethan?"

Her brown eyes pleaded more than her words, but I sat there stunned. Was she embarrassed that we'd slept together? Women usually wanted to tell the world they'd spent the night with me, and now Summer was saying she wanted to keep it a secret, like it was something wrong.

My ego didn't appreciate the hit, and even more, what Summer wanted threatened everything I needed her for. I couldn't decide if I was offended or disappointed.

"Why?"

A sheepish look came over her face, and she looked down at the floor, avoiding my gaze. "Because if my boss found out, she'd fire me."

Then she lifted her head and added, "I can't imagine keeping this quiet will bother you. I never expected to see you again after last night anyway.”

Fuck. Now I definitely felt insulted. Even more, I felt my plan begin to crumble around me. My mind raced. She wanted to keep our rendezvous quiet, and I needed her to make my family believe I'd found a nice girl.

Then an answer came to me. It wasn't nice, but then again, I never claimed to be nice.

“I'll keep what we did quiet if you do something for me.”

She looked hurt as she waited to hear what I wanted from her. “What could I do for you? You have everything and I have next to nothing, compared to you.”

That she thought I was such a dick that I wouldn't want to see her again after our night of incredible sex and then nearly a whole day with just the two of us together on the flight back stung, but I couldn't let hurt feelings get in the way.

“I want you to meet my family. Maybe once or twice you could come out to the house with me.”

“Why?”

Taking a deep breath, I sat back in my chair and confessed the truth. “I need you to make them think I've settled down with a nice girl. If they think we're together and happy, they'll leave me alone and I can live my life as I want to. You do that for me, and I promise your boss will never find out about the night we spent together.”

Now she looked even more hurt. Shaking her head like she couldn't believe what she'd heard, she asked, “Is that why you followed me up to my room? You wanted me to fall for you after a night of great sex so you could pretend to your family that you cared for me?”

“No, not exactly. I didn't plan on sleeping with you, Summer. I just wanted to get to know you so you'd help me get my family off my back.”

“Then why are you blackmailing me with telling my boss?”

Clearly, this situation had gotten away from me, so I stood up and walked over to her. Taking her hand, I tried to explain. "I'm not blackmailing you. I had just hoped you'd help me. You'd have a good time, I'd have a good time, and everyone would be happy."

Her eyes filled with tears, and I thought she'd begin to cry, but then she took a deep breath and forced herself to smile. "Fine. Then I have a demand. If you're going to be pretending to be with me, you can't be with any other women. I won't be made a fool of simply because you want to lie to your family."

She'd forced my hand, so I had little choice but to agree. But it would only be for a month or so. That didn't sound too bad.

"Deal. While we're a pretend couple, I won't go with any other women. But you can't go with any other men, either."

Summer pulled her hand away and shrugged. "You're lucky you caught me between boyfriends. So when does this whole charade begin?"

Knowing my father would question the pilot like he always did after every time I used the plane, I smiled. "Right now. Make sure when I kiss you as we get off you make it look good."

She pointed to her bag and said, "Well, then any boyfriend of mine would carry my luggage. If we're going to do this, we might as well do it all the way, right?"

Happy to act like a gentleman since she'd agreed to my plan, I smiled and lifted her bag as she watched. "As you wish, honey."

CHAPTER SIX

SUMMER

As I waited for Ethan to come around to my side of the car, I questioned why I'd ever agreed to any of this lie in the first place. True, if Julia found out what I'd done, she might fire me and I'd be penniless, but I felt like a complete fraud coming out to meet Tristan and Nina Stone and pretending to be their son's girlfriend.

For his part, he seemed to be as at ease with lying to them as he was with everything else. Nothing ruffled this guy's feathers. Maybe that was because he'd lived such a charmed life, if the looks of the enormous house just outside the car was any indication.

I'd never known anyone who lived in such an opulent home that it required a gate and a guard to enter like the Stones' estate did. I assumed that came along with the billionaire lifestyle, something I knew nothing of.

The car door opened, and Ethan smiled down at me as he extended his hand to help me out. "Welcome to the Stone Family Compound."

Hesitating, I thought to myself I'd never known anyone who called their home a compound.

I took his hand and joined him, gawking at the sheer grandeur of the house as he closed the door and happily began guiding me toward the front door. Clearly, he was used to all this splendor, but I wasn't, and I suddenly became quite aware that I didn't fit in there.

"Ethan, maybe this wasn't a good idea. I feel really out of

place," I said as I literally began dragging my feet along the sidewalk.

"You're perfect. Don't worry. Just remember that we've been dating for two weeks since the Australia shoot. I'll do most of the talking. You just have to look like you're really into me."

I rolled my eyes. God, why had I agreed to this?

"You mean like gazing at you longingly when your parents are watching?" I asked sarcastically.

He shook his head and cringed. "Let's go easy on the gazing longingly stuff. That might feel weird in front of my parents. How about just trying to look like I don't disgust you, which is how you look right about now."

That made me feel bad, so I looked down at the ground and my lame old black shoes I wore for every special occasion. "I just wonder if they're going to know this is all a lie because of how I look. I mean, I don't look like anyone a billionaire's son would date."

Ethan lifted my chin with his forefinger, and I saw him smiling at me. "Don't put yourself down like that. You're a nice girl from Philly. They're going to love you. You'll be lucky if you escape this dinner without my mother picking out her mother-of-the-groom dress."

He took my hand and led me to the front door, but with each step I knew what was wrong. Well, besides the lying. For the past two weeks, I'd pretended to be Ethan's girlfriend, which meant little other than talking a couple times on the phone for a few minutes to arrange this dinner tonight and driving up here from the city. It cost me nothing but my ethics to do this, but I wanted more.

I wanted him to like me for being a nice girl from a town outside Philly, not just his mother. I wanted him to genuinely like me and not just put on a show pretending to care.

Oh, God. This was bad. I was falling for Ethan Stone.

And at that moment, the front door opened and I saw a beautiful woman with shoulder-length brown hair and beautiful blue eyes beaming a smile and a man no less stunning who couldn't deny being Ethan's father, even if he wanted to, they looked so much alike.

Talented, gorgeous, and wealthy, Tristan and Nina Stone welcomed me into their home, and what was I going to give them in return?

Lies.

And the biggest lie wasn't me pretending to be their son's girlfriend.

CHAPTER SEVEN

ETHAN

JUST AS I PREDICTED, MY parents adored Summer from the moment she walked through the door. My mother fawned over her like she was some kind of movie star. I didn't remember ever seeing my mother fangirl over anyone, but she did for Summer.

Even the always cool Tristan Stone turned on his charm and seemed to take a real shine to her. That was saying something since the last time my father had mentioned anything to me about women, he'd snarled and said, "Maybe you can find someone who doesn't look like she's just left the club five minutes before you're seen in public with her."

While I thought that was pretty shitty of him to say, I had been in my dancer phase at the time, so maybe he wasn't entirely wrong.

But with Summer, even he seemed to approve.

Dinner went off without a hitch, and almost on cue as my parents began their after-dinner conversation, I announced we'd have to leave. "Well, it's been great, but we need to get back to the city. Summer's job requires her to be practically on call twenty-four seven."

I had no idea if that was the truth. Hell, all I knew about her boss was she treated Summer like shit, and in turn, her assistant hated her. But whatever it took to get out of that house before anyone else showed up worked for me.

My mother's legendary pout came out as soon as I finished speaking. "No, you can't. Tressa is due here any minute, and I know she'd be so disappointed if you don't stay to at least say hi. Your sisters and we miss seeing you, Ethan, and I'm sure she'd like to meet Summer."

The last thing I wanted was for Tressa to be involved in this at all. I loved my sister, but she had a nose for bullshit that might blow the whole lie for me.

"Another time," I said as I stood from the table and tugged on Summer's arm for her to do the same.

But I'd waited too long.

Behind me, I heard Tressa yell from the hallway, "Anyone home? I'm not too late, am I?"

"We're in here, honey," my mother called out as she stood up to cut a piece of roast beef for my sister.

I looked down at Summer, who had no idea what had just happened, and quickly sat down. Leaning over, I whispered in her ear, "Now might be a good time to start that gazing longingly business. My sister Tressa is a much harder sell than my parents."

Summer smiled, but I saw fear in her eyes. She had every reason to be afraid. Tressa was a pain in the ass and would like nothing more than to expose my lie right there at dinner, no matter who she had to humiliate in addition to me.

My sister appeared in the doorway and stopped dead. Smiling in that way that made her look menacing, she said, "I'm so glad I didn't miss all the fun. I'm starving, and I'm thrilled I got here in time."

"We were just talking to Ethan and Summer about Christmas. It's been unseasonably warm, so we're hoping to get some snow, even if it's just for the holiday," my father explained, unaware that Summer and I wouldn't even be together by that time.

Christmas was nearly four weeks away. I planned to be single and heartbroken by then.

Tressa sat down next to Summer and excitedly said, "So this is my brother's girlfriend. It's so nice to meet you. I never know what to expect with Ethan, but I have to say you're lovely."

As the two of them talked and became friendly, I thought my head might explode as I waited for Tressa to say something terrible meant to humiliate me. It was what she did best when it came to me, so to think I'd make it through this get-together unscathed was expecting too much.

Better for me to escape while I could.

I picked up my plate and silverware and said, "Let me clear the table for you, Mom."

Everyone stopped speaking and turned to look at me like I'd just announced I planned to move to Jupiter. Not surprisingly since I didn't exactly offer to do things like that ever.

"That's so nice of you, honey," my mother said, beaming her happiness.

Whatever it took to get away from that table and the inevitable nightmare that would ensue if I remained.

I quickly gathered up the empty dishes while my mother raved about what a good son I was, and as I walked out of the dining room toward the kitchen, I heard my father say, "I think I'll help Ethan with the dishes."

With my hands full, I found a place on the counter to put everything and tried to think of a way to get Summer away from my family and quick. My father walked into the kitchen with his plate and, without a word, stacked his on the others.

Maybe I'd get away with at least not having to discuss my new relationship with him.

"Ethan, I'm impressed with Summer. She's a very nice girl."

Damn. No escape for me.

Without looking at him, I nodded. "Yeah, she's great. I knew you and Mom would love her."

"A pretty brunette from outside Philadelphia who works in the city. It's almost as if you ordered her from Central Casting," he said in a low voice behind me.

I sensed a hint of suspicion in his tone, but I wasn't sure. Turning around, I studied his expression. He wore that typical

Tristan Stone look I'd seen all my life. Emotionless, his face didn't give any hints to what he thought, but in his dark eyes so similar to mine, I saw some clue how he felt.

Was that pride I saw in them?

"You like her then?" I asked, curious what he thought of Summer suddenly.

A wry smile slowly spread across his lips. "How could I not? I married a nice girl with long brown hair from outside of Philly who gave me three wonderful children and the happiest years of my life. Of course, I want that for you, too, son."

Unable to stifle a chuckle at the thought that he already had me married with children like him, I said, "Well, let's not rush things. Summer's a nice girl, but we haven't even been going out six months yet."

My father patted me on the shoulder and smiled. "Let's hope it works out. I know your mother would be over the moon to see you with a girl like Summer."

As he walked out to return to the dining room, I felt a little bad that all of this with Summer wasn't real. I hadn't seen my father look at me like that in a long time, and I liked making my mother happy.

And if I was a couple years older, I might want to settle down with someone like Summer. I couldn't imagine doing that with anyone else.

I stood there thinking about how that could be a good thing and didn't see Tressa walk into the room. She stopped in front of me and pointed her finger directly at my face.

"Just so you know, I'm not buying whatever this whole thing is with you and that lovely creature you're claiming to be your girlfriend."

How was it possible that someone could look so much like me and be so goddamned different?

"There's nothing to buy, Tress. Summer and I have been together for about two weeks. It's pretty simple. Even you can understand that."

She shook her head before rolling her eyes. "What I understand is this. That girl is so out of your league that I'm thinking you hired her to put on that show out there."

"Whatever. You have no idea what you're talking about," I said as I turned to leave.

But that didn't stop her.

"There's no way someone like her would willingly go with you. Not unless she's been living under a rock for the past few years and has no idea of what you've been up to. The strippers, the models, the wannabes. All of them are enough to send someone like her running for the hills. But since I know she hasn't been under a rock for all your exploits, I have to assume she's either stupid or naïve. The problem is just from talking to her for a few minutes I can tell she's neither. That leaves only one other choice. This is all a lie for Mom and Dad's benefit. You're probably holding something over that poor girl's head so she'll join you in this farce."

I'd never exactly understood how the bond between triplets worked. Ever since we were children, I could literally feel when Diana was sad, even if she was miles away. Tressa never felt sad, but I knew her emotions as well as my own from as far back as I could remember. Mind reading, however, had never been part of any of our abilities. I had no idea how she figured out what I was up to, but I had no intention of letting her ruin my plan.

"Maybe she's just not judgmental like you. Ever think of that?"

Tressa smiled and shook her head. "It's not judgmental to not want to date a man-whore, Ethan. It's just common sense for nice girls, and that girl in there is every bit a nice girl. I'm going to give you fair warning. Mom and Dad like her, and I do, too, and I've only known her for a few minutes. Whatever you're up to, try to remember that real women—you know, the kind who aren't Barbie dolls—have feelings that can be hurt with your games. That includes your mother, too. Remember that."

"Whatever, Tress. I'm glad you like her."

I returned to the dining room and sat down next to Summer as my sister's words echoed in my head. Nobody was going to get hurt because we both knew what we were up to.

The problem was I couldn't help notice the way I got a dull ache in my chest when I thought about her being hurt. I liked Summer, and if I wanted to date just one woman, I could see me choosing her. She had a lot of what I looked for in someone, and as I'd seen tonight, she was able to do something no one else had ever been able to accomplish.

She impressed my parents and made my father look at me with pride in his eyes.

But I didn't want to be with just one woman. Not yet anyway.

WE SAID NEXT TO NOTHING all the way back to the city, and when I pulled up in front of her apartment building, she practically jumped out of the car. All I got was a quick goodbye and she was off.

I quickly found a parking spot and followed her up the front stairs. She was in such a hurry I barely caught her before she got inside.

"Hey, what's up?"

She didn't look at me and shook her head. "Nothing. I have to get upstairs."

Before she could get away, I grabbed her arm to stop her. "Summer, is something wrong?"

"No." She hesitated for a moment and then turned to face me. "Yes, actually. I don't want to do this anymore. You have a great family that cares about you. I don't want to be a part of lying to them anymore. You can tell my boss what happened if you feel you have to, but I'm out. Go find someone else to parade in front of your family, Ethan."

"So does this mean I won't see you anymore?" I asked as that ache in my chest returned.

Summer looked confused by the question. "Why would we see each other anymore? I was never the kind of person you'd date. You wanted me because I was exactly the kind of girl your family thinks you should be with. But you don't want to be with me. You want models who look good or dancers who look sexy. I'm not either of those kinds of women. I'm just me, Summer, a smart, nice girl who guys like you never think twice about after they sleep with them."

"Can't we at least be friends and still hang out?"

"Do you mean hang out like get-together-and-fuck kind of friends?" she asked with disgust.

"No. I just meant friends. I liked hanging out with you on the plane that day and at my parents' house for dinner tonight."

Sadness filled her eyes, and she frowned. "Guys like you don't have female friends, Ethan. I don't think I'm the right kind of person to play these games. I had a great time that night, and it was fun getting to know you on the plane ride back. Maybe we should just leave it at that and go back to our lives."

I watched her open the door to her building and walk inside as a feeling of emptiness came over me. It would be nothing for me to find a woman to spend time with for the night, so why did Summer not wanting to see me ever again bother me so much?

Unsure about everything I was feeling, I knew one thing. I didn't want to lose Summer from my life. There had to be a way we could still spend time together.

As she waited for the elevator in the lobby, I banged on the glass door to get her attention. I didn't know what to say when she came back, but I had to do something to change this. She heard me pounding on the door and walked over to open it.

"What?"

"I don't know. I just don't like the idea of never seeing you again."

"Ethan, this city is full of women who would give their left arms to be with you. You won't be alone for long."

She really did have an exaggerated view of how appealing I was to the opposite sex. I couldn't help but smile.

"I don't know about all of them. I just know I want to be with you."

"Why?"

Damnit, why did she have to ask so many questions? "I don't know why. I just like being around you."

"So what do you want to do? Come up to my apartment and get me into bed? Is that it? Because I don't have any interest in being any guy's booty call."

"No. I just want to hang out. Maybe watch a movie or something like we did on the plane."

"And you want to do this with me instead of hooking up with some model to have sex?" she asked, her eyes wide in disbelief.

I couldn't explain it, either. Until just a few minutes before, I wanted nothing more than to have my plan work and live my life as I wanted to. But now I wanted something else.

Now I wanted Summer.

"Yeah. You can even pick the movie like on the plane."

She seemed to think about it for a moment, and then she gave me one of her shy smiles. "Okay. Just a movie."

Walking with her toward the elevator, I didn't know why not having Summer in my life bothered me so much. I just knew it did.

So for tonight, we'd do a movie. And next time, maybe it would be something more. This whole nice-girl thing was completely foreign to me, so I had no idea what would happen.

All I knew was I liked my life more with Summer in it than not. Now I just had to not screw things up. The problem was that was easier said than done considering my history.

CHAPTER EIGHT
SUMMER

FROM BEHIND ME, ETHAN NUZZLED my neck as I tried to find the number for that pizza place we both liked but could never remember the name. Of course, that made ordering a hundred times harder.

"Giuseppe's. That's the name, I think," he said against the shell of my ear. "Look for Giuseppe's."

The touch of his lips on my skin tickled, and I rolled my shoulders as I giggled. "I tried that already. No good. I think it was Nardone's."

He pulled me to him and hugged me around my waist. "That doesn't ring a bell. Why don't we cook again tonight?"

His suggestion made me laugh. Turning in his hold, I looked up at him and saw he was serious. "Ethan, the last time we tried that, we got nothing cooked and ended up having sex right here in the kitchen. I was still finding rice in my hair at work the next day."

"I know. It was fun," he said, smiling wickedly. "I've got an even better idea. Let's fly to Italy and get pizza made by actual Italians."

"What? Are you crazy?"

"Maybe, but that doesn't mean it isn't a good idea. The Stone Worldwide plane isn't being used at the moment, so why not?"

"Because I have work tomorrow, for one."

He shook his head and then kissed me. "Call in sick."

"I'll starve to death if I have to wait that long to get food, for two."

"Okay, then. Let's head to Chicago and get deep dish pizza. That wouldn't take long."

The way he said that with such eagerness and wonder in his eyes made it hard to say no to him. He'd taken me on a few impromptu trips in the month we'd been together, like New Orleans for the weekend and Dallas for an overnight adventure one Friday night. I loved how spontaneous he could be. That's why I hated saying no to his suggestions now.

But tonight I had to. I hadn't eaten all day, and if I didn't get some food in my stomach soon, I'd pass out.

I grabbed his shirt in both hands and pulled on it as I pretended to be a woman on the edge. "I need food, man! I can't remember the last time I ate, so if I don't consume something in the next half hour, you're going to find me laid out on the floor, and not in the good way."

Ethan smiled, finally convinced of how dire my hunger situation had gotten. "Okay. Let's forget about that pizza place and try the one I saw about two blocks away. At least I know the name of that one. Vincenzo's. So get them going on the pizza, and instead of waiting for delivery, I'll run for it. That way you can get food into your stomach sooner and not fade away on me. Sound good?"

I tapped my finger on the tip of his nose and leaned in to kiss him softly on the lips. "You know, you're not just a pretty face, Ethan Stone. Good looking and brilliant. It's a great combo."

Turning back toward the counter to make the call to Vincenzo's, I found myself pulled against his muscular body. He buried his face in the spot between my shoulder and chin and kissed my neck.

"Mmmm, I think I might just make a meal out of you," he teased.

"Dying here, Ethan. That means you'll have to explain to the police how badly you treated your girlfriend and how you starved her."

He stopped feasting on my neck for a moment before he planted one final kiss just below my ear. "Got it. I'm on a mission. Summer wants pizza, so pizza she will get. Call them and I'll head down there now so I can grab it as soon as it comes out of the oven."

"Thank you. I promise to repay you in trade later tonight," I said with a giggle as he walked toward my apartment door.

Without looking back, he said, "I'm going to keep you to your word, so be ready. Pizza and then wild sex. Just how Thursday nights should be."

I ordered our pizza the way we always got it—sausage and extra cheese—and root beer soda Ethan liked to drink whenever we got pizza before I sat down on the couch to wait for him and our dinner. It had been nearly four weeks since that night he stood outside banging on the front door to my apartment building to tell me he didn't want to never see me again after I reneged on our deal. For the first couple days, I had a hard time believing he wasn't coming around just for sex, so I held out for nearly two weeks to test him. He never complained or made a move toward sleeping together in all that time. We just hung out at my apartment watching movies at night after work, sometimes falling asleep together on the very spot where I now sat.

Of course, when I let him know I didn't expect us to never have sex again and that I would be open to the idea, he didn't wait. Not that I wanted him to. The man had the ability to make me forget my own name from the things he did to my body, so holding out for those two weeks had been practically torture.

But it had showed me something important about Ethan.

Not that we were rushing into anything. Neither one of us had said those three magic words, although if I had to tell the truth, I'd been in love with him since that night we spent together. I hadn't told him that, though, because even I didn't understand how I could possibly think that, but it was the truth.

Regardless of what we had or hadn't said about how we felt

about one another, every night we got together and he listened to me complain about Julia. When I asked him about his day, he usually gave me some vague answer about time between shoots or how he'd be leaving soon for another one and didn't want to think about it. Then we ate dinner before watching TV or a movie.

To some women, that happening night after night would be monotonous, but to me, spending so much time with him made me happy. In two days, it would be a month we were together, but it felt like I'd known him forever. He made me smile when I felt like life was beating me up at work. When we made love, he worked to please me as much as I did him.

Everything was perfect.

Closing my eyes, I thought about him grabbing the pizza and soda off the counter at Vincenzo's and running back, the bottles shaking up and down with every step so when he opened one for each of us, they would fizz all over the counter like they did every time he ran out for food. I'd be ready with a roll of paper towels like I had since that first time he made soda run all over my kitchen and my feet stuck to the floor for two days, even after I mopped three times. He'd smile and apologize, making that same joke about how carbonation wasn't his friend as he scrambled to stop the soda from exploding out from the top of the bottles.

My phone buzzed behind me on the kitchen counter, so I jumped up to grab it just in case it was him texting. Maybe Vincenzo's had run out of root beer or they didn't have sausage for the pizza.

I looked down at my screen and saw a message from Ethan. Opening it, I read the words but didn't understand their meaning.

I'll be there. Don't worry. It's okay. I miss you too.

What did he mean by that?

Scrolling through our texts from the past few days, I tried to remember if I had messaged him anything that would warrant that text back to me. I found nothing.

"The pizza man has returned!" Ethan announced a minute later as he came through the front door. "I swear I didn't shake up the soda this time, so you don't have to worry about it spraying all over the place. I held it close to my body so it didn't get jostled all around."

I set my phone on the coffee table and headed toward the kitchen to get dinner. I'd ask him about that odd text after I got some food in me.

Ethan already had paper plates set out on the counter by the time I reached him. "Chow down. I can't have you fading away on me," he said before kissing me on the cheek.

As I lifted two slices of pizza out of the huge cardboard box, I inhaled the delicious smell of mozzarella cheese, sauce, and sausage. While Vincenzo's wasn't my favorite pizza place, tonight my dinner made my mouth water. The cheese began to slide off the crust, so I quickly plopped the slices down onto a paper plate just as I heard Ethan twist the top off one of the bottles of soda.

I barely had time to grab the roll of paper towels before I heard the all-too-familiar hiss of the carbonation escaping the bottle. Turning around, I watched as he hurriedly tried to retighten the top of the bottle, but it was no use. Soda ran down over his hands onto the floor as he moved left and right trying to find a place to set the bottle down.

"Sink!" I yelled, pointing toward it like he needed help finding the damn sink.

His eyes opened wide. "Right!"

He took two giant steps and reached the sink, but the damage was done. Looking behind him, he saw the trail of soda across the kitchen floor and frowned. "I swear I didn't think I shook the bottles at all this time, Summer. I don't know why, but carbonation just isn't my friend."

I kissed him and smiled. "It's okay, Ethan. It's sort of your thing with soda. It always happens, so it's okay."

"You said okay twice. I think that's the international sign that it's not okay," he said with a pout as he washed his hands and I mopped up the soda from the floor.

"You're lucky you're cute," I joked, tossing the sopping wet paper towels into the garbage before I ripped off another few to finish the job.

Ethan crouched down and kissed me on the lips. "I also rock your world in bed. Don't forget that. I like to think you consider that one of my saving graces at times like this."

I finished cleaning the floor and rolled my eyes. "My landlord should be thanking you. This floor has been the cleanest it's ever been since I began seeing you. I don't think I did a thing with it all last year."

"You send him to me if he gives you any problems. I'll explain I'm the klutz with soda, not you. Now you better get some pizza into you," he said as he stood and held out his hand to help me up.

In all the sticky commotion, I'd forgotten about eating, but now that he mentioned it, I felt lightheaded as I stood. "Yeah, I better. That whole passing out thing wasn't just a threat."

We sat down on the couch with our plates of pizza and two glasses of root beer that were quickly going flat and ate like we did every night. I thought about bringing up the strange text I'd gotten, but before I could, Ethan suddenly stood up and tossed his paper plate in the garbage.

"Hey, I just remembered I have to deal with something back at my apartment. Give me a couple hours and I'll be back. If I'm not back by eight-thirty, just start the movie without me, but I promise I'll be back before you fall asleep."

Nothing in his voice sounded different than any other time, but every cell in my body immediately went on red alert. He was lying. But why?

"What do you mean? What do you have to do?" I asked, staring up at him as I watched his expression carefully in the hopes that my gut feeling was wrong.

"Just apartment stuff. I had a problem with my lock, and the owner of the building is coming over."

Nothing about that sounded right. What was he lying about? "At seven o'clock at night?"

He looked down at the floor and sheepishly answered, "Yeah. You know how busy everyone is."

Never before had Ethan sounded so distant when he spoke to me. If anything, he always chose details over vagueness.

I reached for my phone and found the text he'd sent me a short while ago. Reading it, I said, "While you were gone, I got this strange message. It came from your phone, Ethan. It says, 'I'll be there. Don't worry. It's okay. I miss you too.' What's that mean?"

Looking up, I saw guilt written all over his face and knew right then and there. He was lying about another woman. He shook his head and shrugged like he didn't know what I was talking about, but he knew. I saw it in his eyes.

He knew and he was lying to me.

My chest began to hurt like I was suffocating and I couldn't get enough air into my lungs. My heartbeat pounded in my ears as my emotions began to spin out of control.

I jumped up off the couch and marched over to him. Holding my phone up in front of his face, I struggled to hold back the tears as I said, "You didn't mean to send this message to me. You meant for it to go to someone else, didn't you?"

"Summer, texts and things get mixed up all the time. The world is full of about half a billion cell phones, so it's not surprising. It's not a big deal. I'll be back from my apartment in a couple hours. I promise. Just wait for me. I'll be back."

"Why are you lying to me, Ethan? I can see it written all over your face. The guilt is filling your eyes. You're lying because you're going to see someone else. That's what that message was about. You're going to some other woman's place, someone you miss, right?"

He shook his head and forced himself to smile. "No. I just have to go back to my apartment for a little while. That's it."

I didn't believe him. Reaching around his back, I grabbed his phone out of his pants pocket and began to search through his messages. I'd never done anything like that before with anyone else in my life, but being told such a bald-faced lie made thinking rationally next to impossible. Seeing became difficult as tears filled my eyes, so I couldn't read the names of all the people he'd sent texts to.

"Summer, don't do this. I swear I'm not with anyone else. I swear. You just have to believe me. Now give me back my phone."

Before I could turn away to try to read more names, he snatched it from my hold and stuffed the phone back into his pocket. Humiliated and hurt, I couldn't stop myself from crying.

Tears ran down my cheeks, and I sobbed, "Why would you do this? Was I always just a fool you toyed with? There's been other women the whole time, hasn't there?"

Once more, he shook his head, but this time he tried to reach out to me. I pushed him away as he said, "No! Summer, there's only you. When the hell would I have time to spend with anyone else? I'm here or we're at my place every night. We spend every single night together."

The pleading sound of his words confused me as much as the truth in what he said. We did spend every night together. I didn't know how he fit in the other women, or maybe it was just this one other woman who missed him and whom he missed too. I didn't know. All I knew was he was lying to me, and it hurt so much I didn't know what to do.

"I don't believe you. You sent that text thinking you were sending it to someone else. Someone you miss. And now you're lying to get the chance to go to her. Tell me I'm wrong."

Ethan hung his head and quietly answered. "Summer, I'm not with anyone else. I swear."

"You can't even look at me when you say that! And don't think I didn't notice that you didn't say I was wrong that you're going to see whoever this person is."

Lifting his head, he looked at me with sadness in his eyes. "I wouldn't do that to you. There's no one else, but I don't see how I can make you believe me."

"Then just go. Go and don't come back!" I sobbed, practically screaming the last few words.

For a long moment, it felt like time stood still as the two of us didn't move. All I wanted him to do was tell me the truth, and all he wanted me to do was believe him. But neither of those things happened.

Before he turned to leave, he sighed and quietly said, "I'm sorry, Summer."

And then he was gone.

CHAPTER NINE

ETHAN

THE CONFERENCE ROOM HAD THE largest windows I'd ever seen in my life. Unfortunately, they didn't look out on much. The view of the building next to us wasn't very good since it was just a basic skyscraper like any other, but it teased of life going on that I was missing. Even seated on the side of the table away from the windows, I thought about how easy it would be for someone to push their chair back too hard and crash into the glass. Would it break and send the person and the chair falling fifteen floors to the ground? I had no idea, but at least that person would be free of this never-ending meeting.

As some guy talked about a quarterly this or projection that, I scanned the people in the room. I saw nothing but an array of dark business suits and a rainbow of dress shirts with the singular job of making those suits look like they didn't belong on pall bearers. My eyes fixed on Limmon's red and black geometric tie as he spoke at the other end of the table. It wasn't attractive, per se, but it had the effect of mesmerizing me for at least a few seconds so I could forget where I was for the briefest of time.

He didn't look like he had enough style to pick that. His wife probably bought it for him. Fuck, she probably laid out his clothes every morning.

The booming sound of a hand slamming onto the cherry wood table snapped me out of my daydream about Limmon's frumpy wife carefully putting out his clothes on their bed, and I looked to see my sister Tressa staring down the table at me. I had no idea what had made her so upset, but at the moment, I sensed it was my lack of interest in her underling's presentation.

"Thank you, Ken. Does anyone have any questions?" she asked, looking directly at me.

I had no questions. At least I had none that involved whatever Ken Limmon spent his time doing at Stone Worldwide.

Actually, I did have a question. What the hell did any of these people do before working at my father's company to actually be here? Did they go to college and dream of someday working at a job like this, happy to spend their days in steel buildings with enormous windows that look out on other steel buildings talking about quarterly and yearly projections or did they just find themselves here after a series of unfortunate mistakes like I did?

As the people around me began to talk amongst themselves, my mind wandered back to how it all went wrong and I ended up dressed in a dark grey suit looking like my father did nearly every day I'd been alive. I had a life people envied, and because of a few horrible choices, it all vanished.

The men and women around me stood up out of their chairs, rousing me from my fantasy of being on that beach in Australia living the kind of life I wanted. I saw one of Tressa's assistants shoot me a nasty look as she and my sister's other minions filed out of the conference room, leaving me sitting there staring out those huge windows at the world outside them.

"I'm impressed with how good you are at sleeping with your eyes open, Ethan."

My sister stood with her arms folded at the end of the table next to my father, the two of them staring down at me with far different looks in their eyes. Tressa's said that she hated how little I thought of her meetings, but my father's had a softer, almost hopeful look in them. He wanted me to succeed here at Stone Worldwide more than he could put into words, and I hated that I would disappoint him. Again.

Tressa looked every bit like the kind of person he wanted me to be. She wore that black business suit like a champ. The red blouse underneath exuded power and success, and with her gorgeous black hair and dark eyes, she looked like a million bucks. I'd never tell her, but she was the epitome of what this company needed after our father decided to leave it.

Why he'd want me to be anywhere near it still remained a mystery.

Before I could answer her jab, she turned on her four inch black heels with the red soles and marched out of the room, leaving my father and me alone. For a long moment, we stared at each other like neither one of us knew what to say. We'd known each other for over twenty-five years, and yet there seemed times when we felt more like strangers than father and son.

"How are you getting along with the ad division?" he asked with the clearest sense of hope in his voice. That hope only made how I truly felt even worse.

I hated the ad division. I wasn't an advertising guy. None of them possessed an ounce of creativity, and they only thought of money. But I didn't have a choice, so I nodded and forced a smile. "Great. They're a great group of people. I'm sure we'll be running like a well-oiled machine in no time."

My father's expression darkened just enough to let me know he was worried. "It's only been a month, Ethan. Give them a chance. They're good people. Some of them have been with this company nearly as long as you've been alive."

I hoped that the abject desperation that last sentence made me feel didn't show all over my face. Over a quarter century in this job? I'd kill myself before I made it a tenth of the way through that.

"Sure, Dad," I said, tugging at my tie that had felt like a noose around my neck from the moment I put it on this morning.

"Your mother wanted me to ask you if you'd like to come to the house for dinner this Friday."

I didn't know if I could spend any time around my mother,

especially since she was about to have a show of her sculpture pieces. I wasn't sure I could handle being around art now.

"I don't know. I'll give her a call and talk to her," I said as I moved to leave the conference room. The place felt like a prison, as I always thought it would.

"She loves when you come out to the house. This show coming up means a lot to her, and I know she'd love to talk to you about it. I think she's got some nerves about the whole thing. You know how she is."

That only made things worse. I wanted to support my mother in everything she did. She was the entire reason I ever explored anything artistic. When my father wanted me to play sports in school, she stood at his side explaining that she believed art was just as important as other extracurricular activities. I ended up going out for the football team, and I loved it, just like he said I would. But I loved the art classes she found for me too, so it tore me up not being able to share her joy about this upcoming show because of what happened.

As I headed toward the door, my father said, "Son, it's for the best. This company was always going to be my legacy for you and your sisters."

Angry at the thought of spending the rest of my life in a suit stuck inside a ten by ten office, I spun around and asked, "And how does Diana feel about that, Dad? Because we know how Tressa feels, and unless you're blind, you know how I feel about it. But what about Diana? Do you think she'll ever be able to fit in here at Stone Worldwide? How is it possible that you married someone like Mom and you can't imagine us ever being anything like her?"

He opened his mouth to speak but closed it and sighed like he did whenever he wanted to say something that would only result in an argument. "There are people in this world who would kill to have the opportunities you've had. I swore when you were born that I would do everything in my power to make sure you had the best life possible, and I've kept that promise year after year without fail."

His ability to compartmentalize how he felt about Diana and me never ceased to amaze me. "We don't fit in here, Dad. Tressa does because she loves it, but we don't. Has how Diana and I feel ever figured into your plans for the future?"

For a moment, he remained silent and merely frowned before saying what he hadn't since everything happened with me. "You're here now because as much as I didn't think it was a good idea, I agreed with your mother that you should have a chance to prove yourself with your talent. It's not my fault what happened, Ethan. For that, you need to look in the mirror. Don't punish your mother and me and everyone here for your mistakes."

And that, right there, hurt the most. My father knew that. I didn't deny I'd made mistakes. I'd made a metric shit ton of them, much to his disappointment. What hurt was that he didn't understand that I didn't belong there.

"You can't even talk about her, can you?" I asked, knowing I was way out of line and not giving a damn.

He looked at me and the hurt in my father's brown eyes hit me like knives stabbing my chest. In a low, sad voice, he said, "Let me know if you need anything, Ethan."

I walked out of the conference room and marched back to my office two floors down, careful to avoid Tressa and her office at the other end of the hall. The last thing I wanted was to deal with her, a younger and prettier version of Tristan Stone.

Staring out my office window, I loosened my tie and tossed it across my desk onto a chair. I couldn't spend the rest of my days in this building. It would kill me.

Lost in thought, I didn't hear Tressa come into my office. Looking up, I was disgusted to see her standing there in her power suit and deep red lipstick that made her look like she'd just devoured one of my co-workers. "What do you want? Don't you have some minion to torture or someone's dreams to crush?"

She rewarded me with her usual sneer. "Still wallowing in self-pity, I see. If there's one thing I appreciate about you, Ethan, it's that you can always be counted on to be so self-involved that you don't notice something, even if it's right under your nose."

I hated my sister's way of speaking in riddles. "Christ, Tressa. Do you do this to your employees? They must hate you."

She looked down at me with an expression of pure smugness. "In fact, my employees love me just like they love our father because we clearly want this company to succeed and everyone to benefit, not just ourselves. If you weren't so self-absorbed, you'd see that. But as much fun as it is talking with you about your problems, I didn't come in here for this. I want to talk to you about something serious."

Right there was the main problem I had with Tressa. Everything was serious, and everything was about business. Talk about people being complete opposites.

"And what would that be? Did Stone Worldwide stock take a tumble this morning at the opening bell?" I asked as I leaned back in my chair to stare up at the ceiling.

"No, you jackass. And where the hell did you get the idea that it's polite or even civil to not look people in the eye when they're speaking to you?"

Startled by her anger, I directed my focus toward her. She really did come in here to talk about something serious. Or at least it appeared serious to her, if the way her dark eyes flashing was any indication.

"Fine. What do you want to talk about?"

Tressa folded her arms across her chest and began pacing in front of my desk. "I think you know that I was no supporter of Daddy's bringing you here to work. Stone Worldwide means the world to me, Ethan, and it means nothing to you. Can we at least agree on that?"

Suddenly, I felt like a piece of shit. Maybe my father was right. Maybe I was the one to blame. "That feels a bit harsh. It doesn't mean nothing to me. I just don't want to spend the rest of my life doing this. I doubt you can understand that since you're all business, but some of us like me and Diana want different things out of life."

Tressa's head snapped around so she faced me. "Don't bring Diana into this. She has nothing to do with what we're talking about."

"Well, she never wanted to be a part—" I began to say, trying to explain that our other sister didn't want to spend her life running the family business either, but Tressa cut me off.

"Don't you think you've done enough when it comes to Diana's life, Ethan? Suffice it to say, she'll never have to worry about money or anything she could ever want. I'll make sure of that. But you, on the other hand, I have no interest in carrying for the rest of my days. You don't belong here, no matter how much our father wants to believe you do simply because you're his son. So I intend on making sure you don't stay here long."

My sister's reference to Diana made my chest painfully constrict like it always did when I thought of her, but I couldn't help but focus on what she said after that. I knew how much it bothered Tressa that our father had some paternal fantasy about his only son taking over the business when he had a perfectly wonderful child who could do wonders with Stone Worldwide. Not that he didn't think Tressa wasn't a terrific person to run the company, but he never mentioned her doing that without including me in his future plans, unfortunately.

"Planning on organizing a hostile takeover, sis?" I asked, only half-joking. Tressa Stone had ice water in her veins, and I could easily imagine her doing something pretty fucking awful to get me out of her hair here at Stone Worldwide.

My sister rolled her eyes. "You're always so melodramatic, Ethan. It must be the artistic temperament in you. No, I don't plan to do anything terrible to you, my dear brother. I'm here to propose a plan. You want out of here, and I want you out. So get back to your photography and try not making it a cover for sleeping with anything with legs. You prove to Daddy that you belong in that world, and I will make sure I support your choices with him one hundred percent. Deal?"

For a moment there, I'd had a real hope she'd get me thrown out of the building or something. Clearly in her desire to get rid of me, she hadn't thought this plan through very well.

"It wouldn't matter if I won an IPA or the National Geographic Photo Contest. He still wouldn't think I should spend the rest of my life doing what I love. You're going to have to think harder, Tress."

Frustrated, she stopped in front of my desk and grimaced. "You know, you had a good thing going there and you blew it. All you had to do was keep it in your pants, and you'd still be globetrotting today. At the very least, you should have kept things on the down low."

I couldn't help but straighten her out on the facts. I did not blow it. What happened wasn't all my fault.

"There were two people involved, you know. In fact, I'd say she had more to do with what happened than me. Some might say I was wrongly punished."

Tressa rolled her eyes at my statement. "Some would be morons then. You slept with that girl and she fell in love with you. Then you broke it off with her because you're a fool, which unfortunately is par for the course for your sex. That she chose not to cover your ass with her boss after you broke her heart isn't her fault. It's yours."

I didn't want to hear any more of this. I didn't actually believe it was Summer's fault I was stuck in this office and working for my family's business. I just didn't think it was all my fault.

"Do you hate all men, Tressa? Is that why you're still so very single?" I asked, feeling the desire to needle my sister for her unhelpful comments. She'd made a bad day worse.

My questions had the opposite effect, though, and she threw her head back in peals of laughter. "Don't be ridiculous. God, you artistic types are so emotional. I don't hate all men, Ethan. I love

Daddy and I love you. As for my being single, I know how to keep my personal affairs just that. Personal. You could learn a thing or two from me. You don't see anyone plastering the details of my sex life all over Page Six or any of those ridiculous gossip sites, and you can be sure I do just fine in that area."

My mind flashed the vision of my sister biting the head off some guy she'd just had sex with like some human version of a praying mantis. That would explain why there was never any gossip about her sex life.

Shuddering from the mere thought, I forced my brain to return to her initial reason for coming to see me. "Well, none of this means anything to me ever getting sprung from this prison. When Tristan Stone wants you to do something, you do it. You've lived as long as I have with him as your father. You should know that by now."

That truth seemed to deflate my sister a little. Scowling, she nodded. "True. Our father is a man who makes his wishes become reality, but I like to think I take after him in that regard, and I think you working here is one of the very few bad decisions he's made. Therefore, I'm going to rectify that. You need to do your part, though, so get that camera of yours out and start doing what you do best."

"And how do you know I won't tell him all about this plan of yours in the hopes that I might get in his good graces?" I asked as she headed toward the door.

Tressa stopped and slowly turned around. Smiling, she shook her head. "You know beauty, Ethan. You see things through the lens that most people will never see. I, on the other hand, know people. I know human nature, and I know there's no way you would tell him, and even if you did, you'd only upset him. Tristan Stone prides himself on a few things—the love he has for our mother, the three of us, and Stone Worldwide. You'd be a fool to underestimate how much he loves this company. So no, I don't believe you would tell him what we've spoken about today.

Contrary to common opinion, you're quite smart, Ethan. So get taking pictures."

I watched her walk out and couldn't help but wish her plan would work. I hadn't taken a single picture since the day I got the news that I'd been fired from *Belle* for fraternizing. As much as I wanted to think I could just pick up my camera and take great shots again, as I sat there in that office that felt like a jail cell, I wasn't sure anymore.

CHAPTER TEN

SUMMER

I HEARD THE MUSIC FROM half a block away, and instantly, my stomach clenched in disgust. My two roommates were at it again. Didn't those two ever sleep?

As I slowly made my way back to the apartment, I wondered what the group would look like tonight. For the past week, Amber and Elise had entertained a variety of guys who were a terrible mixture of hipster douchebags and beer connoisseurs. Or at least they thought they were. Each time they came to the apartment, they brought along a different brew and their endless knowledge of the drink. My roommates listened to them as if they were lecturing on the way to make a million dollars in a day, hanging on every word like it was gold. Then afterward, they drank all the beer and proceeded to spend the rest of their time offending everyone in the neighborhood.

Stopping in front of my building, I stared up at the apartment window. The loud music and laughter told me the beer lecture tonight had concluded early, and now they had moved on to the partying portion of the night. My cell phone would soon be ringing with calls from the rest of the residents of our building since somewhere along the way, I'd turned into the designated roommate.

Even if I wanted to try to forget how awful it felt after losing my job and my apartment and being forced to move in with Amber and Elise, each night made the misery fresh again. I tried to stay away from my temporary home as long as possible, but after a full day of job searching, a girl got worn-out and wanted to crawl into bed. Thankfully, I was dead tired all the time or I'd never get to sleep with the noise my roommates and their boyfriends du jour created.

I took a deep breath and exhaled slowly. *I can do this. This is only temporary. I'll get a job and then I'll be able to move somewhere else. This isn't that bad.*

From the apartment, I heard Elise yelp, "Brent, that's so wrong! I love it!"

I shuddered as my mind conjured up ideas about what I'd be walking into just a few minutes after my climb up the stairs to the third floor. To myself, I mumbled, "Please don't let it be anything sexual. Please, God, don't let it be that tonight."

On the second floor, I tried to avoid making eye contact with Angela Radisson, our neighbor directly beneath us, but it was no use. She'd had to deal with them for God only knew how long today, and she'd already had enough.

"Summer, I know they aren't your responsibility, but I just wanted to give you a head's up. The rest of the building has spoken to the landlord about eviction. I spoke up in your defense, but you know how people are. I'm sorry."

Her big blue eyes filled with sadness for me, which made all of this a tiny bit better. At least no one thought I was the problem.

I nodded and just shrugged. "Thanks. I guess I better get looking for a new place. If I can get them to tone it down tonight, I will, okay?" I said sheepishly as I began walking up toward the third floor.

"Cheer up, hon. Things can only get better," she said in a voice filled with forced optimism.

I didn't answer her. I had no idea if that was true. God, I hoped it was because if things got any worse, I didn't know if I'd be able to take it.

As I suspected, I walked into an apartment that stunk like beer and cheap cologne. The guys for the night looked like every other male they'd brought home—bad haircuts, douchebag beards that made them look like Amish wannabees, and cut-rate clothes. I didn't focus on their faces as I walked through the living room. I wouldn't likely see them again, so what was the point?

"Angela from the floor below says that the rest of the building is working to get us evicted," I said without a hint of emotion as I strolled past the foursome sitting on the couch.

"Why?" Amber asked in a high-pitched voice. "We pay our rent on time every month. What's the problem?"

The guy whose lap she sat on echoed her question before Elise said, "That takes months. I know about this kind of stuff. They won't be able to get rid of us as long as we pay our rent on time and don't cause problems, which we don't. So fuck 'em!"

Elise's guy liked her attitude about the whole thing and raised his can of beer in the air. "That's the way to be. Fuck them all!"

I didn't bother joining in their resistance efforts and continued on my way to my room. "Whatever. Night."

Closing the door behind me, I took a deep breath and fell onto the bed with my bag still slung across my body. Here, in my eight by nine foot bedroom, nothing could touch me. At least I tried to convince myself of that as the music in the living room down the hall grew louder.

Before everything happened at *Belle*, I had a great apartment in a much better section of the city. I lived alone and my neighbors loved me. They baked me my favorite blueberry muffins for my birthday and put little candles in the center of them like they were cupcakes. I loved my home, and then I lost it because Julia fired me when she found out about Ethan.

I could have lied when she asked me about the rumors she'd heard. Who wouldn't believe my denials? In a world of gorgeous models, how likely did it seem that someone like me would be dating Ethan Stone?

But I told the truth. What a damn fool I could be!

I answered her honestly and professionally, and she fired me.

Right there on the spot. Boom. Gone. I didn't have time to even get a word in edgewise while she berated me for breaking *Belle* magazine company policies, and then before I knew it, security was unceremoniously walking me out of the building like some unwanted garbage they had to get rid of at the curb.

Looking down my body, I saw my hands clenched in tight fists and then the sharp pain of my fingernails digging into my palms hit me. I released my fingers and stretched them out as I told myself it was all for the best.

I had no idea if that was true.

The next day, I heard Ethan got fired from *Belle* or they tore up his contract or something. That time in my life was all a blur. Whatever happened to him, I knew he'd be fine. He had the Stone family money. He was probably jet setting around the world at that very moment with two or three gorgeous models hanging off him as I lay there listening to my roommates and their boyfriends for the night partying it up.

Like always, I winced at the thought of Ethan relaxing on a beach with gorgeous women with incredible bodies wearing nothing more than string bikinis. The thought of him with anyone bothered me, even though I knew it was ridiculous for me to even care. He disappeared a month after we started dating, just like he probably had always planned to. I was only supposed to fool his family into thinking he'd settled down. I'd never been a long term plan for him.

He's got Daddy's money, so poor Ethan will be just fine. I, on the other hand, am stuck living with two nymphomaniacs who never discriminate not the least little bit.

As I did each night while I lay there in my tiny room, I thought about how I couldn't afford to live in that apartment much longer since my savings were all but used up after two months of trying to find a job. Julia Carmon had made it a point to tell anyone who would listen that I wasn't a good employee, and that nasty woman's opinion seemed to reach up and down the island of Manhattan.

I don't want to turn to my mother and father. At least not yet. I don't want to admit defeat quite yet.

It didn't help to do any of this every night, so I grabbed my phone to scan my email for anything that might be a job offer. Even a rejection would be better than nothing. Well, probably not a rejection. I didn't think I could take much more of that.

Nothing. No emails at all. Julia had done her job of ruining my chances quite thoroughly.

As much as I tried to think of anything else, Ethan crept back into my mind. Even though I didn't want to know about him with someone new, I couldn't help myself and before I knew it, I was staring at my screen looking for news about him.

Nothing on the half dozen sites I checked far too often. Nothing on Page Six.

I sighed, not realizing until that moment that I was holding my breath the entire time I scanned through the gossip page. No new woman. Good. Not that I should care. Because I shouldn't. Even though I did. My eyes slowly moved down the page to see a link with his name and his father's name. Pressing my fingertip to the screen, the words came up and I found out he'd started working for Stone Worldwide as their artistic director in the advertising division.

Must be nice to have a father who will just give you a cushy corner office after you lose your job.

Then, even though I didn't want to, I couldn't help but feel bad for Ethan. The last thing a guy like him wanted was to be stuck in an office job for the rest of his life, especially a job where he was constantly compared to his super successful father. I'd only spent a month with him, but I knew from even that short time that the shadow of Tristan Stone loomed large over Ethan.

Don't, Summer. This is the same guy who disappeared on you a month into a relationship after lying about there being another woman. He'd been in a relationship with her—a real relationship—while he was just using you to lie to his parents, just like he told you he was. He didn't lie about that. He lied about the girl.

My mind drifted back to that night when I confronted him about that bizarre text. The proof was right there on my phone, yet he refused to tell me who she was or what their relationship was. All he did was shake his head and tell me I was wrong about the text. How could I be wrong? For the entire time he'd known me, he'd probably been texting her messages that clearly showed how much he loved her.

How could I possibly believe him when he wouldn't tell me who he'd meant to text when he messaged me instead?

She was probably a model he kept hidden. Did I know her? Had I ever worked with her? They were probably open about sleeping with other people since they both knew none of it mattered because they had a love no one could top.

As my mind began to run away with me, along with my emotions, I tossed my phone aside on the bed and fell back onto the pillow. Whatever I had with Ethan Stone, it was no more. I had bigger problems to deal with, like finding a paying job and roommates who never seemed to want to go anywhere with their boyfriends but the living room.

CHAPTER ELEVEN

SUMMER

I WOKE UP TO MY phone ringing and grabbed it quickly to see who might be calling. I didn't recognize the number but answered it anyway. Desperate job seekers didn't screen calls.

"Hello?"

"Summer, it's Tressa Stone. How are you?"

Tressa Stone? What could she want? Ethan had told me his sister didn't believe we were a real couple, so why would she be calling me?

"Hi, Tressa."

I wanted to say more, but the words got stuck in my head. We hadn't really gotten to know one another enough much in the month I was with her brother, so anything I could say felt strange.

"How are you?" she asked in a stiff voice.

"I'm fine," I lied.

I had no idea why she'd called me, but I didn't want to let her think my life had fallen apart since her brother and I broke up. I had a little pride left.

"Good. I'd thought about calling you before, to be honest."

But nothing about how she said those words sounded the least bit honest, so why was she calling?

"I have to say I'm surprised to hear from you," I said, now fully awake and intensely curious about why she'd called me.

The phone fell silent for a moment and then she said, "I like you, Summer. I'm not sure how my brother found someone like you, but that's neither here nor there. What I like best about you is that I'm pretty sure whatever shenanigans he was up to, you're a straight shooter, so I'm going to do the same. I'd like to meet for coffee and talk. What do you say?"

The first thought that jumped into my brain wasn't that I should be suspicious or even curious about what she would have to say when we met. No, the first thought was that I had the chance to get out of the apartment and away from the orgy taking place in the living room to meet with a normal human being. I didn't get that much anymore since losing my job.

So I said yes. "Okay. When?" I asked, probably a little too eagerly. She likely thought I was hoping to talk about her brother, so I quickly added, "I just want you to know that I'm fine with what happened. With Ethan, I mean. So no worries there."

Tressa didn't jump on the topic, and instead, she simply answered my question. "What about tonight at nine? If you can meet me at the Stone Worldwide building, we can take the car from there."

I hesitated a moment before quietly saying, "I don't know, Tressa. It might be awkward if I ran into your brother there."

Clearly, I wasn't fine with what happened.

"Oh, don't worry. He's out of the building at five sharp like a bat out of hell. He's not exactly the workaholic type. So I'll see you here at nine, okay?"

I agreed and ended the call, still unsure what she could want from me but happy to escape my apartment, at least for a little while.

An hour later, I stood in front of the Stone Worldwide building trying to imagine Ethan working there nine-to-five every day. Even though I hadn't forgiven him for breaking my heart, I had to admit I pitied him. I knew people would kill for a job at Stone, but the reality was Ethan wasn't one of them. Tressa's comment about him being out of the building at five sharp every day told me he wasn't happy here.

Oddly enough, I didn't like that. When we first broke up, I thought seeing him miserable would make me so happy. Now that I had a sense he might truly be unhappy, I didn't like it as much as I thought I would.

"Summer! Right on time. Great! Let's go up to my office and talk," Tressa called out as she held the glass door to the building open.

I'd assumed we'd go somewhere else for coffee, but this was okay. I hurried over to join her, impressed with how stunning she looked in a black business suit and red blouse. She had executive written all over her.

"I'm glad you agreed to come talk tonight," she said as she ushered me into the building.

"Well, you piqued my interest, so I figured why not?" I said as casually as possible, hoping I didn't sound like I desperately hoped to hear about her brother. Which I didn't. Sort of.

We passed a big, burly security guard who gave us a big smile. "Working late, Miss Stone?"

"Always, Mitch. You know me," she said with a chuckle.

Looking down, I admired Tressa's four inch Louboutins. The woman wore wealth like a second skin. I couldn't help but be intimidated for a moment, but then I reminded myself that she had called me.

We rode up in the elevator to the twelfth floor making small talk about how she hoped spring would come early this year and how there hadn't been too many bad snowfalls this winter. We sounded like ordinary people waiting in line at a deli or standing at a bus stop, which made me smile. Ethan had portrayed his sister as something akin to Cruella de Vil, so her friendliness had always surprised me.

"My office is just down here. My brother's is at the other end of the hallway. I think my father did that intentionally. Sometimes his sense of humor escapes me," Tressa said with a hint of disgust.

I looked down at the other end of the wide hallway to see a

closed door and a darkened office. I knew I shouldn't have hoped I'd see him since she'd made it clear that he left work already, but when she mentioned him now, I couldn't help be disappointed.

The last thing I wanted was for her to see that, though, so I forced a smile onto my face as I sat down in the chair she offered me in front of her desk. Whatever this was about, it certainly wasn't about Ethan.

"How do you take your coffee?" Tressa asked as she poured me a mug and handed it to me.

"I'll do black. I need to be on my toes for the trip back to Brooklyn at this time of night," I said and placed the cup of coffee on the edge of her desk.

She smiled and nodded. "I'm the same, except I have about four hours of work to do after this, so I need something to keep me going." Raising her mug, she said, "To working hard."

Her impromptu toast felt particularly appropriate since I still hadn't found a job, and I secretly hoped my efforts the next day would produce at least some opportunities. Taking a sip of the very strong coffee, I let it roll down my throat as I waited for her to explain why she wanted to see me.

Tressa took a drink of her coffee, set the mug on her desk, and sat back in her chair. "Okay. I said I liked you because I thought you were a straight shooter, and I'm the same way, so let's cut to the chase. Ethan's miserable, hates his new job, and isn't seeing anyone."

Her pronouncement stunned me for a moment, making my brain unable to form a coherent response. I truly hadn't thought she wanted to see me to talk about her brother.

When I finally could think clearly, I asked the obvious question. "Why are you telling me this?"

"He seemed happy with you. I have to admit, I liked that. I don't think I'd ever seen him like that with anyone," she explained with a shrug.

Although I had a momentary thought about telling the truth

again and what might happen, I decided then and there I didn't want to lie to her. "It was all a sham at first, I'm embarrassed to admit. He wanted to make you all think he'd settled down, and I agreed to help him. I want you to know I'm sorry for that, and after dinner with all of you that night out at your house, I told him I couldn't do that to your parents anymore because they'd been too nice to me. It doesn't absolve me of guilt for what I did in the beginning, but I just want you to know I refused to lie about things after that."

My face began to heat up as I continued with my confession, so by the time I finished, I was certain my cheeks were beet red. It felt good to get that off my chest, though.

Instead of being upset or offended, Tressa laughed it all off. "I knew it. I called him on that in the kitchen that night. He denied it, of course, but I knew something wasn't right. Typical Ethan."

Curious how she knew, I asked, "Was it that obvious? I hope your parents didn't know. I'd feel terrible about that."

She waved off my concern. "Don't worry. My parents adore Ethan. I swear they think he can do no wrong. My mother's convinced he's the next Michelangelo and my father's convinced he's the next CEO of the year. They bought it hook, line, and sinker because they're blinded by parental love. I knew the whole thing was a sham, though. You were too good for him, and I knew it."

Too good for him? That felt utterly wrong as I sat there in my inexpensive clothes and shoes without red soles. Ethan was the son of a billionaire. Who was I?

"You two did spend another month together after you laid down the law, so what happened?" she asked, tearing me out of my thoughts about how I could be too good for him.

I lowered my head and quietly explained how it ended. "There was a text message he meant to send to another woman but mistakenly sent to me. When I confronted him about it, he wouldn't tell me the truth. Then he just disappeared. He didn't call anymore, and I've never seen him again. He's obviously in love with someone else. You should probably be talking to her, to be honest."

"No way. My brother has not been involved with anyone. Ethan in love with someone else? Impossible. Who is this person? What's her name?"

"I don't know," I answered sadly as the horrible empty feeling of that night came rushing back again.

I looked up to see Tressa shaking her head. "I don't believe it. No way. I'd know about him with a woman and the two of them being in love. Trust me."

Suddenly, I felt horrible talking about this, and even worse, I felt petty too about how it all happened. "I know it probably sounds juvenile of me, but I tried to find out who she was. I took his phone, but my eyes were filled with tears, so I couldn't see how many texts they'd sent back and forth. It was awful. I'm ashamed to tell you this, but it's the truth. When I asked him about whoever she is, he wouldn't admit a thing. He kept saying there was no one else, but I knew he was lying. I know it probably seems like I then derailed his career because I was hurt and trying to hurt him, but it wasn't like that either. Everything just seemed to happen all at once. My boss found out about us being together, and because I was such a mess after finding out he was with someone else, I forgot myself and just told the truth. I swear I didn't want him to get fired."

Looking down at my hands, I couldn't face Tressa at that moment. I sounded sad and pathetic.

When she spoke after listening to my explanation, she didn't seem bothered by any of it. "Let me lay my cards on the table. Ethan is unhappy at Stone Worldwide, like a fish out of water. He hates it here, and I don't want him here. Not to put too fine a point on it, but I've worked very hard for too long to play second fiddle to my brother simply because my father has some fantasy that his only son will take over the family business. He has me for that. Let Ethan go back to his photography or whatever else those artistic types do. But my father will need to be convinced. I have a plan in mind, and part of that involves you. You lost your job at *Belle* Magazine, right?"

My amazement quickly turned to shame. "I did, but I'm looking for another job every day. It's just that my former boss has been so kind to tell everyone in the five boroughs that they shouldn't hire me."

"Well, she doesn't tell me how to run my business, and I need an assistant. I'll pay you well, but your main job is to get back with my brother and convince him to start taking pictures again. What do you say?"

Overwhelmed, I wasn't sure what to say. Then the reality of my finances rose up in my mind. "I'm about to lose my apartment, and it doesn't really matter because I can't afford to live in Brooklyn. Hip neighborhoods cost too much when you're unemployed, so I don't know if I can help you since I'll probably have to move back to my parents' house in Pennsylvania. I appreciate the offer, but I don't have any savings left, so even if you started paying me tomorrow, I wouldn't have enough to pay for a place to live."

None of my sad sack story seemed to faze her in the least. "Leave that to me. Stone Worldwide has an entire hotel division, and I have rooms I use when I'm too tired to drive out to the house. You can use one of those for as long as you need to. Call it a perk of the job."

Even as my spirits buoyed from her offer, another thought came to me. "I don't know if repeating the same mistake as last time is a good idea. Maybe that's why Ethan and I didn't work out. I mean, we didn't begin on the most honest footing. I don't see things being any better this second time if I'm not being true about things."

Leaning forward, she leveled her gaze on me. "Do you care about him, Summer?" she asked pointedly, making me feel like I couldn't lie to her.

"Yes. But what about the other woman? Nothing's changed there."

"Don't worry about that. You care for him, and I think he cares for you. My brother and I don't always get along, but I don't enjoy seeing him unhappy. I can tell you I've never seen him happier than when he was with you. Right now, he's miserable, and I don't think it's just because he has to work in a job he hates. I think he misses you. Since you clearly miss him, I'm giving you a chance to see if things can work out between you two."

I didn't know if Tressa Stone was the best sister in the world or the worst. Was she caring or diabolical? Either way, she offered me something I couldn't say no to.

"Okay, but it feels wrong having the romance be a part of this. I can't promise that. I will do my best to get him back to doing what he loves, though."

Tressa smiled. "Perfect. How soon can you start?"

"The day after tomorrow?"

"Great! You can begin staying at your new hotel room tonight, if you don't want to travel back to Brooklyn. Or I can have the car service take you back to your place."

I sat there stunned at her offer. "Really? That's more than generous of you."

"You're my assistant now. You'll find that comes with a lot of perks, so get used to it."

"Okay. Would it be too much to ask to have the car take me to Brooklyn tonight to get my things and then stay at the hotel tonight? It would give me a chance to settle in before I start work the day after tomorrow."

"Perfect. Just stop over tomorrow and go to HR to fill out all the paperwork. That way we can hit the ground running on your first day."

My mind raced with questions. How I would ever get Ethan to even want to speak to me after what had happened to his life? No doubt he blamed me for losing his job at *Belle*. More importantly, would I be able to be around Ethan without falling in love with him all over again?

Then I realized I didn't even know the answer to the most pressing question. Smiling to hide my embarrassment, I asked Tressa, "I'm sorry that I don't know this, but what do you do here that I'll be assisting with or even pretending to assist with?"

Proudly, she explained, "I'm the VP of Operations at Stone Worldwide. I'd say it's quite a step up from your last job as assistant to the editor of a magazine, wouldn't you?"

My stomach did a little flip at what I'd gotten myself into. I knew nothing of what Tressa did or what anyone at Stone Worldwide did, for that matter. All I knew was I wouldn't be living with Amber and Elise anymore, and my main job as Tressa's assistant was to get Ethan back to photography.

It all sounded like a win-win.

Chapter Twelve

Ethan

Still half asleep at the ungodly hour of nearly nine in the morning, I sat my ass down in my chair behind my desk and closed my eyes. I still had a few minutes before someone from the ad division could want something from me, thank God. The idea that anyone should be up at this time of day and actually productive felt counterintuitive, to say the least. If it wasn't for the largest coffee available on the planet from that coffee shop a block away from the building, there would be no way I'd be able to pretend to be human this early in the morning.

The monitor on the far wall of my office made its all too familiar noise, and I looked up to see my father's smiling face on the screen. Instantly, I thought to myself that whoever merged the idea of the phone and the TV should be dragged through the streets and beaten senseless.

"Good morning, Ethan. How's it going today?" he asked, his smile growing broader by the moment.

"Everything's good here, Dad. Bright-eyed and bushy-tailed and all that," I said, trying to be funny.

"Good. I'd like you to come up to my office. Your sister has an announcement, so I told her I'd bring you in on it too."

I scrubbed the last precious remnants of sleep out of my head and nodded as I worked to focus on the screen. "Okay. I'll be right up. Any idea what this announcement is about?"

My father shook his head. "No idea. She just asked that I

involve you in the meeting. It won't take you away from the office for long."

He had no idea how long I wished I could be taken away from this office. How did forever sound?

"Great. I'll be right up."

Two giant gulps of coffee later, I headed toward the elevator. I downed the last of the giant cup of caffeine on the way up to the executive suite on the thirty-fifth floor. By the time the elevator doors opened, I felt like some semblance of being human begin to come over me.

Stepping out onto the black marble floor, I remembered the times my mother would bring my sisters and me to see my father at his office back when we were little kids. I used to love staring down at the floor and seeing my reflection looking back at me from the shiny black stone. It made me think my father did something magical for him to have floors like this at his work.

As I slowly walked across it now, I looked down at my reflection, but there was nothing magical in what I saw. Just the vague outlines of grown man being summoned to the boss's office for some announcement he most likely wouldn't give a damn about.

My father's assistant, a middle-aged woman named Brenda, smiled at me as I approached her desk. Why was everyone on this floor so damn happy at the crack of dawn? Did they pump happy gas into the executive suite each morning?

"Good morning, Ethan. Your father's in his office waiting for you. Tressa and her assistant are already in there with him," Brenda said in her strangely somber voice that didn't match her happy expression.

I nodded as I had a flashback to the day she started working for him after his previous assistant Michelle left. I'd never heard such a low voice from a woman, and when she bent down to say hi to me, I ran away. That deep voice of hers never fit with how pleasant she always appeared.

"Thanks, Brenda."

Opening the double doors to my father's office, I had the overwhelming urge to announce, "Here's Johnny!" but neither my father nor my sister would enjoy that reference, and my humor would be met with irritated stares from the two of them. Tressa's assistant, a very serious guy whose name I could never remember—Floyd, Boyd, something that sounded like that—definitely wouldn't enjoy it either. So instead, I simply walked in and closed the door.

"So Tressa, what's this announcement?" I asked as I turned around and nearly fell back against the wall in shock.

My sister stood beside my father's desk grinning like a fucking Cheshire cat with the last person in the world I expected to see that morning. What the fuck was Summer doing in my father's office standing next to my sister dressed like everyone else who worked at this place?

No. Please, no.

I locked eyes with Tressa and silently begged her not to do this. I had no idea what she was up to, but it wasn't good. We'd never had the kind of connection I had with Diana, but for once in our lives, I prayed to God she understood what I was feeling at that moment.

Please tell me you're not expecting me to work with her. Isn't it bad enough that I'm here at all? Didn't we just talk about me getting out of here yesterday, and today you bring her here? Why?

All of these thoughts rushed through my brain as I tried unsuccessfully to telegraph my feelings to my sister. But it was no use. She didn't sense how miserable just seeing Summer made me.

Or she didn't care. My sister, the sadist.

"Ethan, you remember Summer, don't you? She's my new assistant. Anything you need, please see her and she'll take care of it."

I kept my focus on Tressa, not wanting to move my gaze a millimeter and make eye contact with Summer. "Okay. If I have anything I need from you, Tressa, I'll deal with your assistant," I said flatly, struggling to keep my emotions out of my voice.

She turned to her new helper and smiled. "Summer, please go back down to my office and get ready for the staff meeting. I'll be down in a few minutes."

As I kept my eyes locked on my sister, Summer turned to my father and said, "It was very nice to see you again, Mr. Stone. I'm really looking forward to working for your company."

"We're glad to have you here, Summer. I think you're going to love working with Tressa. Her staff raves about her."

Every word seemed to take forever as I stood there feeling more trapped than ever before in my life. Not only did I have to work at this goddamned place that felt like a fucking prison, but now I had to do it with my most recent ex-girlfriend right down the damn hall.

I sensed Summer wanted to say something to me, but I never made eye contact, so she hurried out of the office, leaving me standing there with the two traitors. When the door closed, I finally shifted my gaze to my father and hoped he saw how much I hated Tressa's newest idea.

"So you two think this is a good idea, huh? It's not bad enough I'm stuck here doing a job I hate, but now you have to bring her around? Why?"

My father's expression hardened. "Your sister's allowed to hire anyone she wants to be her assistant, Ethan. Summer Carmichael has excellent experience, as you well know."

Clearly, I was going to get nowhere with him, so I looked to Tressa still standing next to him and smiling that fucking smile that told me this had nothing to do with Summer's experience. "There are millions of people just on this island alone, and you felt the need to hire her?"

"I thought it was the least we could do, to be honest. She did lose her job because of a Stone. The poor thing had to move out of her apartment after she got fired from *Belle* because she couldn't afford it. She lost her home, Ethan. Your behavior has consequences, and it doesn't always just affect you. I've given someone immensely qualified a chance to make a good living. What have you done for anyone other than yourself today, this week, or I'll even go back to since the day you arrived here? Anything?"

I opened my mouth to tell my sister exactly what I thought of her and her little charity efforts, but my father stood up and bellowed, "Enough! Now Ethan, I'm sorry you don't approve of Summer's hiring, but your sister is right. She's qualified, and we can always use people like her at this company. Since it's unlikely you'll actually have to deal with her that often since she'll have nothing to do with the ad division, I don't see what the problem is."

My head began to pound. Neither of these people would understand why I didn't want to be stuck in this job with Summer so close by. Fine. My prison now had its own personal torturer.

"I guess there's nothing else to say then. If you're done with me, I'll be going back to my cell now."

My father frowned but remained silent, so I left without another word to either of them. By the time I got back to my office, I didn't know if I wanted to hit something or throw up. Slamming the door shut, I locked it and sat down behind my desk. I had no idea what the hell Tressa was up to, but I didn't appreciate whatever the fuck it was. Summer being there in the building every day just made a bad thing even worse.

As much as I didn't want to, I couldn't help myself from thinking back to the time we spent together. We didn't date for that long, so I didn't know why she made such an impression on me. We didn't do anything particularly unique the whole month we were together. Just a lot of hanging out. We laughed a lot and watched too many goddamned movies.

I hadn't laughed that much in forever. Even as I sat there stewing about my sister's newest way of punishing me, a smile crept onto my lips when I thought about that time Summer and I tried to make dinner and just ended up making a mess and getting silly drunk on some special red wine she'd read went perfectly with that beef recipe. We never did make that meal and instead ended up having phenomenal sex right there in her kitchen instead of eating.

Her kitchen. I didn't like hearing she'd had to give up her apartment because she lost her job. That's not something I had to deal with when I got canned.

I never meant to get her fired. It's not like I ruined her life or anything. We had a good time and then it ended. Why did everyone have to act like I was the villain in all this?

Tired of thinking about the past, I grabbed the remote and called Cole. My friend since grade school, he'd make me forget how shitty things had gotten, assuming he was up at this hour of the day. Club owners didn't exactly do a lot of their living during the day, especially at nine in the morning.

A second later, I saw his face staring back at me and looking strangely awake for so early in the day. Pushing his nearly black hair off his forehead, he laughed when he saw me.

"Look at you, man. You're sad. What do you say to me springing you from that place and the two of us heading down to my place at the beach?"

I shook my head, wishing I could do as he suggested. "I'd love nothing more, but no go. I have things I have to deal with here in a little bit. How've you been, man?"

With his typical grin, he chuckled. "You know me, Stone. Same old, same old. You're lucky you caught me up this early. You know I don't usually head to the club until around noon. Something going on?"

I shrugged, even as I wanted to throw something. "Nothing I can't handle. My favorite sister just hired one of my exes to be her assistant. You remember me telling you about that Summer girl? Now she's working down the hallway from me. It's like this fucking place just gets better and better every day."

Cole rolled his eyes. "Tressa. I swear to God that sister of yours hates you, man. Why is that? Did you try to smother her in her crib when you were babies?"

I shook my head as the thought of smothering her later that day made me smile. "Not that I remember. I can't figure her out. It's like she wants to see me miserable. I mean, bringing one of my exes here to work on the same floor, for Christ's sake? Who does that?"

"Tressa Stone. The woman is your mortal enemy. She has been since you were like ten. At least you have another sister who isn't, though. How's Diana doing?"

That glint in Cole's eye I'd seen every time he'd set his sights on some woman made my defenses shoot up all over the place. "She's fine, and stop looking like that when you talk about my sister, dude. No good."

Caught red-handed, he threw his head back and laughed. "I was just asking. You can't blame a guy for wondering about someone like her, man. You know I always liked her."

"I know, and what did I tell you the first time you told me that?"

Cole twisted his face into a painful grimace. "I don't know. I couldn't hear anything once you landed the first punch. I still owe you for that, you know."

I waved away his veiled threat and chuckled. "Yeah. Feel free to knock me around the first time I say I want to get with your favorite sister."

"I don't have a sister, dude. All I've got are three brothers, as you well know, but you're welcome to get with any of them, if they'll have you."

"Thanks. I'll pass. I have to go. Time to see my sister."

Cole's eyebrows shot up into his forehead. "Time to go let Tressa know what you think of her latest stunt? Good. She needs to be put in her place. In fact, I can come over and do that for you, if you want."

I rolled my eyes. "She'd have you for lunch, man, and then she'd wear your bones as a necklace."

"I'm up for a challenge."

Unlike when he talked about Diana, it didn't bother me at all when he said things like that about Tressa. She could handle herself.

She might literally have the guy for a snack.

"If you're not busy, come over after work tonight and we can have a few beers."

With a smile, he said, "Sounds good. Maybe I'll duck out of the club early. Have the beers ready by midnight."

"I will. See you then, man."

The screen faded to black, leaving me alone in my office again. I knew talking to Cole would cheer me up. I still hated what Tressa did, but I had other things to deal with today.

CHAPTER THIRTEEN

ETHAN

WITH EVERY STEP DOWN THE hallway, I thought about what I'd say to my sister. It had been a while since we really talked. I'd put it off because I was so consumed with my own bullshit, but I needed to get myself out of that place before I got stuck and nothing would get me out.

I stopped at her door and took a deep breath. Whenever we wanted to make sure the other person knew it was us, my sisters and I had a special knock. I tapped on the door once, twice, and then a third time before pausing and adding another three quick knocks. It probably wasn't very special, but when we were little, we liked to think we'd made up something unique to just us, so I always knocked that way for my sisters.

After a few moments, the door opened. My sister stood there smiling at me like she always did when I came to see her. With her hair pulled up in a ponytail, she looked just like she did when we were in high school. She wore a pink sweater and jeans that furthered the impression that she was a teenager.

"Ethan! You didn't tell me you were coming over. Come in!" she said sweetly, opening her arms to hug me.

"I'm sorry I haven't been by for a while. I've been dealing with some stuff, but it's still no excuse."

She pulled me into the room and closed the door. "Let me look at you. Oh, my God. You look just like Daddy in that suit. I love it! Tell me everything that's been going on. What stuff are you dealing with?”

I let her tug me over to the couch and sat down next to her. “It’s nothing. Certainly nothing worth wasting our time together on.”

Her smile faded, and she nodded. “I had a feeling this morning when I woke up that you’re not doing well. Your texts seem happy, but every time you send me one, I get the feeling you’re not.”

Shaking my head, I wondered how she and I could be so in tune with one another and Tressa and I could be like complete strangers. “Well, I’m better now. What’s new with you?”

“Mommy and I just got finished talking. If you had gotten here a minute earlier, you could have seen her. She’s so excited about her show, Ethan. You better go and tell me everything about it. Promise?”

“I promise.”

I didn’t like lying to Diana. Tressa I could lie to all day, but I couldn’t do that with Diana without feeling bad. I just didn’t know if I could go to my mother’s show with how I still felt.

“So what else is new? How is working with Daddy and Tressa? Are you having fun?” she asked with that same hope in her eyes that my father always had when he asked about how work was going.

Hesitating, I tried to think of a way to tell her the truth and not make this visit all about my misery. Diana didn’t need that in her life and definitely not from me.

Before I could answer, she grabbed my hand and pressed it to her cheek. “I know you’re not happy there, Ethan. I’m sorry this happened. You don’t belong there. For what it’s worth, Mommy thinks that too. I know you miss being out in the world and taking pictures. You can tell me.”

I forced a smile. “It is what it is. I can’t change what happened. So what do you want to do? We can do whatever you want.”

“What about a movie? One of my favorites?” she asked, jumping up from the couch to hurry over to the TV.

“Whatever you want.”

I watched as she chose a movie to watch and then came back to the couch to sit next to me. "Do you want popcorn? I can make some. It won't take long."

All I'd put in my stomach was that giant coffee hours before, but I didn't want to waste our time together making popcorn. "I'm good. What are we watching today?"

With a big smile that lit up her entire face, she said, "Beauty and The Beast. It's always been my favorite, as you know, and I'm in the mood to see it today. That okay?"

Ever since we were kids, that had been Diana's favorite movie. She loved the really old cartoon version my mother first showed to us, so that's the one we'd watch today.

"Perfect. Are you going to sing?"

Diana gave me a look like I'd asked the dumbest question ever. "Of course. Ready?"

"Let's do this."

She snuggled up against me as the movie began, and I wrapped my arm around her to pull her close. I loved seeing her happy like this. After all she'd been through, she deserved all the happiness in the world. If I could give her that, I would.

But I couldn't, so I gave her moments like this.

As the movie played and Diana began singing along with the candelabra, I asked her, "Have you gone out recently?"

She tilted her head up toward me, and in her deep blue eyes, I saw the answer. She hadn't.

"You should get out more. It's not good to stay cooped up in this hotel room."

She frowned and looked away. "I get out. Sometimes."

I knew when she was talking about—when our father came to see her. "I mean other times than when Dad comes by."

"Do you want to go out instead of watching the movie? Is that what you mean?" she asked in a hurt voice.

I pulled her closer and shook my head. "No. That's not what I meant. I'm fine with watching the movie. I just wish you'd get out more."

She curled up next to my body and mumbled, "It's cold out, Ethan. If it was nice out, I'd go out more."

If only that was the truth.

While we sat there watching the movie, my mind drifted back to one time when Diana was sick with the flu. Always smaller than Tressa and me, she looked so frail lying in bed tucked under the covers as my mother and father nervously hovered over her day and night. I stared at her from her doorway for hours because they refused to let me in, afraid I might get the flu too.

When my parents left the room at one point during the night, I snuck in and crawled into bed with her. Her skin felt like it could burn me it was so hot, but I still wrapped my arms around her and hugged her to me. She opened her eyes once and looked at me so afraid before she said in the tiniest voice, "Ethan, I don't feel good. Don't go." When my parents found me there, they tried to force me back to my room, but I wouldn't go. I was afraid if I left that she'd die.

Not much had changed since we were kids.

I looked down at her and saw her smiling as she watched the movie. After a few moments, she caught me staring at her and asked, "What's wrong?"

In that moment, even as the rest of my life seemed like it just got worse by the day, I answered the absolute truth of how I felt when I was with her. "Nothing's wrong," I said with a smile, shaking my head. "Nothing at all."

✧   ✧   ✧

"So what the fuck is going on with you Stones? You looked like you wanted to kill yourself this morning, man. I wasn't sure you'd be with us anymore by the time I got here tonight."

Normally, Cole spent most of his time joking around, but I saw in his expression my friend was serious this time. I must have looked pretty bad this morning after my sister's Summer ambush.

Fuck. That meant she saw how much the whole thing had gotten to me too.

"My sister seems hell bent on making my life miserable. She's studied at the knee of Tristan Stone for all these years, so now they're like two peas in a goddamned pod," I answered before taking a long swig from a fresh bottle of beer.

"Two against one. Those aren't good odds. And now Tressa has your ex working for her. Three against one. Not good, Ethan."

"To say the least."

"Maybe if your sister had something other than work to distract her, she wouldn't be so difficult. I could try to help you out there, you know?"

I stared across the room at Cole and decided I liked him too much to do that to him. "You wouldn't come out alive. Trust me. If she can do the kind of stuff she does to me, her own brother, can you imagine what she does to the men she dates?"

A broad grin spread across Cole's face. "I wasn't planning on dating her. What I had in mind was more along the lines of stress release for both of us."

"Watch yourself, man. That's my sister you're talking about."

He put his arms up as if to surrender. "My bad. I thought you were only hyper-protective of Diana. I didn't realize Tressa got that same treatment."

"Could we not talk about you having sex with either of my sisters? I just want to enjoy some beers with a friend and forget how fucking shitty my life has become, okay?"

"Got it."

But I couldn't stop myself from talking about what happened this morning. "I mean, what the fuck is she thinking bringing Summer around to work at the same place I do? Who does that kind of shit?"

"Tressa Stone. Man, I told you. I think she holds a grudge from when you were kids. You took her applesauce one day, and she's never forgiven you."

I thought back to when we were kids and wondered if she held something against me since then. I did steal her Barbie doll once and cut all the hair off it. She was pretty pissed about that.

Cole interrupted my memories with his own suggestion. "Maybe Summer has something on Tressa and she's forcing her to help her get back with you."

So much of that sounded ridiculous that I didn't know where to start. "First of all, Summer's not like that. Tressa would hold things over someone's head, but not Summer. Second, my sister would never allow someone to have that kind of control over her. Trust me. That would never happen."

Shrugging, Cole took a drink of his beer. "Well, then maybe Tressa wants to get Summer back with you and this is her way to do it. You didn't dismiss my idea of her wanting that, I notice."

"Because my sister wouldn't help with that kind of thing. Playing Cupid to help with my happiness is the last thing Tressa wants to do in this life."

Focused on grabbing another beer from the refrigerator, Cole didn't seem to notice my reference to being happy with Summer, thankfully. I didn't feel like explaining that to him, a committed and habitual bachelor.

To be honest, I wasn't sure I understood it myself. She wasn't really my type. Well, at least not the type of woman I'd traditionally spent time with. She had been part of the reason my life had been turned upside down and now I was stuck working in the prison of Stone Worldwide as a pencil pusher. There was no good reason I should even think of her as anything but a huge mistake I shouldn't make again.

Yet still, I couldn't stop thinking of her, even today as she and Tressa ambushed me.

"So what's the over-under on how long you last at the family business before Tristan or Tressa throw you out of the building themselves or kill you? I'd like to get in on that action," Cole joked, shaking me from my thoughts of how much I missed some of the things Summer and I did together.

He sat back down on his stool on the other side of the kitchen island and laughed at me when I threw him the finger. "I'm just wondering. You don't find too many sure bets in this world, so when you do, you jump on them."

"Maybe I'll just leave on my own," I said with all the false bravado I could muster.

The truth was I couldn't just leave. I'd made a deal with my parents, and as much as I hated the fact that they'd called it in when that whole *Belle* business went bad, I lived up to my word.

"Maybe. But since I don't understand why you went there in the first place, I sense that you got yourself into something that's keeping you in that building every day nine-to-five."

Nobody but my parents and possibly Tressa knew about the deal I'd made back when I was twenty. I never told a single friend about it. I never thought I'd have to. I may not have been the best photographer in the world, but I knew what I could do with my talent combined with my mother's contacts and a dash of my charm. At least I thought I knew back then. So I made the deal with them.

If I could make a living on taking pictures professionally that would enable me to pay for the Upper East Side place I wanted, then I wouldn't have to go to work at the family business. But if I ever couldn't, there would be no turning to Mom and Dad for help. I'd have to work at Stone Worldwide.

And the week after *Belle* got rid of me, I knew for sure that time had come since there wasn't a magazine around that wanted to work with me. Summer had been right. Julia Carmon was nasty. More than nasty. I had other words for her the day I found out what she was telling everyone at other magazines, and bitch was the nicest of them.

That was two months ago, the longest two months of my life. Well, the second longest.

Cole poked me on the arm, and I looked up still lost in

thought. "What?"

"You've got a call coming in," he said, pointing toward the living room wall where the TV hung.

"Fuck. I didn't put the away message on. Why the hell do I never seem to remember that lately? I swear to God if it's Tressa, I'm not holding back."

Egging me on, Cole jumped off the stool to follow me into the room. "Get her! Show her who's boss!"

Just before the person's image came up on the screen, I turned around to see him laughing. "Fuck you, Cole. Remind me again why I asked you over tonight?"

With that smart ass grin of his plastered on his face, he raised his bottle in the air and said, "Because I'm a fucking good time, and you sorely need that in your life right now. By the way, my money's on you in this fight, man. You can take her."

"Fucking ass."

I turned back toward the screen to see not my sister but one of the models I'd spent time with back when my life involved beautiful women and beaches and not the misery of nine-to-five behind a desk. Ilsa Stanton's gorgeous face in HD paled only to seeing her in real life. Tall enough to nearly match my six foot two height, she had green eyes the color of moss the camera loved, a perfect mouth, and a body that didn't quit. We'd gotten together a few times after I shot her for a cover of a European magazine early in my career, but I hadn't heard from her in a few years.

"Ethan, it's so great to see you again. How are you?" she asked with a sexy lilt in her voice.

I had no idea if she knew about what had happened to me, but I'd heard she got engaged to some Swedish businessman. Was she married?

"I'm good. I haven't seen you in way too long, Ilsa. What's new?"

Her mouth formed a pout, and she tilted her head to the right so her hair fell over her face. "I heard you got fired. That's so wrong, you know? You were so sweet, not like those other photographers who were all handsy all the time. I mean, everyone involved was always an adult, so what's the problem? Americans can be so provincial sometimes."

So she had heard. Great. That meant I had to play it casual, as if having my life ruined was cool, which meant I had to fall back on that rich boy shit I hated.

"You know how it is, Ilsa. Don't worry about me. You know my story. I'll be fine with or without that world. So what brings you to me tonight?"

None of that bullshit was true. I never liked to throw my family's money around as proof that I didn't care about not being able to do something I loved, and not just because it was a lie. I didn't like it because I hated the idea that people thought of me as simply some trust fund fucker who didn't care about anything or anyone because I'd been born into money. Anyone who thought that about me was dead wrong.

"I need some new headshots, so of course I thought of you. Can you help me out? I'll make it worth your while," she said in a way even the dumbest man could understand was an invitation to sample the goodies.

As much as I hated to admit it, I missed this. The flirting with beautiful women was definitely one of the perks of my former job.

"I thought I heard you were engaged to be married," I said with a chuckle.

That pretty pout of hers appeared once more. "I was, but he wasn't for me. He was so serious. No more businessmen for me. He wanted me to give him babies immediately, and I had to break it off with him. No babies for me yet."

Pleased to hear she wasn't off-limits, I smiled. "I'm sure I can do something to help you out. Let me call you later in the week."

Ilsa's perfect mouth transformed from a sultry pout to a broad smile full of straight, white teeth. "I knew you would help. Thank you, Ethan. I'm so happy now."

The call ended, and I turned around to see Cole staring at the screen with his mouth hanging open. "Dude, you look like some high school nerd who can't get laid."

He pointed at the screen and shook his head. "That woman was gorgeous. Holy fuck! I knew you used to hang around beautiful women, but that's more than just beautiful. I think I might be in love."

Cole wasn't wrong. Ilsa was stunning. If he saw her half-naked in a tiny bikini that barely covered those perfect tits, he might fall over dead. But as I thought back to our time together, I remembered why she and I didn't stay in touch. The woman brought nothing but drama to everything. Other women hated her, ex-boyfriends were evil, and no one truly understood her.

Nothing but drama. No fun. Just good sex and way too much hassle outside the bedroom.

"What's that face for? You look like you just tasted rotten food. What kind of guy makes that face after talking to a woman like that?" Cole asked in disgust.

"She's hot, no doubt, but she comes with a lot of bullshit too. Drama like you've never seen," I explained as I grabbed another beer from the refrigerator.

"I'd take that kind of drama. In fact, I'd take it first thing in the morning, for a lunchtime snack, and then later at night," Cole joked with a grin.

I saw his point, but Ilsa's drama had been too much for me. I needed more. "Yeah, I guess, but I swear to God I never laughed even once all the times I was with her."

Cole twisted his face into a look of disgust and confusion. "Never laughed? Who fucking cares about laughing with a woman like that? That's what you have friends for. TV. Movies. A million other things I can't think of at the moment, but not women. Women aren't for laughing, dude."

I swallowed the rest of my old beer and tossed the bottle in the garbage. "Yeah, you're right. If I want to spend time with a clown, I can call you."

He laughed at my insult and threw me the finger like old friends did, but I couldn't help but think how much I liked feeling comfortable enough with a woman to be able to laugh with her.

Chapter Fourteen

Summer

I SAW THE ELEVATOR DOORS closing and ran full speed down the hallway, praying to God with every step that I didn't twist my ankle in my heels and go careening to the floor like a fool. Nothing like making an impression that you're a clumsy idiot on your second official day of work at a new employer.

"Please hold the elevator!" I cried out as the doors came within an inch of one another.

A hand grabbed hold of one of them and I breathed a sigh of relief as they slowly began to open. That relief was instantly replaced with utter anxiety when I saw who that hand belonged to.

Ethan.

Quickly, I tried to compose myself as I stepped into the elevator with him. A bead of sweat trickled down my neck from my hallway run, making me squirm as I pushed my shoulder blades together to stop it from running all the way down my back. Thankfully, Ethan stood staring straight ahead and didn't bother to look over at me as I gyrated like a damned idiot.

That he couldn't even meet my gaze bothered me, but at that very moment, I had to admit I was thankful for his refusal to admit I existed. Once I solved my sweaty back problem, I had less patience with his rudeness, though.

"Thirty-fifth floor," I said as he stood there waiting for some direction.

That was a lie. I wasn't going to the executive suites. Why the hell would I be going up there? It wasn't like Ethan's father and I had anything to discuss without Tressa standing there. God, this man still had the ability to make me crazy months after we stopped seeing one another.

My gaze floated over the back of him as he stood ramrod straight in front of me. Like everything else, the dark grey suit he wore looked incredible on his muscular, toned body. His hair looked a little longer in the back and came over the collar of his white dress shirt. I had to resist the urge to run my fingers over his hair to see if it still felt as soft as I remembered it.

Floor after floor passed as we stood there in silence with me perched at the back of the elevator and Ethan hovering near the doors like he couldn't wait for them to open so he could bolt out away from me. By the twenty-fifth floor, I couldn't stand it anymore. I had to say something.

And what came out of my mouth?

"For such a nice building, this elevator sure is slow."

It really was a wonder why anyone at all spoke to me. God, why didn't I say something interesting?

He didn't utter a word in response. I didn't even get a perfunctory, fellow employee polite nod to acknowledge he'd heard me. Just complete silence of the deafening variety.

So I nervously cleared my voice and tried again. "Not that that's a bad thing. Time away from the office can be nice."

There was no device created to measure how little improvement that was from my first statement. For Ethan, though, neither one caused him to even flinch the tiniest bit.

As the seconds ticked by, my blood began to boil. We might not ever be anything but co-workers, but this ignoring people was downright rude. Stepping forward, I looked up at him as he continued to stare ahead at the silver metal doors in front of us and waited for him to look at me.

But he didn't. Not even the tiniest movement to acknowledge another human being was standing next to him. A human being he once spent an entire night making love to and then served breakfast in bed when she told him she didn't think she could walk ever again. That human stood next to him and still he couldn't even glance over at me.

A few seconds more of his brand of shunning and something inside me snapped. "I know you can hear me, Ethan."

Still nothing. Christ, this guy had mastered the art of being a complete and utter dick.

"So is this how you treat people who you once slept with? You're a real class act, Mr. Stone. A real class act."

Not even the tiniest movement in response. I watched for anything—two blinks when there should have been only one, a slightly deeper inhale of breath, any sign my words were being heard—but he acted like there was no one standing not even twelve inches away from him.

"Nothing? You don't a single word for me? We spent nearly every night together for an entire month and you can't even say hi or ask how I've been?"

I waited, but he didn't respond, so I snapped, "You know what? Fuck you, Ethan. Fuck you."

A moment later, the elevator reached the thirty-fifth floor, and the doors opened. Ethan bolted out into the executive suite with its shiny black marble floor, and a few seconds later, the doors in front of me closed. The last thing I saw of him was his back as he slowly walked toward Tristan Stone's office.

I pressed the round number one button, making it light up, and hoped no one would interrupt my drop to the first floor as tears welled in my eyes. I shook my head to fight them off, feeling foolish for ever thinking I could be anything to someone like Ethan. He'd told me all I needed to know when he practically blackmailed me to join him in his plan to fool his family, so even though he had turned into the world's biggest dick, I couldn't blame him for doing exactly as he said he would.

The only blame belonged to me for falling in love with him.

As the elevator slowly descended more than thirty floors, I realized I left my gloves at my desk. I frantically pressed the button for the twelfth floor and hoped I could run to my office, grab them, and be back on the elevator before Ethan descended to his office.

Another run down the hallway, this time to my office, and I found my gloves on my desk just where I'd left them a few minutes ago. As I turned to leave for the day once more, I heard Tressa call my name.

"Summer, please come in here. I want to speak to you."

If only I hadn't forgotten those damn gloves. Now if she asked me how I was doing with my real job for her, I'd have to tell her the truth.

I had succeeded at nothing but being an epic failure.

Tressa sat behind her enormous cherry wood desk with the light from the window behind her illuminating her nearly black hair that hung way past her shoulders. As I stepped into the room, her dark eyes focused on me and watched my every move as I inched my way toward her sheepishly. Two days on the job and already I had to disappoint her. Things were not starting off well.

"So, how are you coming along on your assignment?" she asked, her red stained lips smiling as she spoke.

I stopped walking toward her and looked down toward the grey carpet to avoid facing her. "Not so good. I just tried to talk to him in the elevator and he acted like I wasn't even there."

"Typical Ethan. He can be so difficult, but don't worry. I know that look he had in my father's office. I think I might have underestimated how much he cares for you."

Lifting my head, I looked at her in shock. "Underestimated how much he cares for me? He looked like he wanted to kill someone."

"Not in his eyes. In them, I saw how upset he was. That wasn't anger."

"No offense, but I didn't see that at all."

She waved off my real concern that I'd never get him to speak to me again as if it were a mere trifle. "Trust me. Triplets know one another very well. Too well, sometimes. I'm not worried. Keep talking to him."

"Do you think maybe someone else would be better for the job? I mean, I want to keep this job more than you can know, but after what just happened in the elevator between us, I'm not sure he'll ever talk to me again. I'm sure he blames me for losing his job. That might not be something he can ever forgive."

I truly wanted to keep this job, but I was prepared to accept being let go for failing. I'd just have to go stay with my parents for a little while. Maybe that's what I should have done when Tressa approached me with this plan.

But she didn't seem concerned at all. "Don't worry. He'll come around. I have a good feeling about this," Tressa said far more confidently than I felt. "I know what I saw in his eyes. Trust me. You've only been at it for a couple days. Give it a little while. In the meantime, you and I are going to be planning a party for my mother's show that's coming up early next month, so be ready to go first thing in the morning. In the meantime, have faith. I always get what I want, and I want Ethan back to photography and out of Stone Worldwide and I believe you're the person to get him there."

"Can I ask why you think that?"

As if she'd been waiting for me to ask that very question, she immediately answered, "That night when you two were at my parents' house for dinner I got a good feeling from you. You're smart, level-headed, and genuine. My brother has never been with anyone like that in his entire life. Yes, I know he was running some scam, but the fact that you two spent a month together after you told him you wouldn't lie anymore tells me he cared about you. I think he still does. In fact, I think you're looking at this all wrong. It isn't a matter of him wanting you again. It should be a matter of if you want him again after behavior like you just told me about."

The way Tressa talked, I was in the driver seat about this whole Ethan thing, but it didn't feel like I was. "I think you have me confused with someone like you. I'm sure men fall all over you because of how you look and how wealthy you are. I'm nothing like that."

Again, she waved away my concern like she was swatting away a bug. "Nonsense. You're a beautiful woman who has a lot to offer. So you aren't wealthy. So what? No man who marries me will be getting my money, and they find that out very quickly when I begin seeing them. And still they want to see me. So I have nothing more than you do, except confidence, and that can be learned quite easily. Stick with me, Summer. If you want my brother back, I have no doubt you'll have him. And if you don't, that's his loss and some other man's gain. Never forget that."

I didn't know what to say. No one had ever said those kinds of things to me. Maybe Tressa was right. Maybe all I needed was more confidence.

"Now go have a good night and I'll see you first thing in the morning to get working on that party."

I left her office feeling like a million bucks, but not halfway down the hall I saw Ethan's office and everything she said evaporated into the recesses of my brain. With every step, I couldn't escape the truth of why I felt so awkward about him. About us.

His door was unlocked, so I opened it and saw him sitting there staring off in the distance. He barely noticed anyone had come in, but I needed to say some things.

"I just wanted to say I'm sorry for snapping at you in the elevator. I'm sorry. To be honest, I'm sorry about a lot of things. I'm sorry things ended so badly between us. I'm sorry you got fired from *Belle*. I never meant for that to happen, Ethan. I was upset when you didn't bother calling me after what happened, but Julia caught me off guard. I didn't intend on getting you in trouble. It's just that I answered her truthfully when she asked the question about us being together. I swear I didn't mean to ruin things for you. I'm sorry."

He stared at me blankly as I stood there for another moment, but just before I turned to leave, I thought I saw a hint of hurt in his eyes. I was sorry for that too. I never meant to hurt him by lashing out like I did in the elevator.

By the time I hit the chilly February air, my emotions were all over the place and I felt exhausted. These Stones sure were a lot to deal with. Tressa built me up so high I felt like I could take off into the clouds, and Ethan made me want to run back to my hotel room and bury my head in a pillow.

This job was an emotional rollercoaster.

The ten block walk to the Richmont helped clear my head so at least I didn't feel like I was about to unravel like a cheap sweater. I just needed to get to my room, change out of my work clothes, and watch some mindless TV. Always the recipe for relaxation, I was sure I'd feel better after a few hours of some stupid sitcom.

Just as I reached for the handle on the glass entrance door to the hotel, I heard someone call my name. Looking around, I didn't see anyone I knew, but I had heard my name yelled out. True, I had a name that was also a noun, but it was unlikely anyone was yelling about the season in the middle of the winter.

"Summer! Wait!"

That time I heard it even clearer and knew exactly who had yelled. I turned around to see Ethan not even wearing a coat over his suit and marching toward me like a man on a mission. But what exactly could his mission be with me? He looked like he was about to start barking at me right there in front of his father's hotel.

I stepped out of the way of a group of fellow hotel guests who wanted to go inside and waited for him. He reached me in only a few seconds and stopped dead in front of me, his expression downright serious.

"What are you doing here?" he asked angrily.

"Why, hello to you too. Yes, I think it is a lovely day for February. Maybe spring will come early," I answered in my best smart ass tone.

He let out a sigh and drew in his eyebrows in clear frustration.

"I meant did Tressa send you on an errand or something? It just seems strange to see you coming here."

"I would think it's strange for you to see me coming or going anywhere since we aren't together anymore, Ethan."

Another sigh, this one deeper, and then his expression softened and he looked like the man I'd spent that incredible month with again. "So what are you doing here? Does my sister have you doing busy work on your time off?"

I saw a hint of that stunning smile of his when he finished speaking, so I told him the truth. "I live here now."

"What? What do you mean you live here?" he asked, that edge to his voice present again.

God, I hated having to admit to my ultra-wealthy ex-boyfriend that I had to live off the charity of his family.

"I had to leave my apartment when Julia fired me because I couldn't afford it. I ended up moving in with two people I knew from a coffee shop near the *Belle* magazine offices, but that was in Brooklyn and I hated it for reasons I don't feel like getting into now. When your sister offered me the job as her assistant, I told her I couldn't take it because I had to move back to Pennsylvania with my parents because I'd run out of money. She offered me a room here for as long as I need it."

He listened in rapt attention to my tale of woe, and in my shame, I quickly added, "I plan on moving out as soon as I can. I don't take charity. I just had no…"

I didn't finish my sentence. Too embarrassed to finish, I looked down at my gloved hands and wished this moment could end and Ethan would go away so I didn't have to feel like such a loser.

"That Julia is a piece of work, isn't she?" he said, that edge in his voice gone again.

I looked up and nodded. "She's made sure to tell everyone she can what a rotten assistant I was. I haven't been able to find a job anywhere because of her blackballing, but then I guess you know all about that."

"Yeah."

The sadness in his eyes at that one word made my chest ache. Badmouthing me was bad, but I never thought being an assistant to an editor or anyone else was anything more than temporary. Being a photographer was what Ethan was. It wasn't just his job. It was his identity, and Julia had done everything she could to take it away.

Even worse, she'd succeeded.

Suddenly, I wanted Tressa's plan to succeed even more spectacularly. I still wasn't sure about the part involving us together, but I believed in the part about getting him back to taking pictures. It's where he belonged.

I just didn't know how I was going to do that.

CHAPTER FIFTEEN

ETHAN

As I stood there on the sidewalk in front of the Richmont hotel, I wanted to tell Summer the truth about everything. That I wasn't the asshole she probably thought I was. That I had my reasons for not being able to tell her the truth that night.

The problem was then what?

So I did what I did best.

"Well, I better get going. See you around the building, I guess," I said before walking away from the one person I should have stuck around for.

I thought about looking back to see if she was watching me walk away. I wanted to, but I couldn't stand to see the expression on her face indicting me for being exactly the asshole I didn't want to be.

By the time I got back to work, my emotions were all jumbled up and the one that had surged to the forefront was anger. And the person who was going to be on the receiving end of all of that anger I had stored up inside me was my sister, the person who'd created this current issue for me.

I found Tressa behind her desk, as usual. Her claim that she actually had some personal life to keep on the down low seemed particularly suspect considering the fact that she never seemed to leave this damn place. Then again, I didn't want to think of her that way. Better to keep my anger finely tuned and not let it get diluted with thoughts of her as anything but the manipulative snake she truly was.

Slamming her office door behind me, I launched into the conversation with both barrels. "What's your plan with Summer, Tress? You trying to be her savior or something? You give her a job and a place to stay? What exactly do you plan to extract from her that requires that level of indebtedness?"

My sister tilted her head up and stared at me for a moment before she let out a sigh. "Why do you always think the worst of me, Ethan? I'm your sister, for God's sake. Why can't I just be doing something nice that will benefit everyone involved?"

"Because that's not who you are. Don't bother pretending to be all nice and kind. I know you better."

She pushed her chair back from her desk and folded her arms across her chest, never taking her eyes off me. "It's not an act. I like Summer. She's an excellent assistant, to be honest. That Julia Carmon is a fool, if you ask me. And why shouldn't I do something nice for Summer like letting her stay at one of our hotels? We have those rooms for exactly that purpose. I told you the other day that I felt it only right. You were part of the reason she became homeless. Why shouldn't another Stone make reparations for that?"

No way was I buying this act of hers. Nope. I knew Tressa far too well.

"Again, because you aren't kind enough to want to help anyone for nothing in return. So what's your deal? First, you tell me you want me to return to photography and you'll support me with our father, and then you bring my ex-girlfriend around to make things extra awful for me here. Are you hoping that Summer will make me hate being here so much that I go back on my deal with Mom and Dad and then you'll have this place all to yourself and be the favorite child who can do no wrong?"

Tressa's expression twisted into a look of disgust. "Actually, I think you like her being around far more than you want to admit. I'm not sure why you've been such an ass to her, but let me clue you into something you seem to have missed. I liked her since the night we met at dinner. She's smart, capable, and beautiful. Why she wanted to spend time with you I have no idea, but I think you better get used to the idea that women like Summer Carmichael don't come along that often, especially for someone with your history. I think you might find that it's not a matter of when you might want her back but if she wants you back at all because she has other romantic opportunities. Think on that a bit. Now if you're done trying to pick a fight with me for the millionth time in our lives, kindly close the door on your way out. I have work to do."

And with that, my sister left me more stunned than I wanted to admit. I hadn't thought about Summer and me getting back together, but the very mention of Summer possibly being with someone else made my chest hurt. Was my sister planning on setting her up with one of her executive types she hung out with? I hated those kinds of guys with their three-piece suits and shiny shoes who only seemed to be able to talk about their jobs and how the fucking stock market was doing. I couldn't imagine Summer with a guy like that.

I didn't want to imagine her with anyone, in fact. The problem was that I'd fucked things up royally with her and then made things worse today with my behavior in the elevator.

As I made my way out of the building, my sister's words repeated in my brain, torturing me. *She has other romantic opportunities. Other romantic opportunities.*

She planned on setting up Summer with one of her friends. She probably had someone in mind already. Maybe that blond haired guy she brought to the house once. But I thought he was gay. Maybe he wasn't. Christ, I didn't know. All I knew was every minute I thought of Summer with someone else was worse than the previous one.

By the time I got back to my place, I couldn't remember how I'd made it home because I'd spent the entire trip from Midtown to the Upper East Side running through every guy my sister knew. The jackass who sat on some board of directors by the age of twenty-four, which made everyone think he was some kind of wonder boy in business. I'd only met him once, but by the time that little get-together ended, I'd wanted to lay him out with a sharp right after listening to him boast on and on about how much his company was worth. His father's company, by the way, but you'd never know it from how he talked. What an asshole!

Summer didn't belong with the likes of him. Plus he was short with stubby hands. He didn't even stand six foot. What was he, like five eight? What kind of kids would they have?

Jesus. I'd never once in my life thought about what someone's kids would look like, and there I stood in my kitchen drinking a leftover beer lost in thought about Summer and the short jackhole's future children.

I needed to get my head together, for fuck's sake.

Maybe if I called Ilsa. I hadn't planned on getting back to her for a few more days, but I had to get my mind off Summer. That's exactly what I needed. A beautiful distraction.

I waited as her face came into focus and saw that gorgeous smile of hers. "Ilsa, what's up? I was thinking about you and figured I should get back with you to talk about those headshots."

"That's great! I just got home from a meeting with my ex-fiancé. Can you believe he wants his ring back? He's so cheap. My lawyer says I'll probably have to end up giving him the damn thing back, but I don't plan to make it easy for him."

And there was that usual Ilsa drama I grew to despise enough that I avoided anything involving her after our last time together. We barely made it to the second call before she began dumping the crazy all over the place.

"What do you say to early next week for those shots? How does Monday night sound?" I asked, completely ignoring her complaining about her engagement ring dilemma.

"That sounds great! Do you want to do it at my place or yours?"

The invitation in her words was unmistakable, but just in case I missed it, she made sure to wink. My kingdom for a woman who understood subtlety.

Strangely disgusted by the barely veiled offer of a night of sex with her, I quickly answered, "Better to do it here at my place. It's easier, and I have all my equipment here. How about six Monday night?"

Ilsa giggled at my suggestion. "Ooooh, that's early, but I'm up for it. I remember how you are, Ethan, so I'll be sure to bring my sunglasses. See you then, hon."

I pasted a smile on my face until the screen went dark and then rolled my eyes. Her reference to the sunglasses meant she thought she wouldn't be leaving until the next morning. Not that she came up with that on her own. My past with her was riddled with long nights exactly as she planned, but I had no intention of getting involved with Ilsa Stanton again, and this time it had nothing to do with breaking some fucking provincial fraternization rules. I simply didn't want what she was offering.

My plan to distract myself with her in shambles, I paced around my apartment trying to think of something else to do besides the one thing I wanted to do. Back and forth from the kitchen, through the living room, and to the bedroom, I walked a path for nearly an hour trying to convince myself that going to see Summer wasn't a good idea.

It wasn't. But still some tiny part of my brain kept making it seem like something I should do. The rest of my brain kept telling me I was crazy. No matter how much I wanted to think about how happy I was with her, the reality of my life wasn't going to change any time soon. This was why I'd stayed single for the past five years. I couldn't honestly say I could be there one hundred percent of the time for any woman, so better to just be there sometimes and focus on everyone enjoying themselves.

The problem was Summer wanted someone who wasn't just a good time guy. I thought I could be that, but it turned out I couldn't be.

And still I found myself driving toward the Richmont Midtown.

I KNOCKED LIGHTLY AND STOOD waiting at her door, my mind running through all the possibilities why she hadn't answered yet. Maybe she was in there with one of Tressa's three-piece suit guys already. My sister did like to work fast. The image of that short guy with his stubby hands running them all over Summer's body made my stomach churn until I felt like I'd puke.

Knocking louder the second time, I stood there needing to know if my horrible thought was true. Was she with that guy already?

The door slowly opened, and Summer stood in front of me in a pair of black pants and a green sweater. For a moment, I couldn't take my eyes off her, but then I remembered about that stubby-handed guy and looked around her to see if she had anyone in the room with her. Thankfully, I saw no one.

"Ethan, what's going on? What are you doing here?" she asked with a mixture of confusion and panic in her voice.

"I was just thinking about…I was driving down Lexington and thought…"

For some reason, I'd suddenly forgotten how to complete a sentence. The truth was I didn't know how to explain why I was standing in front of her hotel room door hoping to be invited in.

"I just wanted to see how you're doing. Can I come in?"

"How did you find me?"

I couldn't help but smile. "My family owns this hotel. I just asked the front desk clerk."

"Isn't there some kind of federal rule about that?" she asked shyly. "I mean, what if I didn't want you to find me? What if you were some abusive ex-boyfriend who wanted to kill me?"

"I don't know if there's a law, but Maia knows I'm not an abusive anything. She's known me since I was a little boy and came to see my father in the penthouse. Can I come in?"

Summer stepped aside and nodded as she asked, "Your father lived in the penthouse here when you were a child?"

Turning around, I waited until she closed the door and explained, "My father would stay in the penthouse when he had to work late. When that happened, my mother would sometimes surprise him by bringing the three of us down to see him. It felt like an adventure going out at night to the city."

"Oh, that sounds sweet. I can see your mother doing that. She was very nice the one time I met her," Summer said nervously as she walked away toward the mini-bar on the other side of the room.

Why didn't she want to be near me?

"My sister must be trying to pinch pennies. She could have put you up in the penthouse since my father doesn't stay in the city working late anymore," I said as I took a few steps toward Summer.

"Tressa mentioned that she sometimes stays late like your father used to, so maybe she keeps the penthouse for herself. I'm not exactly penthouse material anyway, so this is fine," she said as she searched the mini-fridge for something. "Do you want a Coke? It's all I have."

"They didn't even stock the bar for you? I'm going to have to talk to Maia about that," I said with a chuckle as Summer's unease began to seep into me.

Why were we so awkward around one another suddenly? There wasn't an inch of her body I hadn't seen and enjoyed with more pleasure than I'd ever experienced with any other woman, yet now we stood like two strangers who didn't know what to say to one another.

"Oh, it's stocked. I just didn't feel right drinking any of the liquor," she explained as she held out a can of soda for me.

Jesus. Our first encounter in that Richmont hotel bar in Australia had been smoother than this. I needed to change things up or before I knew it, we'd be standing there talking about the unseasonably warm weather we'd been having this month, and that was the last thing I wanted to do with her.

"I'm sorry you lost your place. I really liked that apartment. I wish I knew. I would have done something."

Summer narrowed her eyes to squints. "Like what? Stand on the sidewalk and watch me cry as my stuff was loaded into a moving van and driven away to my parents' house?" she snapped.

Her anger stunned me for a moment, and I stepped back into the couch in the middle of the room. She put her hand up and shook her head sadly. "I'm sorry. You didn't deserve that, Ethan. I didn't lose my job because of you. I was just as much at fault as you were. Maybe if I didn't feel like I had everything taken away from me right after the holidays like some horrible reverse Christmas gift I would have handled it better."

The image of Summer standing at the bottom of her apartment building's front steps crying as all her belongings were hauled away made me want to say something other than sorry. That just didn't seem like enough.

"I've missed talking to you. Even more, I've missed laughing with you," I said quietly. "Lately, I've been thinking about that a lot."

"Don't, Ethan. Just don't."

The anguish in her voice hurt me more than any yelling or cruel words she could snap at me with. She had her head lowered so I couldn't see her face, but I didn't need to. I knew the expression she wore was just like the one that last night we were together as a couple.

And still I couldn't help but move toward where she stood so far away from me.

"It wasn't all bad. I don't think it was. We had some good times, didn't we?"

My question made her head snap up, and I saw all too clearly how hurt she still was about what happened. The sadness when her eyes met mine made me stop dead a few feet away from her.

"Why are you doing this? No models to spend time with

tonight, so you thought you'd while the hours away with me here in my sad hotel room? Is that it?"

I shook my head and confessed the truth to her. "There's been no one since you."

"Don't lie. You know how I hate that," she answered sharply.

"It's not a lie. I haven't been with anyone. I have no interest in anyone else."

Her blue eyes filled with pain stared up at me. "You wouldn't even acknowledge my presence in the elevator this afternoon. Do you know how that feels to know someone you spent time with doing the most intimate things you've ever done can be standing right next to you and not even acknowledge you're there. It hurts. It hurts a lot, Ethan."

"I'm sorry. I didn't know what to say. I know that's no excuse, but I am sorry."

"No, it's no excuse. We had one fight, and then the next thing I knew, you acted like I didn't exist in the world anymore. You made me disappear from your life. And then the very next time I see you, I don't even get a hello or anything. You just stared straight ahead in your father's office like I wasn't there. And then in the elevator you did the same thing. How are you able to just ignore someone you spent hour after hour with? I mean, I know it was just a month, but you're able to act like it meant nothing to you."

Her voice faltered on the word nothing, and she lowered her head again. Taking a step closer, I touched her shoulder and saw her wince like my hand on her caused her pain.

"It didn't mean nothing to me. I'm sorry. I didn't know what to say in my father's office. I never expected to see you standing there when I walked in. As for the elevator, I didn't know what to say there either. I just didn't have the right words."

She looked up at me, squinting again as she searched my face. "Why couldn't you just talk to me like we did before? For that matter, why didn't you just tell me the truth that there was someone else and there had been the whole long time? Does she know you're here tonight? Or do you two just have some kind of open arrangement that allows you to visit any woman's hotel room you like?"

"There is no one else. I didn't lie then, and I'm not lying now."

The confusion I knew she felt was written all over her face. "The text, Ethan. I know what you sound like when you truly care about someone."

She stopped talking and pushed past me. "Well, at least I think I do. Maybe I was just fooling myself."

"You weren't fooling yourself. I did care about you. Still do."

"And still you won't tell me the truth about that message. We're in the same place we were the night we broke up."

"The night you broke up with me."

Summer's eyes opened wide. "I didn't break up with you! I just needed you to admit that there was someone else. You walked out the door, and then I never heard from you again until right now."

"And I told you I wasn't with anyone else. Fuck, Summer! Why couldn't you just believe me?"

Shaking her head wildly, she turned her back on me. "I don't want to do this anymore. I can't do this. It hurts too much. You should leave."

"Summer, I didn't come here to fight. Look at me."

She refused to face me and continued to shake her head. "I can't do this with you. Ethan. I don't know what kind of woman you're used to with those models and whoever else you spend your time with, but I'm not like that. I feel too much for someone like you."

I slid my arms around her and pulled her to me. Instantly, my body reacted, like it knew it had found what it had been seeking ever since that night I walked out.

"There was no one else. There is no one else. Please believe me," I whispered in her ear. "I swear."

She turned in my arms to face me and looked up into my eyes with tears in hers. "Why are you here, Ethan? Honestly, why?"

Swallowing hard, I took a deep breath and admitted the truth to the one person who deserved as much of it I could give. "Because I miss being happy. I miss smiling and laughing. I miss that with you."

Softly, she said, "You never had to lose it. All you had to do was tell me the truth."

And that was the only thing I couldn't do for her.

"I can't. I can just swear to God on anything you want me to swear on that it isn't someone else I'm sleeping with. It's no one I've ever been with. Can't you just believe that I'm telling you the truth?"

"None of that makes sense. You know that and still you say that just like you did that night."

I hung my head, feeling the same exhaustion come over me as the night I lost her. "It's the truth. Everything I've said tonight is the truth too."

"Why should I believe any of this?" she quietly asked, and I heard hope in her words I seized upon.

Pulling her into me, I cradled her face in my hands and kissed her like I'd wanted to ever since that night. Her mouth quickly surrendered to mine, and for the first time in far too long, I felt truly happy. When I looked down at her, I saw she'd missed me too.

Chapter Sixteen

Summer

My head felt like it was swimming as Ethan's lips pressed against mine in a kiss that made me feel like I was melting away in his arms. None of the questions I had about that text message had been answered, and yet there I stood willingly kissing him back like his mouth held the very breath I needed to exist.

So much for my promises to myself that I'd never fall for him again.

Was it possible that the text message wasn't for another woman? If not, then who was it meant for? Maybe a friend? Had I blown up our relationship because he had been a good friend to someone when they needed him?

My brain sifted through the memories of those words he'd written to whoever the recipient was as I tried to believe he hadn't been seeing another woman the whole time we were together. I wanted to accept what he said. The way he made my body react just by a single kiss made me want that so badly.

"God, I've wanted to kiss you like that every day since we broke up," he said softly against my lips.

I closed my eyes and tried to calm my emotions that threatened to unravel all over the place. Ethan had a way of saying things that made me want to give him everything he could ever want without the slightest fight.

But I couldn't let myself fall for him again so easily.

Stepping back, I opened my eyes and saw that familiar look in his that told me he wasn't ready to let me go quite yet. His hand slid down to the small of my back and pulled me back into him.

"Stay here with me," he whispered in a husky voice.

"I don't know. You have a way of making me feel things I'm not sure I should," I said looking away.

But I wanted things to be like they were before, so I turned back to face him and saw the man I'd fallen in love with. His deep brown eyes stared down at me in that way that always made me feel like he was studying me, like nothing in the world was more important than me in that moment. I ran my finger along his jawline, feeling the first signs of stubble for the day that he always had by the time I saw him each night. He was the same Ethan as before.

He smiled that sexy grin that never failed to make me feel weak in the knees. "I can say the same thing for you, except I want to feel those things."

God, I so much wanted to let myself go with him. Maybe if we took things slower than the first time. We had started out going a hundred miles an hour and then got to know one another.

If we were going to take things slowly, I needed to remove myself from right next to his body because from what I was feeling press against my hip, he was already raring to go. Backing up, I held my hand up to stop him as he followed me.

"Let's take this one step at a time. Remember, you couldn't even bring yourself to talk to me this afternoon. Why don't we sit down and talk?"

"Because that's only going to get us back to fighting," he said with a wicked grin. "If we aren't talking, we can't fight, and I have the perfect thing to do that doesn't involve much talking at all."

Oh, God, this was going to be challenging. He never failed to charm, and tonight was no exception.

"Then if I agree not to bring up the singular subject that results in us fighting, can we just talk?" I asked as he stepped back in front of me so close that I could feel how much he didn't want to talk anymore.

He seemed to consider my offer and then nodded. "Okay. As long as we don't discuss that one topic, I'm up for talking."

Surprised he relented so quickly, I smiled and said, "I thought I'd have to push a little harder on that point."

"I always loved talking to you, Summer. I couldn't have missed laughing with you if it was all about the sex."

"Well, I certainly hope not. As a basic rule, if a man is laughing at you during sex, you're doing something horribly wrong," I joked as we sat down on the couch.

Folding my legs under me, I made sure there was enough room between us so all we'd be doing was talking. Ethan leaned back against the corner of the couch and spread his arm out across the back of it, looking as comfortable as ever.

"So what should we talk about? I think I should warn you that anything to do with Tressa will probably end up bringing out the worst in me. In fact, any subject having to do with Stone Worldwide is one I'd like to avoid."

Nodding, I filed those details away, happy to not have to talk about work anyway. As much as I wanted to spend time with Ethan, I didn't like to admit even to myself that I was on the payroll at Stone Worldwide to get back with him and convince him to return to photography.

Well, officially, I was only tasked with guiding him back to his former career. That I hadn't figured out how I'd do that made me question why Tressa had hired me at all, but now that I'd gotten the romantic part out of the deal, I felt better about my job. I just didn't know how to bring up that life he lost without creating a dark cloud over our first real conversation in months.

Stymied by what to discuss, I went with an old tried and true conversational tactic. The weather.

"It's been a very warm winter, don't you think?" I asked with all the sincerity I could muster.

Ethan rewarded my efforts with a full laugh that seemed to

come from deep inside. "That reminds me of the first time we talked at the Richmont hotel bar after that photo shoot."

"Did we talk about the weather? Wow, you must have thought I was the most boring person in the world," I said as that night flashed in my mind and I blushed.

My memories of that night involved not a single word about the weather. All I remembered was incredible sex, followed by more incredible sex, and then falling asleep with my head on Ethan's muscular chest and waking up too late to make my plane. So not a lot of words at all, in fact.

"I actually was the one who brought it up, so if anyone was boring, it was me."

His attempt at being self-effacing made me chuckle. "I doubt there's a single person on this planet who thinks you're boring. Trust me on that."

Whatever all those women who wanted to sleep with him and the women he'd already taken to bed thought of him, I couldn't imagine they ever considered him boring.

A look of sadness darkened his expression, and I had a feeling he forced his smile since it didn't go all the way up to his eyes. "Maybe in the past, but now with my nine-to-five life, I wonder."

"I had a feeling you weren't happy with your new job. You know, working like the rest of us folks in the world doesn't mean you can't take pictures on your off time. You have a gift you can use whenever you want. I mean, if your talent was throwing pottery, well that would be different."

Ethan narrowed his eyes like he didn't understand where I was going with all this, so I quickly added, "Then again, maybe that wasn't the best comparison. You know what I mean, though. Just because you're stuck in an office for a few hours of the day doesn't mean you can't still be a photographer. It wasn't like taking pictures of gorgeous women in tropical locales was what made you a photographer, right?"

He raised his eyebrows at my attempts to make him feel better and chuckled. "You have a hell of a way of making me think my life is a whole lot worse than I thought."

"I'm sorry. Everything is coming out wrong. All I meant was you're a photographer, so why aren't you still taking pictures?"

"Because it just reminds me of what I lost," he answered in a low voice full of sadness.

"Well, you can lose it forever, or you can make your talent mean something else then. I think those are your only choices."

He winced at my matter-of-fact assessment of his life and then gave me another forced smile. "Well, I think I better go. It's getting late and the grind starts pretty early in the morning," he said as he stood to leave.

Everything in me wanted him to stay, but I couldn't do that again. Not yet anyway.

"Stop by again. Next time I'll try not to be so serious. Maybe I'll even have something funny to bring back your smile for real," I said as I followed him to the door.

"I'm glad I came here tonight, Summer. I promise if I see you in the elevator that I'll be my usual charming self from now on."

He lowered his head and kissed me softly on the lips before leaving me standing there watching him walk down the hallway wishing for so much more. The problem was I didn't know how much I could handle of Ethan's usual charming self before I completely succumbed to his charms.

I SAT STARING AT THE TV screen in front of me but a million miles away in my mind. More like a couple miles away at Ethan's apartment. Was he there thinking of me too? I had no idea, but I couldn't help but feel a real sense of regret that we'd gotten off track that night. Things might have still fallen apart for both of us professionally since I was a notoriously bad liar and probably would have told Julia the truth, but at least we could have been there for one another when everything happened.

A familiar sound stirred me from my daydreaming about what could have been, and I reached for my phone sitting beside me on the couch to see my sister Dawn calling me. Yes, my parents named me Summer and my younger sister Dawn. Such was our fate as children of new age hippies.

I swiped her smiling face on my screen and said, "Hey, you! Don't you usually work late on Thursday nights? I didn't think I'd hear from you until tomorrow night since we both live such exciting lives."

"I am working, but I had a great idea, I think, and I'm hoping you can help me with it."

"Okay. Shoot!"

"The shelter is overrun with animals and needs adoptions before we can take any more rescue pets in. I had an idea that I think might help since other shelters have done it and it's worked. Do you know anyone from the magazine business who would be willing to do a story on the shelter to get the word out?"

The embarrassment over losing my job in that very business washed over me once more. Since I had to send my things to my parents to be stored, I'd had to tell them, but I'd begged them not to tell anyone else. I hadn't gotten around to telling my sister yet, mainly because I didn't know how to and still be the cooler older sister. Her asking me to help with her idea meant this was as good a time as any to be honest with her.

"I lost my job, Dawn. I don't work in the magazine publishing business anymore," I admitted quietly.

"Oh, Summer. I didn't know. I'm sorry. Why didn't you tell me?" my sister asked.

It was a valid question since we were close enough we told each other almost everything. I hadn't mentioned anything about Ethan to my parents or anyone else in the world, except Dawn, and she didn't even know his name. He'd just been a new guy I was seeing.

"I was too ashamed. My boss fired me because I was dating that guy, and that was right after he and I broke up."

"And you didn't tell me that either? Why all the secrets, Summer?"

Again, a very valid question.

"I don't know. It hurt too much to talk about what happened, I guess. It's been a rough couple months, but oddly enough, his sister hired me to be her assistant, so I'm back on the road to fame and fortune," I joked, hoping I didn't sound too pathetic to my baby sister.

"I wish you would have told me. You know I would have been there for you. We could have sat together and gorged on chocolate while we bashed Julia and your ex. You know I'm always good for that."

That was my sister in a nutshell. One minute she was asking for help to make life better for shelter animals, and the next she was offering to talk shit about people who hurt me because she knew it would be exactly what I needed.

"It was all too much at one time, so I didn't really want to talk about any of it. After I had to move out of my apartment, I felt pretty low."

"You had to move out of your apartment? I can't believe you didn't tell me that either!" she exclaimed in justified surprise.

I had been basically living a lie when it came to her for the past few months. I wasn't much of a sister, it seemed.

"Yeah. That's the reason we never video phone anymore. I didn't want you to see where I was when we talked, so that's why I asked you to call on the cell. I'm sorry I had to lie. It was just too humiliating to admit my life was falling apart. It's better now, though. I'm living in a hotel room my new boss let me stay in for nothing, so if you want to, we can go back to talking and looking at one another. I just have to get a connector."

"So you have a new job and a new place, but what about the guy? Do you have a new one of those yet?"

I had a feeling she was teasing me, but with how much I'd been hiding, I deserved it, so I laughed it off. Since I had no idea what was going on between Ethan and me, I believed I was telling the truth when I said, "No new guy yet, so this girl's still single."

"And here I was thinking I had all the problems because of the animals."

A thought popped into my head about how I could make it up to her for all my lying and help those little kitties and puppies she took care of. "What if I could find a photographer to take pictures of the animals for the shelter's website and social media pages?"

Dawn didn't understand what I was trying to suggest. "We have pictures of all the animals already, Summer."

"No, I mean something more. They could be like those glamour shots Mom has from when she was a teenager. You know the ones with her looking like a movie star. You could put the animals in front of a nice background and in little costumes and show the pictures off as marketing tools. I've heard of this done somewhere, I don't remember where, but I think it helped get some of the animals adopted. I might know a photographer who might be willing to help. Do you want me to ask him?"

"Yeah, but the rescue has no budget for this, so we can't pay. I doubt any photographer from the city would be willing to do this for free," she said, sounding dejected already about the prospects of my idea working.

"I know. That will be the first thing I tell him. There's no money in the deal. Just helping out kittens and puppies."

"We do have older animals too, you know. Those are even harder to adopt out, especially the ones with problems like a missing eye or leg. He has to be willing to take their pictures too or I can't even think of bringing this to my director."

Jumping off the couch, I began to pace around my hotel room in excitement. "Of course! I just figured I'd sell it to him with the kittens and puppies, but every one you want a picture of will have their chance to be a star. What do you say?"

"It sounds great! You ask your photographer friend and I'll talk to my director tonight before I leave. I can't imagine she'll say no, but I want to get her permission first before we do anything. As soon as I find out if it's okay, I'll let you know."

"Great! If she gives the go-ahead, I'll ask him first thing tomorrow morning."

"Thank you so much, Summer. And remember, you don't have to hide things from me anymore. I'm a big girl now. I can handle a little truth from you."

I had to give my sister credit. Without me noticing, she'd grown up to be a pretty great woman in addition to being an incredible sister and best friend.

"I promise no more lying. And just to prove that, I'll let you in on a bit of truth. The photographer I'm going to ask to do this is none other than Ethan, the guy I was dating."

Dawn's sharp intake of air told me I'd surprised her. "Really? So you two aren't seeing each other anymore, but you're friendly enough to ask him to do something like this for free? You're not going to be exchanging sex or anything for payment, are you? Because as much as I love these animals, I would never ask you to do anything like that. I hope you know that."

In the middle of my hotel room, I stopped dead in my tracks as my mouth dropped open in shock. "I can't believe you sometimes, Dawn! No, I don't plan on exchanging sexual favors for some pictures of your animals."

"Hey, I don't know what happens in New York. I'll let you know as soon as I find out what my director says. And thanks again, Summer. Love you."

"Love you too, you crazy woman."

I tossed my phone back onto the couch and continued to pace from excitement. If Dawn's boss agreed and I could get Ethan to agree, not only would those kitties and doggies be getting some help. I'd be doing my job, and Ethan might even see why he should get back to what he loved.

Looking over at the mini-bar, I thought I deserved a drink to celebrate this wonderful plan.

CHAPTER SEVENTEEN
SUMMER

I AWOKE TO FIND DAWN'S message on my phone telling me the shelter's director had given her approval for my idea, so it was a go on their end. Happy the first hurdle had been cleared, I made sure to wear my nicest work clothes in the hopes that it would help me convince Ethan to do this huge favor for me. Wearing my black sweater dress that fit perfectly in all the right spots, my black leather boots, and my hair and makeup done as perfectly as I could, I took one last look in the hotel bathroom mirror and smiled.

"Okay, Dawn's little animal friends. I've done my best with how I look. Now let's see if I can add some persuasion to the offer."

As soon as I stepped off the elevator, though, all my plans were shot to hell by Tressa. Waiting for me in the hallway, she slid her arm around me and deftly guided me right past Ethan's office to hers as she talked about how busy we'd be all day planning this party to celebrate her mother's art show. Just before the door to her office closed, I looked back to see Ethan sitting in his office looking as miserable as ever behind his desk.

Pushing my plans back to lunchtime, I took my seat in front of Tressa's desk and listened as she eagerly explained all her plans for the party we were to plan. She'd thought of everything from the location to the caterer who absolutely had to handle it and even to the color scheme she wanted to use for the decorations.

"This party is the most important part of your job this week, so you're going to focus on it exclusively. I want it to be perfect for my mother, and cost is no object. I know it's late, but I've gotten the caterer on board and the site is all approved. The building next to the gallery has agreed to let me use their first floor since it's been recently renovated and their tenant isn't scheduled to move in for another month, so it's perfect. That just leaves getting the invitations to guests and the decorations. I'll email you what I want on the invitations. Oh, also I'll need you to handle the alcohol and floral deliveries. Of course, you'll have the car service at your beck and call since I don't expect you to be hoofing it back and forth between here and the gallery in SoHo. Any questions?"

By the time she finished, Tressa was nearly out of breath and my stomach was in knots. Planning this party wasn't out of my wheelhouse by any means since I'd organized similar parties for Julia before, but knowing it was for Nina Stone put far more added pressure on me to get this right.

"Do you have a preference as to where I get the invitations made and do you want them to coordinate with the gold and royal blue color scheme you've decided on or would you prefer a simpler look with gold and white?" I asked as I struggled to remember where I'd gotten Julia's invitations for last year's summer barbeque party made.

After thinking about my question for a moment, she nodded. "Good idea. Let's go with the gold and white. Anything else?"

"Who should I use to get them printed?"

"Oh yeah. Use the company we always use for Stone Worldwide events," she answered as she began opening her desk drawers. "I know I have the card in here. They'll get them done fast so you can have them sent out ASAP."

She pulled the business card out of the top drawer and held it out for me. "Here it is. Tell them you're my assistant. That'll do the trick."

"Can I hire anyone to do the decorating, or do you have someone in mind? I can do it, but I'm not going to lie. I don't have a great eye for things like that."

"Whoever you want. It's late notice, so you might have to be convincing. Feel free to throw my name around and my father's. I want this to be perfect for my mother, so spare no cost either. Anything else?"

Our whirlwind meeting made thinking of ideas next to impossible, so I shook my head no. "I don't think so. If I have any questions, I'll ask."

"Excellent! I can't wait to see the fruits of your efforts. I've got a shareholders' meeting to attend with my father, but if anything comes up, just message me. I should be back here in the office by mid-afternoon."

Tressa began flipping through papers on her desk, so I took that as my cue to leave. As I made my way to the door, she asked, "By the way, any news yet on the other part of your job?"

Turning around, I smiled. "I think I have a lead on something that might work. If it pans out, I'll let you know."

"Terrific! Let's hope it works out."

BY LUNCHTIME, I'D SPENT NEARLY three hours straight on the phone contacting vendors I needed to get this party set. As I began to see co-workers filing out of their offices to head out to get food, I ended a call to the printer Tressa had directed me to. The invitations would be done later that afternoon, so I could begin sending them out today, thankfully. That only left just under two weeks before Nina Stone's show, but hopefully, that would be long enough for guests to plan to attend.

I stretched my legs and walked down the hallway toward Ethan's office. As usual, he sat at his desk looking bored and unhappy. I took a deep breath and knocked on his door, hoping his being miserable wouldn't stop him from considering my request.

He looked up at me and smiled. "Have you been sent by the almighty Tressa to deliver a message?"

I shook my head and tried to stifle a giggle at his

characterization of my boss. "Nope. This visit is purely Summer driven. I have a favor to ask you."

Ethan's eyebrows shot up into his forehead, and his eyes grew wide with curiosity. "A favor. This is the most interesting thing I've heard all day. What's up?"

"My sister Dawn works as a vet tech at Mended Paws Shelter and Rescue outside my hometown in Pennsylvania. They take in animals, many of whom have problems like they've been injured or they're sick. They're overflowing with cats and dogs and are desperate for adoptions, but they have little to no promotion budget. That's where the favor I want to ask you comes in."

He listened to me as I tried to fit in all the information I wanted to explain and nodded. "Okay. So what do you need from me?"

"Well, I was hoping you'd help them out by taking some pictures of the animals for their social media pages and website." I quickly found the rescue's site on my phone and showed him the pictures the staff had taken of the animals. "See, what they have is pretty lame. I've heard of shelters taking interesting pictures of the animals to gin up interest and get people in to adopt these poor little creatures. They shouldn't have to spend their lives in cages at the shelter, Ethan."

He studied the images on my phone and looked up at me. "I've never shot animals, Summer. Christ, even saying it like that sounds bad. I'm not sure I'm the right person for this."

"Please? I know I'm the last person who should be asking you for a favor, but I'm asking you to help my sister more than me. I'm sure if the animals were photographed in interesting ways that I know you can do that more people would want to adopt them. They just need some help. Will you do it?"

He didn't say anything, and I remembered that I hadn't told him the least appealing part of this favor. "Oh, and they can't pay you. I know that probably doesn't make you want to do it at all, but please do it anyway."

Nodding, he looked up at me and said, "I'll do it on one condition. If I do this, you have to go with me to the shelter."

Thrilled he had only that condition, I eagerly agreed. "Of course! I'd planned on offering to go since I love seeing the animals and it would give me a chance to see my sister."

"Okay. When do you want to do it? I can go today, if my slave driver of a sister will let you off early."

"There's no way I can do it today. She has me planning the party for your mother's show, and I have no less than a million things to arrange so it's not an utter disaster."

His smile faded, and he turned his head to look away. "Oh, the show. Yeah, everyone in my family can talk of nothing else."

"What about this weekend?" I suggested. "I know it's a lot to ask to give up a Saturday or Sunday, but it isn't for me. It's for the kitties and puppies."

Ethan looked over at me and my attempt to look pitiful with big eyes full of sadness for those poor animals. "You don't have to do that, Summer. I'm happy to do it whenever. I'll pick you up at ten tomorrow morning. Sound good?"

Barely able to contain my excitement, I practically jumped in the air. "Oh, that's great! Thank you! I really appreciate you doing this. Ten it is. I better go grab my lunch now and get back to my desk since I have a busy afternoon ahead of me. Those party decorations aren't going to get ordered by themselves. Thanks again, Ethan. This means a lot to me, and I know it's going to help the animals."

"My pleasure."

I hurried out of his office, and when I looked back at him, he was watching me walk away. My face instantly heated so my cheeks felt warm and likely made me look like I was blushing. I didn't know if I liked the idea of him thinking he could still have that effect on me.

As the elevator doors opened and I headed out into the Stone Worldwide building lobby, I texted Tressa with the good news.

Ethan has agreed to take some pictures of the animals at the rescue shelter my sister works at in PA. He and I will be traveling there tomorrow.

Stepping out into the warmer than usual February weather, I made my way down the street to the coffee shop to grab a bite for lunch. Just as I arrived, my phone vibrated and I looked to see a message back from Tressa.

Excellent! Happy to hear this news. I'll be back in the office later today so you can tell me all you've accomplished on the party too.

She wasn't a slave driver like her brother thought, but she certainly did have a way about her that made my days fuller than they'd ever been. I couldn't say anything bad about her, though. She'd given me a job and a place to live, and I'd never forget that.

CHAPTER EIGHTEEN

ETHAN

A LITTLE MORE THAN A two hour drive filled with talk about work mostly and Summer and I arrived at the Mended Paws Shelter and Rescue just outside of Devon, Pennsylvania. My mother had taken my sisters and me to this part of the state a few times when we were young, but I'd forgotten how beautiful the area was, even in the dead of winter.

"So this is where you grew up?" I asked Summer as she unfastened her seat belt. "Pretty nice."

She shrugged like it was no big deal. "It was a good place to be a kid. It's nothing compared to where you grew up, but it was okay."

Before she got out of the car, she said, "While you get your equipment, I'm going to find my sister. See you in a few."

Even though she punctuated that with a smile, I couldn't miss the distance she'd intentionally put between us that morning. We'd sat right next to each other for hours, but emotionally, it was as if a five foot wall had been dropped between the driver's and passenger's seats in my Land Rover.

I knew I deserved it, but it didn't make it any easier to take. In a world full of people, lately I'd missed Summer more than I could say. As I watched her walk toward the door dressed in jeans that definitely reminded me how much I liked the view of her from behind, I couldn't help but be sad at the fact that we didn't share things like that with each other anymore. Back when we were together, I would have walked up behind her and patted her on the ass while I whispered, "Thanks for the show" or something equally as idiotic. She always gave me a smile, though, because she knew no matter how I said it, I meant I liked the parts of her that worried her the most.

I missed those times with her.

As I hauled the last of my gear inside the shelter, Summer brought her sister over to introduce us. Similar looking, Dawn was slightly thinner and wore her brown hair short. I didn't know if she was younger than Summer, but she looked about twenty.

"Ethan, I want to introduce you to my sister. Dawn, this is Ethan Stone. Ethan, this is Dawn Carmichael, my sister."

We shook hands, as Summer gave her more details on me. "Ethan's pictures have been on the covers of *Belle*, *Prima*, and even *Cosmo*."

Dawn's eyes opened wide in what looked like appreciation. "Wow! How did my sister convince you to do this for the animals then?"

"She has a way about her that I can't say no to," I answered and looked at Summer with the hope she understood what I meant.

"Well, whatever brought you here, thank you so much. We really hope her idea works so these poor babies find homes. The truth is we need the space for other animals, sadly. Let me go get a few of the kittens to start off with. They're the easiest to handle."

I began setting up my equipment, curious if Summer had told her sister more details about me than past covers I'd shot. "Does she know we used to date?"

She shook her head. "I didn't have a chance to tell her really. We did only date for a month, Ethan."

The way she said that made me feel like shit. Avoiding her gaze, I went back to setting up the background and lighting, still unsure about photographing animals. The basics were the same as with humans, but animals didn't react to lights and sounds like the models I was used to. Plus, I'd never worried about being clawed to death or bitten by a subject before.

Dawn returned with three black kittens in her arms and set them down on a white sheet I'd put on the floor in the corner of the room. Summer immediately hurried over to meet them and cooed, "What are their names?"

"Midnight, Boo, and Spooky, all girls," her sister answered. "They were born on Halloween to a mother cat we took in last September. Their mom was adopted last month, but we're having trouble finding anyone who wants to take even one of the kittens."

I looked up over my camera and shook my head. "Why? I would think people would want kittens more than a cat."

Summer sat down on the white sheet and picked up one of the kittens. Nuzzling her nose, she said sadly, "They don't want them because they're black, Ethan. Even today, people are still superstitious and don't adopt black cats as much as other cats."

That sounded ridiculous. "Really? This isn't the sixteen hundreds. What's wrong with people?"

Dawn nodded and sighed. "My sister's right. You'd be surprised at how many potential adopters immediately say no when they find out a cat or kitten is black. It's just a reality we have to deal with in shelter world."

While I thought about how stupid people could be, I glanced over and saw Summer playing with the three kittens. Their black fur looked striking next to her pale pink sweater. Climbing all over her, they meowed loudly.

"I think they have me confused with their mommy," she joked. "I'm their big, pink mommy."

Giggling, she lay back on the floor. "I must have mixed up my perfume with catnip this morning."

The scene created the perfect image, so while Dawn teased her about some time when they were kids and their cat used to like to fall asleep on her head, I began shooting without letting either of them know. Summer looked incredible smiling and laughing with the kittens as they climbed on top of her. The shots were candid and real, and I wasn't sure I'd ever seen Summer look more beautiful than at that moment.

"Not to rush you or anything," she said as one of the kittens began licking her face, "but I think she's getting ready to eat me over here. You ready yet, Ethan?"

"Yeah. Ready when you and the girls are."

Summer picked up at little blue ball and began rolling it across the sheet. The kittens chased after it, tumbling over themselves as they raced one another toward where it landed. She moved out of the shot and rolled the ball again, sending the three black balls of fluff back across the sheet. This time, the one named Boo reached it first and clutched it in her little paws like she was holding gold. As I got my shots, the three of them piled into one big fuzzy heap, each one fighting to be the one who finally ended up with the toy.

Dawn handed her sister a pink and white feather, and Summer dangled it over the kittens' heads. Once they saw the new distraction, they immediately forgot about the ball they'd so desperately wanted to possess just a few seconds earlier. I smiled as I watched her draw a figure eight with the feather across the white sheet and two of the kittens watched it carefully, while the third pounced on it without another thought. Their joy and enthusiasm for that simple feather made for more great shots.

"Okay, little ladies, it's time for someone else to get their picture taken," Dawn announced as I took my last picture of the three of them with the feather.

Summer picked up the kittens and kissed each one softly on the nose. When she lifted up the last one, she snuggled her against her shoulder as I secretly continued to shoot the candid moments.

"Thanks for being such great models. You guys were even better than the human ones I've worked with," she said before handing her to Dawn. "I wish I could take all of them home."

She followed her sister to the room where the animals stayed as I looked over the shots I'd gotten. I hadn't planned on including any human subjects in the pictures, but I couldn't believe how great the ones with Summer and those black kittens turned out. My favorite was the shot with Summer sitting on the floor as the black kitten named Boo sat on her shoulder like she'd found her favorite place in the world to rest.

She really took a great picture. I'd never shot a single one of her the entire month we were together, and I didn't know why as I stood there looking at how much the camera loved her. From the moment I got my first camera when I was a teenager, I'd taken pictures of my sisters and my parents until they were so tired of it they threatened to hide my camera if I took any more. I'd taken pictures of Cole until he said the same thing, and every woman I'd ever been with had been happy to have their picture taken by me.

But I'd never even considered taking one of Summer, and I had no idea why. Even though she didn't believe it, she was as beautiful as any model I'd ever photographed. The images in front of me at that moment proved that fact. Yet, still I'd never thought about taking a single shot of her.

Had that bothered her? Did she think that meant I didn't see her as beautiful as those models I spent hours shooting on picture-perfect beaches?

Summer returned to the room, shaking me from my thoughts, and I saw she held a large orange cat this time. He sat curled up against her like he was terrified of what was to come next.

"This is Jack. He had to have his left eye removed because of an infection he got when he was living out on the streets. Once they brought him here, they realized it couldn't be saved."

She held him up for me to see the smooth orange and white fur over where his left eye used to be. Then it dawned on me. This cat's name was Jack?

"Someone named this guy Jack? One-Eyed Jack? I can't decide if that's cute or cruel," I said as I stared at the cat.

Pulling out a piece of black fabric on a black string, she put it over Jack's head to cover where his lost eye had been. "He used to wear this before he got his eye out, so I'm going for cute over cruel.

I don't know how long he'll keep this patch on, though, since cats aren't like dogs. They don't like wearing clothes and accessories, so you better get your shots in while you can."

Little did she know, I'd been taking pictures the whole time she stood there with Jack curled up against her. She held him facing toward me so I could get some of him with his eye patch showing and then put him on the ground before stepping out of the shot.

"Okay, Jack's ready for his close up. Let's make some magic," she said with a chuckle as the orange cat plopped down on the sheet like a petulant model refusing to work.

"I don't think he's in the mood for posing," I joked. "I think he's more a fan of the still life."

The look on Jack's face told me he wasn't going to be as willing as the three black kittens, so I needed to take my shots while I could. He didn't move much, so I had to do the moving, but after a few minutes I'd gotten some good pictures before he decided to simply walk away like he'd had enough and had better places to be than right there posing as my model.

"Oh! I better get him before he gets lost. My sister will kill me if anything happens to the animals," Summer cried out as she chased him around the room, scooping him up in her arms just as he headed for the door.

Alone, I looked through the shots I'd taken of One-Eyed Jack and saw he had way more personality through the lens than I'd seen with the naked eye. His mouth formed what looked like a sly smile as he sat there looking up at me while I took his picture, and combined with that black eye patch, it gave him a devil-may-care kind of look I hoped some potential adopter would like. As much as he didn't seem to enjoy being a photographer's model, he seemed like he'd be a pretty good pet for someone who wanted a mellow cat with a dash of attitude. Hopefully, the shots I'd gotten could help him find that person.

Summer came back in, but this time she had a dog with fluffy brown fur and white paws that made him look like he wore socks. I didn't know what breed he was, but he was definitely adorable and I knew I'd get some good pictures of him.

"This is Pokey. He's a Pomeranian mixed with something else they're not sure of. Someone found him living in their shed last December."

"Pokey? Why wouldn't they name him Sox? I mean, come on. Look at his paws. He looks like he's wearing socks."

She rolled her eyes and sat down on the sheet with Pokey. "I don't make the name choices, Ethan. I just deliver the animals and you make the magic, so let's do this because I've got this problem with dogs peeing on me."

I began taking pictures as Pokey bounced around eagerly on her lap. "You didn't say anything about the cats doing that. Why does this poor little guy get that warning?"

"Because he's a dog. Cats only go to the bathroom in their cat box. They're very particular about that. Dogs will go anywhere, especially on people if they're excited, which I can definitely report this guy is."

"Well, since that's the case, I better get going. If you don't want to be in this, you better move a little to your left," I warned as I moved closer to take Pokey's picture.

Summer quickly scooted away, leaving the dog wondering where his newfound friend had gone. Snapping my fingers above my head, I tried to get his attention, but it was no use. He liked her more than me.

"I think I have a new fan," she said with a sweet smile. "Maybe if I stand next to you he'll look over at the camera?"

"It's worth a try. If not, I'm going to have to get you back in the shot or I'll be left with just his profile in all these pictures."

She came around behind me as Pokey watched her every move. Standing at my side, she waved her hand and called out his name. "Over here, Pokey. Look over here for the nice man with the camera."

Hearing her refer to me like that made me laugh, but it did the trick and the dog stared up at her with rapt interest like he had when she sat next to him on the floor. "That's it. Keep talking to him so I can get a few more."

"Who's a good puppy? Are you a good puppy? Are you going to get a new home because of Ethan's wonderful pictures? Yes, you are. Yes, you are, Pokey," she said sweetly, enchanting the dog and me.

I finished and turned to see her smiling at the little dog. "I wouldn't have been able to do that without you. Thanks."

Shrugging, she moved around me and returned to take Pokey back to the animal room. "It's the least I could do, Ethan. You're doing me a huge favor. I can be the dog whisperer to help you out."

I gave Pokey a little wave as he stared back at me while Summer carried him away. Taking a look at the shots I'd gotten of him, I saw that just like with the three black kittens and One-Eyed Jack, the best ones had Summer in them.

Chapter Nineteen

Summer

After two hours of wrangling animals and trying to get them to sit still for Ethan to take their pictures, I sat down on the floor exhausted. He said little whenever we were alone, but that wasn't surprising since I hadn't said much to him from the moment he picked me up at the hotel. It wasn't that I was angry with him or anything like that. I just didn't want to let myself feel for him again.

My sister returned from the room where the animals stayed in their cages and thanked Ethan once again for his help. "This has been really great of you, but I have to close up now. The shelter doesn't have the funds to stay open long on weekends."

"But what about the rest of the animals?" I asked, knowing that he hadn't taken pictures of at least half of them yet. "We have to do them too."

Dawn shrugged, clearly used to not being able to do all she wanted for the animals she loved so much. "We can only do what we can afford, Summer. There's never enough money for everything."

I stood and looked at Ethan, who had started to put his equipment away. "We can't let half of them not have their glamour shots. What about next weekend? Can you come again then and get the rest of them?"

Out of the corner of my eye, I saw a look of surprise come over Dawn's face. I knew I'd already asked a lot of him already, but if Ethan could spare a few more hours on one more day, all the animals in the shelter could have a better chance of being adopted because of his pictures. What was one more day considering all the help it might do?

She looked over at him and smiled. "My sister has always had a soft spot in her heart for animals. If you can't do any more, please don't feel bad. You've already done us such a big favor."

Ethan simply smiled and said, "I'd love to come back next weekend. Saturday at the same time okay?"

Shocked he wanted to do more, Dawn nodded and grabbed his hand to shake it. "Oh, thank you! That's more than generous to give of your time and your talent on a second day. Next Saturday would be great! I have to go get everything shut down for the day, but I'll be back."

I wasn't surprised he'd agree to do more. As much as I knew he loved traveling to exotic locations to shoot the most beautiful women in the world, I'd seen a sparkle in his eye while he photographed the animals at the shelter. Actually, I couldn't help be impressed with Ethan. Not a single one of the cats and dogs gave him anything those models ever did, and still he seemed to enjoy himself.

"I want to talk to Dawn before we go. Give me a couple minutes, okay?"

"Sure. I'm going to be a few packing up the car anyway, so take your time," Ethan said with a smile as he stuffed his gear into cases.

I found Dawn filling the animals' water bowls and grabbed a few to fill up for her. "I'll have Ethan send you the pics this week after he finishes doing whatever he does to them. I'm sure they're going to be great."

She took a bowl from me and walked it over to one of the cages. Crouching down, she opened the door and set it down in front of a scruffy mutt named Zeb. "I really can't thank him or you enough for all of this. The animals looked so cute getting their glamour shots. I really think this will help us find them homes, and the pictures he took will be a vast improvement on the ones we took here at the shelter."

"Well, next week he'll get the rest of them and then hopefully you'll get something happening for these little guys and girls," I said as I handed her a second filled water bowl.

"Summer, this is the guy you were dating a few months ago?" she asked before heading down to another cage.

"Yeah, but we're not together now. We're just friends these days. Or maybe not even friends. Actually, I don't know what we are."

I so wanted to tell her the truth—that I was still crazy about him, but he'd broken my heart and even though I'd let him in more than I planned to ever do again Thursday night, I just couldn't handle that part of his life he wouldn't tell the truth about.

But I didn't say any of that. Instead, when she said she thought he still cared for me, I laughed it off. "Ethan's just like that. He flirts all the time. I don't even think he realizes it."

She gave me a look like she didn't believe a word I'd said and smiled. "I don't know about any of that, but I saw the way he looked at you when you weren't paying attention. And I'll tell you what you'd say to me if it was me in your place. A man like that doesn't give up a single hour of his weekend for someone he doesn't want to be with."

"A man like that? What does that mean?" I asked, curious to know what she saw in him that I hadn't.

"He's gorgeous, Summer, and he's a successful photographer. I don't think I'm exaggerating by saying he could be with those models he takes pictures of for those magazines. He didn't come out here because he cares about shelter dogs and cats. He did this for you because you asked him to. Whatever happened, he's still crazy about you."

I rolled my eyes even as I secretly wished that was true. "Whatever. We tried dating and it didn't work. I better go. I'll see you next Saturday. Tell Mom I'll call her this week, okay?"

"Sure. Have a nice ride back to the city with that guy you're just friends with," Dawn said in a singsong voice.

Sometimes little sisters were a royal pain in the ass know-it-alls. Too bad this time she was wrong.

ETHAN DROVE OUT OF THE parking lot of the Mended Paws Shelter and Rescue, and we headed back to the city without saying much. After only five minutes on the road, he looked over at me and asked, "Are you hungry? I could go for a bite to eat."

I hadn't considered food in all the thoughts going through my head as we rolled down the road silently, but now that he'd mentioned it, I could eat something.

"Yeah. There's a little place about a mile ahead that used to have good food. It's no four-star restaurant, but you won't leave hungry. Assuming it's still open, that is. I haven't been there in a long time."

"Sounds perfect! Just let me know which way to go," he said as he pressed down on the gas, pushing me back against the seat.

"It'll be on the right down the road a little ways. It's called Deston's."

He looked downright pleased to hear about the little diner I used to go to as a teenager after high school football games. I didn't know what he might be expecting, but it certainly wasn't much compared to the places in the city. I thought about warning him not to get his hopes up too high, but he seemed so thrilled about how I described it that I didn't want to burst his bubble.

I saw the restaurant's sign on the side of the road up ahead and pointed to it. "That's it. Right there. They look open, so we're in luck."

"Great! I didn't eat much breakfast this morning, so there was no way I was making it back to the city without getting something in my stomach. This place looks perfect. Do you think they'll have pie? I can't tell you the last time I had pie in a restaurant."

Although it seemed like a strange question, I thought back to what I remembered about Deston's and nodded. "They always had pie back when I went here in high school, so you might be in luck."

He parked the car in an open spot in the half-paved and half-dirt parking lot and grinned like a little boy. "If I can get meatloaf and pie for dessert, I think I might be in heaven at this place. Ready?"

Maybe it was because he had never eaten at Deston's or maybe it was that I had more times than I could count, but I couldn't help but laugh at how excited this little diner on the side of the road got him. I'd hoped he wouldn't think it was a hole in the wall, but that didn't seem to matter to him.

A woman wearing a black skirt and white blouse with her hair up in a bun greeted us as we walked in and sat us at a table near the window on the left side of the restaurant. Handing us enormous laminated menus, she said with a broad smile, "Your server will be Jenny. Enjoy!"

Ethan looked over the top of his menu and said quietly, "I was wondering if this place was going to be one of those throwback places. You know, with the Formica tables. I think I'm disappointed there's no red Formica in sight."

Shaking my head, I knocked my knuckles on the wood table. "Nope. Just plain old wood. I think they're going for an early modern thing. The whole colonial thing is very big in this part of the country," I said as I began to skim the menu.

After a few minutes of sitting in silence since we were the only customers in our part of the restaurant, I lowered my menu. "I wonder where the server is. Any idea what you're going to get?"

He smiled, and it went all the way up to his eyes, lighting up his expression. "They have meatloaf, so I'm set. And I saw a case with pie on the way in too. What about you?"

"I think I'm going to do a club sandwich. If I remember correctly, they were always pretty good here."

Looking around, he found someone and waved them over. With mischief in his dark eyes, he leaned forward toward me and grinned. "Hopefully this is Jenny."

It was, and after apologizing for letting us sit there so long, she took our orders and walked away, leaving us alone. Like we had in the car, we didn't seem to know what to say to one another.

Feeling awkward after a minute or so of silence, I said, "It's really nice of you to do this for a second weekend, Ethan. I know my sister was very impressed that you agreed to come back next Saturday."

He gave me a slight smile and asked, "And you?"

"And me what? I'll come again too."

"No, I mean were you impressed like your sister?"

His brown eyes stared directly into mine as he sat there waiting for my answer like it meant something to him. Looking down toward the wood table, I said, "Sure, I was impressed too. I know you have a million other things you could be doing on a Saturday."

"I have nothing better to do. I spends most weekends trying to forget what I do Monday through Friday, so this was a nice change."

Looking up, my gaze met his and I saw sadness in his expression that made me feel bad for him. "Well, thank you for doing this. I know my sister appreciates it. I do too."

"I didn't realize you were such an animal lover. I guess since you didn't have any pets, I didn't peg you for one."

"I couldn't have any in my apartment, and after that…" My sentence drifted off into silence because I didn't want to rehash all that had happened regarding my living arrangements. Instead I changed the subject.

"You were pretty good with them yourself. Did you have a cat or dog when you were growing up?" I asked, realizing at that moment I knew very little about Ethan before he came into my life last fall.

"We had a dog, but it was my sisters' dog, not mine. They found it wandering on the road one day after school, and after we couldn't find an owner for it, my mother said they could keep it.

He was just a mutt. Nothing fancy, but he never liked me much."

"Well, those shelter animals thought you were pretty great. Not a single one ran away from you or tried to bite you."

Ethan laughed at my attempt at a compliment. "That's the litmus test I use for humans too. Anyone who doesn't run away or doesn't try to bite me is someone who must like me."

"Did you have a good time taking pictures again?" I asked, hoping to take advantage of his good mood to encourage him to get back to photography.

His smiled faded a little as he nodded. "It felt good to do it again. I got some pretty incredible shots. I'll send them to your sister after I take a look at them and clean up any issues so she can post them and hopefully get more people interested in the animals."

"Thank you, Ethan. Really. There aren't a lot of people who would give up their time and talent for free like you are. It means a lot to me."

A pained look crossed his face for a moment, and he said quietly, "It's the least I can do, Summer. Really, you don't have to thank me."

I didn't know what he meant by that. The least he could do for what? As much as I blamed him for us breaking up, he didn't owe me anything now. We were just two people co-existing in the world.

That I had to fight my feelings for him every moment he was near me didn't change that.

We didn't say much more at the restaurant and our conversation on the two hour ride back to the city consisted of small talk about work and the animals at the shelter. When we got back to the Richmont, I wished we hadn't broken up because the Ethan Stone I'd fallen in love with before had made me fall in love with him all over again.

Looking over at me, he smiled but I knew it was forced by the way it didn't go all the way up to his eyes and make them light up like they did when he was truly happy. "I guess I'll see you at work on Monday."

"I guess. Thanks again for everything."

As the sound of car horns honking around us filtered into the car, I thought about inviting him to my room, but I pushed that thought away as the memory of that text replaced it. No matter how much I cared for him, nothing had changed regarding that.

"Thanks, Ethan. Bye."

I hurried out of the car so I didn't have to see the look in his eyes I knew was there in them. That look that told me he wanted the same thing I did, even though it would never work.

By the time I reached my room, my emotions were a tangled mess of need and desire and regret. If only I could believe him about that damn text message!

I threw myself onto my bed and took out my phone to send my own text.

Just got back from PA. Ethan took a ton of great shots. He had a good time doing it too. We're going back next weekend to do more. See you at work.

After I sent it off, I closed my eyes as the thought that maybe I shouldn't be reporting this back to Tressa crept into my brain. I felt guilty, like I was betraying him. I didn't have a choice, though. I'd agreed to help him find his way back to photography for Tressa. She'd let me go on the romantic part of our deal. She wouldn't let me out of this part and still let me keep my job at Stone Worldwide.

And that was the hard truth. I needed that job, so if it meant I'd give her details on how the photo shoots with the shelter animals went, so be it.

He had his secrets, and I had mine.

CHAPTER TWENTY

ETHAN

SOME COMMERCIAL ABOUT HUMP DAY came on the TV, and I thought about how much I'd hoped to see Summer by this time in the week. Tressa seemed to have her rushing around every minute of the workday planning that party for my mother's show, so even though I'd watched for her every chance I got, I hadn't seen her a single time since I dropped her off at the hotel four days ago.

I flipped through all thousand channels and found nothing that could take my mind off her. Was she nowhere to be found at work because Tressa had her running around town on errands for the party, or was she avoiding me?

Or had my sister set her up with some executive type and Summer didn't even work for Stone Worldwide anymore?

My mind filled with thoughts of her with that stubby handed douchebag. I couldn't remember his name, but it was probably something like Brett or Brent. Whatever his name was, to me he was simply some douchebag who didn't deserve Summer.

Not that I had any right to decide who deserved her. I'd proven that in spades already. But that didn't stop me from hating every one of my sister's asshole male friends on the chance that any number of them could be circling around Summer like sharks.

Douchebag sharks.

Maybe if I stopped by her hotel room I'd find her alone. I liked that idea. We could talk like we did last time. I missed talking to Summer. I missed everything about her.

Who was I kidding? The same issue that made me not call her after our fight that night was still part of my life, and that wasn't going to change anytime soon. Missing her didn't make that go away.

Pacing around my apartment, I began to feel like a caged animal. I needed to get out, but I didn't want to go to some club to socialize. I wasn't in the mood to meet people. Hell, I'd barely made it through dealing with Ilsa a couple nights before, and I knew her. She got here all ready for good times, and I kept having to put her off so I could take those damn headshots she wanted me to shoot. She even asked what was wrong with me, like not wanting to sleep with her meant I had some fucking defect.

Maybe I did. I didn't know anymore. I just knew I had to get the hell out of that apartment before I went out of my mind thinking about Summer.

I KNOCKED LIGHTLY ON THE hotel door and wished that by some happy coincidence Summer would be coming out of her room at that exact moment so I could see her. As the seconds ticked by, that didn't happen, though, so by the time Diana opened the door, it took everything in me to pretend I was happy to be there.

Happy to be anywhere.

It didn't take me long to see my sister wasn't having a good day. I had no idea what had happened, but the sadness in her eyes was evident to even someone as miserable as me.

"Ethan? What are you doing here?" she asked quietly as she stepped back to let me in.

"I just wanted to see my favorite sister. That's all," I said, my voice full of fake cheerfulness.

She gave me a tepid smile and closed the door behind me without saying anything about my attempt to be cute. Walking past me, she disappeared into the bathroom as I sat down on the couch and stared at a dark TV.

I was used to Diana's moods and knew this one wasn't good. I didn't know what caused her to sink into the darkness that took her over that night, but I suspected it was the same as usual. Maybe she'd gone out and it hadn't turned out well. Or maybe she wanted to but couldn't get the courage to do it herself. She hadn't called me for help, so it might have been something else too. All I knew was she wasn't doing any better than I was at that moment.

When she finally came out of the bathroom, I saw she'd taken her hair out of the ponytail she usually wore when she was in the room. She never wore her hair up when she went outside. She was too self-conscious about the scars, even though after all the surgeries they were barely noticeable.

"Daddy came by today and we went shopping," she announced flatly as if she felt pressured to say something to me.

I hated when she got like this. I knew I had no right to feel that, but I still hated it. I didn't know what to say to make things better, so I usually sat by helplessly watching her, wishing I could say or do something to make her happy again.

"Want to show me what you got?" I asked as she pushed past my legs to sit down on the couch next to me.

"It's nothing special. You know. Just the same old stuff. I made the mistake of forgetting to put my hair down, so we weren't out for long. Daddy wanted to go for lunch, but I told him I wasn't feeling well, so we came home early."

So that's what happened. I thought about my father trying his hardest to make her smile as they were out shopping that day. He probably wore the same disappointed expression he so often had on his face when I was around. The difference, of course, was that he felt more sadness than unhappiness when it came to Diana.

Fuck. No wonder he loved spending time with Tressa so much. She gave him things to smile about.

"Do you want me to run out and get us some dinner? I know it's a little late, but I can. Or I can get the kitchen to make us something. You know, I'll throw the Stone name around for good for once and have them whip us up a five-course meal," I said with a smile, hoping either of my suggestions might cheer her up.

Lowering her head, she mumbled, "I'm not hungry, Ethan. I'm sorry I'm not going to be very good company tonight."

My heart broke seeing her like this. Pulling her close, I held her and smoothed her hair down her back. "You're always great company to me. I don't need to eat anything. We can just sit here together and relax after a long day. How does that sound?"

She rested her head on my chest and curled up against me. After a few minutes, I felt her body shake and looked down to see her crying. I didn't know what had happened that day, but whatever it was, it had broken her.

"It's going to be okay. I promise it will," I whispered.

She shook her head and sniffled. "Why are people so cruel? Why do they think they should ask awful questions when someone is just looking at a rack of dresses? Why, Ethan?"

So that's what happened. Some ignorant salesperson had noticed the scars on the side of her neck or the faint one on her right cheek near her ear and rudely said something to her about them.

"Because they don't know any better. They don't understand how much it hurts. I know. I know it hurts."

I felt her sigh heavily against me and then start to cry again. "I thought he was nice. He talked to me and smiled and I thought he liked me, but then he saw my neck and asked me what happened like I was some freak or some monster or something. Why did he have to say that?"

Instinctively, I tightened my hold on her as the thought of some guy flirting with her flashed through my mind. Diana didn't have the kind of experience with men necessary to understand we were basically thoughtless assholes ninety percent of the time. We didn't mean to say the wrong thing or fuck up. We just did. But where the hell was our father when all of this was happening? He knew better than to let her go off alone.

"I'm sure he was just some ignorant guy. Don't let what he said bother you. You're beautiful, Diana. He just didn't know what to say to someone like you."

She sat up and pushed her brown hair away from her face to reveal the beautiful blue eyes that never failed to remind me of how innocent she truly was. When I looked in the mirror, I didn't see the same eyes I saw when I was little, but Diana's eyes had never changed. They were the same as when she was a girl and the same as they were that night she looked up at me in terror and begged me not to leave as I held her on the side of that road and prayed to God someone would find us.

"I'm not beautiful. I'm a mess. I live in a hotel room because my family wants to pretend to let me live on my own, but I don't really. I'm afraid to go out. I'm afraid of going in cars. I'm afraid all the time. If it wasn't for Daddy and you and my doctors' appointments, I might never leave this room. No man is going to think that's beautiful."

The sadness in her voice tore me apart. She had no idea how truly beautiful she was.

"Don't say that. The right man will. Forget about the rest of them anyway. We're mostly a group of shitheads, and you deserve better than that. You're strong and smart, and you're beautiful on the inside and out."

She shook her head and said sadly, "Ethan, no one is ever going to want someone with so many problems."

I reached out and moved her hair back off her shoulders. "We're all fucked up, Diana. Everybody is. So what if you are? That doesn't mean you're not beautiful and the sweetest person in the world. That's what men want. Someone who's kind and sweet."

"I'm sorry I'm like this. I don't want to be, and I know how this makes you feel when I'm like this."

Her eyes filled with tears at the mention of how this made me feel. After all that had happened, she still worried about how her sadness made me feel.

I pulled her to me and held her close. "The only thing I feel is happy that I can spend time with you. After all you went through, I'm just glad I have that."

"I'm sorry, Ethan. I didn't mean to bring up that night," Diana whispered low against my shoulder. "I don't blame you for anything."

She may not have blamed me for what happened, but I blamed me. I always would.

I LEFT MY SISTER'S WITH my emotions all churned up. Diana was a mess, and no matter what I did, I couldn't change that. I wanted to more than she could ever know. I just couldn't.

As I walked down the hall, I didn't even think about where I was going. Part of me knew where to go, and the rest of me went along. I didn't think about what might happen. I just let my heart decide what I needed at that moment.

I stopped in front of Summer's door and closed my eyes. All I wanted was to feel good again. To smile and maybe even laugh. Nothing else. Just to feel happy with the one person I missed having in my life.

She answered after the first time I knocked, and I didn't say a word as she stood there looking out at me. I simply stared back at her, happier than she could ever know to see her after four days.

"Ethan, what's wrong? You don't look right. Are you okay?"

"I wanted to see you. To tell you I missed you," I croaked out, my emotions threatening to spill out all over the hallway.

"You said that the other day. What's happened?" she asked, but I couldn't explain what was wrong. "Do you want to come in and talk?"

Her invitation made my heart feel lighter for at least a few seconds, and I walked in to that hotel room hating that it was nothing compared to the apartment she lost. She closed the door behind me, and before I could stop myself, I said, "I'm sorry you have to stay here and you lost your place. I really am sorry."

Summer walked around to stand in front of me and looked up with confusion in her eyes. "I know. I don't blame you. It's okay."

"It's not okay, Summer. None of it's okay. I break things and then other people are left to clean up after me. That's not fucking okay."

Before she could say another word, I stepped toward her and took her face in my hands. I didn't want to feel like this anymore. I didn't want to keep fucking up and then feeling sorry for ruining people's lives. I wanted to be the person I believed existed inside me somewhere. The kind of person who people like Summer and Diana thought I was even though I'd shown them differently.

"What's wrong, Ethan? Why are you saying these things?"

I couldn't explain why to her, as much as I wanted to. I wanted to tell her about that night and how I never meant to hurt Diana. How I tried to escape even thinking about it by running away to any distant place I could find.

But I couldn't.

"I never meant to hurt you, Summer. I need to know you believe me about that."

I wanted her to understand that there was never anyone else when I was with her. That there was never anyone else until she came into my life, even if I couldn't explain some things about me.

She nodded and gave me a sweet smile. "I don't think you did. I don't think you're a bad person. I don't."

"I loved being with you. I wouldn't miss you so much if I didn't. You made me happy."

Summer cupped her hands over mine on her cheeks and looked into my eyes. "Why aren't you happy now, Ethan? From where I stand, you have everything a man could possibly want, so why aren't you happy?"

Her question hung in the air between us as I tried to think of an answer, but it was no use. I didn't need to search for why I wasn't happy. The truth was standing right in front of me.

"Because I don't have you."

Lowering her head, she said, "I don't know why that should matter. It didn't matter enough to call me after we had one fight. I think you're confusing losing your livelihood and losing me."

I tilted her face up so she had to look at me. "I can take pictures any time I want. You told me that. Fuck, I barely do any work at Stone Worldwide, so it isn't like anyone would miss me if I walked out every goddamn morning and didn't come back for hours. But I still don't have you."

"What do you want from me?"

"I want you. That's it. Nothing else. No one else. Just you, Summer."

"And you'll tell me the truth?"

"I've never lied to you after we got together. Never. I swear."

I waited for her to voice that same demand as before, but it didn't come. For the first time since that night I lost her, she didn't ask for what I couldn't give her.

And then quietly, she said the words I'd longed to hear. "I miss you too, Ethan."

Pressing my lips to hers, I felt a rush of happiness wash over me that made me feel lightheaded. I slid my tongue into her mouth and felt hers meet mine as eagerly.

She missed me.

Summer ran her fingernails along the back of my neck, sending strings of pain across my skin. I deserved whatever she did to me after all she'd been through, and as she tore those nails over me harder each time, I reveled in the reality that she was mine again.

CHAPTER TWENTY-ONE

SUMMER

SILENTLY, I PRAYED TO GOD that I wasn't making a mistake as I slid Ethan's shirt off his shoulders to reveal that perfect body I couldn't help but adore. Our first time I'd been drunk. The first night we made love once we were dating I'd decided I didn't want to wait any longer to enjoy him again.

This time? I had no good reason for letting him back in. He hadn't told me the whole truth about that text, and even though I wanted to believe him, a tiny part of me couldn't because of what I'd read.

And still, there I stood tugging at his pants to get them off as he sent the most delicious sensations racing down my body with his tongue on my skin. At least if it was just about fucking, I could think to myself that I was safe. Sex was just sex with some people, after all.

That wasn't the way it was with him, though. Even if I wanted to be detached, the way he stared into my eyes as he pumped into my willing body made me betray that desire to keep him at arm's length, at least emotionally. With Ethan, sex had always been all-consuming, and I knew tonight wouldn't be any different.

He murmured my name next to my ear before his hands cupped my breasts and squeezed just hard enough to send a ribbon of need directly to my pussy. I finally unbuttoned his pants to find his cock hard and ready to go.

Tugging my head back, he looked down at me with a

wickedness that always seemed to come out in him at times like this. "God, I need to be inside you, Summer."

Implicit in his words was something of an apology, though, like he wished this time could be romantic but all he had inside of him was pure need. I didn't need hearts and flowers tonight either. I just needed him.

I wrapped my hand around his cock and smiled. "Then don't wait."

In a flash, he kicked his pants and boxer briefs away and lifted me in his arms. I wrapped my legs around his waist and clung to his neck while he walked us into the bedroom, his muscles tensing with each step he took.

"I've missed you like this," he groaned as he lowered me to the bed and followed a second later.

Before I could tell him how much I missed feeling him next to me and worshipping every inch of him, he lay his body over mine and reared back. Grabbing a handful of hair, he tugged hard in that way that never failed to make me run wet with desire and then thrust his hips forward, filling me in one swift push. It took my breath away so only a tiny whimper escaped my throat as he began pumping into my body.

He stared down at me with brown eyes utterly filled with need—need to possess me, need to find that happiness he'd always found with me. Need to escape whatever he'd been running from for so long and find solace in my body.

His gaze practically hypnotized me and made me forget how much he demanded as his cock stretched me each time he slammed into my body. I lifted my legs to wrap them around his waist, tilting my hips to take every delicious inch of his cock inside me. The change in position elicited a low moan that sounded like it came from deep inside his chest.

"Oh…fuck…just like that," he said breathlessly before filling me completely once more.

I watched him watch me, entranced by how his focus never

faltered. He fucked me like a man on a mission to utterly possess me, and I loved every second of it. My body reacted as it always had with him, and I felt the first hint of my orgasm begin to form deep inside me. He sensed it too and changed his motion from hard and fast to slow and easy.

"Not yet," he groaned. "I don't want this to end yet."

"You can always make me come a second and third time," I whimpered, desperate to feel my release.

A wicked smile formed on his lips. "I know, but I always love the first time you come the best," he whispered while he slowly eased out of me, leaving my body feeling empty.

I nudged my heels into the base of his spine to bring him back. "I love it too, so since we're in agreement, why don't you give me what I want?" I playfully begged.

He filled me again inch by inch until our bodies joined and kissed me sweetly. "I love it when you whine like that as I'm fucking you. It makes me want to tease you even more."

My lower lip pushed out into a pout. "Not fair."

"All's fair in love and war," he said with a grin as he thrust into me.

I arched my back and closed my eyes when he hit a spot no other man had ever reached on my body. "Which one is this?"

Ethan slid his hand from my hair to around my neck and pushed hard into me. "It's not war," he whispered against my lips.

I opened my eyes to see something different in his eyes now. They seemed softer, even as his hand gently squeezed my throat and his cock once again pounded into me.

My body reacted to the way he looked at me, and I knew I wouldn't have to wait much longer to come. Tilting my head back, I closed my eyes and hung on to his shoulders as my release washed over me. His hand closed in around my neck to let me know the feel of my body tightening around his cock was inching him closer to him coming too, and seconds later, he plunged into me one last time.

I didn't know how long we lay there together, our bodies still joined as intimately as possible. Ethan breathed heavily next to my head, and when I turned to look at him, his eyes were closed and his long dark eyelashes fanned out on his face.

On those nights when we would drift off in one another's arms at my apartment, sometimes I'd wake up and see him sleeping beside me. He looked so peaceful and sweet, just as he did at that moment in my temporary bedroom at his family's hotel.

Reaching out, I ran my fingertip over his cheek. His eyes slowly opened, and just like always when I woke him, he smiled at me.

"I missed you," he said in a low voice that hit me in that same place his words did as he made love to me.

"I missed you too."

He closed his eyes for a moment before opening them again. "I love you, Summer."

Surprise rushed through my brain, and before I could stop myself, I said, "You love me?"

Ethan nodded. "I didn't realize it until I saw you with those kittens the other day. I'd been so busy first being angry at you and then missing you more than I could bear that I guess I hadn't realized everything I was feeling was because I love you."

I stared at him as if to see if he was telling the truth. From the moment we met, I struggled with why a man like him would be with me. I slowly realized with each minute we spent together that even though he seemed to have been blessed with everything life could offer, for whatever reason, Ethan Stone wasn't happy. And that's what he found in me.

Happiness.

But still I could never be sure if he felt what I felt. I'd never said it to him for fear I'd scare him away, but now that he'd spoken those three little words, I finally wanted to say them too.

As he stared at me waiting to hear what I'd say in return to him, I kissed him softly and whispered, "I love you."

With my eyes closed, I felt a smile form on his lips and then I heard him sigh and say, "I promise I won't make you regret saying that."

He had no idea how terrified I was that he'd do just that.

I PUSHED MY HAIR OFF my face and looked for Ethan on the other side of the bed, but he wasn't there. Sitting up, I glanced down at my naked body and instinctively pulled the sheet up to cover my breasts.

"Why do you do that?" I heard him ask and looked up to see him standing naked in the doorway, perfectly comfortable in his skin as usual.

"It's in every movie I've ever seen with post-sex scenes. I guess I'm impressionable. Why don't you ever think to put a stitch of clothing on when you walk around other people's places?"

He laughed and shrugged at my suggestion. "Who's going to see me? You? You've seen everything there is to see more than once, and this time you were even sober, so I don't know why I'd cover up."

"You make it sound like I was drunk every time we had sex before tonight. I was drunk the first time, and I wasn't even really drunk. Just buzzed and a little out of my head."

He walked over to the side of the bed and leaned over to kiss me softly on the lips. "I'd say you were a bit more than a little out of your head that night. I thought I was getting a nice girl, but that idea was blown out of the water about five minutes in."

Looking down at his cock stiffening as we spoke, I rolled my eyes. "Are you ever not ready to go?"

He followed my gaze and then lifted his head to look at me with a devilish glint in his eye. "He knows what his job is, and he's an overachiever. What can I say?"

"What time is it?" I asked, suddenly worried I'd overslept and would be late for work.

Casually, Ethan checked his phone on the night table. "A little after one. Do you have somewhere you need to be?"

"No, and would you get back in bed, please? I feel weird with you standing there pointing that thing at me like that," I said, lifting up the covers for him.

He chuckled at me and slid under the sheet next to me. "Okay, I'm here. Do with me what you will."

God, he could be so cute at times!

"What makes you think I want to do anything?" I asked, pretending to be disinterested in him. "We've had a few sessions already, and that shower was so hot it pretty much knocked me out. Maybe I just want to sleep."

Smiling, he slid his hands down my back to cup my ass and pulled me to him. "I know. Remember, I was the guy in there with you when your legs started to give out? I think for the future, shower sex with us needs to be with cooler water."

"I love how you just ignore my claim that I might want to sleep."

Ethan nuzzled my neck, sending ripples of need through my body. "Well, I'm hoping that was you just teasing me."

"Don't you ever get tired?"

He leaned back and shook his head. "I'm making up for lost time. Not having sex for months makes me this way."

"Don't lie, Ethan. You don't have to do that with me," I said in a serious voice, unable to believe he didn't go with anyone while we weren't together.

"I'm not lying. I wasn't with anyone since the last time we were together. By the way, my hand and I were getting a little too chummy, so I've decided to break up with him. That leaves things up to you. Just thought you should know."

While I had a hard time believing Ethan had forgone sex with other women for the cold comfort of his hand during the months since we were together, his cute way of talking about him masturbating make me giggle.

"Please tell your hand I'm sorry. Maybe he can find another

cock to make happy."

"I don't think so. He's a one-cock hand, and he's officially retired."

The way he looked at me with such innocence in his brown eyes while he talked about sex and his one-cock hand made me love him even more. "Well, if that's the case, I guess I better get to work."

I pushed him onto his back and pulled the covers back to reveal his naked body all ready for what I planned to do. Straddling him, I leaned down and kissed him long and deep. Surprised since he thought my hand was going to take over for his, he pulled me down on top of him and angled his hips to enter me.

Lifting myself off him, I moved down his body. "Uh-uh. I have something else in mind, so you lie back and enjoy yourself."

He put his arms behind his head and grinned wickedly. "I like where this is going. Do continue."

Ethan's body was truly something to enjoy. I ran my hand over his muscular arms and chest covered in tattoos down his torso to those washboard abs punctuated with that beautiful V that seemed to point directly down to his cock. A light dusting of dark hair trailed through the middle of that V. I traced it with my fingertip, making his skin quiver beneath my touch.

I'd never been with anyone so gorgeous who seemed oblivious to his appearance. Or maybe he was just so comfortable with how he looked that he never thought about it. Whatever it was, I loved to look at his body as the work of art it was.

His cock stood at attention and ready for my mouth, so I flicked my tongue over the crown as a tease. Ethan's eyes rolled back in his head, and he let out a deep moan.

"This is already way better than my hand, I want you to know."

I looked up and met his gaze with a fake look of irritation before taking his cock in my hand to stroke it. "Shhh. I'm working my magic here."

He bit his bottom lip and moaned again. "Oh, yeah…"

My gaze fixed on his expression of pure ecstasy as I slowly took as much of him as I could. My hand held him tightly at the base the way he liked, and I began to slowly move my mouth up and down his cock, flicking my tongue as I made my way along the shaft.

Above me, he groaned low and deep as I sucked the head like a lollypop. I liked to tease him a little before giving him what he wanted, and when he stuffed his hand in my hair, I sensed he'd had enough of my teasing.

I looked up at him and saw the playfulness had left his eyes, replaced by that look of complete need that made him look so incredibly sexy. Clearly, the time for games had ended.

"Summer…you're driving me crazy here," he said in a voice that didn't even sound like his.

"I guess you want something more, huh?"

He stared down his body at me and nodded. "Yeah, and if you don't do something fast, I'm going to flip you on your back and fuck your brains out. Your choice."

As I slowly stroked his cock, stopping each time I hit the tip, I licked my lips and smiled. "So impatient."

Narrowing his eyes like each moment caused him pain, he said, "It's been months since you had my cock in your mouth, so yeah, call me impatient. I'm not going to be responsible for my actions in about two seconds, Summer, so make your choice."

As much as I loved the cute Ethan, I adored this version. Taking his cock in my mouth, I slid down until my lips met the top of my hand stroking the base. The head hit the back of my throat, but my body remembered how to please him. I stared up into his eyes watching me pleasure him the whole time as he grew closer to that moment he so desperately craved.

The look he wore changed from need to power as I sucked his cock. I literally had him in the palm of my hand, yet he stared down at me like he had all the control. And he did. I wanted to please him. I wanted to see him wince in that sexy way he did whenever he came from my mouth on him.

I wanted to give him this because he wanted it. It was as simple and pure as that.

A low moan escaped from his mouth and then I saw that wince as he came. His hands tugged at my hair to keep me on him, but he didn't have to force me. I wanted to do this as much as I wanted him in every other way.

Chapter Twenty-Two

Summer

MY ALARM WOKE ME FROM a sound sleep, and I sat bolt upright in bed to find my phone and turn off that horrible chiming sound. After a few seconds, I saw it through bleary eyes on the nightstand and got rid of the noise that had interrupted the soundest sleep I'd had in weeks.

I lay back down next to Ethan and hated that I had to leave that bed to go to work. He inched over toward me and wrapped his arms around my body, making me hate what I had to do even more.

"You don't seriously get up to that noise every day, do you?" he asked in a groggy voice.

"Yes. I don't have my alarm clock anymore, so I have to use my phone's alarm. That's the best one out of the bunch, but I'm not usually so unhappy to hear it. I can't tell you how much I don't want to get out of this bed right now."

"Then don't. Call in sick. I'll do the same. Trust me. Stone Worldwide will go on just the same without the two of us," he said as he snuggled his face into the space between my shoulder and my chin, tickling me with his new beard growth.

"I wish I could, but I can't. I have too much to do, and it's already Thursday."

"I think it's National Take Off Work and Fuck Like Bunnies Day. Yeah, I think I saw that on my desk calendar the other day. No way you can go into work now. We've got bunny work to do."

His sleepy joke made me smile, and I rolled over on my side to snuggle with him. "This bunny needs her job, Ethan. Don't you have a job to be at too?"

He opened his eyes and grimaced. "Trust me. I could never show up again and nothing would happen. You're far more important to that place than I am."

"That's why I have to go to work, as much as I hate leaving you and this bed."

Tightening his hold on me, he smiled. "Only if you promise that by five-thirty we'll be back in this bed just the way we are right now."

I kissed him and said, "It's a deal. I'm a little surprised you didn't suggest a lunchtime quickie, to be honest."

He shook his head and his grimace returned. "I know my sister too well. I'm guessing you barely get enough time to grab a bite to eat. There's no way you'd have time to get back here and have some fun. Your boss is a slave driver."

"I better get going. You getting up?"

I slid out from underneath the covers and headed toward the bathroom as he mumbled, "Nah. Today they get slacker Ethan who doesn't show up until ten or so. I'm hoping that leads to me getting fired."

EXHAUSTED AFTER A LONG DAY of work, all I wanted to do was crawl into bed with Ethan and sleep until tomorrow. Tressa had kept me busy running all over town practically from the minute I arrived at the Stone Worldwide building, and although the car service was certainly easier on my feet than walking block after block to complete her errands, the end result was the same tired me.

I'd hoped to see Ethan on breaks, but since I didn't get any, that meant I hadn't spoken to him since I kissed him goodbye that morning as he lay naked in bed. He'd texted me a few cute messages, though, and the plan was to meet back at my hotel room after work. Too bad I'd had to work well past five o'clock.

Pushing open my door, I stepped into my hotel room and saw him sitting at the table in the corner that now had a white tablecloth draped over it. Dressed in a blue dress shirt and jeans, he looked fresh and clean compared to how I must have looked. The table was set for dinner, but a quick look around and a few sniffs for the scent of food told me there wasn't any.

"She kept you this long? Man, she really is a slave driver," he said as he walked over to greet me at the door with a kiss.

Ethan took my bag and tossed it onto the couch as he guided me over to my seat at the table. Still confused about why it would be set if there was no food to eat, I looked around again to see if I'd missed some take-out bag, but no. Nothing.

"This looks great, but I think something is missing," I said, not too tired to make a little joke.

He smiled and rolled his eyes. "Patience. I've got a plan here. There's a hot bath waiting for you, so go get into it and relax. The food will be here in about a half hour, so that should be enough time to soothe your aching feet, which look like they're in agony in those shoes. Then we'll have a great dinner made especially for us by the chef here at the Richmont and relax after a long day at work."

My mouth dropped open as I sat there in shock. He'd done all of this for me? Wait a second. I worked late, so how was the bath water still hot?

"How did you know when I'd get back? I worked hours after I was supposed to."

Ethan guided me toward the bathroom. "You can thank the security guard in the lobby at work for that. Seems the guy is a true romantic at heart. Who knew? I didn't. Hell, I didn't even know his name until this morning. But when I told him my plan to surprise you, he was happy to help. Now go relax and when you're finished, we'll have dinner."

Still stunned by all of this, I didn't say another word. He kissed me again, and then closed the door behind me, leaving me in my hotel bathroom lit with candles Ethan had placed all around the tub and vanity. It may have been the most thoughtful thing anyone had ever done for me.

Twenty minutes later, I felt like a new woman. My feet didn't ache anymore, and I didn't feel like the dirt of the city clung to me. That bath was exactly what I needed.

The scent of dinner drifted in under the bathroom door as I dressed in a Richmont hotel robe Ethan had laid out for me. I smelled lemon and some kind of herb. Whatever it was, it made my mouth water.

He sat at the table waiting for me and lifted the silver domed lid covering the main dish to reveal salmon. Smiling, he said, "Did you know these things have a name? It's called a cloche. I had no idea. I thought they were just covers."

"You learn something new every day," I said, sitting down in my chair across from him. "You did all of this for me, Ethan?"

Looking up from cutting a piece of salmon, he nodded. "Yes. Do you like it?"

"Of course I do. Who wouldn't love having someone do this for them?"

My answer made his smile grow bigger. "Good. I think you're going to love this dinner. I can't remember all the things the chef told me about it, but just smelling this salmon is making me want to devour it."

He served me a piece of salmon with asparagus and boiled baby red potatoes with rosemary and then put some of the meal on his plate. Before I could ask him if he wanted a can of soda, he abruptly stood up and walked over toward the mini-fridge.

"Almost forgot the beverage for this fine meal. I feel like I should give full disclosure here," he said as he leaned down to get us our drinks. "I don't usually drink wine of any kind, but according to the chef, I'd be committing some kind of culinary crime if I drank anything but this with the meal he prepared. I didn't feel like telling him I'm not a wine drinker, so I just took it. If you don't like it, I'm sure everything will taste just as wonderful with soda."

Ethan poured each of us a glass of the white wine the Richmont's chef had chosen for us and handed me one. Lifting his in the air, he said, "To you, after a long day working far too hard for whatever she's paying you."

As I watched him sample the wine, I felt a twinge of guilt pinch at me. Tressa had hired me to basically seduce her brother and get him back to photography so he'd be out of Stone Worldwide. I had told her I wouldn't include the romantic part in the deal, but that left me being paid to convince him to return to his previous life. As I sat there with that beautiful meal he arranged all to make me happy, I couldn't help but feel like what I was doing for his sister was wrong now.

"Don't you like it? For white wine, it's not too bad."

His question roused me from my guilty thoughts, and I quickly nodded. "Oh, it's wonderful. All of this is. I can't believe you did this for me."

"Why? You deserve it, and this isn't the first time I've cooked for you. Remember those nights at your place when we tried to cook what that guy was making on that show?"

I laughed at the memory of the two of us trying to follow along with that cooking show host's directions. "We never seemed to be able to get the dish right. I think they skip steps in the commercial breaks."

Ethan smiled and I saw that sexy look fill his eyes. "Well, the fact that we'd start goofing off halfway through probably didn't help, and I'm pretty sure none of that guy's recipes include what I did that one night. It's no wonder you didn't measure the ingredients correctly with me between your legs."

My cheeks involuntarily warmed, making me blush at his mention of that night, and I looked down at my dinner. Ethan continued to eat and said, "I love how cute you get when I say something that embarrasses you. Your cheeks get all pink."

"I don't know why that still happens. I'm old enough that I

shouldn't be blushing at things anymore."

He reached his hand over and touched mine. "Look at me, Summer."

I did as he said and saw him smiling at me. That sexy look in his eyes had disappeared, replaced by the soulful look he always got in them when he was serious.

"I love that you still blush. I don't care why you do. I just think it's sweet. Don't feel bad because you're sweet. There should be more sweet people in the world."

And just like that, I fell in love with him all over again for the hundredth time.

✦ ✦ ✦

ETHAN TURNED OFF THE CAR and leaned over to kiss me. "I'll be there in a few after I get my gear, so you can pick out the first model of the day."

Chuckling as I thought back to all the human models I'd dealt with in my time at *Belle*, I said, "I think today we'll start with dogs since we started with cats last time."

"Whichever you like. You're in charge of the shoot. I'm just the guy taking the pictures. Just like the first day we met."

"I'd rather deal with animals. They don't do stupid things and then have to be coaxed back to their marks."

Turning to open his door, he nodded. "Me too. I think the only thing the human models have over the animals is that they don't drool."

"Aw, come on. What's a little slobber between friends? Anyway, they don't drool on you. I'm the one who has to deal with that."

I didn't mind a little doggy drool. It was a small price to pay for helping out the animals. After all I'd had to deal with from human models, I'd take it.

While Ethan unloaded his equipment, I found Dawn getting ready for us. Thrilled I'd been able to convince him to come back a second time, she excitedly ran up to me and gave me a big hug.

"You were right! The pictures have been working their magic. We've already had people calling here to ask about the animals, and guess what? The black cat sisters Midnight, Boo, and Spooky went to their forever home two nights ago! This was such a great idea, Summer!"

Happiness rushed through me at her news. My idea had actually worked. "Oh, my God! That's great! I'm so happy those little kittens got to stay together."

"As soon as the little girl who came with her mom saw them together, that was it. The mother told my director that her daughter saw the picture and couldn't stop talking about how beautiful the kittens were. She'd only planned to take one, but when the little girl met all three, she begged her mother to keep the family together. I'm telling you it was the picture we put up online. Ethan sent me a bunch of them with the black kittens, but he suggested one with the feather was the best, so that's the one I told my director to use. It worked!"

I turned at the sound of the door opening to see Ethan carrying his equipment into the building. Thrilled at the news, I said, "Dawn just told me your picture of the three black kittens helped them get adopted this week! Isn't that great?"

He smiled and nodded. "Did they use the one with the feather? I thought the colors and their black fur contrasted perfectly."

"They did, and it worked! They all went home to one family. I'm so happy this is working."

"Well, give me a couple minutes and I'll be ready to do more. Have you picked out the first model?" he asked as he walked toward where he wanted to set up.

"Not yet. Let me go now and do that."

Dawn and I hurried to the room where the animals stayed. Grabbing my arm as I made my way down past the cages, she said, "Something seems different about you guys today. What's up?"

I turned to face her and couldn't help but smile. "Shhhh. I don't want him thinking I'm in here gossiping with you about us.

We're back together. It happened the other day. We said I love you. I have to admit I feel like a fish out of water with him sometimes, though."

God, I sounded like an insane person rambling like that.

"Why? It's obvious he's crazy about you. What guy gives up his Saturday to take pictures of shelter animals for free unless he wants to impress the woman who asked him to do it? I'm surprised you didn't see that yourself, Summer."

"I don't know. I mean, we were together before and it was incredible, but then it fell apart. I didn't want to get my hopes up. Maybe he was just being nice. But I think things are different this time. He seems different."

A slow smile spread across my sister's face. "So who said I love you first?"

Looking around to make sure he didn't hear that, I whispered, "Not so loud. He did. I didn't expect it, and then bam! He said it and I didn't know what to say. I fell in love with him the first time we were together, but I never told him. I told him this time, though."

"Who wouldn't fall in love with him? He's gorgeous, worth millions, and he's clearly super sweet when he wants to impress someone. He doesn't happen to have a brother a little younger than him, does he?"

"No. He's a triplet, but the other two are sisters. One of them is my boss now, in fact. We better get going. I think we should start with a puppy today, so let's find one and get out there."

Dawn directed me to a yellow lab with only three legs. He'd lost one when a car hit him, and the shelter's director found him lying on the side of the road dying one night. She used her own money to pay for the surgery and to nurse him back to health, and he'd just arrived at the rescue in the past week.

I carried Butterscotch out to the other room where Ethan had already set up everything we needed to get started. Introducing him to our first model, I said, "This little guy's name is Butterscotch and he's had it rough, so I'd love to be able to help him find a nice warm home to call his own."

Ethan's gaze focused on the area of the puppy's missing leg. "Poor little guy. He can get around on three legs? That's pretty incredible, so let's see if we can make that obvious to everyone who sees his picture."

He pulled a piece of navy blue fabric from his back pocket and flattened it to get the wrinkles out. When he turned it over, I saw it had a big S decal printed on it like the cape Superman wears.

"Where did you get that?" I asked, and immediately wondered when he got it. Other than work, we'd spent every other minute together since Thursday.

"I found this pet boutique about a block away from my place the other day. I never even knew it was there. I found a bunch of stuff I thought might work, so let's see if Butterscotch will wear this cape so everyone can see how super he is."

As Ethan tied the cape around the dog's neck, Dawn and I stared at each other, our mouths open in amazement. When he finished, he stepped back and smiled.

"Now the trick is to get him in place where I can get the cape and the S in the shot. This might be tricky, so Summer, I need you to get down on the ground with him and hold him for a minute while I plot this out."

I did as he asked and watched as he walked around in front of us getting ready to take the pictures. Smiling down at me, he said, "I wish I could use something to make the cape fly out behind him. I think you're going to have to do that and I'll crop you out after."

"That's fine with me. I'm not anyone who should be in front of a camera anyway. Just tell me what you need me to do so Butterscotch gets his glamour shot."

Crouching down, he gave the dog a quick pat on the head and leaned in to kiss me sweetly on the lips. "Okay, I need you to hold the cape out behind him so the S is showing. I doubt he's going to sit still for much of this, so I'm going to make this quick and hope I get some shots I can use. Ready?"

I nodded and leaned over to whisper to Butterscotch, "Okay, little guy. It's time for your close up."

Ten minutes and a few mishaps later, including one involving me having to chase after the three-legged dog who moved much faster than I thought he could, Ethan had a few shots he thought might work and the yellow lab was done with his part in the photo shoot for the day. I carried him back to his cage and then Dawn pointed out an older dog that had been at the shelter even before she started working there.

I looked in his cage and saw an old dog with sad eyes and scruffy brown and black fur staring down at the floor. He didn't even react when we stopped in front of him.

"What's wrong with him, Dawn?"

She shook her head sadly. "Nothing. He's just old. He's been here for so long I don't think he knows anything else, Summer. After seeing what Ethan could do for Butterscotch, I'd love to see him try something cute for Trooper. He deserves to have someone see him as more than just an old mutt nobody wants. He could be a great dog for someone older. He's calm and very patient. I think he's just about given up on life, though, so if Ethan could take a few glamour shots of him, that would be great. Maybe someone would finally give him a place to lie his head for his final years."

Crouching down in front of him, I opened his cage coaxed him out. "Trooper, you're about to be famous, my friend. After we're done with you, people are going to be begging to take you home."

I walked that sad old dog out to the other room and positioned him on the white sheet on the floor. Looking around, I didn't see Ethan anywhere, so I gave Trooper a little sweet talk while we waited and even got him to wag his tail once or twice.

The door to the outside opened and Ethan walked in, but I instantly saw something had changed. Staring at his phone, he frowned and then stuffed it into his pocket.

"I have to go."

I looked up in shock. "We aren't done yet. This dog has been here for so long he doesn't know what life is outside a cage. Just take a few shots of him and if you need to go, then we can go."

"I can't, Summer. I have to go," he said flatly like he didn't hear a word I said about Trooper.

Standing up, I walked over to him as tears welled in my eyes. "It's the same as before! You're not really with me because there's always that other person who's more important. That's why you were looking at your phone when you came in. They messaged, and now you have to leave. Why can't they wait for a few minutes more? It will take only a few minutes to take a couple pictures of this dog. What's a few minutes?"

But all he did was shake his head. "I have to go, Summer. I'm sorry."

"Fine. Go!" I said, turning away from him as tears began to roll down my face. "I'll find my own way back to the city."

He silently began packing up his equipment as I grabbed Trooper and ran out of the room before he could see how much this hurt me. I'd believed in him when he promised me he wouldn't make me regret telling him I loved him. He was wrong. I did regret it. I regretted ever thinking I could trust Ethan again.

Minutes later, I watched as he drove away, tearing out of the dirt parking lot like a bat out of hell. Whoever they were, he cared about them way more than he cared about me.

"What happened?" Dawn asked as I sat crying with old Trooper.

"Nothing's changed. I thought he did, but the first time he had a chance to choose me, he didn't."

"What do you mean?" Dawn asked as she sat down beside me on the hard concrete floor.

"It's the one secret part of him he won't let me know. He gets these messages and no matter what we're doing, he has to leave to go to that person, I guess. It's probably some gorgeous model he sleeps with but can't really be with. I'm just some poor girl he bides his time with. A nice girl he can present to the world."

"That's crazy, Summer. He's obviously into you."

I didn't want to admit the truth to my sister, but it wasn't as crazy as it sounded. We had started out that way, after all.

Chapter Twenty-Three

Ethan

I arrived back at my place to see Ilsa waiting at my door. After what happened with Summer, I didn't feel like talking to anyone, including the beautiful woman who I knew hadn't come by to talk about the weather. She stood there with a big smile on her face wearing a full-length black fur coat and holding a bottle of something out in front of me. The old Ethan would have taken advantage of the offer, knowing full well she more likely than not didn't have a stitch of clothing on underneath that coat.

"God, Ethan. You're a hard man to find, you know that?" she said with a giggle. "You should know I don't wait for just any man."

"It's not a really good time, Ilsa. Sorry."

She took a step toward me and opened her coat wide to show me her perfectly tanned and naked body. "Still think it's not a good time?"

My cock had never been able to resist such temptation, but even he didn't want any part of what Ilsa had to offer. I shook my head and forced a smile, hoping to avoid any drama.

"It's a great offer, but I've had the day from hell. You know how it is."

Running her hand down the front of my shirt, she tugged on my belt and licked her lips as she gave me her best seductive look. "I can make it all better, baby. You know that."

The elevator doors opened and I turned just in time to see Summer step out into the hallway. She stopped dead when she saw

Ilsa and me, and the look of pain on her face made my heart skip a beat. I looked back at Ilsa to see she hadn't closed her fucking coat, making the entire scene look entirely something it wasn't.

Turning back toward Summer, I started to explain, but before I got a single sentence out of my mouth, she ran back into the elevator. I ran toward it to catch her, but the doors were just closing as I reached it and all I saw was her standing there with tears rolling down her cheeks.

"Ethan, where are you going? I'm sure your neighbor will be fine. She just didn't expect to see us standing out here in the hallway like that. Now let's go inside and have a good time like you know we always do," Ilsa whined as I thought about how I could make it down to the lobby before the elevator did.

Ignoring her, I ran all the way down the hall to the stairs and raced down them, praying I didn't miss Summer before she made it out of my building. Out of breath by the time I made it to the first floor, I burst through the metal door but didn't see her.

I ran out to the street but she was nowhere in sight. Fuck. Now she'd never believe me that the texts weren't from another woman I was sleeping with.

By the time I got back to my apartment, I was in no mood to deal with Ilsa and her offer of sex. She stood waiting like before, but this time I just shook my head as she described what kind of fun we could have. I didn't want to have fun with her.

"I'm not interested, Ilsa. Go find someone else."

"What's happened to you, Ethan?" she asked, moping as she closed her coat. "You used to be such a good time. Now you're all moody. Fine. I didn't want to spend the night with you anyway. There are good times to be had in this city, sweetheart, and if you're not going to give it to me, I'll find it elsewhere."

I didn't bother to say another word to her and simply walked into my apartment before closing the door behind me. Whatever good times there were, they weren't for me. I'd made sure of that.

THE BEER I'D HOPED WOULD make me forget only helped to make me remember things I didn't want to think about. I didn't want to feel what I felt either. So much for getting drunk. I couldn't even do that without fucking it up.

I looked through the pictures of Summer and the animals from the shelter for the hundredth time that night, fully understanding that wasn't the way to get over her. In some sick way, it made me feel better. Sort of like when you poke your fingernail hard into a mosquito bite. It hurt, but it was a good hurt.

Yeah, I was fucked up.

She looked so beautiful sitting there with those three black kittens climbing all over her. She hadn't put on extra makeup or anything special that day thinking she'd be part of the shoot, and still she lit up every one of the pictures with her smile and her genuine concern for those animals.

I moved on to the shots of her and One-Eyed Jack with his eye patch and felt my chest get tight. She sat there nuzzling his face and telling him how cool he looked with his patch on. It looked like he understood her in the one where he pressed his forehead to hers as if to say, "Thanks for making me look good, Summer."

The one of her and Butterscotch where she was sitting behind him and holding his cape out made me smile as I thought back to her cheering him on. "You got this, Butterscotch. Three legs are just as good as four. You watch. Once people see your picture as a superhero, you're going to get a home faster than you can say fetch."

I didn't want to have to leave. I would have given anything to stay there for hours with her and those animals. If only I could have.

Like the last time, I wouldn't call her. It was better this way. I couldn't tell her what she wanted to know, so why call? Even worse, everything she'd feared had been on display when she got off that elevator, thanks to Ilsa being there.

Fuck.

I hadn't thought about what would happen at work until that moment, but what did it matter? She'd never forgive me for doing this a second time anyway, and after seeing me standing there with a model wearing only a fur coat and obviously offering herself up to me, what could I say? If anything, she'd probably be avoiding me at work.

The only thing I couldn't handle thinking about was seeing her with someone else. Seeing her and knowing we didn't talk anymore was bad, but her with another man made me feel fucking sick.

When Tressa found out what happened, she'd have Summer set up with those douchebag guy friends of hers in a heartbeat. If I knew my sister, she'd make sure I found out in some horrible way, like at the next family dinner I attended. Even worse, I wouldn't put it past her to invite the happy couple to dinner just to rub it in my face.

I closed my eyes as my imagination ran away with me and my mind conjured up scenes of me forced to endure Summer sitting inches away and in love with some dickhead friend of Tressa's. Whatever. She had a right to be happy, even if it was with a douchebag with stubby hands.

The truth was I couldn't be the kind of person she deserved. I'd made sure of that a long time ago. I could buy her virtually anything, take her anywhere in the world, and give her practically everything. The problem was she wanted something that wasn't mine to give away.

For nearly two hours, I sat staring at those pictures I'd taken of her and the animals and wished things could be different. They couldn't for Summer and me, but maybe they could be for those cats and dogs stuck in cages at the shelter.

I took a chance my father would be at the house and called, hoping I didn't get my mother instead. Seeing her face-to-face and having to lie about why I wouldn't be at her show wasn't something I could handle tonight.

Thankfully, my father answered, and even though he looked

surprised to see me, I had a feeling this call might do some good. At least I hoped it would.

"Hey, Dad. Do you have a few minutes to talk?"

He nodded and didn't answer for a long moment before he asked, "Are you okay, Ethan? I'm not used to you calling here, especially at nearly midnight."

I hadn't thought about the time. Damn. But my father never seemed to sleep much anyway as long as I'd known him.

"Sorry about that. This won't take long if you're going to bed."

"No, I'm not. I'm thinking you know your mother isn't up, though. Is that why you're calling at this time of night?" he asked, leveling his gaze on me.

"I'm not trying to avoid her. Honest. I just don't think I can handle going to her show the way I feel now."

My father sighed. "Okay. You said you wanted to talk to me. Is this about work?"

"God, no. I have nothing to say about work that I haven't said before. This is about shelter animals."

A look of confusion settled into my father's face, and he narrowed his eyes to a squint. "Shelter animals?"

"Yeah. I was wondering if you'd be willing to give Andrew Mason a call and ask him if he'd consider running a piece on the Mended Paws Rescue and Shelter in Devon, Pennsylvania. They could use some help getting the word out about what they do there and getting people to adopt the animals. They have no budget to speak of, but they take in as many animals as they can. I just figured since Andrew has that newspaper of his in that part of Pennsylvania that maybe if you let him know about the shelter that he might send a reporter out there. I've got pictures of some of the animals I'd be happy to release to them for an article."

"You were at an animal shelter taking pictures?" my father asked, still clearly confused.

"I went out there a couple times as a favor for Summer. Her sister works there and Summer thought if I could take some pictures of the animals for their website that people would be more interested in adopting them. She calls them glamour shots."

That made my father's eyes light up, and he chuckled like I'd said something funny. "Glamour shots, huh?"

"So will you talk to Andrew about it? I'd do it myself, but I don't know how much of what Julia Carmon's been spreading around has reached the Philly area," I admitted with more than a hint of shame, knowing how much my father disapproved of my getting fired from *Belle*.

"I didn't even realize you liked animals. You never liked Shaggy."

"He didn't like me either, so the feeling wasn't one sided. He was Tressa and Diana's dog, not mine."

My father leaned in toward the screen and whispered, "Between you and me, I never liked him either. He didn't like males. He only liked your mother and your sisters. Every time he passed by me, he growled."

That my father and I had secretly disliked my sisters' dog all those years made me smile. Other than looking like him, I rarely felt like we had much in common. This wasn't anything important, but for some reason, it made me happy.

"I never thought I liked animals, but the ones at the shelter are great and they deserve to have homes of their own, so I was happy to help them get noticed. Taking pictures of humans was way easier, I have to admit, but taking animals' pictures is more rewarding, strangely. Three black kittens I took shots of last weekend already found a home because of the pictures I took."

My father's eyes filled with that look of pride for me I rarely saw. "Really? Those must be some pictures."

Shrugging, I said, "All it takes is the right subject and some good lighting. The shelter had some pretty lame pictures of the cats and dogs before, so anything would have been an improvement."

"Don't downplay your talent, Ethan. You did something good there. I'll call Andrew in the morning and see what I can do to get him interested in that shelter. Message me the name and address so I have it for him when I call tomorrow."

"Thanks, Dad. I appreciate it. I'd love to see them get some publicity and hopefully then people would give the animals a chance."

"So you and Summer are getting along again?" he asked with a hopefulness in his dark eyes I hated to crush.

I shook my head and sighed. "No. We were, but I had to leave early to get back to Diana because she messaged me this afternoon. That made Summer upset because I won't tell her why I have to go and then…" I didn't finish my thought about Ilsa because my father didn't need to know I'd screwed up there too.

"It's probably not going to happen between us."

Hope turned to pain in my father's expression, and he frowned in that sad way he always did when we talked about my sister. "I don't think you'd be betraying Diana if you told Summer the truth. Is that why you two broke up a few months ago?"

"Yeah. Diana made me promise I wouldn't tell anyone about her. It wouldn't be right to do that to her. If she ever met Summer, she'd know and I can only imagine how hurt she'd be. She's not ready for that kind of thing."

"You can't let what happened do this to your life, son. Nobody would blame you if you let yourself be happy with someone. If that someone is Summer, then don't ruin it. Diana has all of us to help her. It's not all on you."

I shook my head but said nothing. I'd heard this from my parents for years. It didn't matter what they said. I couldn't tell Summer about why I needed to go to my sister when she messaged me without telling her about Diana, and I wouldn't do that to my sister. Not after I promised her I wouldn't.

"Ethan, you made a mistake. You don't have to punish yourself for the rest of your life for it."

"I'm not going to be into work Monday, Dad. I have something I need to handle. I hope you understand. Tell Mom I love her and I hope her show goes great."

My father frowned but didn't say anything. I didn't know what he was unhappy about. My not going to work? Or maybe my not going to my mother's show. That frown might even have been for my past misdeeds since I'd done so much to earn that frown a hundred times over.

"Night, Ethan. I'll let you know what Andrew says after I call him in the morning."

The screen went dark, and I sat back wondering if he'd ever not wear that frown when he looked at me. Maybe not tonight, but someday I hoped to see that hint of pride I sometimes saw in his eyes again.

✦ ✦ ✦

AS I STOOD WAITING FOR someone to answer the door, an icy breeze whipped past me and I chastised myself for not calling first. Surprising people sometimes went well, but what was I thinking driving up to the shelter first thing on a Monday morning without even asking what hours they were open? The damn sun had barely come up over the horizon, for God's sake.

I definitely should have called. I knocked a second time and waited, hearing the dogs inside barking at the noise.

From behind me, I heard a voice say, "Ethan? Is that you?"

Turning around, I saw Dawn walking toward me. "Hey. I drove out on the off chance that I'd be able to pick up where I left off the other day."

Her eyes opened wide. "Sure! I'm just surprised you came out this early. You must have started out before five." She stopped talking and looked over toward my car. Disappointed, she turned back and quietly said, "I thought maybe Summer was with you. I guess you guys didn't make up after the other day?"

I shook my head. "Sorry about that. I didn't want to leave, but I had no choice. That's why I'm here again this morning. I'd like to take some more shots of the animals, especially that old dog."

Smiling, Dawn opened the metal door and welcomed me into the shelter. "Trooper? That's wonderful! I'd really love to see him finally get a home."

"Great! I'll get my equipment and set up so I can get started."

As I walked toward the car, Dawn asked, "Does my sister know you're here?"

I looked back at her and shook my head. "No, and if you could keep this between us, I'd appreciate that."

She didn't answer, and I had a feeling Summer would find out before I got back to the city. It wouldn't change anything between us. I knew that. All I could hope was what I did today would change something for these animals.

A few minutes later, Dawn walked that scruffy old dog Summer had pleaded to be photographed over to where I'd set up my equipment. He tilted his head and looked at me with nothing less than suspicion in his brown eyes. He had a right to. Other than Dawn and the other people at the shelter, the rest of humanity had let him down, including me already. That would change today.

"I have the perfect thing for you, buddy. You're going to charm all the folks when they see you."

Taking out a red and black bandana from my bag, I tied it around his neck and gave his rough fur a pet. He looked up at me like he didn't know if he liked his new look, but I had a feeling he liked the attention.

"Okay, let's see if he'll stay without you holding him. If he starts to bolt, I'm going to need you to stay in the shot," I said to Dawn as I stepped back to eye him through the lens.

She moved away, and after looking back at her for a moment, Trooper turned his head to face me and just sat there staring straight ahead like he'd decided to tolerate what I wanted to do, at least for a few minutes.

"I guess he's okay with it," she said quietly.

As I began to take his picture, I smiled. Trooper was a natural. Without even looking at the shots, I knew they'd be great.

More than an hour later, Trooper, two other dogs, and a black and white cat named Tux had become immortalized on film. While I packed up my gear, Dawn took the last of the animals back to the cages and then returned to thank me again for all my help.

"It's my pleasure. I wanted to help. I'll send you these later today and you can use whichever ones you like."

She studied me for a long moment and said, "You know, my director got a call from the Philadelphia Beacon while you were taking the pictures. They want to do a story on the shelter. You wouldn't know anything about that, would you?"

I smiled and shook my head. "Coincidence, probably. You know how it is. Once people start talking about something, that's all it takes sometimes. Probably someone who saw the pictures you already posted."

Dawn didn't seem to know whether to believe me or not. "I guess. All I know is what you've done has already helped, so thank you, Ethan."

"My pleasure. I better get going. As soon as I get the shots ready, I'll send them to you like last week."

"I'm sorry things didn't work out with you and Summer. You seem like one of the good ones."

My response was a smile but nothing else. Looks could be deceiving, and things weren't always what they seemed. Either were people.

Chapter Twenty-Four

Summer

Tressa had kept me waiting for nearly twenty minutes, and each one felt worse than the one before. My stomach seemed hell-bent on purging the orange juice and blueberry muffin I'd had on my walk to work this morning, and I worried that if she made me wait much longer that my nerves would get the best of me and I'd spew my breakfast all over her desk.

Not exactly the best way to begin what I had to tell her.

"Charlie, I know what we used to do, but my father and I are in agreement on this. We want the Richmont brand to be the gold standard, so let's get the designer in here and see what they've got. Contact my assistant later today with the details and she'll set up a meeting."

With that, Tressa hung up her office phone and sat back in her chair with a sigh. "It's like you have to fight these guys tooth and nail. He acts like if he doesn't get the word from on high on stone tablets with Tristan Stone's name on them that my father isn't on board. I mean, what do these people plan to do when my father walks away from Stone Worldwide and they have to deal with me? They better hope I have a short memory."

I gave her a supportive nod like I was supposed to as her assistant. "I don't think you do, so I think they're in trouble."

She gave me a wide smile and nodded in return. "You're smart, Summer. You figure people out. I like that. You're going to go far in this world."

And that was my invitation to tell her what I'd come to her office to discuss.

"About that. I'm afraid I have to give you my notice. I can't do this anymore."

Tressa pursed her lips and then nodded once again. "I'm assuming you don't mean answer phone calls and set up my appointments, so what happened?"

Looking down to avoid facing her, I said, "I really don't want to talk about it. I thought about this all weekend, and I just can't do it anymore. Ethan and I aren't going to be together, but he is back taking pictures. That's really all I was supposed to do, so it's not like I'm quitting so much as my job has effectively ended."

"Well, you were the best assistant I've ever had, so you should be proud of that. You've done everything I asked of you, so now there's just one more thing for you to do."

I lifted my head in surprise. "One more thing?"

"Yes. You have to attend my mother's party."

The mere thought of seeing Ethan so soon after what happened made my stomach begin to churn again. Shaking my head, I tried to keep my composure as panic raced through me. "I don't think I can. Your brother will be there, and I just don't think I can be in the same room with him yet. Please, I hope you understand."

"Not to worry," she said in the most sympathetic tone I'd ever heard come from her. "He won't be there. He's already told my mother."

"But he's back to what he loves to do. Why wouldn't he go now?"

Tressa shrugged. "I have no idea how these artist types work, but my mother claims she understands. She says it would be hard for her too if she'd gone through what he has. Personally, I find it irritating as all hell that he thinks his problems are more important than our mother's achievement, but she and my father seem fine with it, so I'm the odd man out, I guess."

Since I wouldn't be involved with the Stone family much more,

I had to ask about her sister in all of this. "How does your sister feel about Ethan's not going? Does she agree with you?"

Closing her eyes, Tressa took a deep breath and sighed. When she opened them again, she said, "Oh, no. Ethan can do no wrong when it comes to my sister. In her mind, the sun rises and sets on him. Always has. No matter how many times he's messed up, Diana's right there standing beside him ready to defend him. She's his biggest fan. Everyone in this world should have someone like my brother has with Diana. It must be nice to have someone think you can do no wrong, right?"

I didn't know if I heard sadness in her tone or anger, but clearly, Tressa was the odd man out among the Stone children.

"Must be nice," I mumbled in agreement. How nice would it be to always have a cheerleader in life no matter what?

"So no worries about my brother being at the party. I want you to see the fruits of your labors too. You deserve a night out to enjoy all you've done."

I didn't really have a choice, but as long as Ethan wouldn't be there, I believed I'd be fine. His mother would be too busy with other guests to even notice me, and it was the least I could do to thank Tressa for giving me a job.

"Okay. I'll go."

"Please don't worry about moving out of the hotel quickly either. Trust me. We have rooms just for that purpose, so take as long as you want."

Her offer made me feel strange, even though I knew she meant it to be nice. That room would forever remind me of Ethan, so the sooner I left there, the better. I needed to do everything I could to forget him.

"Thanks. I better get back to work. I want to check a few last things to make sure your mother's party goes off without a hitch."

Thankfully, she didn't stop me as I moved to leave her office. I didn't know why, but all of a sudden, my emotions were all over the place, and if she mentioned another word about Ethan, I may have burst into tears right there in front of her.

First puking and now crying. I really needed to get myself together.

✧ ✧ ✧

EVERY MINUTE I SPENT AT my desk made me terrified I might see him in the last few hours I had to work for Stone Worldwide. I didn't know how I'd avoided running into Ethan in the past few days, and I'd even considered stopping at his office after hearing from Dawn that he spent Monday morning taking pictures of Trooper and the other animals, but I stopped myself from making yet another mistake with him. She told me he didn't want me to know, so better to let him think I didn't hear about it.

Lost in thought, I didn't see Tristan walk into the office until he was standing in front of my desk. I looked up and for a moment my heart skipped a beat he looked so much like his son. If it wasn't for that touch of grey at his temples and a few wrinkles near the outside corners of his eyes, I would have mistaken him for Ethan.

"Hi, Mr. Stone. I'm sorry. I didn't see you there. I guess I was daydreaming. Sorry."

He smiled and held up his hand to stop me. "It's okay. I hear you're leaving us after today. Tressa has raved about your work, so if you ever need a letter of recommendation, I hope you'll remember us."

"I will. Thank you. Everyone's been great here. I just think it's time for me to move on."

Whether he knew what had happened with Ethan and me or not, I sensed in his expression that he understood how I felt. For as imposing a figure Tristan Stone certainly could be, in that moment he was just that man who had sat across from me at his dinner table quietly listening as his wife and I talked about growing up in the suburbs of Philly.

"I hope to see you at the party tonight. I know Nina would love to see you again."

"I'll be there. I'm hoping it will be something she'll love. Tressa has worked very hard to make it wonderful."

He arched a single dark eyebrow and gave me a look that said he saw right through my humility. "Everywhere I turn I run into people downplaying their good work. You and my son are very much alike in that way. I'm sure the party will be great, and when it is, I'll know who to thank for that, Summer."

He walked away into Tressa's office leaving me sitting there wondering exactly what he meant by his comment. Not that it mattered. However Ethan and I were alike, we differed too much to be together.

I HEARD THE CROWD NEXT door in the gallery and wished I could go over there to see the pieces in Nina's show, but I first needed to make sure everything was perfect for the party. The decorator, florist, and caterer had all done their jobs, so after one final check, I'd be done with my job as Tressa Stone's assistant.

Silver trays of hors d'oeuvres and royal blue plates and napkins sat on pub height tables situated around the room, along with champagne and fluted glasses enough for all the invited guests. On each table sat a large postcard announcing Nina's show in a gold frame that the designer had suggested would look great. I'd doubted her idea, but now that I saw it, I had to admit she'd been right. After a quick check of the music set up for the night, I was done.

I stood at the back of the room and took one last look at my work. *You did good. If only you could get paid for organizing parties, your life would be set. Well, at least your work life.*

Happy everything had turned out as I'd planned, I turned to walk toward the door that led to the art gallery and nearly ran into Nina Stone herself. Looking around at the room, she smiled.

"You did a lovely job, Summer. Thank you."

"It was my pleasure, Nina. I know Tressa wanted your big night to be perfect."

She tucked a lock of hair behind her right ear and leaned in toward me. "Between you and me, it's not that big a night. I'm thankful people like my sculptures, but they're more a labor of love than anything else. I just do it to remember my mother. Now there was an artist."

Her husband's words about downplaying things rang in my ears. "I'm sure you follow in your mother's footsteps."

Nina looked around and shrugged. "Sometimes. I think Ethan is more like my mother than I am, though."

Just the mention of him made me nervous, and I looked around to see if he'd changed his mind and come to the show anyway. She saw me and shook her head.

"He's not here. My son's having a hard time dealing with all he's lost. I can understand that, even if my husband and his sister can't."

I didn't know what to say now that the conversation had made the full turn toward talking about him. I didn't hate him. In fact, I was still crazy in love with him. But I needed to get over that so I could move on with my life.

"Congratulations on your show, Nina. I think I'm going to find Tressa and let her know I have to go."

"You know, I came over here because I wanted to talk to you away from everyone else. Do you have a minute to listen to what I have to say?"

Unsure where she could be going with this, I nodded and quietly said, "Okay."

Like her husband, Nina had a way about her that could be intimidating. Maybe it was because she had seemed so relaxed and casual that night at dinner that her serious tone now unnerved me.

"I'm not going to make excuses for Ethan. He's a grown man who can handle himself. To be honest, I thought when you and he came to dinner that time that you were too good to be true. A young woman from a small town outside of Philly with long brown hair? I wondered if he had simply asked you to play the part of his girlfriend so we'd all stop bothering him about settling down. That would be a thing Ethan would do."

She stopped for a moment, so I took the chance to make a full confession of my guilt. "He had," I said, hanging my head.

I looked up at her and continued, "But for what it's worth, I told him after that night that I didn't want to do that anymore. You and your family were too nice to me, and I felt guilty. So even though that night we weren't technically really dating, we did begin dating after that. I'm sorry about that, Nina. I don't know if it makes a difference, but even though he didn't feel anything for me that night, I did feel something for him, even that far back."

She nodded, but I didn't get the sense my confession angered her. Smiling, she poured us both glasses of champagne and took a sip.

"My son has always had a way of getting people to do what he wants. I've worried about him because of that ever since he was a small child."

"Why did you worry? Isn't that what powerful people have that makes them successful? The ability to persuade people to do their bidding?"

I cringed at my poor word choice, but Nina didn't seem bothered by it.

"Things came very easily to him. Everything came easy. Too easy. He was athletic, so he succeeded in sports. He was handsome, so girls lined up to get his attention. He came from money, so he wanted for nothing."

She stopped and lowered her head as if she felt embarrassed. "That last one is partly my fault. As the only boy with two sisters, I may have spoiled him a little."

As I listened to her talk about him, I had to admit I'd never thought of him as spoiled. Ridiculously blessed, yes, but not spoiled, strangely enough.

"When he was almost twenty, he and his sisters came into the first part of the trust their father and I set up for them. Tressa naturally invested it or did something with the stock market."

With a chuckle, I said, "Naturally. Can't take over the world on a shoestring budget."

Nina winked and chuckled too. "You know my daughter well. Diana put most of it in the bank but went on a trip to Europe with her friends too. And Ethan? Well, he bought himself a car. The fastest car he could find for the money. I hated that car from the moment he raced up the driveway with it. I worried he'd get killed in that red sports car, but he loved it."

"Does he still have it?" I asked, sure I'd never seen him in a sports car or even heard him mention one.

She frowned and shook her head. "No. On the night Diana got back from her trip, Ethan was waiting for her to take her for a ride. She's always been much closer to him than Tressa, who hated the car just like I did but for different reasons."

I knew exactly why Tressa would have hated a flashy red sports car. It screamed cocky male, something she hated.

"Tressa was always the planner. She was acting like an adult when she was ten years old. Diana was the smart one. She did better in school than either Ethan or her sister. Ethan was the wild child. I think it was because everything came so easily to him and he never thought he'd have to worry about anything. He was so proud of that car and couldn't wait to show Diana, and her eyes lit up when she sat down in the passenger seat. After promising me to be careful, like every other time he got into the car, they drove away so he could show off his new car to the one person whose opinion mattered."

Nina stopped talking and took a deep breath before sighing. "They didn't get very far before something happened. To this day, we don't know what. He might have taken the turn too fast. An animal may have run out into the road. We don't know. Not that it matters much now. The car became airborne and went careening into a yard about a mile away from our house. Ethan walked away from the accident with just a broken arm, but Diana wasn't as lucky. She was thrown from the car. The police told Tristan and me when they arrived on the scene they found Ethan lying on the ground holding Diana in his arms. She was unconscious and had terrible lacerations on her face and all over her body."

Hearing this story broke my heart for everyone in the Stone family. Nina took another deep breath and continued while I listened to what she had to say with a lump in my throat.

"Diana was in a coma for a week. We didn't know if she'd make it or not. I can honestly say those were the worst seven days of my life. I watched my one child lie in that hospital bed hooked up to all those machines not knowing if we'd lose her and my other child sit by her side day and night, refusing to leave her because he couldn't bear the idea of what he'd done to her. She came out of it, thank God, but she had to endure physical therapy for a year to help her walk again since she had a broken pelvis, a broken hip, and two shattered femurs. And then she had to endure all those plastic surgeries to fix what the glass from the windshield did to her face. All the while, Ethan blamed himself for every horrible thing she had to go through."

Tears welled in my eyes for both Ethan and his sister. "I had no idea. He never told me anything about Diana. The only sister he ever talks about at all is Tressa."

"The two of them have always had a bond he just doesn't have with Tressa. I don't know why, and I don't blame her for feeling left out sometimes. But as bad as it was dealing with Diana lying there in the hospital in a coma, things got worse when we were informed that the police planned to charge Ethan for the accident. He could have gone to jail. I couldn't bear that, and my husband knew it. So Tristan paid off the owner of the land for the damage, and although he's never said he did, I think he paid off the local police too so they wouldn't charge our son."

I didn't know what to say to her as she tried to force herself to smile. I'd thought their family had been so blessed. I never considered that there could be another side to their lives.

"Please don't think badly of Tristan for what I just told you. He's devoted to his family and couldn't stand to see our son go to jail because of what happened. It was bad enough we almost lost one child. We couldn't stand the idea of losing our son to prison. But all that did was make Ethan feel like he has to make up for his crime, so whenever Diana needs him, he does whatever he can to be there for her. His firing from *Belle* wasn't just because he was with you or any model. He missed shoots entirely because he'd have to fly back to be with his sister when he was supposed to be halfway around the world."

Her story stunned me. So that's who he ran to whenever he received one of those messages.

"Is Diana okay now?"

Nina shook her head and sadly admitted what I already guessed. "Not really. She lives in the Richmont in Midtown because she wanted to live on her own, but she can't really. She's physically fine, but life for her hasn't been easy after the accident. She has what some might call PTSD. She's afraid of so many things that she doesn't go out without one of us with her. She can do it, but she's just too afraid. To see her now, you'd never know how horrible the accident was, but she doesn't see that when she looks in the mirror. All she sees are scars."

Diana lived in the Richmont? Had I seen her in the hallway coming or going while I was staying there? I wondered and thought about who she must look like—Ethan or Tressa?

"I'm sorry, Nina. I had no idea. Ethan never said a word about any of this. He never spoke about Diana at all, in fact."

She smiled and gently touched my arm. "He wouldn't. To talk about Diana would mean he'd have to talk about how guilty he still feels about what happened. We've tried to make him see that he doesn't have to make up for anything, that it was an accident, but he still feels like he ruined her life."

I looked away, ashamed at what I had to admit. "We had a big fight the first time we broke up, and then again the other day after we got back together because he wouldn't tell me who the messages were from and why he had to leave anytime he got one. I feel awful, but I didn't know and he refused to tell me anything. He just kept asking me to believe him that it wasn't another woman. I couldn't, though. I kept thinking it was some model, someone prettier than me that he wanted but couldn't be with all the time."

"You remind me so much of myself, and not just because you have long brown hair and grew up near where I did. I always doubted that Ethan's father could want someone like me because he was so wealthy and could have any woman he wanted. He didn't want anyone else, though, but it took me a long time to get over my insecurities. I think you're a lot like me that way. My son is a lot like Tristan, especially in that I think he wants to be with someone who's down-to-earth. Maybe he could have models and actresses, but he was never happy until he started spending time with you."

I had a hard time imagining Nina Stone as insecure, but maybe when she was younger she was a little like me. I liked that idea, actually.

"Do you care about Ethan? I mean, really care about him enough to accept that he comes with some real issues that involve his sister that might never get better until she gets better?" she asked pointedly.

I didn't have to even think about my answer. "Yes, I do."

"Well, I'm certainly not unbiased by any stretch of the imagination, but I care about him too and I'd hate to see him lose out on someone like you because he's too ashamed to tell you what happened."

"I don't know if he'll even want to talk to me. It ended pretty horribly," I admitted sheepishly. "Maybe he's decided it's too much trouble being with me. I think he might already be with someone else too."

Nina smiled and squeezed my hand. "I know my son, and I'd be willing to bet that never crossed his mind. Knowing Ethan, he's sitting in his apartment wishing he knew some way to be the brother he desperately wants to be and the boyfriend you want him to be."

I hoped she was right because I'd never done anything like I planned to do that night. "Please tell Tressa I had to go. I hope she understands. And thank you. And congratulations on your show!"

"Nevermind all that. Just go and good luck!" Nina said, pushing me toward the door.

Without thinking it through, since I knew I'd talk myself out of going, I did as she said. I just hoped I wasn't too late.

CHAPTER TWENTY-FIVE

ETHAN

FOR THE FOURTH TIME THAT hour, I picked up my phone to check the time. Nine-thirty. The party was still going on. If I hurried and got dressed, I could get there in time to at least make an appearance.

Christ, I should go. It wasn't every day my mother had a showing of her work.

But then I thought about dealing with Tressa and Summer would probably be there since my sister was a slave driver but she had manners. She wouldn't have had her do all the work to arrange the party and then not invite her.

I couldn't handle seeing Summer this soon. Not that I thought she'd make a scene or even start an argument with me. That wasn't her style. No, it would be even worse than that because she would probably just turn away when she saw me. I couldn't deal with that yet. A couple weeks, maybe a month. Maybe longer. But not tonight.

Then again, how shitty a son was I to let my fucked up personal life get in the way of celebrating my mother's artistic achievements? The woman had never once not supported me one hundred percent whenever I tried anything in life. How could I not at least make an appearance to show her how proud I was? It would hurt like hell since my artistic achievements could be summed up as he took some pictures of beautiful women in nice places, but that wasn't my mother's fault. She didn't deserve to be punished for my bad choices.

I had to go. No matter how bad it felt to know I'd failed or to see Summer and know I'd never have her, I had to go to my mother's show.

After I threw on a grey dress shirt and found a tie that would work with it and my black pants, I took a glance at the mirror and ran my hand through my hair. I may have felt like shit, but I cleaned up nicely. At least I could do that.

I headed down to the lobby to grab a cab, and while I made small talk with the doorman, out of the corner of my eye I saw her. She wore a black dress that made her look as beautiful as any of the models who graced the magazines I'd shot for, and if I hadn't fucked things up with her, I would have been all over Summer at that moment.

But I had, so I stood silently pretending she wasn't there, just as I had in the elevator that day. I knew it was stupid and immature, but I didn't know what to say.

The doorman sensed something was wrong and made an excuse about having to go outside to look for my cab, leaving me to face Summer alone. I couldn't, though. Nothing had changed, and it didn't matter how much we talked things out. I couldn't explain to her why I had to leave the first time back at her place all those months ago or why I had to on Saturday at the shelter.

And that would never change.

"Ethan, please at least acknowledge I'm standing right beside you. It hurts that you can act like I don't exist, even though you're not doing a very good job of it tonight. Your shoulders look like they're about to swallow your head."

I hadn't realized how tense I felt until she said that, and immediately I relaxed and lowered my shoulders. "I don't know why you're here, Summer."

"I wasn't sure I should come either. Where's the naked woman in the fur coat?"

At least I had a chance to clear that up. "Nothing happened

with her. I didn't leave because of her. Not the first time and not the other day."

"I know."

Confused, I turned to face her and saw her smiling up at me. "You know what?"

She touched my arm, sending a rush of sensation across my skin as my body reacted to her being so close. "Your mother told me everything. Please talk to me."

I had no idea what my mother had told her. Whatever it was, I didn't want to talk about it. "I'm not sure what you're talking about. I'm heading to her show, so I'll ask her when I see her, I guess."

My words weren't those of a man who desperately missed the woman trying to get through to him but those of a dick who spoke like he barely knew Summer. The iciness in my voice was intentional, even though I knew how it hurt her.

And still she didn't give up.

"She told me all about what happened with Diana. It's your sister who you leave to help, isn't it? Why wouldn't you tell me?"

Rage coursed through me at hearing her say she'd heard what I'd done. I never wanted her to know about that. Better for her to think I was some asshole who might cheat on her than someone who nearly killed someone he loved.

I needed to get away from Summer before I said something I'd regret. Storming off toward the elevator, I left her standing in the lobby and went back to my apartment as my brain whirled with anger and guilt. What the fuck had my mother been thinking telling Summer about Diana? We didn't tell anyone about her. She knew that.

As slid my key into the lock, Summer caught up to me. "Ethan, please stop. Talk to me. Please."

"There's nothing to talk about. My mother shouldn't have told you anything. I have to go."

I walked in and pushed the door to close it, but Summer

followed me. "So this is how we're going to act toward one another? You tell me you love me and you won't make me regret telling you I loved you and days later you want to slam your apartment door in my face? Why won't you talk to me?"

"There's nothing to talk about. Whatever you think you know, trust me. You don't," I said, still refusing to look at her while I marched back to my bedroom.

She didn't stop and wait for me. Instead, she followed right behind and slammed my bedroom door shut behind her. "Then tell me what I don't understand! Why are you acting like this toward me? What did I do wrong? I know what happened and I came here to tell you I understand."

I slid the tie from around my neck and tossed it on the bed before spinning around to face her finally. "You don't understand. You couldn't. Now go back to the party and back to your life and leave me alone."

Summer shook her head and frowned. "No. I'm not leaving. I deserve to hear the truth from you, at the very least. You owe me that much."

Hearing her say she deserved the truth made something snap inside me and I marched over to where she stood. She didn't want the truth I had to offer because she had no idea. But now she'd get it.

"You deserve everything you want, Summer. I'm just not the man who can give that to you. I can give you some of what you deserve, but when it comes down to it, I can't be there when you might need me. I just can't. You deserve to be with someone who can say he'll always be there for you. I can't."

My emotions churned inside me like some toxic stew of guilt and rage and sadness. The woman I loved stood right there in front of me, and I couldn't promise her that no matter what she needed, I'd be there for her. And no amount of money or success or looks would change that.

Summer reached out and took my hand in hers. Her touch

made me want so much to take her in my arms, but I fought against what my heart wanted because my brain knew differently. We'd already tried twice. There was no point in going through that again.

"It's okay, Ethan. I know what's going on."

Looking down into her beautiful face, I saw hope in her eyes. I had to make her realize there was no hope for us. "No, you don't. Whatever my mother told you, she didn't tell you everything. You should go now. Go and find some stable guy who can give you the life you deserve."

"But I don't want anyone else. Why do you keep pushing me away even though I've told you I understand why you had to leave when your sister messaged you? It's okay. I understand."

"Why do you keep saying you understand?" I barked, frightening her. "Because Nina Stone told you something? Well, she didn't tell you everything. She couldn't because she doesn't know. My mother prefers to keep this fantasy up that what happened was just some unfortunate accident that no one could have prevented, but that's not true."

"Then what is?" Summer asked quietly, still clinging to my hand.

I tried to pull away from her, but she wouldn't let go. "The truth is way uglier than what my mother told you."

"Are you afraid that if I know the truth that I won't love you anymore? Is that what this is?"

"I never wanted you to know the truth. I thought I could live in both worlds—the one where I'm happy with you and the one where I take care of the one person I can't hurt again—but I can't. This can't work, so please, just go."

"Not until I know the truth, Ethan. I promise if you want me to leave after you tell me the truth, then I'll go, even though I'll still be in love with you. That's not going to change. But I have to know the truth. I can't spend the rest of my life not knowing why I lost you."

"The truth is I'm fucking careless and hurt people. Until I met you, I slept with women simply to get off. I cared enough about them for long enough to get them into bed. I didn't care about what they felt or what they wanted out of life. They were there to give me what I wanted. Period."

I watched for the look of horror to come across her face, but she simply shook her head. "Well, that's not the truth, and you know it. Oh, I know about the women who came before me. Anyone who can read gossip knows about you and women, Ethan. But you're not going to chase me away with your past as a manwhore. That's got nothing to do with the truth I want to hear from you. Tell me what I have wrong about what happened to your sister."

Hanging my head, I finally gave in and told her what she wanted to know. "I was careless and she paid for it. She's still paying for it even today five years later. What happened was no accident. I was screwing around and driving too fast, and even when she begged me to slow down, I just floored it. She started to cry because I was scaring her, and I ignored her because I wanted to show off."

"That doesn't mean it wasn't an accident, Ethan," Summer said softly. "You were a punk kid with too much money and a too fast car. You didn't mean to hurt anyone."

"When I missed that turn and the car flew into the air, everything went silent except for Diana's scream. Music had been playing the whole time we were in the car, but no matter how hard I try to remember, all I can think of is the sound of her screaming my name. And then the car landed and all I heard was the sound of metal splintering apart. By the time I found her, she was lying in a heap on the ground, her head covered in blood so she was barely recognizable. She kept saying my name until I reached her, and as I held her in my arms, she begged me to stay and not let her go."

I'd never told a single soul what really happened that night. My parents had created a story out of their love for Diana and me that said it was an accident on a dark, winding road, but the truth was what happened had been completely preventable if I hadn't been so careless.

"So now whenever she needs you, you drop everything to go to her. That doesn't make you a bad person, Ethan. It makes you someone who cares about making up for what he's done."

I sat down on the edge of the bed, exhausted from the guilt I felt about Diana and now Summer. "You deserve someone who can be with you one hundred percent. I can't, no matter how much I wish I could. What I did to her that night means I'll always have to be there for her."

Summer sat down next to me and rested her head on my shoulder. "So you have to be there for her. That's not a horrible thing. Maybe I'll feel put out sometimes. Maybe you'll feel bad, but we can deal with it if we're honest about things with one another."

"You deserve someone who doesn't have to divide his time. Why would you be willing to take less than one hundred percent of what you should have?"

She looked up at me and smiled. "You keep saying I deserve, I deserve. I bet your mother didn't get one hundred percent of your father for a long time, and they turned out fine. Women married to powerful men rarely get one hundred percent of them. If I got involved with any of those friends of Tressa's she suggested I date, I doubt I'd get all of them."

Damnit. My sister had tried to set Summer up with one of her successful douchebag male friends.

"I remember all those nights my mother putting the three of us to bed without my father anywhere in sight. She likes to romanticize things, but sometimes she looked sad. I don't want you to be sad because of me."

Try as I might, I couldn't seem to convince Summer that I wasn't the guy she wanted. She continued to smile like she'd considered all of this and still thought I was the one for her.

"Real life is sometimes sad, Ethan. What you call romanticizing by your mother about those days is probably just her remembering the good things and forgetting everything else. Nobody's perfect.

Being with someone is a matter of give and take. We just have to tell one another the truth. That doesn't mean things will always be good, but at least they'll be honest. We didn't start out telling the truth to anyone, including ourselves, but that doesn't mean we can't start now."

"What did you lie to me about?" I asked, my heart slamming into my chest as my brain raced with all the possible answers she might give.

Her mouth turned down into a deep frown, and she looked toward where our hands sat joined on her leg. "I fell in love with you on the flight back from Australia. I didn't think you'd ever feel that for me, though, since you had dated all those beautiful women. Then when we broke up and you wouldn't tell me who that text was for, I figured you decided I wasn't pretty enough for you."

Her confession made my chest hurt as I thought about her focusing on what could be wrong with her when it was me who had the problem. Taking her face in my hands, I tilted her head up so she could see the truth in my eyes when I apologized.

"You couldn't have been more wrong, but I'm sorry what I did made you think that. I never meant to make it seem like you weren't good enough. That never crossed my mind because I was so consumed with the guilt I always feel about Diana."

I leaned down and kissed her softly on the lips. "I love you, Summer. I wish I knew when I fell in love with you, but it just feels like I've always loved you."

She smiled sweetly. "I love you, Ethan."

Taking a deep breath, I sighed like I had years of unhappiness to let go. "Well, we better get going if we want to get to the party before it ends," I said as I reached back to grab my tie.

"Your mother is going to be so happy you're coming."

"I have no excuse now. I didn't think I could handle seeing you, but that's all changed now, and I didn't think I could be around her success at the gallery, but things are changed with that too."

Summer stood from the bed, clearly confused. "Have you decided to go back to being a photographer shooting models?"

"Not exactly. I'll tell you about it in the car on the way to the party."

CHAPTER TWENTY-SIX

SUMMER

I OPENED MY EYES AND saw Ethan working on his laptop in bed next to me. We'd fallen asleep after getting back from the party just after midnight, and I looked around for any hint for how long I'd been asleep.

Craning my neck to see the time on his computer, I struggled to focus my bleary eyes on the tiny numbers in the corner of the screen. Five-thirty? Why was he up so early?

"Good morning. Or is it good night since it's still dark out?" I asked as I sat up next to him. "How long have you been up?"

He leaned over and kissed me. "I couldn't sleep. Too many ideas running around my brain. I didn't wake you, did I?"

"I don't think so. What are you doing?"

"Someone from the Philadelphia Beacon emailed about getting some shots for their story on the shelter, and I'm trying to decide which ones I should send," he said matter-of-factly as he stared at the pictures of the animals on the screen in front of him.

"So it was you who got them to come out to Mended Paws? Dawn told me you denied having anything to do with it, but I knew that couldn't be true. I didn't think they'd just somehow seen the pictures you took and became interested."

He turned to look at me and smiled. "Yeah, it was me, but I didn't want anyone to know. I asked my father to contact the owner of the paper and tell him about the shelter so they could get some press about what they do there. My father's been Andrew Mason's friend for years, so I figured he might be willing to help if he heard about it from his old buddy Tristan."

I kissed his cheek and shook my head. "So you're stunning to look at, a god in between the sheets, and have a good heart? I must be dreaming."

Ethan's eyebrows shot up into his forehead as a playful look came over him. "A god in between the sheets? I'll take that compliment as an invitation."

He set aside the laptop on the nightstand as I slid my hand down over his chest. "You should."

Rolling me over onto my back, he ran his hands up my sides until he cupped my breasts and kissed me long and deep. With my feet, I tugged his pants off to find him naked underneath.

"Going commando these days?" I asked as he tilted his hips so his hard cock grazed my pussy.

He looked down at me and smiled in that wicked way I loved. "I didn't think sitting with a laptop on my cock was a good idea, but when I got out of the shower last night, I didn't feel like putting on underwear. So I compromised and put on pajama pants instead."

Pressing my heels into his lower back, I urged him toward me. "Feel free to eliminate that extra step and make things easier anytime."

"I'll keep that in mind," he said low and deep in my ear in that voice that never failed to make me want him so badly it hurt.

Ethan sunk his teeth into my earlobe, biting down just enough to send a string of need racing through my entire body as he slowly slid into me, filling me completely. I arched my back, desperate to feel every inch of him against my skin, and he groaned my name into the pillow next to my head.

"God…Summer…you feel so fucking good."

My fingernails scratched the silky soft skin on his back, exciting him with that touch of pain I knew thrilled him. He responded by stuffing his hand into my hair and tugging hard.

He lifted himself off me and looked down into my eyes. "Fuck.

You know how hot that gets me when you do that. I'm not going to be able to hold back and I'd hoped to make this slow and easy first thing in the morning."

I didn't want slow and easy now. I wanted Ethan wild and free like he'd been when we met, not the buttoned-up suit and tie man he'd been forced to become.

"Good. Don't hold back," I whispered and then kissed him with everything inside me.

His dark eyes filled with that sexy look he got in them that I loved, and the next thing I knew, he filled me completely again in one hard thrust that touched that single spot no other man had ever reached. It took my breath away, but I wanted more.

I wanted everything Ethan offered. His sweetness and the laughter. The darkness that existed in him because of his past. The sensual creature who never failed to thrill me more than any other person in the world had. The good and the bad, I wanted it all.

His cock pistoned into me hard and fast, slowly torturing me with pleasure as my body ached for the sweet release I knew he could give me. I watched his body tense and relax with every thrust, his muscles straining beneath his tattooed skin.

I tilted my hips and moved my legs further up his back to change position, and his eyes grew wide as he slid even deeper into me. I knew how to excite him, even if I didn't have a perfect body and I'd never look like the women he had before me.

Pulling him down to me, I whispered in his ear, "Fuck me. Don't hold back."

He said nothing but held me tightly and fucked me just as I wanted. He didn't hold back, and when he came, it was only after I'd come twice. When he wanted to go again a half hour later, I climbed on top of him and rode his cock until he came again.

Ethan brought out the wild in me, but hours later as we lay in each other's arms in bed, I knew he didn't need his wild brought out by the woman he loved. He needed the good that existed inside him brought out, and even though I didn't know how, I did that for him.

"I WANT YOU TO MEET someone. I thought we could do it this afternoon," he said quietly above me.

Lifting my head off his chest, I saw how much this meant to him and nodded. "Okay. Who am I meeting?"

"My sister Diana."

A rush of fear ran from my brain through my body. I'd met everyone else in Ethan's family, and they'd liked me. I wanted to believe they liked their son and brother with me. But Diana was different. She meant more to Ethan than anyone else.

"Oh, okay. I don't think I have anything to wear, though. My hair could use a good cut too. I wish you had given me a couple days to get ready."

At any moment, I knew I'd begin rambling, so I quickly rolled out of bed and ran to the bathroom. Diana was the person he'd already warned me he'd have to choose over me. She meant more to Ethan than anyone else. What if she didn't like me?

He padded up behind me as I stood staring at my reflection in the bathroom mirror and wrapped his arms around me. Nuzzling my neck, he kissed me just below my earlobe. "Trust me, this is going to be great. You've already met the tougher sister. Diana is crazy about me, unlike Tressa, who I'm pretty sure enjoys seeing me suffer. She's going to love you because I do."

I turned in his hold and looked up at him. "What if she doesn't? What then? You've already told me how much she means to you. What if she doesn't even like me? Will we be finished? I guess at least I'll know why you don't want to be with me this time."

He kissed me before my insecurity spiral could spin out of control. Smoothing the hair back off my face, he said, "I don't need anyone's permission to love you, Summer. That's not what this is. And it's not an audition to see if you get the part of the woman I love. You already have that role. That's why I want you to meet her. Because you're the woman I'm madly, crazy in love with."

Closing my eyes, I admitted the truth. "I just worry that she'll think I'm not enough. I'm sure she's seen all those women on the covers of magazines you've been with. What if she thinks you deserve someone like that instead of me?"

Ethan pressed his lips to my forehead and kissed me softly, whispering against my skin, "You've met everyone else in my family. Do you really think there's a chance that the one member of the Stone clan I like best would think that?"

I looked at him as the reality of our past flashed back into my brain. "They wanted you to settle down with a nice girl. Maybe she thinks you should live the life you used to have. I don't know. I'm just worried."

"She wants me to be happy. That's it. And you make me happier than I've ever been before in my life. Well, except for when I got that motorized Jeep that I drove around the yard until the gardener complained about my tearing through the flower beds and my parents took it off me. That was a very happy Ethan."

Unhappy with his poking fun at me, I lightly jabbed him in the side and moved past him. "Stop teasing. I'm worried about this, and you're talking about toys."

From behind, he scooped me up in his arms and began walking back toward the bed. "Enough talk about being worried. She's going to love you and you're going to love her."

Ethan tossed me down onto the mattress and sat down next to me. Suddenly, his expression grew serious. "I do need to tell you a few things about her, though."

His tone worried me, and I listened as he explained what Diana had physically gone through because of the accident. Each word sounded so full of regret that by the time he finished telling me what I needed to know before meeting her he looked like a different man than the one who'd just be joking around in the bathroom.

Taking him in my arms, I held him and said, "You're a good

person, Ethan. Don't ever forget that."

I SQUEEZED ETHAN'S HAND AS the seconds ticked by and we stood at Diana's hotel room door waiting for her to answer. Even though he'd assured me she'd love me, I still worried she wouldn't. What if, unlike the rest of her family, she didn't think I was right for her brother? The guilt he felt for that car accident might make him want to believe her, and then what would happen?

He sensed my worry and leaned down to kiss my cheek. I turned to see him smiling so confidently. "It will be fine. Don't worry. She's going to love you as much as I do."

Quietly, I said, "I hope so."

Just then, the door opened and I finally saw the third Stone triplet. For a moment, I stared at Diana, surprised by how much she looked like her mother since Ethan looked like the spitting image of his father and Tressa resembled Tristan Stone more than Nina too. But Diana had the softness that her mother possessed, and in her blue eyes I saw the same kindness I'd seen in Nina Stone's. Her chestnut brown hair was a little lighter than mine but much longer, nearly down to the bottom of her back. It hung in long waves that framed her face and hid the scars Ethan had told me still faintly existed on the side of her cheek and on her neck.

"Ethan! I'm sorry it took me so long to answer. I was fixing my hair." Diana turned toward me and smiled. "You know how it is. Any other day it would look fine, but when you have someone special to see, it never looks the way you want it to. I'm Diana. You must be Summer."

I extended my hand to shake hello, but she pulled me into an embrace instead, surprising me. "It's so nice to meet you. When Ethan told me he wanted me to meet you, I was so happy."

She stepped back and opened the door to let us in. "Come in, come in! I'm sorry. I forgot my manners having you stand out in the hallway."

Ethan followed me into her hotel room, which looked like the mirror image of mine, and as she closed the door, he said, "I didn't forget about the pictures from Mom's show. I thought it would be nice if we looked at them together later."

"Was it wonderful?" Diana asked with hope in her voice as she offered us a seat on the couch.

He looked at me and smiled. "It was. The show was great, and the party Summer organized was perfect."

"I can't wait to see the pictures! I bet Daddy stood off to the side near one of the windows for nearly the whole thing, didn't he?"

Before I could tell her she was right, she explained, "Our father is very supportive of our mother, but he's not a huge fan of spending time at art galleries, so he always goes to shows but he does his best to keep out of the limelight so she can be center stage."

Ethan laughed. "When we were kids, my mother would take Diana and me around to show us her pieces and my father and Tressa would stand off to the side patiently waiting for us to be done."

A look of concern came over Diana. "But please don't think my father isn't a great husband. He has this tradition whenever she has a show. At the end when all the guests have left, he walks up behind her and gives her a hug. Then he says, 'Now it's time for your biggest fan to tell you how much he loves what you've done.' When I was a little girl, the show wasn't over until my father said those words. It's his way of telling her he loves her and he's proud of her."

Smiling, Ethan nodded. "Tristan Stone isn't much for the whole art scene, but he loves our mother more than life itself. Tressa too. They just aren't huge art fans."

"But Tressa had me arrange that whole party," I said in confusion. "She'd seemed to care a great deal about your mother's show."

Diana looked at her brother and then smiled at me. "Tressa loves parties. She loves anything where she can schmooze people and talk business. Not that she doesn't love our mother or respect her talent."

They joked around about Tressa and their father's tolerance for art being about two hours tops as I watched Ethan and Diana together in a way I imagined had never happened with Tressa. The dynamic intrigued me, especially how relaxed and happy he seemed around this sister compared to how I'd seen him around his other sister.

After a little while, Diana said, "Ethan, I ordered food from that little restaurant I love. I told them two o'clock, so would you go pick it up? Summer and I will spend the time getting to know one another better."

"Only if you promise not tell her all the bad things about me growing up," he said as he stood to go. "She doesn't need to know about the awkward middle school years."

He kissed me before he left and whispered, "You'll be fine, but if she breaks out those middle school pictures, I need you to remember what you said about me being a god in bed. No kidding. Those were rough years."

I watched him leave, desperate to see those school pictures after that warning. No sooner had he left, Diana sat down next to me on the couch. Now I'd see if she really liked me.

She carefully smoothed her hair around her face before she spoke. "As you can tell, I love my brother very much. Ethan and I are much closer than Tressa and I are, and I can tell even without him saying it that he's madly in love with you. Do you love him?"

Her directness wasn't rude or intrusive but seemed to come from a place of genuine concern and innocence. I liked that, so I answered in the same way.

"I do. I love him more than I thought I could love anyone."

A gentle smile made her face light up. "Good. I had hoped he'd find someone who made him happy. And can I tell you something else? I love your name! I wish mine was something interesting like Summer. It's almost magical. I love it."

And just like that, all my worries disappeared into thin air. "I wish I had a name like Diana. It's so classic and dignified. I worry sometimes that I'm going to be a very strange old lady with a name like Summer."

Diana giggled at my joke like she truly enjoyed it. "Ethan was right. You are sweet and funny. Well, I love your name. If I ever have a little girl, I want her to have a unique name like yours."

When Ethan told me about his sister, he mentioned that she rarely left the hotel room and hadn't dated anyone since the accident. Just hearing that made me sad, but now that I sat there with her in that room, I wondered if he'd been mistaken.

"Do you think your boyfriend will be okay with a hippie name like mine?" I asked, but I instantly worried I'd overstepped my bounds, so I added, "I have to admit my father never liked it or my sister Dawn's name, but my mother insisted on naming us like that."

Lowering her head, Diana quietly said, "I don't date. I haven't for a long time."

"Well, I bet when you decide to that you'll have men all over you. You're gorgeous and sweet. Trust me. You wouldn't be single for long if you didn't want to be."

My compliment made her smile. "Thank you for saying that, but I'm not sure I'd know how to even talk to a man now."

"Just like you talk to Ethan. I bet once you got talking to men, you'd realize it's not hard. I was a little intimidated when I first started talking to your brother, I have to admit, but after a few minutes it was fine."

My confession made her laugh. "I'm so happy he brought you here today. I knew when he said that he wanted me to meet you that you must be special since he's never introduced anyone to any of us before. I told my mother he was bringing you here and she said you were exactly the kind of girl she hoped he'd settle down with. I want to tell you I agree with my mother."

I sat there stunned by what she said. Ethan had never brought any of the women he dated home to meet his family? They were world-famous models.

Like she could read my mind, Diana said, "You're the first girl he's ever had me meet. The same with my parents. He never even mentioned girls to us before you. That's how I knew you must be someone very special to him."

Before I could say anything, Ethan knocked at the door and Diana jumped up to let him in. His arms full of bags of takeout food, he walked past me to put it all on the table as I watched him with a new appreciation for how much I loved him.

Turning to look at me, he asked, "She didn't show you those pictures, did she?"

"No, but since you've brought that up three times already, I'm thinking I really need to see them," I answered with a chuckle, teasing him.

"Just remember the sex god thing and that you love me if she breaks them out. That's all I ask."

I walked over to where he stood unpacking foil packages of food from the brown paper bags and kissed him sweetly on the lips. "I like the idea of you looking less than stunning at some point in your life. It makes you more relatable to us mere mortals."

He smiled just as Diana came up behind us with forks and plates and said, "You know I have those pictures somewhere. If not, I can just ask Mom to send them to me and we can be looking at them on my TV in minutes. Say the word, Summer, and we'll be looking at Ethan in his chipmunk stage."

"I think that might be cute," I answered, squeezing his arm. "They can't be that bad. I'm sure you were an adorable chipmunk."

Diana set off to look for those middle school pictures as Ethan opened up the tins of Italian food that smelled delicious. Bending down, I inhaled the smell of garlic and onions rising from the containers.

"What's in these? They smell incredible!"

Ethan pointed at the container closest to him and said, "That's penne with vodka sauce." Then he proceeded to go around the table, saying, "The one over there is rigatoni with meat sauce. That one is vegetable lasagna, and there's regular lasagna next to it. And that other one is garlic bread."

A look of sadness came over him. "My sister loves Italian, but she didn't know what you might like, so she went a little overboard. She does that sometimes. It's just how she is."

I shook my head and smiled at how thoughtful Diana was. "I think it's great. She's an incredible person, Ethan. Thank you for bringing me here to meet her."

He pulled me into his arms and kissed me. "I'm glad. I better get all my kissing in now since we're going to stink like garlic in about two minutes."

"That's okay," I said, standing on my toes to kiss him back. "We'll both smell like it so it will cancel itself out."

From the bedroom, Diana squealed, "Found them!"

Ethan cringed. "I can't believe she found those pictures."

"Well, you brought them up. I would have never known about them if you didn't mention them."

"Well, since we're playing it that way, I have a few pictures you might be interested in. After we get settled, I'll show you. I think you look great in them."

My mind raced with what pictures he could have taken of me. I'd never posed for him. Panicked, I whispered, "Ethan, what are you talking about? Please tell me you're not about to show your sister pictures of me in any compromising position."

He laughed at my suggestion and handed me a plate to get my food. "Is that what you think I do when you're sleeping?"

His answer didn't make me feel much better about these pictures. "Well, no, but what are they of then?"

"You'll see."

THE THREE OF US SAT on the couch as we ate our Italian takeout food and Ethan showed Diana pictures from the party the night before. We all laughed at the one he'd taken of Tristan standing near the window with Tressa next to him. I guessed some things never changed.

"It looks like it was a fun party, Summer. You did a great job," Diana said as she stood up to put the disc of Ethan's middle school pictures into the TV.

He took our teasing about his chipmunk cheeks in stride, never saying a word when his sister and I giggled about his middle school look, and when we'd looked at all the pictures, he walked over to the TV.

"What can I say? I had some rough years. These pictures, though, aren't rough at all. The last couple I love the most."

Ethan sat down beside me as Diana began scrolling through the pictures he'd taken at the animal shelter. With each one, I told her the animal's name and their story. Then she got to pictures of me and the animals, and he whispered in my ear, "Now you'll see why I love these."

I couldn't help but be embarrassed as I sat there staring at myself sitting with Butterscotch, One-Eyed Jack, Midnight, Spooky, and Boo and giggling as I tried to get them to pose while they licked my face and climbed all over me. He'd taken pictures of me that I didn't hate at all, and I always hated how I looked in pictures.

In fact, I loved these more than any picture anyone had ever taken of me. I didn't know how, but he'd found a way to make me look as beautiful on the outside as I felt on the inside.

CHAPTER TWENTY-SEVEN

ETHAN

SUMMER SAT IN THE PASSENGER seat with a look of concern on her face. She didn't have to worry. Everything would be fine.

"It's going to be okay. I don't know why you're worried," I said in my best supportive voice as I grabbed her hand to squeeze it.

"I know. I'm not concerned as much as anxious. I don't want you to get in trouble."

Turning to face her, I saw concern in her eyes. "If I get in trouble, which I'm not, then we'll just move. I could go for a place out of the city anyway. Somewhere he can get a good run in."

"But you're only allowed to get small dogs. I don't want you to get in trouble because you think I want him."

"You do want him to come home with us, don't you?" I asked, already knowing the answer was yes.

"Of course, but what if you lose your home because of this?"

"Then we move. It's that easy. I can relocate my photography business to practically anywhere. If we all want to move to an island, I could even do that, although that would mean flying a lot. I'm okay with that if you two are, though."

Since I'd decided to go into the business of taking pictures of animals, I'd been overwhelmed with how many people were willing to pay good money to have pictures of their pets, pictures with their pets, and every combination of both. There was gold in those furry faces, and I planned on mining it for all it was worth. So far, it had been successful enough for even my father to compliment me on my business savvy. I didn't bother telling him I actually liked working with four-legged models more than two-legged ones.

"I don't want to move to an island, Ethan. You're missing the point. I'm just worried that my talking about him so much has made you agree to something that's going to get you in trouble."

Summer really could be the world biggest worrier sometimes. I had a feeling if we ever had kids that she'd be in a constant state of stress, especially if we had a boy like I was growing up.

Leaning over, I pressed my forehead to hers and sighed. "Here's the thing. I don't love that apartment one-millionth as much as I love you. You want to adopt him, so we're adopting him. Don't make it difficult when it's a simple and good thing. So, are you ready to go in?"

She appeared to want to still discuss the issue, but after a long moment, she smiled. "Okay. Let's go get him."

We walked hand-in-hand into the Mended Paws Shelter and Rescue where her sister waited for us with the newest member of our family. He still wore that black and red bandana I'd given him that day.

"Trooper, are you ready to go home with us?" Summer asked as she crouched down to give him a kiss on his head.

He looked up at me, and in his eyes, I thought I saw a glint of real happiness as she fawned over him. I knew how he felt. She had that effect on me too.

"When I told him he was going home to his forever home this morning, I swear he perked up," Dawn said. Handing me Trooper's leash, she smiled. "Thanks for everything, Ethan."

Summer gave him another kiss on the top of his head and looked up at her sister. "Have there been any more adoptions?"

"Oh yeah!" Dawn said with excitement. "Jack and Butterscotch are going to their new homes this afternoon, and Muffin the kitty who got her picture taken on that Monday morning went home with a little boy and his dad yesterday. Even better, we've had an increase in adoptions across the board, and I'm sure that will continue once the article comes out in the Beacon next week."

Summer stood and smiled at me. "And it's all because of you."

I shrugged and pretended like all of it was no big deal, even as I liked how it felt to know I'd helped. "I just did what I could. The animals did all the hard work."

"Well, you two are doing a great thing giving Trooper a home. Send me pictures when he gets settled in. Everyone here at the shelter is going to miss this guy."

"I will. I'll send them when I call you later this week."

Trooper tilted his head to the side and barked like he wanted to tell us it was time to go and start his new life. "I think he wants to get on the road," I said with a chuckle.

After saying our goodbyes to Dawn, we piled into my car to head back to the city. I looked up at the rearview mirror and smiled at Trooper as I drove out of the shelter's parking lot. Reaching over, I took Summer's hand in mine and brought it up to my lips for a kiss.

"Are you happy?" I asked.

She smiled in that sweet way that never failed to charm me. "More than I can say."

"What about you, Trooper?"

From the backseat, he barked twice.

Summer leaned over and pressed a kiss onto my cheek. "Did you ever imagine you'd be settled down with a girlfriend and a dog?"

I thought about that question for a moment and smiled as I looked over at her. "Honestly, I can't imagine it with anyone else in the world."

So I was wrong about nice girls. I should have known better. I'm the son of a nice girl.

Businessman, dog owner, and former bachelor in love with a beautiful girl from just outside Philly. I was becoming more and more like Tristan Stone every day. I would have never guessed it, but maybe that wasn't such a bad thing after all.

SET IN STONE

CHAPTER ONE

TRESSA

TWO HOURS LATE BECAUSE I had to work on the London Richmont redesign project, I rushed around the penthouse trying to find my favorite black stilettos. Had I left them at the house? No, that couldn't be. I'd worn them to some event in the past few weeks since I'd been staying in the city every night.

Summer sat on the couch ready to go because she hadn't gotten waylaid by an overzealous designer hell-bent on having her way. Leaning back, she watched in amusement as I raced from room to room looking for my damn shoes.

"Are you like me and stuff things under your bed when people come over so it doesn't look like you're a total slob?" she asked, stopping me dead in my tracks.

I leveled a stern gaze on her face and slowly shook my head. "No."

Used to how serious I could be, she laughed off my quiet reprimand. "I didn't think so, but I figured it couldn't hurt to mention it."

That no one had been to the penthouse other than Summer and my parents in so long I couldn't even remember wasn't a detail I felt compelled to mention. I did prefer to keep my personal behavior on the down low, but recently, there hadn't been much to hide. Work had kept me far too busy to be engaging in any of the sexy stuff, except for one night a while ago.

As I marched back into my bedroom to run my foot under the

bed just in case my shoes had somehow found their way there, I cringed at how long it had been since I'd been with anyone. Had it really been four months?

Then again, how important was something like sex when I had the world to conquer? I'd have time for all that once I proved to the world that being given the COO position of the Richmont hotel chain hadn't been a mistake borne out of a father's love and good old fashioned nepotism.

My pinky toe snagged on the back of a shoe, and I crouched down in surprise to find my favorite Louboutins sitting on the floor under my bed. I must have kicked them off when I got home that night and they ended up there.

"Found them!" I announced as I slid my feet into the shoes.

"Where?" Summer yelled back with the clear sound of relief in her voice after being forced to wait for me for hours.

"Back in the closet," I lied. "Ready to go?"

I stopped in the doorway and gave her a quick once over while she did the same for me. I could trust Summer to tell me the truth, even if it hurt and even if I lashed out because of it. My brother had not only found a wonderful person to be with, but I'd found a good friend in her too.

"That black dress looks incredible on you," she said with a smile. "Every woman in New York, including me, would kill for legs like yours."

Laughing, I motioned for her to spin around so I could see the back of her to make sure her light green dress looked perfect. "I'll make sure to keep my wits about me then tonight," I joked, and then added, "You look great! That dress is so cute on you."

Summer turned around to face me and shrugged. "I do cute quite well. It's my thing."

I had a feeling Ethan had fallen in love with her far earlier than even she suspected. No wonder. Smart, funny, and cute as a button, she was the whole package. Now all my brother had to do was not mess things up with her and someday soon I might have a sister-in-law and my best friend all in one.

"My brother is very lucky. I hope you never let him forget that."

"He knows," she said with a smile.

"Good. Where is he tonight?" I asked as we made our way to the elevator to leave.

"He's photographing a Great Dane on Staten Island."

"Without his assistant?" I asked, surprised he'd gone without the half of the business that actually handled the animals at the shoots.

"I told him I had a prior engagement to attend," she explained as the elevator doors opened. "You should have seen his face. I think he thought I had a date or something. He got a look in his eyes like I had told him I didn't love him anymore. I had to explain to him right then and there that I was going to the pediatric cancer event with you and we'd planned it for weeks."

I pressed the button for the lobby. "Keeping him on his toes. Good. Don't let him get complacent with you."

Summer smiled and chuckled like she did whenever I warned her about how to handle my brother. "Don't worry. I won't. I just hope that Great Dane doesn't take his head off. Ethan's not usually the dog whisperer."

As the elevator descended to street level, I secretly hoped my brother didn't end his career as a photographer that night. He'd finally found a way to do what he loved and do it in a way that didn't involve sleeping with women across the world. I didn't know what he'd do if that all came crashing down.

Hearing the worry in Summer's voice, I reassured her. "He'll be fine. Ethan can charm the birds out of the trees. I'm sure one dog won't be difficult for him at all. I'll tell you what, though. If you want to duck out of the event early after we make our presence known, you can do that and take the car service out to join him."

"See? This is why I tell him he's wrong about you. He's convinced you two are mortal enemies," she said as the doors opened to the lobby.

"Not anymore," I said with a chuckle. "When my brother and I stay in our appropriate spheres in this world, I feel nothing but sisterly love for him. It's only when we wander into places we shouldn't that we get into trouble."

"I'll have to tell him that."

"He knows I love him," I said with a wink. "We're just total opposites. Always have been."

And that right there was the absolute truth. My brother would feel perfectly comfortable walking into this charity event tonight more than an hour late, and he'd fully expect everyone would just be happy he showed up. I, on the other hand, knew I'd spend the entire car ride over there thinking of excuses for anyone who asked why I was late.

JUST A FEW STEPS INTO the ballroom at the Stilton Hotel and I couldn't help but be impressed by the work the organizers had done for the event this year. The crowd seemed much larger than in years past. Each May, the Pediatric Cancer Foundation went all out to celebrate their highest donors, of which Stone Worldwide certainly was, but because Summer and I arrived late, we'd missed that portion of the event. I vaguely remembered seeing something about an auction on the invitation, so I hoped we hadn't missed that entirely. While I didn't really travel in antique circles, I thought I might pick out a good piece if I saw something my mother may like.

"I'm going to get a drink. Do you want one?" I asked Summer as I looked back toward the bar.

Her eyes widened and she nodded. "This is incredible. I thought we were going to be sitting at a table like every awards dinner I've ever had to attend. Is that a runway? What's that for?"

I shrugged but didn't bother to look at whatever she'd become fascinated with. I needed a drink before any fascination could happen for me.

"No idea. White wine?"

Again, she nodded, so I headed off to get us two white wines. Thankfully, the line for the bartender's attention wasn't long, and after pushing through a crowd of people that seemed to suddenly crop up behind my back as I waited for our glasses of wine, I finally reached Summer again.

"Where did all these people come from?" I asked as I handed her the glass.

Still taking in the scene happening around us, Summer shook her head. "I don't know. I guess something big's about to happen."

Something big at a charity event to celebrate major donors? Highly doubtful. I'd attended dozens of these kinds of events, first with my parents when I was younger and then on my own when my father finally decided he could bow out of obligatory events on behalf of Stone Worldwide because I could step in, and never once had anything big happened at any of them. It was always the same, staid event, just at different locations around the city.

Looking at all the people standing around us in the Stilton Hotel's ballroom at that moment, though, I had to admit tonight felt different. I just hoped I wouldn't have to give a speech extemporaneously. I hated those, so I avoided them like the plague. Now that I was there, I couldn't avoid it if it happened, though.

Maybe I needed another drink. Tipping my glass back to finish my first wine, I let it dribble down my throat and then turned to Summer. "Want another?"

She looked at me with surprise. "No. I barely took two sips out of this one. Since when did you become a big drinker?"

"It's been like ten minutes since I gave you that drink," I said with a chuckle. "If you weren't spending all your time people watching, you might want another one too. I'll be right back."

Nearly fifteen minutes and a line twenty deep later, I began walking back to where Summer stood near what I now recognized looked like a dais and a runway. People chattered loudly, making me wonder if I'd missed something. Were they having a fashion show or something tonight? I thought the invitation had said auction, but I'd just glanced at it.

The lights of the crystal chandelier in the center of the room dimmed, and all of a sudden, bright white spotlights focused on the dais at the back of the room. As I wondered what could be happening, people began to cheer and a voice came over the sound system announcing the auction would begin.

All this excitement for what? A rocking chair George Washington may have sat in a few times? A pen Bill Gates may have stuck in his pocket back in the seventies?

With the lights dimmed, finding Summer became next to impossible. Everywhere I turned, I ran into someone and spilled not only my drink but the one I'd gotten for her too. As the crowd roared for something, a man announced over the loudspeaker, "Ready to start big?"

Everyone around me yelled and clapped, so I became disoriented and couldn't find Summer in the sea of people with their arms raised. The screaming grew so loud that the voice of the man running the auction became drowned out. I had no idea why the hell all these people were so excited at a charity auction, but I wanted no part of this craziness.

Raising my arms in the air to salvage at least the half of each glass of wine I held in my hands, I pushed through the crowd toward where I'd last seen Summer and hoped to find her there. Focused on reaching her, I ignored all the madness around me like I'd always had a knack for doing and soon got to her.

"Where did you go?" she yelled as she grabbed a half-empty glass of wine from my left hand.

I leaned down so I didn't have to yell back at her and said into her ear, "This place is crazy. What the hell are all these people screaming about?"

She didn't answer and instead simply pointed at the dais as I realized this was no ordinary auction of boring antiques. Standing there with all the lights trained on him was a man more beautiful than I'd ever seen in my life. He stood well over six foot and filled out the tux he wore perfectly. My eyes slowly scanned his body from his feet up, and by the time I got to his light brown hair that just barely hit the collar of his white shirt, I'd forgotten there was anyone else in the room but him.

Who was this man?

Then before I could turn to ask Summer, he began walking down the runway and my instant admiration for him quickly cooled. Sure, he was gorgeous, but as he basked in the attention of the crowd of screaming people I now noticed was mostly female, I saw someone who had no problem drawing attention to himself.

Of all the character flaws a man could possess, that was the worst.

Too bad. Other than his being an attention whore, I would have liked to find out more about this stunning specimen of manhood. Disappointed, I wondered what kind of man allowed himself to be involved in a bachelor auction.

Nobody I'd want.

He walked out to the end of the runway and winked at someone, which caused the crowd to erupt again. All it did for me was make me feel more disappointed because up close he was even more attractive with pale green eyes and dark lashes that made him look exotic. For a moment, I fantasized about what kind of perfect body existed under that tux, but that served no purpose. He wasn't anyone I could ever be with.

As he turned to walk back toward the dais, he looked down at where we stood and suddenly it felt like time stopped. Those incredible green eyes stared into mine, and even as my mind dismissed this man as the attention whore he clearly was, my body reacted quite differently. That familiar ache between my legs I hadn't experienced in far too long and thoughts of how good he'd feel satisfying that ache made me instinctively sink my teeth into my lower lip. He smiled and ran his tongue over his bottom lip, and for a moment, nothing in the world existed but him.

I felt an elbow crash into my side, tearing me out of my imagination, and Summer yelled into my ear, "Oh, my God! Do you realize who you were just giving the eyes to?"

Shaking my head, partly to answer her and partly to get rid of the incredibly sexual thoughts still lingering about what I wanted to do with him, I stood there speechless, not able to say a thing.

"That's Killian Brenton!"

She said that like I should know the name, but it didn't register. Who was Killian Brenton?

Summer's eyes opened wide, as if she'd heard the dumbest thing ever spoken in the world. "He's the new quarterback for New York. He was traded from Miami this spring. He's the biggest thing in town, and you were just checking him out like you wanted to sink your teeth into him."

I waved off her ridiculous comment. There was nothing wrong with appreciating a good looking man, even if he was an attention whore I'd never sleep with.

"Two thousand! Do I hear three? It's for a great cause, ladies!" the announcer said in an amused voice.

Summer leaned over and asked, "Why aren't you bidding like everyone else?"

I shook my head and waved the question away.

"But it's for charity. You don't have to marry the guy."

After I watched him flirt with another woman in the audience, I turned to her and said, "These things aren't even real. No one expects either party to follow through on the deal."

"Then why not bid for him?" she asked, practically goading me to do it. "It's for a good cause."

Clearly, I couldn't deny that, so I raised my hand when the announcer said five thousand dollars. Turning to look at Summer, I smiled. "Happy?"

"Yes. Do you know that he signed a contract for over three hundred million dollars guaranteed and much more in bonuses?"

Three hundred million dollars? For that much, he should just stop parading around like a peacock and simply donate to the charity. But as I watched him interact with the women in the crowd, I saw he was incapable of not being in the spotlight and letting people fawn all over him.

It's a character flaw. He's an attention whore, and that I cannot abide in a man.

I'd met many men just like Killian Brenton in my time with Stone Worldwide. They believed they were God's gift to everyone on the planet but especially to women. I'd enjoyed proving them wrong whenever I could. They preferred women with few thoughts in their heads who wanted to do nothing more than worship them.

No thanks. I had bigger plans for myself than simply adoring a man for the rest of my life. No matter how gorgeous he may be.

Lost in thought, I didn't see him come over toward us until he stood directly in front of me on the ballroom floor. Craning my neck to look up at him, I couldn't help but be mesmerized by those pale green eyes. God, he was beautiful! He smelled incredible too, and I took a deep breath of air into my lungs, fighting the urge to close my eyes he smelled so good. Was that cologne? I had no idea, but the man was nothing short of delectable.

But why was he smiling like that, like a cat that just ate a canary?

Before I could ask Summer what was going on, he lifted a microphone to his mouth and said in a deep voice that rolled over me like silk, "Congratulations. You're the lucky lady who gets to spend a night with me."

He stood staring at me as I looked up at him speechless and utterly unaware of what was happening. All I knew was I couldn't turn away, or maybe I didn't want to. Whatever it was, this man had an intoxicating effect on me I couldn't explain.

Then he ran the tip of his tongue over his bottom lip and smiled before turning to step back onto the runway. I watched as he took a bow while the crowd went wild and his words finally sank in.

Horrified, I lowered my head because of what everyone would think. How could I have let this happen?

Summer nudged me in the side and asked, "Oh, my God! What just happened there?"

"I don't know," I answered, still shaken by what he made me feel.

"You outbid everyone at ten grand for a date with Killian Brenton!"

Summer's words filtered through the haze in my brain, and I shook my head. "Five thousand, and I have no intention of going anywhere with someone like him."

Summer pointed up toward a big screen behind the stage and the image of Killian with the number $10,000 under him. "You raised your hand when they called for the next bid. I figured you were in the spirit of the evening and decided to be extra generous."

Ten grand. Thank God it was for charity. I didn't care about the money, though. It was only money, after all.

"Five or ten, it's a good cause, right?" I said as casually as I could manage.

"You're going to go on the date with him, aren't you?" Summer asked eagerly. "I mean, I guess you could just say no, but since you paid that much money for a night with him, you might as well."

"I did not pay for a night with that man!" I protested, needing at least Summer to know that. "It was a charity auction. I would have contributed to anyone asking for a donation to cure childhood cancer, for God's sake."

Ten thousand dollars. How could I have been so lost in thought fantasizing about the delicious and decadent things I'd do with him that I bid ten thousand dollars for a date with a man?

As reality sunk in, I gradually realized everyone near us was staring at me. Jesus. How must all this look? I made a point of living as low-key a life as possible, acting professionally when I stepped out in public, and now I'd succeeded in blowing up all I'd worked for, and for what?

A date with a man. An attention whore. How embarrassing.

I watched as the people around us turned to look toward the stage. I followed their gazes to a huge screen showing a picture of Killian and me looking at each other right before he announced I'd won the bid. Anyone with eyes and a smattering of brain cells could see as clear as day what I was thinking about as I stared at him. I practically had a bubble over my head with the caption, "This man is beautiful. God, the things I would do with him."

My stomach began to churn from the disgust coursing through my body. Mortified, I turned to leave and said to Summer, "This has been fun, but I'm going. Feel free to stay if you want."

I couldn't get out of that room fast enough. With each step, I felt people's eyes staring at me like I was some kind of fallen woman. My head reeled from humiliation.

Summer ran up behind me and said, "You're not staying for the party? You love these kinds of things. What's going on? Are you sick?"

Flustered, I kept walking, my eyes firmly focused on the doors. "No. I'm fine. I just don't feel like doing this tonight."

Summer jumped in front of me in the lobby and stopped me. Smiling, she said, "You're blushing. Oh, my God, you're actually blushing! I've never seen you blush before. What's going on?"

"Stop being melodramatic. I think you've been spending too much time with my brother. I'm not blushing. It's just stuffy in here."

Shaking her head, she grinned like any of this was at all amusing. "No, it's not. It's actually chilly in here. I think they went a little overboard on the air conditioning, to be honest. You're blushing."

"So what if I am? It's not every day I'm publicly humiliated by a perfect stranger in a room full of people I'd hoped to chat up."

"How did he publicly humiliate you?"

I stepped around her and hurried toward the front doors. "I don't want to talk about it. God, who does he think he is?"

Summer rushed to keep up with me. "I think the question is who do you think he is because from where I'm standing, you like him. So are you going to go out with him?"

Again with that damn question. I rolled my eyes in disgust. "For the last time, no. Now let's go. I need some fresh air."

Behind us, the crowd began to cheer again as the announcement that the second bachelor to be auctioned off would be coming up next. For me, I'd had enough of the event already.

We reached the doors, and even though all I wanted to do was get out of there, I looked back and saw Killian standing at the edge of the catwalk staring at me. An attention whore man who craved the adulation of a crowd like that? No way was I going anywhere with him.

CHAPTER TWO

KILLIAN

MY BODY HUMMED FROM A lack of sleep and something else I hadn't felt in a long time. It had been years since a woman made me want her more than for just a quick fuck, and one look from Tressa Stone had me worried that crowd at the Pediatric Cancer Foundation charity event might see the effect she had on me. She practically undressed me with her eyes right there in front of all those bluebloods and society types. I did like a woman who threw caution to the wind, though.

Not that I didn't want to fuck her. You bet I did. How had I lived in this town for two months and not heard about her before? I couldn't decide if she was new money or old, but there was money there, no doubt. She practically oozed wealth. She had that icy thing women with fortunes had going on, but the question was whose money was it?

These ideas swirled around in my brain, among others, like was she as icy as she seemed? I bet she wasn't. She looked like an ice princess, but I knew for a fact she had heat beneath the surface. I felt it right there in that room as we stared at one another. She virtually melted in front of me.

My mind constructed exactly how she looked as she stood looking completely fuckable surrounded by all those people. Dark brown eyes and long dark hair I had a feeling fell exactly the way a woman's hair should when she was on top of me, caressing my skin as she undulated back and forth on my cock, the bottom of her hair teasing my chest with every roll of her hips.

Oh yeah, this date was going to be fun. She'd paid ten grand for me, so I intended on giving her every dime of her money's worth.

I needed to know more about her before our date, which I planned on happening this week. Grabbing my phone, I called my publicist Sherilyn and sent it to the screen on the wall across from my bed.

Her cheery face popped up on the display like always when I called her. I had a feeling I may have interrupted something since her dark blond hair looked disheveled.

"Good morning, Killian. Not that I'm not happy to hear from you, but do you know what time it is?"

Shaking my head, I thought about her question for a moment and came up with nothing. "I have no clue, actually. Were you busy with someone?"

She rolled her eyes and held up a hair dryer. "I was busy getting ready for my day. What are you doing up at five in the morning?"

Then her blue eyes opened wide in terror, and she tossed her hair dryer back onto the bed behind her. "Oh, my God! What happened? What do we need to clean up? Give me the details quick so I can get on it!"

She began to frantically pace back and forth across her bedroom floor, waving her arms in front of her. "Just tell me it's nothing illegal. It's next to impossible to get illegal stuff taken care of on a Sunday. If it's something like that, I'm going to have to roll out some of that big news we keep for times just like this. Let me see. What would work best?"

As she spun out of control right there before my eyes, I sat up in bed and waved my hands to stop her before she ran off to announce to the world that I'd secretly been visiting hospitals or something equally as saintly. "It's nothing like that, Sherilyn. Why are you jumping to the conclusion that I got arrested?"

Stopping to answer my question, she twisted her face into a

look of confusion. "Who calls their publicist at five in the morning on a Sunday if it isn't that you were arrested? I know Mike would have gotten you out, but then you'd call me to smooth things over. If it's not that, then what's up?"

Leaning back against the pillows, I folded my arms behind my head. "I want you to tell me everything you know about Tressa Stone."

Sherilyn sat down on the edge of her bed, and her shoulders sagged as she realized she didn't have to start her day in PR high gear since I just wanted some information. Still confused, she asked, "What? Who do you want to know about?"

"Tressa Stone. She paid ten grand at that charity auction for a date with me last night. I want to know all about her. Everything you can tell me."

Looking up, my publicist seemed to search for the information on her bedroom ceiling. When she finally returned her focus to the screen, she shrugged. "I don't know a lot. She comes from a very wealthy family. That I do know. I have no idea of anything about her personal life because she keeps her life very secret. She must because I've never read a single word about her in the gossip pages or on any sites, and as you know, I read them religiously so I can be up on everything. I remember her brother being mentioned in them a lot a while back. He was some kind of photographer. Good looking man, but that's not surprising."

"Well, I want to know more. I need you to find out everything you can about her. I want to be prepared for this date."

Sherilyn shook her head, sending her half-wet, half-dry blond hair swinging around her shoulders. "You know, Killian, those things don't always happen. Everyone involved understands that the important part is giving to the charity. I wouldn't be surprised if she has no interest in going out with you at all."

That sounded ridiculous, especially considering how Tressa looked at me last night. "Trust me. She's interested. No woman pays that much for a date she has no intention of going on. Just find out everything there is to find out about her and get back to me, okay?"

"Okay, Killian. Just don't be surprised when she says no. I'll let you know what I find out."

The screen went black, leaving me sitting alone in bed thinking about Tressa Stone. She wouldn't say no. Christ, if all those people hadn't been around, I had a feeling she would have dragged me to a corner of the ballroom and climbed on top of me right there. I knew how to read women, and that woman wanted me. That I was sure of.

Just daydreaming about fucking her made me hard as a rock. Instead of calling my agent like I planned, I slid out of bed and headed into the bathroom to grab a shower. I wouldn't be getting any more sleep this morning, so why not rub one out and get going on my day?

A LITTLE WHILE LATER AT a time I knew my agent would be awake, I made my second call of the morning designed to help me make my date with Tressa Stone perfect. Mike never let me down, no matter if it was negotiating a contract or helping me navigate my new city. A born and bred New Yorker, he seemed to love giving me suggestions about where to go and what to eat, so who better to ask where to take a beautiful woman on a date?

Dressed in his usual golf shirt and pants, Mike looked like he perpetually was heading out to the links. If he didn't do such an incredible job on getting me the biggest contract for a quarterback in the league, I'd think the guy just spent his entire days goofing around and golfing.

He smiled as his face came into view on my screen and pointed at me in that way he always did whenever he saw me. "Killian, how are you doing?"

"Good. I need suggestions on where to go to get a good meal. Nothing too loud or popular. I don't want to have to deal with the press. Well, not much anyway."

Mike thought about how to answer for a moment. "Let me mull it over and I'll get back to you. I'm more interested in talking about that charity auction event last night. I saw some pictures already this morning. It looks like you're fitting into this city perfectly."

I ran my hand through my hair and headed over to the window that looked out over the city. Scanning the horizon, I had to admit New York was my kind of place and the weather wasn't anywhere as hot as Miami, thankfully. "I told you I'd be fine. With enough money, I can be fine anywhere. Hell, you could have gotten me the deal with Minnesota and I'd have been fine. Bored to fucking hell and colder than a witch's tit, but fine."

"I hear some woman paid ten grand for a date with you. That's a lot of money for one night."

"She gets to go out with a man who's one of a very elite group of men in the world. Seems about right to me," I said.

"So is that why you want restaurant recommendations? When are you planning on doing this?"

Turning away from the gorgeous view out my bedroom window, I nodded. "I like to strike while the iron's hot, so something this week. I got her number from the organizer last night, so I'm planning on calling her today. So say Tuesday? That's why I need to know where I can take her today."

My agent let out a big laugh. "You do work fast. It's already Sunday morning."

"You didn't see this woman. I would have gone last night if I could have."

"Actually, I did. It's all over the news. You're a hot topic around here, and that charity event is a popular news story every year. Check out the local news. You'll see."

I turned on one of the New York channels and saw Mike hadn't exaggerated. The press had been out in full force, but I hadn't expected this much coverage. I figured New York had more interesting things to concern itself with than some football player hauling in ten grand at a charity auction.

Then I saw the picture of that moment when I walked up to Tressa and our eyes met. Definitely something there. Beneath that perfectly icy exterior, that woman sizzled. I'd bet a good million on it.

"You keep behaving yourself and this town is going to love you. Well, behaving yourself and taking New York to the big dance," Mike said.

I had more confidence in my getting my new team to the championship than I did in my behaving. I'd been a good boy in the time since I moved to New York, but I had no intention of living like a monk for the rest of my life. All behaving and no play made for a very boring Killian.

But I planned to change that with Tressa Stone.

"Well, I can't make any promises about behaving, but you have to admit that charity event helps."

Mike nodded but his toothy grin faded just a bit. "Be careful with this woman. You don't need any problems like that here."

"Like what? I'm single, and if she's single, what's the problem?"

"I don't know her, but I do know the Stone name is important in this city. You don't want to make any powerful enemies here, Killian. This isn't like Miami. New York will chew up a man and spit him out before he knows what's happened. Yes, charity events like the one last night are good, but don't negate all the benefit you get from it by becoming a permanent fixture in the gossip pages."

"Well, you know what Sherilyn says. There's no such thing as bad publicity," I said with a laugh.

But my agent didn't find anything about what I said funny.

"You know my opinion on that. I can get you the world with the talent you have, but if you become a distraction or a problem for your team, I won't be able to get you a deal selling fucking athlete's foot cream, much less anything good."

I could tell any time Mike got hot about a subject when he

started dropping F bombs. Since I had no intention of becoming a distraction for anyone other than Tressa Stone, I needed to calm him before he began to get worried I'd fuck up all his hard work.

"Don't worry. I know what my job is here. This whole thing with one woman isn't going to make me lose focus. It's just a date."

Mike arched one eyebrow to show me how skeptical he was about my claim. "I've seen that look before in you. Just remember once workouts start, you need to be all football all the time."

"Have I ever not been?" I asked, knowing the answer to that wasn't exactly no.

But that was when I was a rookie in the league. Now at twenty-nine, I knew I had just a few more years left before it all could slip away in one season. I had no intention of leaving my football career before I wanted to.

"Just remember what you told me when you came to me all those years ago, Killian. You said you wanted one single thing in this world, and that was to play football. As my grandmother used to say, you chase two rabbits and you'll catch neither."

"Got it. You don't have to worry about me, Mike. It's just a date with someone who paid ten grand for some time with me. The least I can do is take her to a nice restaurant."

Mike didn't look convinced. "Yeah. Well, let me think about it. I'll send you over some ideas later today."

The call ended, and as I stood in my bedroom alone again, I thought back to those early days of my career. Christ, I was such a naïve kid. Straight out of college and barely twenty-two, Miami started me halfway through the season when Sterling tore his ACL. Too green to even realize I should have been scared shitless seeing that happen right in front of me on the field, I ran in and huddled up with the players, ready to be the phenom everyone said I was since the first touchdown I threw in college.

By the end of my first season, I could do no wrong. Everything came so easy. Money. Women. Success. And for a few years, life was all I'd ever dreamed of.

Then one day it wasn't. Then one day I was in my late twenties and hurt. Nothing too bad, but bad enough for Miami to want someone new, someone younger. So when New York needed a new quarterback, Mike made the deal and I became the highest paid quarterback in the history of the game.

Now all I had to do was show them I was still the best in the league.

The screen on the wall made a noise to let me know a call was coming in, and I turned to see Sherilyn smiling at me. Her hair didn't look like someone had taken a blender to it anymore, and she wore makeup like she usually did when she worked.

"I'm glad to see you're up and dressed, Killian. I never know how I'm going to find you when I call," she said, blushing as she finished.

I couldn't blame her. More than once here and in Miami, she'd caught me buck naked in bed or standing in front of the monitor. I never had been able to remember that goddamned away message.

Not that it mattered. I imagined she'd seen people naked before me.

"Showered and dressed like a normal person, for once. I don't think I've been up this early on a Sunday when I wasn't playing in years," I said as I sat down on the edge of my bed. "So what did you find out about Tressa?"

Sherilyn looked down at her tablet and scanned the information before looking up at me again. "Tressa Stone is twenty-seven years old. Never married. She has no children. I thought you'd like to know that right off."

"Not married is good. I like kids well enough, so it wouldn't matter to me if she had some rugrats. What else did you find out?"

"She's a member of the Stone family. Very influential family in this city."

"So I've heard."

"She's not a frequent topic in the gossip pages or even on the business page because of her work for Stone Worldwide, her family's company. She's a VP at Stone Worldwide and the newly minted COO of the Richmont hotel chain."

"Nice. What's this company make?"

"There are dozens and dozens of subsidiaries inside the main company. The Stone name is on things from a line of outerwear under the Storm name, a high end restaurant chain under the name brand Harrigan's Chop House, and dozens of other companies. You probably know their Richmont hotel chain the best, though."

I filed all this information away for our date. "So, she's a business executive? I can see that. She gives off that vibe."

Sherilyn shook her head and frowned. "No, you're misunderstanding. Tressa Stone isn't just a powerful businesswoman. She's also an heiress to a huge fortune. She's set to inherit billions when her parents die, along with her brother and sister, and even now is one of the wealthiest women in all of New York. And the family is old money, not nouveau riche."

"So what are you saying? Someone like her would never lower herself to go on a date with a lowly football player? I'm not exactly a pauper here, Sherilyn."

"I'm saying that maybe she isn't exactly the type of woman you date. Usually, I mean."

The way Sherilyn said that made me wonder if she hadn't told me all she'd found out about Tressa. What was she hiding?

"Is there something you're not telling me about this woman?"

Sherilyn slowly shook her head. "No. You saw her. Does she look like the type of woman who spends her time with athletes? My guess is she's more of a three-piece suit kind of woman who likes men who are like her, if you know what I mean."

I'd known my publicist longer than I knew my agent, so I couldn't believe anything she ever said to me wasn't meant to be helpful. We'd been together through thick and thin from before I even signed with a team, and she'd seen me at my worst and my best. I knew what she was seeing in Tressa Stone, but I saw something else.

Something more than just a businesswoman who projected an icy façade to the world. And I planned on finding out if my hunch about who she was behind that cold mask was right.

"Well, it's just a single date, Sherilyn, so you don't have to worry about me."

"Oh, I'm not worried about you, Killian. I know you. You'll be the same charming man you always are with women, and if she doesn't like that, at least it's just a few hours of your time and it's for a good cause."

"Thanks, Sherilyn. I can always count on you to help me. Talk to you later."

Now that I knew some details about Tressa, it was time to make that date with her.

CHAPTER THREE

TRESSA

AFTER OVERSLEEPING NEARLY TWO HOURS, I sat at the table in my living room and stared out the window that overlooked the city. I squinted at a ray of sun that chose at that very moment to shine into my penthouse, turning away as I prayed my morning coffee would start to do its job. So far, it hadn't done a damn thing to make me wake up, and I couldn't function well until the caffeine kicked in.

The chime from the TV told me someone had made the mistake of thinking they should call me this morning, and I turned to look at the monitor as the person's face came into focus. Ethan. Ugh. Not this morning. Please, God, not this morning.

But he had other ideas.

"Good morning, Tress. How are you feeling on this fine and sunny New York morning? Feeling famous or would it be infamous?" he chirped away with that ridiculous smile on his face.

Wishing my coffee would kick in at that very moment, I mumbled, "I don't have the time to deal with you today, Ethan."

His stupid grin grew even larger. "It's a wonderful day, so why not make time? The birds are singing in the trees, and the newspapers are out with all the news we fine citizens could possible need. Want to see the highlights?"

My brain attempted to figure out what the hell he was referring to, and just as the memory of the charity auction popped into my head, he pointed to the pictures of Killian and me at the charity auction last night that popped up in succession to frame his face on the screen. Each one showed me gazing at the man like some lovesick schoolgirl, or worse, like some horny teenager looking like she wanted to jump him right there in front of everyone in the ballroom.

"I love how you keep things on the down low, Tress. Just how low is that now? I mean, I guess it could have appeared on the front page of the Post and the Times. That would definitely not be keeping it on the down low like you are now with it on Page Six, all the gossip websites, and even on the local TV news."

His teasing made me want to lash out, but I was too exhausted, and honestly, it was all so embarrassing. Ethan had me dead to rights on this mess, and there was nothing I could do about that, so I just snapped, "What are you doing up so early? Did you lose your girlfriend? Did she finally figure out she could do better?"

My brother simply smiled at my sharp attack. His smugness knew no bounds, and justifiably so. He'd waited all his adult life to get me back for all those times I'd chided him about how he conducted his personal life. I didn't begrudge him this payback. I'd do the same thing myself. I just wasn't in the mood at that very moment to trade verbal jabs with him.

"Summer and I are perfectly fine. I just wanted to check in on my sister who preaches about keeping things on the down low. That seems to be working pretty well for you. I do have to hand it to you, though, Tress. You definitely chose someone perfect for your debut on Page Six. Just wait until Dad sees you standing with Killian Brenton."

I groaned in misery. The thought of my parents seeing me ogling some football player at the charity auction made this morning one hundred times worse. I'd always prided myself on being the consummate professional, and now this would ruin everything I'd so assiduously worked for.

"If I find out you called them about this, I swear to God, Ethan, I will be merciless in my revenge."

He threw his head back and laughed like he was having a grand old time. "They don't live in a cave, Tress. They're going to find out eventually. It's all over the news. One of their friends probably showed them those pictures over breakfast."

Oh. God. The very thought of one of my parents' friends calling them up over coffee and muffins on a Sunday morning just to show them those pictures made me feel like I'd be sick.

And just when I thought I couldn't feel any worse, I saw my father calling.

"Ethan, go get back to your life and leave me alone. I'm busy."

More laughing at my misery was followed by more taunting. "I've waited for years for this day. I'm not going to let it just go like that. How about we talk about that ten grand you paid to spend the night with Killian? That was how they said it, spend the night, right? I'm loving this down low thing you have going on. You should give lessons on how to keep your private life private, Tress."

"Go to hell."

I hurried over to the TV and ended the call with Ethan to answer my father's. Before I said a word, I immediately assessed how he looked. No frown. Good. No pacing. That was definitely good. When my father was upset, he paced. Maybe he hadn't heard, but then again, if he hadn't, why would he be calling me so early on a Sunday morning?

Plastering a smile on my face, I effected my happiest voice. "Hi, Dad. It's early to see you this morning. Everything okay?"

Oh, God. That sounded panicked, not chipper, like I wanted it to be. Hopefully, he didn't hear the fear in my voice. I had to stay cool. Nothing bad had happened. This whole Killian Brenton thing would blow over by the time Monday rolled around, so I just had to keep things in perspective.

"Oh, yeah. Everything's fine. How was the charity event last night? Did you have a good time?"

My father had never been the teasing type, but his questions sounded oddly taunting, similar to my brother's. Had Ethan already gotten to him? If he did, I would kill him for this. Or even better, I'd torture him. There would be no end to my vengeance.

"It was a very nice event, but they always are. You know how they are. You spent enough years attending them. You haven't spoken to Ethan yet this morning, have you?"

Damn. My words tumbled out of my mouth so quickly my father had to suspect something wasn't right.

My father shook his head. "No. I haven't spoken to him in a few days. Is anything wrong?"

Good. There was my chance to steer the conversation in the direction of my brother. I needed to build on that inherent worry he always had that Ethan had done something wrong.

"No. I mean, you know how he is. You can never tell what he's going to do. One day he's taking pictures of dogs, and the next who knows? That's just Ethan, I guess."

Nodding, my father said, "Your brother has been known to have some wild times. I guess I expect it from him. Now you, on the other hand, I don't expect it from." He stopped talking and pointed to a box at the top of the screen he'd put there as he spoke. "Imagine my surprise to find out my daughter is going out on a date with the new quarterback for my favorite team. You don't even like football, do you? Not that it matters to go out on a date, but you've never wanted to go to a game like your brother and sister."

My stomach dropped to my feet, and I cringed as I looked up and saw the picture of Killian and me staring at each other like long lost loves. Oh, who was I kidding? That wasn't even remotely true. Only I was staring at him like that. At least he hadn't put up the one of me staring at him like some oversexed schoolgirl.

"I think I must have had a reaction to the allergy medicine I took yesterday afternoon, Dad. The pollen has been terrible this spring. Did you see how much of it was in the air this week? I think it made me a little loopy—the medicine, not the pollen—and then I had a few sips of wine right after I got to the event. It must have been that. Honestly, it looks much different than it was in actuality.

It's really not a big deal."

Nice job rambling, Tressa. That will convince him everything's fine. Anytime anyone in the history of the world said something wasn't a big deal, those very words told everyone it was so much a big deal.

None of what I told my father sounded even plausible and didn't explain why I was gazing up at Killian Brenton like some pathetic schoolgirl with her first crush. I didn't even have allergies.

God, how was I going to show my face anywhere ever again?

My father smiled sweetly at me like he always did when he saw me worrying about something. "You don't have to explain having a good time, honey. You're a grown woman, and a very competent woman at that. And Killian Brenton is a big deal. I'm not surprised you'd be more than a little impressed with him. The amount you bid to the charity for him all goes to a great cause, so I think you must be feeling pretty good about things."

I wasn't impressed by him. He was nothing more than an attention whore who loved the limelight. That kind of man was nothing but a turn off. I couldn't tell my father that, though, since he didn't see me like that. To my father, I was his overachieving daughter who would someday take over Stone Worldwide. I acted the way I was supposed to, as opposed to my two siblings, and he appreciated that.

So if he knew what had been going through my mind at the moment that picture of me gazing longingly up at Killian Brenton was taken, I'd be too embarrassed to face him.

"It was nothing, Dad. Just some allergy medicine gone wrong. I'm happy to make the donation to the pediatric cancer association, though. At least that went right."

"When are the two of you going out? You did bid on a date with him, right?" my father asked a little too eagerly.

"We're not," I answered, grimacing at how tawdry the whole thing sounded. Thank God it was for a worthy cause. It was truly the only saving grace of the entire situation.

"Why not? He's the talk of the town," my father said with a deep frown, sounding downright disappointed by my announcement that I wouldn't be going out with Killian.

"I prefer my dates to grow out of organic circumstances, to be honest, Dad. I'm sure Mr. Brenton will be fine with my declining his offer. He has other things to occupy his time with, I have no doubt."

"Oh. Well, if you want to do it that way, that's fine. I just think it's a shame you aren't going because if anyone deserves a night out, it's you. I know how hard you work every day. I wish you'd reconsider. I hear he's a great guy."

Ethan had been right. My father did want me to go out with the quarterback from his favorite team. What was it with these men and football that made them think such ridiculous things?

I needed to change the topic or I'd have to explain my dislike for Killian Brenton to my father, something I really didn't want to do now or ever. "I have to go, Dad. I have work I need to get done today, and I'll never finish it if I just sit around all day. Tell Mom I said hi. Are you two just relaxing today?"

Leaving that horrible discussion of my misadventures the night before, my father's eyes lit up, and he smiled. "No. We're coming into the city to take Diana out for lunch. You're welcome to join us. Ethan and Summer said they might come too. We'd love to have you there too."

My sister had recently started leaving the hotel more because of Summer and Ethan's efforts, but I didn't feel right crashing their family time. Diana and I were too different to spend much time together. Every time we did, I seemed to say the wrong thing and upset her.

"I wish I could. Tell Diana I said I'm sorry I couldn't come this time but maybe next time. Tell her I'll stop over to see her this week."

That hopeful look in my father's eyes made my chest ache because I knew as soon as I said those words that I wouldn't go to see my sister anytime soon. I couldn't. Being around her made me too sad because I always thought back to who she was before the accident. It broke my heart to know she'd never be that person again.

"Okay, honey. Have a good day, and Tressa, remember that you deserve to relax and have a good time every so often."

"I love you, Dad. Don't worry about me. I'm having a good time doing what I love, which is working at Stone Worldwide and making it the successful company it is."

The screen turned black, leaving me alone in my misery once more. Feeling a headache beginning to form, I pinched the bridge of my nose and tried to push the memory of those images of Killian Brenton and me out of my mind. So far this day had been utter shit, so it had to get better. Maybe if I took a shower and got dressed. That might make me feel better.

What would really make me feel great would be if someone could invent a way to wipe my mind and the mind of every person in New York of the sight of me looking up at Killian Brenton like I wanted to devour him. That would be perfect.

CHAPTER FOUR

KILLIAN

WHY WERE MY PALMS SWEATY? It made no sense. I'd dated hundreds of women. Well, maybe not hundreds but I'd never had a problem with getting any woman I wanted. There was no reason to think Tressa Stone would be any different. For God's sake, she'd already basically given me the green light the way she looked at me last night. She was probably waiting for me to call at that very moment.

Rubbing my hands together, I took one last glance at the card the woman from the pediatric cancer foundation gave me. Tressa Stone, one date with Killian Brenton. My eyes drifted over her number for the tenth time. For a few moments, I closed my eyes and let my mind linger on that look in her eyes when she was staring up at me. I'd had women check me out before, but that was different.

She was different. And I intended on finding out every way that was true.

I'd take her to one of the restaurants Mike suggested. Maybe the Italian one. Or French. I'd decide once I talked to her. Then we might go for a drive. One of my teammates had told me about this place he bought last year upstate. A nice drive on a gorgeous spring night would set the stage, and then I'd bring her back to my apartment. Or hers. Either would work.

I remembered how she looked up at me when our eyes met. Those dark eyes possessed an intensity I had a feeling I'd enjoy once she was naked and riding my cock. Oh yeah, this was going to be a night she'd never forget.

Eager to get things rolling, I made the call to Tressa Stone I'd delayed for nearly an hour and waited for her face to appear as I wondered what she'd be wearing at barely ten o'clock in the morning. Was she a T-shirt and shorts or silk pajamas kind of woman?

That was easy. Silk pajamas.

A second later, I saw I'd been wrong in my guess. Tressa stood in the middle of what looked like a luxury penthouse in a pair of black cotton shorts and a pale pink T-shirt wearing no bra. Pleasantly surprised, I had to admit even in something as casual as that, she looked incredible. Her dark hair was wet, as if she'd just come back from a swim, and clung to her T-shirt just above her breasts, making the shirt damp so I could see her nipples. Overall, it was quite the beautiful sight I hadn't expected at all.

She stood staring in shock for a long moment before rushing over to grab a white towel off the back of a chair to cover herself. The whole action made me smile at how cute she could be.

"Don't cover up on my account. I like what I'm seeing."

"How did you get this number, Mr. Brenton?" she asked, clearly flustered as she struggled to cover herself with the towel.

"The woman at the event last night gave it to me since I'd have to call you to arrange that date we're going on."

Shaking her head, Tressa put her right hand up to stop me as she clutched the towel near her neck with her other hand. "Oh, no we aren't. I'll be sending the money to the charity first thing tomorrow, but we won't be going on any date. Sorry you made the effort when it wasn't needed."

"What do you mean we aren't going on the date you paid ten grand for?" I asked with a chuckle. "I'd think any woman who paid that much would be chomping at the bit to make plans."

Clinging to the towel as it threatened to expose her wet breasts again, she shook her head. "No offense, but I thought I was paying five, not ten, but that doesn't matter. It's for a good cause, so all the better. But I have no interest in going out on a date with you, Mr. Brenton."

Was this woman serious? My ego was beginning to feel bruised. Why wasn't she interested in going on a date she paid ten thousand dollars for?

No worries. I knew I could charm her into it. Maybe she was intimidated by my fame. That happened sometimes. "Please, call me Killian, Tressa. For the amount you paid, you can at least call me by my first name."

But even that dose of charm did nothing to make her warm up. Drawing her eyebrows in, she said sharply, "Mr. Brenton, I have to get to work today, but thank you for calling. Please feel free to consider yourself unobligated to have that date with me. I'm sure there are many women who would take my place, so choose one of them. Good day."

With that, she gave me one last glare and that was the last I saw of her before the screen went dark. I stood there in the center of the room in shock. Did that just happen? Last night, the woman couldn't see enough of me as I walked down that catwalk, and this morning, she acted like I was some fucking leper she couldn't get away from fast enough.

Now my ego was more than bruised. Who did this woman think she was? She paid ten grand for a date with the highest paid quarterback in football. It didn't matter if she thought she was only paying five thousand, although I couldn't help but feel that a night out with me was worth more, especially considering all the proceeds went to charity. She acted like I was some fucking janitor who had offended her by asking her out.

Nope. That wasn't going to be the last word on this. No way. Why the hell didn't she want to go out on a single date with me?

Immediately, I called back but got her away message that in a delightful tone I hadn't gotten the pleasure to hear a minute before now told callers that she was busy and couldn't talk at the moment.

There was no suggestion to leave a message or ever call back again. I was sure I'd never heard such a dismissive away message before in my life.

What was the problem with this woman?

Frustrated, I stood staring at the dark screen in front of me still stunned at what just happened. Or maybe I was angry. I couldn't tell at the moment. All I knew was I'd never met anyone who could run so hot and cold. This woman wanted me last night, and now she treated me like I disgusted her.

This wasn't over. Tressa Stone wasn't going to have the last word on this. No. I didn't know who the hell she thought she was, but this wasn't over. Not by a long shot.

Irritated, I called my publicist to find out what more she'd learned about Tressa Stone in the past few hours. Her answer? Nothing.

"What do you mean nothing? This woman isn't some kind of ghost, Sherilyn. She's a VP at a major company. She's a member of one of the most important families in the city, and you can't find out a damn thing about her?" I barked as my frustration began to overtake me.

Sherilyn's eyes grew wide at the bellowing sound of my voice. "I'm sorry, Killian. I can't just make up information on this woman. I can't help it if she's kept her personal life very personal. For most people, the first time they've seen a picture of her was this morning. She's just not like you."

"Does she have something against football players, for Christ's sake? She didn't last night, so I don't know what I could have done between then and this morning to change her opinion. We didn't even speak for the first time until five minutes ago."

My publicist nodded in her sympathetic way she thought helped when I got angry. It didn't help, but I appreciated the attempt.

"I don't know why she wouldn't want to go out on the date with you. Did she say if she planned to not give the money to the pediatric cancer foundation too? I can't imagine why she'd do that."

I shook my head as I began to pace back and forth across the room. "No, she's not doing anything like that. The woman isn't a monster. She's also not stupid. Going back on that bid would be a PR disaster for her and her company. No, she's more than happy to pay the ten grand to the charity. She just has no interest in going on the date with me, which incidentally, was supposed to be the prize for the highest bidder."

Sherilyn looked down at her tablet. "Let me see if I can find anything now. Maybe this morning's news blast about her has jarred some tidbit of information loose. Give me a second."

As she scoured her sources, I continued to pace. Maybe she thought she was too good for someone like me. She was a rich girl. That explained the temper tantrum she'd had a few minutes ago. Between being born with a silver spoon in her mouth and being a corporate bigwig, she was probably used to ordering people around.

None of that turned me off her, to be honest. I liked powerful people, and I'd found powerful women made for incredible sex because they were happy to tell you exactly what they wanted. Unlike other men, I appreciated that. It also made for some really hot talk while I was fucking them, just as I suspected it would with Tressa. The spoiled, rich girl thing I could do without, but the allure of a powerful and sexy beautiful woman overruled that character flaw in my mind.

As I marched past her, Sherilyn looked up and smiled. "I did find out something interesting about her father, though. Tristan Stone is a huge New York football fan and has had a box at the stadium for years. There was even talk a few years back that he considered buying the team when it was last up for sale. Keep that in mind if you're thinking about doing anything with his daughter. Your new team wouldn't appreciate you alienating one of the organizations' biggest supporters."

This was good news. Having a family member of Tressa's who was a huge football fan could only help.

I stopped pacing and thought about how to use this information. "Is she close with her father, or is this one of those dysfunctional families where every member is trying to oust the others in some money grab?"

Sherilyn shook her head. "No, I don't think the Stones are like that. Every picture I'm seeing with her father they look happy. She's worked at Stone Worldwide since college and all through her graduate school years when she was earning her MBA. From what I can gather, she's the heir apparent to the company since neither of her siblings work there."

"Okay, then. This will be my plan: Get in tight with Dad."

Sherilyn scowled at me. "Don't be so cynical. I've met Tristan Stone on a number of occasions. Despite his reputation for being a shark in business, nearly everyone likes him. He lost his entire family in a plane crash when he was young, and I hear there's some family tragedy with one of his children. His wife is some kind of artist, if I'm remembering correctly. I don't see why how her father feels about football changes anything anyway. She's a grown woman, Killian. If she doesn't want to go on that date with you, maybe you should just gracefully accept that and back off."

I looked at her through squinted eyes, not believing what I was hearing. "No way. This is a matter of pride now. The woman basically acted like she was too good for me. Nope. We're going on that date. I have no intention of having people at that charity asking me why the date isn't happening and why the press they're expecting isn't happening."

"Fine, but I don't understand what you plan to do with the information about her father and how he's a fan of the team."

"Let's say I like to know everything that's going on around me, on and off the field. Send me the information about where I can find Tristan Stone tomorrow."

Without missing a beat, she said, "Oh, that's easy. The thirty-fifth floor of the Stone Worldwide building in Midtown. I'll send you the address."

That she knew the man's exact location so quickly impressed me. "Do you carry that kind of information around in your head?"

Sherilyn laughed. "No. Well, I guess yes. Before I became a publicist, I was a reporter on the business beat. I interviewed him at his office a few times. Unless something's changed, he'll be in his office tomorrow morning like he always is."

"Good. Send me the address. Oh, and let's see what my new employer might have to offer one of the team's biggest fans, okay? I wouldn't want to go see him empty-handed."

Sherilyn nodded and began making a second call even before our call had ended. "I'm on it. I'll let you know what I hear."

"Good. Make sure it's something impressive."

The picture went dark as I continued to pace back and forth across the room. A little visit with dad tomorrow morning would do the trick to soften her up. Since her father was a huge fan of the team, she'd see that living up to her end of the deal regarding our date was the least she could do.

I winced at the reality that I had to do any of this to get the woman to go out with me, but a deal was a deal, and I had no intention of looking like some fool who could reel in ten grand for a charity but couldn't get someone like Tressa Stone to have dinner with him.

After all, who the hell said no to dinner with a star quarterback?

CHAPTER FIVE

TRESSA

MONDAY MORNING I AWOKE WITH the singular hope that the world had forgotten about me with that damn Killian Brenton. I'd been the name on everyone's lips all day Sunday, enough that I couldn't even leave the penthouse to go out and enjoy the nice May weather. After the fifth or sixth time I saw the pictures of us, I turned off the TV to spend the day working from my bedroom.

But even that didn't stop the day from being devoted to what happened. I ended up fielding calls from people far and wide, some of whom I hadn't heard from since high school, because my picture had been in every paper, magazine, and gossip site up and down the East coast. Why they all seemed so damned interested baffled me.

I walked out of the Richmont to start my workweek only to find the press and their cameras lurking around on the sidewalk waiting for me. A few of them yelled questions about my relationship with Killian, to which I wanted to yell back, "There is no damn relationship! Go away!"

Thankfully, I was able to duck into the car the service had waiting for me at the curb and drove away before they could descend upon me like a swarm of locusts. However, I ran into a group of reporters outside the Stone Worldwide building when I arrived to work, which meant I had to dash through the lobby in four inch heels to get to the elevator. As I tried not to break my ankle racing across the marble floor, I silently cursed that bastard Killian Brenton.

I hadn't planned on a run so early in the day, especially in my favorite work shoes. A few of the paparazzi had gotten pictures, but I had a feeling they hadn't expected me to tear off like I did.

As I rode up in the elevator to my floor, I couldn't believe all of this nonsense had been added to my life because of that man. I already hated him, and I'd only known he existed on the planet for less than forty-eight hours!

How did people live like this, being hounded by photographers day and night because of who they were with? I'd never even had a full conversation with him that any of these people knew of, and still they hurled questions at me about the nature of our relationship.

The very idea made my stomach roil. That man and I would never be anything to one another. He was an attention whore, pure and simple, and of all the things I hated in people, that was the worst. Attention whores thought the world revolved around them. Their narcissism never failed to make them truly ugly on the inside, no matter how impressive the outside was.

I couldn't deny that he had something I liked. More than liked. Fine. Something I really liked and possibly would have desired.

So he was stunning. All right. He was. The man was gorgeous from head to toe. I'd never seen any man in the world who looked so sexy in a tux. Most of them looked like overstuffed penguins in tuxes, but Killian had worn his in a way that told me what those black pants and white shirt were hiding was nothing less than perfection.

So what? So I ogled him. I did. I'm a grown woman who knew a good looking man when I saw him. Was it a crime to appreciate beauty now? I had no idea why everyone was making such a big deal about how I looked at him. Some of the articles said it was a look of love. Love! God, everyone in the world was so melodramatic.

I liked what I saw and didn't hide it when I checked him out. Period. Full stop. That's all it was.

As for Mr. Brenton, I'd been very clear with him about how I felt about this date I'd won. No thanks. Why would I go on a date with a man like him? So I could listen to him drone on about how important he was and how much money the team paid him just to come to New York?

I'd pass, thank you. The idea that someone playing a game was paid three hundred million dollars made me question the sanity of anyone associated with that sport, but that was neither here nor there. I didn't need to sit through a meal listening to him brag about how worthy he was to receive that amount of money to throw a ball down a field.

The elevator doors opened as my phone began to ring, tearing me from my thoughts about that man. I looked to see my father calling.

"Hi, Dad. What's up?"

"Can you come up to my office?"

This was exactly what I needed to get my focus back. My father and I would discuss something—maybe he wanted a progress report on the redo of the Richmont in London—and I'd get back to being my normal self instead of this distracted mess I'd turned into in the past two days.

"Sure, Dad. I'll be right up," I happily answered.

I'd even take some talk about his time with my mother and Diana yesterday. Not normally my favorite topic of conversation, at least it would get my mind off Killian Brenton and the upheaval he'd brought to my once idyllic life.

My father's assistant smiled at me as I walked across the black marble tile on the thirty-fifth floor where the executive offices were at Stone Worldwide. Although I'd been made a Vice President and the COO of the Richmont hotel chain, I chose to stay in my office on the twelfth floor where I started with the business for now, even though my father had offered to have the executive suite completely redesigned to accommodate me. My father would retire someday, and I'd be here soon enough. He deserved to be the only Stone on this floor until that day.

"Good morning, Tressa," Brenda said in her low voice.

I nodded and smiled as I wondered if anyone else ever found the way she sounded jarring. "Good morning. It's a beautiful day, isn't it?"

"It is. Your father is waiting for you. There's coffee in there, but I can bring in tea, if you like."

I waved off her suggestion. "No, coffee's great. Thanks, Brenda!"

Opening my father's office door, I walked in feeling great and then instantly felt like someone had sucked all the air out of my lungs as I stopped dead. Standing there in front of me, I saw Killian Brenton with my father talking and laughing like they were the best and oldest of friends.

Son of a bitch. What was he doing here?

For a moment, the memory of what I did to Ethan with Summer flashed through my mind and I finally understood why he still to that day called it an ambush. The difference, though, was that he cared for Summer even then. I didn't even like Killian Brenton.

I needed to get the hell out of there and quick. "Oh, I'm so sorry. I didn't realize you were in a meeting. I'll come back later," I said as I turned to leave, grabbing the handle to open the door.

Before I could escape, my father said, "Tressa, please don't go. I believe you know Mr. Brenton."

Closing my eyes, I wished the floor would open up and swallow me whole at that very moment. Unfortunately, it didn't, so when it became obvious I'd have to stay and be professional, I turned around, all smiles for the two of them. "Not really. We've only met once, but it's very nice to formally meet you, Mr. Brenton."

Killian smiled and walked over to shake my hand. He seemed to glide across the floor and reached me in two steps. Seeing him up close like this, I realized how much bigger than me he was. I'd never stood next to a professional athlete, other than at the auction, and I couldn't help but admit Killian was impressive. Even in jeans and a basic white dress shirt, he looked incredible, and what I'd guessed about his body hidden beneath that tux had been one hundred percent correct.

In fact, it wasn't just his size that was impressive. Somehow, in the light of my father's office, he looked even better than he had at the charity event. His gaze focused on my face, his green eyes studying mine so intensely that I was thankful my father couldn't see how this man looked at me.

I silently pleaded for my face not to show how uncomfortable I felt at that moment, praying I wouldn't blush so my face turned beet red. God, he smelled incredible, just like he had that night. Once again, I had to fight the urge to take a deep breath in and close my eyes to revel in the scent. What was that? Something musky with a hint of citrus? Was there vanilla in there too? Whatever it was, it made him practically intoxicating.

"It's a pleasure to get to finally meet you somewhere we can talk without hundreds of people standing around us. I wanted to thank you for contributing such an incredible amount to the pediatric cancer care organization. They've joined forces with me this year to promote the cause to as many people as we can. Normally I wouldn't be caught dead at a bachelor auction, but I'll do anything I can to get people to give to cure cancer in kids."

Damn. I couldn't be rude to him after that little speech. Was that for my benefit or my father's? I wasn't sure, but I plastered a smile on my face to show my graciousness.

"I'm always eager to help out worthy causes, Mr. Brenton, and I can't think of a worthier one than curing cancer in children."

Our eyes locked, and I couldn't help but think his pale green eyes with those dark lashes were stunning. A woman could get lost in those eyes, and for a moment, I did. But then I remembered how he acted at the auction, strutting up and down that platform while all those women hollered at him and he ate it up. The man standing there in front of me in my father's office was no different simply because there were no screaming crowds adoring him. He was an attention whore, a playboy, the kind of man I actively avoided.

"Please, call me Killian. May I call you Tressa?" he asked in that deep voice of his I didn't want to like, not even a little. Except I did and more than a little.

From behind him, my father's gaze met mine, and he nodded eagerly, like my giving this guy my permission to be nice to me was important. Feeling like I didn't have a choice, I said, "Of course."

My father walked over to join us and said, "Killian came here to thank us for our donation and to invite us to a benefit the team is holding next weekend. I'd love to go, but your mother has me booked for a trip to see your Aunt Jordan and Uncle Gage in Palm Springs from Friday to Monday. I'm sure you can go alone, Tressa, can't you?"

I loathed when my father played matchmaker. I knew he always had the best of intentions, but I still felt uncomfortable whenever he did it to me or either of my siblings. I'd watched him do his Cupid act with Ethan half a dozen times when we were in high school, and my brother hated it each time. My father had only tried it on me one time with some guy from Cornell in my junior year of college, and that date had been the worst of my life. I couldn't even remember his name, but I distinctly remembered he drank more than any guy I'd ever met, much to my father's dismay that night when I arrived home in a cab. Now he wanted to try a second time, and I doubted this attempt would end up any better.

As much as I wanted to say no, my father giving me that look that said he really wanted me to do this made declining impossible. So I forced myself to give Killian my best smile and said, "I'll see what my schedule looks like. I'm sure it will be delightful."

I only ever said the word delightful when whatever I was being forced to do was anything but delightful. My father knew this as well as anyone, and over Killian's shoulder I saw his expression change to that hopeful look he wore whenever he wanted his kids not to disappoint him. I was used to seeing him look like that with Ethan and even Diana, but rarely ever me.

Damnit. I'd barely been formally introduced to Killian Brenton and already my father was giving me that hopeful face like he did with my sister and brother who routinely disappointed him. So far nothing Killian brought to my world had been good.

"I look forward to seeing you there, Tressa. Are you a football fan like your father?"

Arching my eyebrow in disgust, I shook my head. "Not really."

My father quickly said, "Tressa works so much I doubt she's gotten to be a fan of anything much in the past few years."

While the two men in front of me joked about how everyone was busy, I felt my disgust for Killian grow by the second. Now he had my father making excuses for me when it came to not liking football? Since when did that make a damn bit of difference?

"Well, please excuse me, but I have work to get back to."

"Please, let me walk you out," Killian said before I could turn to escape. Pressing his hand to the small of my back, he said, "It was great to meet such a supporter of New York football, Tristan. I look forward to seeing you again."

"Of course, and thank you for the wonderful offer to attend the event. I'll have to make sure I ask Tressa all about it."

As Killian gently guided me out of the office, I looked back at my father and gave him the death stare I'd only used on others in business negotiations before. I didn't appreciate my own flesh and blood serving me up for this Cro-Magnon's delight.

The door to my father's office closed, and I immediately moved away from Killian's hold. Spinning around, I shook my head as I glared at him. "I'm not sure what all of that in there was, but I don't like it."

Before I could continue, Killian tugged on my arm to move me. "Unless you want to have this discussion in front of your father's receptionist, I suggest we continue our talk somewhere else."

I looked back and saw Brenda quickly try to make it seem like she hadn't been listening to every word we'd said. Furious over the way this fool had already made me look in front of two people I knew, I stormed away toward the elevator.

Killian caught up with me just as the doors opened and I marched in. Before I could press the button for my floor, he pushed his finger into the button that stopped the elevator from moving.

"Now, let me explain."

Cutting him off, I tried to push him away so he didn't stand so close, but I couldn't budge him. Christ, was the man made of bricks?

"No, let me explain, Mr. Brenton. I don't like people manipulating one of the people I love more than life itself simply to further their goals. I'm sure your agent or your PR person did a little digging and found out my father loves football. I'm sure you know he's had a box at the stadium for as long as I've been alive. Maybe longer. So you thought you could just waltz into his office and sweet talk him so you could get to me. Well, forget it. I'm not interested in going on any date with you. I had the money sent to the charity this morning, so the transaction is complete. Now if you don't mind, I have work to get to."

Killian simply grinned, like anything I'd said could be misconstrued to be something even slightly amusing. "Why don't you want to go out on this date with me? I'm a decent looking guy. I've got money. Not as much as you, but a good amount. I've been the toast of the town since I arrived in this great city, so what's the problem?"

"Right there. I have no interest in a man who can't get enough of the press taking his picture. You're an attention whore, Killian, and that is the last thing I want in any man I spend time with."

"So you do like the way I look," he said, stepping forward so the space between us shrunk to almost nothing. "I thought you did Saturday night, and I'm usually pretty much on the mark with things like that."

I liked the way he looked—way too much for my own comfort. He had a presence about him that emanated power like no other man I'd ever met. It had an intoxicating effect on me, and that was nothing to say of what he made me feel when he stared at me with those incredible eyes of his. Then there was his mouth. His lips were nothing less than inviting and made me wonder what they'd feel like against mine. They looked soft, and something deep inside me craved to know just how they felt on my mouth…on my skin…between my legs.

Yes, I definitely liked how he looked far too much already.

Get it together, Tressa. Remember why you didn't like this man in the first place.

Right. His ego. It made wanting to even stand there with him for another minute impossible.

Twisting away from him, I pushed the button to get the elevator to move again. "You're perfectly fine, and I'm sure many women appreciate how you look, Killian. I just don't want to go out on that date with you."

"We're making progress," he said from behind me in his low voice that made me instinctively close my eyes. "You called me by my first name. I liked the way it sounded coming out of your mouth too."

My eyes flew open as I realized I was letting myself be seduced by him. Oh. My. God! This man was infuriating!

I turned around and glared at him. "Does this work on other women? Are there really females who think this thing you do is charming?"

A slow, sexy smile showcased his beautiful white teeth and perfect mouth. "I don't know if they think it's charming, no. It has been known to work on women, though, charming or not."

"Well, it's not working on me."

That was a lie. I knew it. He probably knew it too.

"Not even a little?" he asked, staring deeply into my eyes.

God, all I wanted to do was get out of that elevator without saying something I'd regret. I wasn't sure if he had some ability to hypnotize with those gorgeous green eyes, but whatever he was doing with them as he stared at me, it was working.

I couldn't let it.

And then just when I didn't think I couldn't stand him looking at me that way a second longer, he opened his mouth again and broke the spell.

"I'm not a man who gives up easily when I see something I want, Tressa."

The elevator punctuated his statement with a ding, like it was announcing the end of a round of boxing, and I snapped back at him as the doors opened, "I am not a thing. That was your first mistake. I don't give second chances after a mistake like that. Good day."

I marched out of that elevator with the silent approval of every woman who had ever wanted to tell off some smug guy who knew he was hot and used it to get whatever his heart desired. I felt his stare on me as I walked to my office and didn't look back, even when he yelled down the hall to me.

"Tressa, remember what I told you. I don't give up easily. We will have that date."

No, we won't, Killian. This time you lose.

CHAPTER SIX

KILLIAN

AFTER MEETINGS WITH THE TEAM all day, I headed back from the stadium with Tressa on my mind. Our encounter in the elevator on Monday morning showed me she had fire for sure, but that fire wasn't fueled by dislike for me, by any means. I didn't know why she didn't want to admit to liking me, but nothing I'd seen so far had given me anything but a green light with her. I'd never shied away from a challenge before. I wasn't about to start now, especially with the promise of something so incredible if I conquered it.

I checked to see if she called since I'd sent her flowers earlier. Nope. Sitting back, I watched as the lights on the highway flew past the car and wondered why she hadn't at least sent me a message to thank me. I'd never met any woman so difficult, but after what I'd felt when we were in that elevator together, I couldn't give up getting her to go out on that date.

Maybe the flowers hadn't been delivered. A quick check on the florist proved that wrong. They'd been signed for by the woman herself.

So she wanted to play hardball. Okay. I could do that too. I'd hoped she'd come around on her own, but I wasn't above going low to get what I wanted.

Time to go in for the kill.

A few seconds later, I was looking at Tressa standing in the living room of her penthouse. As always, she looked gorgeous, even dressed in a loose blue dress that hid what I imagined was an incredible body. She frowned when she saw me, so I knew didn't have much time to get out what I wanted to say before she'd end the call.

"You again? I think you'd be considered a stalker now."

"Well, this is a serious call. I'd hate to have to tell the organizers of that event the other night that you refuse to go on our date. Would that be considered fraud? They did advertise that the winning bidder would go out on a date with me. I think that's sounds a lot like fraud."

I watched with pure enjoyment as Tressa's mouth dropped open. I'd found her soft spot.

"It's not fraud. Don't be ridiculous. God, you are a piece of work, Killian Brenton."

Putting on my best sad face, I continued, "The rules charities have to follow are pretty serious. Charges of fraud could get them shut down. I'd hate for that to happen, wouldn't you? They help so many kids with the money they get people to donate. That's not going to be easy to make up, and I think we both know cancer isn't just going to stop because they go out of business."

Tressa's shoulders sagged and she hung her head. "You're not going to let this go, are you?"

"No."

Looking up, she seemed almost defeated. I saw it in her dark eyes. I didn't want to see her like that. This was never about beating her at something.

"Why? Why does this mean so much to you? I already sent the charity the money I bid. What does it matter if we go out on a date or not?"

For a moment, I didn't know how to respond. Her frustration with this whole thing confused me. It was just a date, and I knew she liked me just as much as I liked her. Why did she still want to fight me on going out for one damn dinner? Leaning back against the driver seat, I turned to watch the cars as mine passed them and figured now was the time to be serious with her.

"This charity means a lot to me. My foundation works with them to help in the fight against pediatric cancer. I wouldn't usually let myself be auctioned off, but for this charity, I'd do anything."

Tressa nodded and then sighed. "Can this date be somewhere low key? Please?"

I shook my head no. "The PR is important to helping them bring in more money."

"You're the one everyone wants to see, Killian. Not me," she said in a pleading voice.

"Seeing me with a beautiful and successful businesswoman who's from New York would be impressive, Tressa. You're no fool. You know this."

After a moment of hesitation, she finally relented. "Fine."

Success! I knew she'd give in and go on our date. Even though I wanted to celebrate, I controlled myself and coolly said, "How about tomorrow at eight? I'll pick you up. Just tell me where."

"The Richmont Midtown," she said flatly.

"Great! Cheer up. It'll be a good time. We'll have dinner and a few laughs."

She nodded and then the screen went black. I had to admit I felt good. I knew she'd agree. Thankfully, I'd made reservations earlier that day. It always paid to think positive.

✧　✧　✧

JUST LIKE BEFORE I CALLED Tressa the first time, my palms suddenly grew sweaty as I pulled up to in front of the Richmont hotel at quarter to eight Wednesday night. I'd been playing football since third grade, and never once had my palms gotten sweaty before or during a game. In fact, I couldn't remember any time I had sweaty palms other than when I called her for the first time and right now.

"Stay cool, Killian. It's a date, not a lifetime. One night, and if things go to plan, a night that will end with this woman in my bed. Nothing to be nervous about," I said to myself in the rearview mirror as I checked out how I looked one last time.

I looked good, so now it was show time. Tressa walked toward the car dressed in a knockout red dress as the press that had been hanging out around the hotel for days began to rush her, so I quickly jumped out of the car and ran up to her.

Putting my arms around her shoulders, I shielded Tressa from the reporters already swarming around. "Enough. The lady is just trying to go out to dinner, and you guys rush her like she's holding the secret to life here. Give her some space."

"Are you two dating?" one young guy with a camera yelled out from behind another reporter busy sticking his phone in our faces to get a comment.

"How long have you been together? Miss Stone, does this mean you're leaving Stone Worldwide? Killian, does this mean you're off the market?"

Tressa's head spun toward the reporter who asked about her quitting her job, but I pushed him away and said in her ear, "Don't even listen to them. They ask questions that don't make any sense sometimes. Just ignore them."

"Why would they think I'm quitting Stone Worldwide? Who would have told them that?" she asked pointedly, clearly thinking I'd had something to do with it.

"It's nothing. Don't worry. Just get in and you'll be fine."

I opened the passenger side door and held off the reporters as she got into my sports car. Satisfied I'd been able to protect her and still have the press get their pictures, I smiled at the reporters to give them a good shot.

"Thanks, guys. She's not used to all of this, so try to take it easy on her."

One woman with glasses yelled as I walked around the car to open the driver's door, "Does this mean you're off the market, Killian? Are you still single?"

I simply waved and flashed them a smile before getting in and driving off. All they really wanted was a good picture to put with whatever they planned to write about anyway, and I knew my part in all of this.

Looking over at Tressa, I saw she truly didn't like the attention of the press. Her frown told me our run in with them had started our date out on the wrong foot. No worries. I'd fix that.

"Sorry that got a little wild back there. I'm glad I was around to protect you, but remember, they're harmless."

She turned to look at me as her frown grew deeper. "Protect me? You're the reason they're out there day and night in the first place. If you would have just left me alone and not insisted on going on this ridiculous date, I would have never had to deal with them at all."

The car stopped at a red light as I said, "To be honest, they're out there because of the picture someone took of you looking up at me at the auction. I didn't have anything to do with this. It's because of you, actually."

I heard something like a growl come out of her at my explanation. Not exactly fixing things. I had to switch gears, so I said, "I think you're going to love the place I picked out for dinner. My agent tells me great things about it."

"Where are we going?" she asked, only slightly less infuriated than she was a moment ago.

"The National Club."

My car took that as an opportunity to inform me of the important details about our ride. "Dinner reservations are for eight, sir. I'll call ahead and let them know you're on your way and to have the valet look for the closest spot near the building as it's going to rain in approximately two hours and thirty-one minutes."

Tressa looked at me and arched her eyebrow. "Approximately? I think your car doesn't understand the meaning of that word."

I smiled, and the car answered, "I understand every word in every language known to man, Miss Stone. I simply like to be precise whenever I can be. I don't want you to get wet on your date with Mr. Brenton. We will arrive at the National Club in fourteen minutes. Please sit back and enjoy the ride."

The light turned green, and with that, the car continued on its way as I turned in my seat to face Tressa. "So have you ever been to the National Club?"

"No offense, but your car is a know-it-all. I turn all that off, and more often than not when I drive, I actually perform the act."

I couldn't help but be charmed by this woman. Even cranky, she had a way about her that made me want to be around her. At the moment, she looked downright unhappy to be there with me, though, but that would change.

"I like an old-fashioned woman. It seems like nobody drives anymore."

"Well, I do. My brother does too, along with my father. My mother never liked driving after an accident she was in years ago, so she was more than happy when self-driving cars became available."

"You are an interesting woman, Tressa Stone. I want to know more about you."

For the first time, she smiled. "Why don't you ask your car? I have a feeling it can find out anything you like about anything in the world."

I shook my head and laughed just as the car began talking again. "Sir, Miss Stone is twenty-seven years old. She is the daughter of Tristan and Nina Stone. She is one of the few people on the planet who can say they're a fraternal triplet. Less than one percent of the population is a triplet, according to the latest information from the National Center for Health Statistics. Her brother's name is Ethan, and her sister's name is Diana. Tressa is named after her paternal grandmother. When she was four, she—"

Leaning forward, I quickly pressed the button to turn off the sound of the car. "Enough of that. Since you're an old-fashioned girl, I'll learn about you the old-fashioned way."

Amused, Tressa chuckled. "Then you won't learn much since this is going to be our one and only date. I think you're going to have to go back to talking to your car on this one."

"We'll see. I'm hoping to impress you with my charm so you'll at least smile in the pictures the press gets. You're truly a beautiful woman when you aren't scowling."

"And when I am?" Tressa asked sharply as her expression instantly returned to unhappy.

I studied her face for a moment and smiled. "I'd guess most people would say you're intimidating, but I have a feeling you're more frustrated with things than unhappy."

She rolled her eyes and sighed in disgust. "Frustrated, huh? Typical man. I bet you think if I just had a dose of your magical penis that I'd be a perfectly happy woman, don't you?"

"No. All I meant was you know what you want out of the world, and you work hard to get it. When those around you don't work as hard, you get frustrated."

Tressa looked away and after a moment quietly said, "Oh. Well, color me embarrassed. I'm sorry I said all that."

"No problem. I'm tough. I can handle it."

As she stared out the window, I knew for sure now she was definitely not disinterested in me. No woman mentioned a guy's cock if she hadn't thought about it at least once. I had a feeling I was exactly the kind of man Tressa Stone would enjoy. Men had let her down because they weren't strong enough to handle her. But I was, and I intended on finding out just what it took to make her happy.

"So you're a triplet?" I asked, just realizing what the car had said minutes earlier.

For a moment, Tressa didn't answer, and I figured I'd have to keep asking her questions in the hopes of starting a conversation both of us might enjoy. But then she turned to face me and gave me a little smile.

"I am. Two girls and a boy."

"I thought triplets were always identical. I guess I learned something today," I said with a chuckle.

"No, not when there aren't all the same sex. My brother meant we'd be fraternal instead of identical."

"So do you and your sister look the same and he just looks different?"

My question made her genuinely laugh, and even though I knew she was laughing at me, I didn't mind because for that moment, she didn't look like she wanted to slap my face or bark at me anymore. She looked happy.

"No, it doesn't work that way either. My sister looks like my mother, but my brother and I resemble my father more, as I'm sure you noticed when you were there with us the other day. I'm just the female version of Tristan Stone. My brother could be his twin."

"I've never met anyone who was a triplet. That makes you unique, Tressa."

She shrugged like that didn't mean much. "I think I'd rather be unique because of something I've done after I was born."

"Twenty-seven years old and already the COO of a major hotel chain? That makes you pretty unique. VP at a successful company like Stone Worldwide too? Again, pretty unique, and trust me, I know about being unique. I'm one of only a handful of people on the planet to do what I do at my level."

Narrowing her eyes, she stared at me and asked, "Your car didn't tell you all of that, so how do you know about me?"

"Maybe I asked it about you on my way to pick you up."

"Did you?"

I didn't want to lie to her, so I shook my head. "No. I asked around. I wanted to know about the woman who paid ten thousand dollars for a date with me. By the way, I promise to make it worth every penny."

My answer made her blush. "I swear I thought it was just five thousand. Every time you say that number, I sound more and more ridiculous."

"Why?"

As the car stopped in front of the National Club, she winced like what she had to say made her uncomfortable. "No self-respecting woman would pay that much money for a date, Killian. I looked desperate."

"You looked like the most beautiful woman in the room, Tressa. Trust me. There's nothing desperate about you."

For a second time, she blushed, and I had to admit this side of her made me like her even more.

CHAPTER SEVEN

TRESSA

THE MAÎTRE DE AT THE National Club escorted us through the main dining room of the restaurant dimly lit with candlelight and wall sconces. As we walked past other diners already at their tables, I saw their reaction to Killian as he followed behind me, his hand gently brushing my arm as if he was protecting me somehow. Their gazes passed right over me and then they smiled up at him and said his name, while others pointed and whispered about his being new to town and how much the team paid for him. I looked back and saw him smiling in return like he truly enjoyed their attention.

When we were finally seated at a secluded table near the rear of the restaurant, I couldn't help but notice that Killian had chosen the chair with his back facing all those people who'd just adored him as he walked by. While he scanned the menu, I sat transfixed by how much they actually cared about him being there with them.

"Does it ever bother you to feel people's eyes on you?" I asked as I watched one man point in our direction.

Looking over his menu, Killian shook his head. "No. It's just something you get used to. They're like the press. I figure if I wasn't doing something right, they wouldn't give a damn about me or what I do."

"I don't think I'd ever get used to it. The fact that people keep turning around and looking at us seems so intrusive."

Killian lowered his menu and flashed me one of his stunning smiles. "They're probably looking at you."

Suddenly, I felt completely exposed. Holding my menu up in front of me to hide everything from my eyes down, I said, "Why? Because of those pictures everyone plastered all over the papers and online?"

"No. Because you're gorgeous and wearing that dress."

I looked down at my red dress that I'd bought for last year's Christmas party at work. I'd debated on wearing something that showed a little cleavage since I didn't want to give Killian the wrong idea, but as I stood in front of the mirror modeling it earlier that evening, I loved how it looked next to my dark hair and how it always made me feel beautiful.

Now I wondered if I'd made a mistake.

"Is there something wrong with my dress?" I asked, happy to be hidden behind the menu.

He shook his head and smiled again. "Not as far as I can see. You do understand people stop and look at beautiful women, right? I can't believe this is the first time in your life you've been stared at by strangers because of how you look."

"That's not who I am, so I have no idea what you mean."

Lowering his menu, he leaned forward and whispered, "Tressa, these people aren't looking at me anymore. My back is to them. If they're staring over here, it's because of you."

"You're just trying to make me think that we're similar, when it's obvious we aren't. If I was alone at this table or with any other man, no one would give us a second thought. They're looking at you, and you love it."

His response to my indictment of him was to shrug. "Any idea what you're going to get? I hear the swordfish is great here. I'm not much into that, but my agent raved about it."

Killian's sudden change in conversational topics caught me off guard. I'd planned on keeping him on the one about him being an attention whore, but he didn't seem to want to talk about that anymore.

Not that it mattered. It didn't change the fact that he loved the attention and I hated it.

We sat in silence staring at our menus until the waiter arrived to take our orders. As I watched Killian order steak and asparagus, I couldn't deny this felt like any other date I'd ever been on. I even had to admit that it was probably better than any I'd been on since he was definitely more attractive than any man I'd ever dated.

After I ordered and we were once again left alone, the silence returned. Not that I'd expected we'd have much to say to one another anyway. We had nothing in common, and he was a football player.

"So tell me more about this old-fashioned streak you have."

I looked across the table at him and tried to determine if he was making fun of me, but he seemed sincere. I didn't know why he wanted to know much of anything about me since this whole date was just the fulfillment of that auction so the charity could never be guilty of defrauding anyone.

"I'm not sure there's much to tell. I actually drive cars instead of letting them drive me. I guess my use of phones would be considered old fashioned since I would prefer not seeing the people I'm speaking to most of the time."

"Why's that?"

"Because I'm not superficial. I don't judge people on what they look like. I judge them on what they do and how they act."

Killian leaned back and leveled his gaze on me. "See? We're not that different, you and me. I'm the same way."

Somehow I doubted that. I would never admit it to him, but I looked up some of the women he'd dated in the past few years. Every girlfriend was stunning, each one more gorgeous than the last.

When I didn't respond to his ridiculous claim, he continued. "I judge people on their abilities. On the field, a player is valuable if he does his job well. Off the field, people's behavior dictates whether or not I spend time with them."

As much as I wished I could let that go, I couldn't. Something about this man brought out the fight in me.

"So the women you've spent your adult life surrounded by were carefully chosen based on their behavior and not on their looks? I'm sure they're all deep thinkers and people working to change the world, right?"

Instead of taking the bait, Killian simply smiled. "Women are different."

"Oh? Why is that?"

"Because maybe I don't get to meet many deep thinkers and women looking to change the world."

I didn't know how to respond. The way he said that sounded strangely disappointed, like he wished he did meet more women like that. I doubted that, though. Women who dedicated their lives to intellectual pursuits and to changing the world would have no place in Killian Brenton's life. How would they look for the camera?

"What made you go to the charity event the other night? You've already made it perfectly clear that it wasn't to meet me, so what was it?"

"I go to those kinds of things all the time. I like to support charities whenever I can."

"Me too. My foundation works with the pediatric cancer organization. It's one of the charities I support. I bet you didn't think I did that, did you?"

I saw in his expression he was sincere and not just lying to impress me. What I didn't understand is why he was bothering.

Leaning forward, I looked him straight in the eye and said, "Killian, let's lay our cards on the table. You don't have to make me like you. That's not necessary. You wanted this date to happen, and it is. I'm guessing it was some kind of conquering thing you athletes have in your DNA that made you practically blackmail me to come tonight. Or maybe it was an ego thing. You couldn't handle the idea that any woman wouldn't be interested in going out with you. Whatever it is, you don't have to work to impress me. After tonight, we'll never see each other again, so relax and have a few drinks. Maybe go talk to your fans. I'll be fine here. Really."

He said nothing for so long that I wondered if something in his brain had short-circuited and he couldn't speak anymore. I watched as he nodded like he understood and then leaned forward so our faces nearly met in the middle of the table.

In the dim light, I saw a sparkle in his green eyes that seemed entirely out of place with what I'd just said to him. Maybe he hadn't understood me.

Then he spoke and I was the one left speechless.

"Tressa, at first I thought you were simply beautiful but shy. Then I decided you were a nasty bitch, plain and simple. Now I see neither of those were entirely right. You're beautiful, you have a streak of bitch a mile wide, but you're not shy and you aren't nasty. I'll admit my ego was a bit bruised when you refused to go on our date, and yes, I manipulated you to come here tonight. I'm guilty of those things just like you're guilty of all your faults. That said, I know what I saw when you looked at me Saturday night. I wasn't mistaken then, and I'm not mistaken now. I don't know why you want to pretend you aren't attracted to me, but as I told you already, I don't give up when I meet someone I want."

My heart beat wildly as the words came out of his mouth so calmly yet so forcefully. No one had ever spoken to me like that. It wasn't rude or offensive. It was simply strong and straightforward, and I couldn't help but like Killian more than even before.

And it didn't escape my notice that he'd changed his way of talking and I wasn't a something he wanted anymore but a someone.

Killian Brenton and I would never be anything romantically, but I couldn't deny he'd impressed me. He wasn't just a pretty face and a great body.

"So now that we got that out of the way, maybe we can enjoy ourselves?" he asked with a sexy smile that made my stomach flip.

"Okay. I can appreciate someone who's a straight shooter like me."

The waiter brought our food, and for the next hour while we

ate, I genuinely had a good time there with him. I hadn't expected him to be smart or funny, but after we both said what was on our minds, it felt like a wall had come tumbling down between us.

And then some reporter with a camera showed up on our way out to the car and everything changed.

Chapter Eight

Tressa

"Killian, you seem to be taking New York by storm. A new team, a new city, and now a new girlfriend. What do you want your fans to know?"

I instinctively stepped away from the blond woman and her photographer, leaving Killian to deal with them. It felt like they'd been lying in wait for us while we enjoyed our dinner inside the National Club. We'd had such a good time during the last hour that I'd forgotten who he was, but no sooner had this woman approached us and her cameraman began taking pictures, he morphed into the same old person I'd suspected he was all along.

An attention whore.

He answered her questions with a flirtatiousness that made me wish I was anywhere else in the world than there at that moment. His cute way made her ask more questions, and all the while I wondered if he even remembered I was standing next to him.

It was like he couldn't get enough attention from this stranger he'd just met when we walked out the door. As the seconds ticked by, I found myself turned off by him once again. I didn't know why it disappointed me because he was exactly what I thought he was from the moment I laid eyes on him strutting around on that catwalk, but it bothered me.

I'd let myself think he wasn't this preening fool so eager to pose for pictures and talk about himself incessantly, and I felt stupid.

When the blond woman turned to ask me a question, I pushed

past her with barely a smile. "Excuse me."

Thankfully, she didn't care enough to ask any follow up questions or chase after me. When I reached the car, the valet kindly opened the door for me so I didn't have to stand there waiting for Killian. He finally joined me after I sat waiting for a few minutes, and as we drove away, I simply stared out the window watching the cars we passed by.

"I have to admit I was a little surprised when that reporter approached us."

Without bothering to look at him, I said, "I don't know why. Wasn't the whole point of the date to get press for the charity? I guess I should be thankful you didn't invite them to the table to have dinner with us."

"I made sure to tell the maître de that we weren't to be interrupted. I knew you didn't want to deal with that. I slipped him some money to make sure he took care of business," Killian answered, sounding quite pleased with himself.

What may have been a nice gesture before now felt like another manipulative ploy. As much as I liked the Killian I'd spent the last hour talking to, I didn't like the version of him I'd seen outside the restaurant and nothing he could do would change that.

I'd gone on the date I paid for. Now I just wanted to go home.

By the time the car pulled up to the Richmont, I couldn't wait to get away from him. When he asked if I wanted to go for a drink, I shook my head and opened the door to leave.

"Thank you for a nice dinner. Goodbye, Killian."

I heard him say something, but I didn't stick around to find out what. The disappointment I felt nearly overwhelmed me. I'd been foolish to question my gut feeling about him, and as I hurried into the hotel, all I wanted to do was be alone.

As I rode up in the elevator, tears welled in my eyes. I didn't know why because I'd never wanted to like him in the first place. But for a little while there, I'd let myself think he was the kind of man who I could be with and who would want to be with me.

We were too different, though.

The doors opened and I walked out into the private hallway outside the penthouse. Taking a deep breath, I let it out slowly, hoping all my likes and dislikes concerning Killian Brenton left with it.

From behind me, I heard a sound and turned to see him walk out of the elevator. Stunned he'd followed me, I was even more surprised when he asked, "What's the problem? We had a great dinner, and I know you enjoyed the conversation. Why are you all icy again?"

My disappointment and sadness evaporated, replaced by anger. How dare he fucking call me icy simply because I didn't want to smile for the camera or give some cute answer to that reporter's idiotic questions?

I spun around to face him. "I bet you think every woman who isn't draped all over you like a bitch in heat is icy. Well, let me help you out, Mr. Brenton. You aren't that wonderful that I should warm up at all for you."

Opening the door to go inside, I couldn't believe when he walked in behind me. Stunned at how presumptuous he was, I said, "What...that wasn't an invitation."

He didn't answer and stepped forward toward me so there was no space between us. "You know you were having a good time. Why are you in such a hurry to get me to leave?"

"What on earth could you possibly want from me now, Killian? There are no cameras here to memorialize this moment."

Suddenly, he appeared to understand and smiled. "Ah, the press bothered you. It couldn't be avoided. You know that."

Hating how obtuse he was acting, I shook my head as I prepared to set him straight. "No. The press doesn't bother me. They have a job to do, and they do it. I admire that, in fact. It's how you crave attention that bothers me. I don't like men who are attention whores, and you're the biggest one I've ever met. I'm sure there are women who don't find that to be a character flaw, so why don't you go find one of them?"

"I guess I could lie and tell you that dealing with the press is just part of my job, but the truth is I like being me. I like that the press follows me around because of who I am."

"Good for you. I suggest you go find them and leave me alone," I said before I turned to walk away toward my room.

"What is it with you? So I like being famous. What's so wrong with that?"

Fine. He wanted my opinion. Now he was going to get it. I spun around and stared into those gorgeous green eyes so he'd know I meant every word that was about to come out of my mouth.

"What's wrong with it is someday you won't be. The press and the cameras will be gone, and then what will you be? A man is only worth what he inherently is. What are you on the inside, Killian? What are you when the cameras and the press and the throngs of adoring fans are nowhere to be found?"

He looked like I smacked him across the face. He didn't seem to know how to answer my questions. That didn't surprise me. Sadly, though, I already knew the answers.

But then he walked over to where I stood and shook his head. "I saw the way you looked into my eyes the other night. I saw the way you reacted when I told you the truth at dinner tonight. You love the idea of a powerful man finally being able to handle you. I'm guessing no man ever has. Whatever I am to the rest of the world, I'm exactly what you want when it's just the two of us."

"Fuck you, Killian. Fuck you and your superficial bullshit celebrity nonsense. Go find yourself a woman who thinks you're something because I don't."

For a moment, it felt like time stopped. We stared each other down like two opposing fighters each refusing to give up, and then he slid his arm around my waist to pull me to him, holding me tightly with his hand firmly against the small of my back. Before I could protest, he leaned down and pressed his mouth to mine in a kiss that made my head swim and took my breath away.

I should have pushed him away. He'd barged into my home and into my space. I'd never said I wanted him to kiss me like that. Men needed to get my permission to get something as intimate as a kiss from me.

But I didn't want to push him away. I wanted to inhale how incredible he smelled so my mind would forever remember this moment. I wanted to feel his lips on mine as he kissed me like no man had ever kissed me before. I wanted him to take me in his arms and give me what I'd wanted from the first moment I saw him.

Even more, I wanted exactly what he said. A man who wasn't too weak to handle me. Every man I'd ever dated had been too weak. When I opened my mouth, they grew small. I wanted someone who could meet me eye to eye and not flinch when I was strong.

But even more, I wanted someone who would be strong when I couldn't be. The way Killian made me feel made me think he could be that kind of man.

His tongue teased mine with the promise of future delights, making my pussy run wet with desire, and a tiny mew of need escaped my throat. He slid his hand down over my ass and pulled me into him, tilting his hips forward so his cock pressed against my abdomen. So much bigger than me, he threatened to overwhelm my body with his if we continued standing there in the middle of my living room.

Breaking our kiss, I tried to form a coherent sentence as my mind reeled from how much I wanted him. Motioning toward my bedroom, I mumbled, "Let's go in there."

He had other ideas, though, and in one swift movement he pushed my dress up around my waist and lifted me up to straddle his hips. I tried to slip off my panties, but his hand holding me to him made it impossible. Never had I hated wearing the damn things so much as at that moment.

Killian's gaze drifted down my body, and he smiled. "Little red silk bows? Do they untie, or am I going to have to rip these beautiful underwear off you."

His green eyes danced with delight, like he relished the idea of tearing off my clothes. I shook my head and reached for the bow on my left hip, but he covered my hand, stopping me.

"No. Let me."

Tugging on the end of the silk bow, he unraveled it instantly. In seconds, my white silk panties with the adorable red bows I'd bought especially for tonight ended up on the floor beneath me.

He lifted his head and looked into my eyes. "I like them. I'd like them even more in black."

I felt like I was melting there in his arms. "I don't have them in black. I got them a while back and don't think they even carry them anymore," I lied.

Why I lied about something so insignificant I didn't know. At that moment, all I truly knew was I didn't want to talk about my underwear. I didn't want to talk about anything.

Leaning in, he nuzzled my neck and whispered against my skin, "Even better would be if you wore nothing."

The feel of his lips brushing the shell of my ear made a rush of need race through me. I felt him moving his free hand beneath me, and I prayed to God he was unbuttoning his pants.

He gently sunk his teeth into my earlobe, sending my body into overdrive. I dragged my nails across the nape of his neck and moaned, "Oh, God…" as I arched my back. What was taking him so fucking long to get his pants open and his cock out?

"Someone's eager," he groaned as he finally unzipped his pants and I felt his cock press against my ass.

I rolled my hips in an effort to speed up what Killian clearly wanted to drag out, but he stopped me by pulling my body to his and holding it there. I knew he wanted me as much as I wanted him—his rock hard cock was evidence of that—so why was he taking so long?

"Look at me, Tressa," he ordered in a low voice tinged with as much need as I felt.

I did as he commanded and saw in his eyes the sparkle I'd seen a minute before when he asked about my panties. I stared into them and felt myself get lost in the pale green color I'd never seen in anyone else's eyes before.

"There's that look I saw at the auction. I knew I wasn't wrong," he said low and deep, his voice resonating against my chest as he pulled me to him.

He hadn't been wrong. I wanted him like I'd never wanted any man that night, and I wanted him even more now. In those seconds as he held me to his body and we gazed into one another's eyes, he saw the truth of how I felt about him.

"No, you weren't," I admitted quietly in a voice barely above a whisper.

"What do you want, baby?" he asked, grinning as I tried my hardest to fight against his strength and roll my hips to feel his cock against me.

He knew exactly what I wanted. My wet pussy rubbing against his stomach told him. The look in my eyes told him.

And yet still he asked what I wanted.

"Is this some kind of triumphant conqueror thing for you? You knew I wanted you from the moment I saw you, so now that you have me in your arms, you want me to say what I want so you can feel like you won?" I asked playfully, not bothered at all to tell him exactly what I wanted from him tonight.

The corners of his mouth lifted ever so slightly, and he repeated his question. "What do you want, Tressa? Tell me."

I felt his hand stroke the full length of his cock beneath me, as if he needed to remind me what my reward would be for finally admitting the truth to him. Leaning forward, I ran my tongue along the outside of his ear and grazed my teeth against his earlobe.

Dragging my fingernails lightly over the back of his neck, I whispered, "I want you to fuck me. I want to feel that cock of yours you've been teasing me with fill me. That's what I want, Killian."

I didn't care that my voice verged on pleading with him to fuck me. Never in my life had I sounded like that with anyone, but it didn't matter. This man had something that made me want to lower my defenses, and I wasn't even afraid of my vulnerability.

The muscles in his neck and shoulders twisted, and a second later our foreplay ended. He stuffed his hand into my hair and tugged my head back so we once again faced once another. The look in his mesmerizing eyes was different now. Gone was the sparkle of delight, replaced by a stare of pure, unadulterated need. Now I'd see the truth of who Killian really was.

He staggered over to the wall and lifted me a few inches higher before lowering me down onto the tip of his thick cock. I clung to his neck in anticipation of finally getting what I'd wanted since the moment I first saw Killian Brenton.

Watching me intently, he slowly entered my body, inch by delicious inch, until there was no space between us. A tiny whimper escaped from between my lips when he finally filled me, and he stayed still, merely watching me for a moment.

"I'm not hurting you, am I?" he asked sweetly and began to ease out of my body.

"No. Don't stop," I answered, urging him with my words and my body to return to where he'd been so I could feel completely full once again.

Our bodies joined, and once more, it felt like time stopped. But that ended quickly, and Killian groaned low and deep like some wild animal before kissing me hard as desire overtook him.

And then he began to fuck me. His mouth devoured mine as he plunged his cock into me over and over. Each time he entered me, he touched a spot that sent my body to a place I'd never felt before. After just once, I craved that feeling more than my next breath. Each time his cock left me, I eagerly pushed down to have him back inside me. I didn't care that I looked too enthusiastic or that I might want him more than he wanted me. I'd always worried about that when I had sex with men before, but with Killian, all those fears disappeared, replaced by the most incredible sensations my body had ever experienced.

He fucked me like no man had ever fucked me. God, he fucked me better than I'd ever read in any magazine or book. I didn't know if it was his size or that once he began in earnest, he fucked like a man with the singular goal of making me come, but whatever it was, he made my body surrender to his every thrust like it was made for him to do as he chose.

It wasn't just what he did with his cock, though. Everything about him focused entirely on me. With each moment, I wanted more of his attention. The feel of his hands on my body worshiping me as they held me so I didn't fall. The sound of his voice when he murmured my name into my ear like the word held meaning for him. The taste of his lips as he feasted on my mouth like it held something necessary for him.

No man had ever acted like this with me. I reveled in him and how he made me feel like the only person in the world who mattered. I hadn't expected it and couldn't really understand it considering how he usually acted, but I couldn't get enough of it.

I couldn't get enough of him.

And then just when I didn't think I could feel any more incredible, my release raced through me and I tightened my legs around his waist to keep him from moving out of me again. I wanted to feel every wonderful inch of his cock inside me when I came.

My pussy milked his cock through my orgasm, and Killian moaned low in my ear, "Fuck, you feel so fucking good."

I didn't know how long my body enjoyed what he'd given me, but finally, my thighs began to hurt from squeezing him between them. As I eased them open a tiny bit, he gently pressed me against the wall one final time and came, his body sagging against mine as he held me in his arms.

We said nothing to one another while we stayed there in that place in the corner of my living room as the tremors from our lovemaking still rolled through us. Killian nuzzled my neck and let out a sigh of contentment against my skin. I gently ran my hand across his shoulders, feeling the thin sheen of dampness, and kissed next to his ear.

"That was nice," I whispered, knowing that was the understatement of the century.

He lifted his head and flashed me a sexy smile that told me he knew how much nice undersold what we'd just done. "Definitely nice."

God, I was in trouble. Not only was he gorgeous and sexy, but he succeeded in the one thing no man ever had. I wanted more than just one night with this man.

CHAPTER NINE

KILLIAN

SLOWLY, I OPENED MY EYES and looked around as my brain woke up and tried to figure out where the hell I was. Looking down my body, I saw Tressa's dark hair spread out over my chest and stomach. Below that, her gorgeous long legs intertwined with my tanner legs, making us look like two parts to a single whole.

Our date definitely had gone better than I thought it would, and I'd had pretty high hopes for it. As usual, we'd had sharp words for one another, but after that, holy fuck. I'd thought it would take to at least the second date to get her into bed.

Not that I had a problem with us fucking on the first date. We were both grown adults, so why not? It was just that she fought me so much just to get her to go out to dinner that I thought she'd fight me more on getting her clothes off.

As my memories of the night before began to filter through my brain, my cock got hard. That thing she'd done with her tongue. Fuck. I needed to experience that again for damn sure.

Pushing her hair back to see her face, I had to admit she really was incredible once she let her guard down. I hadn't thought she'd turn out like that.

Her eyes opened and she looked up at me sweetly. Still so beautiful, even first thing in the morning.

Then her expression changed, and her dark eyes grew wide. "Oh, my God. How did this happen?"

I smiled down at her. Definitely the same Tressa. "Well, I

kissed you and you kissed me back and our clothes fell off. From that point on, it was just nature."

Tressa covered her face. "Don't make jokes. This isn't funny. The press is going to know you stayed here and I'm going to have to deal with questions all day. Oh, my God! What time is it?"

She rolled off me to look for her phone, but it wasn't on the nightstand. The sight of her perfect ass made my cock grow even harder. Reaching over, I slid my hand around her waist to pull her back.

"I think you should bring that beautiful body back here so we can continue what we left off with when we fell asleep."

Leaping out of bed, she hurried around her bedroom looking for her phone. Folding my arms behind my head, I watched her and loved how sexy she looked running around naked.

"I don't think the sun's even up yet, so I'm sure you're fine," I said as she bolted out of the bedroom.

She returned a minute later with her phone in her hand, shaking it in the air. "Four calls missed already! I can't believe I let you convince me to sleep with you last night."

"Just curious. What part of what I did convinced you? You know, for future reference. Was it the kiss or something else?"

"Stop making jokes. As the Chief Operating Officer of the Richmont hotel chain, I'm responsible for every hotel around the world. There could be a problem in one of the London locations. They called twice already."

I patted the bed next to me and smiled. "Come back over here. You can call them from bed, can't you?"

Just then, Tressa looked down and her eyes grew wide again. "Ugh! I have to get dressed and get to the office."

She rushed off to the bathroom, so I followed her and found her turning on the water for a shower. Leaning against the doorframe, I watched, loving what I saw, and asked, "Are you always this stressed out after a night of incredible sex?"

Turning to look at me, she let her gaze run from my head to

my feet and frowned. "Please stop asking me questions. I might have a crisis on my hands, and you're standing there with the world's biggest hard on."

I glanced down at my erect cock and smiled as I looked back up at her. "I don't know if it's the world's biggest, but thanks for the kudos. Seriously, are you usually this stressed out in the morning? You're not going to make it to thirty if you keep it up like this."

"Please let me take a shower so I can get to work," she said as the water began spraying from the showerhead.

She stepped into the glass shower and wet her hair as I watched her, impressed with how beautiful she truly was. She really did have to relax, though. The woman had only been awake for less than five minutes and already she was functioning at prime stress level.

I followed her into the shower and grabbed the shampoo bottle off the shelf. Tressa opened her eyes and looked up at me with an expression of pure exasperation. "You don't know how to take no for an answer, do you?"

"You haven't told me no since last night. Now turn around so I can shampoo your hair."

"Shampoo my hair?" she asked, obviously surprised by my offer.

I squeezed some of her orange shampoo that smelled like citrus and coconuts into my hand and began to work it into her long brown hair. "Yeah."

Leaning around her, I saw her smile as I gently massaged the shampoo into her hair and scalp. "Then I'm going to do something else to take the edge off."

"And if I say no?"

I kissed her cheek and continued to shampoo her hair. "You won't. Now relax. You're going to like starting your day like this so much you're going to be begging me to take showers with you every morning."

"You think so?" she said with a chuckle.

"I know so. Stop fighting this. You know you like it, so just let yourself enjoy it."

She started to say something in response but stopped and leaned back against me instead. As much as I loved the feel of her body pressed to mine, it made shampooing her hair impossible, so I gently pushed her off my chest and turned her around to face me.

"I promise once I'm done here we'll get back to that," I said with a smile as I smoothed her hair off her forehead.

"Should I close my eyes or are you good enough that I can leave them open?" she asked with a smile.

"Better close them. I don't think sex with a crying woman is a good thing."

She followed my instructions and giggled. "So women don't routinely cry when you're fucking them, Killian?"

I tugged her hair and tilted her head back to kiss her. "No, and I would think you'd already know that since we've already had sex nearly four times."

Tressa's eyes flew open just as a stream of shampoo rolled down from the top of her head. "Eyes closed," I said before pushing it off her face.

"Sorry. But I don't understand the nearly four times. By my count, it was only three. The first time out in the living room and the second and third times in my bed. Where's number four coming from?"

"You started sucking my cock but fell asleep. Don't worry. I'm not holding that against you. Okay, time to rinse."

She opened her eyes and smiled up at me. "You're a very bossy hairdresser, sir."

I stepped around her and waited as she moved under the water. She really was beautiful, even with her hair soaking wet and with no makeup on her face. When she finished, she opened her eyes, pushed her hair back, and looked down to avoid my gaze.

"This isn't exactly the way I want anyone to see me. I must look like a drowned rat."

Reaching out, I snaked my arm around her waist and pulled her to me so her body pressed against mine. "You look as gorgeous as you did last night. Next up is conditioner."

"Conditioner?"

I pointed at the bottle on the shelf next to us. "Conditioner. You wouldn't have it here if you didn't use it."

"I'm just confused at how you know anything about all of this."

Squeezing a glob of conditioner into my palm, I smiled before rubbing my hands together. "My mother had a salon when I was a little boy. Ready?"

Tressa looked down at my hands and shook her head. "That's not going to be enough. My hair is way too long and needs about five times more."

I slid my hands over her hair down to the ends. "Trust me. This is enough."

She stared up at me in disbelief as I began to massage the conditioner in. "You are a very bossy hairdresser for sure."

"Shhh. I'm working my magic here."

"I guess I'll just have to keep myself busy some other way," she said with a giggle as she reached out and palmed my cock.

The feel of her hand stroking up and down my shaft felt so fucking good that I forgot what I was doing. My hands stilled in her hair for a moment, but when she cupped my balls and gave them a gentle squeeze, I grabbed a handful of hair and tugged as need coursed through me.

"Enough conditioner. Rinse," I bit out.

With a pout, she let go of my cock and stepped under the water to do as I ordered. A minute later, she was finished and we could get down to business.

"Now as for that stress relief I promised."

"Let me guess. A deep conditioning treatment."

Her teasing made me smile. I ran my hands down her sides and cupped her ass. "I don't think I've ever heard it called that, but we can use that for our secret code."

"Why do we need a secret code?"

I leaned down and nuzzled her neck, nibbling on her skin. "You never know. We might be in public somewhere when the need to fuck you comes over me."

"Mmmm…so we're going to be in public now? I don't see how that will work since cameras follow you everywhere," Tressa said as she slid her hands down over my abs to palm my cock once again.

Lifting my mouth from her neck, I kissed her lips. "I'll make sure they don't. Deal?"

She looked up at me and smiled. "Deal."

"I should warn you that the need to fuck you will be happening quite often."

"Oh? You can see into the future?" she asked as she slid her hand from the base of my cock to the tip.

Fuck, her touch made it nearly impossible to think straight. Enough of this playing games.

I lifted her up and held her over my ready-and-waiting cock. She wrapped her legs around my waist, eager for what I was about to give her, and slid her arms around my neck. Steadying my feet on the wet tile, I lowered her down onto me and gave my hips a single thrust, filling her completely.

Tressa moaned softly, and I saw in those beautiful dark eyes how much she loved this. For all her fighting and iciness, the truth of who Tressa Stone was could be found in her eyes as she rolled her hips each time I pushed my cock into her perfectly tight cunt.

She truly was unlike any other woman I'd ever been with. As difficult as she'd been before last night, as soon as we kissed, everything else but desire melted away in her. The transformation shocked me at first since I'd suspected she wanted me but never thought the woman beneath the feisty façade could be so sensual and yet so sweet.

"Oh, God…don't stop," she whimpered in my ear in that voice that bordered on begging and made something deep inside me want to make her mine.

I couldn't have stopped, even if I wanted to. The need to please her took over my mind and body, and I pumped into her in search of that moment when she'd whimper as her orgasm raged through her and her cunt milked my cock to my own release.

She rode me as much as I fucked her, the two of us desperately needing to come. Our eyes fixed on one other with an intensity I didn't recognize from anyone I'd ever been with. In hers, I saw desire and passion and something else I couldn't place.

Was it fear? Why would she fear me?

As I watched her bite her lip as her body began to give in to me, I saw whatever that was in her eyes disappear, replaced by pure satisfaction as she came hard on my cock. The feel of her walls squeezing me pushed me over the edge a moment later, and I buried my face in her neck.

We stood there in the shower, the water hitting her back as I sagged against the cool tile wall behind me. My eyes remained closed, and I reveled in the pleasure we'd given one another and how good she felt in my arms. Tressa gently ran her fingertips across my back and shoulders, softly stroking my skin while she sighed in contentment.

"That was...incredible," she said quietly before kissing my cheek.

I lifted my head to see her smiling. I liked seeing her like this. Relaxed. Happy. Satisfied.

"See? I told you it would relieve your stress."

Looking away, she blushed so adorably I couldn't help but be charmed. We'd had sex in half a dozen positions and shared the most intimate parts of one another since last night, and my lame joke about sex as stress relief embarrassed her.

"What?" I asked, needing to know why she blushed at that.

Tressa lifted her head and met my gaze. "Nothing. We better get out of this shower or we're going to be pruney for days."

I kissed her, letting my lips linger on hers to avoid ending our time together so soon, and then lowered her to the tile floor below. She quickly turned off the water and opened the glass door, grabbing a white Richmont hotel towel to cover herself before handing me one.

"If you need more than one, there are more in the cabinet over there," she said, pointing toward the vanity and tall cabinet on the other side of the room.

She hurried out of the bathroom, leaving me standing there in the shower alone wondering where the woman I'd had sex with last night and again a few moments ago had gone. The Tressa Stone who'd fought me every step of the way since the first time we met in her father's office seemed to have returned, but I had no idea why.

And I had to admit I was disappointed.

I dried off and wrapped the towel around my hips before heading out to her bedroom. I found her combing her hair as she sat on the bed. Taking a seat next to her, I said nothing but waited for her to speak.

Finally, she turned to look at me and said, "I can't sit around here all day. I have to go to work."

"Nobody's stopping you."

"You're stopping me. You keep making me want to stay," she answered with a cute smile.

Reaching out, I touched the ends of her hair and kissed her softly on the shoulder. "Then stay. Tell all those people who think they should be bothering you twenty-four hours a day that you're taking a day off."

The smile faded from her face and she shook her head. "I can't. That's just not who I am."

"Is that why you're back to icy Tressa?"

Her mouth turned down into a deep frown and her eyes filled with sadness that made me instantly regret my words. "Please don't describe me like that. I would think after all we did that you'd know I'm not icy."

"I didn't mean that as anything bad. I just noticed something changed in you after we finished in there."

Tressa shook her head, but the sadness remained in her eyes

even if the frown left her face. "Nothing changed. I'm the same person I've always been. And you're the same person you are."

That sounded ominous. I didn't like where this was headed.

"Whatever we are with the rest of the world, we're pretty damn good when it's just the two of us, don't you think?"

"Can that ever be enough, though?" she asked, cutting to the heart of things like always. "You're famous and those cameras and the press aren't going anywhere. I don't want to live my life on the gossip sites with strangers dissecting the look on my face or the clothes I wear or if you really care about me because of the way you hold my hand. I'm the wrong kind of woman for that."

"I told you. I'll make sure that won't happen."

Tressa turned her body to face me and I saw that promise wouldn't be enough. "You love being famous. You told me that last night. You like being someone the press follows around. I won't ask you to give that up."

I took her hand in mine and brought it to my lips. Kissing it, I looked at her and smiled. "You don't have to ask me to give it up. I'll have that and when it's just us, they won't be around. I'll make sure of it. Trust me. It's not as big a deal as you think. Today, I'm a big story in this town. Next week, someone new will come along and I'll just be the quarterback for New York. It really happens that fast."

The look of hope that had flickered in her eyes for a moment dimmed, and she asked, "Then why hasn't it happened already? You've been in the league for years."

"Because I never had a reason to not look for it until now. I'm twenty-nine, though, and my days as a quarterback for any team are numbered. I think it's time I look for something else."

"And I'm that something else?"

I'd never lied to any woman before, and I didn't want to start with Tressa. "Here's the thing. If you haven't heard about my past already, you will, so let me tell you the truth. There have been a lot of women, but none who made me think of them more than the game. Until you. Now maybe it's because I've met you late in my career, or maybe it's because you're you. I don't know. And I don't know what's going to happen with us. All I know is from the moment I first saw you at that auction, I haven't been able to stop thinking about you."

"I can't live my life in a fishbowl, Killian. I hope you understand that."

"You won't have to," I said and then pulled her onto my lap. "It's not like I'm going to impress you with dinner at fancy restaurants and public things like that. You'll get the private Killian that no one else gets."

Looking into my eyes, she asked, "Will that be enough for you?"

I chuckled and kissed her. "Trust me. From what I've seen so far with you, I'll have more than enough to keep me busy."

Tressa's cheeks blushed that pink color that made her look sweet. Whatever happened with us, I liked the challenge of making her happy enough that she felt comfortable letting this side of her come out. I had a feeling she didn't do that for most people.

CHAPTER TEN

TRESSA

AFTER A LONG DAY AT work, I arrived back at the penthouse to find a bouquet of twenty-four red roses in a crystal vase waiting for me on my living room coffee table. I lifted the small, white envelope out of the flowers and smiled when I read the card.

Redeemable for one shampoo.

This thing with Killian could never work out. I knew that. I knew our differences were too much for either one of us to overcome, no matter what we told one another. Still, I couldn't deny the man did something no man had ever accomplished.

He made me happy. I hadn't realized how much I wanted that until he came into my life. I couldn't deny I had a good time with him last night. He was incredible in bed, and when there was no press around to take his picture, he was attentive like no other man I'd ever met. He also could handle me and rocked my body like no one else ever had.

I closed my eyes and remembered how I felt in his arms. An ache formed between my legs as the memory reminded me of how he knew just what to do to please me.

But it was useless to think about what might be when it couldn't be. He wasn't going to change who he was, and I wasn't going to change who I was. We were just too different.

I should call him to thank him for the flowers. No, that would be a bad idea.

What was the point? We'd talk, he'd make me want to see him

again, and that just wasn't something I should do.

He was going to eventually call, and I didn't want to intentionally avoid him by putting on the away message again. After the time we'd spent together, he deserved better than that. Maybe I could go out. The press had left the front of the hotel, and I had a feeling I had Killian to thank for that. So I could go somewhere.

But where? Summer was on location with Ethan taking pictures of Kiki Anderson's prize show dogs out in LA, so she wasn't available. Prize show dogs. How ridiculous. But I had to give Ethan credit. For all the doubts I'd had about him, he was a natural businessman, after all. He'd turned something he cared about into a viable business.

That business, however, kept my best friend on the other coast at the moment. I couldn't go see my parents, even if the drive out to the house might do me some good. One problem. They both knew about Killian, and I had no doubt that the entire conversation would be about him. That was the last thing I needed.

The idea of going to see Diana crept into my brain, and I instantly dismissed it. We hadn't spent any time together in ages. What would I say to her?

I walked over to the window to look out over the city as guilt began to fill me. She was my only sister in the world, and I never saw her, even though we lived in the same hotel.

Turning away from the world outside, I glanced up at the TV. He'd be calling soon. I felt it, like the time we'd spent together had made us close enough for me to know how he'd react to my not calling to thank him for the flowers.

Without thinking about where I was going, I left the penthouse and a few minutes later found myself standing outside of my sister's door. Not even a suite, it was just a regular hotel room. I'd never understood why she insisted on living there.

Don't do that, Tressa. She's been through enough. Don't say the wrong thing and upset her. She wants to live here, so leave it alone.

I knocked on her door as doubt about what I was doing began

to make me want to leave. I didn't, though, and when the door slowly began to open, I made sure to put a smile on my face.

Her reaction to seeing me wasn't what I hoped, though. Tears filled her blue eyes as she asked, "What happened? Is it Mommy or Daddy?"

Immediately, I put my hand up to stop her from jumping to the wrong conclusion. "No, nothing's happened. Everyone's okay."

Diana's fear and sadness that I'd bought bad news were replaced with a look of confusion. "Then why are you here? You never come to see me."

Anyone who thought I was the only Stone who could be blunt was seriously mistaken, but I deserved that. Forcing myself to smile, I said, "I wanted to talk to someone. Any chance you have some time for your only sister?"

She returned my smile with one that lit up her entire face. "Of course, Tressa. I always have time for you. Come in."

I walked into her room and a feeling of disgust washed over me. The Richmont had suites she could choose from. As the daughter of the owner and the sister of the COO of the Richmont hotel chain, she could have her pick. Yet still she insisted on living in this regular hotel room.

As I looked around at the light tan walls every basic room in the hotel had, Diana said, "Please, sit down."

Turning around, I saw her already seated on the couch, so I sat down at the other end. All that space between us made me feel like we were strangers.

"What's going on that you wanted to talk about?"

"Oh, nothing much. Just thought it would be nice to catch up."

Diana smiled sweetly. "Even though Summer and Ethan have been taking me out a lot more lately, I don't leave this hotel room much, Tressa, so this is going to be a short conversation on my part."

I couldn't help but look around the room and frown. "Why

aren't you in a bigger room? Didn't Daddy tell you how much nicer you'd feel in a suite?"

"I know this hotel has suites. It has a penthouse you've been living in for the past few months too. I like this room. It's cozy, and it's mine."

The defensiveness in her voice made me hang my head. As always, I'd said the wrong thing, even if I did have the best of intentions. "I didn't mean anything bad. I just wondered if you'd like more room to move around in. That's all."

"It's okay, Tressa. I'm happy here. Daddy told me about your big news. Congratulations!"

Oh, God! My father had told Diana about Killian. Had he been going around telling everyone? "It's not that big a deal. Really. Whatever he said, take it with a grain of salt."

"I think you're downplaying it. Becoming COO of the Richmont hotel chain is a big deal."

Relief washed over me, and I burst out laughing at my mistake. "Oh, that. Thanks. I'm proud of what I've accomplished with Stone Worldwide."

We sat silently for a few moments before Diana asked, "Then why were you minimizing it?"

"I wasn't. I just got confused about what you were referring to."

"What did you think I meant?" she asked, leaning forward, curious.

Figuring my sister wouldn't tell anyone, I said, "I thought Daddy had told you about this guy I bid on at a charity auction the other night. We had our date last night."

Diana's mouth dropped open and she stared at me. "I've never seen you like this. What's his name?"

"Killian and what do you mean like this? How am I acting?"

Diana smiled and shook her head. "Like you like him. Like you like him a lot, in fact."

I waved my hand to dismiss that immediately. "No, I don't. It's nothing big at all, in fact."

"Then why are you blushing?"

Touching my cheeks, I felt them heating up against my fingertips. "I am not. It's just hot in here. Why is everyone in this family so convinced I'm always blushing?"

"Because you are. You like this Killian. Is that why you wanted to talk?"

I shrugged and shook my head. "There's nothing to say, really. He's nobody special. Just a guy I had to go out with. We went out and that's that. We've got nothing in common, so it can't go anywhere."

"Oh, okay," Diana said quietly like she was disappointed. "I was hoping you'd come to talk about a guy. You've never talked about any with me."

"That's not true. Remember Corey Adams? I talked about him day and night in eighth grade. I'm embarrassed to think how much I talked about him, in fact."

"Eighth grade? That was over a decade ago. I meant since we became grown adults who didn't spend our time talking about how gorgeous some boy looked in his corduroys."

Her memory of Corey's corduroys made me giggle. "I did have a thing for those corduroy pants he wore. What were they grey or brown? Either way, I doubt it was a good look for anyone, including poor Corey Adams."

Diana didn't answer, and the way she stared like she was studying me made me nervous. "Why are you looking at me in that funny way?"

"It's so nice to hear you giggle like you used to. I've missed that."

"I've never been much of a giggler, Diana. You were always the one who giggled."

She nodded and gave me a tepid smile as I thought about the last time I giggled before now. Killian. He made me giggle. He said such silly things sometimes. How could I not giggle at him?

"I've missed you, Tressa. We used to be so close."

My sister's words hit me square in the chest, like someone pressing on my heart. We were close. Never as close as Ethan and she ever were, but I always knew I could tell her anything and she'd understand. I missed that.

"We still are," I lied in a voice full of forced cheeriness. "Things just got busy. That's how life is, but we'll always be sisters, no matter what. Nothing changes that."

"I guess."

Diana's expression morphed into the one she always made when she was upset. Ever since we were children, whenever she was sad, she pressed her lips tightly together and drew in her eyebrows toward her nose. It never failed to make every one of us want to do whatever we could to make her happy again.

I always screwed up like this. This is why I rarely came to visit her because I ended up saying something stupid that hurt her feelings. I didn't mean to. I never meant to hurt my sister. I just didn't know how to behave around her.

Hoping to cheer her up, I blurted out, "Would you like to see what Killian looks like?"

It didn't take even a nanosecond to regret saying that. I knew if she saw me staring at him up on her enormous TV screen that she'd know I liked him more than I wanted to admit to her or anyone else.

But Diana's eyes lit up with excitement at my offer, and she jumped up off the couch to turn the screen on. "Yeah! Definitely. What's he do for a living? Is he an executive like you?"

"No. He's an athlete. A quarterback."

My sister's mouth dropped open in shock. She had every reason to be surprised. I'd never dated anyone other than businessmen and executives. Even in high school, I had no interest in the jocks everyone loved, including Diana. Killian definitely wasn't my type.

"A quarterback? The new one for New York? I read about him. He's supposedly just what the team needs."

She sat down next to me as I stared at her, confused how she knew all this. Turning to face me, she said, "What? Don't you remember Daddy taking Ethan and me to the games when we were kids? I don't know everything about the sport, but I know New York needed a quarterback and Killian Brenton is supposed to be how the team plans to get back to top form."

"Then you know what he looks like already, so we don't have to find a picture," I said, grabbing the remote from her hands.

She took it back from me and pointed it toward the screen hanging on the wall in front of us. "No way. I want to see this man you say you bid on. Like for a date? How much did you pay?"

"It was for a charity, so please remember that, okay? It's not like I'm in the habit of paying men to date me or anything."

Diana grinned at my pained explanation. "Got it. So how much was your winning bid?"

"Ten grand," I admitted sheepishly.

Her smile disappeared as a look of shock registered on her face. "Ten thousand dollars! Even for charity that sounds like a lot for a date. Where did you two go?"

I felt my cheeks getting warm again and knew I was blushing. Looking away, I said, "The National Club. It was nothing big."

As I attempted to hide my obvious interest in Killian, Diana said to the TV, "Pictures of Killian Brenton, quarterback."

A second later, dozens of images of the man popped up on the screen. Some with women, some alone, some with him in a tux, some of him in his Miami uniform. He looked phenomenal in all of them.

"Tressa, he is gorgeous! Are his eyes green? Wow, those are beautiful eyes. Are they as nice in person?"

I lowered my head so I didn't have to look at all the pictures of the man who had rocked my world multiple times last night and this morning. "They're pretty nice. The green is very light, like a color I've never seen in anyone's eyes before."

"And his tanned skin makes them even more beautiful," Diana said as she stood up to walk over to stand in front of the TV.

Looking back at me, she smiled. "He really is a gorgeous man."

"Yeah. He's all right. I mean, he wears a tux pretty nicely. You know how most men looked awkward in a tux? He doesn't," I mumbled.

"I see. You look pretty incredible in this picture I found too."

My stomach sank at her mention of how I looked. That meant she'd found one of the pictures of the two of us at that charity auction event. Dread filled me, and I covered my eyes with my hand. "God, that isn't the one where I'm looking up at him like I want to devour him, is it?"

"No. Look. It's a nice picture of the two of you. He's looking down at you and you're looking up at him but not like you want to devour him. It's more like you want to know more about him. Tressa, I promise it's not bad. Look."

Lowering my hand, I focused on a picture in the upper left hand corner of the screen my sister pointed to and realized I'd never seen that shot before. Unlike all the others the press had circulated, this one focused on Killian's point of view instead of mine. He looked stunning as always, but I saw in his eyes something that said maybe he hadn't exaggerated when he told me that morning that from the moment he saw me he couldn't stop thinking about me.

"Yeah, well that's him," I said in my best casual tone, hoping to hide how much I liked that picture and what it told me.

"When are you seeing him again?" Diana asked as my eyes scanned the rest of the pictures on the screen. Whether he was in his uniform or in a tux or anything in between, the man never took a bad picture.

And as that thought went through my head, another one did too. How many women had he been with? Had he been photographed with every single one? In front of me, I saw no fewer than ten of his ex-girlfriends, each one stunning as they hung off his arm.

"Tressa, did you hear me? When are you seeing him again?"

I moved my head so I didn't focus on all those women and

looked at my sister. "I don't know. Probably never. It was just a charity thing, you know, so I did my part and went out to dinner with him."

Diana returned to her seat next to me on the couch and tilted her head like she couldn't believe what I'd said. "I don't understand you. I've never even seen you two together, other than that one picture, and it's obvious to even someone like me who is as socially backward as they get that you like this person. Why are you acting like you don't care?"

"We're just very different. What's the point of trying to date? Look at the man. He's an attention whore. I'm the exact opposite. I keep my private life private."

My sister didn't buy my excuses. Shaking her head, she said, "You're not the exact opposite of him. I am. You are a normal woman who's had incredible success in business. People know your name, Tressa. They may not want to take your picture every time you step outside this hotel, but you're well-known in this city and around the world. So what's the real reason you're acting this way?"

There again was that bluntness we shared. Even Ethan didn't get to me like Diana could with her candor. No one else had a way of cutting to the truth like she did.

Well, no one other than me.

"I haven't been successful with men, Diana. At some point, I just figured out that I'd have people I slept with from time to time and that's all I'd ever have when it came to relationships. I don't think Killian Brenton is going to be any different."

She took my hand in hers and gave it a gentle squeeze. "Maybe he could be if you let it happen. You don't have to push everyone away, Tressa. He could be the guy who has just what you want in a man, but you'll never know if you don't give him a chance."

Everything she said made sense. I hated that, but it was the truth. Nothing I could say would change that.

Diana lowered her head and added, "I know you probably are thinking that I'm no one to give advice since I don't have anyone in my life. That's true, but so is the fact that you don't have to push people away, Tressa."

"You don't either, Diana."

She looked at me, her eyes full of tears, and smiled. "That's nice of you to say, but I don't have any of the things you have going for you. You're beautiful, smart, successful, and confident. If you want Killian Brenton, you can have him. I know you can."

I didn't know what I wanted when it came to Killian. All I knew at that moment was my sister had no idea how great she was.

"Well, I better get going. I have a ton of work to do. You know how I am. Work, work, work," I said awkwardly as I stood to leave.

She followed me to the door and touched me on the arm. "Come back again, okay? I like seeing you, Tressa. And don't work so much that you don't have fun."

Taking her in my arms, I hugged her close and felt that sense of happiness I'd missed from her. "Maybe the two of us could go out sometime like you do with Ethan and Summer?"

Diana smiled and nodded eagerly. "I'd like that."

"Good. We can do whatever you want, okay?"

I turned to leave and heard her say, "Next time I'm going to ask for details on Killian, so you've been warned."

In a flash, my face heated up from a blush, and I looked back to see her smiling. For all that had happened, Diana wasn't as awkward and strange as she thought she was. She was just a normal person working through some things. I'd forgotten that for too long.

Chapter Eleven

Killian

Two days. It had been two days since I last saw Tressa. I'd kissed her long and deep before walking out the door of her penthouse and missed the feel of her next to me before I reached the elevator. Then I'd sent her two dozen red roses I knew she'd received since I already checked with the florist.

I'd never called fucking florists to check on flower deliveries. Then again, I'd never had to. No woman had ever gotten flowers from me and not called for two days. Hell, no one had ever gotten flowers and not called five minutes later to thank me, usually with an offer I couldn't resist.

Not Tressa Stone. Nope. She received the flowers the day I ordered them at eleven-fifty-eight. I knew she'd worked all day, but even assuming she didn't get back home until that night, she'd still had those fucking roses for over thirty-six hours by now and I hadn't heard a damn peep out of her.

I'd called her no less than four times in that thirty-six hours too, each time getting her away message. That infuriating away message that made me want to throw my fucking phone off the edge of my balcony.

She couldn't be avoiding me. No way. Not after the night and morning we had together. She had a good time. I knew it. A man knows when a woman is into him. There'd been no faking orgasms with Tressa. I'd made her come until her thighs shook. She had a good time.

We both did. Fuck, we both had an incredible time. I knew there was a soft side to her, and I got to see it in all its glory that night and in the shower that morning. She was open and sweet and downright submissive at times, while at other times she was practically ravenous in how much she wanted me.

I hadn't been able to think of anything but her since. If I didn't know better, I'd swear she'd possessed my mind. The memory of how she felt beneath me and how she sounded when she whimpered right before she came haunted me.

And yet she was able to not call me at all. She knew I'd called and she'd gotten the flowers. What was with this woman?

I tried to call her again, and again I got that damn away message. Pacing back and forth across my living room, I forced myself to think of anything but Tressa Stone. The first game I played in the pros. The day I was drafted by Miami. My first game in college. Those were the memories I always went to when I needed to focus. All showed I was a winner who'd been blessed time and again in life.

Yet this time, none of those helped. My mind kept drifting back to the other night with Tressa at her penthouse. Why the hell was I so obsessed with this woman? She wasn't the most beautiful woman I'd ever been with. For fuck's sake, I'd dated supermodels, actresses, and beauty queens.

I stopped in front of the glass doors that led out to my balcony and stared out at the lights of the city. This had nothing to do with how she looked. Tressa was a knockout from head to toe. She rivaled any of the women I'd been with.

No, this had to do with something else she had that other women didn't. I could find a woman who wanted me anywhere I looked. She made me work for every second I got with her, but even though I loved a challenge, this was beginning to piss me off.

Fuck. I needed to get my mind off her or I'd end up going crazy. Needing something to distract me, I called Sherilyn. As usual, she answered immediately. If only Tressa was like my publicist that way.

"I was just about to call you. I need an answer about that premiere for Athena's movie. I was supposed to tell her people if you were coming two days ago."

Athena's new movie. I wanted to fly out to LA and spend the night with my ex at some stupid premiere for another one of her movies like I wanted to rip my arm off and beat myself with it. The first few times were sort of fun, but after a while, movie premieres all became the same.

"When is it?" I asked, wondering if a quick trip out of town might help me clear my head.

"Tomorrow night. I know it's Athena, but you know how she loves having you on her arm at these things. It doesn't hurt you either to have the public see you at events like this. I know you've got a lot going on here in New York with the team, but it would only be a quick flight out, a few hours at the premiere and after party, and then a quick flight back."

New York to LA was never a quick flight, no matter what she wanted to say. Even worse was flying out there and then practically turning right around and flying back to the East coast.

Then again, I could use a change of scenery. I was supposed to go to that event I told Tristan about, but since Tressa clearly had no intention of attending, I didn't feel like showing up either.

"Fine. Tell them I'll escort her to the premiere. I don't want to spend more time than I have to out there, so forget the after party and be sure to get me on the first plane back after the premiere. Make sure she knows I can't stay too."

Sherilyn beamed a smile and nodded. "Of course. I'm so glad you're attending this premiere, Killian. I think it's a good promotional move for you. It keeps you in the public eye, and it shows you and Athena are still close."

"We aren't still close," I said, rolling my eyes at the thought that Athena and I felt anything now. "She just knows I make her look good since her last two boyfriends were drugged up wastes of space. If she had a decent man in her life, I'd never hear from her again."

My explanation of the true relationship between my ex-girlfriend and me seemed to disappoint Sherilyn, and she twisted her face into a grimace. "Well, it keeps you in the public eye, so that's a good thing."

"Make the arrangements and send me the information."

"Great! I will. By the way, how did your date go with the woman who won the auction the other night?"

Sherilyn's chipper voice suddenly irritated me. I opened my mouth to vent my frustration but decided against it and simply ended the call. Even though she knew me better than nearly anyone else in the world, I didn't need her trying to make me feel better about the whole situation. That would only make things worse.

I returned to pacing for another fifteen more minutes and then tried Tressa one more time. At the first sound of her voice on that fucking away message, something snapped in my brain, but instead of tossing something through the TV, I decided I needed to take matters into my own hands.

AFTER A QUICK KNOCK ON her door, I waited for Tressa to answer it, reminding myself to stay cool and not let her see how much she'd gotten to me. The fact that I'd taken the chance and come over even though I knew she was avoiding me already made me look a little more eager than I liked.

She opened the door a crack and glared at me with a look of disgust. Not exactly the response I'd hoped for after the night we'd shared.

Without saying hello, she said, "How do you make it past security? I pay people to make sure no one gets up here."

"Your security guard is a football fan. I was on his fantasy team last season and made him a fortune. I could have talked him into selling his mother for that," I said with a smile.

"Ugh. I'm really busy, Killian."

I noticed she hadn't returned to calling me Mr. Brenton anymore. That was progress. Not that she should after the all night fuck session we'd had.

Leaning in toward her face, I asked, "Did you like the flowers?"

She drew her eyebrows in and sighed. "Yes, I did. Thank you."

"I just wondered since I never heard from you after they were delivered."

Looking down toward the floor, she mumbled, "I was busy."

We stood there in silence for a long moment before I finally said, "I feel sort of stupid standing out here in the hallway, Tressa. Can I come in?"

"No."

Suddenly, jealousy filled me, and I craned my neck to look around her to see if she had another man in there with her. "Why?"

"Because I can't spend another night with you like last time. That's why."

Her answer made all the worry ebb out of me. Smiling, I said, "Another night like last time?"

"Please, Killian. This isn't going to work. I'm not really the kind of woman to just have one night stands with men, and I'm definitely not a woman to have a relationship now."

The way she pouted when she said that made me want to kiss her through that tiny crack in the door. "That doesn't leave much room for you to relax and have a good time."

"I don't have time for either, to be honest."

"I get it, Tressa. You have a world to conquer. But there has to be some time when you leave work and let yourself have fun. Trust me, I had to learn that the hard way."

She didn't answer me, so I nudged the door open a bit more. "You know you like having fun, Tressa."

For a moment, I waited to see how she'd react and then gently pushed the door open a little more. She didn't fight me and reluctantly stepped back to let me in.

"This will never work between us."

Stopping just inside the door, I kissed her. "It already has worked pretty damn well. Neither one of us is looking for forever, so why can't we enjoy ourselves for a little while?"

"Because a little while turned into an all-night marathon last time," she said with a skeptical look in her eyes.

"I was doing my best to impress you since it was our first time together," I said, chuckling at how hard she wanted to make this on the both of us.

Tressa closed the door and turned her back to me to walk away. "I don't know why you keep trying with me. We're as opposite as opposite could be. Polar opposite, actually."

Following her into the living room, I found her sitting on the couch. Nothing that indicated she'd been working sat nearby, like a tablet or computer or even her phone. I didn't see any paper or a pen either.

"Busy, huh?"

She scowled and folded her arms across her chest. "Why are you here, Killian?"

Leave it to Tressa to cut to the chase and jump right over all the sweet talk I had planned. Fine. Somehow we'd returned to being blunt, so that's what she'd get.

"Because it's not nice to receive gifts from people and not say thank you, Tressa."

My scolding tone irritated her even more, and she stood up to walk away from me. "Don't speak to me like I'm a child. That might work on other women you know, but it won't work on me."

"Then don't act like one. That might work on other men, but it definitely doesn't work for me."

Even though I enjoyed this kind of verbal sparring with her, the way she spun around and glared daggers at me told me she didn't like it as much. Without any emotion, she pointed toward the door and said, "I'm really busy, Killian. I think you should go."

Fuck. With every word she spoke, it was like I could see

another layer of the wall around her going up. What the hell was wrong? We'd had a great time together the other night. What had changed since then?

Maybe verbal sparring wouldn't work tonight. Maybe I needed to use another tactic with her.

I walked up behind her as she stood staring out the window and gently wrapped my arms around her. Resting my chin on her shoulder, I said, "You're clearly not busy, Tressa, so what's going on?"

She took a deep breath in and blew it out in a rush before her entire body sagged beneath me. "I'm not the right kind of woman for you. I don't know why you don't see that."

"Isn't that for me to decide?"

Closing her eyes, she hung her head. "We're too different. Why won't you admit that?"

I squeezed her in my arms and nuzzled her neck. "I'm not worried about our differences. I like our similarities a lot more."

Tressa turned in my hold and looked up at me with worried eyes. "What similarities exactly are you talking about? The only thing we have in common is that we're good together in bed."

"You say that like it's a bad thing."

My joke fell flat, and she returned to scowling at me. "I'm not the kind of woman to be some guy's fuck toy. Sorry. It doesn't fit with my personality."

"That's not what I think of you, Tressa."

Folding her arms across her chest, she shook her head. "Then what do you think of me? You said you couldn't stop thinking about me ever since you saw me at the auction. What does that mean? You saw a woman you wanted to sleep with and that was your goal? Well, you achieved the goal, so why do you keep coming around?"

I took her face in my hands and knew I had to tell her what I'd realized on the ride over there. I didn't really understand it myself, but it needed to be said and she needed to hear it.

She looked up at me with fear in her eyes as I tried to find the right words for what I wanted to tell her. I had a feeling she'd heard a lot of bullshit lines from guys before me. Maybe that explained why she ran so hot and cold. She'd figured out from them that letting a man know she cared for him got her hurt, so she intended to hurt first so she never had to deal with that pain again.

"Have you ever thought one thing, but then when the time comes and you're given everything you want, you see that you wanted something else?"

Talk about saying nothing in as many words possible.

Her eyes grew wide as what I wanted to say came out all wrong. "What?"

I'd gone from verbal sparring to verbal fumbling in just a few sentences. I needed to find the right words before she slapped me across the face and threw me out of her life forever.

"Wait. That wasn't what I meant. Let me try again. I thought I couldn't stop thinking about you because you were gorgeous and the way you looked at me that night made me want you. Then I thought I couldn't stop thinking about you because you wouldn't even call me to say thanks for sending you flowers. Neither of those are true, though. I don't know why you've gotten under my skin, but you have and I can't think of anything else but you. And I don't mean just sex with you. I mean you, Tressa. The way you look when I joke around. That cute way you blush at things. The way you giggle at things I say."

"So this isn't about you just coming here because you want sex?"

I shook my head, still pretty amazed at that fact myself. I'd never been the decent guy type when it came to women. Tressa was different, though. I didn't know why, but unlike her, I didn't feel the need to examine that question.

"No. I'm not going to lie. The sex is phenomenal, but that's not the only reason I want to be around you. Now if you'd stop fighting me at every turn, we could have a good time, sexually or non-sexually."

The look on her face told me she still didn't believe me, so I took her hand and led her back over to the couch. I expected some kind of resistance, but thankfully, she didn't argue. We sat down and I moved her so she could lie back against my chest while we talked.

Leaning forward, I moved her hair over her left shoulder so she wasn't resting on it. "Comfortable?"

"I guess," she answered tentatively, like she expected me to begin undressing her at any moment.

Not that I wouldn't have been all for that, but instead, I wrapped my arms around her and leaned back against the couch cushions to relax. I couldn't remember the last time I just sat and talked with a woman once we'd slept together, but it felt nice to be there with her and not have the expectation of anything but some conversation.

"So how was work today, dear?" I asked with a smile.

Tressa sighed. "Horrible, but thanks for asking."

Moving my hands up, I began massaging her shoulders, which were as tight as drums. As I attempted to ease the stress out of her body, I said, "Horrible isn't good. Want to talk about it?"

Another sigh made her body sag against my torso. "No. Maybe. I don't know. I'm sure you have no interest in hearing about the problems I'm having with a designer who thinks she knows best and who's being overpaid for having taste in her mouth and that's it."

"I'm all ears. We're just hanging out here trying to relax, and if that means telling me about this horrible designer, then do it. Whatever makes you feel better."

Tressa turned her head to look up at me. Still suspicious, she narrowed her eyes and asked, "Is this some kind of new seduction technique of yours?"

"Nope. Just me giving you a chance to vent after a bad day. Want me to start first? I sent flowers to a beautiful woman and do you know she never even sent me a message to say thanks?" I said with a smile.

Her expression softened and her eyes grew wide. Smiling, she said, "She sounds like a complete and total bitch. You should forget about her. You know, other fish in the sea and all that."

I shrugged and shook my head. "If only I could. I don't know what this woman has, but I can't get her out of my mind. It's maddening, to be honest. I'm just going to have to keep trying to convince her that I'm a good guy."

"Maybe she doesn't deserve you. I mean, if she isn't even polite enough to say thank you when someone sends her flowers, maybe she isn't worth it."

Pressing a kiss to the top of her head, I felt her soft hair caress my lips. "She's worth it."

For the first time since we lay down, she squeezed her arms against mine and smiled. "Well, if that's the way it is, I'm sure she'll warm up to you eventually. Some people just take longer than others."

"That's fine. I've got nothing but time."

Looking away, Tressa asked in a voice barely above a whisper, "What about all the other women, though? Maybe you'll want to spend your time focusing on one of them instead."

So that was the problem. Or part of it. I had a feeling a woman like Tressa Stone had layers of resistance to someone like me.

"As much as I'm sure it would surprise the world, there aren't other women to focus on. Just the beautiful woman who seems to hate my flowers."

She didn't respond for a long time until she finally said, "She doesn't hate them, and she doesn't hate you. She's just difficult."

"I'm not sure difficult is the right word. I have another word for her. I think of her as challenging, and there's nothing I like more than a challenge."

I felt her body tense up against mine and knew I'd said something wrong. A second later, Tressa pushed herself up off me to stand up. I didn't know why she was running away since we'd been having a pleasant conversation, but I planned to find out.

Following her into her bedroom, I found Tressa standing near the window that overlooked the city. I walked up behind her and tried to slide my arms around her, but she pushed me away.

"What's wrong?"

She shook her head and wouldn't look at me, turning her back so I couldn't see her face. The truth was I had no idea what I said, but at least I knew I'd said something wrong. Silently, I gave myself points for that.

"I don't know what I said or did, but can you at least tell me so I don't have to spend the rest of my life wondering how I fucked up?"

"I'm not interested in being some goal for you to reach, Killian. That just makes me sound like another notch on your bedpost."

"I don't have a bedpost, and even if I did, I can't imagine cutting a notch into it even once, forget multiple times."

My lame joke meant to get a response did just that, and she turned around to face me, her expression twisted into a look of disgust. "This isn't funny to me. Why do you have to make a joke when I'm being serious?"

"Because I want to see you smile."

"I don't want to be a challenge to you, Killian. Challenges are things you overcome."

"You'd rather be thought of as difficult?"

Tressa looked down toward the white carpet on the floor and shrugged. "This is why I'm not a good fit for you or anyone, for that matter. Maybe there's no word to describe what I am. Maybe I'm just a bitch like I said before."

I took a step toward her and then another. Opening my arms, I brought her to me and hugged her tightly. "You're so focused on fighting this thing between us. I don't know why, but you'll tell me when you want to. Until then, I'm not giving up on you. Just giving you fair warning."

She tilted her head up and gave me a tiny smile. "I'm always going to be difficult. I just am. I want to believe you're an okay guy, but my experience with men says otherwise."

God, I had no idea what she'd gone through with men before me. I could only imagine. Weak-ass men afraid of strong women were everywhere, unfortunately, and in her dark eyes, I saw she'd had more than a few run-ins with that kind of asshole guy.

I wasn't one of them, though. For all my faults, I wasn't the type of man who feared a strong woman. Exactly the opposite, in fact, and I planned on proving that to her in spades.

At the moment, though, all I wanted to do was make her happy. "Well, first things first. I'm way better than okay. I would think the reviews of our night together show that. Secondly, I do cute romantic things like send flowers. That's got to be a sign I'm more than okay. I guess if I went out and picked them that might be more impressive, but I have a feeling if I stole my neighbor's flowers, she'd call the cops. That's another point in my favor. I don't steal flowers."

As much as she fought it, a smile lit up Tressa's beautiful face and she giggled in that adorable way I couldn't help but love. This difficult woman who insisted on putting me through my paces and pushed me away over and over giggled at my stupid jokes.

"You say the silliest things. You know that?" she asked as she cradled my face in her hands.

"I'm disarming. It's one of my best traits."

I leaned down and pressed my forehead to hers. "And I'm not going to give up on you, so you're just going to have to find another way to deal with me."

Chapter Twelve

Tressa

Crossing my legs in front of me, I sat on my bed and scanned the designs for the London Richmont hotel the designer sent a few minutes before. As my eyes roamed over the images, I ground my teeth in frustration. I hated each one more than the last. All she could think of was remaking the hotel with a retro design. The woman couldn't talk about anything else since she joined the project.

The problem was I didn't want it to look like something out of the 1950s. I flipped through the pictures again. The furniture looked skimpy and boxy, and what was with those wooden spindle dividers that hung from the ceiling cutting up the lobby area and that enormous red lamp that looked like some horrible swollen tentacle lurching out into the middle of the seating area?

I should have never agreed to let her show me anything retro. Christ. Of all the decades she wanted to emulate, why that one?

Disgusted, I set my work aside and closed my eyes. This meant we'd have to have another meeting so I could explain once more what my vision for the hotel redesign was. Hopefully, she'd listen this time and not ignore every point I mentioned in favor of wretched pinks and yellows, geometric prints, and hideous lighting.

I could have simply hired someone to handle this, but I wanted to do it myself, even though I was the COO. I wanted to put my mark on the Richmont chain. Now I wondered if that had been a mistake.

Pushing all the hassle with the designer out of my mind, I took a deep breath in and tried to relax. All of this would work out. I just had to make sure she knew what a Richmont hotel should look like and how the chain presented itself. Once she understood that, everything else would go smoothly.

At least I hoped it would.

Relax, Tressa. You can handle this.

I smiled as the thought of what Killian would say to me at that moment popped into my head. He'd make some stupid joke so I'd smile or say something cute to make me giggle. Even when I wanted to remain upset, he knew how to lighten my mood.

That thought led to another. I shouldn't have let him in last night. One night was enough.

Who was I kidding? One night was never going to be enough. I knew that from the minute he kissed me the first time. The man had the ability to make my head swim with just a single kiss. And that said nothing about how he made me feel during sex.

God, I didn't want to think that way. I wanted to believe we wouldn't work out. We were so different, so how could we?

But that wasn't the truth. The truth was I enjoyed being with him. When it was just the two of us, he was a great guy. But when the cameras were around? I hated that kind of publicity, and the fact that he loved it bothered me.

I leaned back against the pillows as the memory of the last time we were together settled into my mind. No matter how hard I made it for him to get close to me, he didn't give up. I walked away, and he followed. I pushed him away, and he came back with his arms open wanting to hold me.

He wasn't going to give up, and I loved that. I didn't want to admit it to anyone, even to him, but I secretly wanted him around.

As I got lost in thought about Killian, my phone rang. My heart skipped a beat at the idea that it might be him, but one glance and I saw it was Summer calling.

Without saying hello, she asked in a voice full of concern,

"Tressa, what's going on?"

"Nothing I'm working. Why? Is something wrong? Are you and Ethan okay?"

My mind instantly traveled to the idea that Ethan had fucked up. If he did something to break them up, I was going to march right up to his apartment and let him have it. Or maybe he was hurt. Animals weren't like humans. Maybe one of them attacked him.

As my brain raced with every conceivable stupid thing my brother could have done, Summer said, "Everything's okay. Ethan's fine, and I'm good. I'm just wondering how things went with Killian the other night. I never heard back from you after I returned home from the shoot."

I breathed a sigh of relief before answering her question. "They went," I said.

"That's not much of an answer, but if I didn't know better, I'd swear I can practically hear you smiling. You had a good time, didn't you? Is he nice?"

Nice? No, nice wasn't exactly the right word to describe Killian Brenton. Other words came to mind, though.

Sexy. Fucking incredible in bed. Distracting.

"I don't know if I'd call him that," I said with a chuckle. "We had a good time, though."

My comment was met with silence for a long time before Summer squealed, "Oh my God! You slept with him, didn't you? I can hear it in your voice. That's the sound of a woman who had great sex with a gorgeous man!"

"Don't be ridiculous."

"You did! Just admit it. It's not like I'm going to ask about the personal details, unless you want to give me them, of course. It's okay. You're two grown single adults. Why can't you have sex?"

"Please stop. I swear you and my brother are two of a kind. Is there nothing off limits with you two?"

"I won't tell anyone, Tressa. Not even Ethan. I just think it's great that you had a good time. That's all I was saying."

"Well, it's not a big deal. Two people had dinner and a nice time. It happens all the time."

Summer didn't seem to be buying my dismissal of the whole Killian thing, though. "Sure, although you two aren't just two ordinary people. He's a star quarterback for a New York team that's looking to have their best season in five years, and you're the COO of Richmont Hotels and a VP at Stone Worldwide. Not exactly just two people."

"Well, I have no idea if any of that makes a difference. It was all for a good cause anyway."

"Yeah. The pediatric cancer foundation. Definitely a good cause, although I don't think they expected you to sleep with Killian," Summer said with a giggle.

"God, you're so much like Ethan! This conversation is over, and don't tell anyone about this, Summer. Promise."

"I promise, Tressa, but no one would have an issue with this anyway. You're allowed to be happy. I think most people would say you've earned it."

Summer sounded so much like Diana it was scary. "Well, I have to earn my salary by working, so I'll talk to you later."

I ended the call and tossed my phone off to the other side of the bed. I loved being friends with Summer, but sometimes she could be so silly. Then again, it would have been nice to be able to tell her about my time with Killian. I hadn't had a good old fashioned gossip fest with another female in a long time.

Grudgingly, I returned to the redesign of the London Richmont hotel, making detailed notes on exactly how I wanted the hotel to look. A few minutes later Summer called a second time, and now she sounded frantic.

"Hey, how did you and Killian leave things after your date and whatever else you did?"

"I told you I didn't want to talk about this, and don't you ever say hello when you begin a call?"

"Hello. I'm just wondering if you two decided anything."

"Decided anything? No. But I have to admit I am enjoying seeing him."

"So you've seen him more than just that date for the charity?"

I finally relented and shared the details with Summer. "Yes. Okay. Yes. You're right. We slept together. More than once. God, I didn't realize how much I wanted to share this with someone, so I hope you're not going to get all provincial or anything on me. As you said, we're grown single people, right? Why can't we have a good time? And yes, I know he's a huge attention whore, but we're not doing anything in public, so it will be fine."

My confession was greeted with silence for so long that I wondered if Summer was still there. Nervously, I said, "Of all people, I didn't think you'd be so judgmental about all of this. I expected you to be more supportive."

"Uh, Tressa, are you watching TV right now?"

"No. Why? What does that have to do with what I just told you?" I asked as I searched the bed for the remote control.

"I think you better turn it on. Go to the Premiere channel," Summer said in a tone that sent a chill racing down my back.

Oh, God. Please don't let him be telling people about us on worldwide TV. Please, God. He seemed to understand how much I hated the spotlight. He wouldn't do that. Would he?

Afraid of what the answer to my question could be, I asked Summer, "Why? What the hell channel is the Premiere channel? Is it a sports channel or something? Is Killian on a sports talk show or something?"

"It's up in the low three thousands," Summer answered in a somber voice. "Thirty-one twelve."

I pressed the numbers into the remote and a moment later on the screen, up popped Killian with a stunning platinum blonde. Tall and willowy, she had the most perfect breasts I'd ever seen, and they were practically spilling out of the black evening gown she wore. I had no idea who this woman was, but they looked beautiful together, like they were made for one another.

Then a thousand questions raced through my mind. Where were they? Why was Killian dressed in a tux and with this woman? Who was this woman? Clearly, they knew one another well, if the way she draped herself over his arm was any indication.

"What am I looking at, Summer?" I asked, hating how much hurt hung off each word.

"I don't know. Who is she? This is the movie premiere for One Lucky Day, some movie about a guy winning the lottery and then having some horrible things happen to him. She's in the movie, I think."

None of that answered the real question I had about the scene playing out in front of me.

"Is this live?" I asked, unsure why that would matter.

"Yeah, I think so."

With each passing moment, my stomach twisted into a knot as I watched Killian walking the woman down a red carpet, basking in the attention as photographers took pictures of him and the beautiful actress hanging on his arm. I knew I shouldn't be jealous. Why would I be jealous? We had no commitment between us. I'd made it perfectly clear to him that I didn't want anything like that.

Then why did every moment I watched him with that woman make me feel like someone was hollowing out my insides?

Swallowing hard, I forced myself to sound like this didn't bother me at all. "The man can wear a tux. I'll give him that. And whoever she is, she can wear a black gown like nobody I've ever seen."

"Maybe they're just friends," Summer suggested, but it sounded like a sad attempt to be helpful.

"I have to get back to work. I'll talk to you later."

Summer began to say something, but I ended the call without another word as I stared at the TV screen in front of me. Killian looked happy with all those people clamoring to get his picture or his date's picture. Whichever it was, he looked right at home in that scene.

I watched for a few moments more before turning off the TV. I had no idea if this woman was just a friend of Killian's, like Summer said, or if she was something more serious. It didn't matter.

Or did it?

Slowly, my disappointment and sadness turned to anger that he'd been cheating on this actress with me. I'd seen her with him in some of those hundreds of pictures I'd found. She was someone he'd dated before.

Or maybe they'd never broken up? Regretting every moment I spent with him, I chastised myself for ever giving him a chance.

You should have gone with your gut, Tressa. Why did you ever doubt yourself?

CHAPTER THIRTEEN

KILLIAN

THE REDEYE FROM LA TURNED out to be even worse than I thought it would be. Three hours seated next to some guy who smelled like he'd bathed in twenty dollar cologne and in front of a woman who quietly sobbed the entire time from the moment the plane took off to the moment the plane landed in New York. I'd tried to relax and get some sleep, but between his smell and her sadness, it wasn't happening.

Stepping off the flight, I squinted at the daylight and inhaled a deep breath of fresh air, thankful to be away from that guy. Sherilyn had arranged to have a driver waiting for me, and I found him standing outside the terminal. At least that would be good. I could count on her for that.

I slid into the back seat of the black Town Car while the driver talked about it being a nice day in the city, according to some weather forecast. Interrupting him, I said, "Take me to the Richmont hotel in Midtown."

As the car rolled toward its destination, I thought about trying to call Tressa again but decided against it. I'd called her three times before getting on the plane, but each time I'd gotten that damn away message of hers.

I couldn't help but wonder why she hadn't answered. When we saw each other the night before last, we hadn't even had sex. We spent the whole time talking, and I thought we had a good time. I thought I'd finally succeeding in showing her I wasn't just some attention whore athlete, and even more, I wasn't some asshole guy like the ones she'd dated before.

So why that goddamned away message again?

The car ride felt like it took forever, but we finally reached the Richmont and I jumped out of the backseat as I yelled back at the driver, "I'll be back in a few minutes!"

I saw the night security guard who let me up to the penthouse last time, so I flashed him a smile and made a beeline for him. A few well-placed words and if Tressa hadn't left for work yet, I'd be upstairs to see her in a matter of minutes.

"Hey, Charlie! Do they keep you here 'round the clock?" I asked with a laugh, only half kidding.

He responded to my lighthearted teasing with a stony look and gave me his prepared speech like last time. "I'm sorry, sir. I can't let you go up there."

Time for the charm offensive.

Pulling the slightly overweight man aside, I patted him on the back like we were long-time friends. "Charlie, I get that she has you telling everyone that, but she doesn't mean me. Trust me. I'm guessing it just slipped her mind."

The security guard looked around to make sure no one was nearby and then whispered, "She gave everyone orders to not let you or anyone up there, but I'm going to tell you the truth. Miss Stone isn't here. She had the car service take her away in the middle of the night around three a.m."

Three in the morning? Why would she leave at that time? Instantly, my mind went to another man.

"Where'd she go?" I whispered, sure he wasn't lying to me but also sure I had no idea why Tressa would go out in the middle of the night.

Unless it had to do with some guy.

"That I don't know. It was all very hush-hush. All I know is she isn't here anymore."

"Was she going to her office?" I asked, hoping that was the

answer and not that Tressa was spending the night with some other man.

Charlie shook his head. "I don't think so. She had a bag like she takes when she's going on a trip."

A trip? Granted, we weren't at the point in our relationship that we told one another everything. I hadn't told her about my quick trip to the West coast, so maybe my gut feeling was misplaced. The problem was I couldn't shake the idea that something was wrong.

"Any idea when she's scheduled to come back?"

The security guard shook his head. "No idea. She just came down at right after eight o'clock last night and told us no one was to be allowed upstairs, including you, and then she came down again at three this morning with her bag. She got into a car waiting for her and left."

Quickly, I seized on that car as jealousy coursed through me. "Was it the usual car she uses from the car service or was it someone's car, like someone she was traveling with?"

Holding his hand up like he wanted to stop me from jumping to the wrong conclusion, Charlie smiled. "She got into a car service vehicle like she always takes. In fact, the only other car I've ever seen her get into is yours, Mr. Brenton."

"Okay. Thanks, Charlie."

As I turned to leave, he gave me a pat on the arm to console me. That was what my life had come to because of Tressa Stone. Now security guards pitied me.

By the time the car dropped me off at my apartment, I didn't know if I felt angry or disappointed. I still had no clue as to where she went, and even though I couldn't think of a single reason why she'd be avoiding me this time, I had a sneaking suspicion something had happened to change her mind about me.

Had she tried to contact me while I was in LA? I checked my phone and found no calls from her. Since all calls were directed to my cell, she wouldn't have gotten my away message. I wondered if she'd come over with the idea of surprising me. That didn't sound like Tressa at all, but a quick check with the security in the lobby of my building and I crossed that idea off the list of possible reasons she'd be upset with me.

After a quick shower, I called her office and her assistant gave me a very vague answer that she wasn't in today. If anyone knew where Tressa was, it was that woman, but her very businesslike way told me she wouldn't be offering any additional information on her boss's location. When I asked when she'd be back, the woman claimed she didn't know.

So much for that route. I ended the call and had to admit that I shouldn't have expected anything more from Tressa's assistant. She was as cold as her boss appeared to be.

No worries. I had another way I could get around the assistant's stonewalling. Why not go straight to the top and ask Tristan Stone where his daughter was?

The woman who had been all smiles the day I was there to see the man in person tersely told me to hold and then left me waiting for nearly five minutes. Finally, she came back and transferred the call to her boss.

"Killian, how are you doing? I saw on the news yesterday that you guys might be getting another wide receiver. That could make New York practically unstoppable, don't you think?" Tristan asked in the same jovial way as when I'd met him in his office.

That felt like a good start. I had no idea why everyone else at Stone Worldwide was so icy this morning, but at least Tristan seemed his usual self.

After discussing how a wide receiver would shore up the offense and make the team a powerhouse, I segued to the real reason I'd called him. "Sir, I called because I'm trying to find Tressa. We've been seeing each other, and I just want to make sure she's okay."

"You two have been dating?" Tristan asked, clearly surprised.

I hesitated for a moment to call what we'd been doing dating since I doubted it would technically be considered that, but then I answered, "Yes. We've seen each other a few times this week. When

I returned from LA this morning, I found her gone and no one seems to want to tell me where. I've called her a few times, but it always goes to her away message."

"That sounds like Tressa is avoiding you, to be honest, Killian. Only you'd know why."

But I didn't.

"I honestly have no idea. We did have a misunderstanding after our first date, but we cleared that up a couple days ago. I don't know what could be wrong."

"Well, as much as I wish I could help you, I think my daughter is the one to deal with. I will tell you this. She's not in the country at the moment, but I expect her to return within the week. If I talk to her, I'll be sure to tell her you've been trying to contact her."

Disappointed, I thanked him for his help, but just before I ended the call, he said, "If it helps, Tressa isn't treating you any differently than anyone else, Killian. This is how she is when she's upset about something. She's been like this since she was a little girl. I don't know what could be the problem, but this isn't unusual for her. Give her time. I bet she comes around."

I thanked him again and tossed my phone onto the kitchen counter in frustration. Where the hell could Tressa be and why was she avoiding me this time?

Knowing that she routinely did this to others, even her family members, didn't make me feel any better. For fuck's sake, we'd had a good time the other night. What did I have to do to make this woman understand I wasn't just some dick like other men she'd known?

After becoming more and more frustrated by the whole damn situation and pacing for an hour, I made sure all my calls would go to the videophone and sat down to watch some TV. I didn't have to be at any meetings until afternoon, so hopefully, I could find something to take my mind of Tressa.

A few minutes later, I heard the familiar noise alerting me that I was getting a call. My stomach tightened and my heart skipped a beat as I hoped it would be Tressa, but it wasn't.

Disappointed, I sat back as Sherilyn showed up on the screen all smiles. "How was the premiere?"

I shrugged. I'd completely forgotten about the premiere until that moment. "Good, I guess. The movie was shit, but I pretended I liked it. I have a feeling Athena knows it's bad, though. No need to pile on when someone's down."

"You looked good, Killian. Black tie affairs always work for you. I have no doubt when you're done with football that modeling or even acting is in your future."

I stared at her utterly confused. "What do you mean? You weren't there, were you?"

"No," Sherilyn said, laughing as if anything I'd said was funny. "We have this thing called TV now. I saw you on the Premiere channel. I'm still amazed they have an entire channel dedicated to movie premieres and after parties. But then again, there are thirteen game show channels, three channels dedicated to dogs, and an entire channel for needlepoint, so why not? To think people used to think fishing shows were ridiculous."

"What the fuck are you talking about?" I asked as the idea of a channel for needlepoint ran through my head. Who the hell would watch that?

"The Premiere channel. Are you okay? That flying out and back in one day must be messing with you."

"What channel is this Premiere channel?"

"Thirty-one twelve. They're going to be replaying the whole One Lucky Day premiere and party around the clock, I'm sure. You can see. You looked great. Athena did too, but she always does."

I pressed the buttons on the remote to go to the channel, minimizing Sherilyn into the corner of the screen. Two women dressed in black gowns and talking about who attended some party appeared in front of me.

"How much of it do they show?"

"Everything. I can't believe you've never heard of this. It's been around for a few years now. I've seen you at a couple of them on that channel. They start with the stars walking down the red carpet, and then if you pay, you can see the film right when it premieres. Then they have a team of people who mill about at the after party interviewing the guests."

Just then, I saw the beginning of the One Lucky Day premiere show. I watched as the star of the movie and his girlfriend walked down the red carpet and posed for pictures. Then right behind them I saw Athena and me walk toward the press. At least now I knew why Tressa wasn't answering my calls.

Then I heard the commentator say, "It looks like Athena Rogers and Killian Brenton are as close as ever here tonight for this premiere. I have to say they always made a gorgeous couple."

Fuck. Tressa had seen this and jumped to the logical conclusion that I was even worse than just an attention whore athlete. Thanks to these assholes and their comments about Athena and me, she thought I was with another woman.

I began pacing again as the commentator continued talking about useless shit like who the designer of Athena's dress was and who designed my tux. Who the fuck cared about those kinds of things?

"Sherilyn, I need to find out where someone is. Any ideas on how to do that?"

"Uh, here or international?" she asked.

"Out of the country. I don't know where, though. Left in the past few hours."

Sherilyn nodded. "All pilots have to file flight plans. If you know where the flight left from, assuming the person is on a plane, that could be one way. Which airport?"

"I don't know. I need you check all of them. I'm guessing it's a Stone Worldwide private jet she took. I need you to find out where Tressa Stone went."

Sherilyn stared at me, clearly confused about all of this. "Why don't you just call her?"

"I tried. She's not answering my calls. I keep getting her away message."

"Maybe she's sleeping. Not everyone keeps the hours you do, Killian."

"I want you to find out where she went, Sherilyn."

Still confused, she shrugged. "Okay. Give me a little while. I'm not even sure flight plans are public. I'll do what I can."

"Good. Find out as soon as you can and get back to me."

I ended the call and sat back on the couch. Tressa saw me with Athena and jumped to the wrong conclusions. Of course she did. With the way Athena was hanging all over me, like she always did, most people likely thought we were back together even without that jackass reporter talking about it.

As I sat there waiting for Sherilyn to call back, my mind moved from how much I hated this fucking Premiere channel to how much I hated the fact that I had to keep chasing after Tressa. Every time I wanted to see her, I had to fight tooth and nail to get to her. She had to be blackmailed into going out on that damn date she paid ten grand for. Then I didn't even get a thank you for the flowers, and when I went to see her, I had to charm the damn security guard to get to the penthouse. And after all that, she still kept me standing out in the fucking hallway where I practically had to beg her to let me in.

Why did she have to be so damn difficult?

A few minutes of that shit and I had to reel myself in. The truth was I liked Tressa, and the work I had to do to be with her wasn't anything more than I'd ever done with anyone else. True, most women didn't make me work so hard to see them, but the drama and bullshit I had to deal with once we were together were just as difficult to deal with as the hassle Tressa put me through.

And when I finally did get to be with her, I had a good time, and not just with the sex. When she let down her guard, she was fun and even sweet. I liked that. I didn't understand her dislike of the public eye, but getting to be around her privately made up for that.

I'd never shied away from a challenge, and Tressa Stone was just that. I wasn't ready to give up on her quite yet.

Sherilyn called back a half hour later, and I knew instantly she hadn't been able to find out what I needed to know. "No luck. She didn't fly out of any airports in the area. Maybe she went on a cruise?"

"Doubtful. Okay, thanks."

The screen went dark again and I closed my eyes. Where could she be? I didn't have a clue, so I had no choice but to wait until she returned home. I just hated not being able to tell her that what she saw wasn't what she thought she saw.

CHAPTER FOURTEEN
TRESSA

THE CAR ROLLED DOWN MANHATTAN'S streets on the way to the Richmont hotel as I prayed to God Killian wouldn't be waiting there for me when I arrived. After such a successful trip to London, the last thing I wanted on my return home was to deal with him after what I saw on that ridiculous Premiere channel.

Pushing the memory of him and that blonde with the most perfect breasts I'd ever seen out of my mind, I focused on the London redesign. I'd expected to have to fight with the designer, but as soon as we sat down and I calmly explained in the nicest terms how I hated her American midcentury designs for the hotel, she thankfully agreed and we started fresh by discussing exactly how I wanted it to look.

If only every facet of my life could work so smoothly.

I took a deep breath in and closed my eyes as I let it out slowly. *Don't think about him. Don't. You made a mistake, but now you're going to fix it and be done with Killian Brenton.*

The car stopped and the driver said, "The Richmont, miss. Would you like me to help you with your bag?"

Opening my eyes to thank him for the offer, I saw a nightmare awaiting me outside the car. Dozens of reporters milled about in front of the hotel. Damnit! Why were they here? Did that mean Killian was inside waiting for me? How could he know I was returning now?

I didn't answer the driver and opened the car door to see the press rushing toward me. I barely stepped onto the sidewalk before they swarmed, yelling out questions like a crazed mob, all of them about the same topic.

Killian Brenton.

"Tressa, are you and Killian dating?" one asked as I began to push through the crowd.

I kept my head down and my bag in front of me to carve a path through them. I wanted to answer their questions by announcing how much I wasn't dating goddamned Killian. I also wanted to tell each of them to go away and leave me the hell alone.

None of that came out of my mouth, though.

"Is it serious? How long have you been together?" another one yelled as I passed by him.

I cringed at the description of us as serious. Hadn't any of these vultures seen him with that blonde woman just a few nights ago?

Just then, one of them yelled out, "Killian was just with his ex Athena Rogers the other night at the premiere of her new movie. Did you know they're seeing one another again? How does that affect your relationship with him?"

My heart sank at each word. Was I considered the other woman he was cheating with, or was I the foolish girlfriend who didn't realize she was being cheated on? Both sounded horrible, and under my breath, I cursed the moment I laid eyes on Killian.

I finally reached the glass front doors and saw the portly security guard named Charlie waiting just inside. Opening them for me, he did his best to chase away the reporters, stopping them as they tried to get into the hotel lobby.

"Miss Stone, I'm so sorry you had to return home to this. I promise you not a single one of them will get into the hotel, though."

Spinning around to face him, I glared at him and didn't even try to hide how furious the scene outside had made me. "No one is to be allowed upstairs, and that means no one! And if a single one of those reporters or anyone else gets up to my penthouse, you'll be fired quicker than you can say your name! Got it?"

The man's round eyes opened wide and he nodded quickly. I turned on my heels and marched over to the elevator to take me to my home. I'd planned on relaxing tonight, but I had something else to attend to now, and I didn't want to wait until I cooled down.

As the elevator passed each floor, I grew angrier and angrier. Balling my free hand into a tight fist, I pressed my fingernails into my palm to keep my rage at a fever pitch. When the doors finally opened on the top floor, I stormed out toward the penthouse, throwing my bag onto the couch before I turned toward the screen on the wall next to me.

"Call Killian Brenton now!" I demanded and waited impatiently as the piece of electronics did its job.

A few moments later, he appeared on the screen looking as pleasant as always. But I wasn't in the mood for pleasant. In fact, I doubted I'd be anywhere near pleasant in the next week.

"Tressa, I'm so happy to see you."

I held up my hand and shook my head. "Don't speak. I'm not listening. I am, however, furious about the mob of reporters outside my hotel crowding me as I return home from a business trip and asking me questions about the two of us dating. You did this, didn't you? I couldn't have been clearer about how I felt about being in the limelight, and still you told one of them we were dating, which we aren't. Why? Why would you do that? What purpose did it serve?"

He flashed that sexy smile that I couldn't resist, which only frustrated me more. "I guess we haven't done much of what dating entails, but you wouldn't want reporters to be asking if we're fucking, would you?"

"I hate you. Do you know that?"

Killian shook his head and smiled even more broadly. "No, you don't."

"Despise you. That might be more appropriate. Loathe you. Yeah, that feels right. I loathe you for what you've done. Goodbye,

Killian."

He leaned forward so his face was all I could see. "Which thing do you loathe me for? I'd like to know just for future reference."

God, the way he looked at me with those green eyes. No. I shouldn't look at him. I needed to focus on my loathing of him.

"I just told you. There are reporters outside my damn hotel bothering me. I can't even leave, for God's sake! I'm trapped here, and it's all because of you telling them we're dating, which I feel the need to repeat, we are not. We. Are. Not."

"Oh, okay. I thought it might have been for that whole movie premiere thing, which you know would mean you don't hate me at all but like me an awful lot. At least that's what it would look like, you know, if you were loathing me for that. Which you aren't, I guess."

My cheeks began to heat up, and I turned away so he couldn't see my face. "I'm not having this conversation with you. I don't know what you're talking about, so you're making no sense. You better get whoever you told we were dating to retract that right now."

"So the loathing isn't about the movie premiere? Good, because that was just me doing a friend a favor."

I spun around to see him staring at me and grinning. God he was infuriating! "I don't care what or who you do, Killian Brenton. Actually I do care what you do. Tell whoever you have to that we aren't dating right now so I can leave my hotel room."

"I had a feeling you cared. You come off like some kind of ice queen, but I know what's smoldering underneath that cool façade, Tressa. I've seen the real you, so I knew you cared. But it wasn't anything to worry about. Athena isn't anyone to me anymore. We're just friends, and she asked me to attend her premiere with her. Nothing else to say."

What was wrong with this man? Hadn't he heard a word I'd said? And what kind of name was Athena? Did parents who named their children after Greek goddesses know ahead of time their daughters would look like that blonde Killian had hanging off him just a few nights ago?

God, my mind was racing! This man made me crazy. None of that mattered. All that mattered was Killian getting those damn reporters with their cameras out from in front of my hotel.

"You're not paying attention, Killian. I don't care who you do or what she looks like, goddess or gargoyle. I only care about the reporters outside my hotel waiting for me to comment on what you told them, so tell them the truth right now."

He leaned back away from the camera and folded his arms behind his head like this was a casual talk we were having. "I'll tell you what. How about I come over and tell them in person? That way no one can misquote me. What do you think of that?"

Hanging my head, I sighed as the frustration began to make my head pound. "That will only make them think we're together, which we aren't, Killian. There are a million other ways to let them know we aren't dating. Use one of those."

"I don't know if there are a million. Maybe a dozen. That might be an overestimation, actually."

Clearly, he wasn't taken this or me seriously, so there was no point in continuing this conversation. "Fine. Goodbye, Killian."

Before he could utter another idiotic syllable that would only make my head hurt more, I turned off the videophone and the screen went black. I stood there staring blankly into space as my frustration and misery overwhelmed me. Covering my face with my hands, I tried not to be upset with everything that had happened—seeing Killian with that women named after a Greek goddess, having to travel to London and back in three days, coming home to a swarm of reporters waiting for me, and finally dealing with the man who had been the cause of all my misfortune since the moment I saw him—but it was no use.

My life was a mess, and it was all his fault. I hated him. Loathed him. Yes, that was better. Loathing sounded more righteous, and if anyone had a reason to be righteous about Killian

Brenton and the havoc he wreaked on people, it was me.

Since I was now trapped in my own home, I had to do something to relax before the stress of all of this made the top of my head blow off. Stomping into the bathroom, I ran a bath and poured nearly an entire bottle of bubble bath into the tub.

Just as I stripped down to my bra and panties, I remembered I hadn't put the away message on. Fuck. I didn't want to have to deal with Killian calling back, or even worse, my parents asking about my love life.

Which I didn't have with Killian Brenton anymore, as much as that made me even more miserable to think about.

So I marched out to the living room and fixed the only problem I could before stomping back to the bathroom and slamming the door behind me. I tossed my bra and panties aside and slid into the tub to cover myself with bubbles up to my chin, and when the water nearly came up over the sides of the tub, I stretched my foot out to turn off the water with my toes.

"God, give me the strength to get through this madness and come out the other side still standing strong," I mumbled as I sank under the water completely.

AN HOUR LATER, I STILL loathed Killian, but at least my headache had subsided. Hoping to take my mind off him and everything about him, I sat down on my bed and closed my eyes to do that yoga thing Summer claimed helped relieve stress. It had never worked before for me, but I was desperate, so I slowly breathed in and held the air inside my lungs before letting it out slowly and counting to ten each time. I couldn't deny that it calmed me a little, but every thought that filled my empty mind was about Killian.

And people wondered why I rarely dated. This was why. Romance meant nothing but misery for me. Always had and always would. I just needed to accept that and acknowledge that I'd be alone for the rest of my life.

That idea made me wince, throwing off my breathing and making my stress come rushing back. I didn't enjoy living alone. That morning when I woke up and saw Killian there with me in bed hadn't been bad. It had been sort of nice, actually.

But maybe some people were meant to be alone. I freely admitted to being a difficult person to deal with. Perhaps that meant being alone.

I didn't want to think about any of this tonight.

A knock at my door tore me out of my thoughts. Hopefully, some food would make me feel better. It had taken the kitchen long enough, though. As I walked toward the door, I told myself not to bark at the person with my dinner. I wasn't angry with them, and the restaurant was busy at this time of night.

I opened the door and there standing in front of me wasn't a member of the hotel staff but Killian smiling at me.

"Oh, my God! I'm going to have to fire that security guard. Do you realize you just made that man unemployed?" I asked as I moved to shut the door in his face.

Killian stuck his foot into the space to stop me from closing the door. "I'm here to take you away from all the madness. And you can thank the security guard because he's making sure the reporters stay out front while we sneak out the back."

This man had lost his mind, and if I wasn't careful, he'd make me lose mine too.

"I'm not going anywhere with you. Go away. You've lost your mind if you think I'm going to spend another minute with you. Goodbye."

He leaned in toward my face and said, "You keep saying that word, but I'm not hearing that you really want me to go."

The way he looked at me made it difficult to focus my justifiable anger at him, but I had to. Avoiding his gaze, I said, "I do really want you to go. Since I first laid eyes on you, you've been nothing but trouble. I don't need this in my life. I had a perfectly good life and now it's all upended because of you."

Killian propped himself against the door frame and smiled confidently. God, he was cocky. "You do need this in your life. Admit it. You and I have a good time together."

Now I had to look at him because he was clearly not understanding what I was saying. Maybe if he saw my true feelings in my eyes, he'd finally get it. "We do nothing but have sex, Killian. Do you think you're the only man on Earth who can give me that? Your ego needs a check."

Lifting his hand in front of my face, he put up one finger and then two. "One, that's not true. We had a great time just hanging out and talking the last time we were together. And two, while there are other men with cocks on this planet, they aren't me and my cock."

"You're ridiculous. Stop talking about cocks. I'm furious with you, so the last thing I want to think about is any of your body parts."

"I had a fan tell me once that I had great calves. Maybe you want to think about them instead?" he asked, clearly making fun of me and how upset I was with him.

"Enough!" I yelled before walking back into my room. "I can't do this with you anymore. You're driving me crazy."

Killian followed me and came up behind me to wrap his arms around my shoulders. Nuzzling my neck, he said, "I want to drive you away from this place. Come with me."

He certainly didn't lack focus or persistence.

"I can't."

"Yes, you can."

I turned in his hold and looked up at him. As much as he made me crazy, I couldn't deny that I liked having him around. And my body had already kicked into overdrive with just a single touch from him.

But I couldn't forget why I'd been so happy to fly away the other night.

"I don't want to feel things for you, Killian. Do you understand that?"

Hurt flashed in his eyes, and he shook his head. "No, I don't. Why do you want to deny you like me as much as I like you?"

"Do you know what it felt like to sit here on my bed and watch you and that woman walk down that red carpet the other night? I know I had no right to be upset by that, but I was. I don't want to feel that way, and you made me feel that."

He stroked my cheek and leaned down to kiss me softly on the lips. "Athena is just a friend. Actually, she's not even that. We used to date but broke up a while ago. She needed someone to walk the red carpet with her at that stupid premiere. That's all it was. I flew out just in time to do that and flew back the same night on the red eye. What you saw on that stupid show was literally all we did together."

None of what he said sounded like a lie, but the problem was worse than him possibly not telling me the truth. Just feeling that way meant there was the real risk he could hurt me.

I hung my head as all the frustration of the past few hours ebbed out of me. Pulling me into his arms, he held me to him, and as much as I hated to admit it, I felt good for the first time in days.

Killian kissed the top of my head and whispered, "I'm sorry you had to see that and you thought I was just another asshole guy. I didn't know if we were at that place where we told one another things like when we're leaving town."

Looking up at him, I said, "We weren't, and that only made what I was feeling worse."

"Well, I'm sorry anyway. Let me make it up to you. Come with me tonight."

My defenses melted away as he stared down at me with those beautiful eyes and smiled like I was the most important person in the world to him. "Where are you taking me?"

"Anywhere. Everywhere. I've got a car, and we've got the open road."

"I have a job, Killian. Don't you have one too?"

"I do, but I can take a few days away with the only woman I want to spend time with. As for your job, you're an executive at your family's company, so I can't imagine you can't take a few days off too."

Nothing seemed to tamp down his enthusiasm for this plan of his to get away. "I don't have any makeup on and my hair's a mess."

He shook his head. "Doesn't matter and no it's not. Anything else?"

"It does matter to me. I have nothing packed."

Killian kissed me on the forehead. "Then you put on some makeup, and I'll pack you a bag. Don't be surprised if all I pack are socks, though."

I looked up at him and rolled my eyes. "You're insane."

"You have five minutes starting now."

When I didn't move, he leaned down to kiss me and whispered against my lips, "Four minutes and fifty three seconds."

This was crazy. I couldn't believe I was going to run off with Killian for a few days. I'd never done anything like this in my entire life, but something about how carefree he was made me want to do it.

And my gut wasn't telling me no. I just prayed it wasn't making a mistake this time.

CHAPTER FIFTEEN

TRESSA

JUST BEFORE MIDNIGHT, WE DROVE up a long driveway to an enormous old pale blue house on a secluded road in the Catskills. All the way there, we talked about what Killian had done in his career, and I found myself giggling at more of his silly jokes. I'd driven upstate countless times, and never before had I enjoyed it so much.

He parked the car and leaned forward to look out the windshield at the old house. "I hope it has running water."

"I wouldn't worry. You'd be surprised at what these older homes have going for them," I said, knowing from my childhood how houses like this held great possibilities.

Killian looked at me in surprise and then nodded. "That's right. You're an old fashioned girl. I forgot."

"I don't necessarily like houses like this more than my penthouse, but I grew up in one of these older homes. They have some really interested things to them."

"Since I grew up in an apartment above a grocery store in Nebraska, I wouldn't know about that kind of thing," he said with a wink.

"Well, look for cold spots in places and creaky floorboards that make sneaking up on people next to impossible."

"Aren't cold spots signs of paranormal activity or something like that?"

The serious look on his face told me he hadn't been joking.

Rolling my eyes at the idea of supernatural cold spots, I laughed. "Not that I know of. Mostly it just means that the house is old and poorly insulated."

He shrugged at my purely logical answer and leaned over to kiss me. "Well, if we find one, I promise to keep you warm. Of course, it is May, so I don't think there will be a lot of cold spots tonight."

"I guess I'll be on my own to fend off any chills then," I teased.

Shaking his head, he kissed me quickly before turning to get out of the car. "No way. I'll be on the job keeping you warm. Don't you worry."

I moved to follow him and saw he had other ideas. Racing around the front of the car, he opened my door and bowed. "You have to give me a chance to be a gentleman," he said with that sexy smile of his.

He took my hand and helped me out as he explained whose house we were looking at. "It's one of my teammates'. He's one of those people who's all about old things. Houses. Cars. You name it. He bought it last year and offered it to me when I said I wanted to get away. He didn't say anything about what it looks like on the inside, so brace yourself. It could be rough."

I scanned the outside of the blue Colonial style home and had a feeling the inside would be beautiful. There was something about houses like this that held up against the test of time.

"You might be surprised. People pay good money for homes in this area. I'm guessing this has at least four bedrooms and at least a couple acres of land. But I'm a little surprised one of your teammates bought a house all the way out here. It's not exactly a place for a young guy."

Killian took me by the hand and walked toward the front door. "Darius mentioned something about liking how quiet it is here. From what I can see, there's nobody nearby, so it's probably deathly quiet most of the time."

As we walked into a dark entryway, I nudged him in the side. "I'm guessing you aren't a big fan of silence since you called it deathly quiet."

"Not in a pitch black house where I can't seem to find the damn light switch I'm not. Every horror movie I've ever seen has had this exact scene. If I can't turn on the light in about three seconds, we're out of here. We can stay at that motel we saw on the road on the way up."

I clung to his arm as the two of us walked in tandem toward the wall and Killian felt his way in search of the light switch. I hoped he found it before the time was up because by the looks of that motel, I had a feeling we'd be spending the night with a family of roaches sleeping on top of a bedspread that likely had stains from someone's murder still on it.

"Found it!" Killian yelled out just before a light above us turned on and brightened up the beautiful foyer we stood in.

"Hey, this is nice. I like all the wood," he said as we swiveled our heads to look around at the home we'd walked into.

"Let's see the rest of the place. I bet it's beautiful."

We walked into a room to our right that looked like a sitting room or living room. Killian's friend hadn't furnished it with much other than a grey couch and a white wingback chair, so it looked pretty empty. The lack of even a rug highlighted great hardwood floors, though. Like in the foyer and hallway, woodworking all along the walls with wainscoting decorated the room, but in here, it had been painted white instead of remaining the original dark wood.

Killian looked around and said, "It feels like a farmhouse. Or what I think a farmhouse would feel like since I've never been in one. Let's find the kitchen and get a drink."

After walking through what seemed like a dining room that had nothing but a single old wooden chair placed in the corner, we reached a kitchen that instantly took my breath away. Unlike the other rooms we'd seen so far, this one had been completely modernized with stainless steel appliances, including a chef's stove, and a black granite countertop that made the white painted wood cabinets stand out stunningly.

I stopped just inside the doorway as Killian headed directly for the refrigerator. "Wow."

Peeking his head around the door, he smiled. "Now this is what I'm talking about. I can do old if a house has a kitchen like this. And even better, Darius made sure the fridge is stocked. Check it out!"

Killian hadn't exaggerated. Looking in, I saw enough food to feed an army. "Are we going to be joined by other people? That's a lot of food."

He turned around holding a bottle of red wine in his hand and flashed me a devilish smile. "No one but the two of us for as long as we want to stay. Time to find a corkscrew and get this getaway started."

"I thought it already started. You know, with the drive up?"

As he rummaged through drawers to find the corkscrew, he laughed. "No. That was getaway foreplay. This is the real thing. Where the hell does he keep the damn corkscrew? He has wine but nothing to open it."

I began opening cabinet doors to help in the search, but a minute later he announced he'd located the all-important corkscrew, lifting it high above his head as he said, "Found it! It was in a drawer with those holder things you use to hold ears of corn and are shaped like ears of corn."

Killian poured us both a glass of wine and as the first sip slowly eased its way down my throat, I felt my body warm. I didn't know Darius, but he knew good wine.

"So, tell me where did you fly out of when you went away?"

I hadn't expected that to come out of Killian's mouth after he took his first drink of wine. What a strange question. "That's odd. I don't think I've ever been asked that."

Killian leaned against the countertop and took another sip of wine. "Well, I like to think I offer firsts in a number of areas."

"Teterboro. My company's private plane always takes off from there. Why?"

"Because my publicist couldn't find any flight plan for any plane from Stone Worldwide flying out of the New York area. Where's Teterboro?"

"I have to tell you that's got a very strong stalker vibe to it that right there. Why would she want to know that?"

He took a sip of wine and placed his glass on the countertop. "Because I wanted to know it and I asked her to find out."

This conversation was making me uneasy. "Why?"

"Because I wanted to know where you went so I could find you there."

"And do what exactly?" I asked, challenging him.

"Surprise you at your hotel. I'd think by now that you'd be almost expecting that from me."

"Yes, a whole week of knowing you and I'm already used to the unexpected from you," I said with a smile as I secretly thought to myself that it had crossed my mind that he'd try to visit me in London.

"Were you disappointed I didn't show up?" he asked in that cute way that told me he wanted to hear I missed him.

But I didn't want to give him that. Not yet.

"I was furious with you, so you should be happy you didn't show up."

He walked over to me and stopped to place his wine glass on the island in the center of the room where I'd been standing the whole time. Leaning down, he kissed me softly on the lips and smiled.

"Well, you know that you shouldn't have been furious with me, so are you disappointed now that I didn't show up in London?"

"I don't even know how to make heads or tails of that, Killian. I think you might be certifiably crazy."

He looked up like he was thinking about how crazy he actually might be and then looked down at me, shaking his head. "I'm not crazy. Well, maybe a little, but only about you."

When he said things like that, I couldn't deny that just being around him made me happy. Something about the way he didn't seem to need to ever hold back on what he felt or said made me want to be that free. I couldn't be, not yet at least, but I wanted to be.

Turning away, I took a drink of my wine and pretended to study the room around us. "I'm sticking with my original diagnosis. You're crazy. My own crazy stalker. I can't decide if that scares the hell out of me or makes me chuckle."

Gently, he took my chin between his thumb and forefinger and turned my head to face him. "You know, not that I'm a stalker, but you pretty much make it so hard for a man that he has to resort to basically stalking you just to get you to see him, Tressa."

"Maybe that's just my way to weed out men who aren't worthy."

Killian smiled and took the glass of wine out of my hand. "Good to know I pass the test."

"Don't you think you're jumping ahead of things?" I asked as he slid his arm around my waist and pulled me to him.

"No. I believe in thinking positively. I have no doubt I'm passing all your tests."

"Do you go into everything in life like that?" I asked, amazed at how confident the man always was. Did nothing ever make him doubt himself?

Nodding, he grinned, his eyes sparkling as he gazed down at me. "Yeah. There's no other way to be. If you have the goods, then all you need to do is use them to the best of your ability and you'll succeed every time."

"I can't decide if you're confident or cocky."

His hands slid down from my waist to cup my ass, pulling me toward his body so I felt his already hard cock press against me. "Cocky is thinking you're good when you're not but you can bullshit your way through it. Confident is knowing you're good because you are. I'm confident."

"Too confident, I think," I murmured against his ear as he dipped his head to nibble on my shoulder.

He looked up and faked a hurt expression. "How could you say that? Haven't I proven more than once that I'm the best at what I do?"

"Are we talking about football or something else?" I asked, loving how he played along with my teasing. "Because if we're talking about something else, I'm not sure I'm ready to reward you with the title of best."

His hurt expression melted away, replaced by a sensual look that told me my time for teasing him had ended. "Then I'm just going to have to prove it to you tonight so you know who you're dealing with."

Scooping me up in his arms, he threw me over his shoulder and began walking through the house as I protested. "What are you doing? Where are you taking me, Killian?"

"Watch your head," he said, completely ignoring my questions, as he walked through the doorway to head for the stairs.

"Put me down! I can walk on my own," I said, lightly pounding my fists against his muscular back. I'd felt that back while he was on top of me more than once. My pummeling him likely didn't even register.

"I know you can walk on your own," he said before slapping my ass hard with the palm of his hand.

While I watched the downstairs disappear step by step, I couldn't believe he pulled this caveman act on me. If he was any other man, I would have screamed and pitched a fit until he put me down, but something in the way Killian did it so playfully made me not hate it.

Still, I couldn't let him think I liked his prehistorical man routine, so I continued to hit his back to get him to stop. "Are you even feeling any of these punches?"

He laughed before he turned at the top of the stairs to walk down the hall. "Not really. It's sort of like having one of those massager things working on my back. You can hit harder if you want. That might feel okay."

I pulled my arm back and hit him as hard as I could, but still I got no reaction. "Don't make fun of my boxing ability."

"You know I can practically hear you pouting," he said with a chuckle as he opened the door to a room at the end of the hallway. "Head down again."

I dropped my head against his lower back and waited for him to put me down now that we'd made it to a bedroom, but instead, he lifted me off his shoulder and threw me into the air toward the bed. I landed with a thud on the mattress, which thankfully wasn't hard as a rock or I'd be crippled.

Stunned, I looked up as he began lifting his black T-shirt over his head. "I can't believe you tossed me onto this bed like a basket of laundry!"

He poked his head out from underneath his shirt and smiled. "Like clean laundry. Nobody ever tosses dirty laundry onto a bed. That's something."

I opened my mouth to say it didn't matter, but nothing came out. The man had a way of making me speechless. Better for me to just watch him take his clothes off anyway. It was definitely a more enjoyable thing than verbally sparring with him.

Killian tossed his shirt at the foot of the bed and unbuttoned his jeans before stopping to face me. "Am I the only one getting naked here?"

Shrugging, I leaned back on my elbows. "I was enjoying myself watching you. Feel free to continue."

Enjoying myself was truly an understatement. Killian's body was as close to perfection as I'd ever seen, much less experienced. All this time I'd had so little respect for athletes. Clearly, I'd never considered how incredible all that working out was for their bodies.

My eyes traveled over his broad, defined shoulders that flared into muscular biceps and thick forearms covered in tattoos of images and words I'd never really looked at before that moment. One on his right arm looked like something tribal, and another on his left forearm said something about success, but as I tried to read it, he unzipped his pants and my gaze focused on his washboard abs and his lack of underwear beneath his jeans.

"Do you always go commando?" I asked as he stepped out of them and tugged on my legs to drag me toward him.

He didn't answer my question, instead removing my shoes first. When he moved up to the white capris I'd chosen to wear with my favorite blue T-shirt, he ran his hands over my calves before answering, "No, but I had a plan for tonight, so underwear weren't really needed for this job. I gave them the night off."

As he pulled my capris down my legs, I helped him by wriggling out of them. "A plan? What plan?"

I had no doubt he'd had a plan. The man always seemed to have something planned for me.

Killian lifted his head to look up at me and smiled. His green eyes had a twinkle in them like that first night we got together, and I had a hunch I knew what this plan of his had entailed just by that look in his eyes.

"Well, I was either going to get you to come up here with me, or I was going to spend the night at your penthouse. Either way, I didn't need underwear."

He slid his hands up the outside of my legs and hooked his thumbs through my underwear, tickling me and making me giggle. "That seems pretty presumptuous since I'd told you not more than an hour earlier that I hated you."

In one swift movement, he yanked my panties off and tossed them over to where he'd deposited his shirt. "Loathed. I think it's important to get the sentiment correct."

"Loathed. I remember. Still seems pretty presumptuous."

Pushing my legs apart with his knee, he lowered himself down on top of me. Staring deep into my eyes, he said, "The word you're looking for is confident, remember?"

He thrust his hips forward slowly, and in seconds, his cock filled me completely. Whatever it was called, Killian was that and so much more.

CHAPTER SIXTEEN

KILLIAN

TRESSA WRAPPED HER LEGS AROUND my waist and tilted her hips to take all of me on my second thrust into her tight cunt. She moaned sweetly in my ear as I began pumping into her, making my body crave her even more.

For hours, I'd wanted to be inside her. When we were together, I knew we could overcome all the differences she was so sure should keep us apart. All of that meant nothing as soon as she let herself enjoy what we had between us.

I loved fucking her. The icy, distant woman who insisted on being difficult with me melted at my touch, turning me on more than she could imagine. The change between that Tressa and this one who moaned my name and begged me to fuck her harder never ceased to amaze me. After that first time together, I wanted nothing more than to figure out how to get the ice queen who put me through my paces to be the woman who wanted me as much as I wanted her.

As I pushed my hips forward to fill her once more, I thought back to the morning after she bid on me and remembered my fantasy about her riding my cock. Sliding out of her, I rolled her over on top of me. She looked down at me and her mouth made that adorable pout I couldn't deny made me want her even more.

"Why did you do that?" she sulked.

With my hands on her hips, I positioned her over me. "I want you on top."

Tressa pulled her T-shirt off and then removed her bra, tossing them off to the side. Leaning down, she kissed me, sliding her tongue into my mouth before playfully sinking her teeth into my lip.

"So you want me on top? I like a change of pace," she purred in my ear.

My cock nudged up against her ass as my need to be inside her ratcheted up another notch and the thought of my fantasy of her actually coming true made me hard as a rock. She rolled her hips to take me inside her, and the next moment I was filling her completely.

Tressa sat up on me and began to ride my cock like her body was made for me. She looked like a goddess fucking me, her long dark hair teasing my chest just like I fantasized. I watched in awe as her inhibitions disappeared with each time she rocked her hips to take me deeper into her cunt. Her eyes closed, she rode me better than any other women ever had, and I loved it.

When I thought I couldn't handle any more, she looked down at me and smiled in the way only a woman who knew her own power could. Her dark eyes fixed on mine, and I reached up to cup her breasts. She moaned loudly and then leaned forward so I could take one deep pink nipple into my mouth.

I sank my teeth into her tender skin and felt her body contract around my cock as she began to come. She bucked against me with abandon as each wave of her orgasm rolled through her. I stuffed my hands in her hair and tugged hard to force her to still on my cock as my release ripped through me, flooding her pussy as I groaned with relief.

Fuck, this woman knew how to give a man what he needed.

Tressa collapsed on top of me and made a sound like a whimper next to my ear. "That was incredible, Killian."

I ran my fingertips over her back as she continued to recover from coming. "I want you to know that was even better than when I fantasized about it."

Lifting her head, she looked down at me. "What do you mean?"

"I fantasized about doing exactly that the night after the auction before I even formally met you. I told you. I couldn't stop thinking about you from the moment I laid eyes on you."

A slow smile lit up her face. "You're the first man to ever say anything like that to me."

Kissing her, I whispered against her lips, "Trust me. Other men have thought it too. They just didn't have the balls to tell you."

"I'm glad you did."

"That's what you get with a confident guy. Confidence has its perks."

Closing her eyes, she nuzzled the space between my jaw and my neck and moaned, "Mmmm…I see that."

A few seconds later, she took a deep breath in and moaned again. "I need to know what cologne you wear. You smell delicious. It was one of the first things I noticed about you that night at the auction."

I shook my head and laughed. "I don't wear any cologne. That's all me."

Tressa sighed and kissed my neck. "Mmmm…"

As we lay there naked in one another's arms and me still inside her, it felt like Tressa had been a part of my life forever. I pushed her hair back and glanced down at her face. Her eyes closed, she looked so sweet.

"I wish I'd grabbed our glasses before you went all Cro-Magnon on me," she said with a smile. "I could really go for a drink of something right now."

"Me too," I said as I started to move out from underneath her.

But she stopped me, clinging to my neck and refusing to let me go. "Not yet. I can handle dehydration for a little while. Just stay here."

"Okay."

I wrapped my arms around her and heard her sigh next to me. I liked the fact that I could give her this momentary contentment I doubted she found much of in the rest of her life. Not that I was usually so interested in how anyone I slept with spent their time when I wasn't around. As I lay there while Tressa traced her fingernail over my collarbone, I couldn't remember anyone who'd made me care like she did.

In a quiet voice, she whispered next to my ear, "I think you've hypnotized me or something. I'm guessing it's your eyes. That's how you did it, isn't it?"

Sometimes she could be so cute.

Leaning back, I lifted her head so I could see her face. She looked up at me with a dreamy feel to her eyes like I hadn't seen before in her.

"Why do you think I hypnotized you?"

Tressa drew her eyebrows in toward her nose in an expression that seemed strangely unhappy considering the orgasm I'd given her and that she hadn't wanted me to leave the bed just a minute ago. Confused, I waited to hear her answer as a lick of worry flickered inside my brain over what she'd say.

"Because the Tressa I usually am would have never let you take me away. She would have never spoken to you again after the other night and that premiere. So I can only conclude you've somehow hypnotized me, and the only way I figure that could have happened is with your eyes. I thought they had a hypnotic quality to them when I first saw you up on that stage, so my guess is you did something that night and I've been under your spell ever since. I haven't been able to determine how you keep me under it when you aren't around, though, I have to admit."

I shook my head and tried not to laugh at how cute she sounded trying to understand why she was happy. "I don't think I have that power, honestly. I have a lot of skills, but hypnotism has never been one of them that I know of."

She ran her finger over my cheekbone and pointed at my eye. "Well, there's something going on because I don't run off with men or give them second chances. Ever."

"Don't think about it. Just enjoy it."

Rolling away from me, she turned her head so I couldn't see her face clearly. "I can't help it, Killian. That's what I do. I think. It's just who I am."

"Aren't you allowed to have fun? There's got to be room in your life for that."

I saw the corner of her mouth turn down, and she said, "I think I might be one of those people who can't have fun. Not the way others do."

"What do you mean?"

Instead of answering me, she slid out from under the sheets and walked out of the room, mumbling, "Nothing. I'll be back."

I lay there confused as to how that had all turned bad so quickly and wondering where the hell she planned to go without even a pair of underwear on her body. Looking around, I saw no way there could be a bathroom attached to this room. That must be where she went.

And then a few minutes turned into ten and then fifteen minutes. She had no clothes on. Where the hell had she gone to? And what was that noise that sounded like someone had turned on a waterfall outside in the middle of the night?

A quick walk down the hallway gave me my answers. The door to the bathroom stood open showing the light on, so I peeked in and saw her sitting in the tub, her arms hugging her knees as the water filled up around her.

"Just figured it was time to grab a bath?" I asked with a chuckle.

Tressa looked up at me and gave me a tiny smile. "I came in here to go to the bathroom and just felt like taking a bath. I never do, even though I have that gorgeous tub in my own bathroom. I'm always in such a hurry to get in and out of the shower every day."

Leaning up against the doorframe, I reminded her that wasn't always true. "Not with me. We stayed in there until our fingers got all waterlogged."

"Okay, not always. I just wanted to take a bath."

"Sounds good. Move up," I said as I stepped into the tub and sat down behind her.

The warm water sloshed up around us and over the side of the tub as I stretched my legs out in front of me. Tressa stared back at me in shock.

"What are you doing?"

Gently, I pulled her back so she reclined against my body and wrapped my arms around her. "Taking a bath. Didn't we just have this conversation? I'm beginning to think you have short-term memory loss, you know that?"

Turning her head, she stared up at me. "Do you do this with everyone?"

"Take baths? I can honestly say the answer to that is no. In fact, this might be the first bath I've taken since I was a teenager. I'm more of a shower guy."

"You know that's not what I meant."

I kissed the top of her head and quietly said, "No, I don't, Tressa. I've never chased anyone like I've had to chase you, but I'm not going to let you ruin a good thing because you want to run away."

She sagged against me and closed her eyes. "You'll get tired of chasing me."

Weaving our fingers together, I splashed water against our bodies and squeezed her in my arms. "Then don't run."

"It's who I am," she whispered, like it was a secret I didn't already know all too well.

"Then I'll keep chasing. Don't worry. I'm an athlete. I'm used to working day and night for the prize. A little chasing doesn't bother me at all."

We sat there silently as the bathwater lapped at our legs, hers long and white and mine longer and much tanner, and I knew we'd just told the truth about who we were together. She needed a man to show her he thought she was that prize, and I needed someone worth working for. We'd found what we needed in one another, and even though she wasn't sure about it yet, I was.

Tressa was the ultimate prize, and I had every intention of winning her.

CHAPTER SEVENTEEN

KILLIAN

AFTER TWO DAYS OF BLISSFUL time in the country where Tressa's phone only rang half a dozen times, I knew we had to return to the city and get back to real life. I didn't plan on letting it sidetrack us again, though. I'd had her for two whole days without too many interruptions and without a single reporter screwing up what I was trying to do, and I intended on keeping that progress going.

She'd still run and I'd still chase, but after our time at Darius's house, I believed her running away wouldn't happen as much. Or at least I hoped that would be the case once we returned to the city.

Tressa stood in the entryway looking up at the ceiling and then at the rooms on both sides of the hallway just before we left. With a smile, she said, "This house reminds me of the house I grew up in. I know it sounds strange, but I think I like something old like this more than my penthouse."

Looking at me, she shrugged. "Crazy, right?"

"Not at all. You're an old-fashioned girl. I knew that from the first time we talked."

An expression full of skepticism settled into her face. "I think you're already remembering our history incorrectly, Killian. The first time we talked didn't tell you I was old-fashioned. That phone call told you I was difficult."

I couldn't help but laugh at her insistence to be thought of as something most women would have hated. "Difficult. Old-fashioned. What's it matter? All I knew was you weren't like anyone

I'd ever met before. Let's say you were unique."

She considered that description of her for a moment and nodded. "I can go with unique."

Leaning down, I kissed her just as her phone rang. "Do these people not understand I was going for a moment in time there?"

"They have no respect for romance," she said as she quickly opened her bag and rifled through it to find her phone. "This won't take more than a minute. I promise."

When she finally fished it out of her bag, she smiled. "It's just my father. Hang on."

Stepping a few feet away, she said, "Hi, Dad. What's up?"

I watched as her expression changed from happy to serious, and by the time the call had ended, I knew something was wrong. "Hey, everything okay?"

As she put her phone back in her bag, she forced a smile. "I'm sure it will be fine. Do you mind if we take a little detour to my parents' house? I promise it won't take long there. I just want to talk about a few things with my father, and I'd rather do it in person."

Why she thought I wouldn't want to see her father again escaped me. The man was a huge fan of my team. Why wouldn't I want to meet him again?

"Not a problem. You just tell me where and we're on our way."

LESS THAN AN HOUR LATER, we rolled up to a house that looked nothing like the one we'd just left. Darius had purchased an older home with some land. The place where Tressa grew up was an estate complete with security manning the main gate and a home that resembled a mansion.

"I think your description of the house you grew up in needs some work," I joked as the car came to a stop in front of the enormous home.

She looked out the window and then at me. "Your friend's house had a very similar feel to this one, but I get your point.

They're both older homes, though, so I was right on that."

I moved to get out of the car, but Tressa clamped her hand down on my forearm, stopping me. Turning back, I saw pure worry in her dark eyes.

"What's wrong?"

She hesitated a few seconds before sighing. "My mother is going to ask you questions about our relationship. I feel like I should warn you. Sorry."

"Why? I'm sure she'll be great."

Tressa screwed her face into a grimace. "Well, it's just the way she is. My mother's an artist, so she works a lot on the emotional level of things. Think of the exact opposite of me, pretty much."

I leveled a stare of disbelief at her. "You're not emotional? Since when?"

Rolling her eyes, she sighed. "My mother doesn't do icy. I get that from my father. My mother does chatty and feely. I thought you should be forewarned."

"So what do you want me to tell her? The truth or something nice?"

"What's the truth?" Tressa asked.

I smiled before kissing her and said, "That I'm crazy about you and might be a stalker, but that's not entirely my fault because you make it hard on a guy."

She laughed and shook her head. "And the something nice?"

"That I'm new to the city and you're the only woman who will talk to me and that's just because you paid ten grand for me."

A sound like a growl came out of her, and she said, "I don't like either of those choices. Maybe you should just leave the talking about us to me. I know my mother better. I can maneuver around any of her questions."

I shrugged and opened the car door. "For the record, I liked both of those answers, but since this is my first time meeting your mother, I'll let you take the lead this time. But eventually in the future at some point I'm going to let it slip that you played hard to get, but I did the work a man was supposed to in order to have a woman like you."

Looking back at her, I winked and added, "Or I might tell her that I have an addiction to women who are wild in bed and you fit the bill perfectly."

She blushed in that way that looked so cute, and I knew I'd calmed her worries for the moment. When she was like that, Tressa was downright sweet.

FIVE MINUTES AFTER WE WALKED in the door, Tressa and her father hurried off to his office to discuss work, leaving me alone with her mother. It didn't take me long to see Tressa hadn't been wrong about how her mother would want to know about our relationship.

Taking my arm, she guided me to the kitchen as she asked, "Would you like a drink? We have water and iced tea, and there might be soda in the refrigerator. I can look."

"Water or iced tea works, thanks."

She said nothing more and a minute later handed me a glass of iced tea. "It's sweetened."

I took a sip and smiled. "Thanks."

Somehow, the feeling between us had turned, even though she still wore a smile. I couldn't put my finger on why, but I had a sense Tressa's mother didn't like me. I hadn't said much at all since we got there, so I wondered if she'd heard something about my past. It wasn't like any of it was a secret, unfortunately.

"My daughter seems to like you, Killian."

I waited for her to continue, but Nina stopped speaking and simply stared across the kitchen island at me. In her eyes, I saw a look very similar to Tressa's. She'd been wrong when she said they weren't much alike. I had a feeling behind the kind blue eyes and friendly smile was a sharp woman as bright as her husband and daughter.

So I decided to be straightforward with her as I had been with Tressa and Tristan.

"I hope so. I like her. A lot."

"I'm curious how you got her to warm up to you."

Nina had clearly decided to be frank with me too. Good. I liked people who didn't pull any punches.

"I'm not exactly her type?" I said with a chuckle before taking a sip of sweet tea.

Nina shook her head. Arching a single eyebrow, she said, "Not at all. My daughter is a very serious young woman, and from what I've observed, you're the exact opposite of her. She tends to date equally as serious young men."

From the small amount Tressa had told me about her past, I could only imagine the kind of men she usually spent her time with.

Feeling there was more Nina wanted to say, I offered her a chance. "Observed? I'm guessing you don't mean seeing us together for five minutes today."

"No, I don't mean that. When my husband told me you and Tressa had been dating, I checked out who you were. I'm not someone who follows football like Tristan, so I had no idea who Killian Brenton was. It didn't take long to find out, though. You're someone who photographers love. Picture after picture of you. I could still be looking at them right now there were so many."

I had a feeling charm wasn't going to work on Nina Stone, but I smiled and said what she hadn't. "And most of them with women, right?"

My question hung in the air between us for a long moment before she said, "My husband tells me that quarterbacks are very intelligent athletes. Is this true?"

"I like to think so. I can't speak for all quarterbacks, but I think I'm pretty intelligent."

"My daughter isn't like the women I saw on your arm in those pictures. Tressa is…"

Nina stopped for a moment as if she was trying to think of the right way to describe her daughter, but I knew exactly what she was saying. Smiling, I finished her sentence for her.

"Difficult. At least that's what she says she is. I think a better word for her is unique."

My description of Tressa made Nina's eyes open wide, but then she nodded. "I can't deny that, but I'd say she's challenging. I like that better than difficult. Challenging and unique are exactly what Tressa is."

I leaned forward toward where she stood on the other side of the kitchen island and said, "Well, if I'm being honest here, she puts me through my paces at every step of the way. I told her I'd probably wait to say this until some day in the future, but I might as well say it now because it's the truth. She requires a lot of work, but she's worth every bit of it."

A slow smile lit up Nina's expression. "I like that, and I hope you two do have a future together. I have to admit I never thought I'd see her of all my children so relaxed and happy."

Before I could say making her happy was my only goal, Tressa poked her head into the kitchen. With worry filling her eyes, she asked, "What are you guys doing in here?"

Nina gave me a knowing look before turning to face her daughter. "Killian was telling me about how quarterbacks are intelligent and hard-working."

Tressa stared at her for a moment before turning to look at me as if to get confirmation that was actually what we had been discussing. I nodded and shrugged my shoulders. "Intelligent and hard-working. That's me."

"Well, Dad and I are finished with work, so we need to head back to the city now."

That less-than-subtle hint that she wanted to leave meant my time with Nina had ended, so I took a final sip of my iced tea and held my hand out to shake hers. "It was very nice to meet you."

Instead of shaking my hand, she wrapped her arms around my body and hugged me like we'd known each other for years. I saw

Tressa's eyes open wide in surprise at her mother embracing me and smiled at her. I seemed to have won her over.

"It was great to meet you too," Nina said as she stepped back away from me. "I hope this won't be the last time we see each other."

As we all walked toward the front door and Tristan pulled Tressa aside to tell her something he'd just thought of about work, Nina said in a low voice only I could hear, "I can see why my husband and Tressa like you. Just remember that even though my daughter is clearly a fan of yours, she's not the same kind as her father."

Tressa kissed her mother goodbye while I wondered what she meant by that. That Tressa and Tristan weren't the same kind of fan or they weren't the same kind of person?

Chapter Eighteen

Tressa

By the time Killian stepped foot on the field for his first season game as the New York quarterback, we were officially a couple for just over four months. In that time, I'd grown a little more comfortable with the press around him, and although I didn't know for sure, I had a feeling he'd done something to make sure they weren't in our faces twenty-four seven. Like he promised as we sat together in that bathtub at the house in the Catskills, he hadn't stopped chasing me.

Even though I'd tried to run away a few times.

The press tried to make us out to be some high powered super couple, but the truth was we were just Tressa and Killian. I worked my job, and he worked his. I didn't go to see him play, despite my father offering me prime seats in his box for each home game. I didn't feel like I belonged in that part of Killian's world because of how I felt about dealing with the press. I knew he would have loved to know I was there, but I wasn't ready for that just yet.

That didn't mean I didn't watch him play and love every second of it, even though I had no idea about the rules of football or a clue about any of the other players around him on the field. It didn't matter. I was only watching him anyway.

He had a game in New Orleans on the first Sunday in December, and as I turned on the TV to watch, I thought about doing something I'd considered for the last game he had out of town. I'd been spending more time with Diana over the past few months, so I wondered if she'd want to watch with me.

I knocked on her door and waited for her to answer. When she opened it, she smiled and pulled me inside her room.

"Look who's here!"

I saw Ethan stand up from the couch, and I looked around for any sign of Summer. She hadn't mentioned spending time with Diana this weekend when we talked the other day.

"Am I interrupting? I can come back later," I quickly offered, knowing how close my brother and sister were and not wanting to intrude on their time together.

Ethan waved me toward him and sat down on the couch. "I thought you'd be in the Big Easy this weekend. Isn't that where Killian is today?"

"I don't travel to the cities where he plays. I don't even go to the games here in New York," I sheepishly admitted as I made my way to where he sat.

"Why?" he asked with confusion in his voice that matched his expression. "Isn't that a perk girlfriends of major sports stars get?"

"Maybe. I don't know. I spend very little time in that part of Killian's world. You know how I am about publicity."

Diana hugged me from behind and then joined Ethan on the couch. "We were just hanging out. Come sit with us!"

"Oh. I don't want to intrude. I just wanted to come down and ask you if you wanted to watch the game with me upstairs. It's okay, though. You guys had plans, so it's okay."

Once the words left my mouth, I felt awkward standing in that hotel room. I didn't want to feel that way around my siblings, but it had been a long time since the three of us did anything together, and now that I'd said that, I felt like it might have been a mistake.

Diana and Ethan exchanged glances, and then she turned to face me. "We'd love to! Want me to bring anything?"

Her answer made me genuinely happy. Even though I knew she was only doing it because she had Ethan to come too, it felt like the old days when we all did things together.

"No, I've got stuff to drink, and we can order from the kitchen if we get hungry," I said as my excitement grew for our afternoon watching Killian play.

Ethan stood from the couch and laughed. "I don't know if lobster with clarified butter is really game day food. Why don't we order a couple pizzas?"

As they say, when in Rome, do as the Romans do. I had no idea what to eat as we watched the football game, so I agreed with him since he seemed to know better than I did.

"Okay. We can order pizzas and anything else you guys want."

"Great! Let's go so we can be at your place by kickoff," Diana said, happier than I expected at my offer.

HALFTIME CAME, AS DID THE pizza, and even though I'd had a good time with Ethan and Diana, it was patently obvious I didn't know a thing about the sport Killian played. When my brother mentioned how mobile he was out of the pocket, I couldn't find any sign of anything that even looked like a pocket on his uniform. Diana commented about something involving a screen, but I didn't know what that meant either. At least I was able to figure out what they were talking about when they kept saying he was dropping back.

Ethan tossed a piece of crust into the box on the coffee table and sat back in his chair. "This is nice. I can't remember the last time the three of us sat around and shared some pizza."

"It was that night Mom and Dad went with Aunt Jordan and Uncle Gage to that wine tasting. Remember? We ordered pizza and breadsticks and more soda than the three of us could consume in a year," Diana said as she grabbed her second slice.

I thought back to that night and remembered it slightly differently. My brother snuck his girlfriend into his bedroom, and when I saw the lights from the car coming up the drive way, he had to practically push her out the window while Diana and I distracted our parents by bombarding them with questions just as they walked through the door.

"What's that face for?" Ethan asked, tearing me from my memories.

"I was just wondering if Mom and Dad ever knew you'd brought your girlfriend over that night. Do you remember how she had to climb out your bedroom window?"

A sly smile spread across his face, and he threw his head back in peals of laughter. "I can't believe you remember that! Damn. We were right in the middle of having some fun when you yelled up about Mom and Dad pulling up the driveway. Poor Shelby. She twisted her ankle climbing down the lattice, and by the time I got down to her, she was in tears. I had to carry her all the way to the back of the estate before we snuck through the fence and she hobbled the four blocks to her house."

"And you had to run all the way back while we kept Mommy and Daddy at the front door talking about wine tasting and how Aunt Jordan and Uncle Gage were doing," Diana said with a giggle. "Daddy kept looking at Tressa and me like he suspected something, but he never asked. Thank God, because he would have seen in my eyes that I was lying."

"Then I would have had to give him my serious face because he always trusted my serious face," I said. "You still owe us for that, Ethan."

He smiled and nodded. "I know. I owe you guys for a ton of stuff from back when I was a teenager. What can I say? I don't know what I would have done without you two."

For a moment, we all looked at one another like we used to when we were younger, and it felt good. We'd drifted apart in the past few years, but I could never forget that my brother and sister were my first best friends in the world.

And then Ethan, in his usual funny way, looked over at me and said, "Are you ready to start asking questions? Because it's pretty damn obvious you had no idea what was going on in the entire first half of this game."

Leave it to my brother to point out how painfully lacking I was with the one thing Killian excelled at. I lowered my head and quietly admitted the truth.

"I honestly have no idea. Like where is this pocket in his uniform you guys keep talking about? And why can't I see the screen you keep mentioning when he passes the ball?"

My questions were met with silence for a few moments before the two of them burst into laughter. Diana leaned over on the couch and hugged me in my embarrassment.

"Don't feel bad, Tressa. Ethan knows all about football because he played it, and I know a little from those Sundays when I went to the games with Dad. But don't worry. We can help. We have a whole second half for you to ask whatever you want."

I looked up to see both Ethan and Diana eager to help me understand the game. That's what they'd always been deep down, no matter how strained things got among us. They were my brother and sister, and for good and for bad, we were family.

✧　✧　✧

THE TOUCH OF SOMEONE'S HAND on my shoulder startled me, and I sat bolt upright in bed to see Killian next to me wearing a big smile and nothing else. While my heart returned to its normal beat, I wiped the sleep from my eyes.

"Sorry. I didn't mean to wake you up. I just got back and came directly here. I figured I'd surprise you in the morning."

"It's okay. How did it all go?" I asked, knowing even in my groggy state that the team had won against New Orleans hours before.

"Twenty-eight, twenty. I had an interception, but other than that, pretty good. We're eight and two and now we're on a bye week, so I'm all yours until next Wednesday."

I stared at him, amazed at how cute he got whenever he talked about football. "I'm sorry I'm not more fun. You're on vacation, and I'm all knocked out."

Killian slid his arm around me, pulling me to him. "Shhh. Go back to sleep. We can talk more in the morning."

My nose pressed against the skin of his neck, and I inhaled, loving how he smelled so clean, like soap and water that had washed away the remnants of his day. Curling up next to him, I sighed, perfectly content to be there with him at that moment. If there was anything like bliss that existed in the world, I experienced it in his arms at times like this.

My eyes fluttered closed as Killian slowly ran his fingertip up and down my arm, lulling me back to sleep.

"BOYD, I'M ON VACATION THIS week, which you and I both know means I only want you to call me if it's an absolute emergency. The fact that there's a strike at a factory in the UK which is going to hold up the reupholstering of the lobby chairs at the London Richmont is not an emergency."

My assistant stared at me in shocked silence, which wasn't surprising since he'd never seen me take a vacation before this and he'd grown accustomed to problems always being emergencies. Both of those were my fault, but now I wanted things done differently.

"Tressa, I'm sorry. I thought you'd want to know about this right away," he said, his eyes wide with fear.

He had every reason to be afraid. The old Tressa all too often found a reason to bark at him for just about anything.

"It's okay. You don't have to apologize. The chairs in the lobby of the London Richmont will get reupholstered when they do. In the meantime, hold down the fort and only call me if there's something you can't handle that comes up. I have faith in you, Boyd. It will be fine."

I smiled because I knew he was as capable an assistant as anyone had ever had. He'd never let me down before, and I believed he'd do a great job this week while I stayed away from the office.

"Thank you, Tressa. I won't let you down."

"I know. I'm sorry I don't tell you that more often, but I've always known."

The fear in my assistant's eyes melted away at my kind words, and he visibly relaxed on the screen in front of me. "Have a wonderful vacation. I'll see you next week."

I ended the call and leaned back against the chair. From behind me, I felt Killian's hands slide over my shoulders, and I looked back at him.

"Did I wake you up with my call? I didn't mean to. It was just Boyd calling about some issue with the lobby chairs in the redesign in London."

"I heard," he said with a smile. Leaning down to kiss me, he added, "I also heard you tell him you're on vacation and not to bother you. Who are you and what have you done with my Tressa?"

"Funny. We've had this time off planned for months. The company can do without me for a week."

He walked into the kitchen and yelled back, "Again, who are you and what have you done with my Tressa? The woman I fell in love with was a hyper Type A who never took time off and worked day and night. Vacation was a four-letter word to that woman."

I sat there in my chair stunned at what he'd said. Love? Neither one of us had ever used that four-letter word before in all the time we'd been together.

Killian returned to the living room and sat down on the couch to drink his coffee as I wrestled with how I should respond. Was I supposed to tell him I loved him too? I did and had for months, but I'd never said the actual words to him. Should I just not say anything and act like I hadn't heard him say he loved me for the first time?

Lost in thought, I didn't notice he'd said something until he tapped me on the knee, tearing me from my mental tug-of-war about what to do. "What? I didn't hear you. What did you say?"

"I asked if you were okay. You looked a million miles away. Something wrong?"

Shaking my head, I tried to think of a good lie so he wouldn't know all I could think of was that he'd said he loved me, but my mind went blank.

He seemed satisfied with my non-answer answer and leaned back against the couch to close his eyes. If only I could relax after hearing those words.

I definitely loved Killian. I had for so long that I just took it for granted that he knew. I didn't know why we never said it before today. There had been hundreds of times in the past months when I could have said it. The man had pursued me when I fought him at every turn. He made me smile when no one else could, mostly with his stupid jokes and refusal to let me wallow in worry or negativity.

"You're uncharacteristically silent today, Tressa. I'm not sure I like the vacation you. I'm used to the Tressa who talks more. What's going on?"

My brain short-circuited, and I blurted out, "You said you loved me. That you fell in love with me. You've never said that before this morning."

He smiled in that sexy way that never failed to make my stomach flip and shrugged. "I've found that coming at you from a place you aren't expecting usually works best. So I didn't tell you I loved you when I first wanted to. I just decided to work it into a conversation one day. Today happened to be that day."

"I really am that difficult, aren't I?" I asked, sad that the man I loved felt like he needed to sneak his declaration of love into a conversation so I didn't give him a hard time about it.

Killian shook his head and leaned over to kiss me sweetly on the lips. "Not difficult. Unique. You've just got some walls up around you, so I decided to tunnel in instead."

Looking into his green eyes that I'd once thought might have the ability to hypnotize me into caring about him more than I wanted to, I said the words I should have said months before. "I love you, Killian."

He shrugged, and with a smile, made a joke just when he knew I needed one. "I know."

"And you love me."

"Of course I do. I've been in love with you for months. If I didn't think you'd bolt, I would have told you when I first realized it."

I hung my head and quietly said, "I'm sorry for being so…unique."

Kneeling in front of me, he smiled up at me. "Don't be. You keep me on my toes, Tressa. There are men who wouldn't appreciate that, but they're not me. And we didn't have to say the actual words I love you to feel them."

I ran my hand through his soft brown hair, and he laid his head on my thigh as I admitted the truth of how I felt. "I've loved you since that night up in the Catskills, you know that?"

"You run, and I chase you. And even after I caught you, I still chased because you'll always want to run. That's okay, though, because I'll always chase."

That was who we were. I didn't know if it would work with any other man for me or any other woman for him, but it didn't matter. It worked for us.

CHAPTER NINETEEN
TRESSA

REACHING AROUND HIM, I ADJUSTED Killian's tie as I looked at the two of us in the mirror. Just like with his tux, he wore a suit better than any man I'd ever seen. "You clean up nicely," I joked as I finished fixing his tie.

"I do, don't I?" he said with a sexy grin as he leaned forward to admire his look.

"You're so cocky, Killian. You know that?"

He raised his eyebrows in fake surprise and laughed. "Confident. Cocky doesn't have the goods to deliver. I do."

I stepped in front of him and pushed him away from the mirror. "You've done enough fawning over yourself for one night. I need to check myself out to make sure I'm ready."

Rolling his eyes, he walked over to the bed and sat down on the edge as I examined my black dress for any imperfections. I loved Killian more than I could say, but I didn't love some of the things that came with being with a man like him.

Actually, I just disliked one thing. Attending events with him where there was sure to be press in droves. He loved having his picture taken, as he always had. I still hated it, no matter how much I tried not to. I'd gotten a little better in the time we'd been together, and I didn't freeze in terror at the sight of a camera anymore, but given the choice, I'd avoid any event if I could.

From behind me, I heard him say, "You look incredible. You always do. I don't know why you worry about these things."

I ran my hand over my cheekbones wishing my makeup looked better. "I worry because I want to look good. You should care about that since every picture they take tonight will have me standing right next to you."

"You act as if that would ruin them, Tressa. You're gorgeous. You make me look better, if I'm being honest. You're the real draw anyway since there are a million pictures out there of me by now. Since this is only the fifth event we've done together, you're the one who's the new thing. I wouldn't be surprised if they asked for you and told me to step away."

Spinning around to face him, I shook my head as the mere idea of that happening filled me with terror. "Don't you dare leave me like that, Killian Brenton."

He stood and walked over to me. Taking me in his arms, he kissed me and whispered against my lips, "Uh-oh. She used my full name. This must be serious."

"Promise me you won't step away, even if someone stupidly thinks they should take a picture of me alone."

Killian's expression grew serious. "I won't step away, Tressa. Not tonight. Not ever. I promise."

I breathed a sigh of relief and the fear subsided. "Okay. Good. Now let me make sure I look perfect since we have to leave soon."

Taking a lock of hair between his fingers, he lifted it away from my head as he walked away. "You're always perfect."

I leaned in toward the mirror and wished that was true. My makeup never lasted for more than a couple hours before it started to look stale. Whipping out the mascara wand from the tube, I gave my lashes a third coat and wished I had gone with the false eyelashes this time. Frustrated, I tossed the mascara into my makeup tray and sighed at the face staring back at me in the mirror.

Why did people need so many damn pictures anyway?

KILLIAN SQUEEZED MY HAND AS the car slowly stopped in front of the Manhattan Room. One glance out the window told me the press had come out in force for the NYCBest! launch party. Dozens of people rushed the car in the few seconds we sat there, and I swallowed hard as fear swirled inside me.

He smiled sweetly and kissed me on the forehead. "This is going to be great. You look beautiful. I've got you. Remember that. I'll have your hand the whole time, so it's just like we're going out for dinner or a few drinks, right?"

Taking a deep breath, I let it out slowly as I tried to calm my nerves and racing heart. "Right. Just like that."

"I love you, Tressa," he whispered as he pressed his forehead to mine. "Thank you for being here with me tonight."

All it took were those few words, and in a second, I relaxed and my anxiety about what awaited us outside that car melted away. I squeezed his hand in return and took another deep breath.

"I love you. Let's go do this magazine launch and show them why it was a good idea to choose you as their cover model."

Killian rolled his eyes. "You sound like Sherilyn now. She's been calling me that for months since she found out they planned to put my picture on the front of their magazine's first edition. I'm not a cover model. I play football."

"I think it would be a cover model and football player as of tonight. Don't downplay this. You love it, and you know it," I teased him, knowing everything I said was true.

He did love it, and even though I still wasn't someone who appreciated the limelight, he did so I supported him.

"Fine. I like it," he grudgingly admitted. "Now let's go out there and have a good time."

A second later, he opened the car door and all I saw were reporters and cameras. Killian held my hand securely in his and helped me out of the car, standing in front of me so I had a few moments to get my bearings. Men and women barked out questions before the car door even closed behind us, but I attempted to block out the noise and focused on keeping a smile on my face as the two of us began walking toward the front door of the club.

They asked the usual questions about how he felt the team was doing and if he thought they'd go all the way to the championship. Every so often, one asked about us and our relationship, but after six months together, very few reporters seemed to focus much on that anymore. I silently thanked God that they didn't because the last thing I wanted to do was be the center of attention at any event I attended with Killian.

He was the star quarterback, the one who enjoyed the spotlight. They should focus on him and his career. We were just two people dating who'd finally said I love you a few hours before. Nothing to see here. Go find some starlet with man troubles to bother about her relationship. We're just two happy people in love.

By the time we walked into the Manhattan Room, my hand hurt from holding onto Killian's so tightly. He didn't seem to mind, though, and when I pulled mine away to stretch out my fingers, he immediately sought it out, even as he made small talk with a man standing in front of us.

When the man turned around, I leaned in next to Killian and whispered, "My hand's cramping up. I guess I was pretty nervous out there. I figured you might like your hand back for a few minutes."

"You sure? I got you. Don't forget that."

"I'm okay," I said as I continued to stretch my fingers out. "Let's celebrate your big night."

We finally made our way into the club to see balloons and streamers in the magazine's blue and red signature colors hanging from the ceiling and tied to every chair in the room. As he said something to me about balloon overkill, Sherilyn hurried over to us and latched onto his arm.

"You have to come over and meet the people who started NYCBest!" she squealed in her usual excited way. "Have you seen the enormous life-sized picture of the cover on the wall over there? Just wait until you see it!"

I'd always found Killian's publicist a bit much for my tastes, but he'd explained even though she did tend to be a little over the top sometimes, she'd been with him since his college days supporting his career in any way she could. She rarely spoke to me, and when she did I had a feeling she had to force herself to, but since I'd had to see her only a handful of times since we started dating, I put up with her and always had a smile on my face when she was nearby.

Killian looked at me and smiled. "Life-sized picture of me. Are you ready for that?" he joked.

As if she just noticed me standing by his side, Sherilyn turned her head to face me and with a big, toothy grin I felt quite certain was forced and may be causing her pain, she said in a far less excited voice, "Oh, hi, Tressa. I didn't realize you were coming tonight. Killian's told me how much you hate these promotional things. I thought you might beg off since this one surely would have more cameras and press than others because NYCBest! is a media outlet."

I didn't need to have spent the last five years at my father's side learning the ins and outs of business to know that hadn't been an enthusiastic greeting. I felt Killian take my hand in his and give it a gentle squeeze, and the desire to explain to his publicist that I supported him no matter how many cameras and reporters were around faded away.

That didn't mean she'd get anything more than the icy Tressa that always existed inside me for just these occasions, though.

"It's so nice to see you, Sherilyn. Are you here with someone or alone?" I asked with my nicest smile in my sweetest voice.

Killian brought my hand to his lips and kissed my finger while I watched her eyes grow big at my comment. I took that as approval for how I'd acted and simply smiled when she said something about being there to work and not socialize before she made some excuse about needing to speak to someone and hurried away.

"Wouldn't all a PR person does be considered socializing?" I wondered aloud as we walked toward the life-sized picture of Killian and the inaugural cover of NYCBest! Magazine.

Pulling me close to him, he leaned down and whispered in my ear, "Most women would want me to say something to Sherilyn, but I like how you handle it all by yourself."

I saw in his green eyes that he had approved of the way I dealt with her and stood on my toes to kiss him. "I don't need anyone to fight my battles for me, Killian. I don't understand why she doesn't like me, but as long as you like having her as your publicist, I'll have to be around her. She gets from me what she gives, so I promise if she ever becomes nice, I'll be as sweet as pie with her."

"No way. Only I got sweet as pie Tressa," he said in a hurt voice I knew wasn't genuine.

"Well, then she'll get cordial Tressa. How's that?"

"Perfect. Brace yourself. There are about to be two life-sized me's in front of you. Are you ready for that?"

I giggled at his joke and walked with him into the room to see the other version of him that graced the cover of the magazine. I stopped dead as it came into view, surprised to see Killian not in his uniform or in a tux or anything like that. The picture they'd chosen showed him in a pair of jeans slung low on his hips and barely hanging on and wearing nothing else.

Everywhere it seemed was his naked and tanned skin.

His muscular shoulders. His broad chest. His perfect washboard abs.

That spot just below his belly button where I dragged my nails across when I went down on him because it drove him crazy.

I knew it was silly, but seeing him so exposed like that to all those people milling around us felt embarrassing, like they shouldn't see him practically naked right there in life-sized form.

Opening my mouth to say something—anything about how great it looked—I couldn't get a single word out. They were trapped somewhere between my brain and my mouth, spending time with a fair dose of shock at what I was looking at.

Sherilyn came bouncing toward us with a smile that spread

from ear to ear and clamped her hand down on Killian's left arm. "Isn't it great? I know you weren't sure, but at least it's not nude like they first wanted. I personally don't see why you didn't want to do it nude since they were never going to just show all of you on the cover anyway. But this still looks incredible, doesn't it?"

Nude? He was supposed to do that photo shoot nude? He never mentioned that when he told me about it. Granted, that was only a few weeks after we began seeing one another, but I'd remember if he told me the magazine wanted to take a picture of him nude and put it on a cover where millions of people would see him.

I felt my fingers involuntarily squeeze his hand as the thought of Killian on that cover in front of so many people made my head swim. When he'd told me about it, I had in my mind him in his uniform or something classy like a suit or a tux. The man could wear anything and looked fantastic, so naturally I assumed he'd be wearing clothes. Or at least something other than the hint of a pair of jeans that looked like his hipbones were doing their very best to keep them hanging onto his body.

"Nude wasn't ever going to happen, Sherilyn. I told you that the day you pitched me the cover. A pair of jeans worked out fine anyway. The cover looks great."

As my brain grappled with my boyfriend, the man I loved and slept with, being out in the world with practically no clothes on, I had a sense that his statement about how great the cover looked was directed toward me. Looking up, I saw him staring down at me like he was waiting for me to finally say something about that cover.

Opening my mouth, I squeaked out, "It's nice. Very nice."

"Nice? I think you can come up with a better word than nice. It's spectacular!" Sherilyn gushed far too loudly for my comfort. "There's not going to be a woman in this country who doesn't love Killian Brenton after this magazine cover starts appearing everywhere."

I had a feeling my smile had faded and a look of disgust had settled into my face, so I forced the corners of my mouth up high and nodded. "Spectacular. Definitely spectacular. Will you two excuse me? I need to find the ladies' room."

Killian's hand clung to mine, but I tugged my fingers from his hold and hurriedly walked through the crowd hoping to find an exit that wouldn't be clogged with people waiting to take someone's picture. I needed some fresh air and peace and quiet for a few minutes while I convinced myself that the cover of a single magazine wasn't a big deal.

I found a door at the back of the club and pushed it open. Outside there was a small place to stand on top of a set of stairs, so I shut the door behind me and closed my eyes. This wasn't a big deal. I wasn't sure, but I had a feeling many people had seen Killian in various stages of being dressed.

Of course they had. The man had been photographed thousands of times. This wasn't any different.

But all I could see when I closed my eyes was that cover and all of him out there for the world to see.

"You don't own him, Tressa. He's a grown man with a great body. He can show it off to whoever he likes," I mumbled to myself.

But I didn't want him to be showing it off to anyone but me.

"Don't be ridiculous. Everyone knew how he looked before this cover. Not everyone has what you have with him."

I opened my eyes and hoped I wouldn't see anyone standing nearby who could hear me. I knew how stupid my reaction to this cover was. I didn't need some stranger knowing too.

Behind me, the door opened and Killian walked out to join me on that tiny landing. The look in his eyes told me he was worried, but that only made me feel worse. I didn't want to make this about me. This night was about him, not my stupid reaction to some picture because I was possessive and jealous.

"Why did you walk away like that?" he asked as he pulled me to him. "Everything okay?"

I wrapped my arms around him and leaned my head against his chest. "I just needed some fresh air. Nothing big."

"Something's wrong. Tell me."

"No nothing's wrong," I lied, praying to God he dropped this so we could go back into the party.

Killian tilted my head back so I had to look at him. "Tell me what's wrong and I'll make it right."

"You can't make it right because it's me. I'm wrong. Let's just go back in and have a good time. I'm sure people are noticing you're not in there. Sherilyn will be tracking you down any moment now."

He put his hand against the metal door to hold it shut and turned his focus back to me. "No she won't, and I don't care who notices I'm not in there. I'm out there where I need to be. So tell me what's wrong."

There was no way I could avoid telling him what the problem was, whether now or later, so I blurted out the truth. "I've come to realize I'm a possessive woman with a streak of jealousy a mile wide. That's what's wrong."

He smiled and nodded like he already knew what I thought I'd newly confessed. "I'm pretty impressed with how long you took to come to that conclusion. Most women realize that before we get to the second date. It's the cover, isn't it? You don't like it."

Avoiding his gaze, I nodded. "I hate it. The only thing that would make it worse is if you were naked, and I think I'd have to hire a crew to buy up all the copies of the magazine if that were the case."

Instead of being upset at my pettiness, he laughed. "It's an online magazine, Tressa."

"Then I'd have to hire someone who could disable their server."

"Look at me."

I did as he ordered and saw him smiling down at me. "This body is just the outside. It's the stuff that gets on magazine covers. You get to see it all the time, but you get all the inside stuff from me too, and no one gets that but you. That's the important part of me, isn't it?"

"Yes. I know that. I know you're only with me, Killian. I just never realized how the rest of the world looks at you."

"Pretty much like you did the night you first saw me at that auction."

I cringed at the memory of my staring up at him on that stage and thinking of how much I wanted him. "That doesn't help. Not one bit does that help."

Killian cradled my face in his strong hands and gazed down at me like he only did when it was the two of us alone. "I love you, Tressa. I haven't been able to think about anyone else since the night we met. Still to this day, you're all I think about when I'm not out on the field or practicing. I am completely and utterly yours in all the ways that count, and even in the ways that don't count, like how I look on that cover. You have every part of me all to yourself. You don't have to worry what the rest of the world thinks because the only person I care about is you."

I took a deep breath in and felt a sense of calm come over me. Everything he said was right. I'd been jealous and stupid about this cover, but even now he didn't make me feel foolish.

The rest of the world could have their pictures of Killian. I had what mattered.

CHAPTER TWENTY

KILLIAN

I HELD TRESSA'S HAND IN mine as we walked back into the party and began to mingle with the other guests. Her jealousy had surprised me at first, especially since she never showed me any hint that my popularity bothered her like that. As we chatted with some executive at NYCBest! Magazine, I wondered if that's why she hated coming with me anywhere the press was.

She didn't have to worry. Whatever I showed the world in pictures or interviews, no one ever saw the private me. Only Tressa got that.

Out of the corner of my eye, I saw Sherilyn practically running across the room toward us. She didn't have her usual smile on, and by the time she reached me, I wondered if she was in pain by the expression on her face.

Tugging me by the arm, she said, "We need to talk."

"About what?"

"There's an issue we need to handle."

"Whatever it is, I'll handle it tomorrow. Tonight, we're enjoying ourselves. Go get a drink and try to have a good time for once."

Sherilyn shook her head and tugged on my arm again. "No, we need to handle this now."

What the hell was she talking about? The fear written all over her face combined with the fact that my publicist would never consider me passing up a chance to be seen in public told me something serious had happened. But what could it be?

Relenting, I began guiding Tressa toward a quiet spot at the back of the club, but Sherilyn stopped me. "I think this is something we need to handle alone right now. Maybe you should send Tressa home."

Already tired of her cryptic bullshit, I stopped her right there. "No. Whatever's going on, she's part of it, so let's go."

My publicist didn't argue anymore and followed us to the corner where we could talk. I held Tressa's hand and quickly explained Sherilyn had something she needed to tell me.

"I promise this will only take a minute."

Tressa nodded and then Sherilyn pulled me down to her level to say in my ear, "A reporter just asked me for a comment about a story some gossip website released about an hour ago. Eden claims you two were together for a rendezvous the weekend of the LA game."

Eden? My ex-girlfriend Eden Mitchell? Why would she say that?

I waved away my publicist's concerns. "We haven't even spoken since we broke up last February. It's bullshit. Don't worry."

Sherilyn began searching on her phone and a few seconds later held it up for me to see. "She gave them pictures to prove it."

Staring at the screen, I saw some website named Dirt had posted about Eden's claim we were together again. Quickly, I scanned the article that mentioned my relationship with Tressa and said I'd cheated on her with Eden. Scrolling down the page, I saw the pictures they claimed prove we were together. Grainy and slightly out of focus, they showed a man and woman naked in bed together that I had to admit looked a lot like Eden and me.

But that was impossible. I hadn't been with her for nearly a year.

I pushed the phone away and shook my head. "It's a scam. I don't know why Eden would do this, but I'll find out tomorrow."

Sherilyn's gaze shifted from me to Tressa standing behind me. I turned to explain to her about how this wasn't anything important and things like this happened all the time to athletes like me and felt my heart skip a beat when I saw the look of horror on her face.

"It's nothing, Tressa. I'll get this cleared up tomorrow and it will disappear. I promise."

Shaking her head, she held up her phone and I saw she'd read the article already. She pointed at the screen and said, "She says you two were together the night before the LA game. That was in September, Killian."

My heart sank as I listened to her voice crack as she said those words. She thought I'd cheated on her.

"She's lying. I don't know why, but she is. I'll find out tomorrow. Don't worry. Nothing happened."

Tressa turned the phone to face her and looked at the pictures, enlarging them on the screen. I watched in horror as it became obvious that was me in them with Eden. I didn't know when they were taken or how they'd gotten shots of such an intimate moment between us, but I couldn't deny the pictures were real.

"She says these are pictures taken that night. You cheated on me and had someone there taking shots of the whole thing?" Tressa asked as she continued to stare at those fucking pictures.

I turned to Sherilyn and grabbed her by the shoulders. "I want this handled, so get on it right now. Find out what the fuck is going on and why. I'm taking Tressa out of here, so call me when you have something useful to tell me. Until then, don't fucking call me. Got it?"

By the time I turned back, Tressa had disappeared into the crowd. I barked out a repeat of my instructions to Sherilyn and took off, pushing past people as I searched for her. After looking everywhere at the club, including that little porch thing we'd stood on outside, I rushed out to the street to look for any sight of her, but she was gone.

I knew where she'd run to, so I broke into a sprint down the street and headed to the penthouse. If I was lucky, I'd catch her before she told that damn security guard to keep me out. I didn't have the time or patience to schmooze with him tonight, so if she beat me back to the hotel, I'd just have to use brute force to get past him.

Thankfully, some problem with a hotel patron made slipping past security easy. By the time I reached the penthouse floor, my stomach had twisted itself into a tight knot. I had no idea why Eden was lying, but I saw in Tressa's eyes as she looked at those pictures nothing but pure sadness and pain. She'd always worried about being with me because of my fame, and now that very fear had come back to haunt us.

I opened the door and saw her standing by the window staring out at the city. I practically felt her running away even as she remained in the same room with me.

"Tressa, I want to talk about this."

As I made my way across the floor toward her, she shook her head. "I don't. There's nothing to talk about."

The flatness in her voice made me stop dead in the middle of the room. My chest tightened as the distance between us made me feel like I'd never be able to reach her again.

I couldn't let that happen. Every time she ran, I chased. I never minded doing that. Tressa was worth every step I took to have her, and this time wasn't any different.

"Tressa, this isn't a big deal. I know it seems like it is, but things like this happen all the time with athletes. I have to admit I didn't peg Eden for one of the crazy ones, but obviously I was wrong. I promise I'll get to the bottom of this tomorrow and we'll never have to think about this again. But tonight, I need you to talk to me."

I waited, but no words came. I took a step toward her and slid my arms around her waist as my fears rose inside me that she had already run too far for me to catch her.

"Please talk to me, Tressa. Please."

She shook her head but remained silent. In the window's

reflection, I saw her fight back tears, so I hugged her to me, hoping to do something to make her understand I wasn't the man she thought I was.

"I would never cheat on you. Never. I've never cheated on anyone in my life, and I certainly wouldn't start with you. I love you, Tressa. You're everything to me. Please say you know I wouldn't do what that article claims I did."

In an icy voice, she answered, "I think it would be best if you got your things and left."

Turning her to face me, I shook my head in disbelief. We weren't over. I wouldn't let it happen. She fixed her eyes on my chest, refusing to look up at me, and I watched in sadness as she forced herself to not show any emotion at all.

"No, I'm not going. You run, and I chase. It doesn't matter how far you run. I'm going to be right there chasing you. I promised you I'd never stop, and I'm not. We're going to get past this, even if it means I have to chase you around the world."

For a moment, I saw the sadness return to her eyes before she closed them and in a small voice said, "I don't want you to chase me anymore. Whatever we were is over. I want you to leave."

Her words landed harder than any hit I'd ever taken from a defensive end hell bent on leveling me. I felt like I couldn't breathe, like someone had put a five hundred pound weight on my chest and was pushing down on it. I couldn't let this be the end. I had to change her mind.

Dropping to my knees, I looked up at her working so hard to keep the hurt she felt hidden. It tore my heart out that I had any part in it, and I needed to prove to her I'd fix this.

"Tressa, don't do this. I'll find out what this is all about tomorrow and then I'll make sure the truth gets out. I never cheated on you. I don't know what Eden's up to, but I swear to God I wasn't with her any time since we met. There hasn't been another woman since the night I laid eyes on you. Please believe me."

After what felt like an eternity staring up at her and waiting for any sign she'd heard what I said and was still willing to listen, she opened her eyes and looked down at me. The sadness and hurt was gone, and in their place I saw nothing in her deep brown eyes.

No caring about all we had together. No love for me. Nothing.

"What I believe has nothing to do with this. I want you to leave."

"Tressa, don't do this. I know you love me like I love you. Don't let something like this ruin what we have."

I needed her to talk to me. If I could get her to talk, she'd see we could get past this. I'd be able to make her smile like I always did and we'd be okay. I just needed to get her to talk to me.

But she kept saying those horrible words. I want you to leave.

Standing up, I took her face in my hands and pleaded with her. "Tell me you believe me. Tell me you trust me."

"Whatever I felt is gone, Killian. It left when I saw those pictures. I want you to leave and never come back. Don't send me flowers or bribe the security guard to let you up here. Don't leak something to the press to prove how much you love me. Just leave me alone."

Her words made the weight that felt like it was on my chest disappear, and all of a sudden, my entire body felt like it had been hollowed out. The emptiness of not having her in my life anymore felt instantly unbearable.

"I didn't do this. Please believe me. I wouldn't do this to us. I love you, Tressa. You know that. You run. I chase. I told you I'd never stop chasing you. I won't let this happen. You love me. Don't do this."

For a second, it felt like time stopped as I waited to hear if my pleas had worked. She had to believe me. She ran, and I chased. That's who we were. I accepted it and loved being the man willing to do anything to show her how much she was loved. I never doubted her feelings for me, so how could she doubt mine for her?

She looked up at me with tears in her eyes and said in that emotionless voice that hurt like knives plunging into my heart,

"We're finished. Go find another woman to charm, Killian. There are millions out there, so you won't be alone for long."

Then she turned to walk away, leaving me standing there watching as she cut me out of her life like some part she no longer wanted. I couldn't bear the thought of that, so I grabbed her by the arm to keep her there, to keep her talking so I still had the chance to get through to her.

"We can't be finished. What we feel for one another isn't some passing bullshit like others have that can be thrown away like this. We make each other happy, Tressa. I love you. Why won't you admit that and believe I'd never risk losing you. You run. I chase."

Suddenly, she spun around and pushed as hard as she could on my chest. It didn't move me an inch because she was so much smaller, but she kept trying over and over to push me away when I refused to let her.

"Stop saying that! Stop saying I run and you chase. How could you, Killian? How could you do this to us? Do you deny that's you in those pictures? I know every inch of your body as well as you do, and I know those are your legs wrapped up in hers. I know those are your hands holding her. Touching her skin. Pulling her to you like you do with me."

Tressa stopped and drew a sharp breath in as her angry words hung in the air between us. I couldn't deny any of her accusations, even though I hadn't been with Eden for nearly a year.

"I don't know where those pictures came from or how they made it look like I'm in them with her, but I swear to you on my life I didn't sleep with her. I wouldn't do that to you, Tressa."

"So you want me to believe one of your ex-girlfriends who lives in the very city where you traveled to at the exact time she claims you slept together is making all of this up? Why? What reason would she have to do that, Killian?"

"I don't know. Eden and I weren't serious like you and I are. We dated for a few months after friends set us up. I stopped seeing her long before you and I even met. I haven't talked to her since we ended it last February. I don't know why she'd lie like this, but I didn't do this. I swear."

As tears began to roll down her cheeks, Tressa pushed on my chest and sobbed, "You're full of I don't knows, aren't you? I trusted you, even though I broke every rule that kept me safe to believe we could work. I changed for you. I went to those events that terrify me more than you can ever understand because I wanted to be there for you, to make you happy. And the best you can give me after all we've been through is I don't know?"

I felt her slipping away right before my eyes. I grabbed her hands and held her there, knowing I could change this if I just kept her talking. She'd see that I couldn't do this to her. She'd smile at something I said, and I'd get that chance to convince her to let me prove to her this was all a horrible mistake.

"I know I love you more than anything else in this world. I know you love me. I know how much you hated those events and still did them because of how much you love me and how you held my hand so tightly that your fingers cramped because you were scared and needed to feel me there next to you. I know you're not the kind of woman who trusts easily, but you gave me that gift of your trust and I cherish it. I know those pictures hurt you, and I would do anything to erase that pain from your mind. But most of all I know you want to run now, baby, and I don't blame you. It's who you are, and I love you even for that. But you run, and I chase. I promised you I'd never stop, and I'm not going to."

She yanked her hands away from my hold and shook her head as tears flowed down her face. "Stop saying that! That meant the world to me, and you took it away. You ripped it away, and now you want me to keep believing in you. Stop!"

"Tressa, I didn't take it away. I love you and that means if you run, I chase. I never stopped. Right now, as you're running away even as we're standing not two feet away from one another, I'm chasing as hard as I can because that's what I do as the man who loves you."

"You chased someone else, Killian. You chased her all the way to her bed. I can't get over that. You need to go and don't come back."

Right there was the truth I couldn't stop her from believing. I hadn't been with Eden, but until I found out what was going on with her and those pictures, I'd never be able to convince Tressa that I hadn't betrayed her.

I felt the space between us grow by the second as I stood there watching her cry because of me. My arms ached to hold her, to make her know that the man she loved would fix this and make things better.

But I couldn't reach her, even as she stood close enough for me to touch her. It felt like a unique kind of torture I could only feel with Tressa.

"I won't give up on us. Please don't give up either. I'm going to find out what's going on and who did this. I promise. I don't care how far you run, Tressa. I won't give up on us."

She didn't say a word as I walked away from her, my heart breaking with every step. But I'd be back.

Tressa ran, and I chased. And I had no intention of giving her up to her fears.

CHAPTER TWENTY-ONE

TRESSA

THE IMAGES IN THOSE PICTURES flashed over and over in my brain, each time hurting more than the last. All I wanted to do was forget. Forget what I saw in those pictures. Forget what happened. Forget Killian.

And I couldn't do any of that. I especially couldn't forget him.

I didn't know if I'd ever be able to do that. I'd let down all my defenses for Killian, and now I lay there bare and more vulnerable than I'd ever felt in my life. I didn't know if I should feel stupid or hurt or which was worse.

Stupid stung because I'd promised myself I'd never give so much of me that losing a man would devastate me. Now I was nothing less than that. Devastated and lost without him.

Hurt made me cry at how much I loved him and how hard it was to tell him to go away. My body ached from how much I hurt that I didn't know if I'd ever feel good again. As I lay there in bed hidden under the covers, I couldn't imagine how any good would sneak into me without Killian there by my side.

I lifted the pillow off my head and ran my hand over where he slept every time he stayed there with me all those months. Pulling his pillow to my face, I inhaled in the hope of still being able to smell him. The faint scent of the man I loved still lingered on the cotton pillowcase, and the memory of the last time I saw him lying there when I awoke came rushing back into my brain.

His eyes closed and his dark lashes resting on his cheeks, he'd held me as I fell asleep in his arms, my head on his chest and my ear pressed to the place above his heart so I could listen to its steady beat lulling me to sleep. I'd gotten used to feeling that stability and strength from him, and now that it was gone, I realized how much I needed it as every moment that passed by I felt like my world was crashing down around me and there was no one to protect me.

I didn't want to cry any more. I couldn't understand how I could still have tears left inside me after the hours I'd spent sobbing. But now as I thought about the first day of my life without him, all I wanted to do was cry. I missed him more than I could bear, and all that lay before me in the minutes and hours until I could cry myself to sleep tonight appeared empty without him by my side.

My phone rang for the third time that hour, but I didn't bother to see who it was. Boyd had everything under control at work, so whoever it was calling didn't need me. In truth, they didn't want me in the state I was in. Even if an emergency came up, my assistant could handle it better than I could right now.

I took another deep breath in and smiled even as my eyes filled with tears once more. Part of me loved that I could still smell Killian on my sheets. It made me feel like he was still in my life. But another part of me wanted nothing more than to bleach out the scent of him so I would never experience it and all the memories that came with it again.

Everything in the penthouse reminded me of him. The bed we shared. The couch where we spent hours lying in each other's arms watching films on release days instead of going out to see them. I knew he probably would have preferred going to the movies to see them sometimes, but he never once suggested it. The tub where he'd run me a bubble bath when he saw I'd had a hard day and slide in behind me to wrap his arms around my shoulders so I had someone to lean on when things got rough at work.

There wasn't an inch of my home that didn't remind me of how happy I was with Killian. Now all those parts of the penthouse haunted me with those memories.

As I lay there, I heard a knock at my door. I didn't want to see anyone feeling like I did. Pulling the pillow back over my head, I silently begged whoever it was to leave. Five minutes later, they still insisted on intruding on my misery, so I dragged myself from the bed and slowly made my way to the front door, even as they continued to bang on it.

Stopping to peer out the peephole, I closed my eyes and prayed, "Please, don't let it be him, God. Anyone else in the world but him. I can't do it. I can't see him and tell him to leave me alone again. I don't have the strength."

I opened my eyes and looked out. Standing there was Summer wearing an expression filled with worry. She'd seen the story of Killian and that woman on TV or in the news, no doubt.

Even though I didn't think I could do this, I knew she wouldn't give up. She'd stand out there knocking for hours, if she had to, so better to get it over with sooner than later and not have to listen to that damn knocking for any longer.

I slowly opened the door and looked out at her. "What's up? I'm sick. I think I caught a bug."

Not a single word of that sounded like it could convince a complete stranger, much less the one person outside my family and Killian who knew me best in the world. Summer shook her head and frowned, blowing up my lie without saying a thing.

"Well, come in because I know you want to anyway. Come in and see me at my worst," I said as I stepped back to let her walk past me.

Before I closed the door, I looked out in the hallway, half hoping Killian stood there waiting for me. I knew that was stupid and self-defeating after what had happened, but old habits died hard, and feelings took even longer to fade away. No matter how much I wished I could forget him, one day wasn't enough.

I didn't know if one lifetime would be enough.

"I came by to see if you needed anything," Summer said in a soft voice like a social worker would use.

"Thanks, but I'm fine."

She held up a paper bag and pulled out a white container. "I brought ice cream. Whenever things go to hell with my romantic life, I find bingeing on ice cream makes me feel better."

"I'll get the spoons."

I returned to the living room to find her sitting on the couch with not one but two containers of ice cream waiting for us on the coffee table. Confused, I handed her a spoon and asked, "Why are you having any? Did something happen with my brother?"

Summer shook her head. "Friends don't let friends overeat ice cream because their love life has gone to shit alone."

I sat down beside her and tried to smile at her lame attempt at a joke. She and Killian were alike that way. Whenever I was down, they always tried to make me feel better.

"Thanks, Summer."

"It's what friends do, Tress. I was there the moment you met him. It's only right I'm here with the ice cream to drown your sorrows in now. I've got Death By Chocolate and Rockiest Road. You choose."

I reached for the quart of ice cream on the table directly in front of me and popped the top off. "Those two names alone tell me my life has gone to hell. Death By Chocolate it is."

Leaning forward, she took the other container and we plunged our spoons into the delicious dessert. I hadn't eaten anything all day, so as soon as the sugary chocolate taste hit my tongue, my body perked up like someone had given me a shot of caffeine.

"Wow, this stuff is good, but I don't think it's just chocolate. What's in this?" I asked as I ate my second spoonful of ice cream.

"I think it has espresso in it too. Watch you don't eat too fast or you'll give yourself brain freeze."

Dipping my spoon into the container a third time, I dug out a huge mound of ice cream and stuffed it into my face. Seconds later, the brain freeze Summer warned me about hit, and I scrambled to push my tongue up against the roof of my mouth to end it. The trick I'd heard all my life didn't work, and I dropped the spoon onto the table to writhe in pain from the worst headache I'd had in years.

"Why'd you go so fast? I warned you. Brain freeze is a real thing."

I sat hunched over as my headache slowly subsided, leaving me less interested in bingeing on ice cream and as sad as before. Covering my face with my hands, I admitted the truth to Summer as I began to cry again.

"I really loved him," I said quietly.

She put her ice cream and spoon on the table and pulled me into an embrace as I began to sob. "Oh, I know, honey. And if it helps any, he obviously loved you too."

That didn't help because it only made me wonder why he'd gone with her when he had me. As my body shook from crying, she held me close and let me get it all out.

"Why would he do this, Summer? I loved him. Did he need more? Was I not enough? Did he want someone who adored him like a fan? What did she give him that I didn't?"

Every question that popped into my mind made me feel worse. That last one really hurt. Was she more beautiful? Is that why he was willing to throw away all we had to be with her? Did she have something I didn't that made him happier?

"Don't think like that," Summer said as she rubbed my back. "I'm not even sure men can explain the stupid things they do. You did nothing wrong, Tressa. You loved him. This mistake is on Killian, not you."

I sat up and pushed my hair off my face. Sniffling, I shook my head and wiped the tears from my eyes. "I can't help think like that. He obviously found something in her that he didn't find in me. That's why men cheat. It's rather simple, actually. We just make it more because we want to make ourselves feel better."

"Did he say anything when you confronted him about it? Did he have any excuse? Not that there is an excuse, but did he have anything to say in his defense?"

"I didn't really confront him. I know that must sound surprising, but as soon as I saw the pictures, I ran out of the Manhattan Room where we were at for that party to celebrate the magazine cover he's on. He came here looking for me right after I got back, and he was full of loving words. He loves me. He would never hurt me. All of that. But he never admitted to cheating on me. He tried to get me to believe it was some mistake, but I know it's him in those pictures."

Summer frowned. "Why would that woman say it was him if it wasn't? She's his ex, right? Did they have a bad breakup or something and she's trying to punish him?"

I sighed as my brain tried to process all the questions we had. "I don't know. It makes no sense to me. He says they haven't seen each other since they broke up last February. It sounds strange to me that she'd wait nearly a year to do something to him to retaliate for their breakup. Revenge is a dish best served cold, but that's practically frozen. No, you and I know the truth is far more likely to be the easiest answer."

For a moment, I stopped talking because I didn't want to say the words. When I finally spoke them, they hurt just as much as I knew they would.

"He slept with her when the team had their game in LA in September. For over two months, he's been walking around here pretending to love me when he knew he'd cheated on me."

Then a more horrible thought rushed to the front of my brain. "Oh, my God! Has he been cheating on me all the time since September?"

I tried to remember where he said he was anytime we weren't together. He'd been out of town for games since then, but where? I couldn't remember the damn cities where the away games had been held.

Summer took my hands in hers and gave them a gentle squeeze. "Tressa, don't do this. Look at me. Don't do this to yourself. You'll drive yourself insane thinking about this. You know what you know and you did what you had to do. Don't spend any more time dwelling on what ifs. That's a road you don't want to travel down."

Hanging my head to avoid facing her, I said quietly, "I'm so embarrassed. I thought we were so happy together. How could I have been so stupid?"

"You weren't stupid, Tressa. You were in love."

"I was stupid in love, and now I feel stupid because I still love him."

"It's never stupid to love someone."

No matter how much I wanted to believe she was right, I hated how much regret had seeped into what I felt for Killian. I had been happy, truly happy, and now all that happiness was gone, replaced by sadness and regret.

THE SOUND OF MY FRONT door closing startled me, and I sat bolt upright in bed. Killian still had a key to my penthouse, and even though I hadn't heard from him in the past three days, I didn't put it past him to use it. But I couldn't handle seeing him so soon.

As I sat in bed, frozen in place, I heard a voice say, "Tressa? Are you here?"

A man's voice. It wasn't Killian. It was my father.

I hurriedly threw on a robe and pushed my hair off my face. Rushing past a mirror as I walked out to meet him, I saw I looked like death warmed over.

"Dad?"

Walking into the living room, I saw him smile at me like he did every morning when I saw him at his office. Was there a problem at work? Was that why he was here to see me?

"I think I got a bug," I lied, hoping it worked on my father better than it had on Summer. I had to look worse than I had two days ago, so maybe he'd buy it.

He nodded and looked around before saying, "I came over to

see your sister for lunch, so I thought I'd stop up here to see you."

"Don't worry about me, Dad. I had planned to take a few days off this week, so it's all taken care of at the office. Boyd knows to call me if anything happens that needs my attention. I'll be back in a few days as soon as I get over whatever this is."

My father took a step toward me and smiled. "I'm not here as the CEO of Stone Worldwide, Tressa. I know you have everything handled at work. You always do. I'm here as your father, honey."

Oh, God.

He could have said anything else and I would have been able to keep my emotions under control, but when he said that, I felt all that sadness and hurt I'd been working so hard to keep in check start to unravel inside me.

Covering my face, I sobbed, "Oh, Dad…This hurts so bad. I loved him."

Strong arms enveloped me as I cried harder than I had since I watched Killian walk out my front door days before. I pressed my cheek against my father's chest, loving the familiar feeling of his dress shirt against my skin as he held me to him like when I was a little girl and he comforted me after I skinned my knee playing tag or fell down roller-skating in the driveway.

Above me, he whispered, "It's okay, honey. Let it all out."

"I loved him, Dad, and I thought he loved me. I thought he loved all the things no other man had ever loved."

There, standing with my father in my living room, I needed the first man who loved me in my life to reassure me I deserved love. For all his coolness, my father had been my knight in shining armor for twenty-seven years, and as he held me while I cried for all I'd lost, his strength helped me feel stronger.

"Of course he loved you, Tressa. I don't know why this happened, but I saw the way Killian acted. He loved you."

That answer only made me cry harder. "Then why did he do this to me? To us?"

Holding me close, my father whispered what I wished wasn't

the only answer I had. "I don't know, honey. People make mistakes, and those mistakes can hurt a hell of a lot."

"This hurts so bad. I don't know what to do now," I sobbed quietly against him. "What do I do?"

We stood there quietly for a long moment before my father answered, "You remember how strong you are. I know this hurts now, but you'll be okay. It just takes time. You've got all of us here for you if you want us to be."

"Is Mom coming up now too?"

He kissed the top of my head and chuckled. "No. You and I know how your mother is. I figured you didn't need all that just yet. She's at the house out in her studio. She has been since she heard about what happened. I suspect the art she's creating will have a heavy touch of anger to it."

Looking up at him, I smiled. My father knew me better than anyone else in the world, and he was right. As much as I loved my mother, she'd want to talk about things, to get them out of my system as she liked to say, but I wasn't like her or Ethan or even Diana.

I was like my father, and when we hurt, we didn't want to talk or lash out. We just wanted someone strong there to quietly remind us that no matter how bad things were, we were loved and we'd be okay.

"Thanks, Dad. Tell Mom I love her and I'll call her when I'm feeling a little better."

"Of course. Now what do you plan to do once you decide to leave the house?" he asked with a smile as he looked down at me and slid the pads of his thumbs over my cheeks to dry my tears.

I attempted to fix my hair after days of lying in bed, pressing it to my head to smooth it out, but it was no use. Wallowing in heartbreak had a certain sad look to it, and I had it in full force. "I must look like a bus hit me. Well, no leaving today, but maybe tomorrow. Not that I'm looking forward to having to deal with the crowd of reporters I'm sure is camped outside."

My father nodded as he rolled his eyes. "They're still there. I suspect they're going to be there until they figure out you won't be giving a statement."

"You'd think they'd know that already. Anyway, I'll be back at work on Monday like I planned, so you don't have to worry."

"I never worry about work and you, honey. You're just like me in that respect. I hear the London redesign is shaping up to look pretty damn good. Maybe a trip to see how that's going might cheer you up?"

He gave me a sly look like he didn't want to come right out and suggest I leave town to lick my wounds, but beating around the bush wasn't necessary. I'd already thought about what I wanted to do.

"I was thinking maybe I'd move on to the next hotel I want redesigned. The Richmont in Barcelona needs a redo even more than the London location, so I thought I'd head there for a week or so. The designer and I have come to a meeting of the minds after that initial rocky start, so I'll see when she's available and move from there. If she's busy with another project, perhaps I'll still go to the Barcelona hotel and get a feel for what I want to do there."

In truth, I'd known what I wanted for that hotel for nearly a year, but I loved the idea of hiding away in Barcelona where nothing would remind me of Killian, unlike in this penthouse where everything felt like him.

"I like that idea a lot. I'm sure your mother will think it's a splendid plan. I'll probably have to hold her back from jumping on the plane and heading straight to Barcelona herself," he said with a smile.

"It's okay, Dad. Tell her to come visit me if she wants to. I can't hide away alone forever."

He opened his arms to hug me again. "I better go. I'll be sure to tell the rest of the family that you're going to be fine. I love you, honey."

"I love you, Dad. Thanks for coming over and saying all the

right things."

After giving me a gentle squeeze, he stepped back and pushed my messy hair away from my face. "You're going to be okay, Tressa. I worry the least about you out of all three of my kids because you're like me. No matter how bad things get, we can handle it. You'll handle this. I know it."

"Thanks, Dad."

I just hoped that would be true this time. I'd made a career out of being able to handle things, but nothing the business world had ever thrown at me had hit me like this.

He turned to leave and then looked back at me. "You know you're always welcome to come back to the house if you don't want to stay here anymore. The carriage house could give you some privacy, and I'm sure if I spoke to your mother, she wouldn't visit too often."

With a wink, he chuckled and added, "Well, I can't promise that, but I can tell you from experience that having your mother around when you feel down is a good thing. She does most of the talking so you don't have to say much, and she has a way of making you see that even in the worst of times, you're not alone."

He didn't wait for me to respond and left me standing there knowing one sure thing. I had the best family in the world.

CHAPTER TWENTY-TWO

KILLIAN

THREE DAYS OF TRYING TO get Eden to talk to me had resulted in nothing but her away fucking message being practically tattooed on my damn brain I'd heard it so many times. I'd spent seventy-two hours watching my world spiral out of control like some kind of goddamned bystander unable to do anything as shit just got worse and worse.

Every minute of those three days I thought about Tressa and what she must have been going through. The gossip and sports channels couldn't talk about Eden's claims enough, running stories and commentary every hour like my personal life deserved the kind of coverage the news gave to real events like wars and elections. I just hoped Tressa didn't watch any of it.

Even the team had gotten in on the act. Not twelve hours after the story broke on that damn gossip site, my coach and owner called me in for a talk. Nothing like having to face people you respected after your bare ass had been displayed across the goddamned world.

And after all of that, Eden still avoided talking to me, despite the fact that she had no problem lying to that reporter and handing over pictures of the two of us that I still couldn't figure out. I'd stared at the two of us in that dim light in those grainy pictures until my eyes hurt, and I had no clue how she'd gotten me into a picture supposedly taken in September when I hadn't even seen her since February.

I knew they'd been doctored some way, but the bigger problem was she and I never took pictures of us in bed. We'd dated for a few months, had some good times, and then parted ways because neither of us saw it going anywhere. Hell, we'd only slept together not even half a dozen times because our schedules never meshed. In truth, neither of us made much of an effort to get around our scheduling problems, so when I told her I wanted to end it, she didn't put up even the slightest fight. No tears or recriminations at all.

So why the fuck was she doing this to me now?

I paced back and forth through my apartment like a caged animal as the minutes ticked by. I needed to fix this fucking mess, but if I couldn't get Eden to talk to me, that was going to be difficult.

Frustrated, I called Sherilyn for the second time in two hours to see what she'd found out. Usually helpful, she seemed utterly lost with this problem, though.

Her smiling face popped up on the screen in front of me beaming her happiness that had to be for some other client. "Hi, Killian! I didn't expect you to call back so soon. What's up?"

"What's up? What the fuck do you think is up? The same thing that was up yesterday and the day before. The problem that's turned my goddamned life upside down."

That ridiculous smile of hers faded away, and she nodded like she finally understood how pissed I was. "I'm sorry. I was just trying to keep a positive outlook, Killian. I know this has been difficult, but Mike tells me the team isn't upset about the publicity, so you should be fine there. In the end, remember there's no such thing as bad publicity. You just do the honorable guy thing and don't lash out about what's happened and your stardom will only get bigger because of this."

"I don't care about my stardom. All I ever cared about was playing football, Sherilyn. I'll admit I liked being famous and having the press all over me twenty-four seven, but I'm thinking

Tressa was right. That life is shit. Look what it's done to me and the woman I love, for Christ's sake. What have you found out about Eden and why the hell she's doing this?"

My head began to feel like it would split open from the stress I'd been dealing with since I first saw those pictures and found out what Eden was claiming. Closing my eyes, I took a deep breath in as Sherilyn yammered on about having a hard time finding her.

I opened my eyes in amazement. "What do you mean you're having a hard time finding her? I've never seen you have a hard time finding anyone. You're a fucking publicist. You've made it your life's work to know where famous people are at all times. Eden is a fucking actress. Are you telling me it's hard to find an actress now?"

"Well, she's not at her house in Malibu. I checked there. She hasn't answered any of my calls, and her agent says she's indisposed for an indeterminate time."

"An indeterminate time?" I said, repeating Sherilyn's ridiculous words back at her. "She didn't get into a fucking spacecraft and fly to goddamned Mars. She's a famous actress, for God's sake. How hard can it be to find her? I want to talk to her today. Do you understand me? Today! She's not answering my calls, so you better find a way to get in touch with her or..."

I held back the threat to fire her that sat in my brain ready for me to act on. I hadn't appreciated how my publicist treated Tressa, but she'd been useful in other ways and Tressa had told me she could handle whatever Sherilyn threw at her. Now I regretted that. Her usefulness shouldn't have been more important than how she treated the woman I loved.

Love. I needed to make sure I kept that word in the present tense. Nothing had changed for me because of this fucking mess Eden had created, and when I fixed this all, I intended on marching back to Tressa to convince her we weren't over.

Sherilyn's eyes grew wide and full of fear at my unspoken threat to fire her. "Killian, I always do everything I can to help you and your career. You know that, don't you? I've been with you for longer than anyone else. I love you like you're a part of my family."

The sadness in her voice triggered something in me, and my mind returned to how Tressa sounded that night. Waving away Sherilyn's concerns, I began pacing again.

"Just find Eden and figure out what's going on, okay? I'll be here."

"Okay, Killian. Please don't worry. Everything will work out. This won't hurt your career. I'll make sure of it."

The screen went black as her words rang in my ears. This won't hurt your career. The problem was I didn't give a fuck how this affected my career. My ability to throw a ball and lead my team to the championship affected my career. This affected the rest of my life, the important parts that made everything worth it.

This affected Tressa.

TWO HOURS LATER, I STILL paced back and forth through my apartment and hadn't heard back from Sherilyn. A knock on my door broke me out of my thoughts about the mess my life had become, but I welcomed some reprieve from thinking of Tressa and how hurt she'd looked staring up at me like I'd betrayed everything we were.

I opened the door and stepped back in shock at who stood there in front of me. "I have to admit I didn't expect to see you on the other side of this door."

Tristan Stone slowly nodded as his steely gaze studied me. "I think we should talk. May I come in?"

Stepping back out of the way, he walked past me like he owned my apartment, not turning around to face me but looking around like he wanted to inspect where I lived. The man had a presence about him I had no choice but to respect.

He was also the father of the woman I loved and who at this very moment was heartbroken because of me.

"I'm not thinking this is you coming to see me because of how the New Orleans game went," I said as I walked around to stand in front of him.

"No, it isn't. I just went to see my daughter, and now I want to talk to you about what's going on," he said in a low voice that sounded more than a little ominous.

"Did she…" I began to say and then stopped. "How is she?"

Tristan arched a single eyebrow and leveled his gaze on me. "I think you know how she is. She's devastated."

Hanging my head, I wished I could be there to make her smile. "I'm sorry. I never wanted anything like this to happen."

"She loves you, and I believe you love her. Tressa is a private person, and seeing the man she loves in all his glory with another woman for all eyes to see isn't exactly something that makes her happy."

Looking up at him, I needed Tristan to know the truth. "I didn't cheat on her, Tristan. I wouldn't do that. I'm a lot of things, but I'm not a cheater. Tressa means the world to me. I hope you know that."

He frowned and then nodded again. "I do. For what it's worth, I don't see you as a cheater, so that leads me to believe you're being blackmailed. Is that correct?"

"No. That's the crazy thing. Eden didn't contact me about wanting anything in exchange for not releasing the pictures, which by the way are doctored. I don't know how, but I swear to you they are."

Tristan made a low, guttural noise and shook his head. "That doesn't make sense. If she doesn't want money, what does she want? Is she hoping to get you back with this ham-handed ploy?"

"I don't know. I can't even get her to answer my calls so I can ask why she told that website all those lies."

He narrowed his eyes like he didn't believe me, but then he said, "None of this makes any sense. You're telling me no one tried to blackmail you in regard to these pictures before they were released to the public?"

"No. I had someone threaten to go to the press about a month ago with an accusation that I had taken money in exchange for throwing a game in college, but that was total nonsense. I didn't pay them, and nothing ever came of it."

He perked up immediately and reached into his pocket for his phone. As he dialed a number, he said, "By mail, I'm guessing? If you have that letter or whatever they sent you, get it for me."

Then he said to the person on the phone, "Daryl, Tristan. I've got something for you. This is an ASAP situation, so it needs to happen now."

I didn't hear what this Daryl person said in response, but a few seconds later, Tristan stuffed his phone back into his suit jacket and smiled at me. "I've got my guy on this. Anything you can tell me, in addition to giving me what they sent you, can help."

A minute later, I handed him the letter I'd gotten trying to blackmail me. "I don't even bother the police with these things anymore. Nothing ever comes of them, so why would I? I didn't think this would have anything to do with Eden and those pictures, though."

"I don't know if it does, but my guy will find out. I've known him for years. He'll figure out what's going on with all of this. Eden Mitchell has a house in Malibu and one in Idaho, if I'm not mistaken. Have you tried both?"

Surprised to hear someone like Tristan Stone knew anything about my ex-girlfriend, I stammered out, "I only tried the Malibu house. She doesn't stay in the Idaho place after Labor Day."

"Didn't think I'd know about a world famous actress?" he asked with a chuckle.

I shook my head but said nothing, at a loss for words about much of what had happened since he got to my apartment.

"I had you checked out when you started dating my daughter, Killian. I'm a protective father, and just because you're the star quarterback for my team didn't mean I didn't want to know all about you. That's how I was pretty sure this whole thing with your ex wasn't what it seemed. I'll get this letter to Daryl and let you know what he finds out. In the meantime, take it easy. Things might not all be lost yet."

He didn't give me a chance to ask what he meant by that before he turned and walked out of my apartment, leaving me standing there hoping this guy of his would clear everything up so I could prove to Tressa all of this had been a huge lie.

I SPENT THE NEXT THREE days holed up in my apartment looking at pictures of the two of us and hating every minute I couldn't be with her, couldn't hold her hand and promise her we could get past this. Had she already hardened her heart to the very idea of me so by the time I returned to her with the truth about what Eden had done it wouldn't matter?

Every few hours Sherilyn called to tell me she hadn't found anything out yet, and I listened long enough to be disappointed once more before I ended the call and went back to looking at Tressa and me in better times. These weren't pictures taken by the press since she always looked so stiff and uncomfortable in those that I couldn't help but smile. She'd been so nervous every time we attended those events, but still she was right there holding my hand tightly as the press took picture after picture.

No, the images I loved best of her were the ones I'd taken myself. Some were from quiet moments when we said nothing for long stretches of time and simply sat watching TV, the two of us cuddled together on the couch. I'd take my phone out and snap a picture before she could complain she didn't look good enough or I'd caught her frowning.

Others were of the two of us having fun outside at Darius's house or relaxing at a secluded beach at one of her hotels or a hundred different times when her smile lit up her beautiful face because I cracked a stupid joke. In each of those, she was happy.

I swallowed hard as I stopped on one of just her out at her

parents' estate. My mind flashed back to that day in August right before preseason games began. We walked around the grounds holding hands, and when we reached the fence at the edge of the property, she told me a story about how she'd snuck out to meet a boy from school one night. Tressa had always been the perfect daughter and the perfect student, but that one time she couldn't stop herself from breaking the rules.

She'd blushed in that way I loved as she told that story, so I quickly took out my phone and got a picture of her so adorably admitting to risking everything in her teenage life for some bad boy. I took her in my arms and kissed her after that, charmed by her honesty and vulnerability. She couldn't understand why I liked that story of her so much since in her mind it showed a weakness, but with me, she never had to worry about fearing being weak because I would be strong for her.

And now because of me, all her fears about our differences and how she didn't fit into my world had come true.

The familiar sound of a call coming in tore me from my thoughts, and I looked up to see Darius staring back at me. Our bye week had passed so quickly for me since I'd spent it doing nothing but wallowing in misery and trying unsuccessfully to fix things that I hadn't spoken to him since the shit had started raining down on me nearly a week ago. He looked fresh after the time off, and he'd even shaved.

"Killian, man, what's going on with you? I would have thought you'd call me this week. What's up with that whole story with you and that actress?" he asked in that gravelly voice of his, the only part of him that didn't sound refreshed after nearly seven days off.

"I haven't done much talking to anyone this week. Sorry. The issue with Eden Mitchell is still going on. She unloads her story and those pictures to that bullshit gossip site and since then no one's been able to find her. Nice, huh?"

"Yeah. That's what you get for dating actresses, man. They're the original drama queens," he said, his expression worried as he pushed his blond hair off his forehead.

"Well, if I can get her to admit the whole fucking thing was a lie, I don't plan on dating any actresses ever again. I just have to find her first. I've called dozens of times, but I can't get in touch with her."

"That's just shitty. You know what else is shitty? Looking online for a new jacket and two fucking links later I'm staring at your bare ass."

For a moment, he tried to fight back a smile, but it was no use. He threw his head back and let out a deep laugh I couldn't be angry with. And after days of being miserable, I laughed at this whole thing for the first time.

"Thanks, man. I needed that. Now if I could just get the truth out and get this mess over with, maybe I can get Tressa to take me back."

Darius smiled and nodded like he understood. Of all the people I knew, I had a feeling he did understand how I felt about Tressa. I didn't spend my time telling people how much I loved her because that wasn't what I did with my teammates, but Darius was smarter than most of the men I played with and read people better.

"You know what kills me? It's easily provable that you didn't go with her since the two of us spent the entire night before the game hanging out. Anyone who knows you can attest to the fact that you never break your routine the night before. The idea that you would go off and have some kind of rendezvous with anyone that night is ridiculous."

I sighed, letting the air out of my lungs as the frustration of the whole thing made me want to beat the fuck out of someone. "A picture speaks a thousand words. You know that as well as I do. Ironic, though, that a picture would be the thing that ruins my life. I've always loved getting my picture taken. It was Tressa who hated it. She couldn't understand why I enjoyed it so much. Guess the joke's on me, huh?"

"Well, once your career is over, you could have a second one as a male model. You know the ones who pose nude for art students. You look like you've got the moves down pat," Darius joked.

I laughed again and shook my head at the absurdity of it all. "Fuck you, man. But thanks for calling. Hopefully when you see me next, this whole thing will be over and done with."

"I'm hoping it is. I'll see you Monday at the field. Call me if you need anything."

The screen turned to black, and I sat back against the couch unsure of what to do. I hoped Tristan's guy would have found Eden by now, but it looked like that hadn't happened, so that left me no better off than before.

Even though I knew I shouldn't do it, I found those fucking pictures Eden had given to that online rag and looked at them closely for the first time. I'd avoided them like the fucking plague all week, but Darius's joking about my future career made me want to see if I could recognize anything that would tell me when they were taken. The fact that Eden had secretly done that still surprised me. I'd been dead wrong about her, for sure.

I stared at the first picture up on the screen and had to squint to make out much of anything through the graininess. That was definitely me and Eden. Nearly six feet tall, her legs stretched even longer than mine on my six foot four frame. They wrapped around mine like two pythons. All that could be seen of me was the back of my head and body, but there was no denying it. It was me.

The picture had been taken in her bedroom at her Malibu home, but I knew that the first time I looked at it. Walking across the room to stand in front of the screen, I tried to make out anything that would indicate when the image had really been taken since September was a lie. I saw nothing except the enormous painting of herself she'd always kept on the wall above her bed. On each side of the image was the bedroom furniture she had the entire time we dated.

Fuck, this was frustrating! Like I wanted to be standing in my goddamned living room staring at a picture of me naked and fucking a woman I never loved and currently didn't even fucking like anymore.

Moving on to the next picture with me sitting up and Eden straddling me in her Malibu house bedroom, my eyes were immediately drawn to that gaudy painting behind us. More than once, I'd looked up at it while we were having sex and wondered why anyone would keep that nearby where they slept. The artist had been talented, but the thing was creepy, like one of those velvet Jesus paintings with eyes that seemed to follow you wherever you went in the room.

I pushed that out of my mind and focused on the two of us for a moment. Eden looked like she always did, at least from behind—long blond hair that curled slightly on the ends as it hit the middle of her back and a nice ass. None of that helped to prove the thing was doctored.

Little of me could be seen since she was perched on my lap with her legs on the outside of my hips and her torso covering up my head and face. In fact, all that could be seen of me were my legs outstretched in front of me and my hands holding her waist.

Squinting even harder, I leaned in toward the image so my nose nearly touched the screen. There had to be something to prove these goddamned pictures weren't taken in September and Eden was pulling some kind of scam. My eyes roved over every square inch of her body and then what I could see of mine.

And then I saw it. Or more truthfully, didn't see it. The tattoo I'd gotten on my right wrist in April after she and I ended things two months before. The one to commemorate being traded to New York. Those two black bands with arrows facing opposite directions were nowhere to be found.

I stepped back as the realization that I could prove these images weren't taken in September washed over me. Proof! But seconds later, the happiness morphed into resignation. I could prove I wasn't with Eden any time during that LA trip with a simple statement from Darius or any other member of the team who saw me at the hotel that night. It didn't matter. As I said to him, a picture was worth a thousand words. My proof didn't matter.

Unless Eden agreed to admit she lied, those pictures would remain the only truth anyone believed.

CHAPTER TWENTY-THREE

KILLIAN

As I sat there staring at that picture, Tristan's face popped up in a box at the top of the screen. Compared to the expression he'd worn when he was standing in my apartment three days earlier, he looked excited, so I quickly exited out of the picture of Eden and me and stood up, hoping he had something good to tell me.

"Did you find out anything?" I blurted out, forgetting who I was talking to. "Sorry. Hi, Tristan."

"It's okay. I know you're on pins and needles waiting for news, and I've got some for you." Looking down at his watch, he smiled. "I think you'll want to check out channel eighteen forty. I'm told something interesting is going to appear right about now. I'll wait."

I grabbed the TV remote and punched in the channel number. Eighteen forty. I didn't know what that channel was dedicated to. Hopefully, it was the channel where ex-girlfriends told the truth to the world about how they were lying bitches. I didn't know if there was a huge calling for that kind of thing, but I could definitely get behind it.

Minimized to a square at the top right of my TV, Tristan said, "Watch. I think you're going to like what's coming up."

I waited as some commercial about male pattern balding extoled the virtues of some revolutionary cream that promised to change your life after only a month. Annoyed, I mumbled, "Who the fuck cares about bald guys? Get on with it."

"If you were this impatient on the field, you'd never connect with your receivers," Tristan said in a steady voice. "It's coming. Just wait for it."

If he wasn't the father of the woman I loved, I'd have a few choice words to say about how waiting to see some surprise he sprung on me a minute ago was nothing like my job as a quarterback. Since he was, I kept my mouth shut and hoped this commercial about bald fuckers ended before I exploded.

Then just as I didn't think I had a second's worth of patience left in my entire body, I saw what he'd called about. Eden sat with a dark-haired woman in her Idaho house I remembered her hating in the cold weather and quietly answered questions in what the reporter called an exclusive interview.

Leaning forward, the woman said in a somber voice, "Eden, you agreed to this interview because you wanted to get a few things straight about the article and pictures about you and Killian Brenton. What would you like to say?"

Eden grimaced and then took a deep breath before letting it out slowly. Turning to look at the camera, she said the words I'd prayed to hear for nearly a week. "I want to say that what that article said was incorrect. Killian and I weren't together in September."

Her admission that she'd lied, as vague as it was, hit me like a truck. I stepped back as the reporter asked her why she said she had been with me long after we broke up and stopped as her answer stunned me.

"I was paid to say that. I realize that was a mistake to take the money now, though."

"Is there anything you'd like to say to Killian?" the dark-haired reporter asked quietly.

For a moment, Eden didn't move and I wondered if the picture had frozen. What could she possibly have to say to me? Sorry for ruining your life? I hope it wasn't too much of an inconvenience? Too bad you lost the most important thing in your world?

When she finally answered the question, her words did little to make up for the damage she'd done. "I'd like to tell him that I'm sorry I made such a terrible mistake. I was misled by a bad person."

Well, Eden never had been the courageous kind. I doubted she cared at all what her lies had done to me and Tressa.

The interview continued, but I had no interest in hearing any more of what she had to say. I turned it off and brought Tristan back to thank him since no doubt his guy had gotten her to admit her lies.

"I'm guessing that guy Daryl found her. How did he get her to do that interview?"

Tristan smiled and shrugged. "Daryl is very persuasive. From what he told me, though, she wanted to tell the truth about everything once he explained how her lies had caused you and Tressa to break up. You have a bigger problem, though."

"Bigger than the fact that I lost the woman I love because my ex showed the world phony pictures of us having sex? I can't imagine things could get any worse, to be honest."

"Well, they are. Daryl found out who was behind the payment to Eden to get her to lie. You've got a traitor on your team, Killian."

A traitor on my team? No way. He had to be wrong. Every man who played on my team was one hundred percent behind me as much as I was for them.

"He's got to be wrong. From the coach and owner to the water boys, my team supports me. Tell him to look again."

Shaking his head, Tristan said, "I didn't mean the football team. I'm talking about the people you have around you. The person who paid Eden to lie was your publicist, Sherilyn. She's been paying her for over a year."

I stood there in shock. No way. Sherilyn had been with me longer than anyone else. I loved her like a sister, and she loved me like I was part of her family.

"I don't believe it. Why?"

"You'll have to ask her yourself to get those answers."

That's exactly what I'd do, but that conversation would happen in person. "Thanks for everything, Tristan. Does Tressa know? Did you tell her? I can't wait to see her."

He shook his head slowly and frowned. "No, I didn't tell her, but don't bother looking for her at the penthouse. She flew out yesterday. Give her some time. I'm sure when she finds out the truth that you never cheated on her, she'll come around."

"That isn't how we work. I need to talk to her. Where is she?"

But he wouldn't tell me. He simply repeated his suggestion that she'd come around.

"If you talk to her, please tell her the truth so she knows."

He smiled and said goodbye, and as I stood there wishing I knew where Tressa had gone to, all I could think of was what I told her that night she ended it with me. You run, and I chase.

The problem was this time I didn't know where to find her.

AN HOUR LATER, I STORMED through the front door of Sherilyn's office to find her talking to another client, laughing it up like she hadn't just tried to ruin the best part of my life. I didn't recognize the man on the screen talking to her, but he was better off getting far away from her.

"She'll call you back. Or maybe she won't. I don't fucking care. Find a different publicist because this one's done."

Sherilyn's mouth dropped open, and she began to complain, but I stopped her cold. "I know what you fucking did. Eden did an interview about an hour ago and told the truth. You've been paying her for a year. What the fuck for? To ruin my life?"

She stared at me in shock, like anything I said hadn't been right. "Killian, don't be upset. Everyone benefited. She needed some exposure, and I knew the people she wanted to get in contact with. As soon as I found out Miami was going to trade you, I made sure you two got together. It made for good headlines, so by the time you got here to New York, you were the name on everyone's lips."

"As much as hearing you paid some woman to sleep with me

makes me feel like shit, that doesn't explain why you paid her to lie that we were together this September. What did that do for my career or hers, for that matter? Who benefited there?"

Sherilyn came around her desk and stood in front of me to pat my chest, a move she'd done since the very first time she met me. Back then, it made me feel like someone important was looking out for me. Now it sickened me to have her touch any part of me, so I backed away.

"Answer me! Who benefited? Did you? Is that what this is?" I bellowed so loud she jumped.

Her expression hardened, and she suddenly changed in front of my eyes from a forty year old woman who'd helped me to some haggard thing who'd betrayed me. "You were too involved with Tressa. Your brand is all about sex appeal, Killian. Everything you were was sex. There was no way you'd have any chance at a career in modeling or acting if your brand was tarnished like you seemed intent on doing. The tied-down lovesick guy isn't a huge seller. I was just looking out for your future."

As I watched her explain away the horrible things she'd done, I felt my rage ebb until all that was left inside me for Sherilyn was sadness. She never understood that as much as I loved being in the public eye, it was never about sex appeal or any of that bullshit. All I ever wanted to do was play football and have some kind of happiness off the field.

"You didn't care about my future. You cared about yours. We're done."

She shook her head frantically as she pointed at the pictures of me that covered her walls. "No, Killian, you don't understand. Look around you. You're my most important client. I would never hurt your career. You have to know that."

I looked around at all those pictures of me on and off the field, alone and with ex-girlfriends, and felt nothing for any of them. "You didn't hurt my career, Sherilyn. You hurt the woman I love. Your lies broke us up. Don't you see what that did to me? How can

I ever trust you again?"

Hurrying around her desk, she grabbed her phone and held it up as she stared at me desperately. "I'll call her. Right now. I'll call her and tell her it was a publicity stunt. She'll forgive you. I can do it. I'm happy to, Killian. We can get past this and be a team again."

Sad and disgusted at how the person I trusted most for all those years had sold me out, I hung my head and said, "No, we can't. I don't know what's going to happen to you once the authorities find out your part in Eden's lies, but our time working together is done. Goodbye, Sherilyn."

As I turned to leave, she rushed over to grab my sleeve and began to cry. "No, Killian, we can fix this. No one wants you to be successful like me. You know that. Please, don't do this."

I'd heard enough of her plans for my future. Yanking my arm from her hold, I walked out of her office as she sobbed behind me about what she would do for my career.

She didn't get it. I had the career I'd always dreamed of. Now I wanted more, and I didn't care if that meant the world didn't think I was sexy ever again. All I cared about was getting Tressa back.

CHAPTER TWENTY-FOUR

TRESSA

NEARLY EIGHT AND A HALF hours on a plane left me feeling like maybe running off to Barcelona hadn't been my best idea. Actually, I hadn't run off. No running. I'd left on a working trip. That was my job.

You run. I chase.

Killian's words echoed in my head as I tossed my bag onto the couch just inside the door of my penthouse and headed toward the bedroom. I'd hoped to forget all about him, but I forgot how similar the penthouses were in all the Richmont chain hotels. The Barcelona one wasn't the mirror image of this one, but it was close enough that it made all kinds of memories of him come flooding back every day of the past two months.

When I learned the truth of what that Eden woman had done, I almost called him. I stood there in front of the screen and thought about it, but in the end, I walked away. Those pictures of him supposedly cheating on me weren't the entire reason why I broke things off with him. I'd never fit in with his world. I'd tried, and I'd failed. I liked keeping my private life private. I liked staying at home and curling up with the man I loved as we watched movies, just the two of us.

And I liked the idea of a life away from the limelight.

Killian loved being the focus of attention, and I didn't blame him for that. He had the looks and the talent and the personality, so why shouldn't he enjoy his time in the spotlight? I just couldn't be the person by his side in those bright lights.

So I never called. I hid out in Spain far longer than I'd planned, setting up a working office at the Richmont Barcelona and doing my job as I always had. That's who I was. That there probably weren't too many men who would ever appreciate that was something I'd have to learn to accept.

While I lay there on the bed we'd shared, I heard my phone ring out in the living room. Damnit. I hadn't taken it out of my bag when I got home. It might be Boyd, although I sincerely doubted he'd gotten up to call me at six in the morning on a Sunday. I was a slave driver, but even I gave my assistants a day off once a week.

Dragging myself up out of bed to answer the call, I saw it was my father. Instantly, fear rushed through me. He would never call this early in the morning unless something was wrong. A million horrible ideas raced through my brain. My mother had sounded off the last time I spoke to her. Summer had told me she and Ethan were traveling out to Montana to do a photo shoot with some guy and his horses. Had they been trampled? Was something wrong with Diana?

My heart slammed against my chest as my fear ratcheted up in just that brief moment, so I quickly answered and without even saying hello, I asked, "What's wrong, Dad?"

"Nothing. I knew you were getting in this morning and wanted to see how you were doing. Why do you think something's wrong?" he asked in that baffled voice I'd heard him use with my siblings so many times in our lives.

I took a deep breath and tried to calm my nerves. My father needed to learn that calling at six in the morning meant something bad to the majority of the world.

"I'm fine, Dad. Did you see the pictures I sent from the designer? What do you think? I love the Spanish touches she wants to incorporate in the Barcelona location."

"I did, but now's not the time for business. Rest up because I want you to come with me on a trip this afternoon. The plane will leave at two o'clock. I'll have a car come get you at one, so be ready."

My body sagged at the very thought of going on another plane so soon after my flight from Europe hours before. "Dad, can we do this tomorrow or Tuesday? I'm exhausted from my trip back from Barcelona. I just got in."

"No, I'm sorry, honey. It's got to be today. I'll see you at the plane at two," he said firmly.

With a sigh, I accepted my fate. "Okay, Dad. I'll see you then."

I dragged myself back to my bed and set my alarm for noon. My eyes closed a second later, and I fell asleep thankful I wouldn't have time to think about how much I missed having Killian beside me in our bed.

"YOU'RE ALMOST LATE. THIS ISN'T like you, Tressa. Two months in Europe have changed you," my father joked as I walked toward where he sat on the Stone Worldwide company plane.

"I overslept."

Practically throwing myself into the leather seat, I looked over at him and noticed he wasn't wearing a suit. My father always wore a suit for work. Always. As in every day he ever worked since I was born.

"Why are you dressed like we're going out for lunch? I thought this was a work trip."

He winked and gave me a sly smile. "I never said this was a work trip. Just a trip."

So he wanted to be cute. Okay. I liked seeing my father relaxed, so I'd play along. "I know it's not for my birthday because then Ethan and Diana would be coming with us on this little trip, so what's up?"

"You'll see. In the meantime, just sit back and take it easy. We'll be there in a couple hours."

"Be where in a couple hours, Dad? Is Mom coming or is she

already where we're going?" I asked, utterly confused by his need to be so secretive.

He shook his head and grinned like a little boy. "No, your mother isn't coming and she isn't going to be with us on this trip. This is just you and me. Now, no more questions or you'll ruin this."

I was too exhausted even after nearly seven hours of sleep to verbally spar with him. Whatever he wanted to do on our father-daughter trip was fine with me. We didn't have enough of these together, just the two of us.

LOOKING OUT THE CAR WINDOW, I wondered why Tampa had bumper-to-bumper traffic on a Sunday afternoon in early February. My father and I hadn't talked much since landing and transferring to the limousine. He seemed deeply involved with some paperwork he'd brought along on our trip. Strange since he claimed this wasn't a work trip, but my father seemed to work constantly all my life, so maybe it wasn't odd.

"This town is as bad as New York in the middle of the week. What's going on here today?" I wondered aloud, hoping he'd take the bait and give me a clue as to what we were doing in Tampa, Florida, of all places.

He didn't look up from his papers but answered, "I used to be part owner of a club down here years ago around the time I met your mother."

"Is that where we're going?" I asked, seizing upon his willingness to talk suddenly.

Lifting his head, he smiled. "No. That wasn't a place to take your daughter."

And that was it. He said nothing more, and I didn't ask another question since I'd get nothing but riddles for answers. My father could be cute that way sometimes.

Still groggy after traveling from a different continent, sleeping far too little, and then sleeping two hours on the flight there, I leaned back and closed my eyes. I'd never liked riding backwards in limos, but my father had insisted I sit opposite him, so being a dutiful daughter, I did as he wanted.

The traffic thinned slightly, and then a few minutes later, the car stopped abruptly. I leaned over and looked out the windows, but the tinting made seeing much of anything difficult since the sun was already setting.

"I guess we're here?" I asked as a feeling of nervousness came over me suddenly. I didn't know why, but something felt off.

I pushed it out of my mind, though. Nothing could be wrong. I was traveling with my father.

He stuffed his papers into a briefcase on the seat next to him and nodded. "We're here. Ready?"

"Ready? I have no idea where I am or what we're doing. And by the way, I feel like I'm overdressed in this skirt and blouse since you're in jeans and a polo shirt, Dad. You want to tell me what's going on?"

The car door opened, flooding the inside with the last remnants of daylight and warmth from the weather outside. I watched as my father got out and then followed him. It only took a few seconds to understand what he'd done.

Instantly, my hands began to shake as nerves overtook my entire body. "Oh, Dad. No. This is a bad idea."

With that little boy grin of his, he shook his head. "Nonsense. Are you ready for some football?"

I SAID NOTHING AS EVERY cell in my body screamed, "No!" I wasn't ready for what he'd done.

FOR TWO HOURS, I WATCHED Killian and his team play, still not understanding much of what I was looking at. Yes, I knew what the pocket was, thanks to my brother and sister, but I spent most of the game watching Killian wherever he went on the field, when he moved to the sidelines, and when he ran into the tunnel for halftime. He looked like he always had. So full of life. When they were doing well, he smiled and seemed to command the entire field as if it were his own. When Pittsburgh came back to tie the score in the fourth quarter, his mannerisms changed and he grew serious, like a warrior bent on winning the battle.

And then just as time began to run out, he threw a touchdown to Darius to win the game. The stadium went wild with people cheering, and for the first time, I understood why my father and siblings loved this game.

Even more, I understood why so many people loved Killian. Watching him was exciting, and not only because I loved him. He looked like a god out on that field. No wonder he had so many adoring fans.

I watched as his team basked in the glory of winning their first championship in years because of him. He stood proudly up on the stage rolled out onto the field after the game to accept his MVP award, thanking his teammates for helping him have the best season of his career. He spoke with humility and grace, and I couldn't have been happier for him.

My father sat quietly beside me in the box we now had to ourselves after the owner and his guests left for the post-game trophy presentation, and when it was all over and Killian and the team had left the field, he leaned in next to me and said, "So what did you think? He looked pretty incredible today, didn't he?"

Struggling to hold back the tears from the mixture of pride in Killian and sadness that I couldn't share this important day with him, I nodded and said quietly, "He did. Thank you for bringing me here, Dad."

"You're welcome, honey. I want to talk to Harold Canning, the owner of the team, but I won't be long. You'll be okay alone here for a little bit?"

"Yeah. Go ahead. I'll be fine."

Left to myself, I couldn't deny the strong regret I had that after all that had happened, I wouldn't get to share this with Killian. Did he have a new girlfriend? The mere thought made my chest tighten. Not that he didn't deserve to have a woman to celebrate his big day with. He did. I just couldn't help wish it had been me.

I watched as the stadium emptied out and the workers began to clean where just a short while earlier nearly seventy thousand screaming fans had cheered on the two teams. Every so often, a player would walk out onto the field dressed in his street clothes, and I craned my neck to see if it was Killian.

But it never was.

He had interviews to give and pictures to pose for. Knowing him, he loved every second of that, I thought to myself, smiling at how much an attention whore that man could be.

I stared out at the field wishing I could get just one more glance at him. Behind me, I heard the door open. Reluctantly, I stood from my chair and grabbed my bag, wishing we didn't have to leave yet.

"Did you have a nice time talking to Mr. Canning?"

"Well, he's a pretty big fan of mine right now since I helped bring the championship home to him, but I told him I had someone else I needed to talk to tonight."

My heart skipped a beat. I knew that deep voice so full of confidence.

Stunned, I spun around to see Killian standing there smiling at me like I was the most important part of his day. He looked so good in a simple pair of black pants and a white dress shirt. I'd almost forgotten on incredibly gorgeous he was.

I couldn't find the words to say how happy I was for him, so I stood there simply staring, filling my eyes with the vision of him after so long.

"This reminds me of the first time we met. Remember? You didn't seem to have much to say to me that night either."

I opened my mouth to say congratulations, but suddenly my

emotions overwhelmed me and I burst into tears, sobbing, "That night I couldn't stop thinking of how gorgeous you were. Tonight's different because I want to tell you how happy I am for you but the words wouldn't come."

He walked over to me and pulled me into his arms. "I'm so happy to see you, Tressa. I knew you were here, though. I felt it the whole time I was playing."

"My father told you he was bringing me here, didn't he?" I asked against his chest, loving how safe I felt in his arms again.

"No. He kept that a secret until a few minutes ago. I just knew you were here, though. I can't explain it, but I felt it the whole game."

I looked up at him and quickly moved to wipe under my eyes. "I'm sorry for being such a blubbering fool. You know me. I'm not usually like this. I must look a mess. Nice. You win the championship and what do you get? Some woman crying and getting her mascara all over her face."

Killian shook his head. "You look beautiful. I've missed you so much. I thought about calling you every day, but I didn't know where you were. Your father said to give you time, but I want you to know I never gave up on us. You ran, and I wanted to chase but I didn't know where to chase after you. But I never gave up."

"I'm sorry I didn't call you after I found out that whole mess was a lie. I convinced myself we were too different, and you'd be happier living in the spotlight with someone else. But I realized as I watched you today that I don't care about us being different. I love you."

A slow smile spread across his face and lit up those beautiful green eyes of his. "I've waited to hear those words, Tressa. And I have a confession. I thought I loved being famous, but when I lost you, I realized I loved you more than being loved by fans and having my picture taken by the press. When that's all I had, it felt like I had nothing because I didn't have you."

I stood on my toes to kiss him, pressing my lips to his in a kiss

I'd longed for since that night I told him goodbye. Like always, he took my breath away, and once more I fell in love with him all over again.

Pressing his forehead to mine, he whispered those words that never failed to make me the happiest woman in the world. "I love you, Tressa."

"I love you, Killian."

He stepped back and nodded in a resolute way that confused me. "I know you'd probably prefer me to do this in private, but I don't think there are any cameras around, so here goes."

Then he took a small black velvet box out of his pocket and knelt down on one knee in front of me. Looking up, he took a deep breath and opened the box to reveal a diamond ring more beautiful than any I'd ever seen. "I've had this for a while now. You know me. Always confident. So, Tressa Stone, will you marry me?"

My mouth dropped open in shock, but I knew my answer. I'd known it since the moment I realized I loved Killian all those months before.

"Yes! Yes, I'll marry you, Killian Brenton," I answered as my emotions overwhelmed me and I began to cry.

He slipped the engagement ring on my finger and stood to take me in his arms. In my ear, he whispered, "You run, and I chase. Forever."

Forever.

Chapter Twenty-Five

Killian

Tressa curled up against me on the couch in my living room as we got ready to watch SportsCenter. Although she'd been scared to death to do an interview, she agreed to do her first by my side after we announced our engagement on the network of my choice, so of course, I chose a sports show. I had a feeling that would be easier on her since the reporter would probably spend more time on my career than on gossipy topics like other shows did.

Grabbing my hand, she squeezed it tightly. "God, I'm so nervous. How do you do this all the time?"

I smiled and shook my head at how someone so incredible could be so insecure about this one thing. She'd been spectacular that day as we sat across from the reporter at the television studio. Full of doubt, she held my hand so tightly in the minutes before the interview began that I thought she might hurt herself, but when it came time to answer questions, she was the Tressa I knew and loved. Professional and sweet at the same time, she looked like a natural.

Not that she believed that for a second. Since then, she'd worried about how she looked and if she'd sounded too bossy or too strident. No matter how much I tried to convince her that she'd been perfect, I knew it would take actually watching the interview for her to see she'd done great.

"I told you that day you were perfect. I keep telling you. All these reporters have interviewed me so many times they're going to be knocking down the door to talk to you now. You're the new big thing."

She rolled her eyes at my teasing. "Don't be ridiculous. I just hope my hair looked okay. They did a great job with makeup, but my hair felt a little big. Like country-western star big. Oh, God. Was it big?"

I pulled her close and kissed her to stop her from talking. "It was perfect. You were perfect. I think maybe this needs to be the last interview you do because it's making you go crazy."

A sigh escaped her lips, and her body instantly relaxed. With a smile, she said, "That's the best thing I've heard this week."

I heard the familiar SportsCenter intro music and knew the show was starting. "It's coming on now."

Her hand clamped down on my arm as we watched the host introduce the show and then move into the segment that included our interview. "Oh, God. This is so nerve wracking!"

She had nothing to worry about. Although she didn't believe it, Tressa was a natural in front of the camera.

We watched in silence, and every so often she squeezed my arm when she answered a question or the interviewer asked me about our relationship. Then it came time for my favorite question and answer, so I pulled her close and said, "Listen. I love this part."

"So Killian, I hear you proposed right after the big game. Did you plan it, or was it a spur of the moment thing?"

I watched myself smile and look at Tressa seated next to me before I answered, "I had it planned, but I have to say it went even better than I thought it would."

The interviewer laughed. "Well, she said yes, so that tells me it went great."

Nodding, I smiled. "She said yes and that's all I kept repeating to myself as I hugged her after she agreed to marry me. 'She said yes.'"

A minute later, the interview ended, and Tressa kissed me before letting out a sigh of relief. "That wasn't too bad. I looked okay, and I didn't embarrass either one of us."

"Of course, you didn't."

She pressed my hand against her cheek and leaned into it. "Did you really keep repeating that to yourself after I said I'd marry you?"

I smiled and nodded at her question. "Yep."

Opening her eyes wide in surprise, she asked, "Did you think I'd say no?"

"I wasn't sure, to be honest."

Tressa sat up and looked at me like she couldn't believe what she was hearing. "What happened to all that confidence you always have about everything?"

"Well, you had told me you never wanted to see me again and then avoided me for over two months. Confidence can only go so far."

My answer made her smile, and she cuddled up next to me again. "That's true. But you never had any reason to doubt I'd say yes, to be honest."

"That's good to know," I said with a chuckle. "Makes all those nerves I had when I asked you seem stupid now."

Hugging me, she sighed. "I run."

I finished her sentence for her. "And I chase."

After a moment, I added, "But if we're being truthful, you technically came to me in Tampa, so you chased when it counted."

Tressa tilted her head back to look at me and smiled. "Okay, then. I chased, and you chased. And in the end, we caught one another."

Pulling her to me, I closed my eyes and let that new reality settle in. I'd caught the elusive Tressa Stone for my own, and one day soon, I'd make her my wife.

That was a future I looked forward to.

SILENT AS A STONE

CHAPTER ONE

DIANA

To anyone looking me, I must seem very much like my sister and brother. Tressa is a more glamorous version of me, and Ethan…well, he's what I like to think I might be if I'd been born his brother instead of his sister. Confident and sure, they are every bit the children of Tristan and Nina Stone.

I used to be that way. At least I like to think so. That was so long ago I'm not sure when I'm remembering if my mind is playing tricks on me. Maybe I didn't act with as much confidence as the belief that I had everything in front of me.

College. Boyfriends. Good times.

It all lay ahead of me. After finishing my second year of college, I knew I wanted to go into law. My mind had a sharpness back then that a lawyer needs.

And then everything happened, and my dream of someday sitting on the Supreme Court faded away with every day I stayed in that coma and every day after that. My doctor tells me I'm wrong about that. My time in a coma left no permanent brain damage, so that shouldn't stop me from pursuing my dream.

In fact, the casual observer would say I have nothing holding me back. I'm physically in great shape. Well, not supermodel shape, but my body isn't broken in any way that would make going back to school any sort of a challenge. My legs work. I can write and type just fine. My eyes have perfect 20/20 vision. I have no hearing loss.

Even more, I have the Stone family money, so there's not a

university in the world I can't afford to attend. My God, if I told my parents today that I wanted to go back to school, they'd probably buy me a house and hire a full household staff to wait on me hand and foot in that new home.

No, it isn't physical or mental ability or even money that keeps me from being the person everyone in my family wishes I could be. It's me. Or rather, it's my fear.

See, on the outside, I look like Ethan and Tressa. We're triplets, so that's not surprising. I resemble my mother whereas they resemble my father, but it's obvious with even a casual glance that we're related.

But it's the inside that's different. Some days I try to blame it on the fact that I not only look like Nina Stone but behave like her too. My sister and brother have the competitive spirit that my father possesses. It makes the three of them truly believe they can take over the world, and when they do, no one's surprised.

My mother's different. Softer and kinder, she never wanted to rule the world like them. That she has is a by-product of what she really wanted.

My father. And not for his money or power. She fell in love with the man whose chocolate brown eyes made her forget the rest of the world existed. At least that's what she's always said when she tells the story of how they fell in love.

I've always been more like my mother. That's why my father was so protective of me. Not that my shaky beginning in life helped. While my brother and sister came out ready to take on the world, I didn't have that fighting spirit and faltered on my first day. They weren't sure I'd make it to a second day.

I did, and even though the story of our birth always made me out to be weaker, I never felt that way until after the accident. I'd been the smart one out of the three of us. While Ethan could charm the birds out of the trees and Tressa could outmaneuver anyone she ever met, I had the brains. It was those brains that would lead me to the highest court in the land someday.

Since the accident, all my brain seems to want to do is tell me that I can't do it. Do what? Everything. Go outside. Be in a car. Meet new people. Go on a date.

Be happy.

But I haven't given up. I may look like Nina Stone, but I'm also a fighter like Tristan Stone.

TRESSA AND KILLIAN'S ENGAGEMENT PARTY had been billed as the party of the year by those in the know in the media, which meant it mushroomed into something much bigger than even either one of them had planned. I had to attend since not having her only sister there would be noticed by everyone, so even if I didn't want to, I had no choice.

It never occurred to me to miss it, though, and not because my parents, Ethan, and Summer had to talk me into it, like they thought. I loved Tressa and seeing her happy made me happy, and although I hadn't spent much time around Killian, the few occasions we had the opportunity to talk had convinced me he adored her like she deserved.

That didn't mean I intended on playing the part of hostess with the mostest, moving among the guests and flashing a smile as I schmoozed with them. I left that job to my parents while I stayed on the sidelines near the carriage house. At any ordinary party, my staking out a place so far away from the main house might appear rude, but with the hundreds of party guests milling about on the estate grounds, I just seemed like one who'd chosen wisely and found a shady place to enjoy the festivities.

Killian's teammates, larger than life men who towered over many of the other people around them, showed up in force, much to my father's delight. A huge football fan, he looked so happy to interact with the players that I couldn't decide if that smile he wore was because one of his children was celebrating her engagement or because he got to spend time with his favorite team.

I had to give it to Tressa. She swore all the way back in junior high when boys were all I could think of that she'd never marry until she found someone as strong as her. I always figured that meant she'd be single forever, but in Killian she found that strong man.

She'd spent years pushing men away for not being exactly what she wanted, and now she was getting married. In a strange way, it gave me hope that someday I might have that kind of happiness. I pushed people away, for different reasons, of course, but maybe there was that one person out there for me too.

From across the lawn, someone waved their hand frantically, and I shielded my eyes from the sun to get a better look at who it was. Summer. My brother's girlfriend who should have been his wife by now, she was also as much a part of our family as any of us Stones. After the first time we met, she'd made it her mission to get me out of my hotel room and back into the real world, as she said. My being there at that party was a testament to how successful she'd been.

Dressed in a white dress and wearing her hair up in a bun, she looked as beautiful as anyone my brother had shot in his days as a photographer. Walking toward me, she smiled and waved again.

"You're smarter than the rest of us, Diana! You got the best shady place around."

She stopped in front of me and waved her finger up and down my body. "That dress looks so good. I knew it as soon as you tried it on that you had to get that one. Blue is your color, especially true blue. It brings out the blue in your eyes. How are you doing over here? Do you want me to have Ethan bring you a glass of something?"

Turning back to look at the party, she said, "He's following behind me, or at least he was a minute ago. Maybe he got waylaid by someone."

"No, I'm good. I stashed some iced tea in the refrigerator inside, so I'm set."

Summer turned back to face me and shook her head. "See? I would have never thought of that. You're so smart. So did you see the grand entrance when Tressa and Killian came out onto the lawn? The sound of those football players alone probably made the neighbors call the police with all their hooting and hollering. Who knew guys could get so excited about an engagement party?"

As we laughed at the truth of what she said, Ethan strolled across the grass toward us. Dressed in a black suit I knew he hated wearing, he looked as casual and relaxed as he always did, no matter what he wore. My brother had cool down to an art form.

"How is it you always know where to hang out so you get to enjoy the action but don't have to be a part of it?" he asked me as he stopped behind Summer and slid his arms around her waist.

"You know me, and don't pretend that you don't love being in the middle of things like this. You and Tressa are like identical twins with that kind of thing."

He shrugged and chuckled at my on-the-mark analysis of him. Nuzzling Summer's neck, he smiled. "Fine, but I have to say in my defense that's who I used to be. Now I'm seeing the wisdom of how you two like to live. The unobtrusive life is for me."

Summer teased him about his life before her as I thought about his characterization of how I lived. Unobtrusively. It sounded like a way of life some billionaire would choose to avoid people interested in his money.

If only that was the reason I lived like I did.

"Isn't Killian perfect for your sister?" Summer asked as she looked over toward where Tressa stood in a black sheath dress that hugged her body perfectly. "I can say I was there when they first began. That night at the charity auction. I knew she liked him, even though she refused to admit it. I saw it right then and there when their eyes met."

Ethan shook his head. "From what my future brother-in-law told me, she made him work hard to get her. To hear him tell it, there was no eyes meeting and then they fell in love. Tressa put him through his paces, which I tend to believe more than your romantic story about love at first sight."

Elbowing him, Summer frowned. "I'm telling you I saw it that first night. Tressa is Tressa, so she made him work, but I know what I saw when she first saw him and she was head over heels in love with him that very night."

"Diana, I think we need to clear up some misconceptions about our sister for Summer here," Ethan said with a smile as he hugged her to him. "Tell her about the time Tressa made that guy in high school carry her books home while she got a ride home. And then she cancelled on him because he didn't call at the time he said he would!"

Summer's eyes opened wide, but we all knew how Tressa was. That made her finding someone she could be happy with all the more wonderful, though.

"Your parents look so happy too. Look at that smile on your father's face."

We looked across the lawn to see my parents enjoying the party. My father beamed a smile, and a twinge of sadness pinched at my heart because I knew he never looked like that when he was around me. All his moments with me were filled with worry and concern, never lighthearted laughing and smiling like today.

Nudging my arm, Ethan got my attention and smiled. "Don't worry. The only thing I've ever done to make our parents happy is finding Summer."

"Don't minimize how proud they are of you. No matter what you think, even Daddy is proud of you and always has been," I said quietly.

My brother nodded and forced a smile. Out of the corner of my eye, I saw two people walking toward us, and before I could figure out who it was, Ethan yelled, "Cole! Get over here, man!"

Cole Knight, my brother's best friend since grade school, and now one of the most successful club owners in New York City, according to Ethan. Tall and muscular, he looked every bit the athlete he did in high school when he played football and baseball, although his dark brown hair was cut shorter now and didn't hang in his eyes. Dressed in a dark suit with a white shirt and a black tie, he reminded me of some kind of gangster today, though. Considering his family's history, it seemed appropriate.

"We've got a who's who of New York here today, for Christ's sake. You Stones always did know how to put on a party," he said as he shook hands with Ethan.

"Good to see you here, man. I knew you wouldn't miss a party like this. You're like my father, a businessman through and through."

Cole threw his head back and laughed. "Like I'd have to sell anything here. Half the crowd doesn't do the club scene, and the other half is in my place every night. I'm here because I had to see for myself that Tressa is really getting married."

Summer and I exchanged glances as we waited for Cole to introduce the woman with him. Clearly much younger, she looked irritated about something. Her skimpy pale yellow dress barely covered her breasts, which looked as if they strained against the silky fabric and would bust loose at any moment. A gorgeous woman with short brown hair, she had a sexiness about her I couldn't deny.

For his part, Cole seemed happy with her. At least it seemed so by the way they held hands.

Finally, after he and Ethan got through with their guy joking around, he sheepishly looked around and said, "I'm sorry. Diana and Summer, this is Rachel. Rachel, this is Diana Stone, Ethan's sister, and Summer, Ethan's girlfriend."

"Hi. So this is your family's place? Pretty swanky."

I hated the word swanky. It sounded stupid, and there were so many other words that conveyed how gorgeous my parents' home was.

Smiling, I happily let Summer chat this woman up while I slowly began to hate her as much as I hated swanky.

Then, as if the universe wanted to punish me for my evil

thoughts about how much I disliked Cole's girlfriend, my mother called Ethan and Summer over to meet someone she was speaking to, leaving me standing there with Cole and Swanky Chick. We all just stared at one another, none of us having anything to say, and I imagined they wished someone had called them away too.

"So, how've you been?" Cole asked me in a low voice as the three of us looked at the party going on nearby.

"Good. You?" I answered politely, wishing Ethan and Summer would return and save me from this conversation.

"Good. Good. The club's doing great. You know how it is."

I had no idea how it was. Not a single word of what he said was supposed to do anything but fill the dead space. Each word he uttered was the dictionary definition of meaningless small talk. I knew Cole to be so much more than this boring person standing in front of me, so I couldn't help but be surprised.

Rachel tugged on his arm once and then a second time a minute later before whispering far too loudly, "When are we blowing this place? You told me we'd only stay for a little while."

Cole looked over at me and cringed before he himself whispered loudly, "We haven't been here for that long. I've known Ethan's family since I was a kid. I can't just duck out a few minutes after arriving."

Fighting every urge to turn around and walk inside the carriage house to get away from the awkwardness playing out in front of me, I pretended like I didn't hear anything they said. When she stomped her foot and told him she wanted to leave right now and then stormed away when he said they couldn't, all I wanted to do was run away.

Cole's shoulders sagged. Turning around, he looked at me sheepishly and smiled. He didn't have to be embarrassed. At least he had a date for this party.

"Sometimes the road to happiness is rocky," I said, needing to say something to ease the discomfort between us.

Instantly, he shot down my suggestion. "There's no happiness at the end of that road. That road doesn't lead anywhere," he said with a frown.

"Oh. I'm sorry."

I wasn't sure why I apologized other than that I didn't want to see him so miserable.

Shaking his head, he smiled, but this time it went all the way up to his eyes and made the area near his temples crinkle slightly. "I know what being happy feels like. It's been a long time, but I remember."

Something in the way he looked at me made me think he was referring to that time I hadn't thought of in forever. A time when I wasn't afraid of everything and he wasn't unhappy.

I silently climbed out the living room window and ran as fast as I could across the yard toward the back of the property. The dampness from the dew just forming on the grass for the night touched my feet, wetting my skin and making running in my flip flops difficult. I'd gotten good at navigating across the estate in the darkness to get to the area of fencing with a hole in it that allowed me to reach the nearby town much quicker than taking the main road. I suspected Ethan had cut the fence open at some point to sneak around just like I was tonight.

Out of breath, my heart pounded as I reached that point where I'd meet my partner in crime. That's how I liked to think of him, and even though we technically weren't doing anything criminal, I knew if my parents and Ethan found out what I was up to, they'd make sure I never left the house again, especially once they knew who I'd been sneaking out to see.

Just outside the fence, he stood there in dark shorts and a white t-shirt. He waved at me, hurrying me toward him. "Come on! Did anyone see you this time?"

No one ever saw me. My parents spent most of their time worrying about whatever Ethan was up to, so that left Tressa and me to our own devices. For her, that meant reading or hanging out with friends, and for me, that meant sneaking out whenever I could to see Cole.

I ducked as I squeezed through the chain link fence, careful not to catch my clothes or my hair on the metal. "No, it's good. My parents are watching some movie. They're probably asleep since it's after eleven."

Standing to my full height, I looked up at Cole and smiled. Nearly a foot shorter than him, I barely reached his chin if I didn't stand on tip-toe. He pulled me into him and kissed me with a desperation that marked every moment we spent together.

The son of a convicted criminal could be the best friend of a Stone, but he couldn't be the boyfriend of one.

"I missed you," he said in a low voice that covered me like a security blanket.

"Me too. We only have about an hour because I can't risk being out much longer than that. Ethan is due back at midnight, so he'll wake up the whole house when he gets home."

Cole slid his hands down my back and kissed me again. "Thank God for that stupid photography club and their field trips."

"Did you have any trouble getting out tonight?" I asked as we walked toward the woods where we always went to be alone.

He shook his head and chuckled at my question. Since his father went away, Cole and his three brothers had been living with his grandmother, a woman in her seventies who only paid attention to the youngest of them, Chase. The other three boys ran practically wild, much to the dismay of every parent around, including mine. They'd known Cole since he was a little boy, so while they disapproved, they didn't feel right barring him from my brother's life.

My life was an entirely different story. If they ever found out we were secretly dating, my father would kill him. Without a second thought. And I could only imagine what he'd do to me.

I knew that and still I couldn't say no whenever he texted me and asked me to meet him late at night. How could I? I loved him.

"Diana, are you okay?"

Cole's question jarred me from my daydreaming about the past, and I quickly forced a smile and nodded. "Oh, yeah. Just watching all the fun everyone's having."

"Because for a minute there, you didn't look okay."

As he walked away across the grass toward the party, I thought about how much I hated that question. Are you okay? It was all anyone ever asked me.

The worst part was the answer was always the same. I didn't know if I'd ever be okay.

But I wanted to be. I wanted that more than anyone could possibly know.

CHAPTER TWO

COLE

As I walked through the living room, I saw through the window that Rachel had found someone to drive her from the party. From the looks of the guy, he was some kind of linebacker. With nearly a hundred pounds on me, I guessed he might crush her if she didn't take top.

Whatever. Crush her or don't, dude. She's your problem now.

Scanning the party guests as I walked back outside, I knew I'd have no trouble finding a replacement for Rachel if I cared to. The reality was that I didn't know if I wanted to. For the past five weeks, I'd played boyfriend and girlfriend with her mostly because she'd pushed for it. A committed bachelor, I never looked forward to that whole scene. Women were fun to pass the time with, but I didn't need one around twenty-four seven.

I spied Ethan across the lawn and made my way over to him. Still the same guy since he got together with Summer, he'd probably bust my ass about losing my date, but it could be good for laughs.

"Hey, man. I think you need a leash for that girl. One of Killian's teammates just left with her," he said with a smile. Ethan never disappointed.

Summer's mouth turned down into a pout. "Awww. I'm sorry, Cole. She seemed very nice. I had hoped you guys were moving toward something."

Before I could get a word out of my mouth, Ethan chimed in.

"Yeah, they were headed toward her ditching him for a professional football player. Dude, you're losing your game. You're slipping, man."

Since I didn't have the option of slugging him for that crack, I mouthed, "Fuck you," and flashed Summer a smile as Ethan headed off to grab the two of them fresh drinks. "Your boyfriend's in rare form today."

"I think he's worried about Diana," she said far more seriously than I expected her to answer.

Confused, I felt like I walked in on a movie halfway through. "Why? She looked fine to me when we were all over near the carriage house talking. She even got to see the first act of my breakup with Rachel."

Glancing over, I saw Diana standing alone at the carriage house right where I'd left her a few minutes before. She looked the same as she always did.

"You know how these things are for her. He's just overprotective."

Now I felt even more baffled. Why would hanging out at her parents' house on a beautiful Saturday afternoon in May be a problem?

"Summer, I'm going to be honest. I have no idea what the hell you're talking about. I've known Diana as long as I've known Ethan, and she seems the same as always. What's going on?"

She stared at me wide-eyed for a long moment before tugging me by the arm to a more secluded spot away from the party. Summer had never been shy about talking to me, but at this moment, she seemed unsure what to say.

What the hell was the mystery here?

"Cole, you're Ethan's best friend, so I'll be as nice as I can with this. I get that you're all about being the player and living the lifestyle that goes with that, so maybe you don't care about sensitive things like what Diana goes through all the time and especially at events like this. Fair enough, I guess, and if Ethan tolerates that, okay, but he does care about her and so do I. Minimizing what she goes through every day is a dick move, though. Sorry if that offends you, but there it is."

Being told off twice in the span of thirty minutes hadn't been in my plan for this day, particularly since it was Summer doing it this time. Any other person talking to me like that would either get a quick but nasty response or ignored and walked away from, but this was my best friend's girlfriend, so I had to temper my urge to shoot from the hip.

And, to be honest, she hadn't said anything wrong about the kind of guy I was. Even more, I was more than a little curious about what the hell she could be talking about when it came to Diana.

I tipped my glass to finish the last of my beer and looked around to see if anyone could hear us. Nobody was close, so I leaned down and said, "I have no idea what you're talking about here, Summer. Again, I've known Diana for nearly all my life, and I don't see anything different about her. Is this a jealousy thing because Tressa got engaged before her? Trust me. I'm sure if Diana wanted to be married, she would. She's got everything any decent guy would want."

Summer seemed to stop listening after my question about Diana being jealous about Tressa's engagement and stormed away as she mumbled something about guys being assholes. A pretty general statement of fact, it still didn't explain what the hell I'd done to offend her or what the great mystery was about Diana that she knew about and I didn't. Since she'd known Ethan for a fraction as long as I'd known him, I had to figure he'd told me about what she was talking about and I'd forgotten. It wouldn't have been the first time.

By the time I got a refill of my beer and returned outside, Ethan had found me and looked about as pissed as I expected him to be after my conversation with Summer. Before he even reached where I stood, he snapped, "What did you say to Summer? Not that I don't agree that you're an ass, but what did you do to impress that opinion on her in the last fifteen minutes?"

"I have no idea." I raised my right hand and continued, "I swear. She was talking about how hard this is for Diana, and all I said was I didn't understand why it would be. She told me that was a dick move, although I have no idea why, and when I asked if Diana was jealous because Tressa got engaged first, Summer stormed off and called me an asshole. Those are literally the high points of our conversation, and to be honest, I still have no fucking idea what the hell is going on with you Stones today."

Ethan took a deep breath, and I prepared myself for the punch he'd throw in a moment. I wasn't a high school kid anymore, so he wouldn't be able to take me as easily as the last time he slugged me, but the look of anger in his eyes told me this time could hurt just as much. Nothing like having two women ball you out and then getting hit by your best friend. The afternoon may have been a record asshole outing for me.

He let the air out of his lungs in a frustrated whoosh, and like his girlfriend, guided me toward a more secluded spot away from Tressa and Killian's guests. When he stopped, he sighed and shook his head.

"I never told you about this because I didn't think I should be the one to tell anyone, but I guess it's time you knew since you're practically a member of the family."

"One who's been treated like the red-headed stepchild today," I said in an attempt to lighten the mood between us. It didn't work.

Lowering his head, Ethan stared at the ground as he began to talk. "Remember that accident she and I were in like eight years ago? She had some pretty bad injuries and spent a week in a coma?"

He looked up at me and the anguish in his expression took me by surprise. I'd never seen him look like this in the over twenty years I'd known Ethan.

"Yeah, I remember. But she came out of it and your parents found the best doctors in the world to fix her up."

Nodding, he sighed again. "Yeah, the outside is practically

perfect, except for a few scars from one of the surgeries. The inside's a whole other story, though."

"What are you talking about, the inside? What does that mean?" I asked, wondering what the hell he could be referring to when it came to Diana's insides.

A look of pain settled into his face. "She's never really recovered from the accident. Since then, she's been dealing with a lot of psychological things. She rarely leaves her hotel room at the Richmont Midtown where she's lived for years. Summer's gotten her to go out more in the past couple years, but it's been hard. That accident fucked her up pretty bad, and in the eight years since, she's been a mess. Just being here with all these people is a huge step for her. That's what Summer meant before."

His words stunned me. For years, I thought Diana lived with some guy in some penthouse in the city. Ethan rarely talked about her, and when he did, he made it sound like they were getting together to hang out like any ordinary brother and sister would. I never had any hint that she'd ended up living any other kind of life than the one she deserved.

"I had no idea," I said quietly, suddenly worried that the people a few yards away might be able to hear what we were talking about.

Ethan nodded sadly. "I don't tell anyone, so don't feel like I was intentionally keeping it from you for some reason. You've always been nice to her, so it wasn't that. I just didn't tell people because I didn't want to hurt her again. Don't get me wrong. She's much better than she used to be. It's just hard for her. Something happened after that accident that injured her far more than what the car did to her physically."

My brain worked to process everything my friend had told me so far. It sounded like Diana had PTSD after the car accident. But surely her doctors would have medicated her so she could handle everyday things.

"Didn't the doctor give her something? Haven't the drugs worked?" I gently inquired.

Ethan shrugged and shook his head again. "She won't take them. She's been like that ever since we were kids. Unless she was at death's door, she wouldn't even take cold medicine."

"But they would help her, wouldn't they? Why not take them and feel at least a little better?"

The sadness on my best friend's face deepened. "Because she felt like a zombie when she tried them, and she doesn't want to feel that way. She's caught between the devil and the deep blue sea. If she takes them, she isn't as afraid but she doesn't feel much of anything. If she doesn't, she's not walking through life like she's sleepwalking, but all that fear is there all the time. She can't win either way."

We stood there in silence, Ethan blankly looking past me toward the house while I tried to focus on the carriage house porch to see if Diana still stood there watching everything that was happening from afar, close enough to be a part of the festivities but far enough away to feel safe. I didn't know what she feared, but I guessed being around so many people having a great time didn't help.

I couldn't see her there anymore.

"Well, thanks for telling me. I've always liked Diana. She deserves better than the hand she's been dealt."

That sounded supremely condescending, but that wasn't how I meant it. The problem was I couldn't tell Ethan how much it bothered me to hear this about Diana because he could never know how I felt about her.

Ethan forced a smile and chucked me on the arm. "Thanks. Do me a favor and keep this to yourself, okay? She'd be horrified if she found out I told you."

I wanted to ask why, but that would only lead to a different conversation I didn't want to have.

"Of course, man. Not a word."

"Thanks. I better go find Summer and tell her you're not the asshole she thinks you are."

"It's an easy mistake to make. I'm not exactly the greatest guy in the world," I said, not trying to be self-effacing. I really wasn't a terrific guy most of the time.

As Ethan disappeared into the crowd of partiers, I thought about the girl I knew back when Diana and I snuck around to be together. Sweet and funny, she made me smile at a time in my life when nothing else could. We were so innocent then.

Well, at least she was. Everything my family had been through my senior year in high school stole any shred of innocence I had left, replacing it with an ugly reality that changed me practically overnight.

But when I was with Diana, all the problems I had to deal with disappeared. The ugliness of being Anthony Knight's son faded away for a few short hours when I was with her.

I wandered around the party, smiling at women as I passed them by, and eventually I found myself walking toward the carriage house. Diana stood alone looking toward the party, and although I knew I shouldn't, I felt drawn to her now after what Ethan told me.

"In case you're wondering if you're missing anything, let me assure you. You aren't. You've seen one engagement party, you've seen them all," I said with a smile.

Diana narrowed her eyes for the briefest moment and then shook her head. Smiling, she said, "I've never been to an engagement party. Are they all like this?"

"Pretty much, although I do have to admit you Stones always put on the best parties. I mean, come on. You couldn't order a bluer sky. I'm beginning to think Tristan Stone controls the entire universe."

My playful jab at her father landed just as I intended, and she giggled. "My father did want this day to be perfect for Tressa, so you might be right."

Our conversation quickly dwindled to awkward silence, so I said, "Tressa and Killian seem to be perfect for one another."

"They are. I'm very happy for her. She got exactly the kind of man she wanted in Killian."

I didn't know what to say to that since I'd long suspected Tressa didn't like much of what she saw in men, so I kept silent. I could joke around with Ethan with comments like that, but not Diana.

As we stood there in silence, my mind travelled back to when she and I first got together. Feeling strange after what I heard about her a few minutes before, I found myself wondering if she ever thought of the time we spent for those couple months in high school.

And before I knew it, the words I shouldn't have said had come out of my mouth.

"Do you remember that first night we snuck out and ran across the yard right over there?" I asked, pointing toward the back of the estate.

She blushed and looked down toward the ground. "I can't believe you still remember that."

I couldn't help but be charmed at how sweet she looked. "I had a good time that night. I don't have that many memories that make me smile, so of course I remember that."

Looking up, she seemed confused. "But we never did anything more than just kiss."

"I don't think that matters. I had a great time that night. You did too, if I'm remembering correctly."

I shouldn't have been using any charm on Diana. If Ethan found out, he'd drag me out of there and beat me senseless. And he'd have every right to do that and more. He'd just told me Diana was dealing with things, and there I was talking about a night a decade before when I'd broken every rule he and Tristan had set just to be cheered up by her.

Still, I couldn't stop myself from flirting with her.

Diana blushed again and nodded. "I did. Remember how terrifying it was when we thought Ethan had seen us out near the back of the grounds? If he had found out…"

She didn't finish her sentence, so I did. "He would have killed me. Trust me, I know. He's warned me over and over never to even look at you like you're a female."

She smiled and looked away, but I added, "But I couldn't stop myself. Forbidden fruit is just too tempting, I guess."

I wished she would keep talking, but she begged off and said something about her having to go find her father. Watching her hurry away, I thought about the first time I kissed her. I'd been so afraid to make any move on her, and when I finally did that spring night after the baseball game, it had been as incredible as I thought it would be.

Maybe it was the lure of forbidden fruit. I didn't think so. While Diana had always been off-limits, I never thought of her like I thought of other girls back then. They'd been playthings to sleep with, fuck them and then forget them was the basic motto of how I dealt with females in high school.

But not her. Not Diana. I'd slept with other girls long before that time I spent with her that spring right before graduation, but never once did I try to get into her pants. That's not what I wanted from her.

My life was a mess after my father got sent to prison and my three brothers and I were sent to live with my grandmother. We still got to attend the same high school and still got to hang out with our friends, so everyone figured we'd be fine. And maybe on the outside we looked okay.

We weren't. Our mother had left when I was twelve. One day, we woke up and she wasn't there anymore. I didn't know why, but it didn't matter. All that mattered was she was gone. My father had never been the parenting type either, so when he found himself left with four boys, he did what he'd always done with us.

Nothing. We found our way on our own, aided by his money to act on our worst instincts.

Then with him gone too, we were lost. Lost wealthy boys with too much unsupervised free time and money, a disastrous combination for the best people, and we weren't the best.

But when I was with Diana, I found what I didn't even know I needed back then. That goodness in her made me feel safe in a world that had no stability or security. I needed that more than I wanted sex, drugs, or any of the bad habits I gleefully enjoyed then.

I remembered the way she looked up at me that first night, her blue eyes wide like she couldn't believe I kissed her. I hadn't planned on it or even thought about what I'd do next after that first kiss. We'd just ended up alone when Ethan left with some girl, and since I had no interest in her friend, I agreed to walk Diana home as a favor to her brother. The road was dark, and we cut through the woods at the first chance we got since we'd played in there nearly every day of our childhoods and we knew that place like the back of our hands.

And there in the darkness as we wove our way through the trees just sprouting their new leaves, I grabbed her hand when she tripped over an exposed root on the path. When she steadied herself, I didn't let go, and then my lips were on hers in a kiss I hadn't planned but never wanted to end.

I didn't know what would happen next. All I knew was when she kissed me back, all the terrible things life had dumped on me and all the awful things I did to others disappeared. She was good and pure and I needed that like I needed air to breathe.

By the time we exited the woods near her house, I wanted more of how she made me feel. I could get sex from other girls, but I couldn't get the way Diana looked at me like I was something worthy of a girl like her.

I liked the way her blue eyes lit up at the sight of me. I missed having someone look at me like that now.

Would a woman even look at me like that again?

CHAPTER THREE

DIANA

THE DARK CIRCLES UNDER MY father's eyes told me he and his party guests had enjoyed themselves long after Ethan and Summer had taken me home yesterday afternoon. He was undoubtedly too tired to do our weekly Sunday afternoon out, but still there he stood waiting for me, smiling like always when he came to see me.

"Your mother apologizes, honey. She's not feeling well today. She promises she'll come next week," he said before covering his mouth to hide a yawn.

"It's okay, Daddy. You look pretty exhausted yourself. Do you want to just cancel today?"

His expression grew serious, and he shook his head. "No. We do lunch every Sunday, so I'm here to take you out to get something to eat. Where do you want to go?"

"Let's make it your choice today."

My father would undoubtedly choose a wonderful restaurant he knew I'd love. That's the type of man he was. He probably wished he could be sitting at home in bed resting after Tressa's engagement party where he likely had too much to drink, but he didn't want to let me down, even for a single day.

That was my father. No matter what he did for Tressa or Ethan, he always showed up for me.

Since he could use a good, strong cup of coffee, I said, "What about that place around the corner that has those wonderful pastries with the chocolate drizzled on top?"

Cherries and Cream had become a favorite spot for Summer and me since they opened a few months ago. In addition to the most delicious pastries I'd ever tasted, they had a variety of coffees and tea we loved, and the place was absolutely adorable.

"Sounds good, but don't you want lunch instead of just pastries?" he asked, stifling a second yawn.

I waved off his concern and shrugged. "It's okay. I'll take a chocolate anything over lunch any day."

"I think we went there a couple weeks ago, didn't we? That's where I had that Denver omelet I loved, wasn't it?"

"Yes, that's the place," I said as I grabbed my white sweater just in case they had the air conditioning on so early in the year.

My father took a deep breath and smiled as I approached him. "You look lovely, Diana. Is that a new dress?"

I looked down at my brand new light pink sundress I'd fallen in love with because of the little white daisies that dotted the hem and smiled. My father never missed an opportunity to make me feel like the most beautiful woman in the world.

Lifting my head to face him, I nodded. "I bought it the last time Summer and I went shopping. Aren't the daisies adorable?" I asked, pointing toward the bottom of my dress.

"You and your mother have almost the identical taste. You got your good style from her."

I rolled my eyes. "Says the man who always looks fantastic."

"That's because your mother tells me when I'm about to walk out of the house looking like a mismatched nightmare. If it wasn't for her, God knows what I'd be roaming the streets like."

Tristan Stone had never looked like a mismatched anything a day in his adult life, no matter what he claimed. I'd seen pictures of him before he and my mother met, and he looked just like he did at that moment in my hotel room. A little greyer at the temples than when he was my age and a little sleepier after yesterday's party, but always sharp looking. My mother's help with his wardrobe choices only improved on what nature had blessed him with.

I stood on my tip toes and kissed him on the cheek. "You're always perfect to me, Daddy. Whatever you look like, you're always the same man on the inside, and that's what counts."

"If only the rest of the world thought like you, honey."

As we walked through the Richmont lobby, my father's employees smiled and said hello, making sure to wish me a good day like they always did. I'd never known if he instructed them to do that or if they just tried to be nice because that's who they were, but their effort never failed to make me happy.

Weaving my arm through his, we stepped out into the warm May day and walked the block and a half to Cherries and Cream. The sun felt good on my face, and I tilted my head back to let it heat my cheeks.

The restaurant occupied a tiny, narrow piece of real estate in Manhattan, but the owners made it feel like someplace out in the country with their charming design. The outside of the building had a façade that looked like an old Victorian house. Painted white, it reminded me of the homes in the town near my parents' home upstate. There, in the middle of the city, the restaurant stood as a welcoming spot to enjoy a treat amid all the hustle and bustle of everyday life there.

Inside, the décor featured red and white checkered tablecloths on the tables and wooden spindle backed chairs painted white to match. Shelves with antique teapots dotted the walls that had been wallpapered in a red and white flower print that oddly didn't overwhelm the place or make it feel too busy. On the floor, hardwood planks that had been whitewashed completed the homey look.

As I took in the feel of the place, my father quietly instructed the hostess to seat us near the front window. I pretended to not know and smiled when he thanked her for the best seat in the house, as he always did at every restaurant. He had the best of intentions for making me sit so others saw me. I knew that, so I never said anything in protest, even though it never failed to make me feel awkward to have passersby staring at me as I enjoyed a pastry and a cup of tea.

I scanned the menu for my usual and then looked over at the chalkboard hanging on the wall for any specials since the owners routinely offered something new each week. On it, I saw written in pink chalk the words STRAWBERRY CREAM PIE.

Tugging on my father's sleeve, I directed his attention to the announcement. "Mom is going to be so disappointed! You should take her a piece home."

He smiled and nodded. "That's a good idea. I'll do that. Are you getting a slice? You love strawberries as much as your mother."

"I do, but I love chocolate more, so it's that pastry with chocolate drizzle for me. What about you?"

Sighing, he said, "Coffee and something light and flaky sounds exactly what I need this morning. I think I'm going to go for a biscuit with butter."

"You and mom had a good time yesterday," I said with a chuckle.

A good time was an understatement. I had a feeling my father never stopped smiling from the moment the first guest arrived to the moment the last one left.

"It was quite a party. Did you have a nice time?" he asked, always worried about me when it came to events like that.

"I did. Ethan and Summer hung out with me for a while, and then Cole and his girlfriend joined us. That didn't end well, but it was nice to talk to him again. We haven't spoken much since high school."

For a moment, my father's eyes narrowed at the mention of Cole, but then they softened again and he smiled. "I think I heard your brother mention something about his date stranding him out at the house. I guess that's what you mean by not ending well."

"I don't think it was true love."

My father didn't try to hide his amusement at my comment. Laughing out loud, he shook his head. "Cole Knight and true love.

Now that's a combination I don't think will be happening anytime soon."

As much as I wanted to defend Cole and ask my father why he thought he wouldn't ever find true love, I stopped myself. Asking too many questions about him would sound suspicious, and I didn't want to have to lie to my father this morning.

The waitress took our order and left us alone again to talk. A group of four women arrived and were seated a few tables away from us. Around my age, they looked tired like my father, and I suspected they spent their Saturday doing exactly what he'd done, just in another location.

He turned and watched them for a few seconds, studying them almost as if he needed to remind himself how normal twenty-eight year old women behaved. I thought I saw a hint of approval in his eyes, like he was happy to see them acting like they were expected to.

Unlike me.

When he turned back to face me, that approval faded, replaced by concern my father forever seemed to have in his eyes when he looked at me. I used to find that look comforting. Now I had grown to hate it because it meant I was as broken as I worried I was.

"Tressa and Killian seem to have found that true love," I said, eager to talk about something that would make him smile and make that look leave his eyes.

"I think they have," he said with pride in his voice. "She's crazy about him, and he's obviously over the moon about her. I think they'll be very happy."

"I never thought Tressa would be the first to marry, I have to admit," I said with a sigh.

A long time ago, I thought I would be the first to find someone to settle down with and have kids. God, that seemed so strange now that I thought about it.

My father chuckled. "I don't think if I had to bet that I would have gone with your sister getting married first, to be honest."

"I definitely doubted Ethan would ever be serious with one woman, so maybe I was wrong when I thought he would have been the last to settle down."

Unlike so many other times when I brought up the subject of my brother, now my father didn't get that familiar hint of disapproval in his expression. Instead, he nodded and smiled. "Your brother and Summer have been a wonderful surprise. I think she's had a good effect on him, especially when it comes to business. I always knew he'd be successful. He's doing what he loves and making a good living at it, and I think that has a lot to do with Summer. She's good for him."

I forced a smile as I thought about how happy my siblings were. Both Ethan and Tressa had found happiness and success in their personal and professional lives, and what had I found? I lived in a room in my father's hotel and only went out when one of my family members joined me. I didn't have friends like the women seated at the table across the room. I didn't have a significant other like my brother and sister.

I had nothing.

My father's hand gently covered mine, tearing me out of my thoughts. His brown eyes filled with sadness, he said, "Honey, you're only twenty-eight. It's very early to be thinking you should settle down. Don't compare yourself to your sister and brother, okay?"

Under my breath, I answered, "Especially when you haven't dated for real in eight years."

I knew my father heard what I said, which only made the look in his eyes even worse. He used to get that with both Ethan and me. Now it was reserved only for me ever since Ethan got together with Summer and started his own business.

"It's okay, Daddy. You're right. I'm young. Too young to be settling down already."

But I couldn't help but wish I had at least an opportunity to be serious with someone.

Eager to change the subject, I forced myself to smile and said, "I was thinking maybe I'd take some online classes. You know, just to keep my brain sharp."

My father's face lit up. "That sounds great! What did you have in mind?"

"I don't know. Lately, I've been thinking about how when I was little and you taught me sign language that winter when my tonsils were giving me such trouble. I still remember it all. Can you believe it?"

I watched as he signed the first thing he ever signed to me. *Don't be scared. You're going to be fine, honey.*

When he finished, I signed back. *I love you, Daddy.*

I didn't sign back what I signed that day when I was a terrified little girl in pain.

I'm scared, Daddy.

But that was exactly how I felt as I thought about how alone I'd been for so long and how I had no prospects of being anything other than alone for the rest of my life.

Scared.

Something had to change, or I'd never have a chance at the happiness Ethan and Tressa had found. I had to change.

The waitress placed our food down in front of us, and as she walked away, an idea came to me. If I had to change, then it was up to me to do it.

And out of the blue, I looked across the table at my father and said, "I think I want to move."

The words seemed to hang in the air for a moment before they registered in his brain. A second later, he looked like someone had hit him across the face. Stunned, he sat back in his chair and said in a low voice, "Move? Where?"

Then as if he saw a light in the darkness, he sat up and smiled. "Oh, do you mean back home? I saw you at the carriage house yesterday. Were you thinking you should live there? I think that's a great idea, honey."

I reached over and set my hand on his. "No, Daddy. I mean move, like to somewhere like where Ethan lives."

My father's expression fell, like all the hope he'd momentarily felt collapsed on itself. "What about the penthouse at the hotel? Your sister isn't living there anymore. It would be perfect."

"I'm not a penthouse kind of girl like Tressa, Daddy."

He shook his head and grimaced like I'd said the most ridiculous thing he'd ever heard. "Don't be silly. You're my daughter. Of course, you're a penthouse kind of girl."

I hung my head as I tried to find the words to explain how I felt to him. "I can't live in the hotel for the rest of my life, Daddy. I've been hiding there for far too long already. I don't want to end up alone, and if I don't do something to change that right now, I'm going to. I want to be happy with someone like Ethan and Tressa are. You understand that, don't you?"

My words were met with silence, and I feared looking up and seeing total disappointment in my father's eyes. I hated the worry and concern he always wore in them when it came to me, but seeing disappointment would crush me.

"Of course, I want you to be happy," he said quietly, his voice catching on the word happy.

Still fearful of what I'd see, I looked up. Those deep brown eyes that never failed to make me feel loved and safe when I was a child filled with utter sadness now. Sadness because of me.

"It'll be okay, Daddy. I'm not planning on moving far. I'll still be here in the city."

He tried to smile but his frown wouldn't go away. "I know. I guess I've always known this day would come. I just didn't think you were ready."

"I'm not, but my fear of the world isn't worse than my fear that I'm going to end up alone with my family having to care for me."

"You're not an invalid, Diana. You're just…"

When he couldn't finish his sentence, I finished it for him. "I'm afraid of everything. Of cars. Of people. Of not being liked.

Of crowds. Of loud noises. Of everything. But I can't stay this way anymore."

"Please promise me you won't go too fast. Promise me you won't make any snap decisions, honey. Your mother and I want to help, so keep that in mind."

I knew how hard this was for him to be supportive when all he wanted to do was wrap his arms me and protect me from everything that could hurt me. I didn't want to upset him or my mother, but I had to try to get my life back.

"I promise I won't, Daddy. This isn't about rebelling against you guys. It's about living again."

✧   ✧   ✧

MY FATHER STOOD IN THE door to my hotel room as he prepared to leave. "I'm going to get that strawberry cream pie home to your mother. She'll love the surprise."

I hugged him and whispered the truth of how much I appreciated him and all he did for me as he held me in his arms. "Thank you for today, Daddy. For everything."

"Thank you. I enjoy our Sunday lunches, even when they're more like brunch. I love you, honey. Never forget that."

Squeezing him, I reveled in the security he provided. "I love you. Tell Mom I missed seeing her today. And don't worry. I'll be okay."

My father leaned back and kissed my forehead. "I know you will be. Just take it slow, okay?"

I nodded, preferring not to lie outright to him, but I didn't want to take anything slow anymore. I'd taken nearly the last decade slow, and what did I have to show for it?

"I'll call you tomorrow. I suspect when your mother hears the news I have to give her she'll be calling before that. Just so you know."

"I figured as much. Be careful driving home, and give Mom a kiss for me."

He took one last look at me and nodded before closing my hotel room door behind him. Left alone once more, I could barely stand to be in that room now. I wanted to get out, even though the very idea of being anywhere else terrified me.

I heard the sound of a call coming in and turned to see Ethan's face staring at me on my TV. Had my father called him the second he left to tell my brother about my plans?

"Ethan, what's going on?"

"Just wanted to see how your lunch with Mom and Dad went," he said with a smile I didn't find suspicious.

But his asking about my lunch date I had every Sunday with our parents felt strange.

"It was good, as usual. Mommy didn't come because Daddy said she wasn't feeling well. I don't think he was either since he looked like he hadn't gotten much sleep and barely ate anything."

Ethan laughed and shook his head. "It's called being hungover. They probably celebrated until the wee hours of the morning with Killian and his friends. Those guys can put the drinks away."

"Well, Mommy and Daddy were happy, so don't take that away from them," I said as I sat down on the couch. "So what else is new? How is the puppy picture taking going?"

Rolling his eyes, he sat back and shook his head. "Summer and I had to take a poodle's picture for a spread in American Dog Magazine. You should have seen this thing, Diana. It was huge, like a small pony, and in its white curly hair they had pink ribbons. Let me tell you, that dog did not like having her picture taken, and sadly, the camera didn't love her either. Definitely not a match made in heaven. If it wasn't for Summer, I wouldn't have been able to finish the shoot. I swear that dog hated me."

"Summer is the dog whisperer, so you better keep her around," I teased.

He looked left and right and then leaned in toward the screen. "Speaking of that, I'm planning on asking her to marry me. I wanted you to be the first to know," he whispered.

Suddenly, tears began to stream from my eyes. Ethan was getting married now too?

"What's wrong? I thought you liked Summer. I thought you guys were close," he said with nothing less than real worry that I disapproved.

Shaking my head, I dried my eyes. "No, I'm crying because I'm happy for you. When are you going to pop the question?"

Smiling, he told me about his plan. "I'm going to take her out to dinner at a nice restaurant and then ask her to marry me when we get home." Stopping, he looked around to make sure Summer wasn't nearby and held up a robin's egg blue box. He opened it to reveal a gorgeous engagement ring with a huge, round center diamond and two smaller diamonds flanking it nestled in a black velvet cushion.

For a moment, my breath caught in my chest. "Oh, my God, Ethan. It's stunning! Did you pick it out yourself?"

He smiled and nodded with pride. "The woman at Tiffany's helped a little."

"With a ring like that, you have to make it a memorable night when you ask her to marry you. It needs to be more than just a dinner."

My suggestion seemed to confuse him. "Like what? She's a pretty down-to-earth woman, Diana. I mean, she's not like Tress. Summer and I are low-key compared to them."

"Take her to her favorite place in the world. You can afford it, so do it. She deserves that kind of proposal, the kind she'll never forget. The kind she'll tell your kids and your grandkids."

Ethan shook his head and laughed. "Whoa. Don't rush things. Grandkids seems a bit much."

"Just make it unforgettable like only you can do, Ethan. Promise me you'll do that."

"I will. I promise. Are we still on for lunch Thursday?" he asked.

"Of course. I expect to hear all about how it went. I'm talking about details, brother."

"Well, if I do it right and she says yes, she'll probably tell you all about it before I even get the chance."

"I want to hear the story from both sides. It will make it even better. Now go make that proposal unforgettable, okay?"

Ethan gave me a big smile. "Love you, Diana. Wish me luck."

"You won't need it. She's crazy about you. I love you, Ethan."

The screen went black and I couldn't stop myself from crying again. But not because I was happy for Ethan and Summer. I sat there alone in my hotel room and felt a sadness I'd never experienced before. I was the only one of us who had nothing in her life. No successful job. No one who loved me like Summer loved Ethan and Killian loved Tressa. No one who even wondered about me other than my family.

For the first time since I walked through that hotel room door all those years ago, I hated this place.

CHAPTER FOUR

COLE

MY BEST FRIEND'S PLACE STILL looked the same as it had when he was single, but I had a feeling if I checked the bathroom there would be something frilly or pink to show that Ethan had left the ranks of bachelorhood for good this time. Probably a pink razor in the shower or something like that. He'd never dated anyone for as long as he and Summer had been together, but since he hadn't married her, I'd long thought that maybe she was a passing fancy.

Except for the fact that the passing fancy had been in his life for two years, lived with him, worked side-by-side with him in his business, and appeared on his arm at every social event he attended. Not exactly passing.

Not surprisingly, I'd never been accused of being able to see things clearly when it came to relationships, mine or anyone else's.

As I finished scanning the apartment, this time to see if Summer was joining us, I sat down at the kitchen island on the comfortable new stools he'd gotten to replace the old, purgatorial ones that made your legs feel like someone had separated them from your body. Another effect of the passing fancy not being so passing.

Ethan handed me a beer, and I took a long drink before setting the bottle on the countertop. When he invited me over tonight, he sounded serious, so I braced myself for what he had to say. All day possibilities had run through my head. First and foremost, I wondered if he found out about when Diana and I were together in senior year of high school. That was a decade ago, but he'd never been too keen on me even looking sideways at her, so although a lot of time had passed, I had no doubt he'd still be pissed.

But the idea that he'd found out was pretty unlikely, which led me to my second guess. Something was happening with Summer. But was it good or bad? I studied his expression as he drank down a full gulp of beer and couldn't decide. Maybe they were breaking up. Two years was a record for him, so maybe the whole thing with her had run its course. Or maybe they were getting engaged, taking their cue from Tressa and Killian after their party the other day.

No way. Ethan Stone wasn't getting married. Nope. We were going to remain single forever, just like we said back when we celebrated my twenty-first birthday with the cheerleading squad from whatever that college was upstate. Ethan did not intend on leaving the ranks of single men.

"So," he began, his voice shaky. "What's new?"

I stared across the island at him and knew by the way he looked like someone was squeezing his balls too tightly that what he had to say was exactly what I'd been so sure could never happen.

"So. I'm assuming you called me here tonight to either unmask which of us is the murderer or to tell me you and Summer are getting hitched. To be honest, I'd rather you tell me you've killed someone."

I watched as every ounce of stress left his body. He visibly looked more relaxed as soon as I said those words.

"Don't be an asshole," he said with a smile. "If I killed someone, it probably would have been you."

Twisting my face into a grimace, I nodded. "True. I seem to bring that out in people. So this is the final meeting of the bachelor's club, huh? We better get drinking. Our last meeting can't be conducted soberly."

"Don't be ridiculous. It's not like Summer and I are running off to get married tomorrow. I haven't even asked her yet. I'm doing it tomorrow night after I take her somewhere nice."

"Ethan Stone married," I said, shaking my head. "Now I've

seen everything. You know, this leaves me alone in our circle of friends as the lone single man. I'm not sure I'm up to the task of servicing all the single women in this city. What am I going to do without my wingman?"

He threw his head back and laughed. "Cole, I haven't been your wingman for two years now. That's probably why you turned to dating women like that one you brought to Tressa's engagement party. Dude, what the hell was with her?"

I hated to admit he was right, so I chose to focus on the more positive aspects of Rachel. "I know. Hot, right? I know you're spoken for and all, but you still notice gorgeous women, don't you? Did you check out that ass? Mmmm…"

Ethan took another drink of his beer and shrugged. "Yeah, great ass, but she had the personality of a fucking porcupine."

Opening my mouth to disagree, I had nothing. Not a single word to defend the women I'd spent nearly five weeks with. "What can I say? She was a great lay. She could do this thing with her tongue…damn. I think I'm going to miss that porcupine."

For a moment, Ethan just stared at me in disbelief, but then we both exploded into laughter. "So Rachel wasn't the one for me. Maybe there isn't a one for me."

"At least your usual type knows how to have a good time. This one didn't even have that going for her."

"Rachel wasn't really a serious thing. She was shallow and demanding, and when I said I wanted to stay at the party, she stormed out after telling me we were done. It was all very dramatic. I ended up having to hitch a ride with other people heading back to the city."

My tale of woe didn't elicit any sympathy from my best friend. "Nice choice of a girlfriend, dude. Generally, you want to avoid the ones who strand you out in the 'burbs," Ethan teased.

"Fuck you. Not everyone gets to have the girl-next-door like you. Maybe if I'd been born with a silver spoon in my mouth."

Ethan's eyes grew wide for a moment before he simply laughed at me. "Your parents were multi-millionaires, Cole. It's not like you were a poor kid. If I had a silver spoon, you had at least the same thing."

"Well, maybe if my parents had stayed together I'd attract nice women. I'm sure there's some deep psychological reason I chase women like Rachel. It probably has to do with my mother's leaving just as I was becoming interested in girls. All incredibly psychological. Or maybe I just like nasty women."

"Maybe if you didn't chase nasty women who are just out of high school," he suggested like he was trying to be helpful. "How old was she anyway?"

Smiling, I said, "Twenty-one. And before you say another word, let's reflect back on your history before Summer came along. You were with barely legal girls when you were doing that whole model thing. They may have looked like women in their twenties, but you and I both know they weren't. Hell, if I'm remembering correctly, that one you hooked up with in Bali was barely eighteen, and you were how old?"

The grimace on his face told me I'd successfully driven my point home. "Fine. I won't bust your ass about your taste in women anymore. I'm just suggesting that maybe if you spent time with someone closer to your age that you might not get stuck begging for rides back to the city because your girlfriend had a temper tantrum and left you high and dry."

"Fair enough, but you feel free to point me to a woman our age who doesn't come with a metric shit ton of baggage. You got lucky, man. Most women near thirty have kids, at least one ex-husband who's never really completely gone from the picture, and other problems I don't need in my life."

"I did get lucky with Summer, but I hate to say this and I know they're going to take my player card for this, but maybe you try looking for women in places other than your club."

His dose of reality just hung there between us, a strange truth I knew like every other single guy in the world. I had nothing against women in clubs. Hell, I owned a club, so I'd spent more nights than I could count finding my newest partner in it. But the truth was if a guy wanted to find something more permanent, a club wasn't the best place to search for it.

I'd had enough of this serious conversation about the success or failure of my time as a single man. Tipping my beer bottle to my mouth, I drank down the last few sips and then shook it in front of me.

"Now that we've dissected me and my psychological issues with women, how about you get me another beer? I'm still too sober to deal with the fact that my best friend is getting married, so more alcohol is called for."

Ethan chuckled at what he considered to be a joke, but his announcement that he was soon to be a husband made what I didn't have in my life become all the more real. All through my twenties, I'd scoffed at the mere suggestion that it was time for me to settle down. Why the hell would I do that? I was a wealthy and successful man who had his pick of women. Who traded that life for one with the same woman every day?

I spent my time enjoying single life, and when it had been Ethan and me out on the prowl, I couldn't imagine anything ever topping that. Then he met Summer, and everything changed.

Not that I didn't understand why. I mean, who the hell wants to spend their life moving from person to person, night after night? Even though most people who knew me wouldn't recognize much change in the past two years, I had settled down a little. A couple years ago, I wouldn't have spent five weeks with any one woman, no matter how great she was in bed. Before, I saw the plethora of single women in the city as my personal banquet, and I saw no reason not to gorge myself on every possibility in sight.

So I had changed a little. That didn't mean I wanted to settle down with one woman and find ourselves a house with a white picket fence. That wasn't who I'd ever be. But I liked the idea of finding what Ethan had found in Summer. She wasn't boring, and there was no denying that my friend was happier since she came into his life, and who didn't want to be happy, right?

"Cole? Earth to Cole. You in there?"

I shook the daydreams about happiness from my head and laughed as I took the bottle of beer from Ethan. "Yeah, relax. I was just thinking about Rachel and that ass of hers. I really will miss that, I think."

"You're going to be single forever, man."

After downing a mouthful of beer, I said, "You act like that's a bad thing. Just because you've joined the ranks of the soon-to-be-married doesn't mean there isn't a great life the rest of us get to enjoy."

Ethan's expression grew serious again. "Speaking of me getting married, assuming Summer says yes, can I count on you to be best man?"

Just hearing the words best man made everything so fucking real all of a sudden. I sat back and blew the air out of my lungs. Best man. Holy fuck. Nobody had ever used those words to describe me, not even on my best day.

"Of course. Who else would you ask? We've been friends since grade school, for Christ's sake. I'm the only one who's up to the task of giving the reception toast, which by the way will have some mention of your misdeeds all these years, so there's your fair warning."

"Try to keep it to the minor misdeeds, okay? I don't want to be served with divorce papers on my damn honeymoon," Ethan said with a chuckle.

"Got it. I'll stick to the misdemeanors and stay away from the behaviors that could have gotten you put away." Raising my right hand, I smiled. "She'll never know the worst of you, I swear."

He shook his head. "She's lived with me for two years, Cole. Trust me. She knows the worst of me already."

"But she doesn't know about high school Ethan, I bet. That guy has probably stayed hidden, hasn't he?" I teased.

"That guy doesn't exist anymore, man. I grew up. My youthful indiscretions don't matter now."

I'd wanted to ask about Diana all night, so now seemed as good a time as any to segue our conversation to the topic of her. "Speaking of our youth, I have to say what you told me about your sister stunned me. I had no idea. She was always a sweet girl, so I just figured she'd settled down long ago with some nice banker your parents loved."

Ethan shook his head and frowned. "No. Diana has spent the last few years dealing with the mistake I made."

Damn. I hadn't brought up Diana to make Ethan feel like shit.

"You were a kid. You made one mistake. I'm sure she doesn't blame you for that. She's not that kind of person."

He sighed, blowing the air out of his lungs. "I know, but it doesn't make things any easier for her. I have to say, though, that where the rest of us Stones have failed miserably, Summer has really helped her. Since she's been around, Diana has started to go out more. It's still not great, but I think she's trying."

"So she's just been living in the Richmont in Midtown these past few years? I can't imagine what that must be like," I said, even as my brain tried to do just that.

Diana had been so full of life back when we were in high school. Always there with a smile for everyone, she brightened up any group lucky enough to have her in it.

"It's bad, but I don't want you to think she's a basket case. She's just got some issues because of the accident."

Taking a drink of beer, I tried to lighten up the conversation. "Who doesn't? I mean, I wasn't even in an accident and look at me. I only chase after women I shouldn't want because I have some asinine mommy issues. I bet Diana's going to be okay. She just needs some time."

Ethan rolled his eyes. "You chase after women you shouldn't want because you're a dog. It's not exactly the same thing."

I shrugged. "Maybe not, but everybody's got their problems.

The key is to find someone who doesn't think your issues are so fucking scary that they can't handle them. At least that's what I'm telling myself because the alternative is worse. How's that for some psychological thinking?"

"Sounds like bullshit to me, but I'll take anything that sounds like my sister might someday have the kind of life I wish she'd have," he said before tossing his empty beer bottle in the garbage.

It did sound like bullshit. What the fuck did I know about the things Diana had been going through since the accident?

I wanted to know, though. Seeing her at Tressa's engagement party brought back memories I hadn't thought of in ages but once they came flooding back, I remembered how happy I was when she and I were spending time together. Maybe it was simpleminded to think that time meant anything to her now after all she'd been dealing with, but it did to me.

Even though I risked raising Ethan's suspicions if I asked about her any more, I couldn't stop myself, so as casually as I could, I asked, "So is she at least enjoying the penthouse at the Richmont?"

That sounded about as smooth as forty grit sandpaper.

My friend didn't answer right off but just stared at me like he didn't understand the question. Finally, Ethan said, "No. She's just in an ordinary room. My father gave her one on the first floor."

"Why not the penthouse?" I pushed further, knowing at any minute Ethan would probably ask me why the hell I was even interested in any of this.

But oddly enough, that question seemed to make him want to open up about it, and he answered, "Well, Tress was living there until a few months ago when she moved in with Killian, so it wasn't available. I'm not sure I can see Diana living in the penthouse anyway. She's not that kind of person."

"The kind of person who wants to be left alone and away from people? I'd love a penthouse. It sounds like the perfect place to stay if I have to be in a hotel."

He smiled and shook his head. "And that's why you're exactly the opposite of Diana. In all honesty, I don't remember why my father gave her the room she has. That time is pretty much a blur now. It's hard to think of."

The sadness in his voice told me I couldn't push any more on the subject of Diana, so I reverted back to my joker self to lighten the mood again.

Spreading my arms wide, I grinned. "I'm the opposite of everyone, man. It's part of my charm. Let's say I come by it naturally. My grandmother used to like to say if you have to be different, you better be charming. She claimed that's what made my father so successful. Of course, he went to prison for embezzlement, so maybe I shouldn't base my style on him, huh?"

"How is Anthony Knight these days?" Ethan asked as he stood near the refrigerator and opened a new bottle of beer.

"He's still doing ten to fifteen in a federal prison in the Keystone state, so I think we can safely say he's not doing great."

Ethan sat down across from me again and nodded. "Sorry. I thought there was a chance he might get out for good behavior or something like that."

"It's only been ten years as of last fall, so maybe. I don't know. I leave that stuff up to my brothers. They go to see him. I'm not much for the pilgrimage to the incarcerated, thanks."

And with that, I had a stark and the best reminder why my best friend since grade school never wanted me within ten feet of his favorite sister.

Chapter Five

Diana

THE FAMILIAR CHIME FROM MY TV told me someone was calling, so I quickly straightened up the area where I sat on the couch filled with magazines and my journal and waited to see who would appear in front of me. Seconds later, I saw Ethan's face and knew by the happiness in his expression that he'd popped the question and gotten the answer he wanted.

Before I could even say hello, he blurted out, "She said yes! She said yes, Diana!"

I forced a smile as tears welled in my eyes. My brother was getting married.

"I'm so happy for you, Ethan! Tell me everything, and don't leave out a single detail," I said as I settled into my spot on the couch to listen to his story.

"Well, after I talked to you, I figured I better come up with something other than just a nice dinner and the ring. I couldn't think of what to do, though. Summer isn't a five-star restaurant kind of girl, so I didn't really know where to go. I thought about taking her back to where we first met in Australia, but that didn't feel right either."

So typical of my brother. More than a minute into our conversation, and already he'd buried the lead.

Eager to hear the juicy details of the story and not his deliberations, I leaned forward toward the screen and said, "Get to the good part. I'm dying to know what happened. Did you take her somewhere exotic? I'm sure Daddy had no problem with you taking the plane, right?"

"I thought about that too, but I went a different way. I thought you wanted me to get to the good part?"

Impatient to hear it all, I nodded. "I did, but then I had the idea that maybe you took her somewhere I hadn't thought of. Go ahead. I won't say another word."

His smile spread across his face as he proudly explained what he finally decided. "We've been thinking about buying a house, and Summer's been looking at a place just outside the city. She pointed it out to me a few times last month. It reminds me of Mom and Dad's house, except it's about one-fifth the size. It's got a yard Trooper can run around in, and it's in a nice neighborhood. Again, it's nothing huge like our house growing up, but she likes it and has mentioned it a few times as she's searching for houses."

Ethan Stone, my brother and horrible storyteller. I loved him dearly, but my God, was he bad at this.

"So you got cheeseburgers and drove by the house while you two ate them? What happened?"

"I bought the house two days ago and took her up there to surprise her. I'd had dinner brought in from Farini's and it was waiting for us when we got there. I actually have Tressa to thank for that because she handled the restaurant delivering the dinner since I was busy driving Summer out there. I surprised her with the house first, and then after we finished dessert, I took out the ring and popped the big question. She said yes and cried so much if I didn't know her I'd think she didn't like it all, but since I do know her, I knew the crying was because she was happy."

As I listened to Ethan's story, I could barely believe what I was hearing. Of all the ideas I'd had for his big moment, I'd never imagined anything so thoughtful and sweet.

"I'm so happy for you. I knew she'd say yes, but after what you did, what girl would want to say no? A gorgeous, three-carat diamond engagement ring and a house all in one night? What did

Mommy and Daddy say when you told them?"

A sheepish look came across his face. "I haven't yet, so like I asked Tressa, I'm asking you. Don't tell them. I want to surprise them. Summer and I are going out to the house to have dinner tomorrow night, so we're going to tell them then."

"They're going to be so happy, Ethan. I know they love Summer, and Daddy's going to be beaming at the news that you're getting married. He won't be able to stop smiling for a week, I bet."

As I said those words, my heart hurt at the reality that I might never be the reason my father experienced such happiness. The blissfully happy look on his face the whole time he walked around the party last weekend told the world he was so proud of his daughter, and now he'd have that same expression after hearing Ethan's news. I wanted to think I would be responsible for making that same smile happen after all the hours of worry he and my mother had devoted to me, but at the moment, I seemed like a lost cause.

"I'm worried he might fall over when we tell him. Me, Ethan, his misfit son who took screwing up from a pastime to practically an art form, getting married and settling down in the suburbs. First a girlfriend, then a dog, and now a wife and a house. I'm not sure Dad is going to be able to handle it all," my brother said with a chuckle.

"You were never a screw up. You were just more of a wild child than Tressa and me. I always knew one day you'd find your brand of happiness. I'm so happy for you, Ethan."

"That means a lot to me. Summer's on her way over to tell you what happened, so I better let you go. I love you, Diana. Oh, and you better be ready for when she asks you to be a bridesmaid because she's already got her list written down, and you're on it, naturally."

"I'm ready. Call me after you and Summer go to see Mommy and Daddy, okay? I want to hear how it went and what Daddy said."

"You got it! Talk to you then."

The screen went dark, leaving me alone in my little hotel room as I thought about the phrase *always a bridesmaid and never a bride*. I couldn't even say that about myself. I'd never been a bridesmaid. How could I? Until just a couple years ago, I spent nearly every waking moment in this room. My friends from high school and college had fallen away long ago, first after the accident and then when I couldn't be anything more than a face on their screens. I didn't blame them for forgetting me. In some ways, I'd forgotten me too.

Now, though, with Tressa and Ethan both starting their new lives, I wanted to see if I could too. Mine didn't include anyone in love with me like theirs, but that didn't mean I had to be alone forever, did it?

SUMMER FINISHED TELLING ME ALL the wonderful details Ethan hadn't bothered to include about his surprise proposal, like he had the house furnished by a stager the realtor knew so they didn't have to sit on the floor while they ate their veal piccata before he asked her to marry him and they were planning a June wedding the next year. My brother, like most men, only gave the high points of the story. For the rest, I had to rely on my future sister-in-law.

Leaning back on the couch, she sighed. "I have to give it to him. Ethan can be very romantic when it counts," Summer said with a smile that showed how happy and content he'd made her.

"Even though the rest of my family doubted it, I always knew he had it in him. It just took the right woman to bring it out."

I reached out to take her hand in mine to look at the engagement ring again. When Ethan showed it to me the other day, it looked beautiful, but up close, it was nothing less than stunning. "I can't get over how gorgeous this ring is!"

Blushing, she beamed a smile that lit up her face. "He really did knock it out of the park, didn't he? Just when I think he couldn't be any more perfect, he goes and does something like this and the house. Can you believe it? I feel like the luckiest woman in the world, Diana."

"I'm so happy for both of you."

Summer thanked me and then fell quiet for a moment, her face growing darker than it had been a moment before. "You've become one of my best friends, Diana. Tell me you'll find a way to be one of my bridesmaids. I know it's a lot to ask because even though Ethan and I want a small wedding, I have a feeling once all our parents get involved, the guest list is going to mushroom exponentially and there will be a lot of people around. I wouldn't ask if it didn't mean so much to both of us to have you right there with us on our big day."

The way she practically begged me made saying no impossible. But I never wanted to not be involved in the most important moments of my loved ones' lives. I just struggled with being around crowds of people.

That didn't matter. Ethan and Summer meant too much to me to even think about bowing out of their big day. I did have just over a year before that, so maybe I would be okay.

I squeezed her hand, partly because the mere idea of how being around all those people would terrify me, and shook my head. "I wouldn't think of missing it for the world."

My answer made Summer's face light up, and she squealed in delight. "Oh, that's great! Let's go out and celebrate. We can do whatever you want. Eat, shop, or just walk around. It's a gorgeous day out there, perfect for window shopping. What do you say?"

She had no idea how much I craved leaving that room that every day became more and more like a prison. I didn't need convincing to go out like she wanted. As strange as it seemed, living in a city with millions of people in it felt oddly comforting since nearly all of them never noticed me. The situations that were hard were the ones where everyone's eyes focused on me, or at least I felt like they did.

"I say let's do it!" Jumping up in excitement at the thought of getting out, I grabbed my purse off the nearby table. "We can look for bridesmaids' dresses, if you want, while we're shopping."

Summer stood and began heading toward the door. "I promise I won't dress you guys in those ugly dresses bridesmaids always have to wear."

Suddenly, she stopped and turned back to look at me. "That sounded awful. I didn't mean that the gowns Tressa's having us wear are ugly. They aren't. That woman couldn't pick out ugly in a lineup."

"Oh, I didn't take it that way. Tressa has the best taste of all of us Stones. Well, maybe equal to my father's. Her bridesmaids' gowns are classic, just like her. You can't go wrong with sleeveless, black silk, floor length dresses, especially when you're having eight women lined up in a row in a church."

Quickly changing the subject, I added, "How many bridesmaids are you having?"

"Two. You and my sister, Dawn. Three, if you count Tressa, but she's technically going to be matron of honor since she and Killian will already be married. She's already warned me that if I ever use that term around her, she's going to make my life miserable," Summer said with a nervous giggle.

"Trust me. I know my sister. She will. So no using the word matron ever again," I said with a smile as I guided her out of my room. "You know, just in case because I'd hate to see you slip one day in front of her."

Terror settled into Summer's eyes. "Don't even think it."

We walked through the hotel lobby and said hi to everyone there who knew Summer well after two years of coming by to see me. On our way out, the doorman Albert tipped his hat to us and wished us a good day like he always did when he saw us. My father's employees treated us like old friends, and I appreciated their gestures. I'd miss them when I left the hotel.

"Do you want to go to that shop on Thirty-Seventh Street? I've heard good things about it," Summer said. "I don't think I want to go to the boutique Tressa's going through up in Chelsea."

"Why not? It's not like money is an issue, so I'm sure you could find something there for your gown and our bridesmaids' gowns," I said as we walked along the sidewalk.

"Oh, I know. It's just that we have different styles. Tressa is high fashion. I'm more what you might call low fashion," she joked. "Plus, I don't want her feeling like I'm intruding on her plans, you know?"

I knew by the worry in her expression that Summer was genuinely concerned that her and Ethan's news might eclipse my sister and Killian's. It was understandable, but my parents had room in their lives for two big celebrations a few months apart. Anyway, Tressa and Killian's wedding day was this August, and Summer and Ethan's wouldn't be for ten months after, so it wasn't like they were one right after the other.

Hoping to put her mind at ease, I nodded my understanding. "Don't worry. My sister is marrying a famous athlete. Just that fact will make it huge news for the gossip pages. You don't have to be concerned that your wedding a year later will affect that."

Clearly relieved, Summer smiled. "Okay. Maybe next time we'll head up to that boutique in Chelsea. For today, let's stick to the bridal shop on Thirty-Seventh."

We headed toward our destination, but we didn't get far before I saw Cole walking in our direction. Instantly, my stomach began to do flips. I quickly adjusted my hair so it hung down along the sides of my face and covered the scars on my cheek and neck just before he reached us.

What was he doing there? In all the times Summer and I had gone out, I'd never seen him.

He looked as good as he had at my parents' house the other day, except now he wore jeans and a T-shirt instead of a suit. As handsome as always, he smiled as he approached where we stood on the sidewalk, his eyes lighting up as he spoke.

"Fancy meeting the future Mrs. Ethan Stone out on this fine day," he said with a chuckle before bowing in front of Summer.

"Ethan told you already?" she asked with surprise.

Smugly, Cole said, "He told me before he even asked you. I knew before anyone else, I'm proud to say. Unless he told you first, Diana. I know how close you two are."

Remembering my promise to my brother, I shook my head. "Nope. I'm like everyone else and heard about it after the fact."

"Well, no matter when you hear the news, it's still all good," he said, his charm evident by the way he practically flirted with Summer.

She sensed it too because she waved away his effort to be nice and said, "I know you, Cole Knight. What's with all this today? You're the same guy who probably told Ethan that getting married would be the death of him or something like that."

He pretended to be hurt by her accusation, raising his eyebrows far up into his forehead in shock. "Me? I'd never say that. I knew the minute he started talking about how much he smiled when he was with you that our guy was a goner. It was just a matter of time before he asked you to marry him. In fact, I'm a little surprised he waited this long since he's been off the market for the past two years."

"Why don't I believe you, Cole?" she asked, grinning as she nudged my arm.

Shrugging, he simply smiled in that charming way that never failed to make me weak in the knees years ago, and before I knew it, I said, "So no new girlfriend to replace the one from the party?"

I couldn't believe of all the things I could have said, those were the words that came out of my mouth! I'd been curious since I watched Rachel walk out of Tressa's engagement party, leaving Cole to spend his time talking to the likes of me, but it was so out of character for me to actually ask that question that I didn't know how to act after I said it.

Looking away to avoid facing him, I heard Cole say, "I'm

officially single again, sadly."

Sadly? Why would he say that? Unlike Ethan, I had a hard time imagining Cole Knight ever settling down.

I lowered my head but snuck a look at him and saw he didn't look like he'd been trying to be sarcastic. Summer seemed surprised by his comment, too, but unlike me, she knew how to handle social situations instead of blurting out what was secretly uppermost in her mind.

"You're never anything but single, Cole," she said. "Women come, but they always go."

With a sideways glance, I watched his expression turn to surprise for a moment before he merely shrugged and said, "And with that, I think it's time for me to go. It's nice to see you again, Diana. Summer, as always, a pleasure. I think I'll go work on that best man toast so I can make sure it's just right for your reception."

As he walked away, Summer groaned. "I can't decide if I like him or hate him, you know that? One minute he's nice, and then the next he's issuing that veiled threat about the best man toast, which you know will include every salacious thing your brother has ever done since grade school. I swear if he ruins my wedding, I'm going to kill Cole Knight."

"He'll be fine. I wouldn't worry."

My voice sounded strangely distant as I watched him walk away, and I didn't notice Summer staring at me until she pushed me on the arm. Caught checking him out, I didn't know what to say to her look of suspicion.

"What's going on here?" she asked, making me nervous and wishing she knew about my past with Cole.

"Nothing," I answered, feeling my cheeks heat up with a blush that probably told her everything about what I felt at that moment without my saying a word.

Summer studied my face for a long moment and wiggled her finger toward my nose. "There's something going on with you. I've never seen you act this way. If I didn't know better, I'd say you like him. Do you?"

Unable to keep our secret any longer, I finally told someone how I felt. "I used to. I used to be crazy about him."

"Did he know? Let me guess. He knew, and then he made a jackass out of himself. I can see Cole being like that. No wonder he can't keep a woman."

I couldn't let Summer think that about him, so I shook my head and pleaded his case. "No, it wasn't like that at all. We actually dated for a few months in senior year in high school. Nobody knew because if anyone found out, my father and Ethan would have killed him. We'd meet secretly at the back of the property at my parents' house and hang out in the woods. I was crazy about him."

My future sister-in-law's mouth dropped open in shock. She stood staring at me like what I'd said was utterly unbelievable. I understood why she might think that way. To see me now, no one would guess I could attract someone like Cole Knight, but at one time in my life, I hadn't been such a mess and even a popular high school boy every girl wanted to have for her own was interested in me.

Finally, she squeaked out, "You and Cole? Really? Was he like he is now back then? Because I have a hard time imagining you were anything like the kind of women he dates now."

I thought back to our time together and smiled. "Not really. He was different with me, though. I saw him with other girls all through high school, and it seemed superficial, like everyone knew it wouldn't last. When he and I were alone, he didn't seem fake, like all he wanted was to sleep with me. In fact, we never did. He never tried, and I was too shy to even make a move toward anything like that."

Her mouth dropped open again, but this time she was able to recover more quickly and she said in amazement, "He never even tried to make a move on you? That's a side of him I've never seen. He's always been a player in the time I've known him."

"Nope. Never once. We just spent time together and kissed,

but no sex. He definitely wasn't a virgin by senior year, but I still was, so maybe that's why he didn't want to."

Summer shook her head as her expression twisted into a grimace. "Trust me. It's in men's DNA. They always want virgins, especially the players. It's like some kind of trophy. I can't believe I'm saying this, but I guess at one time Cole Knight wasn't a dog with women. At least not with you."

"I don't know. All I can tell you is he was sweet to me."

We began to walk, and Summer mumbled to herself about not believing the guy she always thought was a full-fledged player had once been a decent guy. I didn't know why he hadn't been interested in sleeping with me, and it didn't really matter much anyway.

Then a sudden flash of fear hit me. If Ethan found out, he'd have a conniption. I might have been a grown woman now, but back then I was his virginal sister and if he ever knew that Cole and I had snuck around behind everyone's backs, he'd do just what he did the last time his best friend even mentioned liking me.

He'd beat the hell out of him. I couldn't be to blame for that.

I stopped and grabbed Summer's arm by the wrist. "Promise me you won't tell Ethan about any of this. It was a long time ago, and none of it matters now anyway. I don't want him to know, so please promise me this will be our secret. You're the only other person on Earth besides Cole and me that knows we ever spent any time together. I need it to stay that way."

Wearing that same sympathetic look she often had when it came to me, she nodded. "Okay. It's our secret. I won't tell Ethan or anyone else. But I don't think he would be that upset, Diana. That was ten years ago. I think he'd be okay with things, but I won't tell him if you don't want me to."

"Good. It's our secret. Now let's go to that bridal shop and find some dresses."

Summer seemed fine with keeping what I told her from Ethan, and as much I hated being the reason she kept anything from him, I didn't want to dredge up the past. There was no reason. Ten years had gone by. Cole Knight was a different person as much as I was. What happened between us all those years ago should stay back there.

We had no present or future, so why do anything to keep that past alive?

CHAPTER SIX

COLE

MY MIND PRACTICALLY BUZZED WITH excitement from Diana's question. Was she really interested in knowing if I had found someone new already?

She had no idea, of course, that I hadn't been able to think of anyone but her since we talked at Tressa's engagement party. I had so many questions I needed answered about her. The problem was I couldn't ask anyone a single one of them.

I had a feeling that if we could spend some time together alone, without the specter of her family being nearby, that we would get reacquainted. I wanted that, but how I'd accomplish it was another story.

For one thing, I didn't even know where she lived. Also, I didn't have her number. That put me at a distinct disadvantage, to say the least. All I knew was she lived at the Richmont Midtown, which was why I just happened to be strolling along the sidewalk and happened to run into her and Summer.

I'd spent over an hour casually walking up and down that block. I was lucky the doorman didn't get suspicious and call the cops.

This whole thing felt ridiculous. A grown man practically stalking someone instead of coming right out and asking her for her number. I silently defended my actions as I stopped walking and tried to figure out my next move.

I'd spied a coffee shop a little ways down the street from the

Richmont, so I headed back there to find a seat by the window that would give me a good view, but not too close so anyone could see me. I figured I'd discreetly follow her and Summer back to the hotel and find out what room she was staying in that way.

While I waited, I'd busy myself with a few phone calls I had to make about the club and kill two birds with one stone. By mid-afternoon, I'd have the information I needed.

LEANING BACK IN THE VERY uncomfortable wooden seat I'd occupied for the past four hours at the coffee shop, I stretched my legs as I once again looked out the window for any sign of Diana and Summer. Like every other time, I saw dozens of other people walking by but not them.

Had I missed them? No. There was no chance. I'd sat there for four hours focused on every soul who passed by, and I hadn't seen either of them.

I tilted the cup to my lips and downed the last drops of my sixth coffee. If I had to, I could probably levitate myself out the door and up to my Upper East Side apartment I had so much caffeine coursing through me.

Maybe I should have grabbed something to eat with one of those cups of coffee. In hindsight, that would have been a good idea, but I didn't want to be away from my seat that gave me such a great vantage point for long.

So now I sat as a jittery fucker watching for two women in what could be described as stalking. I preferred to label it romantic reconnaissance. Yeah, I liked the way that sounded. At least I didn't feel like a complete and utter creep when I thought of it that way.

It wasn't that I wanted this to be the way I got to meet with Diana again. Hell, I would have preferred doing it the normal way by calling her and going from there. I didn't have that choice, though, so I had to get creative. Yes, it had the hint of stalker to it, but I'd known her since we were kids, for God's sake. I dated her for a few months in high school and never even made a single move to have sex with her. If that didn't prove I was at least in part a decent guy, I didn't know what did.

Why didn't I sleep with her, I wondered as I watched some blond woman hobble past in heels too high for her to be anywhere close to comfortable. I'd been crazy about Diana, and she definitely had something that made me physically attracted to her. So why hadn't I made a move on her back when we were together?

My memories of that time struggled to be anything more than hazy, at best. I remembered spending time with her, but my reasons for why I did much of anything in those days escaped me now. Not surprising since that was around the time my father was being hauled off to jail and my brothers and I were hastily transplanted to my grandmother's house.

Not that my not sleeping with Diana mattered to my current situation with her. I slept with dozens of girls in high school and never spoke to them after graduation. Sex or the lack of it didn't mean anything. I didn't even remember most of them now as I sat twitching in my seat while I moved into my fifth hour of watching for her and Summer.

But I never forgot how Diana made me feel when we were together. I had a sneaking suspicion that I'd secretly been chasing that feeling ever since with every woman I dated in the past decade. It had been a wholly unsuccessful effort, sadly. Not a single one of them had ever given me what she did.

I didn't know how to describe it, but as I sat there pondering what exactly it would be called, I had to say the closest I could come was peace. Diana was sweet and caring, but even more, in my world that had been turned upside down by my family's nightmares, she offered me a peacefulness I found nowhere else at that time of my life.

Of course, since I was a teenage boy, I didn't appreciate it as much as I should have. That goes without saying. Teenage boys weren't very thoughtful in any respect, for the most part. Like most,

I was all testosterone packaged in a growing body with a mind that didn't know how to handle either very well.

As I thought about those days, I finally spied my first sighting of Diana and Summer coming down the sidewalk. My mind racing—mostly from the coffee—I wondered what the hell they'd been doing for the past five hours. No one walked around Manhattan for that long. Not even those fitness freaks who seemed to be always running or walking somewhere. How the hell did those people live like that? Always rushing around to stay fit? Buy a goddamned treadmill, people.

We aren't fucking animals. How much do those running shoes cost? They've got to go at least five hundred bucks.

Focus, for fuck's sake, Cole! You just spent hours sitting here waiting for exactly this. Focus!

I shook my head to clear it of the caffeine induced rambling that had started to take over my brain and shrank down in my chair as they passed directly in front of the coffee shop where I sat. The two of them were smiling, and then Diana laughed and threw her head back like she always did when her giggles grew into something more. She used to do that when I told her stories about what we did on long trips on the bus when I was a baseball player.

When they had walked ahead far enough to not notice me leave the café, I hurried out to follow them, concealing myself behind a big guy wearing a cowboy hat. He walked like he'd just gotten off a horse and feared kicking his calves with nonexistent spurs on the back of his boots. I probably should have chosen someone less obvious since he stuck out like a sore thumb in the middle of Manhattan, but I had to think fast and nobody around him looked big enough to hide behind.

Looking around Tex in the City, I saw Summer and Diana walk into the Richmont. I made a dash to catch up with them, hoping that I could just see the room number so I could take it from there. Not that I had the faintest idea what I planned to do once I had it, but without knowing that basic information, the future of my talking to Diana consisted of me spending hours at that coffee shop drinking gallons of coffee and hoping on the off chance that she passed by that I could happen to run into her.

Not exactly the best plan for getting to know her again.

The doorman at the Richmont held the door for me as I stopped sprinting and attempted to casually enter the hotel. I couldn't be sure, but I thought I saw him look at me side eye with more than a hint of suspicion.

No matter. I had more important things to focus on at the moment. Hurrying through the lobby, I saw the back of Summer's head just as she turned the corner near the elevators. I needed to keep my distance so they didn't notice me, but if I didn't know where they were going, all of this would be for nothing, so I raced to catch up to them.

But I was too late. By the time I entered the hallway, neither of them were there.

Quickly, I looked at the hotel room doors. It had to be one of these since they didn't have enough time to walk the full length of the hallway past twenty or so doors. But which one?

Fuck. I'd spent the last five hours wasting my time and had nothing to show for it except the caffeine shakes from way too much coffee.

You're better than this, man. Seriously. Better than this.

My mind raced to figure out what to do next. Ask the desk clerk? Unlikely she'd just give up the room number of one of the owner's kids. Pretend to be a delivery man? They probably would just take the package and handle it themselves instead of giving out a guest's room number.

True, but I could follow the clerk to the room and then I'd know where Diana lived.

Pleased with myself that I'd been clever enough to think of that, I headed back toward the lobby to go buy something to give to her. She always liked elephants, didn't she? I vaguely remembered her having a necklace with a little elephant charm on it. I could get her a gift that had to do with elephants.

Even more pleased with that idea, I strode into the lobby and nearly ran headlong into none other than Tristan Stone himself. Christ, did the entire Stone clan hang out in this place? Next thing I knew, I'd be seeing Ethan, his sister, or his mother.

Scrambling behind a large black marble pillar, I watched as the owner of the Richmont walked in the direction of the hallway where I suspected Diana's room was. For a split second, I considered following him to see where he went, but then my common sense kicked in and I cancelled that idea immediately. The last thing I needed was to have Ethan's father see me and ask what I was doing loitering in his hotel since there was no way I could lie and claim to be a guest there as that could be easily proven to be a lie. Never a huge fan of mine, Tristan Stone would likely be suspicious.

For good reason, of course. I was there trying to get to see his daughter. The fact that I was failing epically at that didn't change the reality of what I wanted to do.

So I'd graduated from stalking Diana to hiding from her father all in one afternoon. Not exactly my most auspicious outing.

Left with few choices and none of them good, I figured my best move was to get the hell out of there and try my delivery guy idea another day. I'd hoped to have more success that afternoon, but absent Diana texting me her number in the next thirty seconds before I walked out the Richmont's front doors, I'd have to settle for at least having a plan for my next attempt to see her.

Turning around, I walked away from my hiding spot near the pillar in the lobby and took two steps toward the door before Summer appeared on her way out. Caught without anywhere to hide, I hurried myself into a nearby chair and sat down with my back to her. Never before in my life had I had a plan go so horribly wrong. If Ethan showed up and sat down next to me, I wouldn't have been shocked in the least considering how this had turned out.

Thankfully, that didn't happen because I had no answer for the obvious question he'd ask of why the hell I was lounging out in the Richmont hotel lobby. Still wired from the excessive caffeinating I'd done to myself, I pressed my hands to my knees to get them to stop shaking as I lowered my head and watched Summer walk out the front door.

One down. One to go. Now I just had to come up with a way to get out of there without Diana's father seeing me. Or the doorman asking me why the hell I was acting like some coked up jackass. Or the desk clerk, who had noticed me lingering about, inquiring what business I had there since I didn't seem to be meeting anyone and I didn't appear to be a guest at the hotel.

Or maybe way too much coffee was just making me nervous and paranoid.

Whatever was happening, I needed to get the hell out of that hotel lobby before Tristan Stone appeared and there'd be no charming him. He'd been less than thrilled with his son hanging out with me in high school, and my choice of career had done nothing to make him like me any more. Owner of a nightclub didn't seem to rank high on his list of reputable jobs. The fact that he'd been the owner of a nightclub years ago when he and Nina met didn't seem to change his opinion of me for the better either.

So coincidentally running into him was the last thing I wanted to do.

Slowly, I stood and looked around to see if the coast was clear. A number of families milled about in the lobby, their children running around as one parent dealt with the check-in process while another parent chased after the kids. An elderly couple walked through the lobby hand-in-hand toward the bank of elevators, and a few stray single men and women sat reading or doing work in an area set aside from the main area near the front desk.

If I could blend in with any of them, I might be able to escape without attracting too much notice. I began walking toward the front door, but a second later, I sat back down and lifted a magazine from one of the tables in front of me to hide my face after seeing

Nina Stone walk through the front doors and make a beeline toward the hallway her husband had disappeared into.

Didn't any of these people work, or did they just gather at Diana's room every day?

Frustrated, I pretended to read a few lines of some magazine about modern art and quickly tossed the magazine back onto the table once I didn't see Nina anymore. Never in my life had I had to dodge so many people in one day. Hollywood stars didn't have to avoid people as much I had this afternoon.

I silently prayed to any god who wanted to help to keep the Stones out of the lobby long enough for me to get myself out of the building and once again looked around to see if anyone I knew was nearby. For what seemed like the tenth time, I took a step toward the door. Then I took another.

So far, so good. Nobody looked at me oddly, as if they knew what I'd been up to there, and by the time I was about ten feet from the front door, I believed I was in the clear.

The afternoon had been nothing but failure, but at least I hadn't been caught and had to stammer out a poorly thought out excuse for one of Diana's parents.

Smiling at the doorman as I approached him, I felt the heat from the air outside rush toward me. I gave him a nod, which he returned as one of the mothers yelled someone's name, but just as I started through the doorway, he clamped his hand down on my arm.

"I think someone wants you, sir."

I shook my head, sure the name I'd heard wasn't mine. "I think they want someone else."

He didn't let go of my arm, though, and for a moment, I wondered if he'd been watching me the whole time I was there and just wanted to detain me until the cops showed up. Not that I had broken any laws, unless loitering in the Richmont lobby was a crime. Tristan Stone did have a hell of a lot of pull in this town.

As my mind kicked into overdrive and thoughts of him seeing

me and immediately calling the police raced through my brain, I heard someone behind me say, "Thanks, Frankie."

Then, in the next second, a woman said, "I almost didn't catch you. Are you leaving?"

I turned around and there stood Diana smiling at me. Not knowing what to say, I mumbled, "I was just…you know how it is. Heat. Just trying to cool off. It's hot for May, isn't it? Really hot."

Nothing I said made any sense. I'd be lucky if Frankie or Tristan didn't call the mental hospital to have me taken away to have my head examined with the way I was talking gibberish.

"I know. It's pretty hot out there today. I think I might have gotten a little sunburn on my nose," Diana said as she touched her cheek. "I was just coming out to see where my mother went and I saw you."

"Yeah. Just popped in. You know, for a second. Cool off. Yeah," I said as Frankie loosened his hold on my arm.

More gibberish. For a man who had been known to sweet talk women into bed with little effort, I suddenly seemed incapable of speaking like a normal human being.

"Would you like to have a drink and hang out for a little while?" she asked shyly, her words full of an innocence I hadn't heard in ages from a woman. With anyone else, the question would have been an invitation for sex, but I had a feeling she meant just what she asked—that she wanted to have a drink and hang out.

"Yeah, that sounds great," I said as casually as I could, reeling from how bizarre this afternoon had been and how great it had turned out.

She beamed a smile and nodded. "Great! We can go to the lounge."

CHAPTER SEVEN

DIANA

EVEN THOUGH I'D LIVED IN the Richmont for years, I'd only been to the lounge twice, and those times were with Summer. We used it as sort of a practice spot to get me used to being around people. Unfortunately, I couldn't muster up the courage to do anything during nighttime when the lounge got busy, so there had never been more than a handful of people around when we went there.

On the positive side, it tended to be dimly lit, which would make talking to Cole easier. And I found the seats comfortable the two times I sat in them.

Cole and I walked through the lobby toward the back of the hotel where the lounge was located. With each step, I felt like every eye in the place stared holes through me. Silently, I told myself this wasn't true. Likely, no one bothered to notice me at all. My anxiety always liked to play tricks on me at times like this.

Not that there had been a single time when I'd gone to the lounge or anywhere else with a man since I moved into the hotel, so I had no real reference as to what a time like this should feel like. All I knew was with every moment that passed by, my palms grew sweatier and my insides began to shake. I couldn't imagine what this would be like with someone brand new. At least I knew Cole.

Or used to.

Ten years was a long time. He'd changed since high school. A little taller and a little more muscular, he was a man now compared to the boy he'd been then.

Oh, God. A man.

I hadn't been with a man since college. Eight years ago. The only men I ever spent any time around were my father and Ethan, and they didn't count. I'd tried online dating when Summer convinced me it was fun, but it turned out to be nothing but disappointment. All the men I met wanted naked pictures of me, and when I didn't send them, they vanished before I could ever meet them in person. I gave up after two weeks.

Since then, I'd worked on trying to meet people's glances and not look away. Being afraid of virtually everything made that far more challenging than anyone could understand. I did it, and sometimes I added a smile and got one in return, but in the grand scheme of things, I hadn't done anything to meet anyone.

That's why when I saw Cole standing there with the Richmont doorman I took a chance and yelled for Frankie to stop him before he left. Trying out my new techniques of meeting people probably didn't count as much with an ex, but I had to start somewhere.

"Do you hang out here a lot?" he asked as we approached the frosted glass doors that led to the lounge.

I wondered for a split second if I should lie and pretend I did spend a lot of time there. It sounded strange for someone who'd lived in a hotel for years to say she never went to the single place in the building intended for socializing.

But I'd never been a very good liar and would likely get tripped up on some small detail, so I simply shook my head and smiled. If Cole wanted to be friends or anything else again, he'd soon realize strange described me in so many ways I practically owned that word.

He smiled back at me, and a memory from one warm spring night toward the end of our time together all those years ago flashed through my mind. Cole had been so different with me than he was whenever Ethan was around. With me, he didn't say much, preferring to listen to me talk about school and any other topic that popped into my head. When he and my brother were around one another, he became just another teenage boy, his behavior crass and graphic and so unlike the person who spent time alone with me. I never understood why he changed so much when he got around me, but it didn't matter. I liked the quieter version of him.

Summer had warned me earlier when I confided we'd dated in high school that the person I knew back then didn't exist anymore. I got the feeling she wasn't a big fan of Cole's. Other than saying he was good looking and agreeing to believe me when I swore he wasn't awful to me, she had nothing nice to say about him. Every story she had involving the man I was about to spend time with centered on easy women and too much drinking.

I'd been warned, but still when I saw him standing in the door with Frankie, I couldn't stop myself. Now I'd see if that had been a mistake.

Cole pointed to a table in the corner away from the bar and made his way there as I followed. We sat down, and I expected us to begin talking, but a look of disgust came over his face. Even in the dim light of the lounge, I saw now that he was alone with me, he regretted it.

I opened my mouth to tell him this was a mistake, but he shook his head and said, "I'm sorry. I don't know my manners sometimes. I should have pulled out your chair for you, Diana."

So he was disgusted by that and not by the way I looked? I didn't know what to say, so I shrugged and shook my head. "It's fine. Really."

"No, it's not. I would have never forgotten that back in high school. My father would have found a way to tunnel out of prison and beat some manners into me if he saw me act like that then."

The mention of his father brought back the memory of him being taken away that day they arrested him. My friends and I had watched from down the road as Anthony Knight was led out of his home in handcuffs like a common criminal. I saw Cole and his brothers watching from the huge bay window in their living room and hated how sad he looked. I didn't know what had happened or what his father had done until later when he told me the story, but at that moment as I clutched my school books close to my chest and stared in rapt attention at the only person I'd ever seen taken away by the police, all I could think about was how devastating it must be to see your father treated that way.

Cole forced a smile and quickly changed the subject. Looking around at the lounge, he said, "This is nice, but I wouldn't expect anything less. It is a Tristan Stone hotel, after all."

"I doubt my father has ever stepped foot in here, to be honest. And if Tressa heard you call the Richmont hotel chain my father's, she'd be the first person to set you straight."

"Oh, that's right," he said, nodding. "Tressa was made COO of the chain last year. Well, that explains the posh feel in here even more. This place screams Tressa Stone."

A quick glance at the black leather booths and chairs and pendant lighting above each table that reminded me of some high fashion design with sharp angles and muted pale green glass told anyone who wondered that the person responsible for the lounge's design loved to be unique. That certainly was my sister. I would have never considered green glass shades for the lighting in here, but it was so Tressa.

"Stark, unique, and an attention-getter. Just like her," I said quietly, suddenly feeling like I paled in comparison and she wasn't even nearby.

"What do you want to drink?" Cole asked, standing to head to the bar.

"White wine, please."

He strode off to get our drinks while I sat looking around at my sister's design choices and wishing anything like them would ever occur to me. Tressa never failed to be bold. I wouldn't know bold if it came up and bit me, which since it was bold likely would.

Thankfully, the bartender didn't have more than one or two other customers, so Cole returned quickly before I could get lost in my head and all my insecurities. Placing the glass of white wine down in front of me, he sat down in his seat and raised his bottle of beer.

"To old times."

As I took a sip of wine, I wondered if he thought of our past like I did. Probably not. He'd changed so much that he likely looked back on those nights sneaking around as quaint or childish.

He didn't speak for a long time, which only made my insecurities kick into overdrive. A man about my father's age dressed in a three-piece grey suit distracted me for a moment, but when I turned my attention back to Cole, something had changed in his expression. Now he looked uncomfortable sitting there with me.

"Is something wrong?" I asked, almost certain I didn't want to hear his answer.

He shook his head no but lifted the small menu from between the salt and pepper shakers on the table and buried his face in it. Was he hiding?

"If you didn't want to be seen with me, you didn't have to say yes when I asked you for a drink."

Cole turned his body to watch the man who'd just walked into the lounge and then turned back to face me. Lowering the menu slowly, he whispered, "It's not that. Really."

Whatever the problem was, I'd made a mistake. Summer had been right. Cole wasn't the person I knew all those years ago. I stood up to leave without saying another word, but he grabbed me by the arm, surprising me.

"What?"

"I thought that man was your father. If he or Ethan see us here together, I have a feeling I'd end up in the hospital with two broken legs."

The way he talked about us having an innocent drink infuriated me. "I'm a grown woman, Cole. My family might think they should make decisions for me, but they don't. For example, I'm moving out of the hotel soon. Did you know that?"

His dark brown eyes opened wide in what looked like shock at what I said. "No, I didn't. I don't really know much about you at all anymore. But I'd like to."

"You would?"

"Yeah."

Happy to hear that, I sat back down with him and took another sip of my drink. "I'd like that."

But then we fell back into silence, like neither of us knew what to say after admitting we wanted to know more about the people we'd become over the last decade. Unsure what to say, I fell back on our past and asked, "Do you remember the first time we kissed after that baseball game? I don't think I've ever been more surprised in my life. It was a happy surprise, but definitely a surprise."

Cole smiled and shook his head. "I must have been a madman back then. If Ethan or your father ever found out, they would have ripped me limb from limb. I was taking my life in my hands, but I'm glad I did."

Was he exaggerating or did my brother and father really terrorize males back then? As I wondered about that, Cole added, "I didn't mean anything bad by that."

"No, it's okay. I was just thinking that maybe the men in my family were the reason why I didn't have many dates in high school. Then again, I was pretty nerdy and spent most of my time studying, so that didn't help, I'm sure."

Cole laughed. "Trust me. Guys never got past thinking about liking you. Most guys, at least. As soon as Ethan even got a hint that someone was checking you out, he let the guy know that wasn't going to fly. That's why I knew we had to keep it a secret or he'd put an end to it."

"Why was he like that back then?" I wondered aloud.

"It's not just back then. I have a feeling if he saw us sitting here, I'd get to feel his fist on my jaw again today."

"Again?" Had he done that recently because he saw Cole talking to me at Tressa and Killian's party?

Rubbing his jawline, he nodded. "Yeah. Again. I made the mistake one time of mentioning you in a carnal way, making it seem like I wanted to hook up, and he leveled me with a shot to my face."

"Oh," I said quietly, relieved my brother hadn't done it lately.

This made me sad. Ethan didn't have to protect me like that. I doubted he ever said a word to any boy who liked Tressa. Maybe that's why she was asked out all the time while I spent most of my nights as a teenage girl at home.

Cole touched my hand to get my attention, and I looked up to see him smiling. "But we're not high school kids anymore, so maybe I'd get a few shots in now."

"I had no idea he was doing that back then. I feel like some kind of untouchable thing nobody can approach."

"Well, I'm glad you caught me just as I was leaving today."

His words made me smile, but then it dawned on me. Cole wasn't staying at the Richmont, so what was he doing there at all? His excuse that he wanted to cool off sounded fishy.

"What were you really doing in the lobby of my family's hotel?"

Suddenly, his closeness to Ethan made his being there this afternoon suspicious.

I pulled my hand away from his. "Are you here spying on me for my brother? Is that what this is?"

Cole shook his head. "No. I swear. He doesn't know anything about this. Trust me. He'd be pissed. He's never wanted me to be with you."

"Then why were you here hanging out in the lobby?"

He looked down at the table and avoided my gaze as he explained, "I wanted to find out where you lived, so I followed you and Summer back here. But I couldn't figure out which room in your hallway was yours, so I hung out in the lobby trying to come up with an idea. Then your mother and father came in, which threw a monkey wrench into my plans." He stopped for a moment before he looked up at me and continued, "By the time you caught up with me, I was leaving after a few hours of failure to find you."

I couldn't believe what I was hearing. "You wanted to find me?"

Nodding, he answered, "Yep. It wasn't easy. I had to resort to some pretty shady stuff and half a dozen cups of coffee."

Now confusion mixed with my disbelief that anyone would bother to find me. "I don't understand. Why so much coffee?"

He smiled and shook his head. "It's a long story. I promise to tell you sometime in the future."

As much as I wanted to know what he was talking about, I liked that he mentioned the future for us. I wasn't sure what would happen, but I liked this Cole as much as I liked the boy he'd been all those years ago.

"I can't believe you would bother to do all of that just to find me."

He took a sip of his beer and chuckled. "There really was no other way. I had a whole plan for the next time since I figured I'd failed pretty badly today. It involved pretending to be a delivery guy, and then if they didn't let me take the flowers to your room, I intended on following the person from the front desk who took them to you so I could find out your room number. Now that I say it out loud, it sounds like a pretty awful plan, but in my head, it sounded like it would work."

I sat stunned at what he said. He would have gone through all of that simply to find me? To find Diana Stone? I never thought about making it easy for people to get in touch with me because I figured no one wanted to.

"There was no one you could ask?"

His eyebrows shot up into his forehead, and he looked at me like I'd just asked the dumbest thing in the world. "Since I'm trying to avoid letting Ethan and your father finding out, I don't know who I could ask. I doubt the front desk of the hotel would have given up that information to me."

I sighed at the reality I'd created for myself. Even when

someone wanted to find me, I was impossible to locate. Cole was likely the only person who ever tried, but I'd made it so hard that he would have been forgiven for giving up after this afternoon.

"I'm sorry you had to do so much to find me. I don't know why my family feels like they should shield me from you either. Even Summer warned me against you."

Cole's mouth dropped open in shock, so I quickly explained, "I know we promised we wouldn't tell anyone about us in high school, but she's my friend and I needed to tell someone after seeing you this afternoon. But don't worry. She won't tell Ethan. She won't. I made her promise she'd keep our secret."

As I talked, he seemed to be convinced that he wasn't in danger of Ethan charging in at any moment to attack him for something he'd done a decade ago. When I finished, he sighed like he felt bad about something.

"I never told anyone, but I think I assumed you did before today. I just figured girls talked more than us guys. So Summer told you not to talk to me again? She's not my biggest fan, I guess."

Feeling bad about what I'd said, I quickly worked to make him see she didn't hate him. "I don't think it's that. It's just that I think she associates you with Ethan being single, and we all know what he was like before he fell in love with Summer. You can understand how she wouldn't want him to be tempted to go back to that life since they're planning a future together."

Cole waved off my excuses for her. "She doesn't have to worry. Ethan was lost the moment he realized she made him smile more than anyone ever had. There's no comparing with that, not even for a best friend of twenty years. Once he decided he wanted that kind of happiness instead of the kind he got from being single, your brother was done for. Whether he knew it or not, I knew it the first time he mentioned he missed feeling that way. I wouldn't try to ruin that for him."

"I think she knows that deep down. She doesn't dislike you. I had a feeling she felt worried when I mentioned you, like I wasn't the right kind of person to handle you."

"Handle me?" he repeated with a chuckle. "What does that mean?"

Suddenly, our conversation became too real, and I averted my gaze so I didn't have to face him when I answered his question. "I'm not like Rachel. I'm probably not like anyone you spend time with, and as much as I wish I meant that in a cool, unique way like I would if I was Tressa, I don't. I've dealt with a lot of things since the accident."

He didn't respond immediately, which only served to ratchet up my fears until I felt certain I needed to run out of the lounge and never look back. But then he finally spoke, and I didn't even have to tell myself to look at him.

"You were never like other girls. Not back then, so why would you be now? You're Diana, and there's nothing wrong with that. You're still as sweet and kind as you always were. Whatever happened because of the accident, that didn't change."

I couldn't help smile as he spoke, coming to my defense against my insecurities. In all the time I'd hidden myself away in that hotel room, every day becoming more afraid of the world outside, I never dreamed hearing words like those could make me feel so wonderful.

CHAPTER EIGHT

COLE

I WATCHED AS DIANA PLAYED with a lock of her hair next to her face, and the memory of how she used to always wear it up in a ponytail came rushing back to me. Oddly, all the times I'd thought about her over the years, I'd never pictured her with her hair up in that cute ponytail. As the memory blossomed in my mind, I remembered walking behind her through the woods and watching that ponytail bounce up and down and sway left and right as her head moved.

When she stopped talking for a moment, I asked, "Do you ever wear your hair up like you used to in high school?"

My question seemed to rattle her, and she leaned back against her chair like she wanted to put distance between us. Frowning, she shook her head. "Only when I'm at home. Otherwise, I wear it down."

The serious tone in her voice indicated she didn't like being asked that, but I had no idea why. Hoping to smooth things over and make her smile, I quickly said, "Oh, because I was just remembering how it would bounce and sway as you walked. It was cute."

My compliment fell flat, though, and she merely shook her head once more. Although I was curious about what I'd said to upset her, I chose not to ask about that ponytail I liked so much anymore.

"So Tressa's wedding is coming up fast," I said, instantly

regretting my comment when I saw it hadn't led to a change in Diana's expression.

"It is," she said, almost as if she felt she had to give some answer.

I didn't know what had happened, but our conversation had ground to a halt. I didn't want to talk about Ethan anymore since that would only remind the both of us how unhappy he'd be if he knew we were even sitting together in that lounge.

Maybe this was a mistake. After all, people changed. Ten years was a long time. We were kids then.

I'd definitely changed. Back then, I was just a teenage boy lost in a sea of uncertainty about who I was and how to act. My whole life was spinning out of control because of my family problems. On top of that, all the normal teenage male issues had hit me like a ton of bricks by the time I dared to kiss Diana that night after my baseball game.

Looking back, I had a hard time understanding that version of me much at all. Now, I was a grown man who knew what I wanted from women. I didn't fear talking to them or leaning in to kiss them. That kid I was then was so unsure compared to me now.

"Did you go to college after high school?" she asked, tearing me from my thoughts. "I don't think Ethan has ever told me if you did."

I chuckled and shook my head no. "I wasn't like you, remember? I guess I could have gotten some kind of scholarship for baseball, but things were so messed up at that time in my life that I probably would have failed out my first year."

"Oh," she said quietly.

I didn't sense disappointment or disapproval in her answer. More like she'd hoped that would be a conversation starter, but I'd effectively smothered it as soon as I could.

Trying to turn things around, I said, "I know you went to college. Everyone knew you would. I mean, you were the smartest girl in high school. It was only natural that you'd go."

My mention of her time in school made her perk up, and Diana smiled for the first time in nearly five minutes. "I don't know if I was the smartest girl in school, but I was valedictorian, so I guess that would be right. I loved school. College was so much fun."

Happy to see her talking again, I asked, "Lots of partying? I've heard some wild stories."

"Yeah, but I didn't do a lot of that. I had a goal, and spending time at parties would have made getting great grades impossible."

Christ, we really were so different. When I thought of college, all that popped into my brain were keg parties and drunk girls.

"I know it probably sounds lame to you, but I wanted to be a lawyer. I dreamed of being on the Supreme Court one day," she said in a faraway voice.

"It doesn't sound lame at all. If anyone could have done that, it's you."

Diana lifted her glass of white wine to her lips and took a sip. "That's all in the past now. I can barely remember my two years in school. It's like a lifetime ago."

Once more, I'd succeeded in bringing up a topic that made the conversation die. Maybe this was a mistake.

But I didn't want it to be. Just being around Diana made me feel the same way I did all those times we snuck out to the woods to be together. At the time, I didn't understand why, but I knew just being around her made me happy.

Now, as we sat together in that dim lounge, I felt that way again. It didn't matter how long you were away from the feeling of being genuinely happy. It could be months or even years, like with me. As soon as it came around again, something inside you woke up and instantly started to crave more.

That something inside me was wide awake now, and even though this first meeting wasn't going as well as I'd hoped, I still wanted to be around her. I wanted to know more about her. She clearly hadn't become some hardened bitch over the years, which had happened with more than a handful of the women I graduated with. Ten years out of high school and they looked let down, like life was supposed to give them more.

But Diana didn't look let down. She looked sweet and kind, like she always did, but layered over those was a sadness I knew came from all she'd been through since the accident. I didn't know just how broken she was, but at that moment as I felt something I hadn't experienced in far too long, I didn't care.

"You know what I remember best about those nights we used to hide out in the woods and hang out? How good it felt to just sit and talk. Crazy, huh?"

She smiled as I finished speaking, and in the dim light, I saw her cheeks grow pink. "You liked just talking? I mean, I loved it, but I thought teenage boys always wanted more than just talking."

I nodded, willing to accept that I'd walked into that. "Well, you know how we are. Perfect machines of testosterone and other hormones making us want one singular thing."

"Why didn't you ever want that from me?" she asked so innocently that it caught me off guard.

For a few moments, I struggled with what to say. I'd been crazy about her from the moment puberty hit me, but she'd been a secret fantasy I never believed I'd get to live out because of her brother. Then when I finally felt brave enough that night and kissed her, taking advantage of no one else being around and the rush of adrenaline pumping through me after winning my game, I didn't think about anything but wanting to know how it would feel just to kiss her.

Later, the thought of more definitely came to me, but I never acted on it. But why?

I didn't want to lie to her, so I took a deep breath and told her the best version of the truth, as far as I could remember from that time.

"You weren't like other girls. You were Ethan's sister. You were Diana, a sweet girl I probably shouldn't have been with in the first place considering my reputation. Sleeping with you didn't seem like something I should even have been thinking of."

She forced a smile and mumbled, "Untouchable."

"I know it isn't what you want to hear, but yes, you were untouchable. You were too good for high school boys like me."

Diana wasn't wrong, but she didn't understand why I had no business touching her then. Or now, for that matter.

I slept with more girls that senior year than I wanted to admit. I was an athlete, looked good, and took advantage of all the blessings I'd been given. Nothing had changed after high school either. Women were to be conquered. Nothing more. They were a prize in a testosterone driven contest I competed in with other men like me. I learned the techniques that would gain me a win in that competition and used them to my advantage.

But a decade of chasing women just to sleep with them had gotten old. Maybe I'd grown up. I didn't know. I just knew it all didn't mean much anymore. So I could get them into bed. I didn't want more with any of the women I slept with, but some part of me wanted more than to just get off.

I didn't know if that's what drew me to Diana after seeing her at Tressa's engagement party. If I hadn't been worthy of being with her because she was innocent and sweet back in high school, could I say I was any more worthy of her at that moment?

As we sat there together but saying nothing, I wanted to think I could be worthy of her. That Ethan was wrong now, even if he wasn't a decade ago.

"Has your brother ever told you I owned a club?" I asked, my need to impress her pressing on me suddenly.

Diana nodded. "I knew that, but I'm not sure how. Ethan rarely talks about you at all. He doesn't talk about any of his friends much."

"He probably thinks if he does that you might like one of us," I said with a chuckle, suspecting my guess about my friend's motives was right on the money.

She nodded again and took another sip of her wine. "So you

have a club? What kind of club?"

I wanted to brag to her about what I did for a living. I wanted her to see I'd accomplished something of worth in the years since she sat with me in those woods and told me how impressed she'd been when I caught that fly ball and tagged that guy out at second.

But would she think much of a nightclub that stunk of a mixture of stale liquor and beer, piss, sweat, and cum by the end of each night? Girls who wanted to be respectable lawyers who could someday sit on the highest court in the land didn't grow up to be women who appreciated the kind of place I ran.

So I embellished. Just a little. Well, more than a little to begin with since I didn't own a club anymore.

"It's a nightclub, but the clientele is pretty high class. Lots of high rollers like politicians, businessmen, and movers and shakers visit my club."

That was slightly more than embellishment. That was a lie, and not only because I didn't own the club anymore. When I did, I saw people from all walks of life, but my average patron was a guy like me out for a night on the town and looking to get lucky and the woman who came out for the same reason and didn't try to hide it.

And if they heard someone use the term clientele to describe them, they'd probably laugh in their face. That sounded like there was ever some type of exclusivity to my place. There wasn't. There was simply alcohol, room to dance near the bar, and spots to get to know people better, whatever that may be. Dark and slightly seedy, it wasn't likely the kind of place someone like Diana Stone would ever consider visiting for any number of reasons.

Hopefully, she never asked Ethan about it.

Interested by my description, she smiled and asked, "What's the name?"

I couldn't lie about that, so I answered, "The Red Line."

Not that I knew what the current owners called the place. I'd heard they planned to change the name, but I had no idea to what. When your creditors came in and seized your assets, it wasn't like they told you much of anything.

That was nearly three months ago. Thankfully, Ethan had been too busy being happier than a clam in his life with Summer to notice that I never seemed to have to be anywhere at night anymore. Not that I had been a slave to running the club when I did own it.

Starting to get the picture what happened? Yeah, it wasn't pretty. Well, it was pretty fucking ugly. I'd seen it coming, though, and if I'd wanted to stop it all from happening, I could have. I just didn't have my heart in running a club anymore. For almost six years I'd done it, and by the time the bills started piling up, I just didn't care.

So I let it go in all senses of the word, and now I was officially unemployed. Between jobs sounded better. I still had some of my trust fund left, so I wasn't poor.

Well, that wasn't exactly the truth either.

I couldn't tell Diana that, though. Better for her to think I owned some seedy joint in the city than the truth.

"So you're the owner and manager?" she asked.

Desperate to change the subject suddenly, I said, "Yeah, but it's not something I love anymore. I dream about leaving it all behind and moving back to the area where we grew up and living a quiet life."

"Why don't you?"

The way she said that sounded so immediate. She made it sound like I could do it in the blink of an eye. If only that were true.

"It's just a dream," I said with a shrug. I hadn't expected her to be so encouraging, and now I felt like I was just digging the hole deeper with more lies.

"I haven't done anything to make it come true." That wasn't a lie. I hadn't.

"You shouldn't wait to make your dreams come true. Trust me. Make every day count or one day you'll wake up and years will have gone by and you'll have nothing to show for it," she said quietly.

The support evident in her words of encouragement disappeared when she said that, replaced by sadness so clear in her voice that I winced. No doubt it referred to her life and not mine, but still I couldn't help but feel it.

Then, as if she'd decided she didn't want me to see her that way, she smiled and asked, "Would you like to see where I live? You made such an effort to find my room today I thought maybe you'd like to see it."

Surprised by her offer but happy, I said, "Sure. Lead the way."

A couple minutes later, she opened the door to a room at the end of the hallway and welcomed me in. I didn't know what I'd expected, but I silently wondered why Tristan Stone's daughter stayed in a room that barely qualified as a suite. More like one-and-a-half rooms, Diana's place had a bedroom and a sitting area with a table in the corner that mimicked a dining table.

Spreading her arms wide, she looked around and said, "This is it. I don't want you to think that anyone made me stay here, like my family forced me to live in this tiny room. They didn't. I chose to do that. It was all me. Now I'm choosing to find someone else to live, though."

"It's hard to start over in a new place. That's pretty strong of you."

She blushed again like before. "I don't know if I'm strong. I'm just focused on doing something new for a change. It's time that I left this gilded cage I made for myself. I was scared of a lot of things for a long time. I'm still scared, but I'm more afraid of losing myself and waking up ten years from now and not having anything but these rooms to show for those years."

Regret hung off every word. I didn't know exactly what scared her, but it still seemed pretty damn strong to leave a place of her choice and not because someone else decided it was time for her to go.

We sat down on the couch in the outer room and I said, "I

understand being scared. I never told you how much being with you meant to me for those few months back in senior year."

"What do you mean? I don't understand what I could have done."

"Everything my father was going through terrified me. I thought I'd have to leave school and might not graduate. I wasn't sure where we'd end up living since the Feds took our house. For a kid who'd never had to worry about anything when it came to money, life became scary overnight. My grandmother was willing to take my brothers and me in, thank God. But that whole time you and I were together, I spent the rest of my time unsure about everything else in my world. Only those hours we were together gave me peace. I never thanked you for that, but you helped me, Diana."

The smile I received in return for my confession lit up her face. "I didn't know a lot of what you were going through back then, Cole. I'm glad I was able to help when you needed it."

Normally at that point in the conversation with a woman as we sat in her hotel room, I'd make a move and we'd head to the bed. I didn't want to do that, though. Not yet, anyway.

"I better get going. It's been a long day, and I'm starting to come down hard from those six cups of coffee," I said as I stood to leave.

"Someday, I hope you explain about that coffee overdose," she said with a smile, looking up at me with those beautiful blue eyes so full of kindness and innocence.

Even though I had no more right to be with her now than I did all those years ago, I didn't care. I liked how I felt when she looked at me like she was at that moment, like I was worthy of her goodness.

"Do you want to hang out again?"

She stood and walked over to the makeshift dining table in the corner of the room. "So you don't have to hang out in the hotel lobby skulking around again, let me give you my number."

Handing me the piece of paper with her number on it, she smiled. "Next time, just call."

I laughed at her poking fun at me. "I will."

Diana followed me to the door, and when I turned around, she wrapped her arms around me in a hug I hadn't expected. All the emotions she'd brought out in me a decade ago rushed back, and I hugged her, loving the feel of her against me.

Against my chest, she said, "It was so wonderful to get to talk to you again, Cole. I hope we can spend time together again."

"Me too."

I wanted to say more, but I didn't know how to put my feelings into words. I couldn't remember the last time I just sat and talked with a woman. There was usually no talking. Just sex. But this was better than sex, somehow.

When she released her hold on me, I backed up a step and smiled, not wanting to leave. "Next time, I'm calling. I'll talk to you soon."

"Talk to you soon," she said sweetly.

As I walked through the lobby, feeling like I was floating on air, I still looked around to make sure Ethan or his parents weren't there. As much as I liked hanging out with Diana again, I knew nothing had changed since we were teenagers. Nobody would want us to be together.

And they weren't wrong. She was still too good for me. But I didn't care this time either.

CHAPTER NINE

DIANA

MY STOMACH FELT LIKE BUTTERFLIES were inside it doing flips. After a decade of not speaking, Cole and I met and had a great time. I didn't get so anxious that I ran away, and he didn't seem to care that I lived in this hotel room like some kind of weirdo.

I couldn't sit still. Jumping up from the couch, I paced the full length of my room, full of energy for the first time in ages. I spent an hour talking to a man, and it didn't turn out a disaster. I'd been so sure it would when it finally happened. But it went wonderfully.

Sure, I'd felt awkward, and I didn't know what to say most of the time, even though I should have since it was Cole. Still, I did it. I sat there and acted like a normal human being. No running away. No breaking down when I thought he was staring at my scar. No saying something stupid because my anxiety got the better of me.

As my mind raced with possibilities for our next meeting, someone knocked at my door. Had Cole returned? No, he wouldn't do that. He just left. But maybe…

I hurried to the door to see if it was him. Looking through the peephole, I saw Ethan standing in the hallway and quickly opened the door to let him in.

"Ethan! I didn't expect you to come by today," I said as I pulled him into my room, happy he hadn't shown up ten minutes ago.

He walked in and headed toward the table on the far side of the room. Usually he sat down on the couch with me when he came to visit. As I closed the door, I noticed he seemed tense, like he was upset.

"Are you okay? Did something happen with Daddy?" I asked as I walked toward him. "Do you want something to drink?"

Ethan shook his head. His mouth turned down in a frown that told me something was wrong.

"Did you and Summer have a fight? We were just out shopping for our dresses today. Nothing happened, right? You're still getting married, aren't you?" I asked while with each passing moment of silence I felt myself get more panicked.

My breath caught in my chest. Cole left not ten minutes before Ethan arrived. Had he seen Cole leave my room? Had he run into him in the lobby and figured out he'd been to see me?

"Ethan, what's going on? This isn't like you not to talk. What's wrong?" I asked as I took a step toward him and reached out to touch his hand.

My brother's silence combined with the unhappy scowl on his face made me more uncomfortable than I knew how to deal with, so I took a deep breath and tried to collect my thoughts so when they came out of my mouth I didn't sound like a madwoman. I knew he'd be furious about the Cole thing, but I wasn't a teenage girl anymore. I didn't need my brother to shoo away potential boyfriends to protect me. Cole and I had done nothing wrong.

I was a grown woman who had the right to speak to anyone I wanted to, including one of my brother's friends.

Ethan marched around me and began pacing like I had just minutes earlier. I watched him stop at the door and then turn around, his expression still a clear indication of how unhappy he was.

"Why won't you talk to me? You came all the way here to see me, but you don't plan to say anything? What's going on?"

He opened his mouth and closed it shut, pressing his lips together for a moment. Then he took a deep breath in and let it out through his nose. "I just talked to Dad. He told me you're thinking about moving. He's wrong, isn't he? You aren't really thinking about moving, are you?"

My body sagged in relief. Ethan wasn't here about my time with Cole or anything like that. All he wanted to talk about was my moving out of the hotel. As a sense of relaxation washed over me, I sat down on the couch.

"That's all you came here for? You looked so unhappy I thought it was something serious. Come. Sit with me. You look like every muscle in your body is twisted into knots."

His dark eyes flashed anger. "This is serious, Diana. Moving out of here is a huge deal."

"You're making a big deal out of this, but it was always going to happen, Ethan. You don't have to worry. I'm going to be fine. I'm going to find a nice place somewhere. Just wait until you see it. You're going to love it. I've already got things planned in my head. When I'm settled in, I'm going to have a dinner party! You and Summer will be invited, along with Tressa and Killian and Mommy and Daddy. I can't wait! It will be my first time entertaining."

All my enthusiasm for my future housewarming party for all my family did nothing to fix his mood. He still frowned like he heard not a single word that made him see how excited I was about this move.

"I don't think this is the right time, Diana. Seriously, I think you should wait."

"Why? It's time. I've lived here for too long already. I need to get back out into the world and start living. You understand what that means to me more than anyone. I was never going to stay in this room forever."

He began to pace again, shaking his head at every word I uttered in defense of my leaving. Why was he so against this?

"I just don't think it's time. You're not ready."

"Why would you say that? I'm more than ready," I protested, feeling under attack by his comments.

I tried to continue speaking, but he cut me off. "Where will you go? You can't drive, so that limits where you can live. The hotel here is centrally located, so you can get to anything you need."

"So what if I can't drive? Most New Yorkers don't have cars anyway. It's the city, Ethan. I don't need to drive anywhere, and if I need to, I can order a car to take me anywhere I want. What's wrong with you? You're never like this. What's really wrong?"

I tried to grab his hand on one of his passes by me toward the door, but he wouldn't let me. I'd never seen Ethan so upset with me. He was my best friend in the world and the one member of my family I counted on more than anyone else, and now he wouldn't even let me touch him. I didn't understand why he was so unhappy about my moving on with my life.

"Diana, you're safe here," he said with his back turned toward me. "Have you thought about that in wherever you plan to go? How safe will you be?"

My chest began to hurt from how he was acting. "Safe from what? I'm not going to move into a place that doesn't have security. If that's what you're worried about, you don't have to be. I promise you that I'll find a place with a doorman and a great security system. I'll be fine, Ethan."

He spun around and glared at me with a look I'd never seen from him before. "How can you be sure? You can't, Diana! You can't!"

I stood up and walked over to him. He didn't move away when I took his hand in mine and said, "It's time I leave here. I know it's scary, but I have to, Ethan. Please understand. I need to move on with my life."

For a moment, I thought I saw in his eyes that he did understand why I needed to do this now, but he just shook his head and walked away. I stood staring at my hotel room door confused why the one person in the world who had always supported me in everything now seemed intent on stopping me from doing something so good for me.

Behind me, he mumbled something about the timing being terrible. I turned to see him standing on the other side of the room like we were enemies fighting on two wholly different sides and felt more alone than ever before in my life.

"Why can't you support me in this? Of all the people I thought would be on board with me leaving this hotel, I thought you would. Ethan, what's going on here?"

He didn't speak for a long time, but finally he sighed and said, "I just think it's something you should wait on. That's all."

My heart broke from his inability or unwillingness to support me when I needed him most, and right there in that place I'd been shut up in for so long, at long last I said what I truly felt. "So only you and Tressa get to be happy? Is that how it is, Ethan? You get to grow and change, but I have to stay that broken thing I was right after the accident. You get to find happiness, while all I get to have are these four miserable walls?"

By the time I finished, my voice had grown so loud I was screaming the words four miserable walls. Tears rolled down my cheeks as the wonderful day I'd spent first with Summer and then with Cole disappeared, replaced by the sadness the person I loved most in this world had brought to me. It made everything else I'd felt that day mean nothing.

My brother stared at me, his eyes wide in shock from my yelling. I never raised my voice. Not with him. Not with anyone. I was always sweet and nice Diana or completely fucked up Diana who could barely get through a day without having her anxiety take over and make her an utter mess.

But never had I been the Diana he saw a moment ago. That person was hurt that the brother she loved so much couldn't be happy for her when she so desperately needed him to be.

"I can't talk to you about this. You don't understand what I've been through, Ethan. You don't understand what it's like to live in this room for years, afraid to even leave without someone holding your hand. And then when you do finally work up the courage to decide it's time to live your life, you hear you're not ready or you should wait. No one else is told to wait, but I have to because I'm not ready. Well, I've never been more ready."

After I finished, I sat down on the couch. His visit had exhausted me. I felt like I'd been beaten down by his negativity, and I didn't have the defenses I needed to deal with that from him. Of all the people I believed would support me in this, I thought Ethan would be the cheerleader he always was for me.

And I couldn't believe how wrong I'd been.

"I understand everything you've been through," he said softly as he took a step toward the couch. "I do, Diana. I just worry about you. I always have. Ever since we were kids. I'd never forgive myself if I didn't tell you that you moving makes me worried."

"It's going to be okay, Ethan. Everything will be okay. It's really not that big a deal, actually. People move all the time. Now's just my time. You didn't think I'd live here at the hotel forever, did you?"

He took another step and stopped. Nodding, he said, "I know. I guess I just freaked out a little when Dad told me you'd decided to move. I just figured there'd be some talk about it first, some discussion about what your plans are and everything. That's all. I guess it just caught me off guard."

Wiping the tears from my cheeks, I said, "I have to get out of this room. It's long past time. I know you say you understand how I feel, but I don't think you do understand. This place is like a prison. I made it myself, and I take full responsibility for that. But I need to leave here."

"Why does it have to be right now? What if you wait a while? You might have to, you know. Finding the right place can be hard. It might take months for that."

Everything coming from my brother made me feel wrong for wanting to have a life. I wasn't wrong. I deserved to live as I chose to, didn't I?

When he continued to talk about how hard it would be to find a new apartment, all I heard were discouraging words. He had been shocked by my screaming, so now he wanted to sweet talk me into not moving.

Word after word of how I needed to be careful and slow down and how much harder moving was than I thought flowed from his mouth, but not a single one that told me he'd be by my side like he always had been. I didn't know this Ethan, and I didn't like how he made me feel.

Suddenly, I couldn't listen to any more negative comments about the one thing I wanted to do with my life. As he continued to try to talk me out of it with his phony words of wisdom, I picked up an empty glass from the coffee table in front of me and threw it as hard as I could at the wall. It hit with a loud thud and then shattered into pieces that flew everywhere.

I jumped to my feet as my adrenaline pumped through me from the shock of how easily that glass broke into a thousand shards and yelled, "Why won't you listen to me? I'm not that girl you wish I was anymore! I'm a grown woman who can make her own decisions!"

Still stunned by my show of anger and then my outburst, Ethan struggled to answer me. "I am. I am listening, Diana."

"No, you aren't! You're rambling on about how hard it's going to be for me to move. Why can't you say one single supportive thing about this?" I sobbed, the tears rolling down my cheeks again.

Instead of comforting me, he went to the one place that hurt the most. "What does your therapist think of your moving? Have you told him yet? I bet he doesn't think it's the right time now considering all that's going on. Tressa's wedding is coming up in a couple months, and then my wedding to Summer. Now's practically the worst time for you to do this."

I could barely see through the tears as I looked at my brother standing there saying those things. "Nowhere in all of that was any mention of me, Ethan. You found your happiness and you're moving on with your life. Tressa found happiness and she's moving on. What about me? Am I supposed to just stay here in this hotel room rotting away day after day while you all chase after your dreams? I have dreams, too, you know. I want to be happy, too. Why can't you see that?"

His expression morphed into one full of hurt, like I'd said something callous to him instead of the other way around. He had nothing to say now. All he could do was hang his head and leave.

There was no comforting embrace like usual when I cried. No telling me everything would be okay. How could there be since he'd been the one to hurt me?

I waited for him to come back and make things better like he always did. We'd disagreed before, but never like this, so I couldn't imagine he'd just let things stand as he left them when he walked out without even saying goodbye.

But he didn't. For hours, I waited through bouts of crying, but nothing. Not even a call if he couldn't find the time to come over again.

I'd never felt so alone in my life. Even when I lay on the side of that road unsure if I was still alive and begging Ethan to stay with me, I didn't feel as abandoned as I did now. I wanted to call someone in the hope that talking would help me feel better, but my brother was the one I'd usually call when I felt low. I didn't know where to turn now that I didn't have him.

The truth of how much the people I needed the most thought I was an emotional invalid who should stay cooped up in this tiny hotel room broke my heart. If I didn't have their support, how could I do this?

I went to bed hours later still devastated by what happened. I felt like someone had come into my life and ripped all the good out of it after dangling the promise that goodness offered. As I drifted off to sleep, I hoped Cole would call tomorrow.

FOR TWO DAYS, I SAT in my hotel room waiting for Cole. He never called. When I couldn't take the hurt anymore, I did what I always did when I couldn't see any chance of happiness again.

Holding my phone, I typed out my message as my hand shook from the fear that I wouldn't get a response, but I didn't know what else to do. I had nowhere else to turn. Like so many times before, the three words were all I could say.

I need you.

I didn't know how long it took before I heard the knock on my door, but it felt like forever as I sat on my couch in my hotel room and waited. I hurried to the door to open it, and when I saw Ethan out in the hallway, the relief I'd so desperately needed in the last forty-eight hours finally came.

He didn't say a word when he walked in, but when I turned to face him after closing the door, his arms were spread to welcome me into the embrace I needed so badly. I wanted to say so much, but I couldn't find the words.

Instead, I stepped forward and closed my eyes as he wrapped his arms around me. Ethan held me tightly, like he feared if he didn't I'd slip away. Maybe that's why he reacted to the news of my moving like he did. I didn't know. I just knew I needed him.

"I'm sorry, Diana. I should have never said those things."

He had no idea how just hearing those words brought peace to my heart after two days of sadness. Sobbing, I said, "I need you to understand why I have to do this, Ethan, but I also need you to be there for me. I don't know if I can do this without your support."

"I understand. I do. I just worry. You've been through so much already."

I lifted my head to look up at him and nodded. I waited until I stopped crying and dried my eyes. "I'm going to be okay. Look at how far I've come already. It only took me eight years, but I'm about to move out on my own."

The sadness in Ethan's eyes made me think he didn't believe I could do it, but then he said, "This is all my fault. Everything is my fault. The accident. Making you feel bad. Ruining your life. I'm so sorry. I messed up your entire life."

"It was an accident, but my life isn't ruined, Ethan. It's just been put on hold for a while. Now I want to start living it again, and I want you to be by my side when I do. I need my family to believe in me."

He smiled in that way that always told me he wanted me to be happy. "We all believe in you, Diana. Out of the three of us kids, you're the one who's always been the smartest. You can do whatever you put your mind to. I guess I was just afraid of what might happen when you do it."

"Maybe it won't be something bad that happens. Maybe it will be something good. You never know. Whatever happens, I have to try to live my life, and that starts with moving from this room."

Ethan took a deep breath and let it out slowly. "I told Summer what happened the other day, and she said the same thing. She said I have to stop being so worried about you because you need to live your life the way you want. She said some other things too, like how I can be a jackass sometimes, but the gist of it all is I need to recognize you're not someone I need to protect anymore."

I stepped toward him and he hugged me close again. "I'll always need you to look out for me. You've been looking out for me all my life. Daddy always says you watched over me from the minute I was born. You're my best friend, Ethan. I might not need you to protect me anymore, but I need you to be there for me when I doubt myself."

My brother squeezed his arms around me and pressed his cheek to the top of my head like he had since we were small. "I love you, Diana. I'm sorry I wasn't there for you when you needed me, but I promise I'll support anything you decide to do."

As I stood there in the safety of my brother's arms, I smiled. My best friend had returned. I didn't know what would happen, but at least I had Ethan standing by me.

CHAPTER TEN

COLE

TWO DAYS OF WAITING TO call Diana had worn me out to the point that I had a feeling once I did make that damn call I'd probably crash and have to take a nap. A grown man nearly thirty years old having to take a nap was bad enough, but something about being nervous about calling a woman made me embarrassed for myself. I'd asked hundreds of women out in my life. Why was this one shaking me up so much?

I knew the answer. Because it was Ethan's sister. If I played this bad, a hard right to my face was the least he'd do. Not that I wouldn't deserve worse. I knew he'd have every reason to beat me within an inch of my life. Or worse. That's why I didn't want to screw this up.

So I'd waited a couple days like I'd read in some magazine at the doctor's office a few years ago. A gentleman, which I generally didn't consider myself to be, waited a few days so not to crowd their potential date.

I'd laughed at that nugget of advice back then, thinking that magazine must have been an issue from the Stone Ages. Who the hell waited when they wanted something? If I met a woman I wanted to get to know more (translation: wanted to fuck), I called her, we got together, and we did what nature intended.

But Diana Stone wasn't just any woman, so when I thought about calling her the day after we met for a drink, I stopped myself as the memory of that crazy, old-fashioned advice popped into my head. I'd give her a couple days and then casually call to say hi. I'd play it cool since I had a feeling coming on to her like I usually did with other women might scare her off.

So as I walked back and forth past my TV checking the time every few seconds, I tried to channel that cool version of me since this impatient guy pacing definitely wasn't rocking the cool thing. I checked the time again. Almost noon. Not too early, but not too late. Fuck, what did that article say about how to approach the first call?

I shook my head to get rid of that ridiculous and antiquated advice. This was Diana. I could call her and everything would be fine. I just needed to take a deep breath and calm the fuck down.

Okay, in through the nose and out through the mouth. Good. Now call her and let's get this going already. Enough fucking pacing, Cole. Time to call her.

A few seconds later, she appeared before me on my screen looking as beautiful as always. She gave me a big smile and a cute little wave I couldn't help but find charming.

"Hi, Cole! I didn't think I was ever going to hear from you again," she said, surprising me.

"Why?"

"Because it's been two days since we got together. I figured when you didn't call the next day like you used to that you decided you didn't want to see me again."

Fucking women's magazines. Ruining men since the beginning of fucking time.

"No, not at all," I hurried to explain, hoping she'd understand. "I just didn't want you to think I was smothering you. That's all. Just something I read once and figured women liked."

Not most women, of course. Just nice ones like her.

"Oh. I guess I was thinking you'd just act like you used to. We're not in high school anymore. I need to remember that."

Diana winced like her admission hurt and then looked down, as if she was embarrassed to face me. Not a full minute in and I'd already fucked things up. Not a good start.

"I was calling to see if you'd like to go out to dinner tonight."

She didn't move or say anything for a moment, and I held my breath wondering if my following that stupid advice had ruined everything. That's what I got for taking life advice from an old magazine at a doctor's office.

Then she lifted her head and smiled. Nodding, she said, "I'd like that. We could do it here, if you want."

"I was thinking we could go out to a restaurant. Would that work?"

Diana's eyes opened wide, and her smile grew bigger. "Oh, I'd like that. I just figured you wouldn't want to risk running into my brother."

I waved away that concern like it meant nothing to me. "It didn't even occur to me."

That was a lie. Of course, it had. Having Ethan find out that I was interested in Diana while we were on a date would be disastrous. Jesus, disastrous didn't even come close to what a fucking nightmare it would be. That's why I made reservations at a place I knew Ethan would never go to.

"Okay. Oh, I was wondering if I could ask you to help me with something."

When she finished talking, she bit her lip nervously. I had no idea what she wanted my help with, but how bad could it be?

"Anything. I'm completely at your disposal."

She hesitated for a moment and then blurted her request out in one hurried rush. "I was wondering if you'd be willing to go look at apartments with me."

After the words had left her mouth, she stepped back away from the screen. Her body language screamed how nervous she was that I'd say no, so I quickly answered.

"Of course. I'd be happy to. But why aren't you doing this with someone in your family?" I asked, too curious not to.

"Because I want an impartial opinion. My family loves me, but they have their own ideas about what I should do with my life. I think you'd be able to give me good advice."

Not that many people in this world had ever thought that of me. I wasn't who most people turned for good advice. I didn't want to let her down, though, so as much as I'd always hated apartment hunting, I smiled and agreed to go.

"Do you have any showings lined up yet?" I asked. "We could go this afternoon, if you do."

I sounded far more enthusiastic than I actually was. Well, that wasn't true. I couldn't wait to spend time with Diana again. If that meant I had to check out a few apartments, then that's what I'd have to do.

"No. Can I call you right back?" she asked and the screen faded to black before I could answer.

I had no idea what just happened, but Diana had always been like that. When she got something into her head, she charged full steam ahead with it, eyes on the prize and her focus squarely on the goal. For all the ways she'd changed since high school, she was the same driven Diana I remembered.

While I waited, the question of whether or not Ethan knew about her moving out of the hotel popped into my head. He hadn't mentioned it to me, but then he rarely said much about Diana when we talked. If he did know, I had a feeling he wouldn't be too happy. As protective as he was, he likely wouldn't be a fan of her moving to somewhere he couldn't reach quickly like the hotel.

Diana's face appeared before me on my monitor, and before I could ask if anything was wrong, she said nearly breathlessly, "Okay. I lined up three I'd been looking at starting at two this afternoon. If you're still game, I'd love it if you'd come with me."

"Wow. Three. You don't sit on your hands when you decide to do something, do you?" I joked.

"I never did. So are you game?" she asked, her eyes practically pleading with me to say yes.

"Sure. It sounds fun. We'll go to get something to eat

afterward. Okay?"

Nodding, she began to move around her room getting ready for when I'd arrive. "That sounds perfect. How long until you get here?"

Caught up in her enthusiasm, I said, "How about an hour? Is that good?"

Diana stopped and smiled at me. "Great! See you then!"

I watched as the screen went dark again and felt strange at how excited I was to be spending an afternoon doing something I hated. At least I'd hated it when I was looking for my apartment. Her excitement about apartment hunting and wanting my opinion on a potential place made me want to go with her that afternoon.

Then it dawned on me. We'd never talked about where these showings were. I'd been so nervous about calling her that I hadn't even considered that. No problem, though. My car would get us wherever she needed to go.

And then afterward, we'd drive to Staten Island and have dinner at that Italian place I'd stopped at one night a couple years ago. I'd been spending time with a girl from there and she suggested we go there for dinner. I didn't remember her too fondly, but Alfredo's still remained one of my favorite Italian restaurants whenever I got out there.

Not that I made my way to Staten Island that often. I picked that place for dinner because it's out of the way. I also chose it because I didn't think Ethan or her parents would ever see us there.

That sounded shitty even when I said it to myself, but what choice did I have? Ethan made it quite clear how he and his parents felt about Diana dating anyone, but especially me, years ago. I didn't imagine anything had changed in that regard.

Better to keep things on the down low, and then if the relationship turned into anything serious, we would deal with her family. I rubbed my face as the phantom pain from Ethan laying me out that time made my jaw ache. That was a long time ago. We were adults now.

Yeah, I was an adult trying to get together with his sister with no job and soon to be not a lot of anything else. I didn't think he'd be convinced by my claim that my wanting to get to know Diana again had nothing to do with the fact that I had lost nearly everything and things didn't look too good for the near future but instead because seeing her with Summer that afternoon made me miss what the two of us had.

Right before he hit me the next time, he'd tell me in no uncertain terms just how much he thought that sounded like bullshit. It wasn't, though. After losing the club, I spent weeks sitting around my apartment thinking I had nothing to even get out of bed for. Then Ethan told me he planned to ask Summer to marry him, and something inside my head clicked. I could pretend I was happy sleeping with woman after woman and never having anything to show for it other than some occasional good sex, or I could find someone to settle down with and maybe be happy like him.

I never set out to get back together with Diana. It just happened. I saw her that day walking with Summer, and before I knew it, I wanted to see her again.

That's what I'd tell him. I'd leave out the afternoon of stalking and the elaborate plans I had to find out what room was hers at the Richmont. Better to save that for years from now when we could laugh about what kind of ass I could be.

Hopefully, he'd understand.

✧　✧　✧

I PULLED UP TO THE Richmont Midtown and saw Diana standing outside in a yellow sundress with big blue and white flowers. Like she said she always did, she wore her long brown hair down, but today it looked different because she'd curled the ends. It made her look even sweeter than usual, if that was possible.

She waved when she saw me, but something in her smile looked wrong. I quickly scanned the area and checked my rearview mirror to see if someone from her family was around, but I saw no one. Relieved, I stepped out of the car and walked over to her.

"Your car is very nice, Cole," she said with a smile I saw was forced now.

Looking back at it, I thought about how much longer I'd have the silver Maserati and that sense of loss I'd experienced when I lost the club rushed through me. I didn't have time to mourn losing this too now. Some other time.

"Thanks. I love this car, but it's nothing special," I said as casually as I could. "Ready to go?"

Diana nodded and took my arm when I offered it, but suddenly she felt wooden against me. Just a few steps away from the car, she grabbed my hand and squeezed it tightly. I turned to look at her and saw all the blood had drained from her face and in her eyes was pure terror.

"Are you okay?" I asked as she tightened her hold on my hand.

She shook her head as tears filled her eyes. "I can't. I thought I could, but I can't go in your car, Cole. I'm sorry. I hoped it wouldn't be a problem, but I can't."

"It's okay. No car. We'll just get there another way. Let me give the valet my keys, and I'll be right back."

"Okay. I'm sorry," she said as she slowly let go of my hand one finger at a time.

"It's fine," I said, waving at the Richmont valet.

He took my keys and seconds later drove away with my car. Diana seemed to calm down now that it wasn't nearby, and I turned to her and smiled. "So no cars. No problem. Driving in the city is a pain in the ass anyway. That leaves trains and plains if automobiles are gone," I joked.

Taking a deep breath, she let it out in a deep sigh. "I think I can do a train."

I thought about it for a second. "I haven't taken a train or the subway in years, so this is going to be new for the two of us. Give me a second and I'll figure things out. Where are we going?"

"Carnegie Hill and Upper East Side."

"Okay. That's doable in one afternoon. When are the showings?"

"Quarter to three and four thirty. Carnegie Hill is first."

"Okay. Let's see what train we have to catch. Give me a sec."

I took out my phone to search for the schedules and then looked up at her with a smile. "Got it." I held out my hand and asked, "Ready? We're going to have to move to catch the train in time to get to Carnegie Hill for that showing."

She took my hand and smiled sweetly. "Okay. Lead the way!"

WE LEFT THE SECOND APARTMENT and walked down the street toward the subway. Diana stayed silent, but I knew neither place had been what she wanted. I didn't understand why since they were both gorgeous, spacious apartments with doormen and security. At both, she pretended to love them but quietly told me she felt they were too small. Since I'd been in her room at the hotel, I couldn't understand why she thought that.

"So onto the third one?"

She shook her head. "I don't think so. It's just going to be like the last two. I think I'm going to cancel. I'd hoped to find something today, but neither one was what I wanted."

"What was wrong with them? They seemed nice. Both were clean, big, and had a lot of amenities. What didn't you like?"

She thought about it for a second. "I loved the high ceilings in the first place. And those countertops were gorgeous. I loved the black. I also really liked the way they disguised the refrigerator and all the appliances the way they did. That was pretty nice. And in the second apartment, I loved the fireplace. I didn't know if I'd like an older place, but that fireplace in the living room changed my mind."

I stopped walking and shook my head. "But you don't like either of them?"

With a shy smile, she answered, "I know this sounds silly, but I want something bigger. Somewhere with more room."

"You mean like a house?"

Her eyes opened wide, and she nodded excitedly. "Maybe I should be looking for a house. A place I can call my own with a yard and a front porch. I love that idea!"

"Well, tell your realtor. Where do you want to live? You're going to have to move out of the city to get a yard. Welcome to suburbia."

She smiled and said, "I don't know if I'm ready for the suburbs, but I love this idea. A house of my own with my own yard where I can plant a garden and sit on the front porch in summer."

"That's definitely going to mean moving to the 'burbs," I joked.

"You must think I'm like an old lady talking about gardening like that. I just think it would be nice to have a yard. I miss that from my parents' house."

"Let's go to dinner and we can talk about it there," I said, taking her hand as we walked to the subway.

I saw her look down at where our hands joined and then up at me. I hadn't thought much of the action, but the expression on her face made me wonder if I'd moved too fast.

"Is it okay? I mean, holding hands? I don't think we'll see anyone we know."

Diana frowned. "You don't have to feel that way. If someone in my family sees us, then they see us. We're not doing anything wrong holding hands and walking down the street."

Leveling my gaze on her, I said, "I know, but we both know how Ethan would react if he saw us."

She tilted her chin up defiantly and pursed her lips. "I'm a grown woman, Cole. I love my brother, but he doesn't make my life decisions for me. If he sees us, I'll make sure to wave and you should too."

I chuckled, imagining a very different scenario of Ethan

catching us together and chasing me down the street while he waved a blunt object and threatened to kill me for touching his sister. "I'm sure there will be waving. I just hope it isn't a gun Ethan's waving at me."

My comment wasn't meant to be funny, but she giggled and lifted our joined hands up into the air. "We're not doing anything wrong. At least I don't think so. Do you?"

In my life, I'd done a lot of wrong things. Too many to count and far too many I wanted to admit to. This didn't feel wrong, though. In fact, it felt more right than anything I'd done with a woman in a long time. Too long.

I shook my head and smiled. "I don't think this is wrong. Your brother would, though. He warned me to stay away from you more than once. The last time we were together way back when, I let it slip what I thought of you and he decked me. I don't think this time would be any better."

"Well, Ethan and the rest of my family are just going to have to get used to the new me. This Diana is moving out of the hotel. She's also holding hands with you in broad daylight, and if that makes me a fallen woman, so be it."

I rolled my eyes and laughed. "I'm pretty sure it takes a whole lot more than holding hands to qualify as a fallen woman."

She blushed at my veiled reference to sex and looked away as we crossed the street. "Well, maybe I'll be doing that too, so they better accept it."

That sounded a lot like the Diana I knew all those years ago. Strong and determined. I didn't know if she felt either of those things about being with me, but I liked the idea that she might.

CHAPTER ELEVEN

DIANA

THE DELICIOUS SMELL OF BUTTERY bread filled the air and made my mouth water, even though we'd already finished our meal. I'd never been to this restaurant, but Cole mentioned it as we made our way to the train and said he'd eaten here once or twice and enjoyed it. I had a feeling he'd had to scramble to find someplace for dinner after I had my anxiety attack and couldn't get into his car without freaking out.

I'd almost expected him to make some excuse to get away from me as fast as he could when he saw the real me, but he surprised me. Not only didn't he react as I thought he would, but he also helped me get through that little crisis. I had a feeling most men wouldn't.

"What do you think of this place? I remembered the food being good, which still goes, wouldn't you say? It's pretty nice, even if it's a little cramped in here," he said looking around at the narrow room filled with tables.

My heart skipped a beat at the mere thought of the number of people that could sit at all those tables. As nice as Castile's was, I didn't think I could handle being in a room so small with so many others.

Cole didn't need to know that, though.

"It's cozy. I like it. There aren't too many people here yet since it's early for dinner, so it's nice."

He smiled and nodded. "It could get a little claustrophobic if every seat was filled, couldn't it? We'll be out of here before the dinner rush comes in. Don't worry."

Cringing at how awkward I felt, I asked, "Is it that obvious?"

But he simply shrugged. "I'm not sure what you mean. I just know that if even half this place fills up before the server brings the check, I'm going to be grabbing you and running for the exits before the oxygen gets limited."

"Thank you."

He gave me another smile and immediately changed the subject. "So it's looking like you're going to have to take your new home search out of the city. Now that I think of it, you told me once you wanted just that—a house with lots of land for your horses. Remember that?"

My mind drifted back to one of the times when we sat in the woods on one of those warm spring nights. Even sitting there in the Upper East Side, I had a feeling if I closed my eyes and inhaled deeply, I'd be able to smell the nature growing all around us then. Leaves and flowers and the dirt under our feet all mixed together to create that unique scent I'd always associate with Cole and the hours we spent together.

"I had such big plans back then, didn't I?" I said as a feeling of loss filled me.

The future held such promise then. Now I didn't see anything definite ahead of me. The blankness of fear made me wonder if any of my dreams would ever come true.

"Of all of us, you, me, my brothers, Ethan, and Tressa, I think you had the biggest plans. I mean, I always suspected Tressa wanted to take over the world and enslave men, assuming that didn't get in the way of being Earth's overlord," he joked, making me laugh.

"My goals were a little more grounded. Be a successful lawyer, become a judge, and sit on the Supreme Court by the time I was fifty. Maybe fifty-five."

I stopped talking as the weight of my unrealized dreams pressed down on me. How many times in the past eight years had I told myself I could still accomplish all of them? That none of them were truly out of reach? Yet every day that passed by, they moved a little further away from me until they were so far away by now that I could barely imagine myself accomplishing one of them, much less all of them.

"You still have time. Twenty-eight isn't exactly old," Cole said, tearing me out of my thoughts about all I hadn't done in the last decade.

"I guess."

"Do you still want to be a lawyer?" he asked.

No one had asked me that question since the accident. They'd all just assumed that dream had been shattered like the windshield of Ethan's sports car that night. I'd thought that too.

Shaking my head, I sighed. "No. I don't think so."

My answer didn't seem to surprise Cole. "I think you're way too nice to be a lawyer anyway. You're too sweet for ruining people's lives. Now I can see you as a doctor. They do good things, and that fits you better. Doctor Diana Stone. It has a great ring to it, don't you think?"

"A doctor?" I asked in amazement. "Really? I'd never thought of studying to be a doctor. After all the time I spent in the hospital, I swore I never wanted to be around one again in my life. But maybe. I'd have to think about it."

"I think you should. You're smart enough. You can afford medical school. Most of all, you're just what a doctor should be— helpful and kind. Let me go pay the bill and let's get out of here. I think I feel the oxygen level decreasing," he said with a smile before he stood and walked away, leaving me to think about what he'd just said.

A doctor. Could I do that? I was just beginning to be comfortable with people, but I could finish my undergraduate degree online. Maybe by the time I would have to begin medical school I would be ready to be in a classroom with people again.

I wanted to believe I could be that person he thought I was. Someone who believed in herself like I did when we were younger.

Before everything happened to make me afraid of so much in life.

As I sat there, I closed my eyes, needing to shut out the growing noise from people at the tables around me talking about work and the subway and all the other everyday hassles they dealt with. I wanted to remember that person I was with Cole ten years ago, that girl who took deep breaths of air in the woods and smiled as she sat with the boy she loved. A girl who dreamed big and lived dangerously, or at least as dangerously as sneaking out with her brother's best friend could be.

Clouds obscured the moon, making running across the back of the property as fast as I could a dangerous prospect. I did it anyway, willing to risk tripping over a broken tree limb that had fallen since two nights before when I ran this same path to get to the fence where I'd meet Cole. Wearing my favorite sneakers and white cotton socks that covered just to right below my ankles, I sprinted through the dewy grass that made the bottom of my legs damp by the time I'd only run halfway to where I needed to be.

I was late tonight, so he may have left already. God, I hoped not. I'd never forgive Tressa and my father for keeping me from seeing Cole if he wasn't right outside the fence waiting.

Of course, just as I was about to leave to supposedly go to a classmate's house to work on a group project that didn't exist, those two decided it was time to discuss college for the eight hundredth time. I didn't understand why either of them thought it was necessary. I'd already been accepted to Columbia, just as Tressa had been accepted to Penn. Why did we have to talk about it anymore? The deal was done. We'd gotten the brace ring.

But the two of them couldn't talk enough about what classes we'd take and what we should be planning for in the final months of high school. All I wanted to think about was Cole, but instead I ended up sitting with them for nearly an hour discussing meal plans, study groups, and how New York was different than Philly, none of which I cared about as much as seeing the one person who made me smile.

I saw the dim outline of the fence in the distance but no Cole. Discouraged, I slowed down to a jog and hoped he was just wearing dark clothes tonight. When I finally reached where he always waited for me, he wasn't there.

"Cole! Are you here?" I whispered as my eyes tried to see more than a few feet ahead of me in the pitch darkness.

I waited a moment for an answer but heard nothing, so again I called out for him, my voice almost pleading this time. "Cole, I'm here."

Sadness filled me, so I leaned against the fence next to the opening and tried to see if he was nearby. Narrowing my eyes, I stared hard into the darkness, but it was no use. He wasn't there.

He probably left because he thought I'd stood him up, I thought to myself. Maybe I could go to his grandmother's house. She was probably asleep already, so I could sneak around back and try to get his attention by throwing pebbles at his window. He slept in a room with one of his brothers, but they wouldn't be asleep yet. It was still early.

I'd never gone there without Cole. He didn't like living there, so he tried to stay away as much as possible. I just needed to see him and explain that I didn't not show up tonight. I would never do that. The time I got to spend with him meant too much to me.

So I pulled the fence apart wide enough for me to fit and carefully stepped through, watching so the metal wire didn't catch on my hair or my clothes. When my upper body was on the other side, I turned to hold the fence open so it didn't snag my leg. More than once, I'd come home after time with Cole and had to clean blood off my legs from the cuts those pieces of metal made when they scraped across my skin. Sometimes my mother would look at me strange when she saw them, but she only once asked what had happened and didn't push for more details when I said I mistakenly ran through picker bushes on the way home from school.

On the other side of the fence, I once again searched for him, just in case I'd missed him before. "Cole, are you here?" I whispered as loudly as I could until my throat began to burn and my voice turned hoarse.

Disappointed, I tried to focus my vision on the area in front of me and took a step forward. Usually when I walked through these woods, Cole held my hand and took the brunt of the tree branches and vines that blocked the path of worn grass that led to the town nearby. Alone, I had to feel my way so I didn't run headlong into anything. I may have been able to explain some scratches on my shins, but I didn't think I'd be able to hide cuts on my face and my parents would certainly ask where they came from.

I heard a cracking sound behind me and spun around in terror. "Who's there?" I asked, barely able to get the words out.

"Who do you think it is?" he said in his smart ass tone he used whenever he thought someone asked a stupid question.

He stepped out of the shadows and came into focus, and I saw him smiling at me as the moon came from behind the clouds. "Cole! I thought you went home because I was late. My father and Tressa held me up. I'm sorry it took me so long to get here."

"I thought you finally decided you didn't want to see me anymore."

Pulling me into his arms, he hugged me tightly to him. "I'm glad you didn't, though."

My face pressed against his chest, and I inhaled a deep breath of air to fill my lungs with his scent. Cole always smelled like a mixture of Ivory soap and whatever brand of laundry detergent his grandmother had bought at the store that week.

I tilted my head back and looked up at him as I wrapped my arms around his neck. "Where were you? I called your name. Didn't you hear me?"

Above me, he chuckled, making his Adam's apple bob up and down. "I was here the whole time." He turned his head to look over at a group of trees a few yards away. "Over there."

"Then why didn't you answer when I called your name?"

Cole shrugged. "I wanted to see if you'd come looking for me."

"Of course I would. I was planning on walking all the way to your grandmother's house."

He smiled and slid his hands down my back. "I found somewhere *new for us to go while I was waiting for you. Come with me."*

I took his hand and followed him as we walked in silence for nearly five minutes. The woods weren't that deep that we wouldn't have run into the town, so I assumed we were walking along the fence to my house.

After a few minutes, I asked, "Why couldn't we just sit where we usually go? My feet are all wet from running through the grass, so my sneakers are starting to hurt."

"Just a little bit farther," he said and then turned back to look at me. "You trust me, Diana, don't you?"

"Yes," I answered in a small voice, unsure why he'd ask that question at all.

I trusted him enough to sneak out of my house and lie to my family and friends to be with him. I didn't trust anyone in the world more.

Squeezing his hand tightly, I held on as we walked up a small hill and Cole stopped at the top. He pulled me up to stand next to him, wrapping his arms around my body to lift me.

"Up you go. What do you think?" he asked and extended his hand like the models on game shows when they introduced the prizes contestants can win.

My gaze followed his hand, and I saw in the distance his grandmother's house. Turning to look up at him, I asked, "Did you build up this little hill so you can see your house?"

Cole laughed and shook his head like my question was a stupid one. "No. I just happened to find it. I figured if some night I couldn't get out for any reason that you could come up to this spot and look to see if I left you a sign, like a candle or something. I could put it in the window."

A jolt of panic tore through me. "You never have a problem getting out. I'm the one who always has to dodge my family. Why would you not be able to come to see me?" I asked, trembling.

Dozens of horrible thoughts rushed into my brain. Was he doing this so he could lie some night and be somewhere else with another girl? Was he planning on telling me he couldn't get out one night when he was actually with someone else? Why would he do that?

"Relax. I don't think I'll have a problem getting out since my grandmother barely knows when I'm there and when I'm not. I just thought it could be cool. Like in that story we read in English class last year. One if by land, two if by sea. Well, our signal could be one candle in my bedroom window to mean I can't come that night, and two could mean I'll be there soon."

As my heart returned to its normal rhythm, I tried to smile to make it seem like I enjoyed his idea even as doubt haunted me. "That sounds great. I guess if your cell phone doesn't work some night, I can come to this spot and look for your signal."

"What's wrong? I thought you'd like that. You love all that stuff they make us read in English. Why do you look like I said something wrong?" Cole asked in a voice full of hurt.

"Do you want to stop meeting? If you do, you just have to say it. You don't have to come up with stuff like signals if you want to spend time with some other girl," I said, hardly believing I had the nerve to say those words.

He didn't answer for so long that I was sure I'd figured out his grand plan. He didn't know how to break things off with me, so he thought coming up with something cute like this would put me off a few times while he made excuses and then eventually I'd get the hint and go away.

Not that I was surprised. I knew the kind of girls Cole usually spent time with. I saw them around school. They were more advanced than me in nearly every way that counted to boys. Not intellectually, but that didn't matter to him or any other boy in high school. Compared to those girls, I was like some backward little girl. That he'd want to be with one of them instead of me was something I'd expected for a while.

It's just that knowing all my fears were true felt worse than I ever thought it would.

I turned away from him and hurried down the hill. I didn't want him to see me cry. He didn't need to think I was a pathetic little virgin who cried when someone told me they didn't like me anymore.

My chest felt like it would explode, and I couldn't get a full breath in, but I made myself run as I heard him yell my name behind me. If only I could get to the fence before he caught up.

"Diana! Wait!"

His words ricocheted around me in the darkness, and then I felt myself tumbling to the ground. I hit hard, my leg bashing off a thick tree root, and the tears sprung from my eyes. I tried to will them away, but it was no use. Between the pain in my knee from falling and the pain everywhere else from knowing Cole didn't want to see me anymore, I couldn't stop myself. I sat on the damp ground hugging my hurt knee and sobbing like some little girl waiting for someone to kiss her boo-boo and make it all better.

"Are you okay? Why did you run away like that?" Cole asked as he crouched down next to me.

I couldn't answer because I couldn't stop crying. When I didn't say anything, he wrapped his arm around me and kissed the top of my head.

"I wasn't saying anything back there, Diana. I don't want anyone else. Why would you think that?"

My words got lost in my sobs for a few seconds before I finally answered, "Because you don't get what you want from me."

"Yes, I do. I get exactly what I want from you."

What did he mean by that?

I wiped my tears and turned my head to see him smiling. "What do you get from me?"

He pressed a kiss onto my forehead and whispered against my skin, "I get to be with you. That's all I want from you."

Like before, what he said made dozens of questions pop up in my mind. Why didn't he want from me what I knew he'd gotten from other girls? Was there something wrong with me? Why did he just want to sit around and talk with me?

Too afraid to ask him, I sat there on the ground and said nothing as he held me in his arms.

I felt someone tap me on the back of my hand as it sat on the table, and I looked up to see Cole standing there. "Sorry. I was lost in thought for a minute."

"We're all settled up, so let's go. It's starting to get a little tight in here."

I looked around and saw all the tables had filled up in the time I'd been daydreaming. Instantly, the restaurant felt crowded, so I stood up quickly, needing to leave. Cole held out his hand, and I took hold of it and followed him out of the building just as I had done that night when he wanted to show me that little hill he'd found.

Right before we reached the door to the street, he turned around and looked at me with worry in his eyes. "We're almost there. Two sardines jumping from the can. Just hold on."

He turned back to focus on maneuvering us between the last few tables, so he didn't see my smile at his lame joke. I didn't think he felt any discomfort at how claustrophobic the restaurant had become, but that he knew I did and cared enough to be concerned about that made me feel protected, like always with Cole.

CHAPTER TWELVE

DIANA

BY THE TIME WE GOT back to the hotel, I'd decided to cancel the third apartment showing since I doubted that one would be much different from the two I'd already seen that afternoon. I wanted something bigger, so I needed to change my search focus before I traveled to see any other places.

I sensed Cole's discomfort as soon as we walked through the Richmont's glass doors into the lobby. He seemed to move away from me, like we were merely two people walking into a hotel instead of two people who'd spent the day together. He didn't say anything about it, but I felt a distance spring up between us.

"Would you like to get a drink at the lounge?" I asked even as I walked in the direction of my room. I didn't want to assume he intended on coming back there with me if he planned to leave.

"I thought maybe we could hang out in your room, if that's okay."

He swiveled his head left and right, looking for one of my family, I assumed. I giggled at how silly the whole thing was. "You don't have to worry, Cole. I'm a big girl. If anyone in my family shows up, it will be fine."

"Sorry. I just don't want there to be a big scene, and I have a feeling that's exactly what would happen if Ethan saw us right now."

I didn't feel like explaining why, but I didn't think that would happen. Not after what my brother and I went through earlier that week. Ethan understood I was a grown woman who had the right to live her life as she wanted, whether that meant moving wherever I chose or seeing who I wanted to see.

"I'm not worried," I said defiantly as I turned the corner and walked to my room.

Cole didn't answer me, and once we were inside, he sat down on the couch as I made a beeline to the refrigerator. "Are you thirsty? Maybe it's because I rarely do so much walking, but I'm parched."

He smiled and shook his head. "No, I'm good, but feel free."

Something about the way he said that made me wonder if something was wrong. He sounded odd, like he wanted to say something else. I grabbed a water and sat down beside him before I took a sip of my drink.

And then there was silence for what felt like forever. We just sat there staring at the black screen on my TV, like two strangers who didn't have anything to say to one another.

Finally, I put my bottle of water on the coffee table in front of me and turned to face Cole. He looked over at me and smiled, but clearly something was wrong.

"Did I say something that bothered you? This feels weird."

He forced a smile and shook his head. "No. I thought maybe the way I acted out in the lobby might have offended you. I didn't mean it like it came out. I just never forget that Ethan has made you off limits to the likes of me."

"The likes of you?" I repeated, hating the way that sounded. "What does that mean, the likes of you?"

"You know. His friends. Guys. Men, in general," he said with a chuckle. "Well, I can't speak for the entire male population, but me. He never liked when I said anything about you."

"What did you say?"

"I mean, when I referred to you as an eligible female," Cole said awkwardly.

"I'm not sure what that means, but I'm going to take it as a compliment and think that you said nice things."

That made him turn his body toward me. "Oh, I did. Always. But even when it wasn't guy talk, he had a problem with it."

Shyly, I pointed out the obvious. "Well, he's not here, so if you wanted to say something nice about me, I'd love to hear it."

Cole stared at me with a strange look in his eyes. "You know how guys are."

I inched over toward him and smiled. "Yeah, but that doesn't mean you aren't nice sometimes, right?"

He didn't respond, and I moved closer to him so our knees touched. My body came alive at the sensation of his body so near to mine. I wanted to feel more of him, so I leaned forward and closed my eyes before ever so lightly brushing my lips against his. They felt soft, like I remembered them, and all at once the past came rushing back to me.

I waited for Cole to kiss me back, but his mouth turned hard as the seconds ticked by. Opening my eyes, I saw him looking at me in surprise before he pulled away.

Instantly, all my defenses and fears raged against the hurt that pinched at me. I felt my eyes begin to fill with tears and turned away, not wanting him to see the effect of his rejection on me.

"You should go, Cole."

My words came out in a painful whisper, nearly choked out of existence by the sob I stifled. I'd thought he liked me again, but whatever I'd convinced myself of this afternoon, I'd misread the signs. The realization that my first real attempt at connecting with a man in eight years had failed miserably was more painful than I'd imagined, and I'd done a pretty good job of worrying how much it would hurt if I let a man know I wanted him and he didn't feel the same way.

He didn't say a thing, likely unable to find the right words to convey that I didn't arouse him in that way. Maybe he didn't want to offer me the "it's not you, it's me" excuse. I should have been thanking him for not recoiling in horror at my timid attempt at seduction. I closed my eyes and felt the couch cushion move as he stood to go, still unable to find a single word for me.

God, I was pathetic. How could I have thought that a man like Cole Knight would ever want to be with a mess like me? All his concern about Ethan and how he'd react if he saw us together was all a lie. He just didn't want to give me the idea that he wanted more, but I'd misunderstood.

From behind me, I heard him twist the doorknob, and the sound went through me like a knife. Taking a deep breath, I willed myself not to cry until I heard the door close. I wanted to preserve some dignity, at least.

"Diana," he said in a low voice. But that was it. Just my name.

"Just leave."

I waited for the sound of the door to open, but I heard nothing. Turning to see if he'd left and I hadn't heard, I saw him standing there looking at me.

Then he spoke and I didn't know what to do.

"I don't want to go."

My heart slammed into my chest at his words as a mixture of happiness and anger coursed through me. I stood up and before I could stop myself, all the words I didn't want to say poured out of me.

"What do you want from me? You do the most bizarre things to find me. Then you don't call for two days. When you do, you agree to go apartment hunting with me, but it was obvious the whole time that it's not something you like to do. Now you say you don't want to go. So what do you want?"

I held my breath in anticipation as I waited for his answer. He remained silent for a long moment before he took a step back into the room and toward me.

"What I want I shouldn't want," he said in a tone that sounded as tortured as mine had a minute before.

But whatever he was fighting, I wanted to hear him say it.

"Why?"

He took another step toward me. "Because you're my best friend's sister. You're supposed to be off-limits."

I wanted to scream at his mention of my brother as his excuse for anything. "Then leave, but stop using Ethan as your justification. Just stop."

Cole took a single step and then another and stopped, shaking his head. "I don't want to leave. I want to kiss you. I want to feel what you made me feel again."

"What did I make you feel?" I asked, needing to hear his answer after all this time.

"Happy. When my world felt like it was coming down around me, you gave me peace," he said as he took another step closer to me and then stopped.

"But now that you aren't that scared boy anymore but a grown man who's successful and can have any woman you want, you look at me and think I'm still that girl you left behind all those years ago."

Cole shook his head. "No. You're wrong. I want that peace again. I need it. More than you can ever know."

"Then why did you react like that when I kissed you?"

He took one last step and reached out to cup my face with his hand. "Because you're too good for me. You're sweet, and I'm jaded. You're goodness, and I don't deserve someone like you."

I closed my eyes and leaned into his palm. "Someone who lives in a hotel room and is scared of going out. Someone who's afraid to go in your beautiful car. Someone messed up like me. You don't have to lie, Cole. I know what I am."

"Diana, look at me."

Afraid to see the look of pity in his eyes, I shook my head. "Just go. Please."

My words came out on a sob I wished he didn't hear. I just wanted him to put me out of my misery.

"Open your eyes. Look at me, please."

I dreaded what I'd see, but I opened my eyes as he wanted. I didn't see pity, though. I saw desire. For so long, I'd dreamed of seeing a man look at me like that.

"You deserve so much better than me, but I promise as long as you want me to, I'll be happy to take the train instead of drive and do what you need me to so you don't have to be afraid."

My emotions threatened to spill out all over the place at hearing him say such beautiful things. Then he leaned forward and kissed me softly, taking my breath away. Fear and need blended together, making it impossible to push one away without pushing the other out of my mind. I wanted to desire him, so for the first time in years, I didn't try to overcome my fear of something.

His hand gently moved from my face to caress my neck, sending waves of need washing through me. I wanted his touch on every part of me, and I had to fight the urge to voice my thoughts, something I'd been taught to do whenever I felt scared.

Cole's tongue slid over mine, teasing me with the promise of what else he could excite that way. I kissed him in return with everything I had—my fear, my need, my craving to be loved as a female after all this time alone.

My fingers tugged at his shirt, pulling it over his head to reveal the same athletic body I remembered. Other than a dusting of dark hair that began on his chest and trailed down over his toned abs, he looked the same as he had back when he played shirts and skins with his friends on the football field.

I needed to feel him, so I ran my fingertips over his soft skin. He quivered at my touch, and I smiled at his reaction.

"Did I tickle you?" I asked, hoping not to ruin the mood with a mistake.

He shook his head and smiled. The look in his eyes made me feel like he wanted to devour me, and as much as I didn't know what to do with that, I wasn't afraid.

"I didn't mean to. I just wanted to touch you," I said softly, suddenly needing to fill the empty space with words.

Cole licked his lips and kissed me. He whispered against my

lips, "You can touch any part of me. I'm all yours."

Leaning forward, I pressed my lips to his neck and inhaled the delicious scent of his skin into my lungs. He didn't smell like soap and detergent now, though. The grown man smelled masculine, and I moaned in response to how it made me feel. I slid my tongue over the area I'd kissed, needing to taste him, to take him into me.

He responded by stuffing his hand into my hair and tightening his fist, pulling back the strands I always kept near my face to hide my scar. I shrank back and lifted my hand to the side of my face, shaking my head while I tried to hold back the tears that threatened to flow from my eyes. I'd been so lost in how he smelled and tasted that I forgot the reality of who I was.

Grimacing, Cole gently pushed my hand away, revealing that horrible scar I hated. "You don't have to hide any part of you."

"The accident…after all the surgeries, I still have scars. I don't want you to…" I tried but I couldn't get the words out to explain.

I stood there shaking in terror as he tucked my hair behind my ear and tenderly ran his finger along the length of my scar on my cheek. Raised and hideous, it never failed to make me feel ugly.

Cole cupped my face in his hands and pressed a soft kiss onto my scar. "This is just evidence that you survived. That's a good thing, Diana."

Closing my eyes, I tried to believe what he said. For so long, I'd seen that part of me as a flaw, but now he was saying it wasn't something awful. That couldn't be true. Could it?

"If you want, I can show you my scars. Mine are just from doing stupid guy stuff, though, so you might not be very impressed."

I looked at him and saw a smile that made all my insecurities begin to retreat back to that place in me where they always waited to ruin my happiness. "I'll be sure to look for those scars."

When he leaned in to kiss me once more, this time I felt no fear or worry. Just pure bliss. I loved that he wasn't treating me like some broken thing he didn't know how to handle. I didn't know if he was like this with other women, but it meant the world to me that he acted like the Cole I'd known and not some stranger afraid of me.

Pulling away, I gathered the courage to say the words I never could all those years ago. "I don't want this to be just kissing. I'm not some untouchable thing, Cole. I'm the same as every other woman in the world. But if you don't want that from me for whatever reason, I'd like you to be honest now because I do."

My thoughts didn't come out like I wanted them to, but at least they made sense. Now it was up to him if we ended up sleeping together or if he walked away.

One second followed another and then another as I waited for his response. I hadn't left him a middle choice. Either we'd sleep together or he'd tell me he didn't want to and he'd leave. The choice was up to him. I knew what I wanted.

His dark eyes focused on my eyes, his penetrating gaze making me feel vulnerable yet again. At any moment, he could say he didn't want me and all I came with. I knew that, but I couldn't look away. I needed to see the truth in his eyes as he answered me.

Slowly, the corners of his beautiful mouth turned up, and he finally said, "I always wanted you, Diana. Just because I was too afraid ten years ago doesn't mean I didn't want you then. Nothing's changed. You still make me happier than anyone else I've ever met, so of course, I don't want this to end with kissing."

Then his smile faded, frightening me. "I can't lie, though. I've been with a lot of women since then. When I say you're too good for me, that's one main reason why."

I reached out and ran my finger along his collarbone. "I'm no fool. I know everyone else's world continued to exist for the past eight years. Wherever you've been and whoever you were with, those experiences made you who you are right now. That's not a bad thing just like what I've been through has made me who I am."

Cole slid his hand against the back of my head and pulled me to him, crushing my mouth in a kiss that made my head spin.

"Then no more talking."

In a flash, he slid my sundress off my shoulders and pushed it down my body until it fell into a crumpled heap at my feet. Then he did the same with my bra and underwear, leaving me naked standing there in front of him.

He kept to his pledge to not say another thing and knelt down in front of me. Before I could feel insecure, he pressed his mouth to me and everything else in the world disappeared but the two of us and his tongue teasing my clit.

I tried to hold out for as long as possible, but it had been so long since I'd been with a man that it didn't take long for me to come. My release raced through me, making my legs buckle as I tugged hard on Cole's hair, but he quickly caught me before I collapsed onto the floor.

Smiling up at me, he licked his lips as my thighs still quivered from my orgasm. "Thank God for good reflexes."

"Thank you for having a talented tongue."

Cole stood up and kissed me hard on the mouth again. "Let's move this to somewhere more comfortable."

He took my hand and led me to my bedroom. Pulling me to him, he kissed me while I hurried to undo his pants and push them down over his hips. I slid my hand over the cotton fabric of his underwear, the final barrier between the two of us, and felt his erection. Cole moaned as I palmed his hard cock and in seconds, he stripped down to nothing.

Everything felt like we were caught up in a whirlwind. We tumbled onto the bed, and I landed on my back. Above me, he looked like a man intently focused on a single goal, and just a moment later, I opened my legs and he slowly moved over my body before he thrust into me, filling me completely.

I arched my back as we settled into a rhythm for our lovemaking. Cole didn't treat me like a delicate flower, which excited me, so I responded to each thrust into me by pushing my hips forward. His cock filling me ignited feelings I'd never experienced before with the handful of men I'd slept with, like every time before had been just a teaser to what being with a man could truly bring out in me. I wanted him to feel as good as I felt.

Cole's head dropped to the pillow next to mine, and I heard his ragged breathing as his hips continued to rock back and forth, pumping his cock into my body. Lifting my legs, I wrapped them around his waist and dug my heels into his lower back, urging him to fill me over and over.

I scratched my nails down his back as my second orgasm began to uncoil inside me, crying out his name when it finally hit. "Oh, God…Cole…"

He moaned something I couldn't make out as I came hard, and then seconds later, he stilled inside me. I slid my fingertips over the back of his neck, feeling the dampness under his hair, as he kissed the shell of my ear and whispered, "Diana."

In that single word, I heard satisfaction. After all this time, I'd finally been able to be myself with a man who accepted me for me.

Lifting his head off the pillow, Cole looked down into my eyes and smiled. "If I hadn't been such a coward, we would have been together like that ten years ago. I wish I hadn't waited."

My cheeks heated from a blush that seemed silly after what we'd just done together. "I don't think I would have been very good back then. Virgins aren't notoriously great lovers, no matter what anyone says."

He nodded and kissed me sweetly on the lips. "I probably wasn't very good back then either. Teenage sex isn't known for being great."

"Then it's good we waited."

Rolling onto the bed, he settled in beside me, and I curled up against his body. I pressed my cheek against the area above his heart and heard it still beating wildly. "Your heart is racing."

Cole wrapped his arm around me and hugged me to him. "That was a workout. I'm not a teenager anymore."

We weren't those kids sneaking off to the woods to spend time together either. No longer teenagers and all grown up, we'd lived very different lives in the past ten years, but we'd found our way back to each other.

One thing had never changed, though. I'd been crazy about Cole as a girl, and that feeling was the same now as it was then.

CHAPTER THIRTEEN

COLE

MY EYES WEREN'T EVEN OPEN all the way before my brain reminded me that I'd spent the night making love to Diana. I'd slept with the woman I'd been told to keep my hands off of. She was literally the only person on the entire planet I wasn't supposed to have sex with, and last night, that's exactly what I'd done.

Multiple times. In multiple positions. Loving every minute of it.

I didn't think it was a mistake. I didn't. But in the harsh light of morning, I couldn't deny that our actions last night could have serious repercussions. For one, Ethan was probably going to do way more than just deck me. That time, he leveled me just for mentioning that I thought she was hot. I hadn't even made a rude comment about her. Just that I thought she was hot, and he'd given me a right to the jaw for that.

We weren't kids anymore, though. Maybe things would be different now.

Looking down my body, I watched as Diana slept on my stomach, her brown hair hiding her beautiful face. We'd talked for hours after the last round of sex. She wanted to know what my life had been like and if I'd found happiness in my work. I didn't want to lie, especially after what we'd done together, but I couldn't bring myself to tell her the truth. Not then. It would have made her think everything between us was a lie, and that wasn't true.

What she made me feel wasn't a lie. That was possibly the

truest and greatest good I'd ever known in my entire life. I couldn't bear the idea of her believing that hadn't been real for me.

I hovered my hand over her head, afraid to touch her because I didn't want to wake her yet. I liked lying there with her on top of me and her breath drifting over my skin every time she exhaled. I wanted to have every single day begin this way.

But how could that ever happen knowing I had nothing to offer her?

Touching the top of her head, I let my fingers glide over her soft, brown hair. I closed my eyes to focus my thoughts on how that felt so I'd never forget, just in case I didn't get to experience that again. I'd lived on mostly memories of Diana for the last decade, even as I went through women like a fish through water. None of them compared to her.

It didn't matter that some had better bodies, bigger tits, firmer ass, or whatever. It didn't matter that most of them were far more confident than Diana or that more than a few were way wilder in bed than her. None of them made me feel what she did all those years ago as we sat together and talked in secret in the woods behind her house.

I'd resigned myself to thinking I'd never get to feel that happy, that peaceful, again. And then that day she stopped me at the front door of the hotel, that happiness returned. Now that it was back, I didn't want to lose it again.

But how could I ever keep Diana once she found out what I really was?

She turned her head and stared up at me as if she'd heard my thoughts, and for a moment, I wondered if I'd spoken them out loud. Then she smiled, and the fear of losing her faded into the background, replaced by the sweetness that came with that gentle smile.

"Morning. Did I wake you up?" I asked as she sat up next to me.

Diana shook her head and rearranged her hair along the sides of her face. "No. I can't tell you how odd it was to open my eyes and be just inches away from a penis."

I couldn't stop myself and chuckled at her candor. "He's up and at 'em like that in the morning."

Her cheeks turned light pink, and she smiled like she found my stupid joke funny. "Are you hungry?"

"Yeah, I could go for something to eat."

Tugging the sheet up to hide her naked body, she leaned over and grabbed her phone off the nightstand. "I'll order breakfast. What would you like?"

"Two eggs, scrambled, two orders of rye toast, and bacon. Two, make that three orders of bacon."

As I rattled off my order, her eyes grew wide in surprise. "That's a lot of food. I usually eat a danish or muffin."

I pulled on the sheet and chuckled. "I used up a lot of energy last night. So did you. You might want to eat something more than a muffin this morning to keep your strength up."

Again, she blushed. "Will I be needing more energy for something today?" she asked innocently, making my cock harden at the sound of her words.

"Likely."

Diana bit her bottom lip in that way that made her look so sweet, even though I had a feeling she did it because she was nervous, and then made the call to order our food. When she finished, I tugged the sheet completely away from her and slid my arm around her waist to pull her on top of me.

"Cole, I need to get up to answer the door when the food's delivered," she protested half-heartedly while I cupped her ass in my hands and squeezed.

"That gives us a few minutes at least. I figured we could start now, eat our food, and then finish after."

I slid my rock hard cock over her clit, and her eyes rolled back in her head. Fuck, she was wet and ready for me already.

Rolling her hips, she dragged her pussy down the length of me.

"I'm not going to be able to hear the knock on the door."

Her protests gave way to her need, and she rocked her hips one last time, taking me inside her with a sweet groan. Stuffing my hands into her hair, I held her head so I could kiss her as she rode my cock. Christ, I didn't know how I'd let her off me if someone knocked right now.

In my head, I quickly added up how long it would take to make our breakfast, hoping the kitchen started from scratch since it was for Diana. By my count, we had about five minutes at least, even if they just had to put the order together. Not exactly a marathon session, but enough to probably get off.

I pushed her up so she sat straddling me. Fuck, she looked incredible perched on me with my cock deep inside her. I slid my thumb over her clit and said, "Ride me, baby."

Staring down at me, she took my command to heart and did just that. Rocking and rolling her hips, she fucked me as well as any woman I'd ever had while looking as sweet as an angel as she did it. I felt her cunt begin to clench around my cock and knew it wouldn't take much longer, so I grabbed hold of her hips with both hands and pushed up hard, ramming into her. She whimpered my name, so I did it again and again until her body tightened around my cock so hard I knew her release had come.

Diana dropped down onto my chest like a limp ragdoll, but I was hell bent on coming before that damn knock on the door interrupted us. Holding her to me, I pistoned into her like a madman, riding the waves of her release to my own. When it finally happened, I thrust into her one last time and groaned as I flooded her with everything I had.

We lay there for less than a minute before the sound of someone knocking on her hotel room door made her roll off me quickly and run to the bathroom. Seconds later, she hurried through the bedroom to answer the door wearing a white bathrobe and looking like a woman who had just been fucked first thing in the morning.

When she reappeared, she had a tray full of food in her hands. "Breakfast is served!"

I sat up in bed and pulled back the covers for her to sit. "Aww, honey. You shouldn't have," I joked as she set down the tray on the end of the bed.

Diana laughed and then her expression grew serious. "I forgot to ask you if you wanted coffee. I'm sorry. I don't drink it, so I didn't think to get any. Do you want me to call down for some?"

"No, I'm fine. I'm wide awake already after what we just did, so I don't need coffee to wake me up this morning."

She sat down next to me, and I saw her blushing again. As I took a plate of scrambled eggs from her, I said, "I think it's cute that you blush like that."

Shrugging, she handed me my bacon. "I don't know why that always happens. I'm not that innocent girl anymore, so I don't know why my face hasn't gotten the memo."

I breathed in the greasy and sweet scent of maple bacon and took a bite. "Delicious. You really know how to make a great breakfast."

"You're silly," she said with a smile and then rolled her eyes.

As we ate our food, I thought about our time together. "You know, I always wished we had sex in high school. Now I'm glad we didn't."

"Why?"

"You know how they say things are better when you wait? They're right. You actually surprised me."

"Surprised you? How?" she asked as concern filled her blue eyes.

Now that I'd started this conversation, I didn't know how to proceed. "I guess I figured…"

Diana waited for me to finish, but when I didn't, she said, "You thought because I stayed here all these years that I wouldn't be good in bed, didn't you?"

The woman never failed to surprise me with her bluntness.

Nodding, I admitted the truth. "Yeah."

A sexy smile lit up her face. "See, this is why boys should always go after bookworms. We learn a lot from reading. You'd be surprised what you can learn just from books."

I took a bite of bacon and asked, "Is that where you learned that thing you did with your tongue when you went down on me?"

She blushed like I knew she would and lowered her head. "No. I guess I'm about to blow up my argument in favor of reading, but I saw that online."

That she could be embarrassed enough by sex talk to blush and then in the next breath admit that she learned how to give a phenomenal blowjob by watching porn online charmed me, as ridiculous as that seemed. Surprised by her admission, I nearly choked on my piece of bacon and could only croak out, "Really?"

"There's only so much reading a person can do, Cole. I may have been afraid to leave here for a long time, but in many ways, I was a normal woman in her twenties."

The sadness in her voice when she said that hit me like a shot to the chest. I hated the idea of her fearing everything so much that she closed herself off from the world. Pulling her to me, I held her and kissed the top of her head.

"You're so beautiful and the thought of you here all alone all that time makes me hate myself for not trying to find you before this."

She leaned back and looked up at me like an angel. "It wasn't that bad. I'm better now, but this place was safe for me when I needed to feel protected."

I gently squeezed her in my arms, wishing I knew what to say. "And now you're going to find a house with a big yard and maybe get yourself some horses like you dreamed of back when we'd talk about all the things we planned to do in life."

Giggling, she shook her head. "I don't think I'm going to go for the horses, but everything else, yes. I want to be able to walk out on my porch on summer days and have a place to read my books and even eat breakfast, if I want to. And if I have anyone over who likes way too much bacon with his breakfast, he can sit with me and eat all that greasy meat too."

That she included me in her future made me smile. I kissed her lips and whispered against them, "And I can give you greasy bacon kisses like that too on your porch."

She made a face like she didn't like the taste on my lips. "My neighbors are going to wonder about me and the man who eats that gross bacon on my porch, but you know what? I don't care what they think. I'll let you eat it all you want."

"I just can't kiss you afterward without brushing my teeth?"

Diana lifted herself up and kissed me. "You can kiss me anytime, Cole."

"I will."

We sat there in her bed surrounded by empty plates after a night of sex I never imagined would ever happen for us. That feeling of peace she'd brought into my life a decade ago had fully returned last night, and I didn't want to think it would ever leave.

She leaned her head back against me and said, "I don't remember what you dreamed of doing after high school. Why can't I remember?"

I pressed my cheek against her to feel her soft hair next to my skin. "I don't know either. I'm sure it was something stupid. I wasn't much for planning out my life like you were then. I was just hoping to get through the next day."

"I'm sorry I never knew how bad things were for you, Cole," Diana said quietly, as if she had anything to apologize for.

"Don't feel you have to say you're sorry. You were the only thing that got me through those days. I may have seemed like I didn't care if you came out to the woods any night, but I did. You have no idea how much I cared. I just didn't know how to express it because I was only a kid."

She turned to look at me and frowned. "I saw when they came to take your father away that day. I couldn't imagine what you were feeling. That must have been so hard for you and your brothers."

I thought back to that day and shook my head as the memory came back all too vividly. "I don't think I can explain how much that scared me. My mother had left, and then they took my father and we were told the house would soon be gone too. I'd lived in that house all my life. My brothers and I had no idea where we'd end up. All I could think was I'd lose all my friends, baseball, and everything I had that came with living in that house. I guess, looking back, it was always the plan that my grandmother would take us in, but in the moment when it was all happening, I felt like I didn't have anything to hold onto, like my world was spinning out of control and nothing tethered me to the earth."

"Is that why you spent so much time at our house right after?"

I took a deep breath as that horrible day began to fade away again. "Yeah. My older brother was able to take care of us until we moved to my grandmother's, but I didn't want to go back to that house. I couldn't get the memory of my father being taken away out of my mind. So Ethan asked your parents if I could stay for a while. I expected them to say no since I don't think they wanted the son of a felon even hanging out with their kid, much less practically living with your family. When they said yes, I was surprised, but you know what the best thing about that was?"

Diana shook her head. "I don't know. What?"

"That's when I started to think I liked you. You probably never noticed how much I paid attention to you in those weeks, but I did. Thinking back, I guess I was stalking you then too. And to think I believed my whole stalking thing just happened in the last week."

"You have no idea how long I had noticed you, do you?" she asked and then lowered her head, blushing.

"In my defense, I did have a lot of shit going on for a teenage kid to deal with," I said, trying to make her smile.

"When we were in sophomore year, you and your friends would play football after school at the field by school. Sometimes Ethan would stay if he didn't have his photography classes to go to, so I'd make an excuse to hang around because I said I wanted to watch him play. But it was you I wanted to see. I liked when your side would play skins the best. You never noticed me because I was always just Ethan's sister and I wasn't one of the girls you hung out with then, but I noticed you."

"Skins, huh? I guess you're right about you bookworm types. I never figured you even saw me since every time I came over to the house before those few weeks I stayed you disappeared."

Looking up at me, her blue eyes wide, she gave me a shy smile. "I knew I wasn't the type of girl you'd like. You always spent time with the cheerleaders and girls who went to parties with you guys."

I lifted her chin with my finger and kissed her. "Again, in my defense, I was a teenage boy. We are historically the worst when it comes to decision-making. That doesn't excuse me for being stupid, but I did get better two years later. I deserve some credit for that, don't you think?"

She nodded and smiled. "Yes. And for what it's worth, I loved every minute of that time we spent together in those couple months we were secretly meeting in the woods."

Wrapping my arms around her, I pulled her to me. "I did too. You saved me, Diana. Nobody else made me think things would be okay, but you did. I couldn't have found what you gave me in any other girl then. When I needed someone, you saved me."

No matter what she thought she knew about those hours we spent together, nothing I said truly explained how much they meant to me. As much as I hated to admit it, now I was little better off than where I was ten years ago, but this time I wanted to be worthy of all she offered.

I just had to figure out how to be that for her.

CHAPTER FOURTEEN

DIANA

MY LUNCH WITH SUMMER THAT we'd planned two weeks ago felt like torture as I struggled not to tell her the wonderful news about what happened with Cole. I wanted to so badly, but was that the right thing to do? I wasn't a teenage girl anymore. By the time someone got to the age I was, they should have been more mature.

But since I'd missed out on most of my twenties, part of me couldn't help but want to share some of the details with her. Another part wanted to tell someone just to show I wasn't some sad, pathetic creature who couldn't attract a man to save her life.

Most of all, though, I wanted to share my happiness with my friend.

Leaning over the table toward her, I looked around to make sure no one at the nearby tables were paying attention to us and whispered, "I have something I want to tell you."

A look of confusion came across her face. "Okay. Is anything wrong? Do we need to leave now?"

"No. I'm fine. In fact, I'm better than fine. I'm thrilled about something I want to tell you about, but I need you to promise me you won't say a thing to another soul, especially my brother. Okay?"

Summer leaned down until her face was next to mine and nodded. "Okay. What's going on, Diana?"

"I slept with someone last night."

It took a few seconds for my statement to sink in, but when it did, Summer practically threw herself back against her chair, her mouth hanging open in shock. "You what? Who? I thought you didn't like any of those guys we were looking at on that site. Who is he? How did you meet him? Have you been able to go out on your own? That's great!"

I couldn't tell what she thought was great—my having sex that clearly had rocked my world enough to want to tell her about it or the idea that I had gone out of my room without anyone with me, which seemed far less impressive in the big scheme of things.

"It's someone you know."

Being cryptic wasn't naturally my style, but I felt like I needed to slow-walk her to my big news of who the man was I'd had sex with.

She narrowed her eyes and stared at me intently. "You slept with someone I know? Who?"

I waved her down to where I hovered over the table and whispered his name. "Cole."

"Cole who?" she asked, and then as if a lightbulb lit up over her head, her eyes grew as big as saucers and she said far too loudly, "Cole Knight? You slept with Cole Knight, Ethan's best friend?"

Instantly, I swiveled my head around to see if any of the other customers at the restaurant had heard her. No one stared at us, thankfully, but if I was going to tell her any more details, she needed to keep her voice down.

"We're in public, Summer! Lower your voice," I whispered.

She shook her head fast. "You just told me you had sex with Cole Knight, Diana! I'm in shock. How did this happen? When? Where? How?" she asked in rapid-fire succession, her voice barely quieter than a few seconds ago.

"If you promise not to let everyone in this restaurant know, I'll tell you. Just calm down. Jeez, you're making a bigger deal of it than I am, and I'm the one who hasn't been with a man in eight years."

Summer took a deep breath and let it out slowly. Once all the air had left her lungs, she shook her head again. "I'm just blown away by this. I want details. This is no time to be modest, so spill them. Start from the beginning and take it slow. I'm just getting used to this, so bear with me."

My future sister-in-law didn't tend to overreact most of the time, so I knew I'd truly shocked her by my announcement. I liked how that felt. She and Ethan were always surprising all of us with their news about his success with the photography business, their engagement, and all their wedding plans, so it was nice to be the one doing the surprising for once.

"I saw him in the hotel lobby the afternoon you and I went to the bridal shop to look for dresses. We had a drink at the lounge and talked, and it was really great. It felt like no time had passed since we used to hang out together in high school. I mean, well, it was a little awkward at first, but he was sweet, so I gave him my number so he could call me."

"And he called and what? You invited him over and wham? You guys leaped into bed?" Summer asked, clearly overestimating my abilities with men.

I laughed and waved away her questions. "Not exactly. He called and I asked him to go apartment hunting with me. We saw two apartments, but I didn't like either one of them. Then we had dinner at a little place in the Upper East Side and went back to my room. We talked for a little bit, and then I kissed him."

"What? You made a move on him?" she asked with a look of amazement.

Nodding, I smiled with pride. "I did. I wanted to know what it would feel like after all these years, so I leaned forward on the couch and kissed him. And it was as wonderful as I remembered."

Summer shook her head. "Unbelievable! So then he made a move, and you just went along with it and slept with him? I don't know what to say, Diana."

"Not exactly," I said with a shrug. "He initially didn't seem to want to do anything, so I told him to leave. I didn't want him to stay if I was the only one in that room who wanted things to go further."

"So you gave him the green light and he marched right in and made a move."

I couldn't help but laugh. God, she was so off the mark about Cole. She had him sounding like he practically attacked me. I needed her to know how wrong she was about him.

"It wasn't like that, Summer. I told him I wanted him, and then we kissed for a little bit and things progressed. I wanted him as much as he wanted me. So we slept together, and I'm not going to lie. It was fantastic."

By the time I finished talking, my smile had stretched so wide my cheeks were beginning to ache. I didn't care. I had every right to grin like a woman who'd had great sex for the first time in ages. Literally.

Summer appeared speechless and kept opening and closing her mouth like she had something to say but didn't know the right words to use. I rarely had this effect on those around me, and I had to admit I liked it. The days of boring Diana who never did anything interesting had ended.

"You slept with Cole Knight," she said like she needed to hear it in her own voice to believe it.

"Yes, and it was fantastic. For both of us, I'm happy to announce."

Her mouth dropped open yet again at that comment. "Wow. I don't know what to say."

"Say you're happy for me."

A look of concern filled her eyes. "Are you okay? I mean, he's not exactly the type of guy I would have suggested for your first time out of the gate."

Her worry made me smile. "I wasn't a virgin, Summer. I have had sex before in my life. Believe it or not, before the accident, I did have a normal life that included sex."

"I know, but it's been a long time. Isn't there some kind of thing where you revirginate after so many years?"

Whether she meant that to be funny or not, I laughed out loud.

"I don't think that's a thing. And even though I'm sure this is moving into TMI range, it's not like that part of my body hasn't been having a regular workout for all these years. I'm a normal woman in her twenties. I just wasn't sexually active with a man until two days ago. And yesterday morning. And afternoon."

Summer waved her hands frantically in a futile effort to make me stop as I spoke candidly about my sex life. "Oh, my God! I had no idea, and I'm not sure I want to know any more, especially about how many times you and Cole had sex. TMI!"

When she finished flailing around, I told her the most important truth the past few days had shown me. "I'm happy. I haven't been able to say that for a long time and truly mean it. And here's another newsflash. I'm moving out of the city. I want somewhere I can have a yard and a porch I can sit on and eat my breakfast in the morning. Somewhere I can close my eyes and enjoy bacon and eggs."

For the fifth or sixth time since we finished our lunch, I'd shocked her into silence. When she finally recovered, she took a big gulp of her water and then sighed. "I've never seen you eat a piece of bacon in the entire two plus years I've known you, Diana. You're moving out of the city? Does Ethan know? Do your parents know? That's a huge step, isn't it?"

"Yes, Ethan knows I'm moving," I answered, knowing I was parsing the truth with that statement. "My parents do, too."

Leaning in toward me, she took my hand in hers and gave it a gentle squeeze. "Are you ready to live alone? I mean really alone. Living in the hotel isn't living alone, technically. There are people there at your beck and call if you need anything. I know you don't have housekeeping come in anymore, but that's not the same as living alone for real. Are you ready for that?"

I smiled, thankful for her concern, but knowing I could handle this move. "I'm going to be fine. Yes, I'm ready for this, okay? And who knows? I might not be alone."

She leaned back in her chair and sighed. "Okay. I need to visit the ladies' room before we go, so give me a couple minutes. You'll be good alone at the table here?"

For so long, that question had been one that needed to be asked, but I hadn't had a problem being out in public alone for months. Summer and the rest of my family meant well, but they really needed to catch on to the reality that I was better now.

Much better.

"I'll be fine. Relax. Go and take as long as you need to. I'm going to sit here and check out some house listings I found this morning."

"Okay. I'd love to see them when I get back, if that's okay."

"Great! We can go back to my room and I'll show you any I plan to see there. The TV is much better than looking at listings on my phone."

As Summer hurried off to the ladies' room, I began scrolling through pictures of what might be my new house sometime soon. I liked the yard, but the porch didn't look big enough to fit a table and chairs for my breakfast and Cole's, if he wanted to eat out there.

Not that I had mentioned any of that to him. We'd only had one night together. Well, one night and a whole day afterward. Smiling, I thought about how wonderful my time with him had been. I hoped we'd have many more. For now, the past few days made me feel like a new woman, and for that, I had him to thank.

When Summer and I got back to my room, Tressa was waiting for us. Surprised to see my sister in the middle of a workday dressed in her black skirt and pink silk blouse that said she clearly had been in the office, I wondered if something had happened with my parents.

Fear tore through me as I hurriedly asked, "Is everything okay? Are Mommy and Daddy okay?"

She smiled and hugged me to her. "They're fine. I had a few spare minutes, so I thought I'd see if you could talk about the bridesmaids' dresses."

My heart slowly returned to its normal rhythm as the fear that something had happened to my parents drained away. "You're in luck because you can talk to two of your bridesmaids since Summer's here. Come in!"

They sat down together on the couch and began talking about something regarding the wedding as I grabbed myself a drink of water. I offered them some, but neither wanted any. They seemed more focused on whatever they were quietly discussing.

"So what's new on the bridesmaids' dresses? I like the black silk ones you picked out. I thought they were a done deal."

Tressa smiled. "I think they are, but I wanted to ask you two about what you thought."

My sister wanting our opinions on the dresses seemed odd. She didn't generally need or want other people's opinions on her decisions, even when they involved making other people do things.

Looking over toward Summer, I said, "I like them. Summer, you like them too, right?"

"I do. I think they're going to look gorgeous," she said.

Tressa clapped her hands together, clearly pleased. "Great! So what's new with you two? I never see you much anymore with all the wedding planning and work."

Summer quickly ticked off what she and Ethan had been up to lately, and then they turned their heads to look at me. Something felt off.

"You know me, Tress. Same old, same old."

My sister and Summer shifted uncomfortably on the couch, and in the silence I knew Summer had called Tressa and told her what I shared with her at lunch. How could she have betrayed me like that?

"You're not here to talk about bridesmaids' dresses, are you?" I asked in a quiet voice, devastated at how they looked at me with such pity, like I was some poor thing that needed their help.

When they didn't answer my question, I looked over at Summer and through tear-filled eyes, I asked, "Why would you do this? You promised me you wouldn't tell anyone. You knew I meant Ethan and everyone else. I trusted you."

Before she could say a word, Tressa stood up and defended her. "She was worried, but I'm more intrigued. I thought you left your crush for Cole Knight back in high school when you and he used to have your secret meetings in the woods. I thought you outgrew him."

My sadness at Summer's betrayal was pushed aside by my surprise that my sister knew all this time and never said a word. "I thought nobody knew. Why didn't you talk to me about it?"

"I knew if you wanted to tell me, you would."

"But that doesn't apply to my life now, evidently. How did you know?"

She smiled in that confident way that told me she knew everything about what Cole and I did back then. "I saw him sneaking around the yard one night, and then you suddenly needed to get some fresh air. I followed the two of you, and let's just say I nearly fell over when I saw him kiss you."

"He was sweet to me, Tressa. He never pushed me to do anything I didn't want to do."

"Well, then you were the only girl in high school he didn't get into bed, except me."

Why was my sister bringing up what Cole did ten years ago? Why did that matter now?

"I don't care what he was in high school. That's a long time ago. We've all changed."

My defense of Cole left my sister shaking her head with that sad look she got whenever she thought I was wrong but didn't want to come right out and tell me. Like I was some clueless idiot who couldn't understand life.

"Honey, do you know anything about him now?"

I snapped, "Obviously, I know something about him. I was with him in this room, and that room, and everywhere else here for nearly an entire day."

Summer quickly stood up and chimed in. "He seems to have popped up out of nowhere, hasn't he?"

Now the two of them were ganging up on me about Cole?

Hurt by her insinuation, I looked at Summer and said, "He's Ethan's best friend. If he wasn't a good person, wouldn't he know?"

They looked at each other and then back at me, neither convinced by my argument.

"We all love Ethan, but it's one thing for a man to like a friend and a completely different thing to say that means he's a good man," Tressa said in her usual commanding tone.

"Why are you acting like this? He makes me happy. I've been alone for years, and now I'm enjoying myself. So I had sex with a man. I'm allowed to do that, aren't I, or am I supposed to live like a nun?"

My sister's mouth dropped open in shock. "You slept with him already?"

I shifted my glare from Tressa to Summer and snapped, "I would have thought you'd have told her that little nugget of information since you obviously told her everything else when you betrayed me by running to the ladies' room to call her. Judas took longer than you!"

Summer frowned and lowered her head. "I'm sorry. I was worried. I never meant to betray you."

I'd had enough of both of their interrogating me about my personal life. "I'm allowed to have sex with anyone I damn want! Who are either of you to say anything about that?"

My sister took a step toward me and stopped. "We care about you. We don't want to see you hurt."

Her attempt to show they cared about me only served to make me angrier about this whole thing. "Can you imagine if anyone tried to pull this on you when you began dating Killian?" I turned my focus to Summer and continued, "Or when you started seeing my brother?"

Neither one of them had an answer for my questions. "I deserve happiness as much as you two do. If Cole makes me happy, why can't you let me have that? All these years everyone has been telling me they just wanted to see me happy again. Now that I am, the first chance you get you come here acting like I've done something wrong."

When I finished, I couldn't stop the tears from coming. I sat down at my makeshift dinner table in my sad little hotel room and covered my eyes, not wanting them to see how devastated their reaction to my newfound happiness made me.

Behind me, Tressa asked in a low voice, "What did he tell you about that club of his, Diana?"

I sniffled and dried my eyes before looking up to face her. "He told me the name, I guess. I can't remember it right now. Why?"

Before she ever spoke a word to answer, I knew she had found out something horrible. The pity was written all over her face. He'd lied or he'd exaggerated, and now I looked like a naïve fool to ever believe him.

"He lost the club months ago. He's broke. Next to go is his apartment. Did he tell you that?"

I couldn't believe what I was hearing. Why did he tell me about his club if he didn't have it anymore? Why say anything about it? I didn't care about how much money he made. I had my own money. Why would he lie like that?

"I'm telling you these things because you're a wealthy woman, Diana. I thought we'd need to have this conversation at some point when you started dating, and maybe I'm to blame for not bringing it up sooner. I told the rest of the family that I'd handle this, and I'm sorry. I should have talked to you about this before."

"Talked to me about what? Do you think I'm so pathetic that I had to pay him to have sex with me? Is that what you think?" I asked in horror at what she was insinuating.

Tressa gave me a gentle smile and shook her head. "No, not at all. He's lucky you cared enough about him to sleep with him. But you and I have a situation that other women don't. We have money—a lot of money—and that means we have to be vigilant when it comes to men."

"He doesn't want my money. That never came up in our conversation. In fact, he never mentioned it at all," I said as I tried to remember every word of my conversations with Cole in the past week.

Money had never really come up between us, had it? I didn't recall, but at that moment with Tressa and Summer looking at me with such pity in their eyes, everything seemed hazy in my mind.

"I thought he cared about me. He said things that made me believe he understood. He made all that effort because of money?" I wondered aloud, unable to stop myself from crying again.

My sister and Summer tried to make me feel better, but it didn't matter. I'd been so happy these past few days, and now that was gone. Had it all been a lie because he needed money?

Didn't any of it mean anything to him like it had to me?

CHAPTER FIFTEEN

COLE

FOR TWENTY MINUTES, I'D TRIED to figure out a way to tell Ethan about Diana and me. Every time I thought I had the perfect way to interject it into the conversation, I either couldn't find the right words or he changed the topic and I lost my opportunity. So while he continued to laugh it up and have a good old time, I had to pretend everything was fine while inside I twisted and turned about how to bring up that I'd slept with his sister, but it was okay because I was crazy about her.

This wasn't going to turn out good.

"So have you heard from Rachel? I thought I saw her the other night near here. Any chance she's sniffing around for another chance with you?" he asked and then laughed.

"No, thanks. I had enough of that. I'm sure she's found another guy to be with," I said with as much macho bullshit attitude as I could force to the surface.

"You really do know how to pick them, man."

His phone rang, saving me from having to talk shit about my ex-girlfriend right before I told him about my newest girlfriend. Fuck. This was a nightmare.

Looking down at his phone, he said, "I have to take this. It's Summer. Give me a minute, okay?"

"Sure." That might give me time to figure out how to word what I needed to say.

I chugged down the last of my fourth beer in search of some

wisdom from being drunk, but none came, as I knew none would. Ethan looked like he was going to be a few minutes, so I headed to the bathroom to handle nature and figure out what the fuck I was going to do. This couldn't go on all night, for Christ's sake. I'd end up drunk off my ass, and then I'd never say the right words.

I washed my hands and stared at my face in the mirror. I was the picture of a coward. Fuck. I was crazy about Diana. Why the hell should this be a problem? We were both consenting adults. High school was a long time in the past. I'd grown up a lot since then. I was his best friend, for fuck's sake. Why wouldn't he want me with his favorite sister? Maybe we'd get married and then I could be his brother-in-law. How cool would that be? Best friends turned family. It sounded good to me.

Okay. You have to tell him before you get all fucked up and start talking nonsense. You can do this. Just remember he's got a right hook that will knock you on your ass if you don't watch out for it.

That's not how this would go, though. Not this time.

As I entered the kitchen, I didn't see Ethan. Time for another beer. I turned the corner to grab a cold one out of the refrigerator and out of nowhere, he hit me like a ton of fucking bricks, slamming into the right side of my head. I couldn't be sure, but I saw something like white flashes as I fell backward onto the floor. There was some kind of noise, which may have been him saying something, but all I could hear clearly was the ringing in my ear. Getting hit in the jaw had that effect.

Instantly, pain radiated up through my cheekbone and eye socket, and my head felt like it might explode. Fuck, that hurt!

Disoriented, I tried to focus my eyes, but the right one was all blurry and the left one didn't seem to remember the only goddamned job it had in my head. Closing them, I tried to get my bearings, but my body was having none of that.

"Holy fuck! Out of all the women in this city, in the fucking world, you just had to bother with Diana. Get the fuck up so I can beat the ever loving fuck out of you!" Ethan bellowed above me.

I opened my eyes and saw pure rage coming off him aimed entirely in my direction. He yanked me up by my collar and even though my eyesight was still blurry, I saw the second hit coming before he landed his fist into my left eye.

Staggering as I tried to keep my balance, I hit a chair and pushed it back until it and I hit the wall. Now neither side of my head was able to work right.

"How could you do that to her? Fucking fight back, you motherfucker! Fight back so I can beat—" he barked until his words just ended in a scream of rage.

I couldn't hit him back, though. I deserved anything he did to me. I knew how he felt about me being with Diana, and still I'd gone ahead and tracked her down. He was right. Ethan was my best friend, and after all he'd told me just a few days ago about what she'd gone through, I'd still slept with her.

"And you lost your fucking club?" he yelled as I struggled to get to my feet. "What the fuck is wrong with you?"

I had no defense. No excuse. I'd been a shitty friend, and whatever he said or did, I had it coming.

"Do you realize how much my sister's been through, you asshole? I do because I'm the one who did it to her, so trust me, I fucking know! All those surgeries and then the PTSD that made her afraid to even leave that fucking hotel room. And you think you should just go in and fuck her like you do with all those women you sleep with? This is my sister, you dick!"

My eyesight cleared up enough for me to see Ethan's expression clearly. I'd never seen rage in anyone like that before. Rage and worry. Not for me but for Diana.

I needed him to know I cared about her. Even if I couldn't get him to listen to anything else, I had to get him to hear that.

"Ethan, I know you're pissed, but I need you to hear me out. It isn't like I just met her and took advantage of anything. I don't know if you know about us dating in high school, but we know each other. We were close then."

I barely finished speaking before he hit me again. As his fist pounded into my jaw, he snapped, "Back in high school? What the fuck are you talking about?"

"We dated. We didn't sleep together, but we hung out for a few months right before graduation."

Now all I saw in his face was hurt. Pure, unfiltered hurt that his best friend had lied to him for ten years.

"What? How is that possible? You and I were together every day around that time. You lived in our fucking house for weeks."

My thoughts got jumbled, so I couldn't remember exactly when it all happened. I wanted to explain things better, but after getting three shots to the head, I could barely get the words out.

The metallic taste of blood hit my tongue, and I rubbed my jaw to ease the pain spiking up into my face. "I'm sorry. I didn't want you to find out this way. But it wasn't some meaningless bullshit. I swear. I care about her. I did back in high school, and I do now."

"She thought you were some big time club owner. You lied to her to get her into bed. That's what you fucking did! Why? Because she was an easy mark? Because you could sweet talk her? What kind of man does that to someone who's gone through everything she's dealt with in the past eight years? It's like I don't even know you anymore, Cole."

I wanted to somehow explain that I lied because I wanted her to think I was successful. I wanted to impress her.

But there was no way he'd ever believe me. Why would he? Ethan had seen me seduce woman after woman all these years. He'd never buy that I cared about Diana. My past showed him time and again I didn't care about any woman as much as I should to be with his sister.

I hung my head and said the only words I thought might help. "I'm sorry. It wasn't what you think. I swear."

He stood in front of me shaking his head and said, "You know what I think? I think you can go fuck yourself, Cole. And stay the fuck away from my sister!"

There was nothing I could say to that. I looked up to see him give me one last look of disgust before he turned and walked out.

I'd fucked everything up, and even worse, Diana now knew the truth about the club. And she knew I lied to her. She probably thought the same thing Ethan thought—that I'd lied to get her into bed.

But that's not why I didn't tell her about losing the club. I had to make her understand that.

FOR THE SECOND TIME, DIANA'S away message played and I sat staring at the screen wishing I could be there beside her to tell her everything in my heart. "I'm not able to take your call, but leave me a message. I promise I'll get back to you as soon as I can."

She smiled when she finished speaking, one of her sweet smiles that went all the way up to her eyes and made the blue in them sparkle. The same kind of smile she gave me over and over that day we spent together.

I looked like shit, but it didn't matter. I couldn't just leave some sterile voice message. I needed her to see as well as hear me.

"Diana, please answer the phone. I need to talk to you. Call me."

Ten minutes later, I called again. And then twenty minutes after that. And ten minutes after that. Each time I tried to convince her to speak to me, to hear what I had to say.

But it was no use. She wasn't out. She was avoiding me.

I knew that and still I left three more messages before an hour had passed and I couldn't do it anymore. I had to see her. I had to at least try to get her to hear my side of the story.

Not that it would sound any better than what she already knew. By now, Ethan had gotten to her and told her all the horrible things about me that only he knew. As I thought about the man I'd been, I couldn't disagree with what he'd done to me. If I had a sister

I loved and wanted to protect, I'd fucking beat the hell out of any guy like me who got within ten feet of her.

But I wasn't that man with Diana. I wasn't that man whore I'd been in high school with her, and I wasn't that guy who went through women without a care with her now. He might not see that, but I had to make her see that.

I drove like a madman from my apartment to the Richmont hotel, barely paying attention to the world around me as I focused on my only goal—to get to Diana. My left eye had swollen shut, and the pain on the right side of my head extended from my jaw up to my temple and throbbed twice as fast as my heart, but I didn't care. I knew there was every possibility that before I could hand the valet my keys that Ethan or Tristan would be there to go for round two with me and I might never get to see her.

It didn't matter. I had to try.

Every muscle in my body tensed up as I pulled up to the front of the Richmont. I swiveled my head right and then left to see if either man lay in wait for me, but I only saw the young guy who was working as valet for the night. I quickly got out of the car and handed him my keys before I headed into the lobby, my body on high alert for another attack that would almost certain come inside.

With every step I took over the white marble floor of Tristan Stone's hotel lobby, I knew more likely than not someone had called security to stop me. I looked like someone had used my head as a punching bag, and more than one guest recoiled in horror as I passed them.

None of that mattered. I had to try to get Diana to hear me out.

I didn't understand how I made it to her room, but staring at that dark wood door, I took a breath and prepared for what awaited me on the other side. She wouldn't be alone. Someone would be there with her and intent on sending me away. I raised my hand to knock and sighed as my knuckles hit the first time.

No matter what they said, I had to at least try to talk to her.

I knocked a second time and waited. Nothing. No sound.

"Diana, please open the door. I need to talk to you. Please, just give me a few minutes to explain. Please."

I waited for a response. Any response. Her telling me to go away. Her telling me she never wanted to see me again. The mere thought of her saying that made my chest ache.

But I got nothing. So I tried again.

"Diana, please. I want to explain. Just give me a chance to tell you the truth. I promise I'll go away if you say you don't want to see me after I tell you everything. Just give me a chance."

My head pounded as I stood there waiting for her to answer. Then things began to get blurry. I didn't care. I had to talk to her. I had to tell her the truth.

The door opened a crack, making my heart race, and I saw her blue eyes full of sadness staring out at me. Slowly, she opened it more, and inch by inch revealed her beautiful face now all blotchy and red from crying.

Because of me.

"Diana, please listen to me. I need to talk to you. Please, will you let me in so we can talk?"

Suddenly, she opened the door all the way and took a step out into the hallway toward me. Lifting her hand to my face, she touched where Ethan had hit me.

"You're hurt. Who did this to you?"

I didn't answer. Either she knew and I didn't have to, or she didn't and I had no right telling her how her brother justifiably beat the hell out of me.

She ran her fingertips over my swollen eye, making me flinch, so I quickly set to pleading my case. "Can I come in? I just want to talk. Just let me set the record straight."

Her touch lingered on my skin as she asked, "Is it true what my sister told me? That you lost your club?"

I lowered my head. "Yes. I lost it a couple months ago."

Diana didn't say anything but took my hand in hers and gently pulled me into her room. I lifted my gaze to see who was there with her, but I saw no one.

"Where is everyone?" I asked, surprised I'd get the chance to talk to her alone.

"They left. I sent them home. I wanted to be alone," she said defiantly.

"Just give me a chance to explain, Diana, and then if you want me to leave too, I will."

Lifting her chin, she struggled to hold back her tears. "I can't believe you lied to me. Did you do that so I'd sleep with you? Because I'm not some desperate thing, Cole. I might have slept with you even though you lost your club. Did you ever think of that?"

I reached for her hand and held it tightly so she couldn't slip away from me. Looking into her watery blue eyes, I said, "I didn't lie just to get you into bed. I know everyone's telling you that, but I didn't. I swear."

"Then why?" she asked, her voice sobbing under the words.

Lowering my head, I admitted the truth. "I wanted you to be impressed by me. I wanted you to think I was successful, because if I was, then I'd be worthy of you. Just like in high school. I wanted you to think I was someone you should be with because I'd done something special."

Tears rolled down her cheeks as she stared at me. "I was crazy about you back then. All you had to do was talk to me and I hung on every word. I told you that I used to make excuses to get the chance to watch you play football instead of going home or to my friends' houses."

Wiping away her tears, she shook her head and pulled her hand from my hold. "You had that entire day we spent together to tell me the truth. You knew I was just as crazy about you now as I was back in school. I showed you with everything I did and everything I said that I never told another soul in this world."

"I wanted to, but it never felt right. Christ, Diana, maybe I didn't want to ruin that day. Maybe something in me subconsciously was afraid if I told you that I didn't have the club and I was losing my place that you'd be disgusted by me. I don't know. All I know is I wanted you to think of me as someone you could be proud of."

Her eyes opened wide, and a look of horror came over her. "What happened to you, Cole? Your business and your home? My family thinks you only came looking for me because you have nothing. How can I ever believe that's not true?"

I scrambled to find the words to convince her that I didn't give a damn about the Stone money. "Have your lawyers draw up whatever document you want that says I don't get a thing. I'll sign it. What I felt for you was never about your family's money. Fuck, Diana! Look what money did to my family. My mother left my father, probably for some richer guy, and my father went to jail for stealing other people's money. Now I'm practically broke and have to start over at twenty-eight. I've spent my entire adult life throwing money around to impress everyone, and what's it got me? I had nothing worth anything real until I found you again. I don't want your money or your family's money. I just want you."

Diana burst into tears and sobbed. Shaking her head, she said over and over, "How can I believe you? How can I when everyone says you're always lying?"

My heart broke that I'd done this to her. I was the one who hurt her, and I was the reason she was crying. I couldn't put her through any more of this.

"I'm sorry, Diana. I know we can't be together now, but I love you and I never meant to do this. I hope someday you can forgive me."

"You love me?" she asked, her beautiful eyes wide with surprise.

I nodded. I loved her. I probably always had and just wasn't mature enough to realize it.

"I love you, Diana. No one else in the world has ever made me feel like you do, like you always have."

She dried her eyes and took a deep breath. "Take me away from here. I can't be here anymore. Will you leave with me?"

"How? You're afraid of cars."

"I'm more afraid of staying in this room and never living like a normal person, Cole. Take me away from here. Please."

As much as I knew what lay ahead of us would be wrath of her family and every accusation they'd make against me, I couldn't say no.

I loved her.

Chapter Sixteen

Diana

Two hours in Cole's car left me exhausted and shaky, but I quietly celebrated my first attempt at conquering that fear while he parked the car in front of his grandmother's cabin. All the way there, he'd held my hand and kept me grounded when I thought I would jump out of my skin. When I rocked back and forth and told him I couldn't stay in the car anymore, he pulled over to the side of the highway and talked me down from my craziness. When I thought I could do it, he got back on the road until I couldn't stand sitting there in that seat for another second and he pulled over again. Over and over for all those miles between Manhattan and that tiny town in the Poconos, he dealt with my fear with nothing but kind words and support.

I looked over at him as he turned the car off and wondered if he regretted saying yes when I asked him to take me away. What man wanted to deal with the kind of emotional baggage I brought with me?

"You okay?" he asked, leaning over to kiss me on the cheek. "Remember what I said about not expecting too much of this place. It's no Richmont hotel."

"That's exactly why I love it already."

"Think cobwebs instead of silk sheets," he said before lifting my hand to his lips to gently kiss it.

"I've never liked silk sheets. I'm more of a regular sheet kind of girl." I cradled his bruised and swollen face and looked into his dark eyes. "Don't worry, Cole. I just need to get out of this car and into the fresh air."

"Oh, God. I'm sorry. Hang on. I'll be right there."

He hurried around the car and opened my door. I stood up on shaky legs and took a deep breath of air that smelled like pine trees and leaves. Closing my eyes, I held Cole's hand and tried to let go of all the anxiety that had churned up inside me.

"Are you okay?" Cole asked in a voice full of worry.

I felt better than okay. Opening my eyes, I nodded and looked up at him. "I love it here already. I love the smell of nature every time I breathe in. I love the sound of the birds up there in the trees. It reminds me of the woods from all those years ago."

Cole smiled and shook his head. "I never paid much attention to all of that. I just remember how damp it always seemed when we met."

"Close your eyes sometime and let yourself enjoy everything here. It's so relaxing, and I need that."

He shut the car door behind me and wove his arm through mine. "I'll have to try that. For now, I want to get you inside. That drive here was pretty rough."

Just as I'd suspected. Seeing my anxiety up close and personal had bothered him. God, why did I have to be such a mess?

I clung to his arm as we walked up the three wood stairs to the front porch of the cabin. Big enough for two yellow Adirondack chairs and a small table between them, it looked out on the road that led to the cabin and woods full of pine trees for as far as the eye could see.

Cole opened the screen door that squealed like it hadn't been used in ages and then turned his key in the front door. It opened up into a large living room designed sometime in the 1960s. A pale green, boxy sofa that looked as uncomfortable as it was ugly sat in the middle of the room flanked by two uglier end tables barely big enough to hold a glass and a book. The furniture reminded me of some of the dreadful designs for the European Richmont hotel redo

Tressa had showed me.

I stopped to take it all in, and Cole said quietly, "I told you not to expect too much. I think my grandmother bought the furniture in here sometime before she first saw the Beatles in concert at Shea Stadium a million years ago."

"It's lovely," I said as sweetly as I could so he didn't know how unwelcome the place looked.

Not that it mattered what the aesthetics of the cabin were. This place meant far more for what it represented. Freedom.

Freedom from the person I was back in that hotel room I'd lived in for far too long.

Freedom from my fears, or at least the chance for me to work on overcoming them.

Freedom to do what I wanted with my life.

"You're a terrible liar, Diana. If you don't like it, we can find some place to spend the night while we figure out what we want to do," Cole said with a smile.

"No, it's wonderful. I'd like to lay down for a little bit, and then when I get up, I need to call my family."

Neither of us had mentioned anything about that on the long drive there. Ethan was like a ghost travelling with us who popped up every time I lifted my head and looked over at Cole's bruised and battered face. The rest of my family were never too far away in my mind as I heard their claims about Cole repeat in my head mile after mile.

None of it changed my mind about going away with him, though. I knew he wasn't perfect. Neither was I. If he could deal with my issues, I could deal with his. As for my family, I hadn't decided what to do yet.

Cole led me to the bedroom, which looked like it had furniture from the 1860s instead of the 1960s, and put my bag down over near the dresser. I'd expected cobwebs and dust, but the cabin was clean, even if it looked like it had been transported through time.

Pointing at the white coverlet draped across the white sheets on the bed, he said, "I can find you a different blanket, if you want. I think I remember that being on my grandmother's bed when I was a kid."

He sounded embarrassed, so I smiled and kissed him on the cheek in the hope of showing him everything was just fine. "I don't need anything fancy. I just want to get my bearings before I call my family."

"Do you want me to leave you alone?" he asked with worry in his eyes that I couldn't place. Was he worried what I thought of the décor of the cabin or about me?

"I'd like the company, if that's okay. That ride was a lot for me, believe it or not. It's the first time since the accident that I've been in a car."

His face lit up from a smile that made him look so handsome, even with his face all busted up. "Okay. Let me lock the door so wolves and other woodland things don't just wander in, and I'll be right back."

While he handled that, I sat down on the softest mattress in the world, nearly falling into the middle of the bed. As I wriggled my body to a sitting position, I laughed out loud harder than I had in so long. Tonight, I'd sleep with Cole on this terrible mattress and I'd love it. It sounded ridiculous, but I didn't care because I was free to choose what I wanted to do, including sleeping on this bed.

Cole stopped in the doorway and kicked off his shoes. "Everything okay?"

"Yeah. It's good. A little soft, so be careful or it might suck you in and never let you out again," I said as I patted the bed next to me.

He sat down far too hard, and the bed nearly tossed him right off the side, but I caught him by the hand and pulled him back before he landed on the floor. "See? This is one crazy mattress. Perfect for me, I guess."

Taking me into his arms, he wrapped them around me and pressed his lips to my ear. "You aren't crazy," he whispered. "You're perfect."

I covered his hands with mine and closed my eyes, loving the feeling of security his arms around me offered. "Perfectly flawed," I whispered back.

"Perfect."

And at that moment, I didn't feel messed up or crazy or anything but safe and happy. Blissfully happy.

COLE SQUEEZED MY HAND, BUT I saw in his eyes real worry. "Are you sure you don't want me here with you for this?"

I shook my head and smiled at how much he wanted to protect me. But this was my family. I didn't need protection from them. They loved me like I loved them. They just needed to see that I wasn't that scared little thing who hid herself away from the world anymore.

"Thank you, but I need to do this on my own."

"Okay. I'll be right in the bedroom. If you need anything, just call my name."

"Everything will be okay, Cole. They just want the best for me. I need to show I know what that is."

He smiled, but concern made it hard for him. I knew what he feared, but he didn't have to worry.

I took a deep breath and inserted the key for my phone into the screen to call each of my family members. One by one, they appeared in boxes on the screen in front of me. Ethan and Summer, Tressa and Killian, and my father. Each one knew it was me calling and quickly answered, their expressions all full of the same concern they always had for me.

"Daddy, where's Mommy?" I asked before I got started on what I had to say.

"She's driving into the city from the house, honey. I don't expect her for nearly an hour yet," he said quietly, always so calm for me.

"Okay. Then I'll have to say this without her. I know you can easily find me just by tracking my phone key, but I don't want you to do that."

Before I could say another word, they all started talking at once. Summer asked if I was okay, and Tressa wanted to know what happened. Ethan said something that sounded like a veiled threat to Cole, and my father began asking what happened to make me leave the hotel so hastily.

Nobody would listen to me at that rate, so I aimed the remote at the TV and put everyone on mute, except for my father. "I'm not going to listen to you all bark questions and comments at me, so you're all on mute. You can hear me, but I can't hear you."

My father sat silently behind his desk in his office at work, stoically waiting for me to say what was on my mind. After I took another deep breath, I began to speak.

"Daddy, I had to leave. I hope you understand."

He nodded, but those deep brown eyes I'd always found security in looked so sad. "I just want to know you're safe, honey."

I'd wanted to be so strong, but now that I faced him, I couldn't stop the tears as they rolled down my cheeks. "I always wanted you to be proud of me, Daddy. I never wanted to be the person I was— so scared of everything that I closed myself off from the world. I got into a car today and didn't fall to pieces. You would have been so proud of me, Daddy."

"Oh, honey. There's never been a day in your life that I wasn't proud of you, sweetheart. If I ever made you think I wasn't, I'm so sorry."

"I just need you to understand why I left. I love you all, but I have to live my own life."

My father sighed, like he carried the weight of the world on his shoulders. "We all want you to be happy, Diana. That's all we've ever wanted."

"Cole isn't making me do anything I don't want to do. If you're angry at anyone, it should be me, not him. I asked him to take me away. He's only doing what I asked him to do."

"No one is angry. We're just worried because we love you, honey. Every one of us."

I hated that I'd done this to them, but especially to my father. "I know, but I need to do this. Please understand. I want to be happy. Cole makes me happy. When I'm with him, I feel normal. I want to be normal again, Daddy."

Scanning the screen, I saw Tressa and Summer crying with me. Ethan, like my father, remained stoic, but I knew my words affected the two of them by the way they winced to hold back the emotion. More than anyone else, they had felt the pain of what I'd gone through all these years. As much as I deserved happiness, I wanted that for them too. I didn't want them to forever see me as someone they always needed to protect because I was such a mess.

"All I ever wanted was for you to be happy," my father said with a gentle smile. "That's all a father could ever hope for his child."

And with that, I knew everything would be okay. As much as it might have terrified him, he wasn't going to come take me back to my old life. Wiping the tears from my cheeks, I smiled back at him. "I love you, Daddy. Thank you for trusting me."

"I've always believed in you, Diana. We all do. Please remember that, and when you're ready, we all want you back in our lives."

For the first time in my life, I signed the words I hoped would make him feel better. *Don't worry. I'm okay.*

My father nodded once more and signed back what he always said to me, the words that had forever given me the strength to go on. *I love you. Always remember that.*

"Tell Mommy I'll call her later, okay?"

"I will, honey."

I turned back to focus on everyone else and said, "I hope you can accept what I'm doing. I love you all very much, but I have to live my life like I want."

Summer and Tressa smiled, and Killian nodded like he

understood. The look in my brother's eyes told me he still worried about me, so I said, "I love you, Ethan. You don't have to be scared for me anymore. I promise. Cole cares for me. Don't worry. I'm okay."

He didn't say anything, but I saw him mouth the words I love you too. Then one by one, each screen disappeared until my father was the only one left. He looked as big as life now staring back at me, but I didn't see worry filling his eyes. Now he looked at me like he always had with Tressa.

With pride.

"Let me know if you need anything. I'll tell your mother you're safe and happy and that you send your love."

"Thank you, Daddy."

The screen turned to black, and I took a deep breath full of old cabin air and let it out in a rush. That call wouldn't have been important to most people, but I had never felt like anything but a helpless child for the past eight years.

Not until now. I knew my family would still worry about me, but I had taken the first step to being a normal person again.

Behind me, Cole walked into the room and said, "It sounded like you did great, but then I got this message from your father."

He handed me his phone and I read the message, my father's deep voice echoing in my head. I'm trusting you to take care of my daughter. If you do anything to hurt her, I'll make your life a living hell. Please don't test me on this, for Diana's sake.

I smiled. That was my father, through and through, and I loved him for it. Handing Cole his phone, I said, "Don't worry. That's just my father giving you a chance."

For a moment, he didn't look convinced, but then he gave me a half-hearted smile. "I guess I better not screw up."

"You won't. I believe in you."

Cole wrapped his arms around me and hugged me to his body. Strong and protective, he made me feel safe. And then he said the words that made me sure I'd been right about him.

"I believe in you too. You and all your perfect flaws."

CHAPTER SEVENTEEN

COLE

DIANA CURLED UP AGAINST MY side as I tried to follow the movie we'd picked out nearly an hour ago. Part western and part mobster movie, it didn't make much sense to me. Every time I looked down to see if she was enjoying it, I saw her intently focused on the screen, though, so maybe I just wasn't bright enough to figure it out.

"Some movie," I mumbled.

I squeezed her close to me, hoping she'd look up and start talking. Her father's not-so-veiled threat continued to rattle around my brain as it had ever since I first read it. Maybe that was why I couldn't concentrate on the western mobster flick playing on the TV.

Diana stretched her legs and turned her head to face me. "I'm not sure what's going on with these people. Are they cowboys or gangsters?"

I threw my head back and laughed in relief. "Thank God you said that. I thought I was just too stupid to understand just what the hell they're talking about."

Frowning, she shook her head. "Why do you say things like that?"

"Like what?"

"That you're too stupid. I don't think you're stupid."

She'd always been so quick to catch things like that when we were together before. I forgot about that. I turned away, unable to look into her blue eyes staring so intently as she waited for my answer to her question.

"I don't know. It's just how I am. Being smart was never who I was."

Diana straightened up so she sat next to me. "You must have been smart. You ran a business. That takes brains," she said softly.

I looked at her and smiled. She had no idea how wrong she was. Oh, it did take brains to run a business well. The well part was what distinguished good businessmen like her father from people like me who ended up losing their businesses.

"The fact that I lost the club is proof that I wasn't very smart or even very good at running it, I'd say."

And then came the moment I'd dreaded since realizing I had to tell Diana the truth about everything.

"What happened? Why did you lose your club?" she asked in that innocent tone that told me for damned sure she wasn't ready for the answer.

But that was the problem. Diana wasn't ready for any of what I came with. My history. My business problems. None of it. She was sweet and innocent. What did she know about the shady dealings of a New York club owner?

"You don't want to know. Trust me, Diana," I said, needing to keep her separate from that world.

She grabbed hold of my hand and brought it to her lips. Looking up at me with those blue eyes so full of sweetness and understanding, she kissed my knuckles and whispered, "I do want to know. I want to know everything about you. All I know is the boy I was crazy about and the man I've fallen for who makes me think I can be normal again. I want to know the rest, though."

Somewhere deep inside, she knew she didn't want to know it all. The way her voice faltered every so often told me she wasn't sure, but she couldn't deny her curiosity. I needed her to, though, or she'd learn how unworthy I was of her.

"That wasn't my finest moment," I said, scrambling to find

euphemisms that would give her just enough so she wouldn't ask for more details. "Let's just say when you lay down with dogs, it's not surprising when you get up you're covered with fleas and other people think you're a dog too."

Diana stared at me for a moment and then made a silly face. "That's not the way that goes," she said with a chuckle.

"Well, you get the gist of it. It wasn't anything I'd ever want touching you in any way."

Leaning back away from me, she twisted her face into a grimace. "You're starting to sound like everyone else in my family. I'm willing to admit that I spent a lot of time away from the world, but I'm not some naïve fool. I know how things work, Cole. You don't have to shelter me from anything."

I pulled her back to me and kissed her, loving how she made me want to be a better man. "What if I want to, though? What then?"

Cradling my face, she gently caressed the area around my black eye. "I just spent years being protected. I don't want that anymore. I'm not that fragile that I can't handle the truth of your life."

She had no idea how wrong she was. Or maybe she could handle it. She had a strength I wasn't sure I possessed. But I didn't want her to handle the mess of my life.

"I don't want you to worry about any of that. It's all behind me."

"Then what's in front of you?"

I smiled, loving how cute she could be. "You."

"What else? What are you going to do now that you don't have the club?"

Inside, a part of me died at that very moment as I knew exactly what my future held. God, the answer I had to give her was so fucking mundane. She sat there looking like something out of a dream, and what was she going to hear? Everyday, common bullshit from a guy who wanted so much more but never quite got there.

"I have prospects, things on the horizon. I haven't decided yet which way I want to go," I answered, swallowing half the words and wanting to choke on them.

"Like what? Tell me," she said sweetly, punctuating her command by placing a kiss on the back of my hand.

There were no prospects or things on the horizon. There was the offer from my brother Chase to work at one of his furniture stores near where we grew up. He needed a manager, and since I'd run a club, he didn't think I'd have any difficulties sliding into the job of running one of his stores. Those were his exact words when he took pity on me three weeks ago and offered me the job. I was scheduled to start in a few days.

Manager of a furniture store. I should have let those loan sharks kill me when they threatened to. Death had to be better than admitting to Diana Stone that the man she sat staring up at with stars in her eyes for was nothing more than a common guy who was about to become far more fucking common.

"I'm considering going into business with my brother on a venture he's got going," I said, every word other than brother a complete lie.

Christ, I didn't want to lie to her. What choice did I have, though? She was Diana, Tristan and Nina Stone's daughter. Beautiful, smart, and talented like her parents, she could do anything, if only she could conquer her fears.

And once she did, how likely was it that she'd want to spend any time with someone like me? When I had the club, the great car, and the incredible Upper East Side apartment, I was someone. Now I was about to become a manager of a furniture store near our hometown.

Fuck. I didn't even want to be with me, so why would she?

"Well, whatever you do, I'm sure you'll be great at it," Diana said with a smile. "What do you say to turning off this weird movie?"

"Yeah. Sure. We can find something else."

She shut off the movie and climbed on top of me. "I was

thinking of doing something else entirely," she said before she kissed me.

I wanted to be with her. God, I'd be a complete fool if I didn't. But what good was sleeping with her when I didn't see how we could have a future together?

Diana sensed my hesitation and frowned. "You don't want to?" Gently touching my still-swollen face, she shook her head. "You're in pain, aren't you? That's why you don't feel like doing anything."

Sliding my hands down her back, I cupped her beautiful ass in my palms. "Of course I do," I said with a smile I hoped she didn't see was forced. "Are you sure you want to do anything with me looking like this? It can't be very sexy."

"I think you're sexy, even like this. I just figure since it's only you and me here in this cabin with no one around for miles, except for the wild animals, that it seems like a perfect time to enjoy ourselves."

"I didn't know if you wanted to after the ride here."

She tilted her head and studied me for a long moment. "Is there something wrong? Did I do something that makes you not want to do this?"

Fuck. Now she thought I didn't want her when I was the problem, not her. I was screwing this all up.

"No. That's not it at all. You didn't do anything. I just didn't want to push you if you weren't feeling up to it," I explained and prayed to God she believed me.

Diana didn't deserve to feel like shit again because of me.

A tiny smile lit up her face, and she leaned forward to kiss me. God, she felt so good in my arms. Why couldn't this be right? I'd never felt this way with anyone else, so why couldn't it?

She kissed her way over to my ear and gently sunk her teeth into my earlobe before slowly dragging her tongue down my neck. My cock didn't suffer from a conscience and immediately sprung to life. If only my brain could be as single-minded as other parts of my body.

Leaning back on the tops of my legs, Diana slid her hands down over my chest and abs until she stopped at my pants. With a grin that was equal parts wicked and innocent, she said, "I bet this would feel a whole lot better if you weren't wearing these."

I nodded and hoped I could shut my brain off long enough to let my cock do all the thinking. She unbuttoned my pants and stood up to tug them down my legs as I slid my shirt over my head.

After she tossed my pants off to the side, she stripped out of her clothes and sat back down on my lap, her naked and beautiful body there for the taking. My brain fought the idea of fucking her, telling me I wasn't good enough for the likes of Diana, but the rest of me wanted her more. When she slid her wet pussy down my shaft, every thought except how much I needed to be inside her disappeared from my brain.

I lifted her off me and slid into her body until nothing separated the two of us. She moaned softly against my lips as I struggled to catch my breath. She felt so fucking good on my cock.

Rolling her hips, she rode me while I held her hips, pressing my fingers into her flesh to keep her from making me come too soon. I barely held on as I watched her so free and innocent fucking me better than I'd ever experienced before.

"You look so fucking incredible like this," I bit out as she took every inch of my cock inside her.

"I saw it in a movie and couldn't wait to try it with you."

I slid my hands up from her hips to her breasts and squeezed her nipples hard when she sat down hard on me, her cunt clenching my cock and making my eyes roll back in my head. "Fuck, that must have been some movie."

Covering my hands with hers, she rocked her hips back and forth, inching me toward coming. "It was. I'm just glad you don't mind acting it out with me."

I pulled her mouth down to mine and kissed her hard, snaking my tongue into her mouth as my cock rammed into her wet pussy. "Anytime. You keep watching them, and I'll keep acting them out with you."

Done with having her ride me, I pushed my hips up off the couch and met her movements with my own thrusts. It didn't take long before I felt her cunt begin to squeeze my cock. Gripping the back of my head, she clawed her fingernails along my neck as I pounded into her, desperate to come. With one last push of my hips, I buried myself inside her.

She sat down hard on my lap, her body convulsing through her release and making me come hard. I took a deep breath and held her to me as her thighs quivered against my sides. Diana cooed her contentment in my ear, and in the haze of my own pleasure, I wished this moment would never end.

"I loved that," she said quietly before she leaned back to look at me. "You look like you loved it too."

Kissing her softly, I smiled. "Loved it doesn't even touch how incredible that was. Thank God for your movie choices."

And just as quickly as she'd become the kind of woman who could rock my world, she turned shy again. Blushing, she smiled and said, "A girl's got to find some way to learn. Firsthand knowledge wasn't possible, so I did the next best thing."

"I love the way you study," I said with a chuckle, adoring how sweet she could be right after fucking me so well.

I KISSED THE TOP OF Diana's head as she lay next to me and quietly slipped from the bed, unable to stay near her because of the guilt I felt for lying to her again. I just needed some time to figure out how to get a better job than the one my brother offered me. Something would turn up.

As I stood in front of the sink with a glass of water trying to think of a plan, I heard a call come start to come in. Looking over to the living room, I saw Nina Stone staring back at me.

This wasn't going to be good. I could tell by the way her eyebrows drew in toward her nose, something I remembered far too often from all the times Ethan and I got into trouble when we were kids.

My feet felt like lead as I dragged myself over to speak to her. Christ, I looked like shit, even though the swelling had gone down a little so I didn't look like the elephant man anymore. A tiny smile broke her expression, so maybe things might not be so bad.

"Hi, Nina. I mean Mrs. Stone."

Christ, I'd called her Nina since sometime in high school, but now that she'd become my girlfriend's mother, I suddenly didn't know how to address her.

"Hello, Cole," she said as she studied my face, probably secretly horrified at how bad I looked.

So far, so good. She hadn't called me any horrible names, but that wasn't her style anyway. Nina Stone didn't just go around calling people goddamned assholes or fucking liars.

I pointed toward the bedroom like it was a million miles away and quickly said, "Diana's asleep. She's tired. She's in there."

Never before in my life had I felt so awkward that another human being might think I'd slept with a woman.

"I didn't call to speak to my daughter. I called to speak to you," she said softly.

But her lack of aggression since I knew she must be upset about what had happened with Diana only served to make me more uneasy. Nodding, I forced a smile as I waited for what was to come next.

"Please, sit down, Cole. I want to tell you a story I think you should hear."

I did as she commanded, fully expecting her to lay into me for everything from dating her daughter to being the one to drive her out of the city and away from her family. For the second time with one of the Stone clan, I didn't plan to defend myself. I had no defense.

"I don't think you've ever heard about when my children were born. Since you're Ethan's friend, he may have mentioned it to you,

I guess, but humor me, okay? When the triplets arrived, Diana was the tiniest. We didn't know if she'd make it she was so weak. Her brother and sister were born strong and ready for the world, but Diana took a little time. I'm sure you remember how often she was sick growing up, don't you?"

Nodding, I said, "I used to think you just didn't want me to come over the house sometimes because you said no so often when Ethan asked that one winter when we were in third grade. Then he told me it was because Diana was sick all the time and you were trying to do everything you could to make sure she didn't get sick again."

Nina smiled. "That's right. Every time we thought she was getting better that winter, she came down with something else. Strep throat, the flu, pleurisy, bronchitis—we couldn't get any of it under control. Things got better, as I know you remember, after that year, but Diana was always sicker than Ethan and Tressa. It took such a toll on her little body, but she got through it all."

"I remember," I said, hearing the worry in Ethan's voice every time he said we couldn't go to his house because she was sick again.

"And then, after getting stronger and getting back on track in school, we found out that when she didn't have to miss half a year, she was bright. I'm not ashamed to admit she's the smartest of the three of my kids. Each one of them has their gifts, and Diana's is her intellect. She wanted to be a lawyer, and she would have been the best the world had ever seen. But just when she had a chance to chase that dream and no doubt catch it, she and Ethan got into that accident."

Tears filled Nina's eyes, so she looked away and cleared her throat before she continued. When she looked back at me, she wore a forced expression of composure I knew wasn't real.

"I know you probably think we overprotected her. We never meant to. We just wanted to let her be independent while still making sure she was safe. We never thought she'd become so afraid that she never left that room."

Regret hung off every word like a sickness Nina now had to fight through. I wanted to help her push that feeling away.

"She knows you did everything you could. I know she does. She isn't doing this to hurt you."

"I don't think she is."

"You think I'm making her do this, don't you?" I asked with more defensiveness in my voice than I'd intended.

For the first time, Nina flashed me one of her broad smiles I knew was genuine. "No. My daughter has been through a lot, but she's a Stone, so she's got a mind of her own. I have no doubt that she was the one who asked you to help her go, just like she said."

I didn't know what to say since I felt like a jackass for jumping on her like that, so I just hung my head and kept my mouth closed. I didn't know where this conversation was going, but I had nothing useful to add to it yet. Better for me to just listen.

"Do you remember when you first started coming to our house, Cole?"

Looking up, surprised at her question, I smiled as I remembered the first time I met Ethan's mother. She looked much like Diana did now. Her eyes were bluer and her hair was a little shorter than her daughter's, but she had that same kindness Diana possessed.

"I was eight."

"You were. You and Ethan were the terrors of the neighborhood. Every day, I'd get a call from someone in town about what you two were up to. Or Tressa would tell me. She always loved reporting back just how much you two weren't behaving," Nina said with a chuckle.

"We were just fun-loving kids. We never meant any harm."

My statement wasn't so much a defense or an excuse as much as a way to say she never had to truly worry about Ethan with me. We didn't cause trouble. We merely were curious.

"I knew that, even if the older ladies whose flower beds you tore up with your bicycles didn't. I used to tell your mother that when she called and asked if we should consider not letting you boys hang around together as much."

Her confession made me sit back in surprise. I never knew my parents considered that. How different my life may have been if Ethan and I weren't joined at the hip from grade school on.

"And then when your mother had to go away, you began spending a lot of time at our house. I know that was hard on you, but I tried to help in every way I could because I firmly believe a boy needs a mother, or at least a mother-figure in his life."

It had been so long since that happened that I'd forgotten how much I'd relied on Nina Stone when my mother left. I wondered if she knew why she'd gone away, but that question would have to wait for another day. Now wasn't the time.

"Do you remember that night when you were twelve and you'd gotten in trouble at school, but Ethan asked if you could stay over? You'd done something with your science teacher, if I'm remembering correctly. Tristan was out of town, so I thought about saying no since dealing with three adolescents was hard enough, much less four, but I said yes."

Thinking back, I remembered weird Mr. Scolari with the thick glasses and cheesy moustache sending me to the office for mumbling under my breath that I didn't have my homework and he could fuck himself. I'd never said that to any adult before that day.

Sheepishly, I nodded. "Oh yeah. Not much of a student then, I guess."

Who was I kidding? I'd never been very good in school, and she knew it as well as anyone else.

"You didn't know this, but your father asked me to take you that night. He didn't know what to do with you and your brothers, and he knew you'd be safe and cared for at our house. We thought of you as one of the family. When your father went to prison, I told your grandmother any time you wanted to stay with us was fine with me. I knew you needed a family, and we were happy to be there for you."

"I think you should get more credit than either of my parents for keeping me out of trouble for most of my growing up," I said quietly, suddenly feeling like I'd betrayed her these past few days.

Nina's expression grew serious, like she thought that too. "I've welcomed you into our home and into our lives because you were Ethan's best friend and you needed the stability we could offer. I'm afraid that didn't transfer to you being an adult, though, did it?"

Clearing my throat, I asked, "How much do you know?"

She sighed and a look of pain crossed her face. "I don't know, but from what my husband's told me, you got yourself into a bit of trouble, Cole."

I hated seeing her look at me like that. Like she was filled with disappointment when she thought of me with her daughter. Like I'd turned out so much worse than she'd hoped I would.

I needed her to see I was better than what she'd heard.

"I got involved with some unsavory people," I admitted, preferring to use the euphemism someone like her would choose instead of the uglier loan shark. "I know I made some mistakes, but they took their pound of flesh. That's why I lost the club. I'm not in that world anymore. I swear."

My confession didn't make the worry disappear from her eyes, though. "I'm happy to hear that, but I'm told you're losing your home and car too. What are you going to do?"

For the second time that night, I had to find a way to make it seem like my life other than being with Diana hadn't fucking unraveled in the span of a few months. Time for the prospects speech again.

"I have prospects, things on the horizon. I haven't decided yet which way I want to go," I said, repeating word-for-word what I'd said to her daughter, except this time I didn't gulp down most of the lie.

Maybe after I told it a few more times people might start believing it. I knew instantly by the way Nina leveled her gaze on me that she didn't, unfortunately.

"Let's try that again. I'm asking you, as a person who has always treated you with kindness and respect, what are you going to do now?"

I sighed and hung my head as the embarrassing truth came out. Every mundane word of it. "My brother Chase has offered me a position as manager of one of his furniture stores. I'm sure if I asked, my brother Cade could find me a spot on one of his construction crews. It's that time of the year, so there would be work," I said barely above a mumble.

When I finished, I couldn't look up. It was too embarrassing to face a woman like Nina Stone after admitting that my future held the prospect of little more than benefitting from family nepotism because I had no real possibilities for anything else.

"So you do have prospects. Good! Why do you look so glum? I know this may not be what you planned to do, but your brothers are happy to help, I'm sure."

I lifted my head and saw her smiling at me. And not an evil smile like she now planned to tell me in some very detailed way how much I didn't deserve to be with someone like her daughter.

"The thought of doing either one of those jobs makes me sick to my stomach. I grew up with a father who moved millions of dollars on a daily basis. Now the best I can see in my future is middle management at a furniture store. I used to think I was better than him because he was in prison. Now I can't even say that."

Nina shook her head and frowned. "Don't say that. You've made some mistakes, but you aren't in prison. And I'll let you know that I came from a middle class background like that middle manager that so disgusts you. There's nothing to be ashamed of if someone is working an honest job and doing his best, Cole. Maybe one day you'll be back to where you were, but for now, there's nothing wrong with working as a manager of a furniture store."

"How can I be with Diana now? I have nothing to offer her," I said, hating the terrible truth but knowing I couldn't avoid it anymore.

Oddly, the one person I thought would agree with me stood

there shaking her head. "Diana doesn't need someone for money. Tristan's family made enough to last generations. She has all she could ever want in that department. What she needs is someone who understands her."

"Is that going to be enough, though? I'll be a guy who can run a store for people to furnish their homes, but I'll never be able to afford one of them."

"Diana can buy and sell most of the homes in this area, so I don't think that matters one way or another. I'm sure she could find someone who has money, but would he be good to her and understand she needs things other women don't? Cole, she's never going to be like the women you've spent your twenties with. They would care what you do for a living. They would look down their noses at your managing a furniture store. She wouldn't because she wasn't brought up to be that way."

As much as I wanted to believe that, I knew the realities of life. Diana didn't need someone with money, but what I could offer wasn't anything that special. She'd be able to find it with some wealthy guy, and then she'd see how much she'd been missing out by staying with me.

My heart sank as I formulated the words I never wanted to say and spoke them out loud. "I know you know where we are, Nina. I think maybe it might be a good idea if you or Tristan drove up here to get Diana. I'll be gone before you get here, but don't worry. She's safe here."

"No, don't do this, Cole. I've spent this whole call trying to show you we approve. Tristan and I approve of you and Diana being together. If she's happy, that's all that matters to us."

"She's happy now, but that won't last forever. She's better off with someone she belongs with. Someone who wouldn't be playacting like he belongs around you and your family. It was only a matter of time before I figured it out. I'm a little dim, so it only took me twenty years, but I see it now."

Nina's frown deepened as she continued to shake her head. "You're making a mistake. If you care about her, you won't do this.

Cole, she hasn't been able to be in a car for eight years. She did that with you because she trusted you. I'm sure it terrified her, but she did it. You have no idea how important that is. Ethan told me she looked like a different person when she called tonight. She looked strong, like her old self. Don't discount how much of that is because of you. Things might not be how you want them to be right now when it comes to your job, but do you love her?"

"That doesn't matter. She deserves better than me."

For the first time, Nina raised her voice, startling me. "Yes, it does! I swear to God it's like you didn't hear a word I just said. It matters because she loves you and wants to be with you. The only thing standing in the way of the two of you being happy is you. We're all fine with it."

"Ethan's not fine with it. My face can tell you that."

She grimaced before sighing. "I'm hoping it looks worse than it feels."

I had to chuckle. It didn't hurt much anymore. Actually, my entire head felt pretty numb. "I'll be okay."

"You'll hear this from Ethan himself soon enough, I imagine, but I know he's torn up about what he did. It's no excuse, but he's always been protective of his sister."

"I know, but that just makes my argument for me." I pointed at my bruised and busted up face and said, "Ethan knows me better than anyone else in the world, and he felt like he needed to do this when he found out about Diana being with me. He's right. She deserves better than me."

"She deserves someone who will love her like she needs. If that's not you, then maybe you're right. Maybe you should leave. Maybe I'm wrong and there are a lot of men who will take care of her like you. I don't think so, though."

"Just get here and take her back to where she belongs with people she should be with," I said sadly as I ended the call.

I'd pretended to be someone for years. Now, my time was up. I couldn't be what Diana deserved.

CHAPTER EIGHTEEN

DIANA

SLOWLY, I OPENED MY EYES to see Cole crouched beside the bed. He stared at me with a sadness I didn't understand, so I tried to push the sleep away from my head and asked, "What's wrong?"

"Nothing. Go back to sleep. I love you."

He was lying. Even in my groggy state, I knew that. The way his voice lowered when he said he loved me told me something was very wrong.

I quickly sat up and looked around the room. Nothing seemed different, except for Cole. Why was he acting so strangely?

"Come back to bed," I said, reaching out for him.

He stood up and took a deep breath in before he let out a heavy sigh. Avoiding my gaze, he said quietly, "I have to run out for a little while. You'll be safe, so don't worry."

"Where are you going? Why do you seem so strange, Cole? What's going on?"

Without answering, he gave me a forced smile and walked toward the door. "You'll be fine."

As he rounded the bed, I knew. He didn't want to be with me anymore.

"You aren't coming back, are you?"

Sighing again, he didn't turn around to face me. His shoulders sagged, and he hung his head. "It's better this way. Your mother will be here soon to get you."

Confused, I tried to understand what he was saying, but none of it made sense. Why was he leaving when he told me he loved me? Did something happen while I was sleeping? Did he speak to my mother?

"Why, Cole? Why don't you want to be with me anymore? Did my family do something?"

Still, he refused to turn around and look at me. "It's just the way it has to be. You'll be okay."

The finality of his words made my emotions explode inside me, and suddenly I couldn't stop myself from crying. I didn't understand any of this.

"I thought you loved me. So you're saying my sister was right? That you only came around to be with me for my money?" I asked, barely able to get the words out as I sobbed uncontrollably.

Cole didn't answer any of my questions. He didn't make a sound. He just stood there a few feet away from me in the doorway to that bedroom in his grandmother's cabin, but with each second that ticked by, it felt like he was drifting further and further away from me.

But why?

"Answer me! Don't I at least deserve to know why you don't want to be with me now?"

His body expanded as he took a deep breath in, and then a second later it seemed to fall as the air left him. "You deserve that and much more. I'm just not the man who can give you any of it."

"Why? Tell me," I said as I jumped from the bed and began to make my way toward him.

"Diana, I need to go. Don't leave the cabin and you'll be fine," he said and then walked out of the room.

With every step he took, I felt him slipping away. I couldn't let him go like this, though. I had to stop him.

So I ran through the kitchen to where he stood in the living room, and in my hurt and anger, I tightened my fists so hard my fingernails dug into my palms before I began to pummel his back to get him to look at me. "Turn around! Tell me why you don't love me anymore! Tell me!"

He finally spun around and faced me, grabbing my wrists to stop me from hitting him. "What's wrong with you? Why are you hitting me?"

"Because you won't tell me why you're doing this," I sobbed. He let go of my arms, and they fell to my side as I stood there exhausted by all of this. "Why don't you love me, Cole?"

Hanging his head, he whispered, "I do. You have no idea how much I want to be the man for you. I'm just not."

I took his hands in mine and squeezed them. "Why? I don't care if you don't own a club anymore. I don't care about anything like that. Please tell me what I have to say to make you understand those things don't matter to me."

When he raised his head and looked at me, I saw tears in his eyes. What had happened to make him so unhappy?

"My prospects are being manager at a furniture store that my brother owns."

He said those words with such disappointment clinging to each one that I instantly knew what was wrong. I brought his hands up to my lips and kissed them, finally understanding what I needed to say to show him he was the man I wanted.

"I don't care about money or what job you have, as long as you're happy doing it. If you don't want that, then do what you want. Money isn't something I care at all about, Cole. Honestly."

"That's because you've always had it. You're a wealthy woman from a very wealthy family. I'm not someone you should be with."

My hands tightened their grip on his because I feared he would turn and leave before I could convince him how wrong he was. "So I've always had money? Did it help me after my accident when I became so afraid of everything? If I didn't have my family's hotel to live in, I would have been holed up in a room in their house, no matter how much money we had. Money isn't anything I think about, Cole. It never was. I didn't fall in love with you when I was seventeen because you had money. I fell in love with you because you made me feel special and I loved how I felt when I was with you."

"Then why did we have to hide the fact that we were together?" he asked pointedly.

He thought I was embarrassed to be with him. How wrong he was.

"We had to because Ethan has always been way too overprotective of me, like I'm his little sister and not born on the very same day as he was. I never wanted to hide what I felt for you. I was crazy about you. I loved you."

"I have nothing compared to you, Diana. That's going to matter someday."

I released my hold on his hands and cradled his bruised face. In his dark eyes, I saw he truly believed that. "All that matters is you love me. Do you?"

"It's not that simple."

Leaning in, I closed my eyes and kissed him. "Yes, it is. Do you love me?"

Against my lips, he whispered his answer as my heart pounded in anticipation. "Yes."

I kept my eyes closed and asked, "Do you understand I don't care about money or things and don't care if you don't have any of it?"

"Yes."

Slowly, I opened my eyes and looked up at his black and blue face. "I might never be as normal as I used to be, but with you, I feel like I could be. You do that for me. I can't put a price on that. It's worth more than you can imagine. So I don't care if you don't make lots of money and don't drive a certain kind of car."

Cole pressed his forehead to mine and looked into my eyes. "The one thing that terrifies me more than anything else is that you will. That someday you'll look at me and think you could have had so much more."

"I promise I won't care, but I might not ever be like the women you're used to being with. I'm afraid you're going to see that one day and not want me."

He shook his head. "Never. I don't want them. I want you."

"And all I want is someone who loves me even though I'm a mess."

Pulling me into his arms, he held me close and whispered into my ear, "You're my mess, and I'm yours."

I'd never felt safer anywhere in my life than right there in his arms. He knew what I was, and he still loved me. And I knew what he was, and I still loved him.

Whatever the rest of the world thought meant nothing. It never would.

Cole gently pushed me away and turned toward the TV. "I told your mother I was leaving, so she's on her way here right now to get you."

"What?" I asked, confused. "Why?"

He fumbled with the remote as he explained, "She called to pretty much tell me what you just said, and I told her I didn't think I deserved you. I told her I was going to leave, so she or your father should come here to get you. She probably left already."

"Did she say she didn't want us together?" I asked as hurt rose inside me that yet another one of my family felt they should intrude on what Cole and I had.

But he quickly shook his head as he called her. "No. She tried to talk me out of leaving. She has no problem with us together."

"Then why did she call at all?"

As the call began to connect with my parents' house, he said, "Because she heard about everything that happened. Even after that, though, she wanted me to know she thought we should be together. We need to find out how long ago she left."

My brain tried to understand what had happened while I slept, and a second later, my mother's face appeared on the screen. Smiling, she said, "Hi, honey. Cole, I see you decided not to leave."

I grabbed Cole's hand and pulled him next to me so she could see us together when I explained to her how I intended to live my life from now on. "Mom, Cole and I are in love. I know all about everything that happened with his club, so please don't try to tell me about the mistakes he's made."

Beside me, he said, "Diana, she didn't—"

But I cut him off. "No, I need my family to know some things, Cole."

My mother shook her head and smiled. "You really don't have to—"

But I cut her off too.

"We're going to stay here for tonight, and then tomorrow we're going to decide what to do. He might take a job working for his brother at his furniture store. Or he might not. We're adults, so we'll choose what we're going to do. In the meantime, I've decided that I'm going to buy a house. I want a yard where I can plant a garden. I want to be able to have windows I can open so fresh air can come in anytime I want. I want to have more than two rooms that I can enjoy whenever I want. And I want a porch, one where I can have breakfast outside at a table and chairs. I'd like your help with finding a house, but if you can't support me moving out of the city, then that's fine too. But I'm doing this and Cole is going to be by my side."

When I finished talking, I saw my father enter the room and join my mother. I didn't know how much he'd heard of my speech, but I intended on repeating it so he could understand our plans too. I loved my family, but they had to see I wasn't that person who'd closed herself off from the world anymore.

"Diana, is everything okay?" he asked, looking more confused than worried, thankfully.

Before I could launch into my ideas, my mother turned to look at him and nodded. "Everything's fine, honey. Diana and Cole are at a cabin enjoying some time alone. This week, she and I are going house hunting. She's moving out of the hotel to a house with a yard and a porch."

I held my breath and waited for my father to say something as Cole's hand squeezed mine. My mother had left out a few important details, but that didn't matter. What mattered was I'd said what I needed to.

When he finally spoke, I couldn't help but smile. My father always knew exactly what to say to make me feel like everything would be okay.

"A house, huh? Real estate is always a good investment. When you decide on a place, we'll get together so the process goes smoothly. Good to see you again, Cole. Did you happen to catch the bus that hit you?"

My mother playfully elbowed him in the side as I let out a giggle at how silly he could be sometimes. "I love you, Daddy. Thank you."

He gave me a wink and a smile, and without saying another word, walked away. My mother rolled her eyes like she always did when he tried his hand at comedy.

"Tristan thinks he's funny, Cole. You probably know that already, but if you don't, you'll get used to his sense of humor coming out at the strangest times. Diana, call me when you're ready to go house hunting. What area are you looking at?"

"I don't know, Mom. Outside the city somewhere. I haven't narrowed it down yet."

"Well, I'm looking forward to going with you. You two have a nice time. Call me when you're ready to go looking, honey."

And with that, the screen went black. I'd expected some kind of resistance. I'd expected to have to defend my choices. But my family had supported me like they always had.

Surprised, I turned to look at Cole. "I didn't think things would go like that."

"I had a feeling they'd be fine with you moving out of the hotel, but I wasn't sure your father would be cool with me after that text he sent me. I guess they're okay with us together."

Standing on my toes, I kissed him and smiled. "Well, I'm more than okay about us. What about you?"

Cole held my face in his hands and pressed his lips to my forehead in a kiss that made my heart feel like it was soaring. "I'm more than okay too."

CHAPTER NINETEEN

COLE

THE HALLWAY FELT LIKE IT went on forever, like some passage in a horror film where the person must run for their life to reach a door to the outside where the killer can't reach them but the door keeps moving and the hallway never ends. Every step seemed to add another ten feet to my destination.

I'd never felt this way about going to see my best friend. I still thought of Ethan in that way, even though we hadn't spoken to one another for nearly a month. In that time, I'd thought about calling him dozens of times. Every time something good happened in my life, I wanted to share it with him. Every time someone said something stupid at the furniture store, I wanted to call him so we could laugh about it.

But every time I thought I would, I remembered no matter what anyone else in Diana's family thought of us together, he'd remained silent day after day. All I had to go on regarding his feelings was the memory of him laying me out in my apartment and Nina's claim that he felt terrible about what he'd done.

I didn't expect him to feel bad. That's not how we were with one another. Men got pissed off. They hit things. Sometimes they hit people. It's how we worked. We got pissed and we reacted, and then we calmed down and had a beer.

This wasn't the first time we'd gotten into a fight. Hell, I'd laid into him pretty good a few times in the past. But this was the first time we hadn't just moved on with our friendship like nothing had changed.

Everything had changed. I just didn't know as I walked slowly down the hall toward his apartment if that meant we weren't friends anymore.

Like losing my mother, the feeling of never getting to talk to Ethan made my chest hurt. Closer to me than any of my family, he had been my best friend for twenty years and like a brother. He knew everything about me. The good, the bad, and the ugly. He even knew about the horrible things I'd never told another human being except him.

No wonder he beat the hell out of me when he found out about Diana and me.

As all this ran through my mind, I reconsidered my plan to talk to him. Diana and Summer had arranged it so he'd be alone tonight, but was I making a mistake coming here? Maybe too much had happened to make being even casual friends possible.

I hoped that wasn't the case, but for the first time since we were both eight years old, I didn't know.

And then, suddenly, I stood in front of his apartment door with a choice to make. Should I try to see if we could still be friends, or should I leave and possibly try again, or maybe never? Summer thought the time was right, but was she just being hopeful when there was no hope left?

I rapped my knuckles on the door and waited with my heart in my throat, wondering if I should be prepared to duck out of the way of a right aimed for my jaw. I hadn't fought back last time because I deserved everything he threw at me. This time was different. I didn't want to brawl with Ethan, but I would now to defend not only myself but my relationship with Diana.

A strange sensation came over me as I waited for him to answer the door. I felt him standing there staring through the peephole at me. A second turned into five and then half a minute passed without him opening the door.

"Ethan, it's me. Cole," I said and then stopped abruptly, not knowing what else to say.

I'd never had to add anything to my name, just like he hadn't for his. I was Cole, his best friend, and he was Ethan, my best friend.

In front of me, the door opened slowly, and I saw him for the first time since that night. He looked like the same Ethan he always had, but when he didn't say a word, I had a feeling things had changed forever between us.

"What's up?" I asked awkwardly, hating how this felt already.

"Not much. What's up with you?" he said, reluctantly continuing the conversation.

"I was hoping we could talk."

He blew the air out of his lungs hard and then stepped back, opening the door all the way to let me in. I walked past him, watching for a fist to come at me, and turned around to face him as he closed the door.

"So this is why Summer just had to go to my sister's tonight and was so interested in me being here?" he asked with more than a hint of disgust in his voice as he walked by me and headed into the kitchen.

I followed him and took my usual spot at the island in the center of the room. How many nights had I stood there shooting the shit with him, drinking beers, and joking around like best friends? Never in a million years would I have guessed that being in that same place would feel so tense and strange.

He opened the refrigerator and then turned around with two beers, one in each hand, like every time before. "You still drink?"

A laugh bubbled up out of my throat at the question. I couldn't tell if he was being snide or just busting ass.

"Of course I still drink. Why would that have changed?"

He shrugged and twisted off the top from one of the bottles of beer before handing it to me. "I don't know. I feel like I don't know much about you, to be perfectly honest."

I deserved that. I'd lied to the one person I shouldn't have for years, so I had that coming.

"Nothing about me has changed. Trust me. I'm the same old Cole you always knew."

Ethan tipped his bottle up to his mouth and took a drink. He took his usual spot on the opposite side of the island, and it felt like hours passed before he spoke again. Christ, this was worse than I'd expected. Well, he hadn't taken a swing at me yet, so maybe it wasn't worse, but it was fucking bad.

"I can't get over the fact that you lied to me for years, man. Years. I thought we were best friends. And you lied about being with my sister, for Christ's sake."

Of all the things I'd prepared myself for, I hadn't thought I'd hear anguish in his voice and disappointment written all over his face when he finally spoke about what I'd done. Anger, rage, and even hatred I'd been ready for, but the sadness he showed gutted me.

"I'm sorry. I don't know what else to say."

He shook his head and frowned. "Just tell me you didn't treat her like all the other girls you hung out with in high school. I can't get that thought out of my head that you did her like you did all those girls back then."

"I didn't. I swear, Ethan. She was different. She and I got together right around the time my father went to prison. My fucking world was coming apart, and she was there to talk to. We never slept together back then. Diana gave me peace I couldn't find anywhere else then. I swear, I didn't treat her badly then and I'm not doing that now."

For the first time since that night he took out his anger on me, he smiled. It wasn't his usual broad smile that charmed the birds out of the trees, but it was something that made me think maybe things weren't beyond repair, after all.

"Everybody in my damn family thinks you're a good guy. They seem to spend every conversation trying to convince me that I shouldn't hate you. If it isn't Summer singing your praises about how happy you're making my sister, it's my mother telling me about how different Diana is now because of you."

I took a swig of beer and said, "She misses you. It's been hard on her not having you around lately."

"She doesn't need me anymore. She's got you. That's for the better anyway. We're adults now with our own lives, so we shouldn't be that close," he said, but I heard how much he missed Diana in every word.

"I'm not her brother. I didn't spend nine months in the womb with her and then twenty-eight years as best friends."

Ethan's eyes opened wide, and I saw the first flash of anger come from him. "Dude, I swear if you use the word womb in another fucking sentence talking about my sister, I'm going to come over this island and beat the hell out of you. Seriously."

I quickly raised my hands as if to surrender. "My bad. Scratch that whole idea. I was just trying to say no matter what I am to her, I can't be what you are because you're her brother. She loves you, Ethan. I don't replace you. How could I? Boyfriends don't replace family."

He didn't answer immediately, and instead took a long drink of beer before setting the bottle down on the counter in front of him. I had a feeling he didn't want to say what was on his mind, but if we ever wanted to be friends like we were again, he had to get it all out.

"Say what you want to say, man. I want us to be able to go back to where we used to be, but that can't happen if you don't tell me what's on your mind. Don't hold back."

Ethan shook his head and a pained look settled into his face. "I don't know if we can ever go back to the way we used to be. You were more than a best friend to me. You were like my brother, Cole. Now I feel like I didn't know you like I thought I did. You lied all that time. You knew how I felt about you even mentioning Diana in any way and still you went there. And then you lied to my face all these years. I don't know if I can get over that."

"I couldn't tell you the truth. Look what happened when you

found out," I said, knowing how lame that explanation sounded.

"What did you expect me to do? I found out you'd been sleeping with my sister who hadn't been on a date in eight years! I know how you are with women, dude. I jumped to the conclusion every other person who knows you would have. Hell, how do you think I felt when all those stories you told me about every woman you've slept with ran through my head and then I saw my sister's face in your own sexual rogue's gallery?"

"I guess I should be thankful you didn't kill me like you said you always would if I ever touched her. If it makes you feel any better, it wasn't about sex the first time we dated, and it isn't just that now. I'm crazy about her. She makes me happy, and you can trust me, living the life of a manager at my brother's furniture store is not anything dreams are made of. But when I get to be with her, I feel happy. Like the kind of happy you feel with Summer."

He hung his head and sighed. Then he looked at me and I knew he meant every word that came out of his mouth. "I swear to God, Cole, if you break her heart, I'm going to fucking kill you. No joke. It's not a threat. It's a promise. Diana has had way too much bad in her life, so if you're even thinking about just playing with her, I'll find you and kill you."

The mere thought of doing that to Diana made my chest ache. Shaking my head, I made a promise I intended on keeping. "I won't do that to her. I'm in love with her, Ethan. She's everything to me, and I can't imagine life without her. I don't have to pretend to be that guy with the club and the great car with her. I get to be myself with Diana, and that's just one of a hundred reasons why I would never hurt her. I promise."

He stared at me without saying a word, and then took a drink of his beer. With a smile, he said, "I'm going to keep you to that. So how's it been being an official part of the Stone family?"

"I kind of felt I was that all those years," I joked. "But it's been okay. Your mother has been really nice. She's kind of a mother hen with me, even more than with Diana. I think she feels like I've always needed a mother since mine bailed all those years ago."

Ethan gave me one of his signature smiles at my mention of Nina. "She's like that with me too. I think it's the mother of a boy thing. She spoils me, so don't be surprised if she does that with you now too. You should see how she is with Killian. Christ, the sun rises and sets on him in the eyes of Nina Stone. She might be even a bigger fan of his than my father."

"Really? I don't remember your mother even being interested in football."

He rolled his eyes and laughed. "She went to every home game last year. Every Sunday the team was in town, my mother was right there in my father's luxury box cheering Killian on. I think she goes to games more often than Tressa, and she's marrying the guy. You should hear my mother talk about the game, too. She's all about the stats. I'm telling you. Unless you've suddenly become a New York fan, avoid getting into any conversation about football with her. You won't make it out alive."

"I bet your sister loves that," I said, trying to imagine Tressa excited about football or any other sport.

"Tress doesn't seem to think of him as one of the biggest sports stars in the world," Ethan said before taking a drink of beer. "To her, he's just Killian. My father still gets that look in his eyes like he's his biggest fan and my mother is definitely a super fan of my soon-to-be brother-in-law, but my sister doesn't seem fazed by all the celebrity stuff that surrounds him."

"What do think of him?"

With a shrug, Ethan said, "I'm like Tress. He's just a regular guy around me. I guess it's pretty cool to say I know the quarterback of the local team and that he's going to be part of the family. We've hung out a few times, and he's okay. I like him, and he seems to be crazy about my sister, so what more can I ask from the guy?"

The conversation seemed to hit a lull, so I looked around at the near empty apartment we stood in. "So, you're really moving out of this sweet place? I never thought I'd see the day."

"Yeah, it's time. When it was just me, it worked. Even when it was just Summer and me, we had enough room, but once Trooper came along, this place started to feel like we needed more room. A dog deserves a place to run, so the house will be good for that."

"I remember the day you moved into this apartment. It was the coolest place I'd ever seen. I just had to get something like it."

He nodded. "Which you did not three months later."

"Yeah. I guess maybe places like this are good for a certain time in your life and then it's time to move on."

Ethan raised his beer into the air to make a toast. "To growing up. We made it through our twenties and lived to tell about it."

I lifted mine and added, "To good friends."

He smiled, and as he tipped his bottle to his mouth to take a drink, he said, "To best friends."

DIANA CURLED UP NEXT TO me on the new couch in her living room and kissed me on the cheek. "So tell me how it went with Ethan today. He called me right before you got here and asked if he could come over and see the house. He's coming over tomorrow afternoon."

I kissed the top of her head, loving the feel of her soft hair against my lips. "It went okay. No hitting and we had a few laughs."

Leaning back away from me, she studied my face for a moment. "You look unbruised. Do you think you guys are going to go back to how you were before this all happened?"

I thought about her question and shook my head. "I don't know. He's always going to be my best friend. Nothing's changed for me on that. I guess we'll just have to wait and see how things go."

As I turned on the movie we'd chosen to watch that night, she snuggled up against me again. "I hope you two are close again sometime soon. I'm sure he's missed you as much as I've missed him."

Diana wasn't wrong. I had missed Ethan being there to talk to and joke around with. When I left his apartment, I felt like I was leaving part of my life behind. We'd had good times there, and now with him moving out of the city with Summer and Trooper, it felt like a chapter in our lives was ending.

For nearly a decade, we'd been single and taking advantage of everything good and bad the city had to offer. We'd lived hard, partied hard, and enjoyed every damn minute of it.

But now, things were different. Ethan settled down with Summer, got himself a dog, and turned himself into a successful businessman. They'd probably have kids someday soon too. He was no longer the player he'd been.

Neither was I. Life had changed for all of us. Diana had her house with a porch where she liked to sit and watch the sunset and a yard where she'd begun planting a garden. Already, just a couple weeks after first putting the seeds into the ground, tiny green shoots had started to come up out of the ground.

I took my brother's offer to manage his furniture store, and while it would never feel as exciting as running a club, I went to work every day and tried to imagine myself doing something bigger in the future. Then every night, I drove over to see the woman I loved and we did things like cook dinner and watch movies.

Someday, when I achieved enough that I could offer her more than my time and my love, I'd ask her to marry me. Until then, the life I had with her came with so much that I never thought I'd experience. The family I'd always admired from afar for all those years was now one that thought of me as one of them.

The Stone clan had taken me under their wing for real this time. I wasn't just Ethan's best friend now. I was the man in love with Diana.

And I couldn't imagine a better life when it came to that.

CHAPTER TWENTY

DIANA

"Cole, check that I put the dip in the bowl, okay? I didn't want it to be out for too long in this heat, but I think I forgot to put it out on the kitchen table at all," I called from the bathroom upstairs.

"Got it! It's almost time. Are you ready yet?" he yelled back from the bottom of the stairs.

"Almost!"

I looked in the mirror and ran my hand over my face as I checked my makeup. Everything looked good. My parents, Ethan and Summer, and Tressa and Killian would be arriving at any minute, so I wanted to look perfect to officially welcome them to my new house.

My long brown hair hung down over my arms, and the temperatures climbing into the high eighties made tiny beads of sweat form along the back of my neck. Fanning myself, I couldn't help but focus on the scar on the side of my cheek that ran down to my neck. It had faded over the years, but my gaze zeroed in on it every time I looked at myself in the mirror.

Turning my head, I watched my finger as I dragged it down along the faint line on my face. For so long, it had made me feel ugly and broken. Not now, though.

Now, I didn't see a scar but proof that I'd survived.

I grabbed a hair tie from my makeup bag and scooped my hair up into a ponytail. Smoothing the hair on the top of my head, I tightened the band until the ponytail hung perfectly down my back.

With one last look, I smiled and hurried downstairs to make sure everything was perfect for my housewarming party.

Cole waited for me in the kitchen, and I saw he'd set out the dip just as I'd asked. Standing on my tiptoes, I kissed him sweetly on the lips. "Thank you. How does it all look?"

He slid his hand along my hair and smiled. "Beautiful. I like when you wear your hair up."

"I'm so nervous. This house is so much smaller than all of theirs, but I want them to like it just as I do."

Suddenly, I couldn't remember if I'd watered the garden that morning. "Can you remember if I gave the plants a drink today? I need to check. I've been raving about my vegetables coming up this summer, but if they're all wilted and dead, that will be impossible."

As I rushed around the kitchen looking for where I'd left the watering can, Cole stopped me and held me still by the shoulders. "Relax. Take a deep breath in and let it out slowly. Your family is going to love this place. No, it's not a mansion or huge estate, but they don't care about that. All they care about is that you're happy here. Everything's going to be great today, so relax. You've got this."

I did as he said and took a deep breath. My therapist had told me not to put too much pressure on myself for this day to be perfect. He'd also reminded me how important it was for me to remember how far I'd come from that terrified girl too afraid to leave her hotel room. I sometimes let myself forget how much I'd achieved.

"You're right. And it's not like my mother and father and mostly everyone hasn't seen the place yet. I just want them to see what I see in this house."

Cole smiled and leaned down to press a kiss onto my forehead. "They will. Don't worry. Everything's going to be great today."

I looked up at him and let myself get lost in his dark eyes for a moment. Whenever I felt stressed out or like I might unravel at some small thing, I found calm in his eyes.

"Thank you for being here with me for this. I probably would have gone off the deep end if you weren't helping. I'm just so excited for them to all be here to see my house and hear my news. I've been practically bursting at the seams for the past three days to tell my mother and father."

"You don't have to be nervous. They're going to be so proud of you, like I am."

I took another deep breath as the sound of a car pulling into the driveway told me the first official guests to my house had arrived. Grabbing Cole's hands, I squeezed them as my excitement began to take over again.

"They're here! Is everything out? Of course it is. We're ready for this, right?" I asked, my thoughts tumbling out of my mouth as soon as they came to me.

"We're ready."

I ran to the kitchen window and looked out to see who had gotten here first. My brother and Summer opened the doors to his black Range Rover, and I turned to face Cole. "Ethan and Summer are here!"

My heart racing, I hurried to the front porch and waited impatiently for them as they climbed the steps to join me. I did one more last minute inspection of the area to make sure it looked perfect and then looked up to see them smiling.

I opened my arms and took Summer into them for a hug first. "Welcome to my new house. I've got food and drink, and I'm so happy you're here!"

She embraced me and then stepped back to hold up a big pink gift bag in front of her. "Just wait until you see what we got you for your housewarming. You're going to love it!"

"Thank you, but you didn't have to do that. I'm just so thrilled you came to celebrate my new place."

Summer rolled her eyes and laughed. "Don't be ridiculous. This is a huge day. That's why I made sure our gift is right for this occasion. I'm going to take it into the house. Is Cole inside?"

I turned to look through the screen door and saw him waiting inside. He and Ethan had talked a few times since that day they got together at the apartment, but this was the first time they'd be together in person. He didn't want to admit it, but I knew he wasn't sure how it would be hanging out with Ethan again, especially with the rest of my family there.

"He's right in the living room," I said as I opened the door for Summer.

She stepped into the house, leaving my brother and me alone for a moment. He didn't say a word before he set the bag in his hand down on the porch and wrapped his arms around me, hugging me like we hadn't seen each other in years.

"I'm so proud of you today, Diana."

I didn't want to cry or get overly emotional, but just hearing him say that to me made holding back the tears impossible. Squeezing him to me, I whispered, "It took me a little longer than I'd planned, but I got here. Thank you for always being there for me whenever I needed you."

Like all those times when I called him to come see me at my hotel room because I needed his support, he kissed the top of my head. "I'm always going to be there for you. I promise."

He stepped back and picked up the paper bag from the porch. Lifting it in the air, he smiled. "Summer has your gift from us, but this is for Cole."

I looked in to see him smiling at what Ethan said. "My brother says he got you a gift."

Cole walked up to the screen door and looked out. "I'm just the dip guy here. I don't deserve a gift," he joked.

Tugging the paper bag off with his right hand, Ethan held up a six-pack of beer. "I couldn't show up without your favorite drink of choice. What kind of best friend would I be if I did that?"

Tears welled in my eyes at him calling Cole his best friend again. Ethan kissed me once more and walked inside to give him a beer, and it seemed like old times again with them.

As I stood on the porch, so happy things had turned out like I wanted them to with Ethan and Cole, I saw my parents drive up to the house. Still the coolest guy I'd ever met or would ever meet, my father parked his silver Porsche next to Ethan's car and popped the trunk, no doubt holding a present on this special day.

Both my parents had already seen the house half a dozen times. My mother and I looked at it first the day I fell in love with it because it had the porch and yard I wanted, in addition to three bedrooms, two baths, and a kitchen with a farmhouse sink I never knew I wanted until I saw it that day.

Then my father had to come see it to make sure it was safe and in good condition, even though the house inspector said it passed his tests with flying colors. I may have been twenty-eight years old, but to Tristan Stone, I would always be his little girl, and I wouldn't have had it any other way. That day, he walked around the perimeter of the house wearing his most serious dad face as I pointed out all the things I loved about the property. Then we toured the inside, just as I had with my mother, who undoubtedly had told him about every inch of the place after she saw it.

But he had to see it for himself, he claimed. I knew that was just him being overprotective, but I loved him for it. When we stopped in the kitchen so I could show him the sink I'd fallen in love with, he nodded and then smiled in that way that told me he loved the place too.

"You have your mother's eye for details, Diana. This house is charming." Then he added, "But a million-two is far too high. I don't care that the train is only a five minute walk and we're just a few miles out of the city. Let me talk to the seller for you. Call it a housewarming present."

I didn't argue with him that day. I knew my father had skills at business I'd never possess, so I didn't fight him on his need to haggle. In the end, I paid far less than asking price for my dream home, thanks to my father.

"Diana, you look so great standing there on the porch like that, and you're wearing your hair up. I love it!" my mother yelled up as she left my father to handle whatever was in the trunk. "Sorry we're late. I couldn't decide which dress to wear."

She lifted the hem of her pale yellow dress and smiled up at me. My mother always looked like the most beautiful woman in the world, no matter what she wore, but today she practically beamed she looked so wonderful.

"I thought maybe it was Daddy who took too long getting dressed," I joked as she walked up on the porch.

"Your father looks good in everything. It's really unfair, actually. I figured he'd have some middle-aged pooch by now. Thankfully, you and your sister and brother seemed to have gotten his genes, although you look more like me than they do. I see Ethan and Summer are here. Did you open their gift yet?"

I shook my head and smiled. "No, but now I'm wondering what this present could be. It must be pretty great if you know about it."

My mother leaned in and kissed me on the cheek. "Summer was so excited about it that she couldn't wait to tell someone. We got you something too. Your father is getting it out of the trunk."

"Thank you, Mom, but you didn't have to do that. You two have done so much already with you looking at houses with me and Daddy negotiating the price with the homeowner."

She waved off my protest and smiled as she looked back at my father. "Are you kidding? He couldn't talk about anything else for days after he got to make that deal with the man selling this house. If you ever decide to get a car, you better not tell him because he's going to insist you let him make the deal. You know how he is."

I nodded, knowing exactly what she meant. As she went into the house to join the others, my father carried an enormous box that hid his entire torso and head behind it. He reached the top of the steps and put it down, and I saw him smile like he was proud of me.

"Your mother may have gone overboard. Just fair warning."

"I'm so happy you're here, Daddy, but you guys didn't have to get me anything. You said helping me with the sale was your housewarming present."

In that charming Tristan Stone way, he winked at me and said, "I lied. It's a father's prerogative to do whatever he can to make sure his little girl is happy." Then a look of worry crossed his face. "I saw Ethan's car. Is Cole here? We're not going to see round two today, are we?"

With a chuckle, I said, "No, Daddy. They're friends again. Everything's okay."

He leaned in and kissed my cheek. "Good. I want things to be perfect for you today. Today's your day, honey. I'm so proud of you taking charge and getting this place of your own."

I couldn't stop myself from crying now, and as a tear slid down my cheek, my father smiled and wiped it away like he used to when I was a little girl. "No crying today. Today's a celebration for you, like your own independence day."

My own independence day. I loved that.

Wrapping my arms around my father's broad shoulders, I pressed my cheek to the spot above his heart and hugged him. "Thank you, Daddy. I love you."

"I love you too, honey," he said above me. "I always knew you'd do it. You just needed to do it on your time and no one else's. You're stubborn like me that way."

I stepped back and dried my tears. "I like that."

"It's a good trait. Don't ever let anyone tell you otherwise."

A black sports car drove up to the house and honked its horn, telling me my last guests had arrived. My father turned around and watched as Tressa and Killian walked up to the porch to join us.

He and his future son-in-law shook hands and commented on one another's cars before Killian helped my father carry the enormous box inside to the living room. Tressa watched them and then handed me a tiny black gift bag.

"I have a feeling whatever's in that box is all our mother's doing since Daddy doesn't shop much," I joked.

She smiled at my all-too-true comment. Dressed in a white sundress and wearing her favorite Louboutin pumps, Tressa looked exactly like what the wife of one of the world's most famous athletes should look like. I'd always wished I could look as put together as my sister always did. Although we looked alike in many ways, especially our long dark hair that she wore down today, we'd always seemed so different.

"This is from Killian and me. I thought since everyone else was getting you housey things that you deserved something purely decadent and utterly not-utilitarian."

Opening the bag, I saw a robin's egg blue colored box from Tiffany's. "I can't believe you went for something so extravagant, Tressa."

She smiled and cupped my cheek with her hand. "Today's an important day for you. I thought it deserved to be celebrated appropriately. You've come a long way, Diana. I'm proud of you. I always knew you'd do it."

"Just on my own time," I said with a smile. "That's what Daddy said. He says it's a Stone thing."

"And it's something you, Ethan, and I share from him. It may take us a while to get where we're meant to be, but when we find out where that place is, God help anyone who decides to get in our way," Tressa said, tilting her chin up defiantly. "You did what you wanted on your schedule, Diana. I'm proud of you for that."

I'd never before in my life felt like Tressa and I were alike when it came to being strong, but now as I stood on my porch welcoming my family to my housewarming party, I saw that we did have that in common. She'd worn her strength for much longer than I had, but I understood why she prized it so much. Being strong felt good.

"Thanks, Tressa. You have no idea how much that means to me."

She wrapped her arm around my shoulders and began to guide me into the house. "Sisters have to stay together. We're the Stone girls. You remember how teachers used to always say that.

Whenever any of them had the two of us in a class at the same time, they knew they were in for it because we were both smart. I was a little sassier and you were a little quieter, but they knew who we were. Those Stone girls. If they could see us now, right?"

"If they could see us now," I repeated, happy my sister could be here to celebrate my day of independence.

Every person I cared about in the world stood in my house talking about how much they loved it and how happy they were for me. We'd weathered the tough times and come out stronger than ever.

Cole held my hand and I took a deep breath in as I prepared to make my big announcement. He knew what no one else knew and gave me a nod, as if to tell me he had my back. But my family would be thrilled at what I had to say, so I wasn't worried.

"Attention, everyone! I want to start off this party by saying thank you for coming here today. I am so proud to show off my house. It's not a mansion or anything close, but it's mine and I love it. I've got food and drinks, but before we get to all that and I give you a tour of the place, I have an announcement."

I saw everyone's eyes grow wide as their gazes moved from me to Cole and then back to me. I knew what they thought, but not yet.

"By the looks on all of your faces, I can tell what you think I'm about to say, but you're guessing wrong, so I'll just tell you. Starting next week, I am going back to college. You're looking at a Columbia University junior, or close to it. I think I'm a few credits short of that level. Anyway, it's been a long road I've had to travel to get to this point, but I'm finally going back to school."

For a moment, my living room filled with a collective gasp, but then my mother rushed over to give me a hug. "Oh, this is the best news, Diana! I'm so proud of you for doing this."

"What are you going to be studying?" Summer asked.

"I don't know. I'm still interested in the law, but I'm also interested in communicating with the deaf. I have been since Daddy taught me how to sign when I was a little girl. For now, I'm just going to start slow and get back into being a college student again. I'm picking up where I left off nearly ten years ago."

Turning to look at Cole, I smiled. "It worked so well the first time I tried going back, so I thought I should try it with college too."

He smiled and kissed me. "Congratulations, babe. You're going to be the best at whatever you decide to do."

My father raised his glass and announced, "A toast. To my daughter."

"Wait, Dad," Ethan said, stopping him. "We need to get everyone a glass of champagne."

Surprised to hear there was champagne for a toast since I hadn't thought of buying any, I said, "Who brought the bubbly?"

My brother smiled and held up the bottle he was pouring from. "I come bearing beer and champagne. Now everyone take a glass and Dad can make his toast."

Once we all had our glasses, we raised them in the air as my father continued. "A toast. To my beautiful daughter, Diana. We never doubted for a second that this day would come. To doing things on your own time."

In unison, my entire family repeated his words. "To doing things on your own time!"

I'd taken much longer than I ever thought I would to come back from the accident. By twenty-eight, I thought I'd already have a law degree and the life I'd planned.

But things didn't always go according to plan.

The years I spent hidden away in that hotel room were years I'd never get back. That's okay, though. I needed that time to show me how much I never wanted to live in fear like that again. I still worried about so much in life and was afraid of more than I wanted to admit, even to the people who loved me the most, but I was getting better with each passing day.

When I looked around the room at my family, I saw happiness.

Ethan had found love with Summer and finally found the acceptance he'd sought from my father all his life. It was amazing how two people who looked so alike couldn't see that all along it wasn't differences that kept them on opposite sides of nearly every issue but their similarities.

My sister also had found what she was looking for all those years. Through Killian, she finally felt secure enough to be her true self. The real Tressa was that girl I loved as a teenager—sassy, smart, and confident, but also loving and sweet. I loved the fact that she'd returned to us.

My mother and father, the example of the truest love I'd ever seen, still gave one another cute looks of love when they thought no one was watching. To the world, Tristan Stone was a successful businessman, but in private, he was my mother's best friend and his children's biggest fan.

Cole slid his arm around my waist and nuzzled my neck. "You look beautiful."

I looked up at him and saw an imperfect person just like me. But I loved his imperfections just as he loved mine.

"Thank you for being here to celebrate this big day with me. You're officially now part of the Stone family. Are you ready for that?"

He pressed his forehead to mine and smiled. "I'm ready for whatever happens as long as I'm with you."

From across the room, I saw my father walk up behind my mother and wrap his arms around her. I'd learned from them what real love was. Every day, they'd showed me it wasn't expensive gifts or fancy things but those little gestures when they thought no one was paying attention.

I'd always dreamed of finding a love like theirs. We all had. It had taken me longer than my siblings, but finally, I could say we'd all found that perfect kind of love.

**AVAILABLE NOW, THE FINAL HEART OF STONE BOOK,
ALL OF ME!**

Tristan and Nina have a fairytale love story, and after twenty years of marriage and three children, they seem to have it all. But Nina worries they need something to keep the spark alive between them, so what better than a date night with her husband?

What begins as a sexy night together turns into something darker neither one anticipated, and their fairytale is threatened by something they have no control over. Tristan won't give up on the love of his life, and all he can hope is she won't give up on him.

All they have together is worth fighting for, but will that be enough to make sure they get their happily ever after?

GET YOUR COPY TODAY!

ABOUT THE AUTHOR

K.M. Scott writes contemporary romance stories of sexy, intense, and unforgettable love. A New York Times and USA Today bestselling author, she's been in love with romance since reading her first romance novel in junior high (she was a very curious girl!). Under her Gabrielle Bisset name, she writes paranormal and historical romance. She lives in Pennsylvania with a herd of animals and when she's not writing can be found reading or feeding her TV addiction.

Be sure to visit K.M.'s Facebook page for all the latest on her books, along with giveaways and other goodies! And to hear all the news on K.M. Scott books first, sign up for her newsletter today and be sure to visit her website at **www.kmscottbooks.com**

BOOKS BY K.M. SCOTT:

Crash Into Me (Heart of Stone #1)
Fall Into Me (Heart of Stone #2)
Give In To Me (Heart of Stone #3)
Heart of Stone Volume One
Ever After (Heart of Stone #4)
A Heart of Stone Christmas (Heart of Stone #5)
Return To Me (Heart of Stone #6)
Forever With Me (Heart of Stone #7)
Heart of Stone Volume Two
Hard As Stone (Heart of Stone #8)
Set In Stone (Heart of Stone #9)
Silent As A Stone (Heart of Stone #10)
All of Me (Heart of Stone #11)
Heart of Stone Volume Three

Temptation (Club X #1)
Surrender (Club X #2)
Possession (Club X #3)
Satisfaction (Club X #4)
Acceptance (Club X #5)
The Complete Club X Series Paperback

If I Dream (Corrupted Love #1)
If You Fight (Corrupted Love #2)
If We Fall (Corrupted Love #3)

Crave (Addicted To You #1)
Adore (Addicted To You #2)
Shatter (Addicted To You #3)
Claim (Addicted To You #4)
The Addicted To You Series Paperback

In The Darkness (Project Artemis #1)
After The Storm (Project Artemis #2)
Behind The Scenes (Project Artemis #3)

Hard Work (Standalone)

K.M.'S BOOKS ARE IN AUDIOBOOK TOO!

BOOKS BY K.M. SCOTT WRITING AS GABRIELLE BISSET:

Vampire Dreams Revamped (A Sons of Navarus Prequel)
Blood Avenged (Sons of Navarus #1)
Blood Betrayed (Sons of Navarus #2)
Longing (A Sons of Navarus Short Story)
Blood Spirit (Sons of Navarus #3)
The Deepest Cut (A Sons of Navarus Short Story)
Blood Prophecy (Sons of Navarus #4)
Blood Craving (Sons of Navarus #5)

Blood Eclipse (Sons of Navarus #6)
Blood Ascendant (Sons of Navarus #7)

Stolen Destiny (Destined Ones Duet #1)
Destiny Redeemed (Destined Ones Duet #2)

Love's Master
Masquerade
The Victorian Erotic Romance Trilogy